# FLIRTING WITH THE LAVENDER LANE

TRYSTAN MICKEL WINDEMIER

Flirting with the Lavender Lane
Copyright © 2022 by Trystan Mickel Windemier

All rights reserved. No part of this publication may be reproduced,
distributed, or transmitted in any form or by any means, including
photocopying, recording, or other electronic or mechanical
methods, without the prior written permission of the author, except
in the case of brief quotations embodied in critical reviews and
certain other non-commercial uses permitted by copyright law.


ISBN
978-1-956161-89-2 (Paperback)
978-1-956161-88-5 (eBook)

# TABLE OF CONTENTS

# CHAPTER 1

# "LIFE" IS SMASHED

I ran up the stairs like a madman, a mixture of dismay, alarm, sorrow, and panic compelling me forward and upward at a frantic pace. My heart pounded, sweat beaded on my forehead, and tears threatened to flow. I could feel the short hair on my head bristle, and I gulped in uncontrollable fear. 'Am I too late?' and 'Lord don't let this happen!' passed my lips as I continued my ascent two steps at a time, taxing even my in-shape body to its limits.

I had been out grocery shopping for Aidan and me at the local produce store. It had been a wonderful evening, I thought, with the brilliant sun slowly setting, warm breezes blowing, and the late October atmosphere warm and a little muggy. When I had left Aidan at home he had been a little down, but not so much that I would have anticipated this development. He had been drinking his usual vodka tonic with avatar and playing Wii. I had no idea he was having this many problems and burdens that would bring this on!

I had almost finished shopping for supplies and my cart was full, when I received a phone call from a strange number. I answered to find I was talking to an Aurora police officer who informed me of the emergency. I was so stunned and upset that I just abandoned my full cart in the aisle, ran out of the store, jumped in my Camarro, and drove like a maniac to home. Unfortunately I had run into traffic problems which delayed me. When I arrived at Candlestick I found the elevator broken. Thus it had come to my current flight up the stairs to reach and save my Aidan.

Flashbacks and memories of one's past with the person in crisis, as well as regrets of opportunities missed, and guilt over possible sins committed crowd one's mind in a situation like this. It was the same for me now as I tore up flight after flight, my mind a jumble of these thoughts.

I remembered the first time I had laid eyes on Aidan on the bus to Aurora from Gurnee, Illinois. He was so hot, so physically and facially attractive. I had fallen in love with Aidan at that moment! I saw in my mind's eye the first time I had touched Aidan quite intimately after he had been assaulted by Jovan the Dominator. I had nursed the welts all over Aidan's body, including his cute, round ass. I remembered the euphoria of our first pledge of love for one another and subsequent first kiss that same day at bed time. I had been confused, ecstatic, yet I had felt guilty too. I remembered the thrill of Aidan defending me from Neils and then nursing my injuries… my first sexual orgasm with him in the shower later… our first time making love on his birthday… our other times of love-making… something over which I still had feelings of guilt in my spirit… I could feel and fondly remember my overwhelming feelings of love, passion, attraction, and desire for Aidan. Then I came to my conflict over the 'Christianity' of my marriage and sexual relationship with Aidan. All of this and more came rushing back, swirling around in a jumbled fashion, stirring my hormones, my emotions, and my body for Aidan… and stirring latent guilt in my spirit over my lifestyle…Is it Biblically okay, or a sin?!

"I'm sorry, Lord, to have these feelings about and for Aidan!" I prayed, frowning. "But I still have not been shown definitively that my lifestyle with Aidan, our lifestyle, is wrong!"

I reached the end of the stairs to the roof. I ran through the open door onto the tar paper. Was Aidan still alive?! Was I in time?! Had he jumped while I was en route to save him?! Had someone else managed to talk him down?! I was shaking with panic, fear, breathlessness, and apprehension. What would I do without Aidan?! I didn't want to contemplate the possibility of losing him!

"Wait a minute, son!" an armed cop intercepted me as I rounded the stairwell. He roughly and painfully grabbed my arm at the bicep. It hurt like hell! I squirmed in discomfort, urgency, and impatience.

"Young man! Where in the hell do you think you're going?! You shouldn't be here! This is an emotional and fluid situation. We have someone threatening to commit suicide by jumping from this roof. You go back down to the street! Now!" the cop who held my arm said as he began dragging me back toward the stairs from whence I had come.

I wanted… I needed to see Aidan and stop him from jumping! Now this burly, blue-suited ignoramus was restraining me and threatening to send me downstairs. Adrenaline flowed as anger and panic rose in my body. I wrenched free of the stupid cop, pain spreading up my arm, and started forward toward Aidan again. I only wanted Aidan to touch me, to hold me again! I wanted to hug him, caress him, comfort him, and feel him! I had to… I *would* convince him not to jump!!

My freedom was short-lived. Once free, I only took three or four steps. The cop turned back and bellowed at me.

"Stop, son, or I will have you arrested!" The officer sounded resolute. "I have my Glock trained on you! Stop! Now!"

"Okay! Okay!" I stopped and slowly turned around. My heart was pounding, and my fear and panic over Aidan caused a wave of nausea. I gagged and wretched a couple of times.

"Don't shoot, please!?" I was now looking directly into the burly police officer's eyes, with only a distance of about three yards between us. I decided to plead.

"I need to see Aidan and talk to him. I know I can talk him out of jumping! I must save Aidan! Please!? Please let me go to him?!"

"Who the hell is 'Aidan', young man?!" barked the officer, as he stopped and kept his Glock pointed at me.

"I mean Andrew! Andrew DiPree! The man who is threatening to jump… Andrew!?" I was losing valuable time here. "I need to talk to Andrew! Please?! I can talk him down and stop him from jumping!"

"Who are you, young man?!" the officer asked suspiciously, his voice still gruff and unfriendly.

"I am his spou… I mean… I mean I am his roommate. I can help! Please, let me go to him?! I can't bear to lose…" I stopped myself before I revealed anything more about my relationship with Aidan. I didn't want any of these idiots to think I was gay with Aidan! I feared they would use that as an excuse to stop trying to solve this situation happily. As long as they thought we were 'acceptable heterosexuals' I knew they would try to save Aidan with all the resources they had.

"Please, sir, let me go to Andrew!?" I looked pleadingly at the officer to let me go to Aidan. By now I noticed two other cops were standing nearby for backup.

"Are you Tyler Belmont?" the officer's attitude and tone of voice suddenly changed dramatically.

"Yes!" I replied excitedly. We were finally getting somewhere! "I am Tyler Belmont! I am his roommate! May I please go to him?! I can stop him from jumping!"

"Well then, why in the hell didn't you say so first thing, son?!" the officer lowered his weapon. "Go! He has been calling and asking for you ever since we got here!"

I didn't wait to see if there were any other issues the officer might bring up, nor did I want to give him a chance to change his mind. I whirled around and quickly finished rounding the stairwell. 'I must get to Aidan, before it is too late!' I thought anxiously as panic caused me to gag again.

I started running the dark length of the building roof toward the lights I saw about 150 to 200 yards away. I was terrified that I was too late! What would I do without my Aidan?! What would I have to live for without my spouse?! Would I want to live on in a world without Aidan's presence, his love for me, without his support, his loyalty, and without our relationship, whether the emotional, spiritual, or the physical? I had contemplated losing Aidan to death only in my worst nightmares, and now I felt like I was living the nightmare.

In a moment or two I could see Aidan, his hot, awesome body illuminated by the many police flashlights shining on him. 'Man,' I thought, 'he is a hunk from the front or the back! I cannot lose him! He cannot die!' Even now I felt a nibbling of shame at my relationship with Aidan. I felt guilty about our love-making; but the sex was so... so... so meaningful, pleasurable, satisfying, and stimulating! However doubtful I was, I justified our relationship because in all its areas Aidan and I meshed, we loved each other, and we were equal in all ways.

"Lord, I'm sorry!" I muttered. "Lord, if I… if we have been living… living in sin… I am sorry, but please help me to help Aidan…I can*not* live without him! Lord, we love each other! Please don't let our love, our marriage end this way! Why can't we love members of whatever sex to which we are attracted and we want without being guilty of a sin, Lord?!"

From my vantage point of running toward Aidan I could see him suddenly whirl around, causing him to lose his balance. He almost fell off the ledge toward the street, and my heart skipped a beat in terror, followed by the feeling of my stomach leaving my body. However, Aidan managed to regain his balance quickly. The thought crossed my mind that he probably had drunk a considerable amount of vodka tonic with avatar before coming here to kill himself. Why was he doing this?! What in his life, our life, was so terrible that he wanted to end it all?! I knew one thing! After this crisis, I was definitely going to put my foot down and demand that he and I get more professional counseling and medical help.

"I want you to get Tyler Belmont up here, you thugs!" Aidan cried out in anger and frustration. "Only he can help me! I want to talk to him before I die!"

Aidan teetered on the roof ledge as he sobbed. My stomach and heart went to my feet again. The flashlights suddenly all shone on Aidan. Aidan stood on the ledge, flanked on both sides by one of the decorative large cement candles about four feet from him. Aidan was in the center of the space between candles, balancing precariously on the ledge.

"Aidan! Aidan!" I called desperately as I tore over the last few yards and came to a stop about twenty feet away from him. "Aidan! Don't jump! Please?! It is Tyler, Dion. Aidan I am here!"

Aidan swayed as he peered through the light trying to see me. My stomach heaved and I almost threw up out of fear for him.

"Dion?! Dion?! Is that you?!" Aidan queried in an accusatory but plaintive tone.

As if on cue, all the flashlights were pointed at me. I was suddenly self-conscious and afraid that the secret of my relationship to Aidan would become public this night. I could feel my face flushing red.

"Yes, Aidan… It is I." I dropped my gaze, very embarrassed by all the police. I couldn't be totally honest, transparent, and loving to Aidan in front of all these people! I therefore began to doubt I could stop Aidan from jumping to his death.

"I need you, Aidan. Please don't do this!" I looked up and pleaded to Aidan with my facial expressions too.

Tears were streaming down Aidan's cheeks as he faced all of us on the roof. I wanted to hug him and comfort him! I wanted to kiss him and tell him it would be all right! I wanted to beg him to stay alive for me, for us, for our marriage! I looked pleadingly at Aidan. I knew I would not be able to show any more love or concern in front of all these policemen. I did not want them to realize I had any 'unnatural' feelings for Aidan. I knew they wouldn't understand the true depth of our love for one another, the correctness of our relationship, and what I considered the natural 'nature' of our love. At the same time I realized that if I did not show Aidan my true feelings like I did in the privacy of our apartment or outside the city of Aurora, he would be hurt even more. That could be a further catalyst for him to jump. What in the hell was I going to do?!

I looked sheepishly and reproachfully at the policemen I could see. None of them seemed to be suspecting my actions or relationship to Aidan. 'I must still be safe!' I thought. To them, it appeared to me as I strained to see as many as I could, this was just another attempt at suicide. This was just par for the course for them as policemen, part of their job. I wanted to scream at them to put all of their guns away, and leave Aidan and me alone so I could be entirely open with Aidan, to get him to come down and stay with me, love me, and continue to make love to me!

A policeman dropped back and pulled out his walkie-talkie. I could tell he was getting the low-down on Aidan and me from the police who had taken up base down in the street in front of Candlestick.

"Aidan, why are you doing this?" I asked. "You have a good life! I know you don't have any really loving family still alive anywhere, except me, and your brother who would like to see you, I'm sure! You also have some good memories of your parents during the time they were alive! You have me, your roommate. You have a good job… we work together on the weekends… we have plenty of money… we have the sporting goods franchises… Why would you want to kill yourself?"

"Dion, I originally lied to you about my 'loving family'…!" Aidan sobbed again. A blond curl fluttered over one eye. "I made them up so you wouldn't blame my past for what I am now! I never knew my biological parents! I have no brother! It was all lies! I have been a foster kid all my life… used and abused… raped! I was a boy toy for the men who were supposed to be my fathers!" his six-pack abs and well-contoured chest jerked as he wept.

"You don't remember your biological parents? You never knew them? You don't have a brother?!" I exclaimed. I was shocked! He had built them up in my mind so much that I felt I knew them.

"No!" Aidan heaved. "I grew up going from foster care home to foster care home. Finally at 16 my foster parents at the time found me in bed with an 18 year old male. For punishment they set so many rules that I just left… I have been alone ever since…!" he looked over his back briefly at the street.

Aidan then turned to the street and teetered. "Bye Dion…!" he sobbed.

My heart raced, and I felt like my stomach was falling to my feet again. I gulped involuntarily. I wanted to run to Aidan, grab him, and then pull him off the ledge to safety. But I was afraid… afraid of causing him to jump… afraid of falling myself… afraid of betraying my intimate feelings for and relationship with Aidan… I hated myself for being ashamed of Aidan and our love in public! I was such a chicken shit, a traitor to Aidan!

"Aidan, what about your good job? You make a good living, and you make a difference at Bear Stearns! What about your mentoring, your…?" I was trying to get his mind on the good things in life, but Aidan's actions interrupted me.

Aidan again turned to face me so fast that he almost fell.

"My good job, Dion? My good job? I am a stripper, waiter, and high paid homosexual whore at a bisexual lounge downtown! That's really something to brag about! It is truly something to write home about! And I don't mentor anyone! Never have. You are just so damn perfect; I had to fabricate something, some lies, to make me sound better than my reality, more than what I am in your eyes! All of my 'life' I made up to impress you, Dion! I made it up so you would accept me… love me!" Aidan's face contorted in a huge breath and then sob exhalation.

"A stripper?" I croaked in surprise and shock. "Waiter? A high paid homosexual whore?!" I was now stunned. Aidan had claimed to be a stock broker at Bear Stearns downtown! I couldn't believe Aidan had gone to such lengths to create a fictitious past, just to impress me. I had been to his 'work place' at the Bear Stearns building… met people he knew … or claimed to know. My head was spinning.

"Aidan, I… I… do not know what to say. I did not know any of this! You told me… you lied to me to impress me?!" I was incredulous, kind of accusatory in my tone.

"My whole life, as I described to you during our first week or so together, is a lie, Dion! Don't you see that? I lied to you, to myself, and to everyone! I lead and have a crummy life, I drink too much, the avatar I take is a drug, I have sex with men for a living, and, in your mind, worst of all, I am… I am… gay!" Aidan paused for a breath and a sob. "Now that I have had to listen to the church and Mr. Hewitt preach about homosexuality being sin, I feel so… so… so cheap… dirty… and lost!" Aidan looked at his sandal shod feet. His shoulders heaved as he sobbed again. "I can't go on like this! Feeling guilty about myself, wondering if the things I do are a sin…! Trying to live UP to your standards, Dion… Trying to live UP to you!"

"Well, Aidan… We still have Viking Sporting Goods! We work hard together there on the weekends…!" I was now starting to panic. I did not know much if any of these revelations about Aidan. How could I talk him down when he kept shocking me?! "Aidan, we have grown Viking Sporting Goods into four stores now… we are very successful… You could quit the bisexual lounge job and we could work Viking full time!"

"Dion, Viking has been one bright spot… in a sea of ink, but we are not making the kind of money I told you! I lied again to make you feel like the stores were making a lot of money. They aren't, and there is no way I can quit my job… no way you can quit yours… to… to work full time at Viking! We cannot afford it! I am a lying failure all the way around." Aidan sobbed some more, as I was reeling about the truth.

"How about the money from your inheritance? Use yours, and I will use mine to prop up Viking…"

I didn't get any further. Aidan interrupted me.

"I don't have any inheritance money left! I lost it all in a rogue gambling session with my co-workers at The Flamingo Lounge!" Aidan exclaimed, his chest heaving. "I have lied to you about still having it because I didn't want you to think me foolish… Dion, I am a total failure! I have lied to you so much that I am not even sure what the truth is! I don't deserve you, Dion!"

My mind was overwhelmed at the magnitude of the deception Aidan had kept up with me just to 'keep me' in our relationship! Didn't he know I would never leave him? I didn't know whether to be hurt, impressed, or angry. At this point, I was just astounded.

"Aidan… I don't know… I am having trouble assimilating…" I stammered around for a response, something wise to say to assure Aidan it would be okay. "Aidan… your job, whatever it is… it has given you a very high standard of living! You have a beautiful apartment, a new car… you support us…" my voice trailed off.

"Dion! Didn't you hear me? I have sex with men for money! I am a high paid homosexual whore!" Aidan sounded exasperated. "Don't you get it?! Everything that I have, everything that I have been up to now, and everything that I am, is due to the fact that I am a gay prostitute!"

"So you've slept with a few guys…" I was still stunned and in denial.

"A few guys?! Dion, try hundreds of guys! I have slept with hundreds of men over the last seven years, Dion!" Aidan sobbed again at the admission. "I'm a dirty, promiscuous homosexual… I don't want to go on… I can't go on living like this…" his voice trailed off. He hung his head and turned again to face the street.

I was stunned, almost speechless, but curious and naïve. I pressed forward.

"Aidan, what about your investment with stock brokers at Bear Stearns, or where ever, that netted us $200,000.00? Wasn't that a good, wise decision of investing your money, where ever it came from? Sure, maybe yours is gone, but we still have my part… I will help you! It is about time I really did so! I owe it to us… I owe it to you!"

"Dion! That wasn't… I had sex… Dion, forgive me!" Aidan wretched and gagged. I thought he was going to collapse. I took two or three steps forward before he recovered.

"Dion! That $200,000.00… that money… it was no… I did not earn it from an investment!" Aidan turned his head as he heaved, shedding tears. "It was money… I earned that… It was money I earned from having sex with an 88 year-old man who was a client of mine at the Flamingo!"

I gagged. I was so astonished, so blown away! I froze. I was completely speechless.

"Dion, I didn't get very far into our session… I was giving him frottage and… and…" Aidan paused and looked pleadingly at me. For my part, I had no idea exactly what frottage meant, but I was so bewildered I didn't respond immediately.

"Dion, we… we were just rubbing each other in the missionary position and he died on top of me! It was disgusting!" Aidan wretched and gagged several times, spitting and drooling on the roof in front of him. "Dion, I am a scum, a lying piece of shit! I am a shallow, weak, deceitful and cheating lover! I will just kill myself and you can find someone better than I. Go get yourself someone like Thad. He is a better person than I!"

I felt like I was in a new nightmare! I could not be hearing these revelations from Aidan in this context. I was transfixed. I could not speak, even though I wanted to assure Aidan I still loved him despite his lies. I forced myself to speak though… I had to do something.

"Aidan, I trust you…You are every bit as good as Thad!" I finally managed uncertainly. "But despite from where the money came, you have shown your love by investing in the chain of sporting goods stores, Viking…"

"Dion! Didn't you see they were from the same man 'Maxson Josiah Wheeler'? Dion! I 'inherited' both from the same 88 year old homosexual client!" Aidan broke down again.

I stood in stark, dumb-founded confusion!

"Dion, the money and the chain store were gifts from my… my client… my dead client! He paid me for the last sex of his life!" Aidan choked again as he gagged.

I wretched, and tears welled up in my eyes. The gravity of Aidan's real job was beginning to dawn on me.

"The 'inheritance', Dion…" Aidan forged forward, "was the gift for giving sex to an 88 year-old man who had spent his life sleeping with men and cheating on his wife!" Aidan slowly and mournfully turned to face the street. He teetered and wobbled like a drunk.

I closed my eyes briefly as Aidan tottered on the ledge. The thought occurred to me again that he was likely drunk. I knew though that Aidan was extremely tolerant of alcohol and avatar. He must have consumed an inordinate amount of a hard liquor to be this drunk. How much had he actually drunk?!

The fact that Aidan was really wasted made my mission even more urgent!

Perhaps I could distract him, and learn some more with which to help Aidan. It was worth a try!

"Aidan, have… are you… did you take… are…" I didn't know quite how to ask this without causing more trouble. "Have you been… been drinking and… taking… taking avatar a lot since I went shopping?"

"What the hell does that have to do with this situation, Dion!?" Aidan whirled around again to face me. "I already told you I drink too much and take the drug avatar. I fail to see how it is relevant how much alcohol and avatar I consumed after you went shopping, or if I am drunk and high right now?!"

"Aidan, it is very important!" I responded as patiently as I could muster, given the circumstances. "If you are drunk and high, you are not thinking rationally! Have you been drinking, Aidan, and taking avatar heavily before you came up here to kill yourself?!"

Aidan hung his head. His sobbing had abated to an occasional quick inhalation and a shoulder jerk.

"Yes, I have been drinking and taking avatar… a lot… while you were shopping. Are you happy?!" he looked reproachfully at me before turning around to face the street again.

"Aidan, I beg of you!" I began. "Don't do this… this thing… killing yourself… when you are under the influence and not in your right mind?!"

There was a weighty pause, during which Aidan seemed to be thinking. His sobs began again, but were muted.

"The final straw, Dion? Do you know what the final straw is that brings me to take my life?" Aidan spoke to me, but remained fixated on the street below.

'There's more?!' I thought to myself. Another sense of foreboding descended on me.

"No, Aidan, I don't know…" I responded hesitantly.

"Do you remember three weeks ago when I came home battered and beaten, with my clothes torn and tattered… I was bloody and filthy… You had to clean me up? You helped me shower and then cared for my injuries?" Aidan turned to face me again, and teetered dangerously. I gulped in fear that he was falling.

"You mean that Friday? You were in a daze and crying? You were in pain all over." I remembered it well. Aidan had come home looking like hell, acting very hurt and scared, and very emotionally damaged. I had been unnerved to the bone. I had immediately nursed him, cleansed and cared for his wounds, held him, and comforted him. I knew something bad had happened, but Aidan had refused to talk about it. Aidan had then refused to make love to me, or allow me to make love to him for a week. He had inexplicably taken a week's vacation despite his boss's protestations. I had been very worried about him, and literally scared! However, I had had to buck up and be strong for Aidan's sake, and I had risen to the occasion.

"Yeah!" Aidan looked directly at me with the same scared, hurt, hunted, and scarred look he had had that night. I became very disconcerted and enervated just remembering it. I shuddered.

"Dion, something terrible happened that evening on my way out of work… I… I… It was humiliating… I…" Aidan sobbed, tears flowing down his cheeks again. I again fought the urge to run to him and try to save and comfort him.

"On that evening… I… I… I left work… I exited the rear door to the parking lot. I… I… I…" Aidan put his hands over his face, as the October breeze blew his gorgeous blond curls across his left eye. I wanted to hold him so badly! I wanted him so badly! He couldn't die!

"I did not see them!" Aidan seemed to draw some reserve strength and plunged forward. "I just did not see them! They were behind the door… hugging the wall of the Flamingo… as soon as the door closed, and I cleared the first… the first… the first line of cars… they came for me…" Aidan paused for what seemed an eternity. He was racked with sobs and tears flowed. During his pause I apprehensively speculated as to what the hell could have happened that would be so hard for Aidan to reveal, and so devastating, that he would be prepared to commit suicide.

"There were three of them… three against one… like there was before… but I had no help that Friday… no one knew they were waiting for me… no one to stop them…!" Aidan broke down to sob for a moment or two. "Dion, I love you… I never meant for it to happen… I fought them, I swear I did!… I didn't allow, invite it, or do it voluntarily. But… but… they were so strong…" He sank to his haunches, and teetered again as he sobbed. I felt sick as I realized he was closer to falling than ever during this evening's crisis!

"Aidan!" I called. "Aidan, I'm here for you! Please stand back up!" I held out my hands pleadingly.

Aidan wavered and tottered, but he stood back up on the ledge. Then he looked at me, begging me to understand.

"Dion! Don't hate me! Please?" Aidan sobbed anew.

I now realized that he was ebbing ever closer toward an admission that he at least had what society would call an 'abnormal' attachment to me. I looked around at the policemen that I could see. They were on guard, but it was a mix, some looking at me, some looking at Aidan. There was no sign of any understanding of our true relationship yet that I could distinguish. I felt safe still.

"Aidan, I don't hate you! I could never..." I said quietly. "What happened?"

"As I passed the first... the first... line of cars, the two bikers and Jaba the Hut came out of the... the... out of the gathering shadows... they grabbed me... they began beating me...!" Aidan stopped again, wiping his hands down over his face and eyes to clear the tears. "Dion! Dion... they... they... they beat me to the ground... then they... they... they stripped me, ripping my clothes... they stripped me naked and then... then... then one by one they... they... they raped me!" Aidan sank to his haunches again, and he lurched and trembled on the ledge.

My stomach was turning cartwheels. Suddenly all of the fear, shock, uncertainty, and concern over and for Aidan had taken its toll. I vomited up my entire dinner. My eyes watered so badly I couldn't see, and I was trembling so badly that I had to kneel whilst my stomach emptied.

I quickly began to clean my face off, as Aidan wavered on his haunches on the ledge. Once I had myself composed again, at least enough to speak, I stood up, shaking, and looked at Aidan.

"Aidan! Aidan... friend!... Please stand up!?" I implored him. "I'm here! I'm listening! But you have to stand up!"

Aidan flinched and then flailed briefly as he stood up. Several policemen gasped. I felt like I would simply die as well! I wished I had stayed home to prevent his drinking and drug consumption. Maybe then we wouldn't be here, Aidan threatening suicide, and I, trying to talk him down. Maybe I could have counseled him. Maybe I could have cheered him up. If nothing else I could have enticed him to a sexual encounter to take his mind off his troubles. If I hadn't gone shopping, maybe we would still be safe in our home talking or making love!

"Dion... Dion they didn't just... they didn't just rape me once each... they wouldn't stop!" Aidan wretched, and I turned my head briefly as he threw up his dinner and alcohol. When he recovered, he looked sadly at me. "I was in such pain... I was so... so... so humiliated! I felt so helpless... and the pain! They wouldn't quit! I was petrified you might find out and reject me...! I could not take that...!"

I thought back to that evening. I remembered that Aidan had been bleeding from several injuries of the skin and flesh around on his body. But I also remembered that he had been bleeding from the mouth, nose, penis, and the anus big time. He had even thrown up some blood. I had urged him to go to the hospital and the police, but he had resolutely refused. I had dealt with and cared for his injuries as best I could. Aidan had then gone to bed.

"Dion... I was brutally raped that evening... raped by three disgruntled prospective clients that... that I had refused to... to service several months ago at work...!" Aidan looked at me, the pain, misery, and humiliation evident on his face. "They raped me repeatedly... they raped me bareback... and as they left me half-unconscious in the parking lot... as they left me cowering in a fetal position on the cement... they said... they informed... they..." Aidan broke down again.

I was reeling! I didn't know what to think. I didn't know what I knew and didn't know with respect to all of Aidan's past. What I did know was that I loved Aidan! I wanted only him. At that moment I resolved first to get him down off the roof. Then we would get him help: counseling for his rape; his past verbal, emotional, physical, and sexual abuse from his foster fathers; and his mental health. In addition, I also would get him to continue counseling with me and Mr. Hewitt about his homosexuality.

I looked lovingly at Aidan, trying to convey my love, loyalty, and trust to him through my gaze. However, Aidan was not done unloading his soul and conscience of the truth.

"As they left, the three bikers..." Aidan trembled. "They told me that Jaba the Hut was HIV positive! Dion... Dion... I might have AIDS! I can't live like this, let alone die that way! That's why I am going to kill myself!"

I stood in stunned silence! My mind was in turmoil again with renewed emotions, shock, and slow understanding of what he had just said. He could have AIDS?! Billows of worry, concern, and fear washed over me! Before this moment, this evening, I was able to assuage myself that I was able to isolate the situation to a problem with which just Aidan had to deal alone. But then it occurred to me! I had given in to my hormones and emotions and had had sex with Aidan six times in the two weeks since

Aidan had allowed it, after he had been raped! We usually used protection. However, thinking back I realized that, of the six times we had made love during the last two weeks, we had used protection maybe twice. I couldn't remember exactly! At any rate, I was equally at risk of having AIDS now as Aidan! I felt like the pillars of my world were crashing down! I looked at my hands and pondered my new reality with desperation.

AIDS?! I realized now it would be prudent for me to join Aidan when he went to be tested for AIDS and STDs each quarter or so.

I was roused out of my stupor by Aidan. He turned back to the street, sobbing.

"Good Bye, Dion!" he said lovingly and softly. "I love you!"

I had to do something. I could tell I was losing him. I couldn't lose Aidan! He was my life!

"Please, God!" I prayed under my breath. "Please help me save Aidan! I love him so! I can't live without him!"

"Aidan!" I thought of another line of reasoning, but I must tread lightly lest I admit to all those waiting on the roof around me that I had an 'unnatural love' for Aidan. "You are like a brother to me. I need you to talk to, to help pay bills, to live with. So you are gay, I don't care! So your job is… is… is not what you have claimed it is! I couldn't care less, Aidan! That in no way changes how I feel about you!"

There was a weighty pause. Aidan looked down toward the street, and one policeman stepped back again into the shadows and began muttering into a walkie-talkie. I heard the policeman ask if something was in place, and then he nodded. I was searching for the words to get Aidan off the ledge. I didn't have to wait long. Aidan had some words for me.

"I'm like a brother to you, Dion!? A brother!?" Aidan turned slowly back to face me. I could tell he was angry. His tears had stopped as he stared at me in disbelief, resentment, and betrayal. He was agape with incredulity.

"Brother, Dion?! Merely a brother!?" Aidan's face was so good-looking, so attractive, his body so buff anyway, but he was also so gorgeous when angry! I felt guilty having these thoughts though, and I shook them out of my head.

"You know, Dion, that is what pisses me off. I'm gay! I admit it. I sleep with guys. I love to sleep with men! You preach to me about how homosexuality is wrong, a sin, and  evil!" Aidan was more than angry; he had just arrived at livid.

"And then you, me, we meet, move in together. It starts out as a move of convenience. But I was attracted to you, I was in love with you from the first sight of your dark, Greek-god looks and fine body! Damn it! I was in love with you from the moment I saw you on that bus! I believe you were in love with me instantly too!" Aidan continued. "We got to know each other, and developed a nice relationship!"

I found myself thinking about how Aidan's well-built and beautiful body was so hot naked; how I loved to sleep naked with him, holding one another! Then my mind and body wandered momentarily to the physical, sexual, and emotional thrill, pleasure, and ecstasy of making love to Aidan… it felt like heaven itself to make love to him and with him! I invoked the name of 'Jesus' under my breath to ward off those lewd thoughts! I forced myself to focus back on reality. If Aidan killed himself, I would not feel him, make love with him ever again! I couldn't bear that!

I wasn't prepared for where Aidan was going with his accusatory soliloquy.

"And then…" Aidan pointed his finger at me. He wasn't crying anymore. "And then you, Dion, Mr. Preacher… better than me Belmont, you make love to me! We have mad passionate sex together, the kind you brag to your friends about! And you loved it! You get right into it and you… you… do it almost as well as I do! I love making love with you, Dion!!"

My face turned bright red, and I could feel my heart race as all eyes turned to me. I could see some faces turning toward that 'now it makes sense, he's a fag too!' look. I had to save my reputation… I had to lie.

"Aidan, I have never slept with you…!" I couldn't say any more because Aidan angrily and dismissively interrupted me.

"You have had hot animal sex with me and loved it, Dion! At least 25 times we have made love to one another!" he still had his finger pointed at me. He ran his other hand through that gorgeous blond hair, staring challengingly at me. I felt the eyes of all those on the roof watching the drama look at me. I blushed red! …I heard myself speak.

"I have not slept with you!" I choked on the lie. I was getting angry now. I was humiliated and ashamed, and it was Aidan's fault! Why didn't he shut up?! But Aidan plunged onward with the truth.

"In fact, Dion, we have slept together 30 times in the last four months!" Aidan sounded pleased with himself. "I keep a diary and I can prove it!"

"It was only 28 times, Aidan! I too, keep a diary." I blurted out before I could stop myself. Oh well, I had to set the record straight! "… And the first time I didn't consent, I didn't know exactly what…what was going on… what I agreed to… I was drunk!"

I knew exactly what the police were now thinking. This whole episode is a fight between two lovers! Let both of the perverts die!

I felt dirty now, sinful. A wave of guilt coursed through my body. This episode was in fact close to a fight between lovers, I guessed.

I saw Aidan bristle. His face got red. You could have cut the emotions around all of us with a knife.

"Are you saying, Dion, that the first time we had sex that… that… that I… 'raped' you?!" He was almost hissing in anger.

"Y…Y…Yes and no, Aidan… I didn't want to…" I stammered.

Aidan interrupted again.

"I remember how the first time came about for us and we had sex, Dion!" Aidan exclaimed furiously. "It was my 26th birthday. I made some moves on you, Dion… and you… you said no!" Aidan choked back tears. "I backed off. You decided to have a drink to celebrate my birthday. The next thing I know, you are all over me! You begged me to have sex with you, Dion! I did not rape you! I love you, Tyler Aaron 'Dion' Belmont, but you keep denying me… denying the truth about… about you… and about us!" Aidan sobbed again.

"Look, Aidan!" I spoke quickly. "This is not important. Okay, we slept together! We made mistakes! But right now you need to get off the damn ledge!" I tried to be as firm as possible when all I really wanted to do was express my love to Aidan verbally and physically.

"A mistake?! We made *mistakes*?! Oh God, Dion! Are you for real?!" Aidan choked again, turned his head and upper torso away from me, and looked down at the street. He tottered there again, and my heart skipped a beat and sank to my feet. There was another weighty pause.

I felt ashamed! My words hurt Aidan and I could tell they did. But I also felt the feelings of disgust and condescension coming from the cops. I felt more ashamed now that my "secret" was out than over what I had just said to Aidan to hurt him. Aidan had just 'outed' me! The thought slammed through my brain like an elephant in a china shop, shattering my perceptions of my reality and faith wantonly.

"You want me to get off this ledge, Dion? You want me not to kill myself?" Aidan spoke quietly and in command again as he turned his upper body back to look accusingly at me.

"Yes, Aidan… Please do not kill yourself?!" I pleaded.

"You know, Dion, from the day that we knew about and admitted our love for each other, you have steadfastly refused to call yourself either 'gay' or 'homosexual'! You have denied the truth about yourself and us!" Aidan was clearly hurt, angry, and ready to challenge me to something. "Then we made our marriage commitment to each other that evening of Thursday, June 7. I expected you would now admit to your homosexuality. But no! To this day you deny yourself, you deny me, and you deny the truth!"

I was still bright red and hot with embarrassment.

"I have a proposition…" Aidan looked at me and spoke challengingly. "If you will admit here in public that you are gay, and that the times we slept together and the times we made love to each other you enjoyed, and that you love me as your spouse, I will come down, I'll live. Then we both can seek whatever helps for homosexuals about which you preach. I will agree to whatever counseling you want. If you cannot say here in public that you are gay, in love with me, and you enjoyed our intimacy, our sex, then I will take it as your rejection of me! I will jump to my death to free you!" he folded his ripped arms across his chest. "So what will it be, Dion?"

I was outraged and stunned! The terms were too much, too costly. Admit I was gay?! I still didn't consider myself gay. I had dated girls. Granted, I hadn't in the four months since meeting Aidan…

"Aidan, I can't… I'm not gay… I…" I found myself stammering. Lying definitely did not come easily for me.

"Okay, Dion…" Andrew turned rather violently back toward the street, wobbling on the ledge, "your secret will die with me." He stuck his foot resolutely over the edge.

I couldn't lose him! In that split second all the strong spiritual and emotional love, the tender times, the mutual support, and yes, the nights spent together and those spent making love to each other came flooding back through my mind. I did love him so! I felt the lovemaking, the sensations, and the intimacy! I had flashbacks of all the good times spent together on trips, the conversations in which we shared common ideas on all issues, the few times we did go to church together. I couldn't lose my spouse! Aidan and I shared a common destiny, a future together! Those things could not end this way!

"Aidan! Wait!" I started to cry. "You're right! I… I…"

Aidan turned to face me. I could see a look of hope, questioning, and anticipation come upon his gorgeous face.

"I… I am… I am g… gay!" I felt embarrassed, but somehow freed! "I… I do love you, and I did enjoy making… making love to you! I loved making love to and with you, Aidan!" I paused. "Truth is, Aidan, I can't live…live without you! I don't want to live without you! I love you, Aidan! Please come down!?"

CHAPTER 2

# MY ROSE-COLORED GLASSES

So many things happen in life that we later discover sculpted the adult that we have become. Sometimes things happen to us that are not pleasant or are downright painful. Ultimately we may just block those bad memories out so that we don't have to face them. In that case we tend to only remember the good times, the wonderful times, and those positive things that happened to us. We ban the bad things and times out of our mind. It is only later that someone or something we encounter forces us to face the memories, and we find that we didn't succeed in completely forgetting the bad times. I didn't realize it, but such was my life. I believed things were all rosy in my past for a long time, at least until the events I relate in this chronicle. Hopefully someone will benefit from my recount, and the recount of the others in this series, of our experiences, our successes, our failures, our sufferings, our ability to endure, and our fun, and we will not have lived, loved, laughed, enjoyed, and suffered in vain.

It all began innocently enough, as I suspect most things do begin. At least I led and convinced myself to believe things were innocent at my house. I was a naïve 'kid' from the farm. I lived, laughed, cried, and played there all of my first 21 years, working and enjoying the farm with: my younger brother, Tristan, who was two years my junior; my older sister, Soenya, who was three years my senior; my mother, Elisabeth, who was 22 years older than I; and my father, Steven, who was 24 years older than I. It was a good life there on the farm, or at least so I had managed to convince myself. My siblings and I worked hard, but we always had time for some fun!

21

My mom, Elisabeth, was a blond-haired blue-eyed lady, with a slender but well-toned feminine figure. She was 5'4" and 130 lbs. in weight, light complected, and very pretty. Mom was a hard worker, and a wonderful cook and homemaker. She was in charge of the house and keeping the inside in good shape. Mom was very kind and loving. She talked with us kids about our troubles, about our faith, and gave us good advice. She was as fine a talker as she was a listener, and she was very smart. Mom was a fine woman. I used to jokingly call Mom June, as in "June Cleaver". In a lot of ways she reminded me of Mrs. Cleaver, and I fancied that she really was June! I found her attractive enough that, when I was little and didn't know any better or understand everything, I used to joke that when I was old enough I was going to marry Mom and take her away from Dad!

My dad, Steven, was a very hard worker. He was a successful farmer who provided well for his family. Although some years' finances became tight, Dad still managed to build us, when I was five, a beautiful old Victorian style farmhouse with large, airy rooms and beautiful architecture. Dad was two years older than Mom. He was a handsome, intelligent man with a stature of 6'and, because of his fine musculature, he was about 210 lbs. He was very dark complected, with brown hair and brown eyes. He was such a looker that Mom used to worry that some other 'beautiful' woman would come and steal him away from her!

Dad had a complex character and had unique habits. He was often aloof from us kids, not one to talk to us as equals or to listen to us talk about our problems. He also was gruff and came across as being put upon when he had to do something for us. It wasn't like he was not a father to us, but it did seem that he had little time to spend with us and nurture us. I fancied him similar to Pa Ingalls in many ways, including work ethic, but totally different from Pa in how he related to us kids.

Soenya favored Mom. She too was blond-haired and blue-eyed, light complected, slender, and really beautiful. At the time of this memoir she had a stature of 5'7" and weighed about 185 lbs. It was hard to nail down her weight because she didn't want any of us to know for sure what her weight was. She was a typical young woman in that respect! Soenya worked with Mom all the time she was at home, helping Mom with all the housekeeping chores and cooking. Soenya was a kind, gentle, and loving person. She took care of us boys when we were little so Mom could get her work done around the house. We loved her dearly!

I am Tyler Aaron Belmont. I looked the most like my father. My mother told me all the time how gorgeously handsome I was and that I reminded her of the handsome 50s singer Dion from Dion and the Belmonts. Her only caveat there was that I was even more handsome than he. I didn't always have very high self-esteem, and I constantly down-played my looks.

At any rate, I was dark complected like Dad, and I shared the most handsome of his facial features, and the most handsome of mother's facial features. I had dark brown short hair in a brush cut on the sides and a wavy longer patch on top that I combed neatly. I had brown eyes, and a nicely buff body with a well-developed musculature that was a visual pleasure, but not grossly muscled. I was 5'11" and 195 lbs. I had graduated from high school as valedictorian, and in school had excelled in academics, honors society, student council, debate team, and some drama. I was physically capable of excelling in some athletics, but I was never interested in sports. I was never interested in hunting either. This earned me some derision from my dad and brother, both of whom liked to hunt.

During the course of each summer I would improve on my highly muscular, lithe, and yet slender body. In the winter I worked out often to keep my figure up. In the summer the sun browned my body to a beautiful darker complexion and the farm work kept my muscles bigger. During the winter I would go into town to tan. I kept myself very dark.

Tristan favored almost a perfect mix of Mom and Dad. At the time of these revelations he was 5'9", weighed 190 lbs, and was very physically fit. He was of average complexion, very handsome, and a strawberry blond with brown eyes. He was very athletic, well-built and sported a very physically attractive body. He was physically very handsome. He was bright and intelligent, a hard worker, and very helpful on the farm.

Tristan was also a ladies' man, courting girls from all over Gurnee and the surrounding areas. He was definitely not attracted to men, and was a vocal anti-homosexual guy, almost to the point of overcompensating. He was almost revolting in his proclamations against and disparaging comments about homosexuals and the gay lifestyle! For some reason when Tristan would go on an anti-gay tirade, I would quickly get angry. However, I kept my mouth shut, most of the time.

I remember a few times that I put Tristan in his place! One in particular sticks in my memory because I really shut Tristan up.

Tristan, while a freshman in high school, fell into the popular fad of calling everything that was bad, or strange, the name 'gay'. Those guys who were teased were called the derogatory gay bashing name 'cocksucker'. Finally, those who were 'cool' would go around and act like the stereotypical 'gay', hitting on other 'cool' guys for fun and laughs. They, including Tristan, thought this was uproariously funny to mock, belittle, and intimidate homosexuals in these manners. I thought it was ridiculous, and insulting in many ways!

One day in the summer after Tristan was out of the ninth grade and I had just finished my junior year of high school, Tristan invited a male friend, Robert, out to the farm to go swimming in our river pool and to help clean some of the barn. Robert was going to stay the night, and, as usual, was going to bunk with Tristan.

That day I happened into the upper floor hay mow of the cow barn as they were talking down in the lower part while they cleaned the stalls. I stopped to listen; yes, I know it wasn't right, but I was snoopy sometimes!

"So, Robert..." Tristan said derisively, "what did you think of the art teacher this year, Mr. DuBois?"

"O, dude!" Robert responded, chuckling. "He was so gay! I don't just mean he was an idiot. I think he is actually gay, dude! I hope we don't have him next year for anything!"

Now, I had had Mr. DuBois for art and economics in high school so far. I had really liked Mr. DuBois. He was nice looking, slender, and tall. He had been an excellent teacher, doing his best to answer questions, help students one-on-one if need be, and to grade everyone fairly. At these two opening comments from Tristan and Robert, I stopped moving hay bales to listen. I got down on my hands and knees and crept to the trap door that we threw the hay through down to the basement. I lay on my stomach and watched my brother and Robert below.

"Yeh! I think he was and is gay too! Literally!" Tristan stated emphatically as I heard him shoveling. "But he was also gay as in stupid, out to lunch, an idiot!"

"Well duh!" Robert replied. I heard the wheelbarrow move outside, and I heard Tristan whistling downstairs as he continued cleaning. There was a two or three minute pause in the conversation.

"But frankly, Tristan," Robert's voice heralded his return, "I think the fact that Mr. DuBois is actually gay, as in being into guys, is the worst thing about him. Willie said that Mr. DuBois tried to check him out at the urinals in the men's room one day! Isn't that so gay!"

"That's nothing!" Tristan piped up. He had a tendency not to want to be outdone. "Ray said he was approached by Mr. DuBois at the fair on the Fourth of July last summer. Ray said Mr. DuBois propositioned him to be his cocksucker, you know, give him a blow job! How gay!"

"I don't believe it!" Robert exclaimed. "Ray is such a liar!"

"I swear on a stack of Bibles that Ray also swore on a stack of Bibles that Mr. DuBois did that! You think Mr. DuBois wears those tight, straight-legged pants for anything other than to show off his package?! He asked Ray to suck his cock!" Tristan stopped and nodded. "I'm serious, dude!"

As I said, I had had Mr. DuBois, and I knew these vicious lies were not true. I was pissed that my idiot brother would fall for them! Mr. DuBois was not even remotely gay, let alone a stereotypical gay. I was getting steamed!

"And those specs of his! How gay! I mean, what the hell, dude! They're Rooster Brands for pities sake! How gay is that!" Tristan snorted condescendingly.

"You know, Tris, Mr. DuBois isn't married don't you?" Robert asked in a manner that made it sound like he had the piece de resistance that proved Mr. DuBois was gay.

I knew my brother wouldn't be outdone. Sure enough!

"I hear he lives with a school board member who himself is unmarried! Now whether or not you are gay, at their ages isn't it so gay to live with another guy?!" Tristan announced.

I knew Mr. DuBois had a steady girlfriend. He was dating Ms. LeFleur, the French teacher, and had been for three or four years. I was really getting angry! These two idiots! I had an idiot for a brother!

"Well, you know Robert…" Tristan copped a lusty, effeminate, and stereo typically gay voice, "we gays just have to stick together, if you know what I mean! We do get rather sticky, don't we!"

They both laughed. I sizzled!

At the time the reason I took offense was that I had a friend in my grade in school who was gay, and had come out to me looking for a supportive friend. If someone saw this junior in school they would swear that he was a heterosexual. He was on the football team and he was captain of the basketball team. He was a very handsome, well muscled, impressive young man. He was nowhere near the stereotypical gay man! I laughed then, and still laugh to this day that no one else knew he was gay! He pretended to date girls when it was required of him, and otherwise went out with other guys secretly on the side. However, some of his dates were 'out' to everyone, and endured some of the most outrageous hazing and treatment from their straight classmates. It was sickening!

I discreetly readjusted my position so that I could see them better. I listened a little more.

"That homework assignment in life skills class in May was so gay!" Robert complained as he worked.

"Yeh! It was so embarrassing to have to carry around an egg as a 'baby' for a whole damn week! How gay is that! I was mortified!" Tristan groaned.

"How did you keep it hidden at school? I never saw you with your egg. I mean we were supposed to carry it everywhere!" Robert inquired.

"I left it in my backpack in a bounce proof case I created that first day after school." Tristan, the ever innovative child, responded matter-of-factually.

"You weren't supposed to do that! That was against the rules!" Robert protested as he stopped working.

"And you are telling me that you actually carried your egg to every class, every day, for a week?!" Tristan snorted and then chuckled. "Man, you are so gay!"

"Shut the hell up, cocksucker!" Robert retorted.

There was a pause as I heard wheelbarrows being filled with manure.

"Still friends?" Tristan asked anxiously.

"Still friends!" Robert said emphatically.

I had my fuel for what I planned to say! I got up on my feet and bent down with my knees in my face. I fell forward into the open door through the floor, grabbing the opposite side. With the agility of a monkey, I swung down through the door and landed on the basement floor just feet from where Tristan and Robert were giving each other a hug. Both of them jumped when I landed and let out a yell. They separated and stepped back from each other, looking angrily at me.

"That wasn't cool, dude!" Robert exclaimed angrily. "How gay!"

"Really!" Tristan added, stepping toward me. "You cocksucker!"

"You know, for two boys who claim to be straight, the two of you seem to be really obsessed with being gay. You sound like two guys who may not be certain of your own sexuality. I think the ones in this barn who are really gay are you two! Have you ever considered admitting and exhibiting your sexual orientation to something other than the animals in here and each other?!" I walked three steps toward the two of them and leaned against a wooden pillar, staring the two of them down with a deadly serious look on my face.

"What makes you think we are gay!" Robert growled.

"Well, it is your conversation, and words you choose to throw around, and sometimes the tone of your voice!" I replied. "For instance, and I quote." I copped a voice like Tristan's. "That is so gay, this is so gay, isn't that gay? Wasn't that gay?" I mimicked Robert this time. "He's a cocksucker, He sucks cock!" I copped a gay voice. "We do get rather sticky, don't we?!" Then I went back to my own voice. "Need I say more as to why I think you both are gay?"

"I am not gay!" Robert proclaimed loudly.

"Neither am I, Tyler, and you know it!" Tristan snarled.

"He who protests most, fits the 'mold' most!" I said, laughing. "As far as Mr. DuBois, boys, he is not gay. He is with a girlfriend and has been for several years. You are so far off base there it isn't funny! In fact, it is actually infuriating!"

"He lives with another older man who is single, Tyler, give me a break!" Tristan held out a hand and sneered at me. "You honestly think two single straight men would live together?!"

"Happens all the time! They are called roommates! And this argument comes from one who is going to sleep in the same bed with his best friend tonight!" I rejoined as I laughed.

Robert and Tristan looked at one another and grimaced.

"We sleep together, Tyler, we don't poke one another!" Robert hissed. "You know that there is no other place to sleep here…!"

"There's the hay mow! But moving on, all guys who have both feet firmly rooted in heterosexuality know how to get out of taking that life skills class and do so. You two had to take life skills and carry around an egg for a week! I rest my case! If it walks like a duck, and talks like a duck, it must be a duck. You, my brother and his friend, are gay want-to-bes!" I turned, laughing, and walked out of the barn to leave them to ponder my words.

I never heard either of them say anything was 'gay' again. The name 'cocksucker' never again was one that they used to berate friends. And, to my knowledge, neither one ever talked in an effeminate, gay voice again.

We all worked hard on the farm and it wasn't easy! We raised everything it seemed like: cows, horses, goats, sheep, pigs, chickens, ducks, geese, and turkeys mostly. We awoke in the morning before sunrise during the fall, winter, and part of the spring times, and shortly after sunrise the rest of the year. We would have a hearty breakfast as a family, although often Dad would be out to the barns already. Then Mom and Soenya would clean up and do the dishes while the men dressed in work clothes and took off to do the chores.

Chores would be done during the next hour or so. Then we kids would hurry back to the house, shower, dress up for school, and get on the bus for a day of learning.

Our days ended by doing our homework and the evening chores, which kept us busy up until around 9:30 or 10:00. It was a lot of work, but then again none of us kids ever got into much of any trouble! We all worked hard, but life was good!

Mom was the consummate match-maker. She found Soenya's husband, and Soenya moved out when I was 20 and she was 23. Mom's favorite pastime was trying to set me up and marry me off. I remember one conversation by heart because it occurred word for word at least once every two to three months.

"Dion, dear," Mom would begin, "you have been working really hard for some time. You must really be lonely here on the farm, and you need a break! There is a social at the church Thursday. Why don't you ask (girl from around the community) and take her Thursday evening with you to attend the social? You and she will have some fun, get to know one another, and you will get a break from all the farm work that you do."

"Mom, I'm busy." I would reply.

"All work and no play will make a lonely and unhappy Dion…" Mom had nicknamed me Dion, after Dion and the Belmonts. At this point Mom would kiss my cheek and hug my neck. "Besides, Dion, you deserve some fun off the farm and in town!"

"Thursday I have to do (some barnyard chore), Mom! I cannot just drop it for Dad to do so I can go and have some fun! Dad will be irate if I do!" I'd plead.

"Dion, (name of local girl) is a nice, kind, moral girl. She's very pretty, very smart like you, and comes from a good family. She is perfect for you!" Mom would continue.

"Mom, (the name of the girl mom mentioned) is way too pretty and smart for an ugly country bumpkin like me. She wouldn't say yes to a date with me!" I'd protest. Usually I would become a bit red-faced.

"You aren't ugly, Dion!" Mom would state in a huffy voice. "You are more handsome and facially and physically appealing than your nick-namesake! Yours is the beautifully sculpted face of a Greek god, or a television star. Your body is brown as a nut, physically attractive and buff! You are a hard worker, honest as the day is long, and you have a bright future in whatever you set your mind to do! Any girl would be a fool to reject you!" Her voice was a firm, comforting purr at this point. I would smile and look bashfully at my strong, tanned hands.

"As for smarts, Dion, schools don't graduate a student grade-to-grade as the valedictorian for their athletic ability! You are top in your classes. You are every bit as smart as (name of this quarter's girl), and more." Mom was ever so sweet.

"None of which changes the fact, Mom, that I have to do (some chore) Thursday evening. If I don't do it, and Dad has to do it, he will be very angry!" I would state softly, but firmly.

It never failed, fortunately or unfortunately for me depending on one's perspective, that every time she pulled this, Mom had anticipated my response to her match-making.

"If that is your only objection, it's all settled then." She would purr. "You and (girl of the quarter) will go to the Thursday night church social. I have it all arranged with her parents. As far as your (some chore), I have told Tristan to take care of it. You are free Thursday night. Now, Dion, you go to the phone and call (girl of the quarter) and ask her out officially!"

Sometimes I would be thankful for Mother's interference, but sometimes I would be irritated that she insisted I date. Either way, she was Mom. I would go to the Thursday night church social with the girl of the quarter. Sometimes the girl and I would date for a while after. But it seemed every time I dated a girl, we would discover irreconcilable differences and break-up.

It never was that I didn't like girls. I had crushes on some of the girls in school with whom I grew up! Some of the girls that Mom fixed me up with I thought were hot, and I admired their various attributes up close and from a distance. I liked girls. I just couldn't find one that met my standards or that had characteristics, morals, and physical qualities with which I could fall in love!

I also had what I thought was a normal, healthy admiration for the physical and personal attributes of good-looking guys. I'd spend time admiring my own body in the mirror. I had some friends who were hot looking hunks, and at times I actually had what others could call a 'crush' on a guy, but I didn't know it. I never discussed my feelings for or interests in other guys with anyone. I just assumed I was a normal guy with normal feelings, attractions, and preferences for both sexes, but primarily girls for me! Any time I had an actual impure thought about a guy I would rebuke it in the 'name of Jesus' and go on.

Sometimes I would notice a particularly handsome brother, or hot male cousin of the girl with whom Mom had set me up that period. I would watch and admire them, become distracted thinking about them, and earn the ire of the girl I was supposed to be dating.

Other times at restaurants where I would take my female date, hot, handsome waiters or other handsome, physically attractive male patrons might draw my eye. I tried not to indulge, and asked God for forgiveness if it were wrong, but it still happened to me.

My younger brother, Tristan, was cute and physically fit like me. He and I worked at our various chores, and I enjoyed seeing his body lightly clothed. I knew though that this was not normal, and I would quickly clear my mind!

My family and I went to church regularly at a Pentecostal Charismatic church. But the church, for whatever reason, preached very little on the homosexual lifestyle and how and why it was a sin. I was looking for current life lessons there, not Bible lessons from the past! As I became old enough to understand that I was not so attracted to girls, but mostly to guys, I expected more guidance and teaching from the church I attended. Their deafening silence on the subject sounded like tacit approval and would prove to hurt me and others later in life.

My father, in his sex talk to each of us kids, spoke briefly about what homosexuality was, how stupid it was, how bad it was, and how unnatural it was, but pointed out only one scripture against it. It seemed to me that no one knew how to prove homosexuality was bad, and that all they could give was their stilted opinions about it!

I knew homosexuality was supposed to be a sin. However, I still thought admiringly of the physical attributes of good looking guys. I still visually 'feasted' upon hot male bodies and I found myself attracted to these guys; especially if they were smart, kind, and facially beautiful as well! I believed that these facts and feelings were normal, young male behavior. I swore to myself in justifying my behavior in this area, that if all males were truly honest, they would have to admit being attracted to a handsome guy at one time or another, or even several times, in their lives!

My life was good, but there came a time when I was offered a good job at a company called Computronix in a city suburbia called Aurora. I began to make plans to move there and take the job, not realizing my naïveté would betray me where I was going. I was gung-ho to go and start making money, live my own life, and be my own boss. I imagined getting married there and starting a family. I had several goals in my mind for my new life!

Before I officially took the job, I had to find a place to stay. For one week I started taking daily trips house-looking around my future place of employment. It was grueling and tiresome. I found many apartments, but none to my liking or in my price range. I was very discouraged. It was on my last trip of my first house-hunting week, whipped, emotionally drained, and frustrated that I met the man who would become an integral part of my life for years to come. I met Andrew.

# I SHOULD BE SO BLESSED!

It was a beautiful spring day. The early sun had already dried the dew as I finished my chores. The balmy spring breeze tickled my scalp as I returned to the house to get ready for my last trek of the week to Aurora to look for housing. I entered our beautiful huge Victorian farmhouse. In the mudroom I disrobed to my underwear, then took the stairs two at a time and hurried to my room. I grabbed my clean underwear and clothes and hurried to the large upstairs full bathroom. Once there I stripped, started the water, and jumped into the shower.

As I washed I admired my body and complexion. I was already developing my dark farmer's tan. To make my body the same color as my torso, I had been tanning regularly. However, there would be no more trips to the tanning salon until I got a place to stay in Aurora and became established there.

I thought of my search for housing. I had been unsuccessful so far at finding a place to live, and I wasn't thrilled at the prospect of returning next week to Aurora to continue looking for housing! It was a pain! I felt like I was begging people for a place to stay, even though I was only answering news ads! I hated this house hunt! I knew I needed to move to Aurora in order to take my job, but still I hated the hunt and then the bartering on the rent.

In no time at all I had finished my shower, dried off, and dressed. I had to hurry. I put on my socks and nice shoes, filled my cargo pants with my essentials; my wallet, comb, Puffs, checkbook, and keys. I left my bedroom in a hurry and headed for the stairs. For old times' sake, and the last time for a while, I hoped, I boarded the rail and slid all the way down the stairs on it. I had done this a lot when I was a child and as I grew up. I landed on both feet facing the stairs on the first floor.

I turned around to head to the kitchen, and gulped involuntarily. There was Dad, scowling at me.

"Uh! Hi, Dad! I ah… I thought…" I stammered. Dad always was an intimidating influence in the family, especially for me! I was scared to death at what he was doing up so early and what he wanted.

"That's the problem, Dion!" My Dad growled. "You don't think well! You know I don't like you sliding down the rail! Yet you keep doing it! Why!"

"Well, hopefully it is the last… the last time… I do it… I did it for old times' sake!" I spit out finally, looking at my hands as my face got red. I looked back up at Dad, whose countenance had now softened some. "Hopefully I can find a place to live today, Dad. Then I will be moving out soon!"

"I know… I know, so… so… I know, son." Dad said gruffly, his voice laced with emotion.

It had been a long time since he had called me son. I about fell over! At the same time I had something nudging my memory for recognition about this man that I needed to face and about which I needed to confront him. I sloughed it off.

"Well, come on, Dion!" Dad said to me in his rough tone. "I'll drive you today to the bus station!"

Again I almost fell over!

"What about your chores?!" I exclaimed, as I was in shock. Dad never left farm work undone when they were on a time schedule.

"Some are done. The rest will keep." Dad stated matter-of-fact like.

I pondered who this man was, and what he had done with my dad! Why this nice gesture all of a sudden?! What did Dad have up his sleeve?! Maybe he would actually talk to me on our way to the bus depot!?

However, our trip to the bus station was silent. Dad did not speak a word. I watched him for any sign of softness, care, concern, or any other emotion that I might grab onto to start a conversation. There was none.

Apparently this was Dad's stiff way of spending some time with me, his son, even though it was spent in silence! I had tried forever to earn his love, why should today be any different than any other day with Dad?! I settled myself to the fact that Dad was different! He had a hard time expressing emotions. I had to get used to that. He loved me, though he didn't know how to verbalize it.

We arrived at the bus station, and Dad drove the pickup right up to the door.

"I should have asked you this at home." Dad said in his usual gruff voice. "Do you have your tickets?"

"Yes, Dad, I do!" I replied brightly. "Actually I ordered them over the internet, so I pick them up when I arrive at the station. That way I don't forget them!"

"That's… I think that… is weird!" Dad said, skeptically. "Isn't technology great."

"Yeh!" I answered. I looked at Dad. He stared straight ahead out the front window. "Good bye, Dad." I said tentatively.

Dad looked at me. His look was strange. I couldn't really describe the emotion… I stared into his face for a couple of minutes. I decided it was a look… a look of… a look of longing, want, and loss? There was something more though! I couldn't place it! Oh well, I decided, he felt a loss at me leaving and not helping with the chores. Maybe he felt longing to take back some of our lost time, and spend it with me instead of away from me. If that were so, then the want was there because he wanted to say so, but he was too uncomfortable to do it.

"Good bye to you, Dion." Dad sighed, and returned to look straight out the window.

I disembarked from the pickup and shut the door. I headed straight for the station doors, and entered the lobby. Inside I stopped and procured a printout of my ticket from the first window that opened up. Then I hurried to the gate where my bus was boarding. I was a little tired already from chores. I would rest on the bus.

I boarded the bus. The front was filling up. I wanted to be alone, or at least in a less populated part of the bus where I was not assured of getting a seat mate. I went toward the back of the bus. It was pretty well wide open. I went to a seat that had empties on all sides, and plopped into a window seat for a rest on my way to Aurora.

I closed my eyes, checking my pockets 'by feel' for my wallet and checkbook. I don't know how long I had my eyes closed, but suddenly a voice disturbed my meditation. It was a soft, firm, and deep voice.

"Is this seat taken?" The voice inquired politely.

I looked up, opened my eyes, and gazed upon a blond Adonis pointing to the seat next to me. I did a double take! If there ever was a guy with whom I could fall in love at first sight, it was this drop-dead gorgeous, handsome, hot man! I felt my heart begin racing! He looked to be a little older than I was, but still in his 20s somewhere. His longer blond, curly hair framed his gorgeous, handsome face, and as I looked down his lithe body sculpted with manly curves in all the right places, I was jealous! He was ripped, muscular, and stunning! I longed for my body to be as sculpted as his was in all the right places that his was. He wore tight pants that showed off the form and curves of his… well… his…his package. His t-shirt showed off the contours of his fine chest, toned and taut, with fine six pack abs… If I had had a glass of water I would have thrown it on him so I could see more…like one could see in a wet t-shirt contest!

"Well?" He inquired again with a hopeful voice.

I was speechless as my eyes returned to his face. His cheek bones were so exquisitely defined; his beautiful dancing eyes, blue like the coastal waters of a Pacific Island in a calendar picture; beautiful, white, properly set teeth; pouty red lips; finely sized and placed mouth; with blemish and scar free skin on his face. His eyes were set evenly on his beautiful face, deeply enough to set off his fine forehead. His smile could set a wet carpet on fire, and I melted at that moment!

"Well?" His voice was gentle but sincere and persuasive. I had to answer it in the affirmative. He had a voice that willed you to obey, to come to him, to tell him everything. I melted again!

I managed to answer this glorious male specimen in front of me this time.

"S… Sure… I yean… I mean yes… I mean no… I mean, it's not taken until you sit down, sir. Seas have a pleat… I mean please… have a seat." I sounded like a blithering idiot, but I managed to get the words out! I stuttered out of sheer fear that my interest in this Adonis of a guy was too obvious. 'Lord, forgive me these thoughts!' I whispered silently as I castigated myself for being so swept away and awestruck with this man.

The blond Adonis sat down beside me, and I was treated to an intoxicating aroma of this man's cologne and deodorant. I closed my eyes and breathed deeply, smiling at the pleasure his scents brought. I hoped the man could smell my cologne and deodorant too. I certainly had put enough on that morning!

"The name is Andrew, Andrew DiPree." He said, holding out his hand. "And you are?"

I shook his hand. The minute our flesh met, I felt a sensation of security, oneness, and unity with Andrew! I couldn't explain it, but I felt so right holding his hand.

Andrew lingered holding my hand after we shook, looking me in the eyes and smiling at me. I felt his piercing blue eyes penetrate my soul, and I blushed.

"Tyler, Tyler Belmont." I answered. I took my hand back and looked out the window nervously. I wanted to visually feast on this man! Why did I suddenly feel this way so strongly? It was disgusting!

"I'm going home to my apartment in Aurora, Illinois. I had a gig here in Gurnee and it's done, so it is back home for me." Andrew settled into his seat. "What about…"

"Oh! You're in a band?" I asked innocently, interrupting him.

"Ah… well… I ah… yeh!" Andrew stopped. He didn't sound too certain. "Yes, that's it! I'm in a band! We are the Megatones! We do bars, parties, front for major celebrity band concerts and so forth. What about…"

"What instrument do you play?" I continued, again innocently interrupting Andrew.

"Ah… the ah… well, I play… I am versatile…" Andrew stumbled around again.

"What is your main instrument, Andrew?" I clarified my question a bit.

"I play… ah… mainly the… drums. Yes, the drums! I am a percussionist!" Andrew looked nervously at me. It seemed like he was hiding something.

"Where is the rest of your band? Don't you have a bus or something to transport you around? And if you travel public transportation, as I asked, where is the rest of your band?" I was really puzzled. Andrew set his jaw, and a certain unwavering look came over his gorgeous countenance.

"The rest of the band decided to stay in Gurnee for a party at a friend of a band member's house. I didn't want to stay. I have to get back to my regular job. They have the bus and instruments and all the rest of the band. I am alone!" Andrew looked at me happily and with certitude.

This time Andrew sounded more certain, more in control, and more truthful. I decided his earlier hem-hawing was due to the fact that he didn't know me, and I was making him nervous!

"In what genre of music does your band specialize, Andrew?" I inquired in a friendly manner.

"Huh?!" Andrew had a bewildered look on his face. "What the hell is 'genre'?"

"Genre means type or style. So my question is, what type or style of music does your band play the best? Rock, metal, classic, oldies, 80s…" I didn't get any further, because Andrew interrupted me.

"Oh, I understand!" He smiled brightly. "We play the 80s hits the best! We also do some of the 60s and 70s music."

"How long have you been in this band?" I asked, trying to keep our talk alive. I didn't want to sit with this hot hunk and be dumb in silence!

"What is this, Tyler, an interrogation?!" Andrew laughed, yet seemed a little annoyed. "Well, now, I guess it has been… well… I started Bears in 2003, and we started Megatones two years later, so… I think… Wow! Tyler, do you know, it has been five years! I can't believe it has been that long that we have been together as a band!" Andrew sighed contentedly and shook his head in amazement.

It was silent briefly as I was a little unsure of asking any more questions based on the reaction I had received from the last one.

"How old are you, Tyler?" Andrew changed the subject.

"I'm 21." I told him. "I just turned 21 on May 8, 2010. How about you?"

"I'm 25. I'll be 26 on June 20th." Andrew stated. "Is it your first trip to visit in the city?"

"Yes," I smiled tiredly, "but I am moving, not visiting. I need someplace to live. It is hard in this Obama Depression to find a place to live, do you realize that? That is what I have been doing all week; looking around Aurora, where my job is, for a house or apartment. I can't afford to lose this job just because I can't find a place to live! Jobs are so hard to find!"

"You have a job in Aurora, and you want to live in Aurora?" Andrew asked incredulously and excitedly.

"Yes." I responded, keeping my head against the headrest and looking sideways at Andrew. "Why, what's wrong?"

"Oh, nothing!" Andrew chuckled. "It's just interesting! As I said earlier when I told you my gig was over and I was returning home to Aurora, Aurora is where I live and work!"

"Really! That didn't register with me when you said it earlier!" I picked my head up and looked fully at Andrew. "We both will live and work in Aurora! What a coincidence!"

The mere thought that Andrew and I would be living in the same city, and maybe would see each other more, made my heart skip a beat and excitement to bubble up in my being.

"Yes!" Andrew nodded his head. "Hey, Tyler, we will have to do things together there in Aurora! I can show you the town! Then we could go to Chicago together and..."

"Whoa! Put the horse before the cart there, Andrew!" I put up a hand to stop him. "You are forgetting I have to find a place to live before any of that can happen!"

"That's true." Andrew's excitement changed to a look of disappointment. He lifted one of his awesome legs up and wedged it against the back of the seat in front of us. "No lodging is a problem if you expect to live there in Aurora. You don't want to live on the streets! That's no fun!"

There was another pause.

"So you have a job lined up to start soon in Aurora? What is it?" Andrew queried.

"Yes, I do. It is at the computer service, manufacturing, and distribution center on Hill Street. 'Computronix' I believe it is called." I nodded my head. " I will assemble computer systems, deliver, and install them. But first I will work in all the other departments. They want me to learn all the stages in their factory and company. Basically I have to start on the bottom rung of the ladder first."

"Most companies want their start-in employees to do that, learn from the bottom to the top." Andrew nodded. "Do you have any aspirations to ever go into management there?"

"Aw! I do not know." I looked out the window. "I haven't really planned that far ahead. After all as you can see, and already know, I don't even have a home yet so I can work there!"

There was another pause in the conversation. I looked out the window. We were getting close to Chicago. We were entering the far northern suburbs.

"Do you have a girlfriend?" Andrew's voice lowered, but it still cut the silence like a knife. He sounded like a spy.

I thought it was a strange question, but I answered anyway.

"No, I do not." I stated flatly. "How about you?"

"No… No." Andrew recovered and looked at me for a minute stroking his chin. He smiled coyly, like he was happy.

"My being single makes you happy, Andrew?" I smiled at him curiously. "Why are you smiling at my 'misfortune'?"

"I'm not smiling because of your misfortune, I am smiling because of my good fortune!" Andrew smiled at me in a sly and deceptive manner. "That is all I will say on that subject!"

We were quiet for a while. I pondered why someone as hot as Andrew wasn't married. In Gurnee he would have been married at 20 years of age at the very latest. All the available girls would have been all over him! It never occurred to me that he might be into guys.

"Do you come from a nice, traditional, all American family? You know, working Dad, homemaking Mom, and siblings?" Andrew asked casually.

"Yeh." I answered. "My dad is a farmer, and he does very well for us and with us. He is 45 years old. Mom is a fine woman, a good cook, and she does care for the house and family well. She is 43 years old. I have a sister who is married and 24 years old. She lives with her husband out of Gurnee. Finally I have a younger brother, Tristan. He is 19 years old."

"I bet your father is really handsome, and your mother very beautiful!" Andrew quietly exclaimed, as he gently and knowingly gave me an elbow and winked at me.

"Why do you say that?" I asked, puzzled by his statement. What did that have to do with our conversation?

"Because you are so stunningly handsome and incredibly attractive, Tyler!" Andrew stated, a look of sincerity on his face. Andrew fixed his gaze on me, like he wanted to see my reaction to his compliment.

"Thank you, Andrew!" I responded, blushing deeply.

"Let me guess! You most resemble… you most resemble…" Andrew reached over the seat arm with his right hand and gently took my chin, moving my face to different positions, and looking intently at my face in each position. As he did so the awesome smell of his cologne and deodorant tantalized and stimulated me. I felt myself growing…

"What are you doing, Andrew?" I queried with a little alarm. Secretly my heart was skipping. I felt limp like wet paper, and I continued to be aroused. It was very disturbing, yet very exciting! I didn't want Andrew to let go of my face, ever!

"I am trying to discover if the dominant features of your face, like your cheekbones, profile, nose, ears, teeth, eye spacing, etc. favor those of males, or if they more favor those of females." Andrew responded, his voice sounding like Detective Goran solving a crime.

"Well, what is your guess?" I asked, intrigued if he would get it right. "Do I have mainly my father's looks, or my mother's looks?"

"Well… based on… yes and you have the…" Andrew pondered my face some more, moving it into all the positions, and then starting over. "Yes, there it is… and your face is… God! You are so damn hot and gorgeous! Oh… I'm sorry! I just spoke my thoughts out loud! Forgive me, Tyler?"

"Yes, Yes! What is your verdict?!" I asked impatiently. If he knew that at his comment I had almost had my heart stop, and my stomach had turned over in elation, he wouldn't be so embarrassed about babbling his thoughts!

"It was hard, but I have it!" Andrew took his hand away from my face, leaving a void there. "You look most like your father! Your mother's features are subdued, but beautifully and artistically mixed with those of your dad to produce the exquisitely handsome and stunning creature that is you! You have the best features from both your mom and your dad!" Andrew sat back and looked at me questioningly. "Well, how did I do?"

I was shocked! It was as if Andrew knew my parents, or had seen them.

"You are exactly right!" I exclaimed in surprise. "I look the most like my dad, but my mom's best features melded with his to make my face and facial features! Everyone has said that all my life!"

Andrew smiled broadly and triumphantly.

"I can't believe you did that?" I enthused. "That's amazing!"

"Oh, it's no big deal!" Andrew said, blowing on his finger nails and polishing them on his shirt. "It is a skill no different than someone reading tarot cards, analyzing handwriting, or predicting the weather!"

I leaned my head back on the headrest and pondered Andrew's skill. The time passed. After five minutes I remembered another question I had for Andrew.

"How about you, Andrew? Do you have the typical, traditional family?"

"I have a brother, mother, and father…" Andrew's voice trailed off.

I wondered why Andrew answered that way. I raised my head and looked over at him. He was looking at his hands and biting his nails. The expression on his handsome face was one of sadness. He looked like a little kid who had just been punished for disobeying his mother.

"Where do you work, Andrew?" I decided to change the subject.

Andrew paused. I thought he wasn't going to answer. He continued to gnaw at his fingers and he continued to resemble a sad child. Finally he spoke.

"I am a stockbroker and day-trader at Bear Stearns. I oversee about 20 company stock accounts and 5 individual day-trader accounts." Andrew smiled at me. He was so gorgeous!

Again I had the thought that I wished he and I could get to know each other in a more intimate way. I prayed quickly for help and rejected the impure thought.

However, my purge didn't work. All I could do was look surreptitiously at Andrew, and dream of being with him, maybe living with him here in Aurora. 'How awesome that would be' I thought with much ecstasy!

We pulled into the bus station. 'Dang!' I thought 'now we have to part! I probably will never see Andrew again!' We both gathered up our stuff and headed to the door of the bus.

"Well, it was nice to meet you, Tyler!" Andrew didn't turn around. That was all right, because I was checking out his cute butt.

'Lord, forgive me?!' I thought, embarrassed.

"Yeh." I replied as an afterthought. "Same here, Andrew. I enjoyed seeing you and talking with you! Perhaps I'll see you around?!"

"Sure thing! Bye, Tyler. I'll look you up!" Then Andrew was gone into the crowd on the platform. I felt such a loss, and in a personal way I didn't want him to go! He seemed nice and I needed a roommate! Oh well, I was hungry too. I headed for the station restaurant.

# CHAPTER 4

# A KNIGHT IN SHINING ARMOR

I stepped through the open door into the relatively dark station restaurant and stopped to let my eyes adjust to the lack of light. Mentally and emotionally I was lamenting my loss of Andrew as though I had lost a well liked… no, more than that… like I had lost a… a… a girlfriend?! I wanted Andrew to come back to me!

I couldn't be feeling this way as a Christian! For a male to be attracted to another male in this manner was, in everybody's opinion that I had known growing up, a sin. I held their opinion too. Why?! I had no scripture, sound reasons, or facts to back up my opinion. Why should I believe it? What little I had been taught about the 'sin' of homosexuality came from my parents. Our church said it was wrong once in an eon. No one could show me the Biblical 'meat' that proved their opinions. I shook my head to clear the heresies causing me to question my beliefs that were beginning to percolate in my mind. I had to stop entertaining these questions and attacks!

In the station restaurant I went to the counter. 'I wish Andrew were here to eat lunch with me!' I thought woefully. I purchased a burger, drink, and fries, placed them on a tray, turned to the dining room, and then found a table. I sat down and put a napkin on my lap. I quickly bowed my head and said grace. I prayed for my food, for a place to live in Aurora, and to see Andrew again. I opened my eyes and looked at the food. It appeared delicious, but all I could think about was Andrew! I was becoming a bit melancholy over him. 'Stop it!' I almost said out loud, trying to shake myself free of the thoughts of Andrew!

I had just started to eat, lost in thoughts and desires about Andrew, when I heard that mellifluous voice again. It was so sexy, soft, and firm, yet friendly.

"Is this seat taken?" Andrew asked.

I felt a wave of joy flood over me, and my heart raced briefly as I slowly looked up.

"Are you kidding? No, it is not taken!" I said excitedly. "Please, join me! I am so happy to see you again!" I am afraid I was grinning from ear to ear, and I was so excited to see Andrew that I was wearing my emotions for and attraction to him on my sleeve! My spirit soared and I was thrilled! My emotions turned all positive, and my hormones raged attracting me to Andrew!

Andrew sat down directly across from me in the booth. He looked me in the face. We just stared at each other for a few minutes, drinking each other in. Andrew smiled and winked at me, and I smiled back at him.

"Hey, Tyler, we have to talk!" Andrew announced presently. "Can I impose on your lunch and talk to you?"

"Any time, Andrew! Any time!" I exclaimed happily. "May I continue eating my fries though? They cool fast!" I laughed nervously.

"Sure!" Andrew chuckled. He paused again and looked intently at me. "I've been thinking, Tyler. I am making payments on an apartment that can be suited for two people. My roommate moved out just last week. At some point I am going to have to have another roommate. I like you, and you like me, I think! We get along wonderfully! You need a place to stay, and I need a roomie. If you want to pay half the expenses, you could move in with me. It's not much, just an apartment in an apartment building called the Candlestick, but we could make it our home! Are you game to try it?"

I almost fell out of my chair. It was perfect! God's timing was incredible! I had just prayed for these things, and God answered all of my prayers positively in a matter of minutes!

"How many bedrooms are there?" I asked with baited breath.

"Mine, plus a study we could fix up for your bedroom. Are you game?" Andrew gave me a smile that would melt Tarzan's heart!

"Yes! I am definitely game!" I excitedly agreed. It was perfect! "That sounds great!"

Here I was moving in with a hunk! My place-to-stay problem was solved! Plus I had a roommate who was nice like a big brother. I had never had a big brother before. The prospect of more in our relationship also perversely interested me. I should have been wise enough to refuse the offer, knowing that I was attracted to Andrew for more than a friend. However, I felt I could handle any unexpected events that Andrew might bring my way. Besides, I would just treat him like a big brother. No one has a lovers' relationship with their big brother!

"Great!" Andrew exclaimed, smiling broadly at me. "It is settled then! You shall be my roommate. We will live together and share expenses. I look forward to having you… I mean being with you… ah… I mean being your roommate!"

"Thank you so much, Andrew!" I said, smiling broadly at him and nodding. "I don't know what to say!? This is an answer to prayer! I too, look forward to being your roommate! You are awesome, Andrew! Thank you for… for your invitation!"

"You're welcome, Tyler! No prob!" Andrew grinned rather… well… lustfully, raising one eyebrow as he gazed at me. "Well, I might just as well eat!" Andrew smiled pleasantly. "I'll be back and we can share our first meal! Then I will take you home with me to Candlestick!"

Andrew left the table and went to the counter to order. I watched him, appreciating the sculpted marvel of his physique. He was nicely muscled but not grossly so. He had a nice, round, cute butt, perfectly muscled, with strong arms and beautiful biceps and triceps. I had noticed too, that he was the same height as I. I wanted his body for my own! I was infatuated with him… I realized! I frowned and looked back at my food. Christian men should not feel this way about other men!

'What a break though!' I thought. A place to stay just landed in my lap! I was thankful, and I breathed thanks in a silent prayer to God. My need for a home was solved! I could take the job, and move out on my own with Andrew. I was ecstatic!

I continued to eat, pondering my plans, and planning my explanation to Mom and Dad about Andrew and our apartment, and my exit from my parents' home. My next step would be to find a way to bring down my bedroom furniture, computer system, my clothes, colognes, deodorants, and other belongings to our apartment in Aurora. I would probably have to borrow money from my parents to rent a U-Haul. I figured I could count on Andrew to help me, and maybe Tristan. I reckoned that hopefully we could move me and my belongings into Andrew's apartment over this weekend, or next weekend.

I looked back at Andrew who was standing at the counter. Again I admired his hot and attractive back, butt, and legs. He picked up his food and turned toward me and our table. I hoped he and I could be like brothers, compadres, and good friends. Yet I also wanted him and me to be more than that, to have a more intimate relationship…

Andrew flashed me a sweet, meaningful smile that caused my heart to leap as he strode to our table. I admired and marveled at his handsomeness and physique again. I could not help myself. He definitely had a perfectly sculpted male chest, which I could see because his t-shirt was so tight. His abdomen was also rippled, and that is how I knew he had pretty well formed six-pack abdominal muscles. I found myself checking out his crotch and package, which I mentioned before were not hidden at all by the tight jeans that Andrew wore. I immediately, however, felt guilty! 'God, please put a guard over my eyes and mind' I prayed. My thoughts, however, of lust for Andrew continued. 'God, where are you? Why do you allow me to have these thoughts? You could clear my mind with one word!' I thought, with a frustrated frown.

Then the thought occurred to me. All I was doing was admiring the perfection, the beauty, and the awesomeness of Andrew's body, which was a creation of God. I was actually complimenting God and the beauty of his design for the bodies of the species known as man! Why should I feel guilty for appreciating and taking pleasure in Andrew's sexually arousing, inviting, and titillating body, which was the handiwork of Father God?

"Well, Tyler," Andrew sat down and organized his food in front of him, "it's good to have you on board! We are going to have such fun and pleasure together!"

Andrew's beautiful blue eyes sparkled as he passed his hand through his blond curls.

He winked at me seductively and licked his lips for me. I blushed as a thrill coursed through my body from head to toe! Was he… ah… flirting? Maybe?!

"It's good to be on board, Andrew!" I reached out my hand to shake his. He extended his hand and we shook. Then we both returned to eating.

"I think that you and I will have such pleasant and enjoyable times together, Tyler!" Andrew stated as he ate. "As I said before you knew you had a home here in Aurora, I will show you the sights around here in the city. We can paint the town red! Then I will take you to Chicago and we can see all the tourist attractions there! Navy Pier, the Museum of Science and Industry, the Adler Planetarium, the art museum, the Sears Tower, and many other attractions, including shopping in the huge malls, await us in Chicago! How does that sound?"

"It sounds great!" I enthused, smiling happily at Andrew. "My family never had any time to take away from the farm, or enough money, really, to go anywhere but Six Flags in Gurnee. We only could afford one trip to Chicago while I was growing up, and we went to the Adler Planetarium. That was so long ago though, that I don't remember much about it. It would be great to see it again, and to see the other sights and sites of Chicago!"

"Great!" Andrew proclaimed. "They are set dates… ah… they are set plans for us for the future then!" He smiled and returned to eating.

I was cautiously excited. Andrew had said that his plans for showing me around were 'dates' before correcting himself! Was he as infatuated with me as I was with him? Did he… was he… did he have… some romantic feelings for me?

As I realized that my feelings for Andrew were indeed romantic, my conscience immediately kicked in, and I castigated myself. Guilt washed over me and I flushed. 'Tyler, you know absolutely nothing about Andrew, except his name!' I told myself. 'For all you know, he could be a serial killer! What are you doing feeling this close to him, and allowing these thoughts and feelings for Andrew into your mind and emotions! You have to snap out of it! It is wrong!'

"So, when will you move your things into our apartment?" Andrew took a bite of his burger, as his voice interrupted my thoughts and caused me to jump.

Andrew must have seen me jump. Through his food he apologized.

"I'm sorry, Tyler! I didn't mean to interrupt your thoughts and startle you! Forgive me?"

"Yeh, it's all right Andrew!" I exclaimed, chuckling. "I am very jumpy when I am lost in thought! It isn't your fault!"

"So, when will you move your stuff from Gurnee into our apartment?" Andrew inquired again, his voice more tender and gentle. He gazed at me expectantly, waiting for my response.

I melted into a puddle of… of… admiration and yes… love for Andrew! He was now saying 'our' apartment, and calling the apartment 'our home'! I was so impressed that he would do so so quickly! He was so giving, so… well… sharing and… loving!

"I'll call my parents and see if they can help me move this weekend. Of course it will depend on being able to rent a moving van and…"

"No need!" Andrew interrupted. He placed his left hand over my left hand. I was thrilled at the chemistry that came from his touch! "I have a friend who owns a moving van, and two other guy friends who will help us move you into our apartment. They all owe me some favors in return for favors or loans I made to them. They'll help us! We'll do it this weekend! In fact, tomorrow, Saturday, sounds good if it is all right with my friends and you! Is Saturday good for you?" Andrew looked at me with an inquisitive, hopeful look.

"Yes!" I was delighted! "Saturday is perfect, the sooner the better!" Then the thought occurred to me that my parents would want to be there and meet Andrew. "I will have to approve it through my parents first though. They will want to be home, and they will want to meet you. You know how parents want to meet and approve their kids' friends! Is that all right?"

"Sure!" Andrew answered. "I look forward to meeting the people who conceived and raised such an awesomely handsome and desirable stud like you! Here! Use my cell phone, call your folks, and get your permission from them now. Then I will call and line up my guys!" He proffered his cell phone.

"I... ah... well, I don't... I've never had a cell phone... I don't..." I stammered, embarrassed. We had never had a cell phone in the family. I didn't know how to operate one!

"Say no more! It's nothing to fret over! I can show you later how to operate a cell phone!" Andrew waved his hand and winked at me. "What is your number?"

I rattled off my home phone. Andrew dialed it, and then handed me the phone.

I heard it ring once, and then Mom answered the phone.

"This is the Belmont residence, Mrs. Belmont speaking." Mom said. "Who is this?"

"Mom! This is Tyler!" I informed her.

"Dion! Are you all right, honey? You aren't hurt are you?" Mom was clearly worried. I could hear the anxiety and fear in her voice.

"No, Mom! I'm not hurt! I am wonderful! I have a place to live lined up!" I gushed, barely able to contain my excitement.

"You do? Well, praise the Lord! Where is it?" Mom's voice still was mixed with worry and concern.

"I will live with a roommate in an apartment complex called... ah it is called..." I covered the mouth net and looked at Andrew for the answer, my eyebrows raised.

"Candlestick." Andrew responded quietly.

"The apartment complex is called Candlestick, Mom! My roommate and I will share expenses and..."

"How is it that you already have a roommate too?" Mom interrupted me. "You just lined up the apartment! How did you find a roommate so quickly, Dion?!" Mom sounded alarmed again.

"Well, the apartment is already in the hands of my roommate." I explained patiently. "He is the primary renter and has been for a long time! I am moving in with him. We will share expenses and I will..."

"What is his name, Dion?! What is your roommate's name?!" Mom asked anxiously, interrupting me again.

"His name is Andrew, Andrew DiPree! He is an awesome guy! He and I hit it off immediately when we met!" I was so excited that I almost told Mom the truth that I had only just met Andrew and had known him only three or four hours. I realized just in time that I should make it sound like I had known Andrew for a month or so, otherwise Mom would be worried sick!

"Andrew and I have talked on line for a month or so, so I knew him over the internet. Imagine my surprise and delight when we met on the bus to Aurora! He asked me to be his roommate, and I need the place to live so I can work here, so I said 'yes'! Doesn't God work in mysterious ways?!" I finished, beginning to feel guilty about my first ever lies to Mom.

"What do you know about this… this Andrew?" Mom queried, her voice cracking with concern and worry.

"Well, he is as tall as I am, blond-haired, blue-eyed, and he is 26 years old. He plays the drums in a band called the Megatones that performs around the area, and at his main job he works as a stockbroker and day trader at the Aurora office of Bear Stearns! Is that good enough, Mom?!" I asked, chuckling.

"At least that is a little relief." I could hear Mom nervously tapping the table in the background. "Seriously, Dion, you need to be careful with whom you become involved! You are moving to the big city! There are a lot of unsavory and downright evil elements that may drag you down in the city! I would feel much safer if you knew more about Andrew before you moved into his apartment!"

"Mom, it's all right! Andrew is a great guy! He is kind, handsome, strong, smart, and friendly! I'll be safe living here with him!" I assured her.

"I'd like to meet him first." Mom decidedly stated. "Can you and he come up to the farm this weekend so we can meet him and get to know him a bit?"

"Funny you should ask that! Actually Mother, that is what I called about. Is it all right if I, Andrew, and three of his friends come up to the farm with a moving van tomorrow, Saturday, June 2, to move all of my things down here to our apartment? At that time you can meet Andrew and assuage your concerns!" I waited with some apprehension for her answer.

"Well, I think that will be fine, Dion!" Mom returned with a sigh of relief. "I don't want you just moving in with a complete stranger that we do not know at least by name and face! I need to know you are going to be safe and that I know your roommate. I need to sound him out a little and feel whether or not I can trust him with you. We'll plan on seeing you Saturday then!"

We passed our pleasantries, and then our good byes, and we hung up. I looked happily at Andrew.

"It's all set with my folks! My mom is looking forward to meeting you! Now it is your turn to call your friends and set it up!" I handed Andrew his phone back.

"Where exactly do you live?" Andrew stuffed some fries into his mouth and took his phone from my hand.

"We live on a farm just outside of Gurnee, Illinois, to the northwest." I replied. "But how much will you all charge me? Any expense and I will have to borrow the money from my folks!"

"No charge. Not a penny!" Andrew flashed a sly smile and winked at me. "Let's just say you owe me, Tyler, and my friends will do it for free because they owe me." Andrew dragged on his pop.

"Gee! Thanks, Andrew!" I was stunned at his certainty and generosity. With that amount of help I could move into our apartment in one day! And it was all free!

"I have to use the restroom, and I will call my friends whilst I do so!" Andrew dabbed his face with the napkin. "I'll be back in a few, Tyler honey. Don't go anywhere!"

Andrew stood up, smiling. He winked suggestively at me. Then he turned and strode off toward the facilities.

Man! His smile was so charming, disarming, and sexually stimulating! It made me want to... Honey! It sank in at that moment that he had said 'I'll be back in a few, Tyler *honey*'! My heart beat faster, and I felt a rush as that reality set in. Andrew must like me a lot already. Did he like me for more than a friend or brother? I wouldn't call my best friend or my brother, Tristan, '*honey*'! I felt giddy with the prospect that Andrew and I might have some romantic chemistry going on.

The guilt set in again. I was playing with fire and the devil by flirting with, dabbling in, and entertaining these prurient feelings about and toward Andrew! At least that is what my parents and other Christians would probably say. I knew they would advise me to flee my growing attraction to Andrew by refusing his offer to be his roommate. They would tell me to bring my mind and thoughts under God's control and deny myself any prurient thoughts about Andrew.

But I couldn't help it! I didn't choose to have these thoughts and desires! They just seemed to be there. Besides, my mind, my hormones, my body, and my heart wanted to know Andrew better, more intimately. He was such a hunk, so gorgeous that I wanted him. My guilt was quickly overcome by curiosity and desire about Andrew.

I quickly finished eating my sandwich and then polished off my drink. Andrew was not back yet, so I decide to go up and order a malted. I stood up and roamed to the counter. I ordered a tropical malt. As I waited I turned sideways and leaned against the counter. My eyes were drawn to a developing scene. I watched a couple on the other side of the restaurant.

A man, probably about Andrew's age, sat with a woman about my age. They were eating lunch and talking. Things didn't appear to be going well however, because every other sentence or so one of them raised their voices, and I could barely hear some of the sentence clear over where I stood. During the times I could barely hear their conversation, whichever one was talking would gesticulate, wave their hands rather violently, and nod or shake their head. It was clear that they were fighting about something important.

Watching them fight, I wondered how God would create man and woman to be so different physically, functionally, mentally, and emotionally, and then expect them to marry, live together, get along together, and work together. It seemed to me to be so impossible, so difficult as to constitute such a waste of effort! Why didn't He create man and woman different physically, but the same functionally, mentally, and emotionally so that we could procreate, but not have the other differences to split us up?

The thought crossed my mind that the logical thing for a man who was looking for a spouse to do would be to hook up with a like-minded man. Who would know more about how to please another man in all ways, including sexually, than another man?! The same goes for women. I quickly banished the thought and said a short prayer! I couldn't keep harboring such thoughts that challenged God's creative wisdom and purpose!

My malt was done, and I picked it up. As I turned back toward my table I glanced over at the couple. I was just in time to see the woman throw her malt into the man's lap, and slap him hard across the face. She then got up and stormed out of the station restaurant, leaving the man sitting there with his arms out, looking bewildered. His lap was full of malted which was by now dripping big time on the floor. His cute face bore a look of growing anger.

I felt sorry for him. He needed a good… a fine… an awesome man… like Andrew. 'Did I say that?!' I thought ruefully. But even as I felt guilty, I realized I would not trade Andrew for any women or girl, even though I didn't know if Andrew was into guys, or if he wanted me romantically.

I returned to our table and sat down, nursing on my malted. As I continued to be lost in thought about why God created men and women to be so different, I heard a rustle next to me. I started to look up and saw Andrew's legs. I jumped again, almost throwing my malted.

"I seem to keep startling you!" Andrew said as he slid into the booth seat across from me. "I'm sorry! One of these days I will have to peel you off the ceiling if I don't be careful! Forgive me?"

"It's all right, Andrew!" I smiled. "As I said before I get lost in thought and I become very jumpy. Apology accepted. What did you find out with your buddies?"

"It's all set!" Andrew smiled and spoke triumphantly. "Saturday they will all come over to our apartment, and we will drive up to your house in Gurnee together. We will load up all of your stuff in the moving van and bring it down here to Aurora. They will help us unload, and then you and I will be responsible for putting everything away here in our apartment! Does it sound good?"

"It sounds great!" I replied, smiling.

There was a pause as Andrew finished eating.

"I miss my family in Florida terribly." Andrew changed the subject. He sounded lonely and forlorn. "Especially my younger brother, Noah. He's 21. Having you living with me will help me adjust. I can pretend you are Noah. Unless…" Andrew looked slyly and longingly up at me and half grinned. "Unless there is someone or something else you would like me to pretend that you are?" He winked at me.

"Well!" I responded, smiling at him. "Perhaps I could be your… well, you… could pretend I… that I am your… boy friend…" I wanted to say lover, but I figured it was too early for that! Besides, I couldn't seem to say it at that point. Something happened that I didn't understand, and I felt a restraint on saying 'lover' yet!

Andrew took the final swallows of his drink and then looked me in the eyes.

"You living with me will definitely be like having my younger brother staying with me. We'll have a blast! Maybe some time Noah can come and visit us and we could show him Chicago together!" Andrew sounded like a teenager enthused about having a friend over. His enthusiasm was catching.

"I'm looking forward to living with you and meeting Noah!" I added happily. "Well, I better go and purchase a ticket."

"What kind of ticket?" Andrew queried with a look of surprise on his handsome countenance.

"Well, a bus ticket, of course! Then I can catch the bus for home, and come back to see you in the morning!" I almost 'no duh'ed him, but instead I just gave him a curious look.

"Nonsense!" Andrew had another godsend idea. "You can spend the night on my couch, and in the morning we will drive up to begin bringing down your stuff. That way you can personally show us where you live without paying for another bus ticket!"

"Oh, I can afford another ticket! It's no problem!" I protested. "I don't want to put you to any more trouble. You are already doing me so many favors, I refuse to impose!"

Andrew waved his hand dismissively and smiled. "It is no imposition. It is settled. You'll spend the night with me, and guide us to your parents' place in the morning. Big brother has spoken!" He smiled brightly at me.

My opposition to the idea disappeared at the sight of that charming smile on his gorgeous face! I was spending the night with Andrew! 'Oooo that sounded so good! I was spending the night... with... Andrew!' I thought as I grinned in pleasure at the mere mention of that prospect. Instantly I felt guilty again. I couldn't have or entertain these prurient thoughts! What the hell was wrong with me! Damn!

# CHAPTER 5

# THE DRAGONLADY OF CANDLESTICK

Andrew and I finished eating, and we both picked up our debris and put it on our trays. I was so thrilled that I would be living with Andrew, someone I 'knew' and trusted! I was on cloud nine! I couldn't help smiling to myself at the prospect of living with Andrew. To have a big brother… to be so close to hot, gorgeous… sexy… Andrew… 'I can't think these thoughts!' I told myself.

We emptied our trays in the trash as we exited the station restaurant.

As soon as we were outside, and our eyes had adjusted to the bright sunlight, I went to the curb and stood. Andrew started down the sidewalk toward the west. As I stopped and took up position on the curb, Andrew stopped, turned, and gave me a pleasantly puzzled look.

"What are you doing?" Andrew walked back beside me and asked curiously, putting his hand on my shoulder. At his touch I felt the strong chemistry, a growing connection again with Andrew!

"Aren't we going to go to your place?" I innocently inquired as I looked up and down the street in front of us.

"Yes," Andrew answered in a confused tone. "But I still ask, what are you doing?!"

"Well, we need a taxi don't we? I am going to signal a taxi! Come on and help me." I responded in a manner of practicality. I waved at a passing taxi, but it zoomed on by.

"Tyler, you've watched too many old movies!" Andrew chuckled. "I don't take taxis anywhere unless my Dodge Intrepid breaks down. Only about 30% of Aurora's population requires taxis for transportation around the city. I have a car. Come on, I'll show you, Tyler!"

Andrew motioned for me to follow him, which I did, surprised at the large percentage of people in Aurora who apparently had vehicles. I saw a couple of taxis drive up, but he was right; not very many people were calling taxis. On the contrary there were parked cars on both sides of the street for two or three blocks. Some had people waiting inside. Others were empty.

I followed Andrew to the parking lot of the bus station, curious to see Andrew's vehicle.

"You've been to larger cities precious few times haven't you, Tyler?" Andrew asked, putting his right hand on my left shoulder, and alternately looking at me and the path in front of us.

"Yes, it has been precious few. As I said, I have been to Chicago once on a family vacation, and every Christmas we would travel to North Chicago to view the Christmas lights. Otherwise I have spent, as you said, precious few times in larger cities than Gurnee!" I looked at Andrew sheepishly. "It is a bit embarrassing, but we were largely homebound because of the farm and finances!"

"Aw! Tyler, it is nothing of which to be ashamed! Don't give me that sheepish look!" Andrew knocked my left cheek with his left clenched fist playfully. "That is something about you that I love and that I find very attractive; you are from a small, provincial town. That means you grew up honoring traditions, morals, and values that people from larger cities and megalopolises have long since abandoned. I want to go back to the old, traditional ways myself! But I want to go back with just the right person, a person who comes from that background, and who can help me learn the ropes!" I glanced at Andrew just in time. He winked at me and smiled warmly.

Andrew took his hand off my shoulder and pointed to a metallic plum colored Dodge Intrepid.

"Thar she be!" Andrew exclaimed proudly. "That is my car! That's my baby!"

"Wow!" I said quietly. "What year is it?"

"It is a model from 2009!" Andrew announced happily, beaming with pride.

Andrew's Dodge Intrepid was impressive! It looked brand new! There was no rust on it. It shone in the sunshine like a gem. It had awesome hubcaps and designer plates. The interior was a beautiful light lavender velour. From what I could see it had everything in the dashboard you could possible want as far as dials, gauges, controls, electronics, and a computer screen.

"She has everything! I had the dealer install all the extras: AC, heat, electric windows, electric seats and locks, a computer, GPS, ABS, automatic shift, remote start and locks. In general it has all the bells and whistles!" Andrew patted his Intrepid's roof affectionately. "She and I have just been looking for the right person with whom to share her abilities and creature comforts. Now we have found him!"

I was so awestruck that I wasn't even thinking about anything except the beauty of the vehicle before me.

"Whom did you find to share her with?" I asked jealously.

"Well!" Andrew smiled and gave me a 'you should know better' look. "He is you, of course! You silly goose!"

"Oh! I'm sorry! I mean… well, thanks! That is awesome!" I replied, kind of snapping to reality.

"That's nothing for which to apologize. You were just in awe of the dazzling splendor of this powerful and loaded babe before you, right?!" Andrew smiled broadly as he gazed expectantly at me.

"Yes, that is exactly it!" I breathed out softly. "I wasn't thinking… about… about an 'us'. This car is awesome, Andrew! I don't know what to say!"

"I assume you are licensed to drive in the state of Illinois are you not?" Andrew asked in a chipper voice.

"Yes, of course." I replied, feeling the smooth finish and marveling at the metallic sheen. It truly was a beautiful vehicle.

"Then what you can say is that you will share this vehicle with me until you buy your own." Andrew declared confidently, slapping the roof gently.

"You mean I can drive her sometimes?! I can drive your car?!" I asked in disbelief.

"Absolutely! I will want to ride along a time or two to test you out and make sure you are a competent driver, but then, absolutely you can drive her by yourself." Andrew winked at me and nodded as he spoke. "Now, let's get in. I want to get you home and show you our apartment."

We both entered the vehicle, Andrew in the driver's side, and I in the passenger side. We settled in our seats, buckled our belts, and Andrew started the engine. It purred to life as I continued to marvel at the beauty of the car's interior.

"She must have cost a pretty penny!" I commented, still in pleasured shock.

"Yes, but I am single, I have a low cost of living, and I have an awesome job that pays very well. I can afford it!" Andrew stated. "I paid cash for it."

"It's all paid for!" I raised my eyebrows and gave Andrew a surprised look.

"Absolutely!" Andrew exclaimed. "I wouldn't have it any other way. You see, I don't do business with or on credit of any kind."

With that said, Andrew drove me to his apartment. While he drove, he pointed out various city buildings, including the Bear Stearns offices where he worked. His workplace was in downtown Aurora in an eight story modern complex. He told me a little about how he had come to live in Aurora and how he had come to work at Bear Stearns.

As we continued to cruise home, Andrew pointed out some good restaurants and promised to take me there to eat. He pointed out Phillips Park Zoo as we passed it, and explained that would be a place he would take me. He pointed out the museum and a few other tourist sites that we would visit. After about fifteen minutes he announced we were almost there. I began really studying the landscape now, instead of just looking at buildings.

"Well, we are here!" Andrew announced a couple of minutes later. "It is that gray stone, 10 story building there." Andrew waved to his right, and I looked at the building. "Across the street there is the parking ramp."

Andrew pulled into the parking ramp and flashed a card of some kind in front of the UPC reader. A ticket popped out, and the blockade rose. Andrew took the ticket and proceeded through the raised blockade. He immediately turned left.

"I have lived here at least six years; therefore I have enough 'seniority' to have an assigned parking place near the entrance." Andrew announced proudly. He went down about eight cars and whipped into a parking place that did, indeed, have his name on a sign on the wall. I was impressed!

"Well, Tyler, let's pile out. Home is a waiting!" Andrew said flippantly.

We undid our seat belts and exited the vehicle. Andrew relocked the doors with his remote starter, and we met at the back end of his Intrepid.

Andrew smiled broadly at me. As I approached his left side, Andrew swung his left arm around my neck and rested his hand on my left shoulder. I tingled with enjoyment at his touch! I didn't realize one could crave something like this, but I craved Andrew's touch! It began to stimulate me sexually even! His deodorant and cologne tantalized not only my nose, but my hormones. I forced my mind to think of other things so I wouldn't become stimulated any further. It was hard keeping my thoughts under control when my hormones and my emotions to a lesser extent were charged and raging for Andrew and his touch!

"Candlestick has a beautiful edifice, as you shall see when we get to the entrance of the parking structure and go to cross the street." Andrew commented as we walked back to the entrance. "The building was built only ten years ago by the partner owners of my employer for an investment property and as a place where their employees could find lodging if they couldn't find any anywhere else. I came to Aurora, as I told you, seven years ago, and I have lived in Candlestick for six years. It is an awesome place to live!"

We reached the entrance and exited the ramp. Andrew used his left hand and arm around my neck to gently stop me. Once stopped he removed his arm from my neck and pointed up.

"Look, Tyler! Look her up and down!" Andrew exclaimed, waving his right arm expansively.

I looked Candlestick up and down in awe.

"What do you think so far?" Andrew asked curiously.

"Well, I'm a movin' on up, to the north side. To a deluxe apartment in the sky!" I sing-sang to him the Jefferson's theme, smiling back. "It's great!"

I looked up toward the sky. Candlestick was indeed ten stories tall. At the top, on the corners and at 10 to 12 foot intervals around the roof perimeter, large ornate cement candles spiraled into the sky a height that looked like about six feet tall. Below each candle on the wall of the building were ornate candle holders molded into the building trim. The candles and the trim were a pretty beige color.

I began scanning down the building. The outside walls were all light gray stone squares with uneven, rock-like surfaces. Each floor had beautiful, top of the line windows, one tall and rectangular, and one tall and rectangular but rounded at the top, off and on every ten feet all around the building. At the bottom of the windows on each level a window ledge traveled all around the building. Each appeared to be about three inches wide, and they too were beige.

As I scanned down to ground level, I noticed that on the ground floor the windows were different. First of all, a large, wide entrance was centered on the front of the building. The entrance sported a handicap entrance, and one large push door on either side. All three doors, and the walls in between and on either side all the way to the entrance walls were made of glass. Once the entrance walls jutted out toward the street, large, round-top bay windows were to be found every ten feet.

Candlestick was a huge building. It was a block and a half in length, and I estimated two-thirds of a block in width. It was symmetrical and magnificent. I whistled in wonderment!

"What are your thoughts, Tyler? Isn't it beautiful? This is our home! Are you going to be proud and happy to live here?" Andrew asked with a glowing smile on his face.

"This is… is… is graceful, lovely, and elegant! Absolutely I will be proud and happy to live here! It is… is… it is just breathtaking!" I couldn't believe my eyes. I was astonished at the beauty. And to think, it was my new home!

"Well, come on bro!" Andrew put his arm around my neck again and guided me to the street. I continued looking Candlestick up and down. As we walked, Andrew told me more about my new home.

"On the first floor there are no apartments. Instead, on the first floor the owners have provided the residents with a large swimming pool, a tennis court, a basketball court, a bowling alley, and two restaurants. On the second floor there are several apartments, a library, and a hall for resident use. You could have a reunion there, a seminar, or a birthday party. All of it is free to residents as long as we keep up our rent! We get cable, phone, WiFi, and high speed cable in all of our rooms! It is awesome!"

It felt wonderful to have Andrew's arm around my neck. His deodorant and cologne were intoxicating (I had to buy some of each scent!), and indicated he was a fragrance connoisseur like me. I had quite a large deodorant and cologne collection at home that I used to help cover up any leftover farm odors when I went out in public, to school, or to any public function. It just felt so good to have at least an older 'brother' with whom I shared so many things in common as I moved to the big city! I thanked the Lord!

We walked across the street, Andrew with his arm around my neck. I didn't think anything about it except it felt good in a 'brotherly love' sort of way. I didn't even think anything of it when pedestrians passing on the sidewalks or crossing the street, and those entering or exiting the parking ramp and apartment complex gave us knowing looks and whispers.

Before we entered Candlestick, Andrew again gently stopped me by tightening his arm around my neck and pulling back on my left shoulder with his hand.

"I have to check you in at the front desk as my new roommate. I'll do so by naming you as my brother, Tyler Belmont, same mother, different fathers. As a family member our rent will be 15% less than if you were a stranger. Let me do the talking, and don't let the bitch behind the counter, Mrs. Kurtz, rattle or upset you. Just remain quiet, let me do the talking, and I will handle this. Ka piche?" Andrew looked hopefully at me and smiled.

"Did you pass your previous roommate off as family?" I asked curiously.

"Yes, I did. But he was a different type of 'family' than you are currently. With him our arrangements were different. No biggie. Will you cooperate with me in registering as my brother?" Andrew squeezed my neck encouragingly and put his face close to mine, giving me a sad puppy dog look as he did so.

For some reason no flags raised at that comment. Looking back, I realize warning flags should have gone up at that point, but I'm not sure now that even if they did, I would have backed out of living with Andrew and whether I would have chosen a different path or not! I was so excited about having a place to live, the fact that the apartment complex was so beautiful and comfortable, and that I had a big brother for a roommate that I was overlooking any warning signs. All I saw were the positives.

I didn't like to lie, but at this point my sense of right and wrong seemed to be on hiatus, so I nodded and smiled at Andrew.

"Sure!" I answered. "I am your brother, same mother, different fathers! I got it!"

Andrew squeezed my neck again, and laid his head briefly against mine. It was so stimulating and loving. My heart skipped at the gesture. Why did I feel this way toward Andrew?!

"Thanks, Tyler! It will save us a considerable amount of money each month." Andrew explained as he removed his arm from around my neck.

Andrew pushed the door open and held it for me. I entered and Andrew followed. Inside the doors was a large elegant lobby, with stairs at the far end to the right, and elevators at the other left end. Marble floors, beautiful mahogany pillars, and potted palm trees finished the gorgeous and comforting ambiance.

In the lobby of the building Andrew guided me to the front desk. He rang the bell, and then said quietly to me:

"This bitch behind the desk is more bark than bite, but like I say, just let me do the talking!"

A portly woman came through the door from a back room. She was short, gray-haired, with black horn-rimmed glasses sitting low on her nose. She eyed us suspiciously, and gave me the once-over without her glasses. Without a smile she returned her glasses low on her nose, and looked at Andrew.

"Yes?" She seemed to be almost glaring at him.

"Mrs. Kurtz." Andrew began patiently and politely, and saluted in a formal way with his right hand. "This is my younger brother from … from…" suddenly Andrew looked at me and motioned below the desk for me to tell my hometown.

"From Gurnee, Illinois." I quickly interjected.

"From Gurnee, Illinois." Andrew picked up. "He will be my new roommate, Mrs. Kurtz. I need to get him registered, and I need a new family discount application." He smiled, and I could tell he was really turning on the charm.

Again Mrs. Kurtz removed her glasses, and this time she looked me up and down. Her face actually registered a brief period of pleasure as she scanned me from my feet to my face. However, she frowned again, and returned her cold, skeptical stare to Andrew.

"Likely story!" She exclaimed, her countenance clouding with anger. "Mr. DiPree, you have pulled some sneaky schemes and fast ones on me and on your fellow residents in your time! Each time you do, you come back to the scenes of your crimes asking for more favors, and trying to charm and flatter your way into more situations that benefit you. Now, Mr. DiPree, you wouldn't be passing this… this…," she glared at me again, "this boy toy off as your brother just to get the 15% discount on rent now would you?!"

She put her glasses back on and returned her fuming gaze to Andrew.

"Tell me the truth, DiPree! Are you pulling another trick on me!?" She barked.

"Mrs. Kurtz…" Andrew smiled broadly in what I would later realize was his beguiling smile to distract his detractors from the obvious. She was still glowering, but Andrew continued. "Would I lie to you?"

Mrs. Kurtz snorted in condescension and sarcasm.

"You would lie to God if it benefited you, DiPree!" She exclaimed in disdain. "Just like you lied to all those guys you double…," Mrs. Kurtz had a point to make, but Andrew interrupted.

"I have never lied to you have I, Mrs. Kurtz?" Andrew took his arms and folded them across his rippled chest. Then he flashed her the smile and look that would make Tarzan's heart melt.

I was puzzled about what Mrs. Kurtz had wanted to say. Why did Andrew interrupt her? Why did she call me a 'boy toy'? What did she mean by that? What 'guys' was Mrs. Kurtz talking about? What had Andrew allegedly done to them? How had Andrew allegedly lied to them? These and other questions arose in my mind, but quickly vanished as I watched Andrew charm his way into getting Mrs. Kurtz's approval for my family discount residency in his apartment.

After much flattery and cajoling, (and Andrew laid it on thick!), Mrs. Kurtz looked doubtfully at me.

"What is your name, young man?" She looked at me over her glasses, scowling. She was so homely and unhappy! I shuddered.

"Tyler Belmont, ma'am." I replied politely.

She stopped scowling, but didn't smile. She turned to Andrew and inquired slyly of him:

"Mr. DiPree, how come you and your 'brother' have different last names?" Mrs. Kurtz used her fingers to make air quotations around 'brother' as though she still didn't believe it.

"We have the same mother, but different fathers." Andrew didn't miss a beat.

"So the mother of you two was a slut, and now you, DiPree, you are a ho…"

"Mrs. Kurtz!" Andrew's raised and slightly alarmed voice interrupted the angry hag. "I know I have never mentioned him before, but Tyler is my half-brother! And, for your information, Mother was not a slut. She was simply married and divorced three times!"

"Hmmm!" Mrs. Kurtz once again looked at me from head to foot. "You look like a fine young man. However, I am not sure I believe you still…." she pushed her glasses up on her nose and reached under the desk.

"Mrs. Kurtz, I am Andrew's brother." I assured her, smiling.

"Well, I have my doubts about that! However, I cannot prove or disprove you, so fill these forms out and return them to me. They will officially register you, Mr. Belmont, in Candlestick. Mr. DiPree, here is your new family discount form." Mrs. Kurtz ordered as she handed me a packet of papers, and Andrew a double sided form. "In the meantime you can move in, Mr. Belmont, and live here, but read the rules of residency so you know the house rules. And Mr. DiPree," she turned on Andrew, "if you ever have parties with your 'brother' like you did with your last roommate, I will tear up your lease and kick you out into the street. I will not tolerate people with such noise and debauchery going on in their apartment, or people who so openly flaunt their alternative lifestyles living in my building. Do you understand?!"

"Yes ma'am!" Andrew saluted again as I folded up the three forms and the rules packet.

"I'll have these back to you by Monday, Mrs. Kurtz." I told her as I turned to leave.

Andrew quickly was by my right side again with his arm around my neck. He used as an excuse to get his arm there the delivering of a "noogie".

"How did I do, passing you off as my younger brother?" Andrew quietly asked, smiling, as we boarded an empty elevator.

I smelled Andrew's intoxicating cologne mixing with my own Curves cologne, and I felt a desire to be kissed by Andrew. I pushed the kissing thoughts out of my head. Andrew kept his arm around my neck, but now he began patting my chest with his hand wide open.

"You did swell, Andrew!" I chuckled. "But Mrs. Kurtz is still not 100% convinced."

"She will get over it." Andrew replied. "In the meantime we remain brothers, and act like brothers around her, okay?"

"Agreed." I answered.

Andrew removed his arm from around my neck. I immediately missed his loving and physical touch!

As we exited the elevator on the eighth floor, I couldn't help but ask.

"What did Mrs. Kurtz mean when she forbade 'debauchery' and 'alternative lifestyles' living in her apartments?"

Andrew looked a little uncomfortable, but he quickly recovered.

"Some tenants have wild parties with alcohol, drugs, and free sex, both hetero- and homo-, on the premises. Mrs. Kurtz wants to stop the parties, and she doesn't want same-sex couples in her apartments. She is on a one-woman campaign to get rid of gays and lesbians and other people with other alternative lifestyles from her apartments." Andrew unlocked his door. "However, the owners of Candlestick have so far prevented her from fulfilling her threats. All they agree to is an occasional change in the house rules."

"Why did she direct such venom on you, as though it were all your fault?" I pushed.

"My former roomie threw his share of wild parties while I worked. He was gay, and his parties were for homosexuals and lesbians. He got me, and basically the whole building, in trouble. Although the parties were not my fault, I was still blamed!" Andrew pushed open his apartment door, and the subject of conversation quickly changed.

"This is it!" Andrew exclaimed, waving his arms open in an expansive motion to the apartment.

# CHAPTER 6

# DYSFUNCTION CITY

For the first 16 years of my existence, my life was a string of one disaster after another. I was born to a Gertrude (Trudie) McKenna and Hans DiPree. I was named after the first of the Twelve Disciples of Jesus, one named Andrew. I didn't know this first hand, obviously, but when the Department of Child Services and Child Protective Services searched my parents' small apartment after their untimely demise, they found documentation to that effect and included it in my file. I saw it years later when I was fourteen, and remembered it with some pride to this day!

My parents, Hans and Trudie, died in a fatal alcohol-related crash when I was three. I had no living relatives willing or able to take me in and raise me, and no neighbors or friends in a position to take me into their home and raise me either. My parents had left no will or other documents directing who could or should assume responsibility for me, and so I was placed in foster care when I was three and a half. I had no brothers or sisters, and so I was all alone in the foster care system. I was told years later by one of the precious few good foster care workers that the first week in the foster care system I never stopped crying and screaming in fear and sadness!

The people who promote the foster care system will sing its praises to you night and day, but I witnessed its reality for the first 16 years of my life. I can summarize it in three words; hell on earth!

The foster care system was and is a miserable and destructive system that allowed the older children to bully, abuse, rape, sexually molest, beat, and otherwise terrorize the younger children. The workers were too busy, too calloused, too scared, too stupid, or otherwise unable to keep order and intervene on behalf of the abused children against the bullies. There were no punishments meted out on the perpetrators, the older children, for their crimes against the younger children! Basically the bullies ran wild, raping and pillaging the foster homes and the younger children, with no effective discipline methods employed by the workers or the foster parents to maintain order. Hell! The foster care system was forbidden by law, and they in turn forbade the foster parents, to employ the most effective method of discipline which is corporal punishment! Foster care system discipline consisted of 'time outs' and removal of 'privileges'! Gee whiz, you mean I have to sit down and rest for punishment! I won't do that again…. NOT! Wow, I don't get to watch TV in the living room, but must sit alone in my room? I'll watch TV there! I won't do that again…. NOT!

It pisses me off to this day that no one in the foster care system intervened on my behalf, or on behalf of the other younger children picked as targets, against the older bullies! I knew many foster children who were raped, molested, and injured during attacks by older, more mature, stronger, and definitely worldlier children. I, myself, was beaten up and sexually molested several times, and raped a few times by older boys and older girls while in the custody of the foster care system, or one of their 'state approved' foster care homes. It is a disgusting, on-going tragedy that only gets worse as the perpetrators become more and more emboldened by the lack of discipline and enforcement. The crimes become worse and more heinous each time a foster care worker or foster parent failed to effectively enforce the rules and punish the perpetrators. I witnessed this phenomenon first-hand too.

Then there were the foster care system workers. I don't mean to dump on the good ones, but none of the workers I experienced were competent at their job. A bigger bunch of disorganized, dangerously lax, lazy, incompetent, untrustworthy, dishonest, and undependable boobs I have never before seen in my life, and I hope I never witness again!

I was told by the worker(s) each time they placed me in a home, that they, the worker(s) would be back for monthly visits to assess my treatment and progress. They would leave, and I would not see them again until they came to remove me to a new foster care home.

Workers would write reports to the next parents who were going to care for me to 'inform' them about me, my attitude, my character, my intelligence, and my progress. I managed to sneak and read a few. A big bunch of lies and bizarre untruths were in those reports, and I say to this day it is no wonder so many foster parents did not give me a chance!

I overheard some of my foster parents at different homes call my foster care worker or agency and request different information or forms be sent to them so they could switch my doctors, dentists, get my Medicaid renewed or switched, sign me up for WIC or whatever other programs they could get, and other sundry requests for help. Nothing would happen for weeks, sometimes months. Meanwhile, often the foster parents would take the situation out on me. I wouldn't get medical care, dental care, enough food, or not the right food, or I would be singled out for particularly harsh and abusive punishments and treatments! They would mentally, emotionally, physically, or sexually abuse me. This didn't happen all the time, but it happened enough for me to live in fear when the foster parents' requests of the foster care system were not answered in a timely fashion.

To add insult to injury, because the foster care system had so lied about my character and behavior, no one in the foster care system would believe me when I reported anything wrong. I finally stopped reporting any abuse or any mistakes for my own good. I didn't want things to get worse!

I witnessed several workers who came to take me back to the foster care shelter until a home could be found, arrive at my current foster care home that I was to leave without my file and without the proper documentation. I was frequently moved from foster home to foster home the first 16 years of my life. Each time, one or more foster care workers or counselors would come to pick up me and my things to move me to either a new home, or a foster care shelter in lieu of a new home. Most of the time these foster care officials did not have my file, any information, or any proper and legal documentation. A brief perusal of their satchels and/or suitcases of materials was like viewing a disaster area. It is hard to imagine they could find anything of importance to anyone's case in the rubble that existed there!

I had to appear in court several times during those twelve and a half years for various reasons. My foster care workers would prep me for court by telling me this would happen, that would happen, judge would do this, judge would ask this, etc. The worker would inform me of the things they were going to say, and the documents they would present. I would go to court fully expecting things to go as my foster care worker said they would. Unfortunately, I would inevitably leave court reeling, because my worker would be late, they would not be prepared, none of the things they said would happen actually happened, and the things they said they would say and the documents they said they would submit also never happened. It was disgraceful and damaging to me!

Then there were the state established standards for how prospective foster parents and foster care homes should be evaluated, approved, and monitored, and the workers charged with enforcing them. I don't know what the hell all their standards were, but every foster home I was placed in missed the bar in several ways of which I did know. At least half of the homes in which I was placed during my twelve and a half years of slavery in the foster care system were outright disasters, where parents were abusive verbally, emotionally, sexually, and physically! They all were real gems, fine examples of your federal and state tax dollars at work! There was not one foster home in which I lived that did not violate at least five standards that I knew the foster care system supposedly had established for care of foster children. The worst examples of foster homes in which I lived, about 24 out of 45 homes and 36 parents out of about 80, violated 10-15 standards regularly and grossly for the whole time that I lived there.

How some of the foster parents that I had ever got approved by the state I will never know. I had foster parents beat me, and almost all of them would verbally assault me. I had several who physically assaulted me and beat the crap out of me. I had at least six fathers rape me and sexually abuse me as a child. It was an outrage! And yet these people had been approved and no one knew, I guess?! As I said, early on I tried to report these abuses by foster parents and workers to the foster care system. However, it was my word against the 'licensed' and 'trusted' foster parents and workers, and the system had made sure I had such a bad reputation that no one believed me. I finally quit reporting anything for my own safety!

At any rate, back to me personally, Andrew DiPree.

For me a typical placement in a foster home followed a pattern I established at the first home in which I was placed. I resented the new "parents"; they were alive and mine were dead. I sometimes refused to obey the house mother, and often never bonded with the house father. I wouldn't even let the house father get to know me. I have to say all of this wasn't my fault because house fathers worked so much they were rarely around. I felt they were absent because they didn't like me, so when they were around I wouldn't give them the time of day. I believed the fathers that were around were more interested in beating me, ignoring me, having sex with me, molesting me, or verbally berating me than in bonding with me in a fatherly way!

My life as a child consisted of: placement in a foster home by an incompetent foster care worker; adaptation to the new home and its expectations; counseling for my problems, including anger management, depression, ADHD, and later sexual identity; rejection by me of the new home, new parents, and the constraints on my life therein; disobedience by me of the foster parents, their rules, counseling rules, and foster care rules in general; and finally removal to a new foster home because the parents of the one I was in wanted to get rid of me. Then the cycle would repeat over and over again. I spent my childhood in up to 45 different foster homes over my life from 3 ½ years to 16 years. Once I reached 16,  I escaped the system and struck out on my own.

At any rate, my disobedience and rebellion, and the rejection and treatment I had suffered particularly at the hands of all of my foster fathers, and to a lesser extent the treatment from the foster mothers, left me isolated, alone, and subconsciously craving male companionship and approval. This craving was hard to fill because: I didn't trust men, having been abused by so many men; I was afraid of men, and I was hesitant to get too close to any man for fear he would hurt me somehow. Yet it was men, or male leadership, influence, and companionship that I most wanted! This left a void in my life that I sought to fill with whatever would provide temporary relief from the loneliness and emotional losses, bad memories, nightmares, and lack of male influence, companionship, and approval that I felt. To fill the void, or at least to assuage me and my inner turmoil, at the age of twelve I began drinking, and at the age of thirteen I began smoking pot.

When I was only in the fourth grade I realized I preferred spending time with and looking at other guys that I thought might fulfill my need for male companionship, approval, and support in all ways. I found myself watching guys in the men's room to see if I could get a peek at their… well… their package. I found myself trying my best to spend time with other boys my age to whom I was attracted. I approached two or three other boys in my grade with the idea that 'if you show me yours, I will show you mine'. We showed each other. Needless to say, at this point girls didn't interest me for anything other than friends.

As I continued through fourth and on into fifth, I continued to grow in my cravings and desires for males to fill my needs. My crushes on other boys in my grades increased. There was more display of our privates between me and several other boys in each grade. I also had my first crushes on two male, young, buff, and handsome new teachers.

By the seventh grade my cravings had turned sexual. I recognized that I was not only having a crush on this boy, that boy, or that male teacher, I wanted to sleep with them. Now, at this age I still did not understand completely how two males would begin to have sex. Even though by this time I had been sexually molested and raped, I didn't yet equate this 'sex' with love between males. I didn't understand that the sex acts that other boys and foster fathers had used to abuse me up to this point were, when done out of a profound sense of love and commitment, the same acts males employed to 'make love' or 'sleep together'! My idea of two males 'sleeping together' was that we would sleep together naked, and just hold one another.

At the age of eleven I had my first consensual sexual experience with a male. There were students that came down from the high school to the various schools of the lower grades to be teachers' aides. They received credit for a work class learning a trade. A blond-haired, blue-eyed, handsome, hot senior boy named Anthony was assigned as a teacher's aide in our math class. From the first day I saw him, I was in love! Over the course of two months I interjected myself into his life and activities as a teacher's aide. I flirted shamelessly, and found ways to let him know that if he were interested, I was interested. Finally he became interested, and he and I met in the bathroom after school and played with each other naked.

The weird thing was that from the ages of eleven to seventeen I tried dating girls. After all, girls made up the majority of my better friends, and I was more awkward and unnerved around boys. The logic I held was that since girls were my best friends, they would easily date me. Further, since I had a shyness and fear around boys, even though I craved and desired them, I felt safe and often very sad that I'd never be with guys as anything other than friends.

Boy was I wrong! No girl would date me once, let alone date me seriously! Hardly any girls would let me get a request for a date out of my mouth before they had to wash their hair, go to class (even though school was long since out!), go home because they could hear their mother calling, or change their feminine utensil. I was rejected at every turn by girls over and over! This forced me to pursue other guys to fulfill my internal emotional, physical, and sexual needs. Thus my internal cravings and desires toward guys that I had felt since fourth grade, all jumbled up inside with the increase in hormones, teenage emotions, and anger were reinforced by my past bad experiences and personal reality with respect to girls.

As I said, at the age of eleven I had my first sexual experience with blond-haired, blue-eyed Anthony, a male senior. It seemed to have fulfilled some of my needs for male approval, male bonding, and male influence. It certainly was very pleasurable, stimulating, and pleasant, and I enjoyed it! I came to believe only a guy would know all the ways to sexually please another guy the best. From then forward I had fondle/play time with various boys of various ages several times a month.

It was after Anthony that I had my first consensual homosexual relationship, that included for the first time oral sex, with a dark complected, sandy-haired fox named 'Mark' from the twelfth grade. Our relationship lasted for about six weeks, and I coveted and enjoyed it! It was also the first relationship I had with another boy where our break-up really broke my heart. I had been head-over-heels in love with Mark, and I thought he felt the same way about me. I was crushed when he ended 'us'.

At the age of 14, getting lanky, handsome, and muscular, I had an affair with a young, handsome, male teacher. It was during this affair that I first went all the way sexually. Mr. Lyons was his name, 25 years old, thick black hair, beautiful body, and handsome! Lord have mercy, was he handsome! Wow! The affair was a torrid, passionate, and lascivious one. Mr. Lyons taught me so many positions and sexual things between men that caused intense pleasure and hormonal rush, that I actually would go days without drinking anything alcoholic. That affair was the first time I decided and admitted I was gay.

From the ages of 14 to 16 I was sexually involved with probably 15 different guys. Eight were fellow male students of various ages. Seven, however, were males age 18 to 35, including a second teacher, a friend's father, my dentist, a doctor, two lawyers and a businessman.

At the age of sixteen my foster parents at the time found me in bed with a boy of eighteen whom I had sneaked into my bedroom through the window for a sheet session. They were very horrified and angry and set several new rules to "deal" with me. They decreed I couldn't go out to after school functions of any kind. In effect I was grounded. However, they would let me go to any church activity. I wasn't interested in religion! They also took away my computer from my room. I was irate and I wanted my freedom!

I left their house and ran away, rebellious and heart set on being independent. I took what few clothes and belongings I had with me, and headed for Chicago. I knew that in Chicago I could find work, and an accepting gay community to help me until I managed to get on my feet. I didn't even think about what dangers might befall me there!

I got as far as Aurora, Illinois, west of Chicago, and I ran out of money. I had to stay on the streets or in shelters for several months.

After several days on the streets of Aurora scrounging dumpsters for food, I was unshaven, dirty, disheveled, and smelly I am sure! I was approached by a well dressed, slender, nice-looking man with graying temples. He asked me if he could pay me for some sexual favors. I agreed, after all I had already done it all to many boys and men already! He offered me $200.00 for an all night session. He also said I could sleep in the bed with him until morning after we were done. Sleep in an actual bed with just sex as my work?! I was totally game! I wouldn't have to sleep in my box! There was one catch. I had to shower, shave, and clean up. This was getting better and better! I definitely agreed then, because I wanted a shower so badly.

Thus began my months of prostituting myself out to males at $100.00 per hour. I had sex with so many men I lost count after about fifty. I always bought and used condoms, and didn't even think or worry about venereal diseases.

Life was rough for those thirteen months on the streets and in shelters, as I turned tricks, and tried to avoid getting beaten up by disgruntled clients and fellow prostitutes. I also had to avoid the police so I wouldn't be arrested. My life consisted of soliciting customers during the day on the streets, in bars, restaurants, and in malls, all the while looking over my shoulders to avoid the cops. At night I would service the customers I had lined up that day where ever they chose as the location for our encounter, and try again to avoid the cops. It was exhausting!

I had many close calls with the cops. I was beaten up by gay and straight males ten times. There were three beatings that would have placed me in the hospital, but I simply refused to go. Some client would take pity on me and help me until I had recovered.

I acquired pneumonia at one point during the winter, and a nice lesbian couple found me almost dead in my alley. They were going to take me to the hospital, but I explained I couldn't go to any hospital or doctor without money or insurance. They reluctantly took me to their home and nursed me back to health, giving me extra antibiotics they had from previous sinus infections and other illnesses they had had in the past. I was so thankful, and I still see them occasionally.

During the thirteen months that I was a male prostitute on the streets, I looked for a different job and a place to live. I saved money like there was no tomorrow. I found bottles to return, ate as little as I could while still maintaining a good health for me and a good physique for my clients, and scrapped metals for extra income.

On the last evening of my thirteenth month in Aurora, I counted my money that I had saved from my prostitution. I was elated that it was enough to rent an apartment and take on some bills! I could leave the streets!

After counting my money and hiding it in my secret place, I had gone back out on the streets. The night had seemed especially long and tedious as I turned several tricks, but I got a break on my final client of the early morning. After putting out to please the client and then taking his money, he told me his name and offered me a job as a male stripper and sex provider in his bisexual bar, The Flamingo Lounge, in rural Aurora. The pay was $12.00 per hr. plus tips thrown on stage, or given for private sessions. He also offered me an apartment in one of the best apartment complexes he owned in Aurora, called The Candlestick. I was ecstatic! A job and a home, all in one night!

However, for me there was one big obstacle to leaving the streets and going to work for Mr. Richard at the bisexual lounge. I had been forced early on into a deal with a pimp, a big guy who promised gang protection and some clients in exchange for 10% of my earnings and four years commitment to work for him. I couldn't just leave him and break my commitment! Who knew what he would do to me if I did?!

When I agreed to work for him, Mr. Richard paid off my pimp for $300,000. In exchange I was to work for Mr. Richard for ten years. Mr. Richard, I, and my pimp worked out details wherein I agreed that if I didn't fulfill my deal with Mr. Richard, I would have to work for my pimp on the streets for my remaining three years as per my original deal with him. I thought that that deal was strange and didn't sound very fair to me. However, I was getting a good job and an apartment from Mr. Richard! My pimp could only promise me customers and I had to live on the streets! Where was the competition in those two choices?!

I now regretted the deal, but it was a done deal! I only had three years left serving Mr. Richard in The Flamingo Lounge and I would be free to go. However, in the meantime I had also found out accidentally why our deal was so strange. I found that my pimp had worked for Mr. Richard for years and received deals like that as kickbacks, as well as some monetary compensation for finding male and female prostitutes to work for Mr. Richard at The Flamingo. That news had pissed me off, but I quickly calmed down as I remembered that Mr. Richard, The Flamingo, and my Candlestick apartment had so improved my life that I really didn't care what underground deals were bringing us working strippers to the lounge! At least I was off the streets, had a roof over my head, and a warm bed in which to sleep.

So it was that I moved into Mr. Richard's ten story, modern apartment complex. My apartment was on the eighth floor, and it was a beaut! It was actually quite large, modeled in an Old Southern mansion style motif.

There was a kitchen, a dining area, a large living room/parlor, one full bathroom with shower, one large bedroom, a laundry room, and a study large enough to be a good-sized bedroom. It was homey, comfortable, and most of all, it was mine!

I moved in on my eighteenth birthday. I had no furniture, but there were appliances in the kitchen. Over the next several weeks I bartered for, pimped for, prostituted myself for, and worked at the strip club for money, furniture, and other household needs.

My job at The Flamingo Lounge, as well as my prostitution, was often a humiliating, albeit a good-paying job. In one night of stripping at the lounge I pulled in anywhere from $300 to $900 in tips, not counting wages. However, I felt degraded part of the time, like a piece of meat for men and women to ogle, use, and abuse. To assuage the negative feelings and emotions I drank steadily, and took a natural drug I could buy at 'happy hippy' stores called 'avatar'.

Before I realized what it would entail, I had agreed in my contract with Mr. Richard to be what was referred to as a 'working stripper'. This meant that I would service clients to sex of their choice in the back entertaining rooms for a set time per person or group. This status earned me the assignment to a dressing room suite, so I had jumped at the idea and agreed to it.

However, I quickly found that it was a lot of extra work and humiliation to do these private sessions. I often had to please male and female customers above and beyond the strip dance. As a consequence of my decision to be a 'working stripper', I had to have sex with any customer who requested it of me. Over seven years I had had sex with probably hundreds of clients, 90% of whom were men. The only beneficial thing to being a 'working stripper' was that I could charge whatever the market would bear for my services of clients in the back entertaining rooms without paying taxes on it, and only giving Mr. Richard and The Flamingo Lounge a 10% cut. At times I even managed to skip paying Mr. Richard his cut.

For all of this I received an hourly wage as a waiter plus tips; for private sessions I charged clients anywhere from $150/ half hour up to $900/ hour. The private session costs varied based on what the client wanted to do during the session, and how many clients would participate or watch. I made good money, there was no doubt about that! But at what cost, I was beginning to wonder at the age of 26?!

At the strip club I often felt cheap, whereas on the street I felt like the master of my prostitution trade. On the street I worked for myself and my pimp, set my own hours and charges, did my own negotiating, and picked and chose whom I would service. Even though I had those benefits on the street, I wouldn't trade it for my lounge job at any price! All those positive things about my prostitution job on the street were wiped out by the fact that I had job security at The Flamingo! Working at The Flamingo also gave me a dressing room. Mr. Richard was a nice employer. At the Flamingo I had such camaraderie with my fellow employees who were my 'family'. I also had a fabulous income that allowed me to buy all the 'toys' I could possibly want, including brand new cars every few years, all the booze I could want, and other things that all Americans desired but many could not afford! I was spoiled working at The Flamingo Lounge. Nope, I had long since decided that overall I highly preferred my job at The Flamingo to my months of prostitution!

I had several roomies at Candlestick over the years, but inevitably they would discover my sexual orientation and move out. The building manager would not allow an unmarried man and woman to share an apartment, even though I was banging her boss. I had to advertise for male roommates. It was a vicious cycle!

It goes without saying that, by the time I was twenty-five, I had an apartment that was fabulously furnished, remodeled, re-carpeted, and had all new appliances. I had a top of the line stereo system, DVD video camera system, top of the line computer system, a Wii system, a top of the line television and entertainment system, and several other high tech toys. I was gay, what else was there to spend my money on but my needs and wants?!

My boss, Mr. Richard, was a great guy. However, he also added to the humiliation of the job by insisting we strippers take turns servicing his desires. The sessions between Mr. Richard and any Flamingo stripper was one for which we would receive no pay. It was put out or get out when we were called upon! Mr. Richard was a pervert, and often forbid the use of condoms during our MSJs, or mandatory service jobs with him. He had many perverse sexual desires, tastes, and fetishes, and we 'working strippers' learned them all. A few I enjoyed, but most I did not.

In almost all other sexual encounters I had, in or out of work, I protected myself with condoms for me and my date or client. However, there were times at work when there was no time for condom application, or the condoms were not available. At those times I went bareback with a client.

At the dawn of my twenty-fourth birthday, Mr. Richard approached me in my dressing room as I was putting on my underwear.

"Son," he said, sipping from his flask of vodka, "do you enjoy your job here?"

I didn't know what to say. I loved the money, but I didn't like the humiliation and moral degradation I often suffered from patrons when performing shows or servicing clients in private sessions. I liked all the weird people with whom I worked, and I even liked Mr. Richard, even though once or twice a month he would pick one of us for a mandatory service job (msj) on his terms.

Should I be honest? Or should I totally lie!? I decided to stake out a middle ground if I could!

"Well, Mr. Richard," I finally spoke, "I enjoy most aspects of the job, and others I don't like. However, jobs are hard to find right now so, I have to… need to buckle down to keep this job. The pay is excellent, and I can live well on it. Overall I am happy and content working here! You take care of us well here, Mr. Richard!" I looked at him and smiled.

"Let's go out to lunch, Andrew." Mr. Richard put on his coat. "I have a proposition for you. We need to talk about it."

I hurriedly finished dressing. I was worried now. What perverse act did he want me to do to him now? Or was it worse? Was he going to fire me? Cut my pay? Was he going to take me off the stage for a desk job like he had done to several other older dancers over the years?

I followed Mr. Richard to his BMW with great trepidation. I was feeling used and abused. This "proposition" couldn't be something good!?

Mr. Richard drove me to his favorite dive, a drive-in across town from the strip club. We parked at a menu/microphone near the kitchen and ordered our food. Mr. Richard even paid for his and my food! This only increased my unease, because Mr. Richard rarely paid anything extra to his employees, or treated us to a free meal.

While we ate, Mr. Richard and I chatted amicably about a new show he wanted to author called "The Gay Frolics". After we finished eating, Mr. Richard cleared his throat.

"First things first, I always say." He turned to me. "Andrew, you've been like a son to me, and I appreciate your work at the club. You bring in a large return clientele. I must say you know how to please men, seduce them, titillate them, and then lay them. Which reminds me, I want you for this month's MSJ date." He put his hand on my inner, upper thigh almost in my crotch.

I shuddered some inside. This was really serious! He was going to use me one more month, and then dump me for a younger blond-haired Adonis! My heart raced in anxiety and I noticed I was also shaking!

"I haven't told you this, Andrew, but you are by far the best gay stripper/dancer I employ. Not only that, you are the best looking, best dressed, and the best audience pleaser with the best physique." Mr. Richard rested his elbows on the steering wheel and looked seriously at me.

I was happy to hear all this praise. Perhaps Mr. Richard actually had 'good' news for me?!

"I enrolled The Flamingo Lounge to participate in a talent exchange to let my best stripper/dancers travel to other cities and other strip restaurants, gay and straight. You will perform at each location. The benefit to you is that you will get more exposure, pardon the pun, and it could lead to some porn movie contracts. The strip joints you are traveling to will pay your travel expenses and room and board. They will pay you what I pay you, and you can keep the tips also, and you would keep what you earn from any private sessions in establishments like ours that offer full service. I would like you to represent my establishment along with our second best stripper/dancer, Marcus, and best female stripper/dancer, Melody. Are you interested?" Mr. Richard had a 'please, please me' look on his face as he posed his request.

I couldn't believe it! An opportunity to travel the country all expenses paid! My only expense was performing a strip/dance act a couple of times at each stop! For that I would get paid my regular wage, I would get to keep the tips, and I would get to keep any money from private sessions! What a deal!

"Interested?!" I exclaimed. "Am I interested?! You bet Mr. Richard! I'm your stripper/dancer to go!"

"Great, Andrew!" Mr. Richard smiled as he sneaked a feel of my package and then patted me on the shoulder. "Like I said, Andrew, you are like a son to me. I can count on my kids!"

As I was rejoicing, the thought briefly crossed my mind that if Mr. Richard thought of me as a son, and yet insisted that I have sex with him on occasion, would he do the same, molest his own kids (if he had any)? However, I quickly forgot that question as I pondered my impending travels!

"How often will I travel to other cities?" I asked.

"Once a month for one week. The exchange program begins this month, and goes for 24 months. You will leave for Seattle on April 20, and return April 27. I have plane tickets for the three of you from a strip/dance establishment in Seattle. Another lounge has paid for your hotel rooms, another has paid for your food, and another has rented two vehicles for your use. While there you three will do shows in each establishment. Any questions?" Mr. Richard pulled out his flask of vodka and took a long drink.

"Nope!" I was still processing the wonderful news!

"Do you want a dreg?" He asked me.

I took a long drink of his vodka as well to celebrate. I was so excited!

So it was that I joined the exchange program. I and my co-performers, Marcus and Melody, traveled nation-wide for two years. We saw many national landmarks, parks, and sights. We met many interesting people, and learned many interesting new tricks to sexual pleasure. It was a blast!

All three of us had a few illicit sexual experiences while touring. During our travels, Marcus seduced me, and we had an on-going sexual relationship throughout the 24 months. To me it was just entertainment sex. I didn't realize Marcus considered it as much more and was falling in love with me!

As usual, all through our travels, I practiced safe sex; the last thing I needed was an AIDS diagnosis or some other STD. I figured it was only prudent since we were having sex with people all over the country, who had slept with God only knows whom! I didn't want the STDs from people with whom Tom in Seattle had had sex when he was in San Francisco.

During our trips our performances were stressful. During the week that we would be in Austin, Texas, for example, we would perform for one bar three nights out of the week. For another lounge we would do two performances one day, and one on another day later in the week. For the final lounge we might perform twice on Saturday, and once on Sunday. That was nine performances, not including any private sessions we may have scheduled. Some days we might put in a full eight hours.

After six months of our exchanges and all this stress that the schedule inflicted, Marcus kind of snapped. He began taking steroids, prescription narcotics, and he began smoking marijuana. He said he needed to take steroids to enhance his performance and keep him bulked up. He took prescription narcotics purchased off the black market and smoked marijuana to relax, so he said. I joined him some in smoking marijuana, but I refused the other drugs.

It was during the exchange program with bars across the country that I realized I did not want to be an exotic dancer/stripper and full service sex provider for very much longer. I was getting to the age where most exotic dancers and 'working waiters' were retired to bartending, cooking, or desk work. I didn't want any of that to happen to me! It would be too humiliating after so many years of drawing clients to The Flamingo because of my figure, my sexual prowess, and my ability to please. It would be even more humiliating than staying with the job I had now as it was presently constituted! I decided that, when I could afford it, it would be better to leave on top, than to have to be retired because I had gradually lost my clientele.

I had saved up a considerable amount of money, and I decided to start on a plan to pursue two goals.

First, I decided to look for a life-long mate. It made sense. I didn't want to grow old alone, so I decided to look for that one special guy I could propose to, that one special guy that would fulfill my life, be my help-mate, my lover, my spouse. Someone with whom I had almost everything in common, or at least with whom I had the important things in life in common.

Secondly, I decided that I was aggressively going to begin building up my savings so that I could quit my job at The Flamingo Lounge and maybe buy myself out of our deal for my employment with my pimp and Mr. Richard. It also had to be enough so I could look for employment elsewhere and have enough money to see me through the Obama Depression while I did so. I wanted respectable work, work in which I could respect myself, work that didn't cause me to feel so used, abused, and cheap!

In April of my 25th year, the first to be exact, Mr. Richard let me know our final exchange was a strip/dance bar just north of Gurnee, Illinois, and would be in the last week of May of this year, 2010. The three of us went and performed, earning a combined $4,500.00 in tips. Finally the exchanges were over! Now we could relax, enjoy our family (if we had any!) and enjoy being home all the time and work at The Flamingo. However, we needed to get home first. The bar at which we had performed offered to pay for whichever mode of travel we chose to go home. As fate would have it, I chose the bus.

# CHAPTER 7

# A LIFE CHANGE

Our last performer exchange had been to a popular yet much hated nightclub in Gurnee, Illinois. Gurnee was quite a conservative family oriented part of the state, and the full service sex club, Neon Red, just outside of town was as much hated by the Christian community as it was liked by its clientele. We had performed three nights and serviced some sex to patrons. Now our two year nation-wide tour was done, and I for one wanted to be finally finished with this part of my life.

The club had generously purchased all of us transportation of our choice back to Aurora. I chose the bus. Marcus and Melody had graciously agreed to take my luggage with them on the private airplane that Neon Red had chartered to return them to Aurora later on this evening. I was therefore footloose and fancy-free to ride the bus home from Gurnee to Aurora.

I wanted to get home as soon as possible to get started on my plans that I had established during the last six months. Marcus and Melody, on the other hand, had decided to stay until this evening so they could attend a party thrown by some clients from the lounge at which we performed last night. They wanted to go and be entertained for a change instead of doing the entertaining. I had no such desire. Another party just wasn't for me right now. I had things to do to plan for and carry out my goals for my future after The Flamingo Lounge.

I had decided to leave early in the morning and walk to the bus station. It was about twelve blocks, but I needed the exercise, and it was such beautiful weather. Besides, I would also save the taxi fare by walking. I would be several bucks closer to my large nest egg!

I exited the hotel where Marcus, Melody, and I had stayed during our engagement in Gurnee. Once outside on the sidewalk I stopped. I closed my eyes and breathed deeply the less polluted spring air of this much smaller community. It was invigorating! I stretched my arms over my head and exercised every muscle in a nice tensing stretch. I smiled blissfully. It felt so good to be alive on such a beautiful day!

I took out of my pocket the instructions I had written down to guide me from the hotel to the bus station. I perused them carefully and memorized them. Then I turned to my right and took off, walking briskly.

As I walked, I decided to review and analyze the conclusions at which I had arrived during the last six months or so of our exchange program.

I was beginning to have serious reservations about my work. I knew, and now admitted, that I was allowing myself, my looks, my body, my emotions, and my spirit to be used and abused by clientele that were only interested in me for sex. They were not interested in me as a person, as a friend, or as a waiter even. They did not appreciate the quality of me, my spirit, my intellect, or my character. They were interested only in my facial beauty and my hot body, and how I could sexually please them. That made me no better than a sex toy! This reality had been the truth for the last seven years, but it was only during the last part of our exchange program that the reality really sank in. I had to believe I was better than a sex toy… a sex tool. I was no longer happy with my work.

I now realized that all of my non-sexual qualities had been usurped by the paramount physical and sexual qualities I possessed that were necessary for my job as an exotic dancer/stripper and full sexual service provider. I had come to realize that I needed to nurture the non-sexual qualities I possessed or they would die. I already felt handicapped when it came to considering employment other than in the sex industry. I wasn't sure I could do any other job, so entwined and dependent had my life become in and on stripping, dancing erotically, and providing sexual liaisons to please clients! The thought of seeking different employment excited me and scared the hell out of me at the same time.

I had also come to realize that my self-esteem and feelings of self-worth had been damaged severely! Any people with whom I interacted at work, other than my fellow employees and Mr. Richard, treated me like a sex slave, a piece of meat, a tool for sex, or a toy for the fulfillment of sexual fetishes. During my last year of exchanges I had come to the realization that I was not just a piece of meat to be cannibalized sexually by clients, or a tool to be used by clients for their self-gratification sexually, or a slave to be kept in subjugation for the sexual pleasure of others. I was not a boy toy upon which clients could fulfill their perverse sexual tastes and then discard me like a worn out play thing! I was a valuable person, with something to contribute to society that was beneficial, productive, and important! I realized now that I had just not selected the right career path that would allow me, or force me, to maximize my potential. That needed to completely change so that I could regain the self-confidence, self-esteem, and sense of self-worth that my prostitution at The Flamingo Lounge, with its perverse clients, was stealing from me and warping and destroying in my mind.

It was also obvious to me now, for some reason, that the labels, stereotypes, jobs, stress, and duties put upon me by my current job were contributing to, if not causing me to be somewhat depressed. I had never thought myself to be depressed or self-loathing, but it had become clear during the exchanges criss-crossing the country that I was depressed and didn't think very highly of myself. The depression and self-loathing led me to seek comfort in vodka and avatar. Why I didn't see that before, I did not know!? I had to leave my job at The Flamingo Lounge sometime in the next one or two years, or I would be permanently scarred and unable to function spiritually and emotionally. If I didn't leave soon, I also realized I might become an alcoholic or a drug addict, if I wasn't already one or the other!

I had pride in my work in that I was the best sexual provider in the Lounge. I was sought out by more clientele than any other working waiter at the Flamingo. I was the best at my craft, the best at sex, the best at seduction, the best at foreplay, and the best at sexually pleasing clients, especially men. Of this I was proud!

However, I was getting older. I did not want to be forcibly retired from the business and relegated to a desk job, bar tending, custodial work, cooking, or non-working waiter. I had decided to strive to work things out so that I could get a new job, and retire from The Flamingo Lounge at the top of my career, rather than on the bottom (no pun intended)!

I had also decided that I wanted to seek and acquire different employment for my mental health, my self-esteem, and my own edification. I wanted a non-sexual job in which I could be respectable, happy, and truly proud of my work.

However, to quit The Flamingo and seek work elsewhere, or to find a job first and then quit the Lounge, all required one thing; a nice size nest egg for emergencies. This I didn't have yet. I had money socked away, don't get me wrong! But I didn't have enough to tide me and a possible lover over until I procured other employment.

So, thus had I arrived at one of my goals from now on. I would aggressively start building up my savings. With the Obama Depression in full swing, I estimated I should have a whole year's worth of 'bill money' saved up just because the job market was so bad. The prospects for finding and landing a better job, same pay, and benies was not good in an economy destroyed by an administration that was clueless on how to facilitate an economic recovery.

My goal for my prospective new job was that it be an intellectual job, a career requiring me to use my intelligence and mental skills. It must be respectable work, not like what I was doing now. I wanted to be able to look in the mirror at night and respect myself. I wanted to be able to throw off the mantle of shame, fear, and hurt that was constantly attempting to cloud in my mind and threatening my well-being and indeed my life, and take on life in pride, happiness, and comfort.

I wanted to end the sex, prostitution, and what I was growing to identify as the depraved part of my life. I wanted an opportunity to restart my career in a different, more wholesome, and legally-sanctioned job. I would still keep my hot body and figure in the quality state it was, but I would do it working out at the gym, not having sex at The Flamingo Lounge for sex-fiend clients.

During our exchanges, I also realized how truly lonely I was. I had never thought about it before, but on the trips throughout the country it seemed like everywhere I went I saw straight and gay couples enjoying each other's company and love. The reality of my loneliness hit home more and more. I had no one in which to confide, no one to whom I could talk, no one to empathize with me, no one to comfort me when I was down, no one with whom to make a marriage commitment, and no one with whom to have committed sexual relations. I was truly in a pitifully lonely state! I wanted someone who was as compatible with me, as they could be. I wanted someone to be my significant other, but more; someone to be my committed spouse. I longed for some man who could truly fill my life with the love, companionship, and monogamous sex that I wanted so badly!

I did realize I had some standards. I didn't want just any guy! I wanted a spouse, a male helpmate who met criteria that I had set for myself, including the following:

I wanted a spouse who was handsome, physically fit, buff, a pleasure at which to look (in other words they would pass the 'eye candy' test!) and a joy with whom to be.

I wanted a spouse that was not an avid hunter/fisherman. Of the great wastes of time in society, hunting and fishing were truly among them!

I wanted a spouse that disliked sports of all kinds, yet enjoyed watching the Olympics.

I wanted a spouse that was a conservative Republican politically like I was.

I wanted a spouse that disliked Obama and all for which he stood.

I wanted a spouse that had similar tastes in music as I did.

I wanted a spouse that loved me unconditionally, who was loyal, true to his vows, honest, and who was in love with me.

I wanted a spouse who could fulfill my life.

I wanted a spouse who could be my helpmate, and who needed me to be his helpmate.

I wanted a spouse who was my spouse, but also my lover, willing to fulfill my every sexual need, as I would be willing to fulfill his.

I wanted a spouse that would not abuse me in any way, and, in return, I would not abuse him in any way.

I knew my ideals in a potential spouse were high, and the pickings were probably slim. However, I had my standards, and I knew someday I would find the right man to fill most, if not all of my criteria for my spouse.

So, I was going to save money aggressively to create a nest egg that would tide me over if I should lose my job, or lose a lot of my income.

I would begin looking for a good job to replace my work at The Flamingo Lounge.

I would begin looking for a prospective male spouse to marry and with whom to spend the rest of my life.

I had a plan, and now I needed to take action! As I walked the last two blocks, I had solidified my life plan. However, I thought the job situation would be answered and made clear first. Little did I know what part of my plan would be achieved and met today.

I rounded the last block and saw the bus station on the next corner across the street. I was relieved. I was getting a little tired. It would be good to rest my tootsies! I strode strongly and determinedly toward the station, emotionally and mentally happy that I had a direction in my life, a self improvement plan. I was taking life by the horns and steering it in a different direction. I was happy that I was finally doing something to change my life for the better!

I procured my bus ticket to Aurora at the counter in the lobby, and watched two or three other male bus riders who were kind of hot. I gave the voucher from Neon Red to the clerk to pay for the ticket, and exited the station to the platforms. The morning spring sun was warming everything, and it was bright and beautiful outside, with the small green leaves giving the trees a beautiful clothing. I had to plan how to find a man who could or would fit my criteria to be a life-long lover.

There were always the obvious pick-up joints for gay men or women, the gay bars. Perhaps frequenting gay bars would give me some prospective spouses?! I had tried gay bars when I was younger. I had looked for a good quality relationship. My experiences had been pretty much universally failures. I kind of nixed that idea, because, in my experience, most gay bar attendees were interested in one thing, and one thing only: one night stands! I didn't go for the one night stand affairs. I knew they led very often to an STD or AIDS. I wanted a relationship, not a deadly disease.

There were other options. I could start going to regular bars. There I could hope to hook up with a man like me who knew the gay bar scene was too promiscuous, but yet longed for a long-term relationship with another male. That might work! It was a possible way to go. However, I knew of no gay couples who had met in this fashion.

I could just get out more often, go places and do things, I thought ruefully. I was pretty much a homebody and didn't prefer to travel too much, especially after the work I did at The Flamingo Lounge! Perhaps I should attend some gay pride events that were coming up?! I could meet other gay men there. I might find a compatible spouse at one of those events. I certainly would meet a lot of other homosexual people. It would be a good boost for me.

Then too, there was the internet. I could register on some of the gay social sites? I knew that on the internet I would get a wide variety of possible men with whom I could have a long-term relationship. It was flush with candidates! However, that thought didn't really appeal to me because I had heard some horror stories from gay and straight friends who had tried to meet people on the internet. They had ended up with creeps, jerks, idiots, and people otherwise completely incompatible with them. Fortunately, all had exited the dating scene with these people safely.

I boarded the bus, planning my next moves toward finding a better job and a life-long lover. I gave the driver my ticket, he stamped it, and I pocketed the stub.

As I turned to move down the aisle to find a seat, I came to a dead stop. My eyes were drawn immediately like a magnet to one of the most beautiful, strikingly handsome, stimulating, and robust sights they had ever seen! My eyes rested on a tanned, dark-haired, facially gorgeous guy sitting alone with his eyes closed. My heart skipped a beat! He was the poem and anthem of the perfect male! His finely sculpted features and honed upper body muscles reminded me of a Greek god. I instantly fell head-over-heels in love with this guy the moment I saw him! I paused… unsure rather to make a move for him… sit with him… introduce myself to him…? Should I put myself out for what could be destiny… was he gay? Did it matter? Could I afford to pass up an opportunity like this?! I decided no, that I could not! Especially since he might be a perfect candidate for my life-long spouse, my help-mate, my lover…! He was so hot!

I made a bee-line for the seat next to him. Was he gay? Could I befriend him? If he were straight, could I swing him to my camp?! I didn't know, couldn't tell. I wanted him in the worst way after just this one look. My body ached for him! I just had to get to know him and find out if he were gay! He would make the perfect life-long partner because he far exceeded the 'eye-candy' test! By the looks of his upper torso, he was slender, yet very buff, with mild muscular curves. Definitely all man! I wanted him to be my man!

He looked like he was conservative, because he was dressed casually, yet smartly. He also looked highly intelligent. I hoped looks were not deceiving!

I stopped at his seat and asked if I could sit next to him. This darkly tanned Adonis looked my body over up and down with a look of admiration and pleasant surprise, thrilling me to my very core as I sensed he was pleasantly impressed with me, my body, and physique. I sensed he too was almost in love with me from first sight.

My heart skipped a beat as he offered me the seat. I sat down next to him and introduced myself. He responded by introducing himself; his name was Tyler. Even his name was attractive! From the instant I sat down, the chemistry and attraction between us thrilled and flattered me. I could feel the electric nature of the connection. As we talked I could tell that Tyler was indeed hot, intelligent, conservative, and available. I was even more in love with him the longer I interacted with him. I wanted him so badly! We were, on the surface anyway, so compatible! He was such a hunk! He would be perfect for my life-long lover.

However, I became more and more convinced of two things. First, I wanted Tyler for my life-long lover. We were most compatible, and our attraction was so strong that I felt nourished by it. We had a chemistry between each other that you could feel in the air. We got along together, and I knew we shared more in common than just what we had discovered in our short conversation.

Secondly, I just knew it wasn't going to work between us because soon we would have to part ways. Once the bus stopped and dropped us off in Aurora, we probably would be like two ships passing in the night, never to see each other again. I had to think of a way to salvage what could be a tragedy!

Why was it, damn it, that any time a good, wholesome, wonderful thing happened to me that it inevitably blew apart in my face!? Why couldn't I have some luck?! Some blessing?! Was I really saying this?! I wasn't one for or against religion! Where did the 'blessing' word come from?!

When we arrived at the bus depot in Aurora, my heart was breaking. I must make a quick, clean break from Tyler before I gave away any more of my heart! I didn't want Tyler to know I was gay, or what kind of a lifestyle I led, and already had weaved several lies about myself and my past. The lies would be hard to keep straight, so maybe it was just as well that we wouldn't be together.

As we exited the bus I said a quick 'goodbye' to Tyler, swallowed hard, and pushed my way a safe distance into the crowd on the platform. I then turned for a last look at Tyler. 'He is a hunk coming and going!' I thought to myself. I watched him from the back. His upper back and arms were manly and well muscled from his parents' farm. He had a nice, round, attractive ass that I wanted to jump now! His figure was perfectly masculine, and I was so attracted to him I couldn't stand it. My body ached to be intimate with Tyler! I watched him go into the depot restaurant. What a shame to lose what could be the love of my life!

I turned to go, knowing I would never see Tyler again. I was devastated, and therefore was not thinking clearly. I had forgotten, in my misery, the fact that I needed a new roommate to replace the one that had just moved out. I couldn't afford all my bills on my own.

Suddenly the thought hit me like a bolt of lightning. My roommate of two years had indeed moved out a week ago! Duh! I needed another roomie to help pay the bills. The match and proposition was so simple I felt a little stupid for not thinking of it on the bus. Tyler was looking for a place to live. Maybe he would like to be my new roomie, and then I could get to know Tyler more! I could be a part of his life, find out if he were gay, get to know him better, and perhaps we would become lovers! Duh! Why did I not think of this sooner?

I quickly turned and followed Tyler into the depot restaurant.

Inside I found Tyler seated at a booth and apparently praying. I waited until I could see he was done, and then approached him. When I first spoke, the look on Tyler's face was one of rapture and extreme happiness. Tyler enthusiastically invited me to join him, and I sat down across from him in the booth. It was at this time that I propositioned him. I offered him room for a half of the rent and utilities. I was so anxious for him to accept and join me in sharing my apartment that I thought I would have a heart attack! However, Tyler accepted enthusiastically, and I was truly in love! We would be roommates and I had a chance to find out if he were gay, and if we could be lovers.

I went and purchased my own food to eat. I was so ecstatic and thrilled! Tyler was moving in with me! I could slowly court him, and try to bring him into my life as a lover. I felt like I was walking on air!

After I returned and began to eat, Tyler and I discussed how to get his things down to Aurora. Tyler mentioned his parents and Tristan bringing them down, or renting a van and having Tristan help him and me move his belongings. The problem was that Tyler's plans were indefinite, and he needed to be down here soon! I wanted him close to me as quickly as possible… I mean, I wanted him here with me in Aurora as soon as possible.

I had a better, more certain way of moving Tyler and his things down to my place in Aurora this weekend. I had a former love interest, a 23-year old named Joshua, who was married but gay on the down-low, unbeknownst to his wife. I had had a sexual lover relationship with him seriously for a few months, but it wasn't going anywhere and I knew there was no future with Joshua. I had been stringing Joshua along for several months now, trading sex for favors from and for him. I wasn't proud of my blatant use of his love and sex, but it served a few needs of mine and got things done.

The first key was that Joshua had a moving van he used to do side jobs to supplement his income. The second key was that Joshua owed me several favors, and he was not accepting of our split. He still loved to have sex with me whenever I would consent, and he was still suffering under the delusion that I was in love with him and would come around to be his lover permanently. I knew this was not going to happen, and had told him so. Joshua, however, still harbored hope. I knew that because he still owed me favors, was still in love with me and sexually attracted to me, and regularly asked me for us to continue our sexual relationship. I knew that he would move heaven and earth to help me.

I was also owed some favors from two friends that were straight. One was married, and one was single. I knew they too would do their best to help me move Tyler and his things down this weekend.

I told Tyler not to sweat it. I would set up his move with these friends from my end, if he would set it up with his family and make sure they would be home. In no time at all it was set that Tyler, I, Joshua, married Steve, and single Abel would move Tyler's furniture and accoutrements down to his new home in my apartment, our apartment, on Saturday, June 2nd. I was thrilled, stimulated, and in love with the idea of loving Tyler! I was euphoric and delirious with the prospect of living with, wooing, impressing, and getting to know him!

We had finished eating, and then I had taken him to our home. He had been impressed with my metallic plum Dodge Intrepid, and in the beautiful edifice that was Candlestick. I had thrown the door open to my apartment, and guided Tyler into his new home. I anxiously awaited his reaction to the comforts, décor, and electronic toys I had accumulated in his new home. My life was looking up big time, and I was so happy!

# CHAPTER 8

# "OUR" NEST

My apartment was really nice, spacious, homey, and very well-decorated. It was finished and modeled in an old Southern mansion style and motif. As I watched Tyler scanning the living room, kitchen, and dining area I could tell he was impressed. His handsome face was lit up in a big smile, and I watched him walk slowly through the living room and into the kitchen. His body moved smoothly, yet strongly like a male figure skater. He was just buff and muscular enough to turn me 'on' every which way sexually and loose, but he was not so muscular that his body was ugly. Oh man! What a cute ass he had! His body was slender and hot! How I longed to get in his pants, to be with him naked! All in good time, I told myself.

"This is awesome, Andrew! What do you call this style of finish and decorating in this apartment?" Tyler exclaimed, as he ran his hand through his longer, thick, shiny dark brown hair on the top of his head. I wanted to run my fingers through his hair... down his chest...

"It's supposedly called an early American finish, but I call it an old Southern mansion style and decorating. Don't you agree it looks more like the pictures you have seen of rooms in old southern mansions?" I asked and gave him a warm, questioning look. He flashed back an adoring, thrilled smile.

"Yes, I agree! It does look more like the décor and style in a classic Southern mansion than it does early American." Tyler replied. "I mean, early American would need some logs in the walls, all wooden furniture, old style appliances, and so forth. This definitely does not fit what I would picture as early American!" Tyler smiled broadly and shook his head in disbelief as he wandered back into the living room. "Andrew! This apartment is… it is awesome! I am… I am awestruck… totally impressed!" He looked back at the kitchen. "It appears your kitchen is fully outfitted with all the latest appliances. Awesome! Do you cook, Andrew?"

"Yes, I do. Being single that is one skill I learned fast." I replied. "How about you?"

"Oh, I have a few dishes at which I am a whiz. I make a wicked meatloaf and escalloped potatoes, for example! On the farm growing up I did my share of cooking. I certainly saw how my mother cooked for us every day." Tyler moved to a cupboard, feeling the nice pine wood finish gently. "My problem is I seldom follow a recipe, so it is impossible to prepare a dish the same way each time I make it!" Tyler shrugged and grinned at me. "However, since I do follow the same basic recipe that is stored in my computer," he tapped his head, "each time I make it, it is good!"

"We can share the meal making responsibilities then." I wanted to begin giving Tyler some signs of my attraction to him. I approached him from behind quietly and tenderly I put my arm around his lower back, feeling with pleasure the beginning of his cute ass. Tyler's deodorant and cologne enticed me, threatening to drive me wild sexually. I longed to blow in his ear, caress his body, undress him, and kiss his face! I guided him back into the living room to show him my entertainment center and appliances therein.

I needed to stop thinking sexually of Tyler in this way and torturing myself! I had to be patient until I knew whether he felt the same way about me as I did about him. I had to wait until I knew for sure if Tyler were gay or not. Sexual stimulation and activity with him would have to wait until I successfully knew the answers to those questions, and until I had seduced him. I did not want to scare Tyler off by pressuring him for sex prematurely. I needed to stop allowing my mind to wander, my eyes to indulge in Tyler's 'eye candy', and my thoughts to lust after him!

I decided to focus on the entertainment center, the computer system, and the amenities in the living room. Finally I would escort Tyler in a tour of the rest of the apartment. These showings perhaps would get my mind off my carnal desires toward my love interest, Tyler!

"What do you think of my entertainment systems, Tyler?" I asked him, stopping us in front of the huge entertainment center unit.

"They look impressive, Andrew!" Tyler whistled. "What are all these components here?"

"Well, I have the room rigged for a brand new 'surround-sound', sound system. This very thin box controls all five speakers for the sound from all the components of this system. This, of course, is a large 52 inch screen High-Definition television. This unit is my stereo with compact disc reading and writing capabilities. This is the radio wave receiver. With it I can pull in several bands of short wave, and regular AM and FM channels in full surround-sound! This box here, and these controls belong to my Wii system. It is a game system that utilizes the television for interactive games. This appliance is the DVD/VCR player. It plays movies on DVDs and VCRs on the television. This book sized appliance is my BlueRay player. And finally, this apparatus is the new version of Play Station." I pointed to each appliance as I talked about it. I was pretty proud of all my new entertainment system components. "This large shelf system in which it is housed was custom made by Amish folks. I had it designed especially for my system and my apartment!"

"You'll have to show me how to operate most of this!" Tyler looked in wonder at the center. "For instance, I have never heard of a Wii system, I don't know what a BlueRay even is, and I have no idea how to operate a Play Station, let alone play it! Even your television and its remote look complex! They are awesome!"

"I will have you functioning and literate with this entertainment system in no time, Tyler!" I smiled and assured him. I then pressed my hand on his lower back and guided him over to the computer system in the corner. "This is my brand new computer system! I had it specially ordered, delivered, and set up last month. Again, the wooden computer desk is made specially to my needs by the Amish. This screen is a 25 inch, top of the line HD, or high-definition screen. I have a hard drive of two terabytes in storage capacity. It has a DVD player, and DVD RW burner. It is flash drive capable, it has several USB ports to operate several peripherals, and you can see I have two printers. One specializes in pictures, and color printing/copying. The other larger printer is faster, holds more ink, and is more for black and white, although it will do color pretty well. It also is a fast copier for small runs." Again I pointed to each part of the computer system as I talked about it.

"What is a terabyte?" Tyler looked at me with a puzzled expression on his gorgeous face. "I have heard of kilo, mega, and gigabytes, but never have I heard of a terabyte!"

"A terabyte is 1,000 gigabytes, Tyler! So my hard drive will hold 2,000 gigabytes of information. Actually it is specially designed to hold a lot of movies that I have downloaded, as well as any games, software, and documents or presentations that I create." I chuckled. "I haven't even scratched the surface of what this hard drive will hold though! I have almost 90% of the space left, and I have already downloaded a lot of material!" I stroked Tyler's shoulder and rubbed his back. "We can download many movies to this computer, Tyler, and watch them, save them, or whatever!"

"You say you have a DVD player and a DVD RW burner. Does that mean you can play DVDs and you can also burn information out to storage on DVDs?" Tyler was asking very intelligent questions for someone who did not know a lot about computers. I was impressed!

"Exactly, Tyler! I can play from, and burn data out to CDs both! I can use CDs as a backup storage sight, like 5¼" and 3½" floppy disks were used ten years ago. This is a much needed and used ability by me!" I smiled tenderly at Tyler as he glanced at me.

"What is a flash drive?" Tyler inquired next, still perusing the system carefully.

"It is this gadget here. It holds several gigs of information and data. You plug it into this outlet on the computer here, and you can save data to it." I pointed both items out, and gave Tyler the flash disk to look at.

"Wow! It's the size of a key chain decoration! And it holds that much data?" Tyler exclaimed incredulously.

"Yep! It holds a lot of data!" I responded as Tyler put the flash disk back on the desk.

"What is the advantage of the flash drive over a burned CD?" Tyler inquired. "Is it exactly what I said, its size, amount of data that can be saved, and the ease with which it can be transported from one place to another that makes a flash drive very convenient and advantageous over a CD?"

"Yes, Tyler, that is the advantage of a flash drive over a CD. The flash drive can literally be carried on your key chain and not break or lose any data." I explained. "A CD can break en route to somewhere else, become scratched and unusable, maybe melt, etc. The flash drive is much more convenient in any number of ways!"

"Will you show me how to use all of these bells and whistles too?!" Tyler asked hopefully. "Or is it over my head?"

"Tyler, if you graduated from high school you will learn this system from me in no time! Of course I will show you how to use it!" I squeezed his lower back reassuringly with my hand.

"I not only graduated from high school, I graduated with honors. I was valedictorian of my class, Andrew! I worked hard for that honor!" Tyler put his right arm around my shoulders and squeezed. He smiled then at me and removed his arm.

I thrilled at Tyler's touch, the feel of his strong arm around my shoulders, the warm flesh, the emotion and meaning involved! Tyler was physical with his feelings like I was! And after the short time that he had known me, for him to touch me in that manner showed he did have strong feelings for me. In addition he was letting me be very physical, almost intimate in some of my touching of him. I was elated, and pretty certain that Tyler was interested in my showing of my affections for him and to him! Perhaps he was gay?!

I guided Tyler around and called his attention to the other furniture in the living room.

"This set of velour love seat, Lazy Boy, and davenport are brand new as of six months ago, Tyler. How do you like what you have seen so far?" I looked at him questioningly.

My living room was furnished quite impressively if I did say so myself, and Tyler's body language and facial expressions told me he agreed! He was all smiles and awestruck looks. His handsome face wore smiles so well! I enjoyed every one of his expressions of awe and pleasure!

"Man!" Tyler exclaimed, whistling. "I love what you have done to the place and what you have! You have all the latest!"

"That's the benefit of being single!" I replied. "I spend my income on what I need and… well… whatever I want! I have… I mean… I HAD no one else to spend my money on. Fortunately that has changed! Now I have you!" I winked at Tyler.

"Oh, Andrew, don't feel like you have to spend money on gifts, food, clothes, or toys for me! You have done more than enough letting me move in here, allowing me to use your toys, and promising you will allow me to use your car! That's more than generous of you!" Tyler shook his head and bore a serious look as he spoke to me.

"We'll see, Tyler! I am a very generous person! There are some things you need, and I intend to see that you get them." I looked seriously but expectantly at him. "Tyler, you are my new friend. I intend to treat you as such… perhaps even spoil you!"

Tyler looked at his feet. Then he gazed at me, his eyes met mine, and he misted up a little. I could sense love, seriousness, and happiness from his gaze. I was enthralled!

"Thank you, Andrew!" Tyler spoke, his voice cracking a bit. "I don't deserve you or all of this! I am truly blessed by meeting you!"

"Tyler, you deserve far more than what I can provide!" I patted his shoulder and then clasped him in a gentle hug. "You are awesome, dude!"

"Where are the bedrooms and bathroom?" Tyler asked, wiping his eyes and changing the subject as we released our hug.

I took his hand this time, which he did not resist, and led him down the corridor, showing him the bathroom, the room that would be his bedroom, my bedroom, the laundry room, and finally the pantry at the end of the hall.

"These rooms are so large!" Tyler exclaimed when we were done with the tour. "I didn't realize that your apartment was so huge!"

"My employers keep us well here at Candlestick!" I returned thankfully. "None of the apartments is small. However, mine is one of the largest apartments because I have… I mean I hold quite an esteemed position in the office!" I fibbed. The reason I had one of the largest apartments in the building was that I was the best full service sex provider at The Flamingo Lounge.

I had released Tyler's hand as we entered the last room for him to look at its interior. Now, as I had finished showing him around, I started back down the hall to the living room, kitchen, and dining room. I heard Tyler follow close behind me, and then he put a hand gently on my shoulder. His hot, sexy, masculine voice stopped me in my tracks.

"Andrew, please… I have something to say to you!"

I stopped and turned to face Tyler. I was shocked to see that his eyes were misty again. Tyler took both of my hands in his and held them, thrilling me to no end! I knew that he must have romantic feelings for me!

"Andrew, I am so thankful that you have opened your doors, your heart, and your belongings to me! I was becoming quite discouraged looking for a place to stay, and worrying about what kind of a roommate I would get." Tyler looked down briefly at his feet, and when he looked up, a tear ran down his right cheek.

Without thinking, I reached up with my left hand and tenderly wiped the tear and moisture gently from Tyler's face.

"Thank you, Andrew!" Tyler spoke fervently. "I appreciate so much all that you are doing for me! I am going to be living high on the hog with you here at Candlestick!"

"Don't mention it, Tyler!" I responded softly and meaningfully. "The pleasure of having you with me is all mine, believe me! I had… I have… well, I am being somewhat selfish in my reasons for inviting you to live with me. But I am happy that you are so happy."

Tyler released my hands, and the two of us walked into the living room.

"How do you keep your apartment so clean and neat, while working full time at Bear Stearns?" Tyler asked, changing the subject.

"I cheat!" I explained. "I have a maid come in once a week to clean. Beyond that I just do a chore here and there, and I don't obsess over it."

"Ahh!" Tyler smiled and turned to face me again.

"I've struck the jackpot!" He said thankfully. "This apartment is perfect. And, Andrew, I really look forward to… to us… to us spending… spending time together."

My heart speeded up as I read into his statement. Maybe he was undecided in his sexuality, and I could exploit and build on that! Besides, he smelled so damn good!

"I also look forward to… getting to know you better, Tyler." We stood looking at each other affectionately for a minute or two. I wanted to grab Tyler and passionately kiss him, but I couldn't yet. I didn't know the depth of his feelings or the certainty of his sexual orientation, and the last thing I wanted to do was scare him away!

Andrew's apartment was awesome! As we stood looking into each other's eyes, I had a strong desire to kiss Andrew. I sensed that he wanted me to kiss him. I shook my head, to clear the impure thoughts. 'Forgive me Lord!' I prayed.

Andrew put his arm around my neck again and we walked into the kitchen. I was glad I had my deodorant and cologne on. I always wore it, but I was especially happy because I wanted Andrew to find my smell pleasant and appealing. I certainly found his cologne and deodorant a sexually tantalizing odor. I found myself carnally wanting to make out and get naked with Andrew…

"Andrew?" I looked at him, our faces so close I could feel him breathing. "I know I've said it twice already, but I really appreciate your hospitality. This is an awesome apartment, and quite close to my job. Thank you!"

"No problem!" Andrew gently tapped my cheek with his fist. "Now, we have you an apartment, a roommate, and we have it all arranged to get your things tomorrow. Would you like to learn some of the entertainment I have available? We have some down time to play some Wii if you would like?!"

I smiled at Andrew as I agreed.

"Wii sounds like it might be fun!" I stated. Then I kind of sheepishly added. "Well, I have never played Wii, or even heard of it. I guess before I say it is fun, you should explain a little about what it is, what is fun and special about it, and what the games are."

"You mean you've never even seen it advertised on television?" Andrew sounded puzzled. "Do you even own a TV…? Didn't you watch it at home? Didn't you have cable?!"

"No, Andrew." I began sheepishly. "We couldn't afford a television for ever so long while I was growing up. Finally, when I was in the eighth grade we got a top of the line color television. It was such a treat!" I paused, embarrassed at my ignorance, and my 'deprived' childhood. "We watched it quite a bit after that at home, but I don't recall seeing or hearing anything about Wii or what it is. As far as cable, Andrew, we were too far out in the country. Cable wasn't available for our neighborhood. Even if it were, we could not have afforded it…" I felt myself blush in shame.

"It is okay, Tyler!" Andrew wrapped his arm around me and we hugged again. "You can catch up here at home. I will love teaching you the love of men… I mean the technology of mankind. I'll catch you up to date!"

"Will… can I learn Wii pretty fast?" I asked uncertainly.

"Sure! You will catch on in no time! Wii is a gaming system to play on the television." Andrew put his arm around my neck again, stroked my chest, and guided me into the living room as he explained. "Would you like a vodka tonic with me before I continue?"

"No thanks." I responded quickly. "I don't drink."

"Well, let me get myself one and I'll continue!" Andrew released me and hurried to the kitchen. He opened the fridge and began fixing himself a strong vodka tonic.

"Wii is a gaming system that has excellent graphics, and requires the players to actually move and be active in order to operate the games, play the sports, or drive the vehicles in the games. If you are playing basketball or soccer, you actually have to 'shoot' the ball, or kick it, by actually making the movements. You get exercise while you play! It's awesome!" Andrew brought his vodka tonic back into the living room as he continued. "If you are playing a racing game, you use the remotes as steering wheels to steer your vehicle, put on the gas, brake, etc. If you are playing a war game, your remote will move your character and allow you to shoot, bomb, or whatever." Andrew picked up two rectangular objects that looked like television remotes. He then picked up two round objects that looked like steering wheels, and plugged the television-like remotes into them.

"Let's start, Tyler, by playing a racing game. I think that will be the easiest for you to learn. We'll play Mario Kart. I think you'll enjoy that!" Andrew exclaimed and grinned lovingly at me.

I blushed at the way Andrew was treating me and being physical with his gestures of friendship. I hoped it meant Andrew felt more serious and deep feelings for me, more romantic in nature.

Andrew had been guzzling and had finished the whole glass of vodka tonic by now. I was surprised but, after all, Andrew was older than I, more worldly, and probably he had been drinking since he was 18 anyway. I determined I would stick with the diet Pepsi that Andrew had brought me with his first drink.

"I need another one." Andrew went out to the refrigerator again. "Sure you don't want one, Tyler?" I watched Andrew fix another glass full of vodka tonic. Curiously he seemed totally unaffected by what he had already consumed. Andrew held up the vodka bottle with a questioning look on his handsome face.

I was tempted. After all, it didn't affect Andrew. Maybe a little wouldn't hurt. I must have shown my conflict by my expression, because Andrew smiled and opened the refrigerator again.

"I don't want you to do anything with which you are not used to or comfortable, Tyler." Andrew put the vodka in the refrigerator. "Sorry I bugged you, Ty." Andrew walked over and put his arm around my neck again, his hand lying flat open on my chest. It felt so good, and Andrew smelled so good. I had to wear his cologne sometimes!

"Come on, Tyler, let's play Mario Kart!" Andrew released me and went to the television and Wii box. "Go ahead and sit down on the couch. I have to insert this cartridge in the Wii console…" Andrew took a colorful cartridge and put it into what looked like a VCR door. The cartridge disappeared. "Now I have to fire up the game!" He began flashing through a few screens, explaining what he was doing as he went. Shortly he came to one screen that had funny characters from the Mario game displayed.

"I've never played Wii." I stated hesitantly. "I won't be very good."

Andrew smiled and looked at me intently.

"There are a lot of important things you've never done, Tyler, that I intend to teach you. Once you learn them, I have no doubt you will perform them spectacularly!" He winked flirtatiously at me. He turned back to the television before speaking again. "At this screen we will choose our characters that we will race. You page down with this button, and when your red flasher is on the character you like, press this key."

Andrew quickly selected his character. I had a strong feeling the important things I didn't know had nothing to do with Wii. Andrew seemed to mean something else, and my heart skipped in my chest. He did like me, didn't he?!

I selected my character, and Andrew moved the game to the next screen.

"Now, at this screen we select our car. You do this the same way using this button to light the vehicle, and this button to select the vehicle you want once it is highlighted." Andrew pointed to the buttons on my Wii wheel.

Andrew selected his vehicle and sat down on the couch as close to me as he could without sitting in my lap. I selected my vehicle, and Andrew moved the game to the next screen.

Andrew finished his second glass full of vodka tonic, and then spoke about this screen that showed several tracks, quite small. Andrew leaned into my space. His deodorant and cologne drove me crazy! I wanted to hold him… to kiss him!

"Now," Andrew began, looking into my eyes, his face a full five inches from my face, "I have selected the easiest track to start. To start your car press two, and to guide your car through the track, use the steering wheel just like you would in a car. If you get stuck, you can steer using these arrow keys." He pointed each out to me as he spoke. "If you want to pop a wheelie, and go faster pull the steering wheel up like this." He jerked the wheel back to his chest. I got a pleasing whiff of his cologne. I was glad he was so close!

"The bananas on the track you want to avoid or you will spin out. The fuel tanks you will want to hit to refuel. These bombs you want to avoid also." Andrew was leaning against me, pointing out objects on the screen.

"Are you ready?" Andrew asked.

"Sure." I shrugged, not knowing what to expect.

Andrew pressed a button on his wheel and a count of three began, after which the race was on. He and I raced down the track. I frequently swerved off the track into the sand or grass, but I quickly caught on. Soon, I was challenging Andrew for first place.

We played for an hour or two, and then I became tired.

"Andrew," I put the steering wheel on the coffee table, "I need to go to bed. I can't keep my eyes open!"

Andrew stayed put, and simply turned to face me, gazing into my eyes.

"Welcome home, Tyler!" He purred. "We'll have a lot of fun living together! I look forward to getting to know more of you, more about you, and everything about you!"

Andrew began to lean forward. I wanted him to kiss me! I leaned forward, and Andrew did too. My heart beat faster. Would he, or wouldn't he kiss me?! The phone rang.

My heart sank, and I quickly sat up straight and sighed as Andrew stood up. He went and picked up the receiver.

"Hello?" he spoke.

I took the remote, found the correct controls, and turned on cable. I turned down the volume on the television.

"But it's nine o'clock, Mr. Richard!" Andrew frowned as he pleaded into the phone.

I wondered what was being said on the other side of the conversation.

"I have a commitment tomorrow. I can't." Andrew stated flatly. There was a pause, and then Andrew sighed unhappily. "Okay, I'll work this evening until midnight." He hung up the phone.

"What's up?" I asked, watching Andrew grab his jacket and shoes.

"Oh, a band member fell ill and Mr. Richard needs me to fill in for three hours." Andrew frowned. "I want to sleep too, but duty calls."

"Before you go," I jumped up and grabbed Andrew's arm, "I need a pillow and blanket for the couch."

"Oh! Yeh! That would help you sleep wouldn't it?" Andrew chuckled and disappeared into his bedroom. When he returned, he had both. "Here you are." Andrew smiled. "I also have these pajamas that I think will fit you. They fit me and I am only a little larger than you. I'll see you in the morning!"

"Good night, Andrew." I said, smiling too.

Andrew grabbed one of my hands. He stroked it gently as he held my hand. He looked what felt and appeared to be lovingly into my eyes and smiled.

"Good night, Tyler. I look forward to coming home and seeing you!"

Andrew strode to the closet, took out a duffle bag, and opened the apartment door. He slipped out, locking it behind him. I missed him already!

# CHAPTER 9

# A FIRST TIME FOR EVERYTHING

Saturday dawned, and with it came the warming sun and clear blue skies. I awoke with the first rays of sun flowing through the window into the living room. I looked around me, expecting for a short time to see my own bedroom at home in Gurnee. When I didn't I panicked! Where was I?! I spent about five minutes reorienting myself to my current location, whose apartment this was, and the fact that I was not living at home anymore, but living with Andrew. The mere realization that I was living with Andrew stirred my emotions to elation, and my hormones to sexual stimulation! Andrew was so facially and physically gorgeous! And he was mine... my roommate. I was thrilled!

Once I was fully reoriented and cognizant on and about my location, the fact that I loved Andrew... (did I say that?!)... and the events of yesterday, I assessed my health. I felt rested, content, and yet exhilarated. I looked forward to the day and to retrieving my belongings from my folk's house. Today I would officially move into Andrew's apartment! Today it would officially be 'our' home, 'our' apartment. I was happy!

I remained briefly lying on the couch, basking in Andrew's luxurious polyester pajama bottoms and wrapped in his soft, good smelling polyester blankets. I felt very close to Andrew wearing his things, and I longed to be closer! The thought that my body was intimately clothed with things that had touched Andrew intimately was sexually arousing to me.

I gazed at the sun dancing on the floor and smiled. A new era in my life was beginning, and Andrew and I would face it together! It was a comforting, exciting, and sexually stimulating thought.

I slowly unwrapped myself from the soft, good smelling, luxurious blankets. I could smell Andrew in them. I breathed Andrew's sexy scent deeply into my lungs and my hormones began reacting to the stimulation. When I was finished uncovering myself, I sat up on the couch and put my bare feet on the floor. Things were a whirl in my mind, and I decided to spend a few moments going over things before I arose and attacked the day.

I thought back to the short time period that Andrew and I had known each other. Even with the infancy of our relationship, Andrew had invited me to be his roommate, and I was now living with a hot, sexy hunk! Andrew and I were perfect together... as roommates. We had planned, with Andrew's friends and my family, a sure-fire way to move me and my things from Gurnee down to Andrew's apartment in Aurora as quickly as possible. Then Andrew had shown me his awesome apartment in which I would be living and was living with him from now on.

My mind continued to go over the events of yesterday and last night. The thought occurred to me that, when Andrew's band leader had called, he and I were leaning toward each other like we were preparing to kiss. Would we have kissed if the phone hadn't rung? Or had I imagined that Andrew was leaning toward me? The thought of Andrew kissing my lips with his lips sent chills of ecstasy... at least it felt like ecstasy... throughout my body. If only that da... I mean stupid phone had not interrupted us! I realized, with some shame, that I longed for a kiss from Andrew... our first kiss.

Then the guilt set in. Why did it matter to me if Andrew was about to kiss me last night? I should be recoiling in revulsion! I knew same-sex love was wrong. It was an abomination to God! I wasn't interested in a more intimate relationship with Andrew, or was I?

I was beginning to feel like I wanted Andrew, like I did want something more involved, something romantic with him. I was even developing some sexual feelings and attraction toward him, and I found his physique, stunning facial beauty, and character so desirable. The fact was, I was infatuated and romantically attracted to Andrew big time! I recognized the symptoms. I had strong feelings of love for Andrew, in other words I had a crush on him! I thought about Andrew and whether he felt romantically toward me all the time since we had met. I was so confused, yet so clear about my feelings and desires toward him! How could that be?! I realized with some shame that everyone had the same questions, feelings, desires, and confusion when they began to fall in love. I was falling in love with Andrew!?

I knew this attraction that I had for Andrew was wrong, wrong, wrong! It couldn't go any further! God condemned same-sex relationships, and that was good enough for me. Besides, I had no conclusive, sure-fire evidence that Andrew was gay, let alone that he was interested in an intimate relationship with me.

I tried feverishly to clear my head of any unGodly thoughts and focus on the day at hand. It was hard because my attraction to Andrew was stirring feelings and hormones that I had never experienced in a serious manner before. However, I made a valiant effort, and was able to go over today's schedule in my head.

Andrew, three of his friends, and I were going to move all of my things into Andrew's apartment. I would gain a place to live, a new job, and a big brother. Andrew would gain someone to help pay the bills, and a new friend, me! I felt it was an even trade, and I even felt like Andrew and I could be considered a 'family'. I felt like it was a great miracle, an answer to prayers, and comforting that God had worked all this out so nicely for Andrew and me!

I had to get off my a… I mean my butt and get moving!

I got up off the couch and went to the kitchen. Andrew's pajama bottoms were a little bit large for me, and by the time I got to the kitchen, they had slipped over my butt and fallen to my knees. I quickly pulled them back up and tied them securely around my waist.

I again found myself sexually stimulated to think that I was wearing some of Andrew's clothes, and that the material that had intimately touched his body was now touching my body in the same places. 'What a sinner!' I reprimanded myself. 'Get your mind out of the gutter!'

I didn't know what I was going to do today. In the morning I was used to a daily shower and change of underwear and clothing. I had no clean underwear, and I had forgotten to ask Andrew for a wash cloth and bath towel.

In the kitchen I decided that, since I could not shower and change my clothes including my intimate apparel, that I would instead look up and make breakfast. I opened the refrigerator, shivering from the gust of cold air as I did so. Inside I found eggs and bacon, perfect for a really good and traditional breakfast. I took both out of the refrigerator and closed the door. With both breakfast foods in my hands, I began to cross the kitchen to the stove and counter. On the way a pile of cloth on the bar between the kitchen and the dining room caught my eyes.

I went to the bar instead of the stove with the bacon and eggs. I set them down on the counter and looked through the cloth. The pile of cloth turned out to be a towel, a wash cloth, a pair of Andrew's clean underwear, and one of his clean t-shirts! A note on top of the pile read:

"I figured you are like I am, a daily shower and clean clothes man. Here is what you will need. Soap and shampoo are in the shower. My under things are clean! Ha! Ha! They might be a little large, but not too much. You will find a large selection of deodorant and cologne in the medicine cabinet over the stool. You should feel free to use whatever you want in our apartment! What is mine is now yours, too! Enjoy! Awaken me after you shower!  Love, Andrew!"

I felt my heart skip and I was again quickly physically and sexually stimulated at the thought of wearing Andrew's under clothes for the day. I took his undershorts and smelled them. I could smell the Downy dryer sheet on them, but I also smelled Andrew's cologne. I smiled as I thought about him wearing them, then giving them to me.

As I collected the shower clothes it suddenly hit me. Andrew had signed the little letter to me with "Love, Andrew!" That could not be a coincidence?! He clearly had some close, more intimate feelings for me! Were they familial, or more intimate, for which I reluctantly realized I longed, more along the lines of a lover's signature?

Clearly I could wear my pants and shirt from yesterday since I had only worn them once and had done no strenuous work in them. Now that Andrew had offered his underwear, shorts and t-shirt, for me to wear, praise the Lord I could shower and change my under clothes for the day! I put the eggs and bacon back in the refrigerator, and headed for the bathroom. I was a 'daily shower and clean clothes' man! That was another thing that Andrew and I apparently had in common!

I turned on and adjusted the tap water to my temperature preference, stripped and jumped into the shower.

Andrew was definitely a lot like me, and had the intuition to know what kind of a guy I was. His gesture to clothe me and his knowledge of me, by giving me underwear of his, and shower supplies was so sweet! I realized he and I were very much 'in sync' with one another.

I washed my body with the cloth Andrew had provided and used the shampoo in the shower. Unfortunately again I found myself thinking how stimulating it was to use soap and shampoo from Andrew! To be close to him in these more intimate things was just bringing out the concupiscence in me and in my thoughts. 'Shame on me!' I thought angrily. 'Why does God allow me to have these thoughts, desires, and cravings if He considers them evil, a sin!'

In ten minutes I was done. I exited the shower and dried off using the towel from Andrew. Then I applied deodorant and a cologne to my body from Andrew's collection, and I put on his underwear. Finally I shaved using Andrew's electric razor, and then combed my hair. I now felt clean, complete, and ready to face the day!

I exited the bathroom and walked in Andrew's underwear down toward the living room, not thinking about the fact that Andrew might be up and watching me. I entered the living room and put on my clothes from yesterday. I now felt so good, and the deodorant and cologne that I had chosen were so intoxicating… I thought fondly of Andrew! I wanted him… I mean I wanted to see him…

Andrew wanted me to awaken him when I finished my shower. I went back down the hallway to his room and quietly opened the door. I stood there for a few minutes gazing at Andrew as he slept. Andrew's clear blue eyes were closed, and he was flopped on the bed, apparently in deep sleep. He was so gorgeously handsome, so cute in slumber! His covers were off, and he had sheer sheets over his body that I suddenly realized in surprise, and a shameful pleasure, were almost see through! I could see through the sheets that he was nude. Because he was lying on his stomach all I could see was his stunning backside and physique from the rippled back down over his tight, round, and cute butt to his masculine muscled legs and his cute feet! I had a strong desire to strip back down to Andrew's underwear and climb into bed next to him. I knew it was wrong, but I wanted to anyway! I again rebuked the thoughts in the name of the Lord!

"Do you like what you see, Tyler?" Andrew's eyes popped open and a mischievous look covered his awesome face.

His voice, though soft and tender, scared the daylights out of me because I was so absorbed visually and mentally feasting on his body, and being lost in thought. I jumped and stumbled backward into the hallway.

"Well?" Andrew pushed himself up to rest on his elbows, smiled, and looked at me expectantly. I sheepishly reentered his room. Clearly he wanted an answer. Should I be honest, or lie? I questioned myself.

"Well… I … I mean…" I stammered. I wanted to say yes, a million times yes! However, I didn't want to give away how I believed I felt when I didn't know exactly how I did feel, let alone how Andrew felt about me! "I feel… I mean I don't normally… I don't appraise guys'… I am not in the habit of rating guys' naked figures…"

"I believe," Andrew interrupted as he rolled over, sat up, and pulled the covers over his waist down, leaving just enough of his hairy pubic 'v' to say he was tantalizing me, "you mean to say 'yes, Andrew, I very much like what I see. Your naked backside is appealingly erotic!'"

He sat there, exposing his bare chest with a stimulating pattern of hair that formed an 'I' over it and then ran down over his stomach and into the pubic area. He held the sheet over his naked lower body, and tenderly smiled and looked me in the face. He seemed to know me completely! That indeed was what I wanted to say. I blushed.

"Yes, Andrew." I recovered, smiling shyly back at him. "I do like what I see." I paused, looking at my feet, and then I finished. "I'll go fix breakfast while you shower." I nervously and shamefully turned to go to the kitchen.

"Why don't you join me…" Andrew said softly and suggestively. "In the shower, I mean. Tyler, I saw you in your… my underwear! You were hot! Your body is awesome, and I would like… I would love to see you in the shower with me!"

My heart rate increased and I felt myself beginning to rise! I couldn't believe he had said what I had heard, let alone that he had meant it! I hoped he meant it! I turned back around to look at Andrew, expecting to see a look of sarcasm on his face. I expected that he would laugh me off with his joke, and that I would be shot down and hurt!

To my surprise and pleasure, Andrew was standing, and when I turned around we were within a foot of each other. There on Andrew's face was a serious, tender, questioning look. He gazed into my eyes with a come hither look, as he slowly dropped the blankets from his body. I received a full frontal view of Andrew naked, and I was not disappointed! His physique, every physical and sexual detail, was poetry in form! Andrew was erect, and I was still rising. A wave of sexual stimulation and desire washed over me!

If Andrew only knew how I was tempted to join him! My prurient desires were wrong, and suddenly made me feel very uncomfortable. Andrew sensed this instantly, and he smiled.

"I had you going for a minute, didn't I?" He patted me on the shoulder.

"Yeh!" I breathed for what seemed the first time in several minutes. "We'll shower together some other time." I laughed nervously, backed out of Andrew's room, and quickly went to the kitchen.

I heard Andrew go into the bathroom and turn on the water. Shortly he pulled the plug to turn on the shower, and I started the bacon and eggs. As I cooked and listened to the water, I sorted through my conflicting thoughts, desires, and emotions about Andrew.

I had never had a close relationship with a guy. My father worked all the time, and I was never very close to him until I reached the age of about 17. When he wasn't working… well, I couldn't remember any times like that! I could remember trying to go out to see him in the fields some days, but most of the time he… ah he… I could only remember that most of the time when I went to see him in the fields he… he sent me home because he said the fields were too dangerous. I felt like he not only didn't consider me important enough to set aside work and spend time with me, it seemed to me he didn't even want to see me. The wave of darkness that came when I tried to remember Dad swept over me and I mentally changed the subject.

My brother was all girls, all the time. He was truly nauseating that way! I had realized early on that I didn't like girls as much and in the same way that Tristan did. Tristan gave up his virginity at the age of 14 when he was in the 10th grade. I wanted to keep my virginity and give it to my wife on our first night together after marriage. I also understood that Tristan had no normal admiration for and attraction to a handsome, hot male with a masculine male physique. I learned early on that I could not have a terribly close relationship with Tristan because we were so different in our relations, relationships, attractions, and our sexual lives.

I decided that my lack of good, wholesome relations with my father and brother, and lack of close male friends at least contributed to the reason why I craved a close, even intimate relationship with Andrew. I wanted a guy's friendship, companionship, and intimacy so badly that the prospect of being with Andrew just felt physically, emotionally, and morally right! He felt like someone I had looked for all of my life, someone who could fulfill me… be a helpmate to… me… I felt safe spending… spending the rest of my life… with him. The prospect of being with Andrew sexually was even sounding… well, sounding very good!

The problem was the intimacy part. I knew that was wrong, a sin. Years of going to church had scratched the surface such that I believed that same-sex activity was wrong, but I didn't know any good reason why! That is why my emotions and desires for and toward Andrew were Biblically wrong and made me uncomfortable. I had this unsubstantiated hang-up that same-sex relationships were wrong, but I could not prove why, and I did not know why except that God condemned it in the Old Testament. The church and my parents had failed me miserably in neglecting their teaching concerning homosexuality, I concluded. Unfortunately, depending on one's point of view, I didn't care. I needed Andrew! I wanted Andrew; at least as a big brother.

My feelings and desires with regard to Andrew were normal, I told myself. I wanted a big brother friendship, and I now had it. My more prurient desires were just normal confusion of a relationship with sexual needs, at least that's of what I had managed to convince myself.

As I put the eggs and bacon on the table I smelled Andrew's cologne and deodorant that I had put on. The scents stirred strong desires deep within me! I smiled. I had chosen a cologne called 'Spanish Fly', and I really had to complement Andrew on his taste in scents! This cologne was awesome!

Andrew appeared from the bathroom fully dressed, combing his curly, damp blond hair. He looked so good… so… so delicious! I smiled at him, and he returned the smile.

"Breakfast is served!" I said happily, placing the last dishes and food on the table.

We sat down to eat. Andrew smelled so good. His cologne was intense!

"What cologne are you wearing, Andrew?" I asked in between bites.

"'Mambo'!" Andrew smiled. "You like?"

"I love!" I purred in a sexy voice as I winked at Andrew. "And I love you!" My guard was down because of the strong desires stirred by Andrew's cologne, and it was out before I could stop it. I was immediately sorry I had said it! I blushed deeply!

"I…I…I mean…Andrew…I…I'm sorry!" I looked down at my plate, and placed my right hand in front of me flat on the table in shame. "I mean… like…we know each other 36 hours…and…and I…I say something… something so stupid like 'I love you'!"

Andrew put his hand gently over my right hand that I had placed on the table.

"Tyler." Andrew's voice was comforting, tender, and firm. "Tyler, stop beating yourself up over expressing an honest feeling. I'm not sorry you said it." He squeezed my hand, and I looked up into his face. He had a tender and serious gaze as he met my eyes. "Tyler." He said quietly. "I love you too! I know it seems impossible, maybe silly, but I do!"

"What I meant, Andrew…" I tried again to rescue myself! "I love you like a brother, or a really good friend! Our love for each other even in that way is really strange because we have only known each other for such a short time!" I glanced secretly at Andrew. He was still smiling at me.

"And I love you in the same way!" Andrew responded, chuckling.

# CHAPTER 10

# MEETING "THE FAMILIES"

I was thrilled, jubilant, and stimulated to the point of 'animal' passion over my progress with my plan to woo over and seduce Tyler to be my life-long lover! So much had happened in just the short time Tyler and I had known each other that I was now probably 70% sure that Tyler felt more for me than just friendly feelings. He had gladly accepted wearing my under things, and he seemed to be curiously 'turned on' by wearing them! He curiously and visibly had enjoyed seeing me completely naked. The pleasured smile he had had as he looked me up and down after I dropped the blankets in front of him had been a joy to see! Then he had admitted to enjoying looking at my naked body. He had fixed breakfast for us. He was wearing my deodorant and cologne. He had complemented my cologne, and in response to my inquiring if he liked it, he had said he loved it. Then Tyler had uttered the magic words that had me in love with him for life. He said 'I love you' to me! Sure it was a mistake spoken by Tyler when his guard was down. I knew though that Tyler must really be harboring love for me in order to say it at all. He had fumbled afterwards apologizing. But I couldn't let him feel like he had to take it back. I had affirmed to him how I felt the same way about him. He had masqueraded his declaration as a love to a sibling, but in my mind the truth of our feelings was pretty much out. However, I still knew I had to go slowly in furthering our relationship! I had, over the years, scared off guys that had been even closer to me than Tyler was now by being too quick to try and establish a lover relationship.

I wanted Tyler to tell me that he loved me for the rest of our lives! I was now so totally smitten and in love with Tyler that I couldn't imagine what I would do if he were killed or if he left me for someone else! I especially didn't know what I would do if he were leading me on, and did not have the love or feelings for me that I harbored for him. The thoughts of these possibilities were so devastating to me emotionally, mentally, and physically that I couldn't bear to even consider them! I attempted now, on a regular basis, to banish them from my conscious mind and subconscious.

Together Tyler and I changed the subject and cleaned up from breakfast. We started dishes. As we worked I told him about my family in Florida, and how important each member was to me. I told Tyler my mother was a beautiful blond model. She was 44, 5'10" and 140 lbs. She had been a good mother, kind and sweet, yet firm and disciplined. My father was a 47 year old strawberry blond construction worker. He was 6'1" and weighed about 185 lbs. He had been a good father, loving, and nurturing to me and my brother. Noah was a 21 year old with light brown hair. He was 6' and weighed about 180 lbs. He and I had been so close in our youth and had shared everything. However, he had kind of dumped our friendship a bit when he found out I was drinking.

I especially talked up my younger brother, Noah, even though he had 'lessened our friendship'. He was cute in my description to Tyler, very nice looking. He was a ladies' man, yet a virgin like me, his big brother, and like Tyler I guessed. He was single, and playing the dating game. He was a CPA by profession, having a college degree in accounting. He was a lot like Tyler, as I described him. I could tell Tyler was taking all of my words in hook, line, and sinker! I felt a twinge of guilt fibbing to him like this, but it was a necessary evil to make me sound as 'good' to Tyler as I could.

I wondered why I was going into detail with Tyler, except that I felt like spinning the yarn to him. He had told me enough about his parents that I felt like I had met them already. I figured I 'owed' Tyler this information. Sure it was all a lie, but Tyler couldn't know what a mess my growing up years had really been! Tyler had to feel I was like him in most aspects of my life and my family life like our growing up years and background, morals, politics, and anything else we came across. It was part of my seduction technique for catching and putting at ease any hard to seduce, somewhat purist prey that I had encountered over the years. Now it was part of my seduction of Tyler, to catch him, reel him in, and make him my lover. I wanted him for my life-long lover so badly that my body had ached Friday night for his body to be next to me! I needed Tyler and craved him so much I could sense it with all five senses. I thus needed to make myself sound as much like Tyler as I could so that he would continue to grow in love with me.

Just as we finished preparing the dishes, loading the dishwasher, and turning it on, the doorbell rang three short bursts. I quickly put away the last clean dish in the cupboards, and then whirled around.

"I'll get it!" I told Tyler as I patted his shoulder and quickly headed for the door. I knew I had to answer it, especially for Joshua! I didn't want him to slip and say anything revealing about us to Tyler. "Can you finish cleaning the table, counters, and stove top, Tyler?"

"No prob, Bob!" Tyler replied cheerfully. He set about the washing and wiping.

I arrived at the door and swung it open. There stood Joshua, the married homosexual on the down-low with whom I had had a sexual affair. Joshua owned the moving van we were going to use today.

Joshua had been a sexual fling for me. The sex had been great, but he had taken our relationship far more seriously than I. He still felt there was an 'us', a relationship between us sexually and emotionally. Now he did whatever I asked of him because he hoped to get me back. I hated to admit it, but I used him, allowing him to think there was still hope for us, while he performed favors for me. I had even had an occasional roll in the hay with him just to keep him on my string. I traded sex with Joshua in return for him owing me favors like the one today using his moving van. I felt a little guilty for this, but I was able to suppress it. It was just business, and it would result today in moving my love, Tyler, into my life and my apartment permanently!

One of the reasons I had decided that Joshua was not my choice for a life-long lover had been that he was already married to a wonderful woman. She did not know that Joshua was gay and having an affair with me. However, the subject of his wife had come up in our relationship many times, and every time he had let it be known to me that he was unwilling to leave his wife or jeopardize his marriage. That fact that he was on the down-low and wanted to stay there and remain married, coupled with many differences in our politics, sexual tastes, and beliefs had doomed our relationship in my opinion. I had bailed out after having a passionate lovers' relationship with him for four months. I had been free of him and putting off 'dating' him, except for the occasional string sex now for the last six months.

Now I was using him to move my newest and hopefully final love interest into my apartment. I felt some shame and regret about this use of Joshua and his love for me, but I assuaged myself with a decision that I would never have sex with Joshua again so that I couldn't expect favors from him anymore.

"Hi ya, lover boy! Long time no sex! I miss you, sexy! How's it hanging?" Joshua exclaimed in a sexy and suggestive voice.

Joshua's boyish cuteness still attracted me to him, but Tyler was my main man now. Tyler was far better looking than Joshua!

I started to fume as I realized again that Joshua was ignoring every pronouncement I had made to him in the last month that he and I were through. There was no emotional or spiritual relationship between us, and now there would be no more sex between us! I pushed Joshua roughly back into the hall and followed him closely. I pulled the door almost closed.

"What is wrong with you, Joshua! Don't flirt with me! Don't talk to me about sex or our 'relationship'! There is none! Especially don't say anything about us in front of …" I hissed angrily as I pointed to Tyler, who was wiping the table, "especially in front of him!... Tyler…" I continued quietly but forcefully. "You and I are done, remember, Joshua!?"

I turned and stalked back into the apartment, trying not to lose my temper with Joshua.

Joshua followed me into my apartment like a lost puppy, his face clouded with confusion. He was slender, a couple of inches taller than I, and had a cute ass. He was dark complected like Tyler, but he was not as handsome, hot, or buff as Tyler was. He was attractive, but now I had Tyler, a hunk!

"But, Andrew!" Joshua protested as I turned to face him in the living room. "I don't understand!? We still have sex off and on…it's so hot and pleasing…"

"Joshua!" I fake slit my throat in the classic 'kill it' motion. "Shut the hell up! I have told you we are over! Don't rock my boat and threaten my relationship with my new guy!"

We both had been whispering in hissing voices laced with emotion, but I was still worried about what Tyler may have heard! I turned 90 degrees to look at Tyler and see what he was doing.

By this time Tyler approached us, a puzzled look on his face.

"Tyler!" I exclaimed with a smile as I put my arm around his neck. "Meet our moving van owner, Joshua. Joshua, my new roomie, Tyler." I rested my open hand on Tyler's muscular breast trying to discretely signal to Joshua that Tyler and I were already sexually intimate. I was trying to get the message across again for Joshua to keep his trap shut! I knew Tyler wouldn't know what my open hand on his chest meant, but I knew Joshua would! …or should, anyway!

However, Joshua had never been too bright about hints like that! Now, either he was playing totally stupid, or he really was not getting the fact that he and I were over and that Tyler and I were a couple!

"Hi, Tyler!" Joshua looked quickly at Tyler and smiled before returning to look at me with a begging look on his face. "I'd like to see you again, Drew." Joshua winked lustfully at me. "When is good for you?"

"Never…!" I hissed again as I pointed discreetly with my free hand at my other hand stroking Tyler's chest.

"You owe me a date…" Joshua said in a sexy voice, "after all, I'm doing you a BIG favor…"

I had to stop Joshua and his trap before he totally spilled our 'beans' to Tyler!

"Can I see you in the hall, Joshua!" I interrupted. I let go of Tyler and pushed Joshua ahead of me into the hall again. I didn't even try to hide my urgency from Tyler! I was so pissed at Joshua and worried about what Tyler might have picked up on!

After I had closed the door behind me rather loudly, I turned quickly and faced Joshua in ferocity.

"Joshua, I have told you several times that a relationship is not in the cards for the two of us! We are through! Kaput!" I waved my arms in frustration to emphasize my words.

"But you and I still have sex sometimes! We have such physical and sexual chemistry!" Joshua pointed out. "You must still love me!? Can't we still have sex occasionally for recreation and pleasure?!" Joshua was pleading. "I need it badly!"

"Yes, I have slept with you a few times since we broke up, but get over it! As the song says, 'what does love have to do with it!' Damn it, Joshua! Our relationship had many rolls in the hay, good sex, and a brief dating fling, but I didn't love you then, I do NOT love you now, nor will I ever love you the way you love me! I got what I wanted from you, and that was good vibrations, sexual pleasure, and loyalty." I was very frustrated that I had to remind him we were through! "I have someone I love now, and with whom I want to live for life! All you are going to have are memories and wet dreams of me, because I won't be sleeping with anyone else, especially you, until I can sleep with my new main man. After that, I am going to be true to him, at the expense of all others, including you. Joshua, you and I are finished!"

"Who is this person that you want? Do you even have anyone in mind that could prevent you and me from… from having sex still?" Joshua had an inquisitive look as he asked.

Before I could think I blurted out the truth!

"It's Tyler, you ninny! Didn't you see me feeling his chest as I placed my arm around his neck!" I was still hissing, speaking ferociously, yet as quietly as possible.

"Tyler?!" Joshua exclaimed, as a light seemed to come on in his mind. "You are after him?!"

I had answered the question about Tyler in a fit of frustration. Now I had to walk the tightrope and hope Joshua didn't do any reverse blackmailing on me with Tyler!

"Yes!" I exclaimed. "I'd appreciate it if you would not flirt with me in front of Tyler! I'm now off limits to you! After today, you can go your own way. I don't want to see you again in any kind of 'dating' situation!" I emphasized my words by punching my right fist into my open left hand.

"Your hand… stroking Tyler's chest… it was for real?" Joshua asked slowly and sadly. "You have… you have slept with Tyler?"

"Yes, I have, Joshua!" I lied angrily. "Our sex is great! It is what I want for the rest of my life!"

"Well," Joshua looked sadly into my eyes, "I won't be helping you today then. I won't be helping you ever again. If there is no hope for us, I have no reason to please you ever again. Goodbye, Andrew!"

I panicked instantly! I hadn't foreseen this reaction for some dumb reason!

I had to have Joshua's help in order to get Tyler under my roof! My mind thought quickly, and I came up with a plan. I grabbed Joshua's arm and restrained him from leaving. He stayed still, but faced away from me and pulled toward the elevator.

"If you don't help me today," I spoke quietly, yet threateningly, "I will tell your wife about our affair, and how you moonlight in the gay community!"

Joshua whirled around and stood facing me in front of the elevator.

"You wouldn't hurt me that way!" Joshua laughed nervously, then stopped. When he spoke again he almost pleaded. "Would you? You wouldn't hurt me that way… You know I love my wife… You wouldn't do that to me… would you, Drew?!"

"Try me!" I growled. "Just try me, Joshua!"

At that moment my two straight friends came off of the elevator.

"Hey, hey, Andrew!" black-haired Abel said, extending his hand.

I shook his hand, and then shook brown-haired Steve's hand.

"Joshua," I pointed as I spoke, "meet Abel and Steve. Steve, Abel, this is Joshua. He has our moving van!" Then an idea hit me. "Joshua, Abel is single and on the down-low." I knew that Joshua knew what that meant, but Abel or Steve wouldn't have a clue, hopefully!

I looked at Abel. I was right! Abel was oblivious. He had a big grin on his face, and was nodding in agreement. I then glanced at Steve. He too showed no signs of understanding what I had said about Abel.

Needless to say, Joshua left me alone to hit on Abel the rest of the day! It was kind of cruel of me to do that to Abel, sic Joshua, a gay man, on him, but it was quite amusing too. Abel didn't always understand Joshua's flirtations, but he did realize something strange was going on.

The four of us went back to my apartment door, and I opened it for everyone to file into my home with Tyler.

I introduced Tyler to Steve and Abel, and we locked the apartment up. We decided Abel would ride in the moving van with Joshua driving (poor Abel!), and Steve would ride in my car as I drove and Tyler guided me to his home in Gurnee. I was to go first with Tyler and Steve, and Josh would follow in the moving van with Abel.

On our drive up to Gurnee, Tyler told me more details about his parents, and brother who still lived at home. He also told how his mother had fixed his sister, Soenya, up with her husband, and what Soenya was like. By the time we pulled into Tyler's driveway, I felt like I had known his whole family forever. Now I would be meeting the family of the man I wanted to marry!

Tyler's family farm was beautiful. I was impressed and in love with it almost instantly.

We all piled out of the vehicles. I rushed around my Intrepid to meet Tyler, Steve, Abel and Josh before the Belmont family came out to meet us. As I did so I heard a cry. I was very surprised and looked for the culprit of the outburst.

I noticed with alarm that Abel was sitting on the ground rocking in pain. Joshua, Tyler, and Steve were already around him, fussing over him.

"What the hell happened!?" I asked as I quickly approached the group around Abel.

"Abel exited the moving van and stepped on this damn rock!" Steve motioned to a rather large, three inch diameter rock in the driveway. "I think he has sprained his ankle!"

Abel sat in the driveway grimacing in pain as Steve tended to his injury. I knew he was in good hands because both Abel and Steve were certified and worked as a team in a para-medics unit. I took Tyler by the elbow and pulled him aside.

"Abel will be fine, Tyler!" I explained quickly. "They are both paramedics and trained in first aid. I need you to give me a primer of topics to avoid with your folks and an idea of how to impress them!"

"Are you sure Abel will be fine?" Tyler looked back at Steve and Abel with a worried look on his face.

"Look, Tyler, I wouldn't drag you away if I figured they needed us. There is nothing that we could do that paramedics don't know how to do better. I am serious!" I gave Tyler a half hug by wrapping my right arm around his shoulders and squeezing him reassuringly. "I need some quick pointers!"

"Well!" Tyler looked at me and frowned, and then began fidgeting. "My family is conservative Republican. They are pro-life, anti-gay rights, anti-liberal, anti-Obama, and anti-national health care. That about sums it up I guess… As long as you are conservative, you shouldn't have any problems!"

I slightly frowned as I realized the anti-gay part would piss me off if that subject came up. I looked back quickly at Tyler.

"How in the hell can I impress them as a prospective roommate of yours in this brief time period in which we will see them?!"

"Be as respectful and polite as possible, and don't offend any of them!" Tyler responded with certitude. "If any of them offend you, let it run off you like water off a duck's back, and don't respond in anger!"

I smiled wanly and uncertainly at Tyler as his family came out of the house to greet us. Tyler introduced Steve and Abel first, and there was a fuss over Abel as Steve treated his sprain.

Then Tyler introduced Joshua, and saved me for last. As he introduced me to his mother, father, and younger brother, I couldn't help noticing his mother was looking me up and down curiously and frowning.

"Mr. Belmont!" I spoke brightly, extending my hand. "Nice to meet you, I'm sure! I am Andrew, Tyler's new roommate!"

"Hello!" Mr. Belmont responded gruffly, shaking my hand. "You had best treat Tyler with the friendship and concern he deserves! I don't take kindly to strangers jerking around my family! If you screw Tyler over or take advantage of him in any way, you'll have me to answer to!" Mr. Belmont gripped my hand so hard I could hear my knuckles cracking! He was obviously very strong from his farming lifestyle. I also noted he was dark complected and handsome. Tyler did indeed have the best, most gorgeous features of both his parents!

"I already respect and have nothing but friendly feelings for Tyler, Mr. Belmont! I will treat him with the friendship, respect, and concern that I and you believe he deserves. Don't fret over it any!" I smiled broadly despite the pain his grip was causing. Fortunately about that time he let go of my hand.

I turned to Mrs. Belmont. She was femininely beautiful! I was impressed.

"Mrs. Belmont, I admire and am a new friend of your son! I am Andrew DiPree, and I hope you will be happy with me as Tyler's roommate!"

Mrs. Belmont was looking at me intently, still frowning. She hesitantly extended her hand. I started getting nervous. About what was she so curious, intent, and obviously not happy?! Didn't she like me? Had I upset her already somehow?!

"Have we met before, Andrew?" Tyler's mom asked me inquisitively as she shook my outstretched hand. "You look so familiar... like I have seen you at a party, social gathering, church meeting, or on a... on a sign somewhere?" A light of dawning seemed to come over her when she mentioned a sign. "Do you do advertising... a male model...?"

When she said 'sign', I briefly blanched! I had been prominently featured on two or three signs outside of Gurnee when I was scheduled to come here and do my strip tease and full sexual service act at the local lounge, Neon Red. What would I say to sway her off her suspicions and doubts, and then to throw her off the trail to find out where she had seen me?!

"I don't believe that we have met, or had any opportunity to have seen one another, Mrs. Belmont." I responded somewhat dishonestly and nervously. "And no, I don't do any advertising or modeling of any kind."

"Hmmm…" Mrs. Belmont said, shaking her head uncertainly. "I know you look familiar! I just can't put my finger on exactly where I have seen you before!"

I quickly decided it was time to rush this job along! I didn't want to give Mrs. Belmont time to remember anything from a few days or so ago that might identify me to her! I had to keep my secret from her because if she remembered that she had seen me on billboards as a stripper and sex provider she would tell Tyler! If I didn't succeed in keeping my job a secret, the Belmonts would take Tyler away from me. I couldn't bear that!

I immediately went into self-defense and self-preservation mode.

"Abel," I spoke authoritatively, "you are injured. You will just focus on driving the vehicle, and moving boxes into place inside the moving van. Joshua and Steve, you will carry Tyler's things from the back door here to the van and load them in for Abel. Any help he needs in re-situating things you will provide. Tyler, you and I and Tristan will carry your things from your room down to the door for Joshua and Steve. Is that agreed as a good plan?"

I looked from one of our party to another quickly. They nodded in unison.

Thus it was decided by me how we would quickly load up Tyler's things from his room into the van so that we could get the hell out of here! Without thinking, I gently pushed Tyler toward the house using my hand on his ass. Out of the corner of my eye I noticed Mrs. Belmont following Tyler and me with her eyes, and she frowned when she saw where I had put my hand on Tyler's body. I quickly removed my hand and put my arm around Tyler's neck instead. Damn! She had seen me on Tyler's ass!

I followed Tyler into the house and upstairs to his room. He had such an awesome figure, and both sides of his body turned me on! It was pleasant following Tyler and admiring his cute ass. By the time we entered his room, I was ready to throw Tyler on his bed and take him there and then! Fortunately I had no vodkas under my belt to hinder my natural patience factor in any relationship, or to remove my reticence and inhibitions to move more quickly with Tyler.

I was stimulated by the thought of being in Tyler's bedroom, just Tyler and I. As I stood with him there looking around my heart skipped in my chest. It was a major turn on that I could soon enjoy all the time once Tyler was living with me!

Tyler's room was neat, tidy, and comfortable. He had a large bureau with a mirror, a beautiful queen-sized bed with a shelved headboard, an overstuffed reclining chair, a computer desk with a complete computer system, two floor lamps, a card table and chairs in front of a large window, and a walk-in closet. A large screen TV rested on a large chest at the foot of his bed.

Tyler walked into his closet and I followed. He had lots of clothes, three pairs of shoes, and a leather jacket. I couldn't help thinking how hot Tyler must look in that jacket!

Tyler had several empty boxes in the closet. He brought them out and put them on the bed.

"We can pack all my clothes and things in these boxes." Tyler said, smiling at me.

"Let's go!" I exclaimed.

"Tyler!" Mrs. Belmont called in a motherly voice. "Would you come down here... alone...? I want to talk to you."

"Ah...I...mom...my mom..." Tyler stammered, looking apologetically at me.

I interrupted so as not to allow the moment to drag on into awkwardness.

"I'll start packing! You go see what your mom wants." I smiled, and gently touched Tyler on the cheek. "It's okay, Tyler."

"Thanks! I'll be back as quickly as I can." Tyler left the room.

I glanced around for Tristan. He was nowhere to be seen. I crossed quickly to the bureau. I wanted to start packing by handling Tyler's underwear. It would be very stimulating! I opened Tyler's bureau drawers until I found the one that held his briefs. I took out the top pair and smelled it deeply. 'Fresh scent Bounce,' I muttered. I sniffed the pair again. 'Tyler's cologne!' I smiled. 'Avatar, I believe!' I started to rise as I unfolded each pair, inspected them, and smelled them again. I neatly stacked them all. I took Tyler's briefs to a box and neatly arranged them inside. Then came his t-shirts, tank tops, and pajamas. Soon I had the bureau empty, and two large boxes full of Tyler's clothes.

I started on his clothes in the walk-in. As I packed his closet clothes I admired all of his casual outfits, nice jeans, button shirts, cargo pants, and farm duds. It was very titillating to touch Tyler's clothing! I felt so close to him while doing so! Soon his closet was also empty. I had another five full boxes of Tyler's clothes.

I moved to his laundry basket. I took a box and began moving the dirty clothes to the box. I whiffed some of them. Along with the occasional barn smell, I could smell Tyler's masculinity, his deodorant, his cologne. They were intoxicating! I found myself getting uncontrollably stimulated and hard. How I wanted to be with Tyler, hold him, feel him, kiss him! I was about to lie down on his bed and take care of myself when Tyler returned. Tristan followed.

"Okay!" Tyler exclaimed. "Where are we in packing?"

"All of your clothes are packed." I told him as I stood up quickly. "Your bureau is empty. We need to do the books, shoes, and small items." I stopped and waved around the room.

"Great, Andrew!" Tyler began stocking a box with books off the shelves.

"Do all of these pieces of furniture move with you, 'us' to Aurora, Tyler?" I waved expansively around the room again and looked questioningly at Tyler.

"Yep!" Tyler paused and smiled at me. "Everything in this room, big and small, comes with me... us! Think we can do it in one day?"

"Oh yeah!" I nodded cheerfully at Tyler. "We'll do it! We'll git 'er done!"

Tyler returned to packing. Tristan began carrying out boxes.

"What did your mom want?" I asked as I resumed packing. "Is everything okay?"

"Yeh." Tyler shrugged, and smiled at me. "Typical mom stuff. She doesn't think I should move out. She wanted to know how long I had known you, and what I knew about you. I couldn't admit I've only known you for a couple of days, so I said you and I had become acquainted a few weeks ago via an internet add. She then wanted to know why I hadn't told them, my family, sooner. I told her I wasn't sure you and I were a match as roommates, so I didn't want to worry them!"

Now, I knew! Tyler definitely wanted to protect our relationship and keep us living together, even if it took deception and lies. I was thrilled! It was another sign out of the way, showing how and to what extent Tyler had feelings for me!

"Did you assure her that you're in good hands?" I picked up a box of Tyler's things.

"Yes, yes I did. Let's get started carrying the boxes downstairs." Tyler grabbed two boxes, and I noticed with pleasure his toned muscles move. I grabbed two more boxes and followed Tyler. Have mercy! What a body he had! I resisted the urge to drop my boxes and grab his ass!

# WATER OFF A DUCK'S BACK

"Tyler!" My mom called in her sweet, comforting voice. "Would you come down here... alone...?! I want to talk to you."

I looked at Andrew, my face flushing a bit. I shrugged apologetically.

"Ah... I... mom... my mom..." I stammered, unsure how to tell Andrew she wanted a private conversation. Would he think it was about him? Was it about him? Why would Mom do this to me now?! It was kind of embarrassing for me in front of Andrew to go and see my mom for a private conversation! Especially if it were about him!

Andrew interrupted me before I could become totally embarrassed and flustered.

"I'll start packing! You go see what your mom wants." Andrew smiled, and to my thrill, gently touched my cheek with his open hand. "It's okay, Tyler!" He finished.

"Thanks!" I exclaimed sincerely. "I'll be back as quickly as I can." I turned abruptly and left the room, not giving Andrew a chance to question me about my mother's possible questions or conversation topics.

I hurried down the upstairs hallway toward the stairway. I had traversed this wood thousands of times as a dependent in my parents' house. What did Mom want? I hoped it wasn't anything bad! I was worried because it was obvious when she met Andrew outside that she wasn't exactly happy with him. I still hoped that she liked Andrew! I would try to remember to ask that myself.

The thought that kept nagging at me, however, was; what should I do if Mom doesn't like Andrew? What could I do?! I knew that I had already made up my mind about Andrew! He was a good man, a good friend, very compatible with me, and he and I would make excellent roommates. I knew too that I had already made up my mind about moving in and living with Andrew. I was going to do it! I was an adult after all! I was old enough to take my own decisions despite what my parents thought or did. Today might be the day when I would have to take a stand for my adulthood and my independence, against my mother.

So, it was settled then! If need be, I would lie to Mom to protect what I had with Andrew. Beyond that, if Mom did not like Andrew and wanted me to back out of our roommate arrangements, then my response would be 'tough rocks!' and 'hell no!' Mom wouldn't like that response, but 'oh well…' I wasn't a child anymore! I had my own decisions to take and my own life to lead, not follow my parents' rules while 'out on my own.'

As I neared the top of the stairs Tristan met me. His strawberry blond wavy hair was unusually tousled, and his face was flushed. There was sadness in his brown eyes. He touched my shoulder and stopped me to talk.

"So, you are moving out officially, Tyler?!" Tristan gave me a questioning and some-what mournful look.

"Yeh, Tristan." I answered, turning to face him. "This is it! I have a job, and I now have a home in Aurora. I'm all set. Andrew, the guys, and I are just getting my things from home and taking them with us to my new home at Andrew's apartment in Aurora. Tristan? You look pale… are you okay?"

"Tyler, I never said it enough growing up. I…" Tristan's eyes were misty, and he gulped involuntarily. "I love you, Tyler! You were and are an awesome big brother, and I loved everything you and I shared together as kids. You were always there for me! You always made me feel important, wanted, needed, and loved. I mean…" He paused a moment. "I love Dad and all, but he was quite distant and aloof from us as kids. You know that. He was the worst to you! You, Tyler, were just the opposite, and I appreciated that. I knew I could always go skinny-dipping with you, play games with you, and go places with you! You…" He again paused, and looked at his hands. "You were both a brother, and sometimes a father figure to me, and I will miss you terribly!" Tristan looked up at the end of his soliloquy and gazed sadly at me. Our eyes met and our souls made a very meaningful connection. I knew I would really miss seeing Tristan daily.

"Tris!" I was misting up, and my voice kind of cracked uncharacteristically. "Thank you for your kind words and expressions of love! Tris, I will always be your big brother! My moving out of our parents' house does not change that! I will always be available to you to talk, visit, and whatever! I love you, too! You were an awesome younger brother, and I will never forget the good times we had together! Never!"

"So you enjoyed, valued, and cherished our relationship as much as I did, Tyler?" Tristan had tears running down his cheeks now. I reached out with both hands and cupped his face in them, wiping tears away with my thumbs.

"Tris!" I responded fervently. "I definitely enjoyed, valued, and cherished every moment of our relationship as kids, and now as adults! We had so much fun, we spent time together, and we had not a lot but enough in common that our relationship and bond became as strong as it is. How could I not hold our relationship precious!?"

"Tyler." Tristan hung his head again as I released him. "I never thought I would feel this way when you moved out! But I am… I am… well, I am devastated! I l… I love… I love you so!"

I was surprised at the seriousness and intensity of Tristan's feelings in this area. I had never realized that he felt this close to me and this way about me!

I was unprepared for Tristan's reaction as well. He grabbed me and hugged me at that moment so tightly I almost lost my breath. I hugged him back, thankful that we were so close in his eyes.

"Tristan, dude!" I spoke seriously. "I love you too! But our relationship is not ending! We will continue to be good brothers and friends into our full adult life. You and I… we… we have a relationship that… well, I pledge… will never die!" Tristan was so sincere, and I was bewildered and pleasantly surprised.

"I know, Tyler." Tristan pulled back, and we broke our hug. "I just hope Andrew doesn't replace me in your life!"

"Tristan!" I exclaimed with a rebuking element in my voice. "Andrew will never replace you in my life! You and I will always be tight. You are my blood brother, Tristan. Andrew is a good friend, perhaps a future 'brother' in spirit but not in blood!"

"Thank you, Tyler!" Tristan put his hand on my shoulder. "You are indeed my blood brother!" Tristan paused, removed his hand, and looked at his feet briefly. "Not that you may care, but I like Andrew. He seems to be a real man's man, and a real woman's man. I dig him!"

"Your opinion of my friend and roommate, Andrew, means a lot to me, Tris!" I gave him another hug.

"You won't mind if I am in and out helping you all load your stuff up? I have some other things I am doing, too." Tristan asked. "I need to pretend this isn't happening right now!" He hugged me tightly again.

"You do what you have to do!" I responded as I gently kissed my younger brother on the top of the head. "I understand!"

Typical of Tristan, he turned and rushed down the stairs two at a time. Tristan was always rushing somewhere too quickly.

I was so impressed that he and I had had this moment. From my perspective my relationship with Tristan wasn't a particularly spectacular and close one. It was a normal brother relationship. We had been 'okay' close during our childhood, teenage years, and until I had turned the age I was now. I had been okay with that. We did things together, talked, went to the movies, and such. But I had never felt as close to Tristan as he had just expressed he felt toward me. I was pleasantly surprised! Tristan had never so succinctly and honestly expressed his feelings about and perspective of our relationship until now! I smiled as some memories of happy times spent with Tristan came flooding into my jumbled mind.

I went down the stairs, crossed through the living room, and entered the kitchen. Mom was there, leaning against the counter. She looked very distressed. I knew this was not going to be a typically amicable, happy chat!

"Mom?" I started, questioningly and cautiously. "What's up?!"

"Dion, honey, sit down please." Mom motioned toward what was their new kitchen table and chairs. They had ordered them from somewhere a month ago, and they must have been delivered Friday when I was not at home.

"Are you all right, Mom?!" I asked nervously, knowing that an invitation to a talk, and a request to be seated by Mother was very serious. The tone in her voice was also disturbing. She was using her serious, loving, and worried sick tone. It did not bode well for me!

"Dion, I am fine. You may not be. Please sit down! I need to talk to you!" Mom again motioned toward a new chair at their fabulous new dining table set.

I sat down apprehensively, worried about what concerned Mom so that she would insist on a private conversation. I didn't know if I even wanted to discover what Mom needed to know or had to say! I decided to try and change the subject of this conversation right off the bat. Hopefully I could distract Mom and get her off track.

"I love the new wooden table and chairs, Mom!" I quipped brightly, smiling at her. "You and Dad took a good choice! They're beautiful! You never did tell me from whom and where you ordered them?"

"Thank you, Dion, we like them too." Mom was polite, but business-like. "They came from the Amish downstate somewhere. They were delivered yesterday while you were gone…"

"Where are the old table and chairs, Mom?" I asked innocently, hoping this track of conversation would keep Mom occupied.

"Dion, I didn't call you down here to discuss our new, or our old furniture!" Mom was curt and to-the-point. "Now stop obstructing and obfuscating the purpose of my talk with you and listen!"

The firm tone in her voice told me she meant business! I was busted! I shut my mouth and looked contritely at Mom.

"Dion, how did you meet this… this… this… Andrew?" Mom stumbled a little bit in her tone and question. She seemed to be struggling already with some developing negative opinions about Andrew such that she couldn't just call him 'Andrew'. I felt another step closer to a precipice, a coming major disagreement with Mom.

I couldn't tell her I had only just met Andrew Friday on the bus to Aurora and had fallen in love… I mean had liked what I had seen. I couldn't possibly convince her that in 12 hours I knew Andrew and that he and I were like brothers, infinitely compatible to be roommates. She wouldn't understand my position of meeting Andrew one day, and moving in with him the next. I wasn't honestly sure I did either, except that it felt so right! I wanted nothing more than to be with Andrew. Here was a time again where I would have to lie to protect what I had with Andrew. It would be hard! I had never lied to Mom about anything this big before.

"Mom, I know what I am doing!" I responded firmly, looking at my hands.

"Dion." Mom replied just as quickly in a serious and expectant tone. "That is not the question I asked. I am not sure you do know what you are doing! I expect an answer to my first question! How did you meet this… Andrew?"

I sat there literally twiddling my thumbs as I furiously considered my next response. Mom was clearly upset about my moving out, and it apparently primarily had to do with Andrew. What was it? Couldn't she see what an awesome guy Andrew was by seeing him and meeting him?! Couldn't she tell he was a real catch for me… for a roommate just by his appearance?! How could I assuage her concerns? What were her concerns? I had no doubt I would find out. She would tell me, but would it be in time to gloss over it from my end?

"Andrew and I met over the internet a few weeks ago, Mom. He was interested in friendship, but at the time he had a roommate." I began as I spun probably the biggest lie I had ever told my mom in my life! I crushed any guilt or remorse quickly as I continued. "I simply shared my situation, a new job, need for housing, and looking for such in Aurora, Illinois, with Andrew over the course of the next month. Coincidentally I met Andrew, the same man, on the bus Friday as he was returning to Aurora from Wisconsin." I knew Andrew had been on the bus returning to Aurora from Gurnee, but something told me to confuse the issue here too!

"By Friday when I ran into Andrew on the bus, he needed a new roommate. We talked on the bus and became acquainted. He asked me to be his new roomie as we ate at the Aurora bus depot restaurant. The rest, as they say, is history to the present!" I shrugged and looked with certainty at my mom. My heart was pounding.

"You didn't know Andrew, except from the internet, when you met?" Mom was firm and commanding. I had only seen her like this in childhood when she was trying to solve family problems by herself, and not involve my dad. I was glad she apparently didn't intend to involve my dad with whatever this discussion concerned.

"Well, I guess… I mean… we…" I fumbled the ball as I looked at my hands, knowing the lie I was spinning! I didn't know if I could continue it. My heart was beating like a bass drum and I felt light headed and flushed.

"Dion!" Mom exclaimed, uncharacteristically sternly. "You didn't know Andrew from anything or anywhere other than over the internet, when you met him personally face-to-face?!"

"I met him over the internet. I never saw, or met him face-to-face before that!" I answered in a burst before my current deceitful personality kicked in again.

Mom didn't miss a beat before plunging on in her talk.

"What do you know about Andrew?" Mom asked, again in a stern tone. "Answer me truthfully, Dion!"

"He's a nice, wonderful guy! He has a life, he's blond-haired and good looking…" I started, trying to slough off Mom's interrogation.

"Cut the crap, Dion!" Mom exclaimed angrily. Immediately she put her hand to her mouth in shame and gasped.

I sat there stunned, my mouth hanging agape momentarily. Mom had never used any semi-foul language when talking or disciplining us as kids, let alone used any foul language! Shoot! She had chastised us kids for using the word 'terd'! For her to use the word 'crap' was big-time. I had never heard her use that word or anything close in my life! I was shocked and chagrined. I buttoned up as I looked at Mom in shocked surprise and concern.

Mom took her hand away from her mouth, and looked at her hands. Then she looked sternly back at me.

"What do you know about Andrew, Dion?! The truth this time! What do you know about Andrew?!"

"I know he is 25, he will be 26 on June 20." I flushed as the truth came tumbling out. I came clean out of sheer shock over Mom's language! "He is a trader and stock broker at Bear Stearns during the day, and in the evenings and on the weekends he moonlights as a drummer in a popular local band. He makes a lot of money, Mom! He rents the apartment we are sharing from his employers. His apartment is awesome, very large and homey! He is not married or involved; his mother, father, and brother, Noah, live in Florida. He is a great guy, Mom! Andrew and I get along like two peas in a pod!" I looked appealingly and seriously at Mom then. "I… well, Mom… I like Andrew! He will make… he will be a good roommate for me!"

Then Mom dropped on me the bomb that was her concern over Andrew.

"Dion, I am concerned about Andrew and his intentions toward you. Specifically I believe he has a… he is very… he is too fond of and affectionate toward you! I believe he is romantically interested in you, Dion!" Mom stared at me firmly as she sat down across the table from me.

'I hope so!' I thought, and almost blurted out. Instead I was surprised, incredulous, and pleased that Mom was reading this into Andrew, his actions, his behavior! Could it be true?! I immediately went into denial mode for Mom's benefit and began defending Andrew, and downplaying her concerns.

"Mom, Andrew is a great guy, and a good friend! He is no more romantically intentioned toward me than… than Tristan is!" I looked nervously at my hands. At that moment I realized that I sensed that from Andrew as well, a romantic intent, but I was happy about it! How could I hide my feelings from Mom!? How could I change her mind about Andrew, and convince her to drop her concerns?! How could I convincingly deflect her concerns when I wanted them to be true?

"Dion, Andrew is too… he is… well, he is too familiar with you for as little time as the two of you have known one another. I am uncomfortable with his obvious love for you, and that familiarity! He puts his arm around you like most men do to their wives. It is quite… It is, well… it is unnatural!" Mom exclaimed with that look of concern on her pretty face.

I smiled and chuckled dismissively, trying to let Mom know how silly her concerns were.

"Dion, this is not funny!" Mom frowned at me. "I am really worried about you… about your faith… about what Andrew intends you to do…

to fulfill for himself... what type of ultimate relationship he wants with you! If he is a homosexual, Dion, you are a sheep dealing with a wolf!"

"Mom," I began, smiling at her, "I meant no disrespect when I laughed! I laughed because Andrew is not too familiar or touchy-feely with me! Sure, he puts his arm around my neck and lays a hand on my shoulder occasionally, but..."

"Dion!" Mom interrupted in a surprisingly angry and frustrated tone. "As Andrew came with you into this house just moments ago he had his hand flat open on your ass!" Again Mom gasped and clapped her hand to her mouth.

"Mom!" I exclaimed in shock. "You are really upset! I've never heard you use this type of language!"

Mom uncovered her mouth a little sheepishly.

"Dion, I am sorry for swearing. However, that does not change my concern and fear for you if you persist in moving in with Andrew!" Her voice was softer but just as firm.

I knew that Andrew and I were being very familiar and touchy-feely with one another, but I enjoyed it, I longed for it! I couldn't let Mom be so concerned that she would insist on me breaking up with Andrew. This would precipitate a larger schism between Mom and me. It was time to lie again to save me and Andrew, and assuage my mom.

"Mom, Andrew's hand on my a... I mean my butt was an accident! Andrew is not too familiar or touchy-feely at home in our apartment. In fact, he hardly ever touches me! Okay?!"

"Dion, I'm sorry for asking you this. However, I have to know for my own peace of mind!" Mom looked at her hands and paused. She glanced furtively at me from time to time.

"Yes, Mom?" I held out my hands palms up. "What is it?" I was scared of what she was going to ask me.

"Dion..." Mom looked up at me nervously but determination shown in her countenance as well. "You and Andrew... Andrew hasn't... the two of you... have either of you... both of you..."

"Mom! You are babbling." I returned softly. "What is it that you want to know?!"

Mom looked me in the face, and I could see her mustering her confidence.

"Dion, you and Andrew have not had… well, the two of you have not… you two have not been… well, you two have not been sexually intimate with each other have you?" Mom inquired, the words coming out in bursts. "Andrew hasn't tried to… he hasn't tried to have sex with you has he?"

I was surprised and shocked. My mom was really wound up and way off on Andrew and me! I could honestly say she was wrong here!

"Mom!" I spoke firmly as I patted one of her hands. "Andrew and I have not had sex or been intimate sexually, nor are we going to be! And no, Andrew has not tried to get me to sleep with him! Mom, I am not a homosexual! Nor is Andrew! Would you stop worrying about me with Andrew!? Anything the two of us do will be done with mutual consent only! And since we are not homosexuals, you don't have to worry about us having sex with each other!"

Mom looked seriously at me, but she nodded.

"Dion, you have never lied to me from the time you started talking until today." Mom stated, still visibly worried. "If you say it, I have to believe you for now. However, I still believe Andrew is after you romantically. If he is not hitting on you now, he will soon!"

I decided to try another tactic. There must be some specific things behind Mother's concerns, and I wanted to know what they were! What did she see that was this 'bad' in Andrew and his actions?!

"Mom, what things do you see in Andrew, what has he done that would make you think and feel this way about him? What… I mean… I am mystified that you think this about Andrew?! How can you think Andrew is gay?"

"Andrew looks very familiar to me, Dion!" Mom began, reaching out and taking one of my hands. "And I finally realized why. Just over the past week I saw Andrew's picture, or at least I am pretty sure now that it was Andrew, on a billboard for the bar/lounge in Gurnee, the Neon Red…"

"Well, that's easy to explain!" I sighed in relief. "Andrew's band played a few days in a bar/lounge in Gurnee after Wisconsin! Of course his picture would probably be on a local billboard! That's how I met him on the bus. He was returning to Aurora from his gig here in town and his gigs in Wisconsin!"

"The billboard was not just for a regular bar/lounge, Dion. It was a strip club, the only gay strip club in Gurnee…it was a billboard for Neon Red!" Mom watched me intently as her words sank in.

"Well… that's… it can't really be… That's ridiculous! I guess his band might play at some questionable places some times, but… it isn't what you think, Mom! Andrew is no stripper for gay men! It couldn't have been Andrew that you saw on the billboard…! I guess the only explanation is someone… someone who looks so much like Andrew that you are just making a mistake in identifying him!" I stumbled around in my defense because I was a bit bewildered at her 'discovery'.

"If it were Andrew that I saw on that sign, Dion, he was not at that… that gay strip bar to play a band gig. He was part of the act!" Mom frowned. "I'm sorry, Dion!"

"I refuse to believe that, Mom!" I was angry, defensive, and rebelling against her concern and… interference! "Andrew is… Andrew works at Bear Stearns as a stock broker! He is a morally upright, upstanding, and a wonderful person, and he wouldn't lie to me about things like that! He has communicated with me via the internet for a month! During that time he and his roommate had a good relationship, but then his roommate went to Arizona. Andrew needs another roommate to make bills. He asked me when we actually met face-to-face on Friday to be his roommate and because of our month-long discussions and conversations, I agreed. It is as simple as that! Don't you understand? Andrew wouldn't be involved in a gay strip act! Whomever you saw on that billboard must have been Andrew's look-a-like!"

My mom wiped her hair out of her face. When she looked back at me, she looked sad and a little haggard. Concern had crowned her face with some beginning wrinkles, and I felt badly for her. Why wouldn't she just drop this nonsense!

"Dion!" My mom spoke firmly, lovingly, and with a sense of resignation. "Dion, are you in love with Andrew right now?!"

I was stunned and incredulous that Mom had arrived at these questions based on some stupid billboard similarity to Andrew! However, I was also at a loss to answer because I was indeed on that road to being in love with Andrew. I couldn't say that! I had to lie and deny, deny, deny. How my life had changed from perfect saint to conniving and lying now that I was in love… tempted with Andrew! I chastised myself, but I knew I must continue to lie.

"Mom! You know me! You raised me right!" I chuckled and snorted in embarrassment, false incredulity, and self-consciousness of the truth. "What makes you think I am in love with Andrew?"

"I think that because every 'evidence' that I bring you that Andrew is gay, is romantically interested in you, and is not who you think he is you shoot down. You manage to plausibly defend Andrew in all things as this impeccable specimen of a perfect, decent, moral, upstanding man and citizen. That is why I want to know, Dion! Are you in love with Andrew right now?!" Mom leaned on her elbows on the table and moved her face sternly closer to mine.

I gulped. I had to… I had to… I couldn't… I had to lie! I was doing it for Andrew and me.

"Mom, I told you I am not a homosexual!" I pleaded my prior testimony. "If I were in love… in love… If I were in love with Andrew that would make me a homosexual! Don't you trust me?!"

"Dion!" Mom pointed her finger at me sternly. "Dion! I want the truth! An honest answer! Are you in love with Andrew right now?!"

I paused, knowing at the same time that the longer I took to speak the more my mom would believe that I was indeed in love with Andrew.

"Mom!" I closed my eyes. I could lie if I didn't look at my mom's honest face. "I am… I am…"

"Dion!" Mom spoke unusually firmly. "Dion! Look me in the eyes to answer me! Open your eyes!"

I gulped again involuntarily. I opened my eyes and looked seriously into Mom's eyes.

"Mom!" I could do this for Andrew! "Mom, my hand on a thousand Bibles, I am not in love with… I am not… I am not in love with Andrew right now!" I spit it out, while mentally reserving my 'crossed fingers' to exempt me from the power of the oath.

My mother sat back with a resignation of belief in my answers to her very difficult questions. She studied me briefly, and then spoke.

"You said Andrew isn't involved with a girlfriend. Is he involved with any other guy like he would be with a girlfriend? Or like he is with you?" Mom asked meaningfully.

"Mom, excuse me, but what the hell does that have to do with anything?!" I blurted before I had a chance to catch myself. Mom had broached the profanity, but I still felt a bit of shame. "I am 'involved' with Andrew in no other way than as a roommate! That's it!"

"There is no need to use any profanity in our talk, Dion. I apologize for using it myself!" Mother said seriously. "My question has everything to do with the reason I am concerned about your relationship with Andrew!"

"Mom." I started in a frustrated but patient voice. "I don't know if Andrew has ever had a girlfriend. I know he has none right this minute. I just know that he has a room and apartment available to share with me in the location of my new job in Aurora, Illinois. I need housing, I have the job! With Andrew, I have the housing. What the hell else is there?!"

I was immediately chagrined at my use of the word 'hell' again! But I was a little angry, and I was quickly losing it.

"Dion." Mom began as she seriously looked at me and set her mien in a caring and compassionate way. "I think Andrew may be a tried and true, bonafide homosexual! I have seen the billboard…"

"Mom! Andrew is a stock broker!" I was now getting mad, nigh on to livid. "They are the most ignored class of people by the press! How would you ever see him, or have an opportunity to meet him? They are never interviewed or seen in the news! I am telling you, if Andrew's picture were on that gay bar's billboard, it was for their band gig, or it is a look-a-like to Andrew! I refuse to believe this about Andrew! It is libelous and salacious, and not as it may seem to you, Mom!" I was uncharacteristically animated as I delivered this rant to my mother, and she did kind of look like one standing in front of a fan getting fake string sprayed in her face.

"You know what, Mom?" I slammed my fist down on the table. "Drop the damn billboard! I am telling you that Andrew isn't that kind of a person! He would not be a gay male stripper! He is a stock broker, a fine man, a gorgeous man… provider, a loyal, trustworthy, honest, moral, and balanced man… citizen! He may have a look-a-like here in Gurnee that is sullying his reputation, but I refuse to listen to it, or even consider it!"

I pushed my chair back and prepared to stand up.

"Dion!" Mom tightened her grip on my hand. "Stay seated! I am not finished!" Her voice, though very firm and stern, was still loving and compassionate. I had to obey!

I sat down, frowning and letting Mom know I wasn't happy about this conversation!

"Andrew is not a homosexual, Mom!" I growled. "Of all the things he might be, 'homosexual' is not one of them. I am not homosexual, and I would feel uncomfortable living with a homosexual man! Mom you have nothing to worry about! I know Andrew as though I have known him all my life, and he is not a homosexual! He is not 'into me' or after me! We are friends and roommates! That is it!"

"Dion, I want you to be on your guard!" Mom began softly. "I may be completely out-to-lunch on Andrew, and I hope I am. However, my intuition and motherly instinct is really concerned that you may be in the process of being maneuvered into a homosexual relationship by Andrew for his narcissistic self-gratification!"

I shook my head, snorted, and kind of chuckled as Mom continued her worries and concerns, damn! This whole conversation was ridiculous! I couldn't get so lucky!

"Dion, I am not blind!" Mom spoke calmly yet forcefully. "Andrew is very handsome, his hair is beautiful, and he has a mega-attractive body and physique! I know that! Andrew flaunts his hot form and figure with tight clothing that shows everything, as well as a flirtatious, charming demeanor and character. But, Dion, you are every bit as handsome, beautiful, and physically attractive as Andrew! From this comes my fear of Andrew's true intentions toward you. Well, that and the fact that he is touching you all of the time!" Mom sat back.

I was fuming and determined that Mom was wrong, but yet I couldn't look her in the eyes! Why did she not shut up and leave me alone?!

"I believe Andrew is looking for someone his equal in looks, appearance, and sex appeal. He found you, and I believe he will start pressuring you for a... well... shall we say... he will start pressuring you for sexual intimacy once you are successfully living with him!" Mom sat forward and grasped my right hand in her hands again.

I was speechless as I searched for something with which to come back at Mom. I had nothing!

"How many bedrooms are there in Andrew's apartment? You and he will not be sharing a room, will you?" Mom spoke before I could interject anything.

This I could respond to.

"There are two fully-furnished bedrooms. I will have one, and Andrew will have one!" I continued to shake my head, disgusted that I had to still partially lie to my mother. I couldn't tell her my room was currently a study, and that Andrew's former roommate shared a bedroom with Andrew! If she knew that she would be more upset and worried about Andrew's sexuality!

"Dion, you make sure you have your own room! And if you do find that Andrew is gay, and wants a relationship with you, realize that you can move back home here, or move somewhere else in Aurora. You do not have to stay in an unsafe environment and immoral home!" Mom squeezed my hand and smiled at me.

"Yes, Mom." I responded, looking at my hands. "May I go now?"

"Dion, look me in the face and meet my eyes!" Mom was firmly commanding.

I couldn't disobey this tone of Mother's voice. I did as she bid me.

"Dion, promise me you will not let yourself get involved romantically with any guy, Andrew, or anyone else too quickly! Aurora is a large city, and it does boast a large gay population. You must be careful at all times with your spiritual life and Christian-walk!" Mom looked expectantly and pleadingly at me.

I realized if she knew that I already wanted to pursue a more romantic and serious relationship with Andrew, she would flip. If Andrew and I did become an item, I didn't know how I was ever going to be able to tell my family. I now feared a relationship with Andrew might trigger a major schism between me and my family! Mom was already apoplectic about my relationship to and with Andrew. Dad had not even been consulted yet. I knew he would hit the ceiling!

"Mom, I promise!" I spoke emphatically. "I told you I am not a homosexual! Andrew is not a homosexual! I am not looking for or into guys! Neither is Andrew! We are just roommates, Mom! Are we done now?" I was pretty exasperated, and tired of this conversation.

"For the time being, Dion, for the time being." Mom released my hand and sat back. Her mannerisms and body language betrayed the fact that for Mom this conversation was far from over.

I stood up quickly and returned to my bedroom the way I had come.

With some anger and resentment I puzzled over my mom's conversation as Andrew and I took down my bed, the bureau, boxes, lamp, tables, and computer system. She had been concerned at the youth of our relationship, the speed with which Andrew and I clicked and were moving in together, and actually how well I did know Andrew. She also shared some bizarre idea she had seen Andrew's picture on a community advertisement billboard as a stripper in a gay bar in Gurnee. I assured her that Andrew was not a stripper and worked instead as a loan officer for Bear Stearns and moonlighted as a drummer in a band. At the end of our conversation Mom had insisted on me promising to watch out for myself. She made me promise not to get involved romantically with any men. I had tried to reassure her, but she apparently was worried and was still concerned that

Andrew was trying to maneuver me into a romantic or sexual relationship. She also reminded me that I was welcome to move back home any time.

As we worked I watched Andrew carefully for any signs that he was gay. It was a really pleasant pastime as Andrew was so gorgeous! However, there were no signs that I could see that Andrew was gay, and Andrew simply continued being familiar with me, which I enjoyed tremendously, for some reason.

Andrew and I packed all of my things neatly in the moving van with the major and deeply appreciated help of Joshua, Steve, Able, and Tristan. I hugged and kissed everyone of my family good bye, promising to visit at least once a month. In no time at all the loose ends were taken care of, and we were back on the road heading for Andrew's… our apartment in Aurora.

On our way back I tried to needle information out of Andrew to verify that he was the type of good person that I believed he was. We had a lively and informative discussion. By the time we arrived at Candlestick, I felt I knew Andrew much better. I totally and determinedly pushed my mom's concerns out of my mind, especially her belief she had seen Andrew on a billboard of a strip joint! What rubbish! Mom was just paranoid.

By bedtime we had all my things in Andrew's apartment. I was home! Some of my things Andrew had put in the living room, some in the bathroom, and some in the kitchen. He had truly integrated our belongings. He made me feel that I was now part of his house and home, and deserved to have room all over the apartment. It was wonderful and a blessing how he took me in and made me feel at home.

Andrew brought the last box of my clothes into my converted bedroom, smelling the clean clothes that were on top. I noticed it with a thrill out of the corner of my eye! I was sitting on my bed looking wistfully at my family picture that I was going to put on the headboard. Andrew put the box on the bureau and sat down closely next to me. He put his arm around my neck.

"Are you all right, Tyler?" Andrew asked gently, putting his left hand on my right arm.

Andrew took the picture from me tenderly. "You have a nice family, Tyler, very nice- looking people. Your parents are indeed a particularly handsome couple. I see I was right on the bus about where you inherited your awesome good looks!"

"I don't think I am especially handsome." I said softly as I turned to gaze at Andrew. I was feeling unsure of Andrew a bit, and questioning why I might attract someone who may be in a gay stripper job.

I was struggling to push my Mom's doubts and claims about Andrew out of my mind, but it was tough! I had trusted Mom implicitly all of my life.

"Not especially handsome!? Dude, are you serious!?" Andrew shook his head and smiled broadly. "You are hot, sexy, gorgeously handsome and with such a fine and desirable physique! You are very beautiful and handsome, Tyler! Don't ever doubt it!"

I blushed, smiled, and looked at my hands. Andrew took one gently and looked at it…

"Strong, muscular, and kind of worn… beautiful hands, but strong and well-worked. From farm work, I presume!" Andrew spoke softly, nodding his head and smiling at me. "Even your hands are sexy, Tyler!"

There was silence again for a while. Then Andrew asked again.

"Are you sure you are all right, Tyler?!"

"Yeh, I'm okay. I just know I'll miss them. I've never lived out on my own before except to spend the night at a friend's house. This is a totally new, strange, overwhelming, yet thrilling experience! I hope I can get used to it, do it, and make it work!" I could feel tears starting to well up. I took the picture and put it prominently on my headboard. Then I turned back around to look at Andrew.

Andrew had another idea. He cupped my chin in his right hand, and held my face to look into his.

"You're a fine young man now, Tyler. Your parents raised you like you are for the day like this day. You and I will do fine, together!" His voice was firm, yet tender.

"Thank you for the compliments, Andrew!" I replied lovingly. "It makes me feel good!"

"You are welcome, Tyler. Besides, you forget something!" Andrew's face was honest, an open book. "You are not alone. You have me, your big brother, to live with!" Andrew let go of my chin, and started tickling and rough-housing with me.

I, unfortunately, was very ticklish. When Andrew attacked he caught me off guard!

We both fell back on my bed as we laughed, wrestled, and tickled each other. I struggled to overcome Andrew. He definitely was stronger than I was. In no time at all he had me loosely pinned, straddling my body with his legs, and mercilessly tickling me!

Suddenly having Andrew so close to me in such tight clothing straddling my body, his legs around my hips, his crotch in mine, the smell of his deodorant and cologne, and his warm, lithe body touching mine, was a big turn-on. A wave of sexual and physical stimulation and pleasure coursed through my body. It felt so right, it scared me! I stopped wrestling with Andrew as he stopped too, and we looked into each other's eyes. So much was said and not said in that moment as we shared our spirits and emotions! I felt confused and embarrassed! It was a moment charged with a chemistry and feelings between Andrew and me that were almost totally new and foreign to me! I liked to feel this way!

Andrew gently ran his right hand through my hair a couple of times to the back of my head as he looked down on me. I smiled at him. He smiled lovingly back.

Abruptly Andrew swung off of me and sat back beside me.

"Come on Tyler. I'll order pizza and we'll watch a movie." Andrew stood up.

He gave me a hand off the bed, and I followed him to our living room.

# CHAPTER 12

# SPIKED!?

I awakened with sunshine flowing over me and my bed. It warmed my body and made me squint my eyes until they became accustomed to the bright light. A wonderfully fragrant spring breeze of lilac and magnolia blew in through the open window on the south wall. It made everything smell fresh and clean. I heard some song birds calling outside my window. For the life of me I couldn't identify them by their calls, but they made awesome wake-up music! I watched two birds pass the window on the ledge. I smiled at the beauty of nature and the wonderfully creative genius of God!

I looked around the room and became confused and a little alarmed. I didn't recognize a thing! The walls were bare. Where were all of my pictures? Boxes were stacked in one corner. My computer desk sat empty along one wall. Where was my beautiful new computer system?! The walk-in closet door was open and I could plainly see it was completely empty. Along the far left wall, from the room corner to the door, my bureau, lamps, bureau mirror, and card table with the folded chairs rested neatly. What had happened?! At the foot of my bed, which I realized with comfort was indeed my bed from home, was my large, flat screen television. However, I still did not recognize the room, or remember where I was! I panicked!

Questions continued to arise and swirl around in my mind. Where was I?! What was this room?! Where was my computer system?! What was in the boxes stacked in the corner?! Where were my clothes, shoes, and personal effects?! Why were the shelves, which were normally filled with books, trophies, and nick-knacks, empty?! Why was my other furniture stacked along the wall?! Where was my overstuffed recliner?!

In a confused and by now frightened state I threw off my covers and quickly sat up. As I swung my bare legs over the left side of my bed and pushed them down to the floor I heard a loud bang and felt a sharp pain in my lower left leg and foot. I looked down, grimacing in pain, and longing to say a few choice words. There, along the wall behind my bed headboard and stretching from my bed to the next wall, were the components of my computer system. I had just kicked my printer! I breathed some relief at that discovery! But the other questions remained! Where in the hell was I?!

I stood up and headed for the door on the left side of the room in which I was, hoping to find the answers to my questions in the area beyond it, whatever that was! As I did so, I happened to glance up above the door. There hung a picture of a blond-haired, hot, gorgeous Adonis! 'Andrew!' I thought with relief. With that recognition, the answers to all of my questions came flooding back. I was at Andrew's apartment… our apartment in Aurora, Illinois. I was in my new bedroom that used to be a study. My computer just needed to be setup and reconnected and it would be copacetic. The boxes held all of my clothes, shoes, books, and other belongings. My furniture was stacked around because I was not fully unpacked. My overstuffed recliner was in the living room. Outside the door was the hallway to the other rooms in our apartment.

I remembered everything now! I sighed in relief. My heart stopped racing and I began mentally calming down.

I was living with Andrew. The thought and the reality of that fact thrilled me to no end! I loved Andrew as a lov… brother. Andrew was a hot, gorgeously handsome hunk, and he was mine… my roommate!

I began slowly turning in place, viewing my awesome new room from all angles. I smiled in happiness!

Suddenly my head pounded, and I became severely dizzy. I quickly turned to go back to my bed and sit down, but my bed was now spinning. I plunged toward my bed, hoping to grab it and stop it so I could sit down before I fell down.

I managed to stumble to my bed, grab the mattress, and throw my butt down toward it. I sat down on the very edge of the bed and promptly almost slid off on the floor. I felt dazed, and I became mentally foggy as I struggled to sit back farther on the bed. What was wrong with me!? I had never felt this way before! Was I dying?! It would be my luck to croak now before I determined whether or not Andrew loved me!

It was then as I sat there reeling, that I discovered two more alarming things. First off, all I was wearing were my under pants, my briefs! I always wore a t-shirt and house pants pajamas to bed. Secondly, in this process I tried to remember what had happened to cause me to neglect putting on my pajamas as I got ready for bed. I discovered that I couldn't remember much after Andrew and I started eating pizza, drinking Andrew's special punch, and watching the movie. What was the movie about? I didn't remember! What had happened the night before?! I could not remember! Why couldn't I remember last night, the movie, or getting ready for bed?!

I still felt majorly dizzy. The pounding had lessened some. Things weren't spinning so fast. I decided I just had to get moving and hopefully it would go away! As I reached for my clothes which were on the floor, I wobbled precariously on the edge of the bed. I managed to grab my clothes without falling face first on the floor, and looked up in time to see beautiful and suave Andrew pop his head in my door.

"Good morning, Tyler!" Andrew smiled his charming, disarming smile, and looked me up and down. My heart thrilled at his inspection! "Are you all right? You are looking veerry fine!" He purred as he gave me a look as though he were hungry.

"Yes, I…I think… I mean… I am fine… I think." I tried to stand to put on my pants, but I fell back to a sitting position because of dizziness. "No, Andrew, I am not fine. I have a headache, I am dizzy, and everything is spinning…"

I paused and closed my eyes. Nothing changed, so I opened them again.

"I always wear pajamas when I go to bed, but I don't remember getting ready for bed. I don't remember what happened during or after pizza and punch last night! I don't remember what the movie was about that we watched last night!" I concluded. I looked desperately at Andrew.

Andrew's face changed to a chagrined look, and he quietly opened the door, came in, and sat closely next to me on the bed. He looked like Tristan when he was caught sneaking a cookie. The fact that he too was clad only in briefs came to my attention, but I was so confused, dizzy, and worried, that I noticed only in passing.

"Perhaps I need to go to a doctor?!" I looked into Andrew's blurry eyes. He was obviously tormented by something. His gorgeous face was tinged with concern and fear.

"What, Andrew?!" I demanded. "What's wrong? What happened?" I was getting worried now! I was suffering, and clearly Andrew was upset about something!

"I was hoping all the symptoms would be gone in the morning, Tyler." Andrew said, looking at me with a look of sadness and guilt.

"Andrew!" I exclaimed with all the gusto I could muster. "Tell me what happened!"

"Tyler, I'm afraid that… well… this is… I mean… I gave you… I am responsible for you… for you having lost your memory last night." Andrew hung his head and, visibly ashamed, stole a glance at me. I could tell this was serious! "Tyler, forgive me?!"

"What did you do, Andrew?!" I demanded in fear, concern, and anger. "What did I do? Did you slip me some drug in the food? How about the punch?!" I was really getting scared!  "Andrew, answer me!"

Andrew turned his head and faced me eye-to-eye. He touched my cheek gently with his right hand and placed his left hand on my upper, inner thigh close to my crotch. Despite my fear of what Andrew had done last night, a thrill coursed through my body at Andrew's most intimate touch so far!

"I didn't slip you any drug, Tyler, nothing like that." He paused, and ran his right hand through my hair gently. He was by now facing me. "Well, I suppose it depends on whether you consider alcohol a drug. Tyler, I didn't do it on purpose!"

Andrew clasped my chin gently with both hands. He looked me directly and apologetically in the eyes. At his full facial touch a chill of excitement and stimulation started in my brain and flowed throughout my body again. I shivered involuntarily. Andrew was such a master at the stimulation of touch! Regardless of what had happened, at the sense of his touch I felt an almost uncontrollable urge to kiss him.

"Tyler, I know you said you didn't drink, and I respect that! I didn't do it on purpose, or for any nefarious reason; I just forgot that my punch is always spiked with vodka. That is, I forgot until you were getting loopy last night. At that point I tried to change your drink and you refused; you said you wanted the punch from the refrigerator. I didn't realize that my punch could get someone so drunk so quickly. I didn't realize your tolerance for alcohol was so low." Andrew let go of me and hung his head again. "You became plastered last night, Tyler! You were so drunk so fast that I…" Andrew looked at me sadly, his blue eyes pleading for me to understand and forgive him.

"Can you ever forgive me?!" He asked sincerely and insistently.

I felt relieved! Spiked punch was not as big a deal as a date-rape drug, other illicit drugs, or something. In addition, it was a mistake according to Andrew. I could pretty much rule out that he may have taken advantage of me, especially since I did not know conclusively that he was gay. I believed Andrew.

I chuckled and put my arm around his neck.

"Yes, I can and do forgive you, Andrew. Just as long as it was an accident and you weren't trying to take advantage of me!" I chuckled again, as Andrew's eyes lit up and he shook his head vigorously. "But I don't understand how I got in bed in my underwear! If I was so drunk I can't remember, then…"

Andrew's face was more relaxed, but he was just as ashamed.

"You were very drunk, Tyler… I … I … I almost had to carry you into your bedroom…" Andrew paused again and fidgeted. He looked at his hands. "I had to help you go to the bathroom by holding you up and aiming you… I was good… I didn't do anything to you, Tyler… I had to undress you and put you into bed… you and I didn't have any clean pajamas that I could find, so I just stripped you down to your briefs and put you under the covers. Is that a problem?" Andrew gazed apologetically, yet hopefully at me.

The thought of Andrew holding me to go to the bathroom, undressing me, and putting me in bed was very touching and sexually stimulating! I was euphoric inside and my heart skipped. Before I could help myself, in a very sexy voice, I blurted:

"No, Andrew, you can do that to me every night if you like!" I smiled, and quickly blushed, hoping I didn't sound as serious as I was. What the hell was I thinking to say something like that?!

"You do forgive me, Tyler?" Andrew asked again quietly.

I didn't hesitate.

"Yes, Andrew, I forgive you!" I assured him. "Just don't spike your punch anymore, or let me know when you do so I won't drink it!" I laughed. I felt relieved. I knew that everything was all right, including that Andrew and I had not had sex, based on Andrew's answers to my questions. He had obviously seen my package, having had to aim me to urinate. That thought was a sexual turn on to me for some strange reason. I felt myself rising.

Andrew smiled mischievously and sighed. He started tickling and rough-housing with me. I immediately fell back on my bed laughing at and fighting his 'attack'. Andrew lay down next to me and continued his 'attack'. We struggled against one another, tickled each other, and rough housed side-by-side for several minutes. I was sexually stimulated by our play! A hormone rush began as I also started hardening.

I was out of breath. Andrew apparently was too because he stopped tickling and rough housing me briefly and lay there smiling at me, mischief percolating in his baby blues. He rolled up on his elbow and looked down at me. I gazed lovingly back. There we lay, in our briefs and naked otherwise, gazing at each other, talking with our eyes. Andrew reached out and ran his right hand through my hair, down around my ear and off my cheek. A chill of joy ran through me again at his touch!

"Oh, you are a sly goon!" He spoke in an incredulous tone, shaking his head and smiling proudly at me. "I was so scared and worried about your being so stone drunk that you couldn't walk, about your passing out as soon as I laid you under your covers. I was worried about your health, and I was scared to death that it might ruin our relationship, and/or our living arrangements. I thought you might hate me, never forgive me, and move out!"

"Andrew! You'd… I mean… you know… I wouldn't…" I stammered as I blushed. "It would take a lot more than what happened last night to make me throw away all the gifts you've given me, Andrew." I finally enunciated gently. "The events of last night are not enough to make me angry with you! You have been too good to me!"

"You, Tyler, are more than deserving of all the 'gifts' I have given you and more!" Andrew propped his head up and looked at me seriously. "I am so happy to have you as a lov… I mean a roommate, Tyler! We are going to have such fun for… well… for a long, long time!"

Andrew's eyes suddenly sparkled mischievously again. I knew something was coming, but I didn't know what. I didn't have long to wait.

Suddenly Andrew was after me again. He alternately tickled and wrestled with me. It was so stimulating to have his body touching, rubbing, and rolling around mostly naked on mine! I was struggling with a hormone rush and a desire to strip completely and be naked with Andrew, but I was laughing so hard and trying to defend myself that these desires were easily ignored.

I hugged myself to try and keep Andrew from tickling me, but he was still managing to needle my sides, my underarms, and my inner thighs. I didn't worry about how close he was to my package. He had seen it and held it already. He could do it again! The next thing I knew, Andrew threw his right leg over me, and straddled my body as he began to pull my arms apart from my chest. It became clear that he was trying to 'pin' me to the bed. His crotch was over my crotch, and it felt really good! He struggled to get both my arms pinned over my head, while locking my legs with his. I, however, was pretty wiry. I was foiling him at every turn.

I was laughing so hard I could hardly speak. I was so enjoying the closeness of our bodies. I grabbed at Andrew to stop his movements so that we could feel our bodies touching intimately in stillness and enjoy it. I wanted to be that way too so that I could assure him that the liquor was no big deal. I lost my grip on his shoulder though, when he went for my open under arm.

"I think you were joking last night about how drunk you were!" Andrew had a big grin on his face as he began making facetious accusations of me so he could continue his attack. "I think you were just trying to scare me!"

"No!" I managed to get out. "I... I... honestly I don't remember... I don't remember anything!"

Andrew continued to wrestle me, trying to tickle and pin me. I couldn't move my legs already because Andrew had them bound with his legs. I writhed and tried to free them, and I tried to throw Andrew off of me.

I was stimulated totally having Andrew on top of me! His crotch in my crotch, his strong, hairy legs wrapped around mine, pinning them in place. His hairy chest was rubbing mine, his face inches from mine. I was hard, and I could feel that Andrew was too.

"Yes!" Andrew laughed. I was managing to tickle him too. "I think you faked being drunk just to get me to aim your hose, undress you, and put you into bed!"

"No, it's okay..." I spoke between laughs, grabbing at Andrew, who was still straddling me, his crotch just above mine now. Unfortunately I didn't realize what exact position he was in and, instead of grabbing an inner thigh, I grabbed his package with my right hand and squeezed. I quickly let go, but not before feeling how hard Andrew really was! I longed to feel him up, but... I stopped because Andrew had stopped.

I had grabbed Andrew firmly enough that he groaned and held himself. He collapsed on top of me, clutching his crotch in obvious pain. His face was on my chest, and in pain he was breathing heavily. It was such a turn on to be in this position; I just wished that Andrew wasn't in such pain so that he could enjoy it as much as I did.

"I'm... I didn't mean... I'm so sorry, Andrew!" I stammered. I quickly pushed him off of me and to the side so I could sit up. As I sat there watching Andrew holding himself and rolling around in a fetal position, I was mortified. At the same time I was tempted and curious to feel Andrew's privates more! Did he know what I was thinking? Did he know how badly I wanted him?! As I watched Andrew writhe in pain I really doubted that he was thinking about whether I wanted to feel and touch his package some more.

Andrew managed to sit up quickly. He was a bit hunkered over, but he was sitting.

"Andrew?" I spoke contritely, sorry for my squeeze of Andrew's delicate package. "I am so sorry! I did not mean to hurt you! Geez! I only meant to… I wanted you to… I was trying to get you still so… I wanted…" I trailed off realizing it was too soon to be so honest about desiring his briefs-only clad body to be still on top of mine.

"It's all right." He smiled, groaning a time or two. "I guess you got me back! But, Tyler, next time you want to feel me up, you're welcome to! However, be a little gentler, eh? It will be a lot more pleasant!" He stood up, faced me, and laughed nervously. "I'm going to take my shower and get dressed. I will let you know when I'm done, and while you shower I will make breakfast!"

"Andrew, you don't have to go to the trouble of making a hot breakfast! We can just have cereal or something! I don't want to put you out. You have done so much for me already! In repayment I grab your privates and give you a squeeze! You probably don't feel much like making the food now, let alone eating it! I'm sorry!" I shook my head and looked matter-of-factly at Andrew.

"Tyler, I am fine! I can fix and eat the food!" Andrew was still a little bent over, and his voice was forced, as though he would rather be groaning instead. "You're not putting me out, Tyler! It will be a pleasure for me to make you breakfast!" Andrew smiled, turned, and left the room rather abruptly.

I crashed back on my bed. I was so attracted to Andrew, definitely for far more than just a brother! I glanced down at my crotch. Yes, my woody testified to the fact that I definitely was turned on sexually by Andrew! However, I knew my emotional, physical, and sexual attraction to him was wrong, Biblically. I couldn't quote scriptures, but I knew it was wrong! Everyone said that loving a member of the same-sex was not Biblical and a sin, anyway. Come to think of it, none of them could quote or quoted any scriptures either! 'God!' I thought as the conflict between my faith and my beliefs, and my physical and emotional desires and hormones flared again. 'Why did you make me this way? Or why do you allow us to have these hormones and desires that you call sin?!' It was so frustrating! God could change this!

In addition there was the thing about how fast things were moving, or at least appeared to be moving. Did Andrew have the same feelings for me as I had for him? Was he emotionally, physically, and sexually attracted to me? Or was I going to scare him off? Why did I always have to say or do the wrong things in a relationship? Did Andrew believe what we had was a relationship? He had said so once this morning, and he had said he loved me (after I stupidly said it to him). He had been so close and kind to me that he must have strong emotions toward me of some kind. I was so unsure of myself, of Andrew, of us. I was increasingly conflicted and confused!

I thought of our wrestling just now. Andrew's body on mine, on top of me, legs entwined, privates touching… it all seemed so right and felt so good. I hoped Andrew enjoyed it!? He was totally aroused so he must have been pretty well into me.

And then it occurred to me again. 'Homosexuality is wrong!!! What the hell did I care for the answers to those questions or any feelings Andrew might have for me!' I told myself. Any relationship closer to Andrew than what we had right now, would be wrong, a sin.

I had to pray to God and concentrate on ostracizing my sinful feelings and desires for Andrew before anything more serious happened between us. I needed to do it, and I wanted to do it, but I also didn't want to do it! I wanted to continue getting closer to Andrew, and think about us together. In my flesh I wanted to push the envelope. I wanted Andrew in any way I could have him, and I wanted him to want me. I wanted to go deeper emotionally and physically with Andrew!

With that I remembered it was Sunday. I needed to find a church around here to attend. Perhaps something or someone there could instruct me, help me to know Biblically the status of same-sex love by verse.

# CHAPTER 13

# MY "MENTORING"

I stood in the hallway outside Tyler's room, still holding myself and rocking as the pain slowly subsided. I was thrilled that Tyler had totally grabbed and felt my package. I just wished he had been gentler and had not squeezed! I shuddered remembering the pain. I took a few sore steps to the bathroom. As I did so, musings of current events, goals, and desires filled my mind.

I had decided I wanted, and I still wanted to settle down with a life-long lover. I didn't want my lonely, narcissistic life I had been living for very much longer. I was growing sick of being exploited only for my physical beauty and appeal and my sexual prowess. Providing physical and sexual pleasure to clients no matter how bizarre, perverted, painful, degrading, and unhealthy was beginning to make me ashamed, sick, angry, and depressed. In addition, I was getting older, soon to be 26, and my goals, desires, and needs were changing from what they were a year ago and before that. I wanted a spouse, maybe to adopt children?! I could accomplish none of this if I continued my current lifestyle, continued in the same muddy rut, serving sex to clients, and living the life of a sex slave. So, I had made a solid decision to work my way out of "The Flamingo Lounge" time of my life. I would save money, search for another job, and I would continue to pursue the perfectly-figured, handsome, and very intelligent Tyler for my life-long lover.

When I had seen Tyler and met him for the first time on the bus my heart and my hormones told me he was the one for me. Tyler was so stunningly gorgeous physically and facially. He was nicely tanned and dark complected. His sexy, nicely muscled, buff body and physique were breathtaking. He was so hot, so appealing and attractive! Everything about him turned me on sexually like no man with whom I had been! I wanted him, and I believed fate had destined Tyler, for my life-long lover. I wanted only him! I dreamed of seducing him into a sexual relationship! I already had become obsessed with dreaming about, planning for, and imagining the sensations and pleasure of my first time having sex with Tyler. I had been almost in a permanent state of physical and sexual arousal over him and physically ready for sex with Tyler since we had met. I wanted to be close to Tyler, to love him forever! Most of all, I wanted those feelings to be returned by Tyler, to me, forever!

Today as I gathered my wash cloth and towel, turned on the water to warm up, and prepared to take my shower, I felt ever more certain that Tyler did have further feelings for me more than just as a brother. Evidence that Tyler had romantic, even lover type feelings for me, was mounting. I felt I had six or seven confirmation items, events, or activities that I could point to to prove that Tyler had romantic feelings for me. After our wrestling and tousling on the bed, our bodies entwined on and with one another wearing nothing but our briefs, I could definitely point to at least seven evidences of Tyler's homosexuality and his falling in love with me. You didn't wrestle and tousle lovingly on a guy's bed wearing nothing but briefs, or grab another guy's crotch on accident! At least, I told myself, any guy I knew didn't do those things at all unless he wanted something more in the relationship, something along the lines of a steady lover or a sexual relationship! In addition, I had been aroused instantly of course, but Tyler had quickly become hard and I could feel him, crotch to crotch. A straight man would not become aroused and sprout a woody if he wrestled with another man in the same situation as Tyler and I had. Since Tyler had become aroused and had become hard as we played and wrestled in our underwear, I had to conclude he was at least very attracted to me. I was thrilled and excited by these developments! I already loved Tyler madly, passionately, and forever. Now I was sure that he was attracted to me and was probably falling in love with me!

I normally would have tried to push a guy who had just felt me up and/ or grabbed my genitals into more serious sexual activity, especially if both of us were dressed only in our skivvies. But it was different with Tyler. On the way up to Gurnee, Tyler had shared how important faith was to him and his family. He had been raised in a Christian home and had gone to church all his life. I knew that this fact would cause a conflict in Tyler over whether a relationship or sex with another man was a sin or not. Any unsolicited and premature pressure from me would scare Tyler off, and I couldn't bear to lose him! Besides, with or without his faith, I sensed Tyler was not ready to go sexual. Since I had already threatened our relationship by getting him drunk, I felt I needed to wait. I had left him in his bedroom quite abruptly for both of our safety so that nothing more would happen. As Tyler had surely felt when he grabbed my package, I was totally hard and fully ready to go sexual with him. I would have had to do so shortly at the time I left him in his room. I was totally hot and bothered and 'raring' to go! Lightning would have struck had I stayed any longer with him on his bed or in his room.

The water coming into the tub was now warm enough to shower. I stripped off my briefs almost painfully because I was still so hard. I stroked myself gently, until I relieved the pressure. Then I turned around. I posed in front of the mirror a couple of times, admiring my nude figure. I only hoped Tyler would love my body and its bodacious physique as much as many men and some women had in my past! I worked hard at the local fitness club maintaining my sculpted form (and checking out hot guys!). Now maybe that was something Tyler and I could do together. We could go to the gym regularly and keep buff and in shape. Then we could shower together afterwards, and we could see 'all' of each other on a regular basis! I had to stop, because fielding these thoughts would not allow me to 'cool' down.

I entered the shower. I had to work today at the Lounge, noon until midnight. I had to come up with a plausible reason for leaving home today at noon for work on a Sunday at a stock market brokerage place, and not returning home until after midnight Monday morning. What brokerage place scheduled Sunday shifts?! I didn't know of any! So what would I tell Tyler?! What excuse could I use that he would believe?! What excuse could I use that was not easily verified or disproved by a curious Tyler?!

My next Sunday night was my mandatory service job with Mr. Richard. I often resented the 'msj dates' with Mr. Richard; it was so humiliating to have to do some of the things he wanted me to do with and to him just to keep my job! However, I had decided to steadily wean off some of my clients until I didn't have any sexual slave servicing of clients and no longer did special private client sessions. Once this was accomplished I would no longer be a 'working' waiter or associate at The Flamingo Lounge. At that point I realized and had determined that Mr. Richard would be my only sexual liaison, my only sexual master. If I could help it, Mr. Richard would be the only client that I would continue servicing until Tyler was mine, and he knew the truth about my past. By then hopefully I could quit the gay stripper job at the Lounge, and find some job more respectable, fulfilling, and acceptable to Tyler. Then we could live our lives together and get married!

As I washed my hair I was thinking hard about my conundrum of what to tell Tyler about why I had Sunday shifts. I knew that Bear Stearns was closed on Sunday. I couldn't use my 'job' there as an excuse because Tyler might try calling there to talk to me, find Bear Stearns closed, and thus discover my lie. I couldn't take that chance! I couldn't be exposed as covering up my past and my present just yet!

The only reason I could think of that Tyler might accept for me having to work so long on a Sunday would be a couple of gigs with my band and then a practice. I lathered my arms, still not happy with giving my 'band' as an excuse for my Sunday work. If I used my 'band' too often to excuse time away from home it would begin to sound like I was spending an inordinate amount of time with the band members working and practicing. In addition, when it became necessary to 'disband' them as an excuse for some of my strange hours at The Flamingo, it would be much harder to 'justify' it to Tyler if I had invested so much time in them.

I began soaping up my legs. I remembered once as a freshman, Mr. Lyons, the teacher with whom I first had total gay sex, had been asked by the principal and my foster mother why I spent so much time with him at his home and at school. Mr. Lyons had told them that he was mentoring me. I agreed with him to back him up and continue our sexually passionate affair. That, in addition to the fact that since the beginning of our affair my grades in all subjects had skyrocketed, proved there were results to Mr. Lyons's mentoring effort. It had gotten him off the hook! The principal and my foster mother had fallen for it hook, line, and sinker. In fact, Mr.

Lyons had a commendation placed in his file for his 'work' in providing me with a fine example of an upstanding citizen! I chuckled. What a crock! Mr. Lyons had been so clever! Calling our animal sex sessions at his place 'mentoring' was hilarious!… mentoring…

Mentoring!

The answer to my excuse problem for Tyler had been answered in a random memory of a similar problem for someone from my past.

I would tell Tyler that sometimes on Sundays I would mentor students in high school at Westchester, Illinois! Today I would be working with… oh… say seven kids. The ten or so hours that this mentoring would take, plus the drive there and back would be about 12 hours. Perfect! Yeh! Since he was a Bible-believing rural man he would accept that as an awesomely altruistic reason to be gone on Sundays! 'That will work', I told myself, 'and it would make sense to Tyler. It will also raise my reputation and my character in Tyler's eyes!'

I lathered and rinsed the rest of my body. Leaving the shower, I grabbed a nice soft cotton towel the set of which had cost an arm and a leg, and dried off. I shaved, applied Axel F deodorant and Lucky Me cologne, wrapped the towel seductively around my waist in case I encountered Tyler, and slipped out of the bathroom. I hurried toward my bedroom to get dressed and pack my duffle bag for work.

Tyler was not in the hall waiting. I glanced through his doorway, and saw him look up from his bed where he lay still in his briefs. I could see by the tightness of the briefs that Tyler was still partially aroused. I smiled. I wondered if he had had to relieve himself as well?!

"Tyler, you can shower now!" I said as I stepped into his bedroom. I smiled at him and longed to lie back down and be with Tyler naked!

"Tyler, are you feeling better now?! Are you back to normal?" I asked next.

"Suddenly I am some better!" Tyler responded in a relieved tone.

Tyler stood up, smiled back, and grabbed a small duffle bag from his bureau. Then he slipped to the door of his room where I stood waiting.

He stood back to let me pass out of his room first, and I was sure he must have gotten a full whiff of my cologne and deodorant.

"You are wearing awesome cologne and deodorant, Andrew!" Tyler spoke in a sexy voice as he slapped me on the ass! Even if I wasn't before, I was now in love with Tyler for life. Surely Tyler had a crush on me at least! I added Tyler's slap on my ass as evidence eight that he was gay and after me.

"Thanks, studly!" I said in a lustful voice.

Outside Tyler's room I turned right toward my room. Tyler turned left toward the bathroom. I stopped and looked back at him long enough to get a good view of his body in briefs again. His masculine body, beautifully muscled and contoured, moved with such alluring fluid grace. It was so tempting! I wanted to feel him so badly! 'Have mercy!' I thought as I watched him walk toward the bathroom.

"I'll fix breakfast." I spoke happily, and Tyler turned around. "Take your time in your shower!" I smiled at him.

"Okay." Tyler smiled back. "I'll be out in a few minutes." He disappeared into the bathroom with his duffle bag.

I hurried into my bedroom and quickly dressed. I put on everyday clothes, but I had to pack my work clothes, three or four sexy outfits in a backpack. I threw in more cologne and deodorant, condoms for later, and a towel. I didn't want Tyler to see me packing stripper outfits, or condoms, for mentoring with high school students! That would look very suspicious! It was hard keeping up this charade of working at Bear Stearns, playing in a band, mentoring, and keeping the reality and details of my actual job and career silent from him, but Tyler was worth my difficult double life. I had to keep it up at least until I could quit The Flamingo Lounge in two to three years hence!

I took my backpack quickly and quietly out of my bedroom, down the hall, and I placed it by the door. Then I set to the task of fixing breakfast. I managed to fix French toast and bacon before Tyler walked out of the bathroom in his underwear and disappeared into his bedroom.

I put the toast on the table, and went to the cupboard to retrieve the plates, glasses, and silverware. I placed the tableware neatly on the table, along with the maple syrup, strawberry syrup, and butter.

Tyler walked out of his bedroom, came down the hall, and entered the dining room. His hair, though still wet, was neatly combed and spiked a little on the top. He was smartly dressed in the sexiest casual outfit I had seen in a long time. He was so hot!

"You set a nice table." Tyler smiled. "And the French toast smells wonderful!" He sat down while I took our glasses and filled them with milk.

"Thank you, Tyler!" I grinned back. "The French toast is an old family recipe from my mom." I couldn't tell him it was a recipe I learned while working at a gay strip club now, could I?

Tyler poured maple syrup over his French toast. Then he cut off a nice bite and put it in his mouth. I wished it was me...

"Yum!" He exclaimed, chewing heartily and nodding his head in approval. "This is delicious!"

"So you like?" I purred happily, winking coyly at Tyler.

"Yes!" Tyler took another bite. "In fact I love it! What is your recipe?"

"I normally don't share my secret recipes with anyone, Tyler." I began as I sat down and poured strawberry syrup over my nicely buttered French toast. "However, since you are my lov... er... I mean brother, I'll tell you."

I kicked myself for almost slipping and calling Tyler my 'lover'! How stupid of me, again! It's too soon for that! I wondered if Tyler caught my blooper?! If he did, what would he do? I looked discreetly at Tyler. There were no signs that he knew of, or understood my near title for our relationship.

"You need bread, obviously." I began. "The 'sauce' is a mixture of eggs, milk, vanilla, cinnamon, nutmeg, and salt. That's it!"

"Sounds easy enough." Tyler smiled at me.

"By the way, Tyler." I continued. "Your cologne is awesome! What is it?" I struggled against the urge to pick Tyler up, throw him on the table, and take him right there in the kitchen. Tyler's cologne was driving me and my hormones wild inside! Kitchen sex was good, too! I had to restrain myself. Self-restraint concerning Tyler was another reason I had decided not to drink until I arrived at the Lounge for work.

"Thank you, Andrew." Tyler smiled at me as I hungrily ate my food and watched him. I paused and chewed my most recent bite as I contemplated my next statement.

"My cologne today is CKuno and I am wearing Light Guard deodorant, called 'Ocean mist' I believe. You're welcome to use it any time! Of course I have to unpack it first!" Tyler winked at me.

"Well, it is very sexy and alluring! I love it!" I exclaimed in between bites.

We ate in silence for a few minutes. Tyler broke the pause in the conversation first.

"I am not the only one wearing great cologne and deodorant! What are you sporting today, Andrew? It is very appealing, attractive, and alluring as well!"

I told him what I was wearing, again inviting him to use any of my deodorant or cologne. Then I decided to get the news of my 'mentoring' over and off my mind so Tyler and I could move on to light talk, or more serious talk, which ever presented itself first.

"Tyler, I will be gone today from high noon until midnight tonight." I swallowed and took a drink of milk. "I shall be leaving here as soon as we finish eating and cleaning up. You will be on your own until probably 12:30 a.m."

"Don't tell me Bear Stearns has work for you to do on Sundays too!" Tyler exclaimed in disappointed surprise. "That… that sucks! I had…"

"No, No, Tyler! I'm not working per se." I smiled at him, happy that he was upset. Must be he had some plans for us or something! "I will be elsewhere doing some volunteer work." I cut up my second piece of toast, poured maple syrup over it, and took a sip of my milk.

"Volunteer work?!" Tyler spoke in an impressed tone. "That's very noble and civic minded of you, Andrew! I am impressed!"

"Well, I don't like to brag." I smiled at my Tyler and blushed. "It is something I do to give back to the community. It is my way of doing something meaningful for others!"

"What type of volunteer work do you do, Andrew?" Tyler took a swig of milk, and then looked admiringly at me with a milk mustache. I chuckled to myself. I wanted so badly to kiss the mustache away. I wanted to kiss Tyler's face, his chest, his abdomen, his… I closed my eyes and forced myself to focus!

"I am a mentor." I took a bite of French toast and bacon.

Tyler raised his eyebrows on his handsome face which now virtually glowed with respect for me.

"Really!?" Tyler continued. "What age of children do you mentor, hon…I mean Andrew?" Tyler blushed and quickly tried to cover up his 'mistake' of calling me 'honey'.

He called me 'honey', before correcting himself! Tyler, letting his guard down in a casual conversation, had called me 'honey'. My heart, mind, emotions, and hormones soared in ecstasy! Evidence nine that Tyler was gay and into me!

"Andrew!" Tyler paused and waved a hand in front of my face. "What age children do you mentor?"

"High school kids! Young people." I answered in a positive beat. I tried not to betray my excitement and deep analysis of Tyler's referring to me as honey.

"Where do you mentor these young people, Andrew?" Tyler beamed at me with what I identified immediately was a look of pride in me and my volunteer work.

"In Westchester, Illinois, at the local high school." I responded. I finished my bacon.

"What do you do with the young people at these mentoring sessions?" Tyler inquired as he finished his last piece of bacon as well. He gazed questioningly at me as he chewed.

"Well, a couple I just take out to eat and we talk about anything and everything." I bit a piece of French toast. "The others I help with their homework and tutor them. I can help and tutor them best in math, English, and U.S. History. However I also do geometry, world history, and U.S. government."

"Wow, Andrew!" Tyler shook his head, smiling. "I am so… so… so impressed with you! You are awesome! That is so cool to give of your time to help others. I graduated valedictorian, as I told you, and I never thought to mentor and/or tutor kids to achieve the academic honors I had received. Andrew, that is awesome!"

"Thanks, Tyler!" I returned, blushing. "That means a lot to me, coming from you."

I felt guilty again lying to my prospective 'lover', but I still had to reel him in. This was part of my plan.

"Can I tag along?" Tyler asked enthusiastically. "I'd like to see you at work and meet your kids. Maybe I could join you in mentoring at the same high school and we could attend weekly together. We could share that ministry!"

I choked and sprayed milk forward to the middle of the table. This was a response I had not anticipated when I had come up with this excuse for Tyler! I had no idea what to say to keep him from coming to 'mentoring' with me. As I coughed, I had to think fast of a reason that he couldn't come to see me 'mentor my kids'. Fortunately, one came quickly!

"I'm sorry, Tyler, but you can't come with me." I swallowed hard. "Your presence would set the kids at a disadvantage and ill at ease. They wouldn't be as open with me. It would hinder my ability to help them. Besides we mentors are sworn by our volunteer agreement to maintain a student/mentor confidentiality. It is kind of like attorney/client privilege or doctor/patient confidentiality. The kids have to feel like they can talk to me about anything, seek advice on any issue in their public, or personal lives without me, or anyone else spreading their discussions around. I'm sorry, Tyler, but no, I cannot bring you along." I looked sadly and apologetically at him.

"Oh!" Tyler responded, looking quizzically at me. "Are you all right, Andrew? From your choking I mean…?" He wiped at the milk droplets with his napkin.

"Yeh, thanks, Tyler, I just choked a little." I answered, clearing my throat. "I hope you are all right with not being able to go. I didn't hurt your feelings did I?" I looked softly and sheepishly at him.

"No, no!" Tyler smiled again. "What time will you be home?"

"Well after midnight." I answered.

"Okay." Tyler finished his toast. "I shall be all right today! I'll stay busy. I will fill out the papers from Mrs. Kurtz. I'll do that after church of course. Then I will go to a gym and workout. Do you know of any good churches around here?"

I frowned. Church was something which I had occasionally attended on the holidays, and then only if whatever foster family with whom I lived went. I could count on my hands the number of Christmases and Easters I had actually been in a church! Never had I gone to a church in between the holidays! Since living at Candlestick I actually had never looked for, let alone been in any church around Aurora. I knew churches would condemn my homosexual lifestyle and look down upon me. I didn't need that in my life! I was proud and accepting of myself, my life, and my accomplishments, or at least I had been. I didn't need anyone dragging me down, judging me or my lifestyle, and calling me a 'sinner'!

"No, I don't." I stated simply and a bit curtly. I finished my toast and rose to put the dishes in the dishwasher. "I never had much use for church, Tyler. They and their attendees are too judgmental and are a bunch of hypocrites generally!"

"Oh! I'm sorry I made you uncomfortable!" Tyler retracted quietly and anxiously.

"No, that's all right, Tyler!" I spoke quickly and smiled at him. "You didn't do anything wrong! What you and I believe, and do not agree on is part and parcel of being different people living together. We don't have to agree on everything, that would be impossible. Even married couples disagree on things! The key is learning to discuss disagreements like adults, respect one another's differences, and appreciate them without letting them cause fights and strife between us, or ultimately allowing them to split us up!" I added that to leave the door open for Tyler and me. I wanted to marry him some day after all!

We arose to finish the morning chores. We put away the condiments in the refrigerator and placed our dishes in the dish washer together. Tyler started the washer and wiped up the table and the counters. I cleaned off the stove.

When I was finished I turned to face Tyler.

"I need to go to Westchester now to my mentoring, Tyler." Tyler sat down as I spoke. "I'll see you in the morning tomorrow." Before I could stop myself I crossed to Tyler, bent over, and hugged him. While hugging him I kissed him on the cheek. It seemed like such a natural thing for me to do, but as soon as I did it, I was worried! Would it scare Tyler off?! Tyler hugged me back.

I flushed in embarrassment and fear!

I turned, crossed to the door quickly, and grabbed my dufflebag of work items. I stopped and looked back, very concerned by my spontaneous kiss of Tyler. How was he taking it?

Tyler was still sitting there at the table as he was when I had hugged and kissed him. He seemed stunned. He had a grin on his face, and waved at me.

I smiled at Tyler, waved back, and quickly left the apartment.

# CHAPTER 14

# FAMOUS LAST THOUGHTS

I quickly closed the door behind me, kicking myself internally. I had just kissed Tyler! Sure, I had only kissed him on the cheek, but it was a kiss just the same. I couldn't believe it! How stupid could I be?! Tyler and I had met on Friday last week! We had only known each other for going on three days, and here I was kissing him. I had a pretty good idea that Tyler was, but I was still not 100% certain that he was gay. Was this kiss going to be too much or too fast for Tyler? Tyler was smiling at me as I left and seemed to have accepted my kiss well. However, Tyler's wild card was his faith! Would his religious faith cause him guilt, shame, and conviction now that I had kissed him?! Would his faith cause him to cut me off entirely? Would Tyler leave me?! Would he just back off, and move more slowly with our relationship? I hoped and prayed… did I say that?! I hoped and prayed that the answer to all these questions was no!! I couldn't bear for any of the questions to come true. I knew that if any one of them did come true, I would be devastated. I realized further that self recrimination over this event was not going to do any good. What I had done was done, history.

I just had to admit and accept that I did not know the answers to these or any other questions. I had to admit too, however, that my kiss of Tyler was just plain stupidity on my part, and a gross lapse of judgment. That I wouldn't contest!

I entered the elevator and pushed the first floor button.

I must slow down some with Tyler, but I couldn't help myself. I wanted him so, loved him so, craved his handsomeness and sculpted muscular male body! I loved everything about Tyler, and I planned that, as quickly as possible, I wanted to express this to him by being intimate with him. That is, if Tyler were gay as well!? I sensed that he was strongly attracted to me. It also seemed from my interactions with Tyler so far that he had many more gay feelings, emotions, and tendencies than he had straight ones. I wanted to know so badly if Tyler loved me, wanted me, and lusted after me! But at this point I only had about nine evidences that Tyler loved me, and my sense that he was strongly attracted to me. Tyler had only once verbalized that he loved me, but there had been question about how he really meant it.

I suspected if I had moved too impulsively, too fast, and had scared Tyler with my kiss, I would hear about it sooner rather than later. Tyler would either be gone tonight, want to talk about it tomorrow, or possibly call my cell. I hoped that Tyler had enjoyed my kiss and would not be upset. Perhaps if he enjoyed it, we could start kissing on the lips. I could only hope and dream!

The elevator ding startled me and brought me out of my worried revelry. It signaled that we had reached the first floor.

The door opened and as I exited the elevator I heard a woman cursing and screaming. I strode past the front desk on my way to the exit doors into the streets. I noticed that the screamer was Peggy Barch, yelling and swearing as she had words with Mrs. Kurtz.

Peggy Barch was a hooker who lived on the sixth floor. Whether she was 'working' on the streets or she was off duty you could always pick Peggy out of a crowd. She dressed 60s retro all the time, miniskirts and knee high fancy boots and all. She wore peace signs and tie-dyed blouses. She wasn't old enough to have actually lived in the 60s, but the decade was her shtick for her prostitution 'work'.

"You old bitch!" Peggy shrieked at Mrs. Kurtz. "This is the fourth time in a year you have raised my damn rent! I can't afford $1,700.00 a month and still pay my other monthly bills! You promised me you wouldn't be raising my rent again this year!"

"Perhaps, you hippy trollop, you should find an acceptable roommate!" Mrs. Kurtz spoke loudly and condescendingly. She was unintimidated by Peggy's anger and language.

I passed the newsstand/canteen and headed for the doors to the street.

"Damn you, old bag! I've tried to clear at least ten women through you for roommates over the last four months!" Peggy yelled in anger and frustration. "You @ing rejected all of them!"

"They were drag queens, Ms. Barch!" Mrs. Kurtz yelled back. "I don't care what you say, drag queens are still men! Unmarried couples cannot live together here at the Candlestick!"

"They weren't drag queens…" Peggy exclaimed angrily.

Mercifully I was at the doors to the street. I opened one quickly and left the lobby for the relative quiet of the parking structure across the street.

Tyler had said that he was going to go to church today. Now I already knew that Tyler was religious. I frowned at the thought. Religion could definitely be a monkey wrench in our relationship! I wanted Tyler to be all right with us holding hands in public, walking with our arms around each other, or even kissing in public. If he started going to church here locally, he might not want to show or share his love for me in public, even if he were gay and in love with me, for fear of being seen, found out, and 'outed' by 'church folk'. If he became too religious he would be divided from acting on his love and feelings for me in public or private, or at all! I knew how the churches viewed two men like us having a committed intimate spousal relationship. I had to hope he didn't allow his faith to interfere with his sexual orientation or activity. I also should make sure he didn't go to a church too close to Candlestick!

I had always resented all churches from the perspective that they wanted to deny a whole class of people, homosexuals, the happiness that they, as heterosexuals, had in their married relationships. Christians wanted to deny, and had denied us homosexuals marriage rights, work benefits, and other forms of happiness for years! 'It pisses me off!' I thought angrily. Any Christian to whom I had ever talked had condemned homosexuality as a sin. However, none of them had offered any cogent Biblical, ethical, moral, scientific, or health arguments against homosexuality. No Christian had ever shown me why homosexuality is a sin! It was frustrating! If no one can prove it is a sin, unnatural, wrong, why should we deny homosexuals all the rights of heterosexuals? If they can prove their allegations about homosexuality and things, the churches should speak now, or forever hold their peace!

I entered my plum Intrepid and started the engine. Then I buckled in, put it in gear, and guided my car from the parking structure.

I had long since decided for myself that, in the area of homosexuality versus heterosexuality, it was more important for each individual to be happy than it was for them to conform to a societal 'moral' and live their life miserably. It wasn't right for society to ask people to live a lie in their life, and yet that is precisely what Christians demanded of homosexuals! As if the wrong of lying actually would cover up one's gay desires and character, and 'cure' them! If homosexuality were in fact 'wrong', then the old axiom came to mind in dealing with homosexuality, "two 'wrongs' don't make a 'right'".

It had long been my opinion and belief, based on some study of the issue, that one did not 'learn' or 'become' gay. I believed one was created and then born gay. Because people were created and born to be gay or straight, a gay person could not be 'cured' of their homosexuality by counseling or therapy to become a heterosexual, any more than a heterosexual could be taught, trained, brainwashed, or otherwise made into a homosexual! To think that any one expert or professional could 'cure' a homosexual and make a heterosexual out of them was analogous to the original theory and practice of forcing left-handed people to be right-handed. It just doesn't compute, nor does it work successfully!

The fact was that I knew some homosexuals who claimed to have been 'cured' or 'saved' from the gay lifestyle. They had gone through this Christian ex-gay program or that counseling to cure homosexuals. They were now living as heterosexuals. I knew, however, based on their DNA and creation as a homosexual that they were still gay. They were just living a lie, denying their true sexuality, and struggling to 'fit their round peg into a square hole'. Some had 'backslidden' and were now as gay as ever, throwing themselves head over heels into the gay lifestyle and society.

I believed programs trying to 'teach' people not to be themselves, gay, were a waste of time, if not dangerous. They perpetuated societal rejection of homosexuality, which could lead to self-loathing and suicide in the gay community.

I chose not to live miserably as a heterosexual and deny who I was born to be, a proud homosexual man!

Which brought me back to mainstream Christian religions and Christianity in general. They taught that God created all of us as children in His image, and all of us He created equal. Yet they denied that homosexuals were created by God, nor were they created equal to heterosexuals. What?! Where was the sense, the logic, the truth, or the Biblical basis for this universally held and believed dichotomy? How dare they deny my rights, salvation, and eternal reward as a child of God based solely on who God created me to be in my sexual orientation?!

That was my long held belief on the topic, and my philosophy as a gay man.

And now, I had to stop thinking about this, or I would become irate and have a nasty day! I would just have to live my life as I saw fit, and be a happy homosexual, and then hope that Tyler would develop the same ideas, character, and opinions so we could become life-long lovers.

I arrived at The Flamingo Lounge early because traffic had been light. I parked the car in the back employee section of the huge parking lot. I stopped and paused for a recovery thought from my anger over Christians and their treatment of homosexuals.

I looked in my rear-view mirror at the façade of the back of the huge Flamingo Lounge. Huge pink flamingos stood on either side of every door, standing in their classic form, neck arched down toward the doors, and standing on one foot. They were gorgeous birds, unlike the flamingos in real life that are kind of awkward and backward. The building itself was warmly decorated with brown stone brick, and gray brick window frames with ornate arches. It had neon lights at the windows of the eating area. Overall it was a beautiful, huge, and inviting business and restaurant. I loved the place and its employees like home and family.

I was beginning to not like my 'working' status as a waiter, having to be a sex slave to everyone who 'wanted' me. I gulped involuntarily as I again realized that for most of my clients I was just a condom, to be used once, twice maybe, and then thrown away for some other condom. I was not even a sex toy! I didn't even have that status to most clients!

I had to think of something else. I had to keep this job for the foreseeable future so I could build up enough money to find a new, better job and apartment for Tyler and me. I had done these full service sexual sessions with clients for years now and mostly had enjoyed it! I could hold out for another year or so. Scrimping and saving, I could hoard the money I needed to move forward in life.

I exited my car, grabbed my knapsack, and locked the doors. I then turned toward the building.

As I walked I noticed three bikers circling the building slowly. I watched them as I made my way hastily to the employee entrance. They were a little creepy, and I eyed them cautiously.

One biker was shorter than the other two. He also was the skinniest, and although one might think he would also be a wimp, I could see his arms, torso, and legs were well-muscled through his tight clothes. The second biker was probably 5' 10", thicker build, with equally tight t-shirt and jeans. I could tell he too was well-built, although he had a small pot-belly, probably a beer belly. The third biker was, without a doubt, the scariest! He was well over 6', with a big build. However his height and build were not his most outstanding characteristics. This biker was huge, heavy, and fat! Rolls of fat protruded in between his t-shirt and jeans. I couldn't see his belt. His upper arms were as big as gallon jugs, his thighs like small tree trunks. He reminded me of Jaba the Hut from Star Wars.

All three bikers wore faded blue jeans, t-shirts, and black faux leather vests. They wore bandannas on their heads in such a way that I could not see their hair.

I shuddered as I hurried to my door into The Flamingo, and kept my eyes warily on the bikers.

Upon seeing me, the huge one who looked like Jaba the Hut began whistling and leering lustfully at me. The other two shouted how they were coming in to @ me. I found myself actually a little scared!

I quickly entered the gay bar/strip joint where I worked, looking at the three bikers over my backpack, and hoping they didn't actually come in and patronize us.

I made a bee line for the dressing rooms. I noticed classic 80s music was the theme of the day. That was good! I liked stripping and dancing to 80s music.

I had a few minutes to kill, so I went to my wet bar and poured myself a vodka tonic. I added a little Avatar for good measure, and began to drink while I casually unloaded my backpack to lay out my clothing and outfits. I lined them up in order of which I would wear them first, second, third, and fourth. I picked out my favorite body tight, black faux leather outfit to wear first. It was my favorite because it showed my hot, sexy, and buff nicely muscled body, my package, and my ass in a way that made me very attractive and appealing sexually, but still had a slimming effect as well. Yep! It was the perfect outfit in which to start my day of serving and servicing!

I took the outfit to my full bathroom. Inside I stripped my civvies off down to my thong. Again I made a few poses in the mirror in my thong. I finished my vodka tonic. I curled my hair a little extra than its natural curl. I redressed in my leather stripper outfit, and combed my blond curls. I brushed my teeth, and put on a tad of blush and makeup. Then I left the dressing room, locking the door behind me.

My first job for three hours was to serve tables in my sexy, tight leather outfit. Usually while serving, my only sexual duty was to flirt with the patrons, male or female. However, probably every fourth or fifth shift I would have patrons that didn't follow the rules. They would grab me, demand favors at their table in front of the other patrons, threaten me, my job, and my life if I didn't please them in every way, verbally and/ or physically assault me, and try to undress me, etc. Those nights were very disconcerting and often intimidating! I sometimes felt threatened bodily on the job! However, I had my job to do, and I brought home so much money from even those shifts that I would just deal with it! I never complained, and only when a patron actually made a scene that required management intervention did I ever report what had happened.

Today it became clear that the patrons I was waiting on intended to break all the rules, and make the shift as humiliating and intimidating as possible. I had no idea that it was going to be a bad night as I entered the restaurant area! I remembered a foster parent saying to me:

"Andrew, man is innately bad, but with the right example, man will become better, and not so hurtful."

This belief was to be severely challenged, if not shattered, on this shift by the patrons for whom I was assigned to work!

# THE SHIFT FROM HELL!

As I approached the first table that I had been assigned, I stopped and froze! I thought I recognized the patrons seated at the table as the bikers who had leered and sexually harassed me in the parking lot. I shuddered, hoping against hope that I was wrong!

I arrived near the head of the table to wait on the patrons there with great trepidation! Upon closer inspection, they were indeed the three sex pervert biker guys from the parking lot. I moaned inside in apprehension! I closed my eyes, swallowed hard, and shuddered. Then resignedly I opened my eyes, took up position at the table, and assessed these three creeps who were my patrons.

The shortest of the three bikers was also by far the skinniest. As I had observed in the parking lot, however, he was nowhere near a wimp. Short Stuff wore tight jeans and a tight t-shirt that showed off his well-muscled arms, torso and legs. He looked very wiry and agile. With his bandanna now off, I could see Short Stuff had sandy hair, neatly brush cut, blue eyes, and a mustache. Short Stuff was alright looking; he wasn't hot, but he was nice looking. If I were paid just by him, for him, I probably would give him a private session.

The middle biker in height and size was, as I had also observed in the parking lot, definitely built heavier than Short Stuff. However, he was still well-figured, and one could see most of his additional weight was not fat. His tight jeans and t-shirt also betrayed a well-muscled physique. Middle Man apparently had one passion that Short Stuff didn't; beer. He had a beer belly that hung over his belt a bit. He too had taken off his bandanna. He was a blond with medium length hair and blue eyes. He was clean shaven and nice looking, but still too large for my taste. He could forget a private session with me under any circumstances!

Then there was Jaba. Up close and personal like I was now, Jaba was even scarier than he had appeared from a distance in the parking lot! He was shaved bald. His beefy, beet red face almost hid his eyes, and his puffy cheeks made his mustache and mouth look unflatteringly tiny. Jaba did not have sense in clothing himself appropriately for his weight. As I had noticed in the parking lot, Jaba wore tight jeans and t-shirt like his compadres. Rolls of fat fell out around his waist and under his arms. His upper arms and thighs were thick like small tree trunks. He smelled of body odor. He was gross! Just plain gross! I made up my mind at first inspection that I would NEVER give him a private session! I had my standards, and my limits! Jaba was way out of my personal job description!

All three had a tattoo or two, and they wore their fake leather vests with pride.

I took a deep breath and began my waiter chores at the biker table. I felt I could almost hear this huge sucking sound as my day went down the drain.

"Good day, gentlemen!" I used the term very loosely. Only Short Stuff appeared to be close to a gentleman. "My name is Drew. I will be your waiter for the next three hours, if you will be staying that long." I spoke cheerily as I laid out the food and drink menus and hoped for the best. "What shall I get for you to drink?"

At the sound of my voice when I introduced myself, all three bikers had at first turned and looked at me angrily because I had interrupted a very animated discussion. As they stared at me and I talked, their angry looks had turned to surprise, and then recognition. By the time I took out my receipt book and pencil to record their drink orders, all three had sly, lurid, and downright disgustingly leering smiles on their faces.

I stood holding my order book and pencil, waiting for their drink orders. I was feeling rosier; my vodka tonic and Avatar were kicking in. I sighed as I felt the buzz and the wave of relaxation wash over me. I could deal with these idiots now!

Middle Man broke out in a lustful, wantonly 'hungry' look with mischievous sparkles in his eyes. He puffed out his chest and licked his lips at me, slapping me familiarly and flirtatiously on the ass.

"Say!" Middle Man purred, looking my body up and down from head to foot and smiling in vivid imagination. "You're the hot, sexy, blond fox we saw just a bit ago out in the parking lot! I complimented you on your smokin' good looks. Do you remember?!" He looked at Short Stuff and Jaba as he finished speaking.

Light had obviously dawned in all of their pea brains as the three of them nodded and looked at one another in agreement. Then all three cast lewd and suggestive expressions at me.

"You are the stud from the parking lot?!" Jaba the Hut grunted, his little mouth barely moving through his fat, beefy face.

"Yes…" I sighed, flushing a little in anger. "Unfortunately I am he! You," I glared at Middle man and Jaba too. "You all didn't 'compliment' me, however, you leered at me like I was a slab of beef! Now gentlemen, what can I get you…" I was trying to get this table over so I could move on, but I was interrupted.

"You are one hot stud, Drew!" Jaba grunted, slapping my ass flirtatiously. "I know what I want for a night cap every night till you're spent, sexy!" He winked at me. At least I think he winked; it was kind of hard to see because his facial fat almost hid his eyes.

Short Stuff laughed and looked me up and down himself. His mouth hung open a lot, annoying the hell out of me, and as he gazed at my crotch, he actually drooled. I stifled a gag.

"Yeh, Blondie, Gus here…" Middle Man interjected, punching Short Stuff in the shoulder and laughing lasciviously. "Gus wants to @ your ass big time, Blondie!"

Gus gleeped as he began to speak.

"So do you, Ben!" Gus leered at the Middle Man Ben as he licked his lips hungrily and winked at me suggestively. "You cat-called…"

"I complimented!" Ben interrupted, winking at me again.

"Okay! Okay!" Gus came back. "You 'complimented' Blondie here and his hot, sexy body out in the parking lot as much as George and me did!"

"To make a long story short, you two pricks…" Jaba grunted at Gus and Ben. "we all want a piece of Blondie's ass…!"

"My name is 'Drew'! Not Blondie!" I exclaimed. I was totally pissed at being talked about as though I weren't present at the table!

"Yeh, George!" Ben exclaimed. "I love blonds! Blond men are awesome @s and the best @ers. Blond men have it going on sexually, dude!" Ben looked at me and rimmed his lips with his tongue, giving me a totally nihilistic, narcissistic, and lustful expression!

Ben stared at my crotch and kept licking his lips. He took his right hand and laid it open flat on the left cheek of my ass. He instantly began moving his hand up and down massaging me. I shuddered and just as quickly became nauseous. I reached around with my left hand and grabbed his hand. I squeezed tightly and jerked his hand off of my buttocks. I dropped his hand and glared at him.

"You cannot lay your hands on the employees unless you schedule and pay for a private session. Then in the private rooms in back you can touch us all you want." I explained tersely. "Now, what can I get you to…"

"Then I want a private session with you, Blondie!" Ben exclaimed, kissing the air in my direction.

I knew that, even if I were self-loathing enough to give Ben a private session, that the pleasure, the acts, and the performance would have to focus on only his sexual fetishes, needs, and pleasure. It all would revolve around him and I would be at his mercy and his command! Again I would truly be just a condom Ben would use and discard! I was not interested in Ben or his money for a private session! I would rather have sex with a woman than I would with Ben.

"I am all booked up today for private sessions!" I lied. It was so easy for me to lie under the current circumstances and pressures. I just hoped these goons would fall for my lie and not continue to request sessions.

I scowled at the bikers.

"I'm sorry… sorry, Ben. But I cannot have a session with you… with any of you, today!" I spoke firmly and looked at them seriously. "What do you each want to drink?"

There was a brief pause as Gus drooled over me, his mouth hanging open. Ben leered at me, and Jaba tried stroking my ass. I grabbed Jaba's hand and tore it off of me. I then threw it at the table. The action caught Jaba by surprise, and I actually hurt him some.

"What can I get you per… jer… ah… gentlemen to drink?!" I managed to ask again as I attempted to remain civil to them.

I had no more than asked the disgusting bikers what they wanted to drink for the second time, than Jaba the Hut grabbed me by the ass using the meat hook with which he had stroked me. He pulled me close to him, my crotch tight to his huge left breast. I immediately smelled his bad body odor! I gagged and stifled an urge to plug my nose. Jaba, one arm wrapped firmly around me, twisted me enough so my right cheek was on his left breast. Then he began feeling and pawing me all over my crotch and ass, and licking my open chest and neck! As I struggled to get away I began serious gagging too. That I could not stop gagging was making my efforts at escape very difficult.

I know what you are thinking! If I had only chosen less suggestive, revealing, and sleazy outfits for my work, then these kinds of attacks, assaults, and mistreatments would not happen nearly as often to me. You must understand that The Flamingo Lounge and my employer, Mr. Richard, required us working waiters to dress provocatively to titillate the patrons and increase private sessions. In fact, while employed at The Flamingo Lounge, my only freedom in choosing what I wore at work was to select outfits from the myriad of 'approved' waiter/waitress outfits on a list. Mr. Richard gave us the list upon employment and updated it every six months thereafter. Believe it or not, I had actually chosen the more conservative outfits on the list for work, compared to what was available! Other working waiters like Marcus and Melody wore much more provocative and revealing outfits than I did.

At any rate, I was being assaulted by one of the most repulsive, if not the most repulsive patron I had ever had to wait on, let alone service! As

Jaba felt me up with his octopus hands and licked me from face to belly button, I fought to extricate myself.

"I don't need a menu, Blondie!" Jaba leered as he groped me all over my private areas, violating all mores of decency in public. "I know what I want! I want my session with a little, blond, male 'ho! I want you, Blondie!"

"My name is Drew! I told you I am booked solid for private sessions today... no time for any of you... men!" I growled as I struggled against Jaba.

At this point I felt like a... a... I... I had no comparison! I felt even lower than a condom, far less than a boy toy for the rich, famous, perverts, and scum. I was simply a thing, a used tool to these men, which they would use to pleasure themselves and then discard. I guessed a piece of trash or toilet paper was equivalent with what I was to these 'men' at this moment. These scum gave all gays a very bad reputation, and that pissed me off too!

"Yeh, you blond bombshell! George here is trying to go on a diet. He is living on sex from young male sluts like you. You will make George very happy!" Ben said, cackling and groping my crotch from across the table. "We'll expect you to be a good little "ho' for us later!" He leered.

"My name is Drew! Once again, I told you I have no time to schedule private sessions for any of you! I am booked solid for this afternoon and evening!" I spoke emphatically as I struggled to free myself from Jaba, and glared at the two 'men' sitting across from Jaba and me. "Let go of me and order your drinks! And... and you, George! Quit licking me! I am not a lollipop!" I fought against George's trunks as he tried to envelop me in smelly flesh.

Now, prior to deciding to pursue a life-long lover and meeting my Tyler, I would have enjoyed being felt up by these men. I probably would have encouraged them to paw me and stroke my body parts. I would have flirted back to them, and later probably would have had a session with one or more of them in a back session room. I never would have cared to have sex with Jaba, but I probably would have given in a few months ago strictly for the money!

Things were much different now, though, with my Tyler in the picture! I no longer desired to please every man at work, especially those of lesser facial and physical beauty, and anyone who was overweight. I knew Tyler, I loved Tyler, I wanted Tyler only, and I had a heretofore unknown desire to save myself sexually and physically for Tyler. Because of this I had decided to slowly wean myself off of sexually servicing clients at work, unless I was forced to continue servicing and doing private sessions by management.

I loathed so-called 'men' like Jaba "George", Ben, and Gus who lived their lives strictly for their own pleasure regardless of how they or their 'pleasure' affected or hurt other people! I also loathed 'men' like Jaba and Ben who put their meat hooks on me uninvited, and then took liberties with me; groping me, fondling me, and molesting me in public. Here I was waiting on their table, and Jaba had me pinned between his huge chest and gut, and the table. I was unable to do my job, I was unable to leave! Both Jaba and Ben were feeling me up all over my body. Jaba was still licking me on every inch of my exposed flesh. I felt totally violated, totally gross, and totally worthless. I was pissed!

Jaba and Ben were both hurting me, grasping my body parts through my clothing, feeling and roughly stroking them, and pleasuring themselves at my expense. All I could sense were body odor, Jaba's sweat soaked shirt, and the hideous mental pictures of having these sweaty, unclean, disgusting bikers in intimate relations with me. I had to get away from Jaba before I hurled!

I was tiring myself by steadily struggling against Jaba. I also realized I would never get free this way. I forced myself to relax for a minute or so and let Jaba and Ben continue to molest me, briefly saving my strength for a final effort at escape. I wanted to hurl! I gagged a few more times. I closed my eyes and moved my head back and forth trying to find some fresh, unpolluted air to breath. Feeling Ben and Jaba's hands all over my body, my exposed neck and chest moist with Jaba's saliva, Jaba's body odor, and my mental pictures of the hell that a private session with either or any of them mixed together to make me physically ill, scared shitless, and angry to the point of losing control!

Suddenly, at the point where I couldn't stand it any longer, I twisted my body and thrust up from the table and the back of Jaba's chair. I continued to twist violently as I fought to free myself from Jaba, and pressed upward with all of my strength. With this rash and violent movement I managed to get free from Jaba's grip. I popped quickly to my feet, and regained my composure at the head of the table. As soon as I was standing straight and at a little distance, I slapped Jaba's hands from my right arm, and brushed Ben's right hand from my crotch.

"Ah,… men…, I…" I spoke as coldly and firmly as possible, but I was flustered. "It is not part of my job description as a waiter in this establishment to be groped by any patron, unless we are engaged in a private session in the back. Kindly keep your meat hooks off of my body and tell me what you want to drink!"

"Shit!" Jaba the Hut responded. "Doesn't our blond 'ho' have a feisty attitude! It's a real turn-on!" He proceeded to sit straight up. Leaning toward me as far as he could, he threw one hand behind my head, and then began forcing me to lean into his face.

"Kiss me, 'ho! Kiss me!" Jaba growled. He licked his lips and drooled a little. His tongue looked like raw hamburger and his breath smelled like it had begun to go rancid.

The last thing I wanted to do was kiss Jaba! I struggled against him again to get his hand off of my head. Jaba managed to manipulate and force my head close enough to his face such that he could almost reach my face with his tongue. Jaba tried to kiss me several times, but I managed to stay just far enough away from his face, lips, and tongue to foil him!

As I fought against Jaba again, dodging his tongue and lips, I contemptuously and thankfully compared fat, ugly, smelly Jaba to my hot, slender, buff, good smelling, sexy, glorious Tyler.

Jaba's breath stank. Tyler's breath always smelled good, like mouth wash. Jaba had a beard and mustache. I could not stand much hair on my face, nor could I stand hair on the face of my lover, boyfriend, or client. Tyler had no hair on his face. Jaba had a pig-tail with hair down to his waist. I preferred hair at a Beatles' length or less, like Tyler's. Jaba was muscular, but also very obese; a major turn off for me. I preferred muscular men on the slender side, like Tyler. Jaba was an idiot. My Tyler was smart, a valedictorian! Jaba wasn't clean smelling; he needed to bathe. Tyler smelled good from deodorant and cologne all the time. He bathed regularly. Jaba was a narcissistic ass. My Tyler was thoughtful to all people and a real gentleman. Jaba was abusive and cruel. My Tyler was kind, gentle, and loving. Jaba was 'over used' goods, likely having had sex with many, many men in his pathetic life. My Tyler was a sexual virgin, brand new, a fact which I found drove me wild sexually! Jaba was no Tyler! I no longer wanted to be or cared to be sexual with just any man. I wanted Tyler! I wanted to save myself for Tyler!

Jaba continued to attempt to kiss me and I vigorously struggled to dodge his mouth. I couldn't seem to fight strenuously enough to free my head from his painful grip. While I writhed and wiggled violently, Ben once again began feeling, stroking, and squeezing my package and ass through my pants.

I almost threw chunks as I became nauseous from struggling against the two bikers. I bowed my head hoping to slip Jaba's grip off of me. Jaba simply grabbed hair, and kept pushing and pulling my head in as close to his body as he could. However, he was now pushing my head toward his crotch. This was serious!

I struggled to get his hand off the back of my head, but that task was now harder because Jaba now had a handful of hair, and it hurt like hell! He was forcing my face ever so slowly nearer to what I could see of his crotch area. I was once again growing weary of the battle. I struggled more as I wretched twice. I contemplated calling for help, but I decided to try one last time to free my head from Jaba's grip. I mustered all of my strength, dropped my recording pad and pencil, and wrenched his hand from behind my head, at great physical pain to myself! Quickly I stood back up, narrowly missing hitting my head on the bikers' table.

"As I said, '*sirs*'..." I gasped as I tried to regain my composure, "my job description does not include being mauled by patrons. My job is to flirt, and take your orders. Orders for drink and food that is!" I straightened my collar and loose tie. I bent over and retrieved my order pad and pencil from the floor, taking two more slaps on the ass from Jaba and Ben.

"Well then, flirt with me, Blondie, you male 'ho'! It takes two to tango!" Jaba the Hut grabbed at me. I managed to step away just in time to avoid being entrapped by Jaba's meat-hooks again.

"What do you want to drink, Gus?" I tried to smile at the men. I then gazed questioningly at Gus.

"You... you little... slut!" Jaba lunged for me again. He connected this time and grabbed my ass tightly. Jaba's hands were so big that his grip held over two-thirds of my ass easily! His meat hooks were so powerful he actually hurt my butt cheeks. Over my dead body would I have sex with this pig!

"Sir!" I breathed deeply and stifled an urge to cuss him out and then run. "It is against this establishment's policy for patrons to sexually harass waiters and waitresses! Get your paws off me, George!" I hissed as I slapped his left hand off of me again. "Now, order your drinks, gentlemen!"

"We'll discuss this later! We are going to have our way with you tonight, Blondie! Voluntarily, or involuntarily... I personally am going to @ your ass until you are raw and unconscious!" Jaba 'George' growled. He reminded me so much of a big slovenly slug-like pig! "In the mean time I want a 'blue motorcycle'!" he blurted, belching.

I shuddered involuntarily. I had just been bodily threatened!

"A 'blue motorcycle' for the... the gentleman." I gulped as I stifled some fear. "And for you other two?" I looked at the other two bikers. "What will you have to drink?"

As I waited I worried about Jaba's pronouncement that they would have their way with me tonight! He said they would have their way with me voluntarily or involuntarily! Was he serious? Would he try to rape me? I decided then and there that I was not giving **any** of these bikers, especially Jaba, a private session this evening or ever in my life! I would have to be dead first! None of them would enjoy a private session as an avenue to carry out any threats to do anything to me!

It was at this time that I realized I was really living a dangerous lifestyle! Because of my enjoyment prior to now of my lifestyle and job it had never really dawned on me. I was really vulnerable to kooks and scum like these bikers! The only way I could protect myself from them  would be to refuse to service any one, or all of these scum, even if I had to refuse a direct order from Mr. Richard!

"I'll have a glass of whiskey. Bring the whole bottle too!" Gus stated in a sexy voice, smirking in his annoying, hyena-like way. "Then I want you, Drew, on the side! I want to sample your dishes!" He used air-quotes around dishes.

"I want a strawberry margarita." Ben said, clasping a hand shake with Jaba George.

I quickly wrote their drink orders down, and thankfully moved to the next table. I was now nervous and anxious about what the bikers might do to me and confounded about how to deal with them. Because of the events that had happened at table one I was apprehensive about the rest of the evening big time! What the hell was going to happen next?! I could tell already that it was a noon to midnight shift from which I should flee, and not look back! I also realized I may have a confrontation with Mr. Richard over my refusal to service any of these scum buckets! So be it! I just wanted to go home and be with Tyler! We could go to the gym together… exercise together…shower together… love…

Four ladies sat at my next table. I mentally sighed in relief. They looked harmless enough! They appeared to be in their early 30s. All of them except one presented as pleasant, polite, and easygoing. The fourth one's only problem that I could see, was that much of her face was covered with metal such as rings, studs, and implants. It was hard for me to tell what expression she had on her face due to all of the bric-a-brac she wore!

"Hello, ladies!" I greeted them as kindly and politely as I could muster after my last table. "What's the occasion that brings you all here today?" I passed out the drink menus.

One of the ladies, clearly a bottle blond and the one whose face was adorned with all sorts of weird jewelry in various piercings on her face, spoke up.

"Hi ya, hunk! This is Flo, this is Bea, this is Patty, and I'm CC." As CC spoke, some of the little chains and different size rings in her face bobbed and pitched. "This is a celebration for Flo's engagement to her boyfriend!" The ladies proceeded to cheer and squeal. CC, the one resembling a potpourri jewelry rack, looked back at me and smiled.

"Congratulations, Flo, on your engagement!" I exclaimed, bringing my order pad and pencil up and ready to write. "Thank you for choosing The Flamingo Lounge as your restaurant of choice for your engagement party!

I am Drew. I'll be your waiter, ladies, until around three. At that time I will be performing for you until six…" I didn't get any further because Patty interrupted me.

"You are going to be one of the strip-tease acts?" Patty enthused, barely able to contain her excitement.

"Yes, but it isn't a strip-tease!" I corrected her. "Here at The Flamingo Lounge we strip all the way!"

The ladies squealed and clapped their hands in glee at my news.

"Can you give us a private dance now? You are so hot!" Patty asked, her hands folded in front of her like she were going to pray.

"No, ladies, I'm sorry, but no. I cannot give you a private show here at your table. I'm not allowed to." I responded. "You will, however, see all of me later when I perform! If you would like, I can reserve four bar stools for you right in front of the stage?!"

"Oh! That would be awesome, Drew! Reserve those bar stools!" Flo blurted, fairly bubbling with anticipation and enthusiasm.

"I will do! Now, ladies, what can I get for you to drink?" I gave each one a food menu and motioned to the drink menus.

"I want a pina colada!" Bea said without perusing her menu.

"So do I!" Patty primped her hair, and then tossed her locks as she winked and looked at me lustfully, licking her lips.

"A strawberry margarita for me!" CC squealed. She looked at me with a big grin on her face. With every movement she made, some of the jewelry in and on her face sparkled and gleamed as it jounced and waved.

"I want whiskey!" Flo announced decisively to the surprise of the others. "I am planning to party hearty today!"

They all cheered again.

I breathed a sigh of relief and smiled. This table would be a bright, easy, and enjoyable, spot in what was already becoming a shitty day. I relaxed some and unfortunately let down some guard.

"Okay, ladies…" I wrote as I talked, "two pina coladas, a strawberry margarita, and a bottle of our finest whiskey coming up!" I turned to go to table three of my set of tables over which I was to be waiter.

CC caught me by grabbing my ass. She startled me and I jumped. I quickly turned around to face her.

"Hey, Drew, you hunk!" She said, standing up and lowering her voice. "Give me a minute?" She motioned for me to follow her a few feet from her table so she could talk to me.

I had a feeling that something bad was going to happen! I followed her two tables away and then I stood waiting, hoping for the best as CC furtively watched her girl friends at table two. Once she was satisfied the girls were busy, she motioned for me to give her an ear. I bent down a little so she could quietly talk in my ear.

"My friends and I want to pay for a private session and get Flo laid before she's married. She has never been intimate with a man so she will be shy. I understand waiters and dancers will do that here?" She winked, or at least I think she winked because her jewelry bobbed. With all the metal in CC's face, I tell you it was hard to tell what her expression was sometimes.

I hated it when my mouth and desire for honesty got the best of me. Ideas, words, and honest responses popped out of my mouth without my thinking about them and giving them final approval. Not thinking ahead of CC's request for a private session for Flo, I actually told the truth.

"Yes ma'am!" I softly exclaimed. "We are a full service lounge. For a large tip you can have your pick of any of six working waiters and waitresses with whom you wish to have a private session. During your private session we will fulfill any and all of your most pleasurable sexual needs or desires."

CC's face lit up, and in the light her face sparkled and glowed like a Christmas tree.

"Great! That's wonderful!" CC whispered emphatically and excitedly. "Bea, Patty, and I have inspected, rated, and decided on Flo's… ah… well we have decided on the staff member that we choose for Flo's only one night stand!" CC paced smugly back and forth in front of me while softly speaking.

"Flo is a lady and she is straight. Those facts eliminate any of the working waitresses here today. We need a man!" CC purred and stopped in front of me. She ran her index finger temptingly around on my chest. "A hot... muscular... all man... specimen...!"

I was beginning to sense danger...

"You, my lovely, gorgeous hunk of man, Drew, are the hottest, most handsome, sexiest, and most sexually appealing of the three working waiters here for work! She loves your blond locks!!" CC's face was six inches from my face now and, with every word dripping with lust and desire, I could feel the puff of her breath and the smell of her grape gum.

I now knew where this was headed. CC wanted me to have sex with Flo! The thought of having sex with the most beautiful woman in the world, let alone Flo, made me nauseous today! Some days I could do the bisexual thing, but not today!

"But CC! I am all book..." I objected, shaking my head. CC interrupted me.

CC kissed her index finger and put it to my lips to shush me.

"You're the hottest guy here. The customer is always right. We want you to ravage Flo this evening!"

She clasped my left hand in a two-handed handshake and I felt paper in my palm. I took my hand back as my heart rate increased in anticipation. I looked in my palm. Five, one hundred dollar bills rested there. I was stunned!

"Just an orgasmic climax or two, Drew!" CC smiled and patted my bare chest. "That's all we ask of you to give Flo!"

I thought quickly, while I looked at Flo. She was cute, but frumpy. She was short and on the stout side. Her breasts were too large for her height and literally looked like shelves. I didn't find her at all attractive or hot sexually. I couldn't even imagine that I would be able to come to my orgasmic climax having sex with her, let alone bring her to climax! I shook my head.

I had done women for tips one-tenth of these bills burning in my hand. However, that was before I met my Tyler. If I accepted this job I could increase my emergency fund. I could pay a month of my car insurance.

I could even treat Tyler to a cell phone and a long time of service. I was tempted to just take the money, the job, and hope for a successful sexual liaison with Flo!

At this point of weakness a full figure mental picture of Tyler in his underwear popped into my head. He was so hot, gorgeous, physically beautiful, and so desirable! I could see his nice-sized package clearly. He was hard in an erection that bulged his underwear out considerably. Tyler looked at me sadly as I considered this job. I wanted to lick...

I remembered I was going to slowly wean off of sexual sessions at work for Tyler and my sakes. I wanted to almost be chaste and a second time around 'virgin' until I could sleep with my Tyler. From that point forward I would only make love with and to Tyler. Besides I had had sex with a large enough portion of the population of Aurora over the years. It was high time I was working toward being monogamous with Tyler. My decision was taken relatively quickly after that.

"Ma'am." I began. "I don't do wom..."

"Oh, Drew! No need to be so formal here!" CC interrupted. "Call me 'CC' please!"

"CC, I don't entertain women in private sessions!" I spoke softly but firmly to her as I clasped her hand and returned her money the same way she had given it to me. "I'm gay. I don't do women." I partially lied about my ability to refuse women, thinking it would end the situation. "I could suggest another..."

"You're a damn fag!?" CC exclaimed angrily, raising her voice. "You are one of those queers!?"

"CC!" I hissed, putting my finger to my lips. "Please keep your voice down! You are making a..."

"You're a cock-sucking fudge packer!" CC turned and walked to her friends and table two. "I can't believe it! We come to a reputable restaurant, full service lounge, and strip club and find out that the working waiters and employees who are supposed to meet and satisfy all of our sexual demands, are actually sexual perverts and cum drinkers! What the hell!" CC whirled around and faced me as I approached to encourage her to keep her voice down, and try to assuage her tantrum.

"What the @ I want to know....!" CC put a finger in my face, her face red as a fire engine. The dangly jewelry on her face was in constant movement now as CC trembled in rage. "Who in the hell are straight people going to hire here for their full sexual service from the apparent gays in tights?!"

I was offended. I was gay, but I was still a person! With whom I preferred to have sex was my business! I shrugged as I decided that perhaps if I left that would be the end of it. I turned around to go to table three.

But CC was not done. She took two steps toward me and grabbed my right arm. I was so surprised and knocked off guard that CC was able to swing me back around to face her. Before I could block her, CC hauled back and slapped me hard across the face. The slap and her words stung badly and hurt me physically and emotionally!

"Don't you turn your back on me or leave my presence you twink while I am still talking. I am not finished with you yet!" CC shrieked.

People were beginning to look at us and watch. Many were murmuring back and forth with puzzled looks on their faces.

"You piece of unmitigated shit!" CC screamed. "You lead me on, making me think you are a normal, straight man, and into women! You dress like a male slut. You let me think you dress that way to entice women. Then, after I try to set up something for Flo, you can't give Flo a private session because you @ men! You are a disgusting, repulsive cocksucker and man pussy!"

I stood there, horrified at the scene CC was making. CC was virtually screaming, and the whole restaurant dining and bar areas could hear her I was sure! I noticed all other talking by restaurant patrons had ceased. All eyes from those patrons within visual distance were glued on me and CC. I cringed. Again my self-esteem plunged and my anger skyrocketed!

"You, man pussy, and your fellow ass wipes should be boycotted! In a perfect world you gay scum would be exterminated... shot! At the very least management ought to can your asses! I want to see the manager!" CC bellowed, pounding the table where her friends, visibly in shock, were still seated.

"CC, if you would just let me refer you to one of our male help who would be happy to fulfill your request I…" I didn't get any further because again CC slapped me hard across the face.

"Get the hell away from my table and send me the manager!" CC pointed toward the other side of the restaurant.

I turned quickly, my face still stinging and my lower jaw hurting from her slaps, and made tracks to the bar. I ran into our manager coming out, and I stopped him to send him to CC at table two. Before I could speak, my manager interjected in a worried tone.

"What the hell is going on, Drew?!" Aaron, our manager, exclaimed with a bewildered look on his cute face. "Who is screaming?!"

"Go to table two, Aaron. But be careful! One of the ladies is throwing a fit!" I replied, rubbing my chin. "She wallops one hell of a slap!"

"What happened?!" Aaron pressed. "What is the situation?! What caused this?! Why is she yowling about homosexuals and poor service?!"

"Her name is CC. She wanted a private session for one of her girlfriends!" I explained. "I have someone special in my life now, and I … I…" I hung my head, a little embarrassed. I was busted! I remembered too late that I was supposed to keep my Tyler a secret from management so as to ensure my continued employment with Mr. Richard. I had let my 'special someone' slip! Did Aaron catch what I had accidentally let loose?! "Well… as you know I'm gay. I declined CC's offer. I let her know I'm not into, nor will I service, women anymore. I told her I was gay. I'm telling you, Aaron, that I am only going to service men, exclusively men from now on!"

"Why?" Aaron exclaimed, a surprised and angry look clouding over his face. "You never have refused to service women before today! What has changed?!"

"I just can't perform sexual services on and for women anymore! They don't interest me sexually. I've discovered that when it comes to having sex with a woman… any woman, I can't attain or maintain an erection to please her, let alone ejaculate for my pleasure. I only get passionately, sexually aroused and pleasured by handsome, buff, and physically attractive men!" I shrugged and gazed confidently and firmly at Aaron. I perused his facial expression to detect whether he would be understanding and supportive, or threaten to fire me. "What can I say? Beyond that I have my reasons." I turned and hurried to the bar/kitchen counter with my drink orders.

I gave the bar tender, Sylvia, my drink orders that came from tables one and two. While I waited for her to complete the orders, I turned around, back to the bar, and watched the manager try and calm CC down. There was quite a shouting match going on. From what I could hear it appeared that CC was very hateful and anti-homosexual. She was probably demanding a straight male waiter. Fat chance of that today! All three of us working male waiters on duty for the shift were homosexuals. I chuckled to myself. The only male waiter that I knew would still service females now that I had decided to drop servicing women was Robbie. Even Robbie only did private sessions with women in a pinch, or on certain shifts. Who knew if he would service Flo today?! I watched the argument discreetly while Sylvia worked on my drinks.

Shortly Sylvia told me my drinks were ready. I gathered them and hurried back to table one, forgetting who was at table one!

I hurriedly brought the bikers their drinks. I was a little distracted as I did so, because I was surreptitiously watching table two. I listened closely while at the same time I gave Ben, Gus, and Jaba 'George' their drinks.

Jaba the Hut slapped my ass and left his hand there for a feel. He took a long dreg of his drink and then added:

"I have a large tip in my pants, Blondie, and it's all for you! You want to see it now, or later?!" Jaba grabbed his belt buckle like he were going to open his pants.

I grinned, declined his offer surprisingly politely, and quickly took the remaining drinks to the ladies' table. I delivered all four in quiet as CC glared hatefully at me. When I was finished Aaron, the manager, pulled me aside to talk.

"I'm switching you to tables five and six and giving the ladies at two to Robbie." He said quietly. "Your table assignments now are one, three, four, five, and six. I don't know what your problem is! What again did you do to upset them so?!"

"I… I… I declined having a private session with their guest of honor, Flo. She is the shorter, stouter, frumpy gal in back." I proffered hesitantly.

"Don't tell me!" Aaron interrupted me angrily. "You refused Flo a private session because she wasn't up to your desires and standards in the area of physical and facial beauty?! Drew, if that's the case I am going to have…"

"No! No, Aaron!" I interrupted, shaking my head vigorously. "That is not why I refused Flo's session. I refused because seriously I am no longer going to do private sessions for or with women!"

"That's better…" Aaron shook his head too. "Finish your story, Drew!"

"After declining their session, I thought if I told them I'm gay that it would end the situation. Instead CC blew up!"

"Okay." Aaron said, rubbing his chin as he frowned. "Why not just do the best you can and have sex with and service the guest of honor? You have bitten the bullet before and serviced women?!" He stared intently and firmly into my eyes with a questioning look on his face.

"I have… I met… I." I stammered to come up with the best response. "Aaron, I told you I can't get it up for women anymore! I want to focus on pleasing only male clients. And…I have my other reasons!"

"Okay. I don't really understand you in this, but you have the highest seniority here at The Flamingo. Your seniority brings you the flexibility to refuse private sessions with one sex or the other." Aaron shrugged. "You'll pick up tables three, four, five and six as I said. Robbie will take table two. I don't know how the ladies will take it since Robbie is gay also, but you can't please them at this point. Maybe he can. Hopefully today is one of his 'on' days when he will do private sessions for and with women!"

I shrugged. Aaron and I went our separate ways. I proceeded to table three.

# SINISTER SEX MAN

As I approached table three I noticed that the patrons there were a couple, a man and a woman, both of whom appeared to be around 30 years of age. Both were handsome, clean cut, and dressed to the 'nines' in fancy casual dress like they had just come from church. They were seated opposite each other, and the woman was facing me as I slowly walked toward them. I purposefully approached my tables more slowly the first time so I could contemplate the patrons and decide early on what difficulties they might pose for me.

The woman sat like a statue, hands neatly crossed on the table in front of her. She was a slender, pretty woman with auburn hair, fair skin, and a curvaceous medium build and height. She was silent, a smile adorning her placid face.

Again, perhaps naively, I mentally put myself at ease. 'Surely this normal looking couple cannot be trouble!' I told myself. 'I can relax now and just enjoy the 'waiting' job!'

I took up my position at the head of the table, menus in hand. I smiled at each of them. The woman turned her head slightly, surveyed my body up and down, and then rested her eyes on my gaze. Her sweet smile never left her face, or changed to a different expression.

"Good afternoon, ma'am, sir." I bobbed my head to each as I addressed them. I gave each a big smile. "I am Drew, and I will be your waiter for part of the day depending on how long you folks stay! What would each of you like to drink?" I gave the man and the lady each a food menu and a drink menu.

"The lady doesn't need any menus!" The man spoke in a brusque, domineering tone of voice, and took the menus from her hands. "I will order for her!" He handed the menus back to me and gave me a piercing, seemingly threatening stare.

The man's demeanor and look at that moment were withering. He was handsome, don't get me wrong. He had short, neatly trimmed, jet black hair and the bangs were combed back in a wave. His evenly set eyes were augmented by high cheek bones and dimpled cheeks. He had thin, perfect lips, a small mustache, and a high forehead. He was clearly slender and nicely muscled. I found him darkly attractive and mysteriously stimulating. I didn't know why! I had a feeling it was because he did seem dark, secretive, and very domineering.

I gazed in surprise at him after his exclamation that his lady didn't need any menus because he would order for her. I was at first a bit turned on and certainly intrigued and attracted some to this 'in charge' man. However, as he looked at me when handing me the menus the expression on his face was challenging, firm, confrontational, and angry. It was his eyes, however, that were most interesting and disturbing at the same time. They were eyes with a callous, dominating quality that blew my hair back and caused involuntary shivers up and down my spine. Yet they were vacant, malicious, uncaring, almost inhuman too, as if the man had no soul. Again I shuddered! But as he looked back at the woman, I realized that the 'after taste' of his gaze was hypnotic, captivating, and beckoning. I was inexplicably fascinated, beguiled, sexually aroused, and drawn to this man. He was handsome, attractive, mysterious, dark, dominant, and bewitching.

I was lost in thought as I assessed and pondered this alluring man, when Tyler popped into my mind. My Tyler! Tyler was far better in all of his assets, handsomeness, character, egalitarianism, physical beauty, morals, and behavior than this man. Tyler was mine! He was the one I wanted and passionately loved!

"I'll have a bottle of your very best whiskey." The man stated demandingly as he opened his food menu and began perusing it. Then he glanced back up and gave me a powerful, commanding, and domineering look. "And I do mean your *very best* whiskey, Drew, I do not want the 40 or 50 dollar shit! I want the 100 dollar-or-more per fifth whiskey!"

Throughout all of this the lady sat demurely, smiling and gazing in pleasure and approval at whomever was speaking. She was eerily like a robot.

"And you, ma'am?" I turned to the lady and inquired, writing down the man's order. "What would you like to drink…"

"I said that I will order for her! I will tell her what she will drink!" The man interrupted in a compelling tone. He put his menu down and frowned briefly at me. He looked at her insistently and threateningly, and then back at me with a compulsory glare.

"She'll have a pint of vodka and a diet coke." The man looked me in the eye, a smirk playing tag on his facial muscles. I realized I was being judged physically by this churlish man as he looked me up and down in an ignoble manner, licking his lips, and suddenly smiling.

The lady looked at me and smiled again modestly, nodding assent.

"Okay!" I said, writing down the order. "I'll be back with your drinks, and you can order any food you might want at that time!"

I turned to go to table four. I managed getting in one step before the man stopped me. He roughly grabbed my arm and heartlessly clamped his hand around my wrist. His grip hurt! I felt the blood flow to my hand cease! I stopped in my tracks. I didn't want to address him, but his hypnotic spell on me and my sexual and physical attraction to him drew me into answering the man. I turned to face him, wriggling my arm to some hold more comfortable.

"Wait a minute, Drew!" The man's voice was firm and coercive, but quiet as well. "Lynette, honey, don't you have to go to the restroom. Your face is kind of shiny." It was more of a command than a question. I stood still and looked at Lynette. I expected some protest or refusal. However, Lynette's expression did not change. I marveled at how domineering this man seemed to be to Lynette. However, what amazed me even more was that she was okay with his treatment of her, and was so submissive.

Lynette nodded assent and arose gracefully. Without a word she left the table, heading for the ladies' room. I turned again to go, but almost fell over backwards because the man wouldn't release his death grip on my wrist.

"Wait!" He said in a firm, commanding voice. "Are you gay like the lady at table two said?" He waved at the four ladies' table, and increased his grip on my wrist.

I was stuck. What did he want? Where was this going?! How was it going to blow up in my face?! The man was alluring, mysterious, and dominating. Yet I sensed danger, violence, and injury for myself in having any sessions or relations with this man.

"Yes, I am." I responded quizzically, and a bit coldly. "Would you release me please? Your grip is hurting my wrist!"

"Oh, yes!" The man released me. "I don't know my own strength sometimes!" There was a dark and dangerous air coming from this man and his cruel eyes as he looked at me without apologizing.

The man smiled wanly as he looked commandingly around the restaurant area.

"This is a full service lounge is it not!" He asked me in a business-like tone. He folded his hands conclusively on the table in front of him. He was foreboding, mysterious, and brooding. I was actually fearful of this man!

"Yes, sir." I responded cheerily, cautiously, but curiously. "This is indeed a full service lounge."

"Are you 'working' today, Drew?!" The man asked, looking at me directly, compellingly, and commandingly in the eyes. His tone was a demand not a request. I became more attracted to him, to his mysterious demeanor, and yet I shuddered again with nervous anxiety.

I was curiously turned on by the 'in-charge' demeanor of this nice looking man. I normally did not like domineering or commanding men, but this guy… well… I was becoming strangely interested and stimulated. I had never really been 'dominated' before. This man scared me, attracted me, sexually stimulated me, and strangely bewitched me.

"Drew!" The man barked as his tone of voice and facial expression demanded an answer from me. "Are you 'working' private sessions today!?"

"Yes, sir!" I exclaimed, flushing a little in embarrassment and gulping involuntarily. "I am 'working' today! I start private sessions at six o'clock!"

"I want a private session with you, Drew! I tip well." Again the man was telling me what he wanted, not asking me like most patrons did. I realized that this man was definitely used to being in charge and in control at all times. He was not capable of any form of submission. I was becoming even more attracted to and curious about this cute man!

The man began fumbling in his pockets for something, probably his wallet. When he didn't find it in the hip pockets of his dressy cargo pants, he pulled a duffle bag up from the floor and began fishing through it. Apparently he didn't find it in the duffle bag either, because he went back to the pockets in the legs of his sexy cargo pants.

"Damn!" He exclaimed angrily and vehemently. "I always forget where I put my wallet! Drew, I want you, I want to do you! You are one hot man and I plan to screw you a new one!"

"But what about the lady?" I queried, a little confused. "Who is she?"

"She's my wife." He stated matter-of-factly, still digging for his wallet somewhere in his cargo pants.

I was shocked! This man wanted a session with me when his wife was present?! What the hell!? What would she think or say?! He had his balls (no pun intended) rubbing his infidelity in his wife's face!

"But sir…" I protested, "Your wife… won't she be angry?!"

He stopped and looked at me with a firm, cold, and compelling look. He effectively interrupted me without speaking a word. His eyes seemed to bore right into my very soul. He pulled out his wallet and looked at me as though he were buying a car. At the same time his eyes still appeared vacant and had an even more empty quality about them, like there was no soul in the man. It was freaky as it seemed I was being given a window into what… window into a man's… into what sin will do to… to a man?!

'Was this guy a man?! Was he still human, or had he become so jaded and desensitized, so lost to his sexual appetites and fetishes as to lose his feelings, ethics, and humanity?!' These thoughts and many questions crossed my mind as I held his gaze, mesmerized by his dominance and demands on my attention. What mysteriously dark behavior was this man hiding? Why was I so attracted to him?!

"You will call me Jovan." The man paused to let this sink in, as he simultaneously bore his dominance and desires into me. I felt weary and scared, yet stimulated still by his demeanor!

"Won't your wife be upset when she finds that you paid for a private, homosexual session with me? That's cheating on your wife!" I was surprised, I don't know why, because I was used to patrons cheating on their spouses with me. But this couple seemed so prim and proper, so much more normal than many of the clientele with whom I dealt, that I was pretty surprised and disconcerted that he was being so blatant about it as to bring his wife to eat and drink at the very scene of his infidelity. "Will she be watching, Jovan?"

"Oh! That!" Jovan sneered and waved dismissively at me. "She is with me most of the time when I splurge and indulge my sexual fetishes at lounges like this!" He paused and looked firmly at me, like he were telling me how to make a Long Island Tea.

"Lynette will not be watching our session. That's why she will drink vodka and diet. After several drinks she'll be so hammered she won't know I'm gone. If she does suspect something, she won't remember it tomorrow as part of her hangover. Here's $500.00. I expect both oral and anal." He paused. "Oh, and I'm on the down low, so this will remain a secret between you and me, or I will be very angry! I am not pleasant when I am angry!"

He glared at me forebodingly, and stood up. He walked threateningly right up to me and stuffed his face and finger into my face, the tip of his index finger an inch from my nose.

"Do you understand, Drew?! You keep this quiet from everyone, management, even my wife! This session is just between you and me in deed, performance, and word!" Jovan's nice looking face was contorted in anger, and he looked almost… almost… possessed!?

"Oh, and Drew, I will be in charge. I will tell you when, what, and how I want you to do things to me, and for me! Just see that you are submissive, obedient, and a hot performer. If you do well, and keep me happy, I tend to tip even more!"

"Sir… I mean Jo… Jovan." I was terribly intimidated by, yet increasingly attracted to Jovan. It was an extreme contradiction! "I no longer am required to service patrons, unless I want to. I'll let you know after you eat if and when I will be available for a session with you…" Jovan sat down. I turned and almost ran to the next table. 'This guy was scary, yet sexy! What a delicious irony that one could be almost scared of a person, and yet find themselves strangely, totally physically and sexually attracted to them!' I thought to myself. I was totally confused as to my true feelings about Jovan! I wanted him too, yet something told me to flee from him! What was I going to do?!

I realized I really didn't have a choice over whether to service the bikers at table one, or this man, Jovan. By my job description and contract I had to do both! However, I was rebelling, and now exercising my own self-will for Tyler's sake. I wanted to begin saving myself sexually for Tyler. Besides, the bikers at table one had threatened me! I would never service their sexual appetites!

I noted with chagrin that I now was lying almost every time I opened my mouth. I knew very well I was contractually required to still service patrons. I felt guilty, but it, the lying, was to save me for Tyler. I would continue to lie, if I had to to protect Tyler, his honor, our relationship, our intimacy, my loyalty, and my integrity! I also wanted to make an effort to cut down the number of clientele I serviced gradually until I stopped altogether. My lying was helping me to do that. I wanted then to save myself sexually for Tyler's first time. It was a romantic dream for me that I admitted may never happen.

Then I reflected ruefully that I was lying to everyone at some level all the time. I had so many people that I had to keep in the dark about one thing or another at one time or another that I was beginning to be confused about who knew this and who didn't, and who did know this but didn't know that. I was becoming unsure of what was reality at times! Who was I telling what?!

I now had four men wanting private sessions with me for at least $500.00. Jaba the Hut was such a fat, disgusting sloth of a guy, but there was a first time for everything. Who knows what he would tip? Then there was the cute, average build, control freak, Jovan, with $500.00 in tips. What to do?!

At the next table, table four, was a group of businessmen in dark, conservative suits and ties. Fragrant herbal cologne smell made the table a pleasant place to be. The men were all young, probably mid 30s, handsome, and they all looked friendly and harmless enough. However, I no longer was ruling out any event, nor was I assuming all would be well. I had as much apprehension over serving this group as a caterpillar might have after seeing a bird!

"Good evening, gentlemen." I forced as charming a smile as I could muster on my face. "I am Drew. I will be your waiter. What can I get you to drink, gentlemen?" I passed out four food menus and drink menus to them, and then looked expectantly around the table.

"I want a Coors beer." The first man exclaimed. "We have some business to discuss."

"We not only have some business to discuss, gentlemen!" One man suggestively winked at each of his fellow table mates. "We have business to do here on our Climax and our tops list!"

I didn't know what the hell he was talking about, but it didn't matter. It was their business, whether it was a car, an apartment complex, or business venture, I didn't need to know!

All around, each one requested a beer.

"I'll be back in a few minutes with your drinks!" I said brightly. I hurried to the bar and placed my order with Sylvia. I gathered up the drinks for tables three and four, and quickly delivered them.

Then I made a bee-line to table five that I had been assigned from Robbie's transfer.

# CHAPTER 17

# THE MELTING POT

Seated at table five were what appeared at first glance to be two heterosexual couples. They looked harmless enough, but my guard was up and I viewed the two women and two men skeptically. As I approached I assessed the danger or problems that these patrons might pose or cause.

One of the men was a bleached white blond with his hair short and spiky. You knew by looking at it he had wax in it. He was tall, cute, and very skinny. It was obvious that he was wearing makeup. Blondie looked to be in his mid-thirties and definitely was acting effeminately. The other man was thicker, yet not overweight. He was of medium height, brown short-cut hair with some curls around the edges. He was pleasantly nice-looking, but nothing spectacular in the looks department. Both Blondie and his 'friend' were attractive and cute, but my Tyler had it all over them in handsomeness and hot, sexy physical and facial beauty!

The two women were smartly dressed in ladies' business suits. One woman was short and petite, cute, with medium length dark brown hair. The other woman was a comely blond bombshell, tall and slender, with a figure that wouldn't quit. Both of the women were a visual feast. If I weren't gay, and were heterosexual, I could definitely be into either one sexually…

As I began to interact with them, the illusion that these were two heterosexual couples was quickly dispelled. Without anyone opening their mouths, I could begin to tell with a closer perusal that Blondie was gay. Blondie was definitely feminine acting, and at least one of his hands never left Browny's body. Blondie was very physical and flirtatious with Browny. Browny soaked it all in.

Likewise the small petite brunette was very physical with the blond bombshell. It was perfectly clear that all of them were gay. Blondie and the brown-haired man were obviously a couple, and the two women were also obviously a couple.

"Good day, ladies and gentlemen!" I mustered some cheer as I passed out the food and drink menus. "My name is Drew, and I'll be your waiter today until three. What's the occasion that brings you folks out to our fine establishment today?"

Blondie, pinkies extended straight out, who was dressed in an effeminate metro-sexual fashion suit, spoke readily.

"Well, studly!" He sounded like a girl. It was sickening! "It's my Carl's birthday. He's forty." Blondie put an arm around Carl's neck, an open right hand in Carl's crotch, and smiled devotedly at him. Then he winked lustfully at me and looked my body up and down, nodding and smiling in approval.

The blond guy was the epitome of the stereotypical gay man! Everything about him screamed; 'I'm gay! Look at me, I'm a faggot cocksucker!' It made me sick to see this kind of 'man' represent the homosexual community. The blond was so effeminate that he was an easy target for anti-gay hate activity. He literally invited heterosexual condescension and scorn, societal discrimination, Christian bias and condemnation, and moral disgust because of everything 'gay' and effeminate about him. He was so prissy, so girly-like that I felt embarrassed for him. I cringed every time Blondie opened his mouth.

Now I'm gay, and by definition I prefer to date men over women. I prefer to have sex with men, not women. However, I prefer manly, masculine men, not 'girly' men. If I wanted 'girly men', I would date women! I've never understood the manly men who are gay, and their attraction to men who might just as well be women based on their mannerisms, characteristics, speech, makeup, and sometimes physique. I cringed physically at this blond spectacle while marveling that Carl was his mate!

"These gals are our best friends." Carl spoke, his voice deep and masculine. He obviously was the man in his relationship. "May and June. My man here is Eddie." He waved at each as he mentioned them, smiling politely at them and then me.

"Happy birthday, Carl!" I smiled and nodded. "As I said I will be your waiter until I perform at three. What…" I got no further, because Eddie perked up, smiled flirtatiously at me, and interrupted.

"You are one of our strippers, stud muffin?" Eddie wiggled his ass in the booth at me and winked. 'His pinkies couldn't possibly rise anymore straight out!' I thought with some disgust. Eddie was almost flitting and flying around the restaurant he was so fairy prissy.

"Yes." I smiled. "What…" I was interrupted again.

"Do you strip… all the way to your birthday suit, Drew?" Eddie inquired, his prissy voice getting even more 'girly'.

"Yes." I replied, struggling to go on. "What…"

"That, I look forward to!" Eddie prinked. "Don't you, girls? Drew, you are soooo hot! Your nicely muscled physique, your cute round ass… Your handsome face… Your package… I'm getting hot…" Eddie fanned his face and was actually panting! I thought, with a small sense of propriety, that Eddie could probably look at me, describe me physically, and have an orgasm right out here at the table in plain view of everyone. Some horny hetero and homo sex perverts were exhibitionists that way!

Both girls had smiles on their faces as they gazed at me.

"I certainly look forward to it, too!" May, the blond, exclaimed.

"I would pay money to see you strip, Drew!" June, the petite brunette exclaimed as she cat growled me. "Oh! I forgot! We already are going to!" The two girls and Eddie laughed.

"Thank you, all." I smiled. "Now, what…"

"I better be your number one stripper, Eddie!" Carl protested, leaning toward Eddie.

"Oh, you are, big guy! You will always be my number one, Carl." Eddie gave him a kiss. "But we can still enjoy watching this stud muffin strip." Eddie gave me a leering look, a prissy smile on his made-up face.

I shuddered. I just didn't understand any man being attracted to a 'girly man' with make-up on his face! I didn't care how handsome 'he' was!

"Thank you." I spoke quietly. "What can I get you all to drink?"

"I want a Fuzzy Navel!" Eddie sang. "Make it a double!"

"I'll have a Bud Lite." Carl grunted, giving me a pat on my ass as he peered back at Eddie.

"We'll have Pina Coladas!" June exclaimed, nudging May.

"Okay!" I sighed in relief. "I'll bring the drinks in a few minutes. You can decide on your food and I will take your orders when I come back with the drinks."

I left table five finally, and geared up for table six.

As I approached table six I summed up those seated there. Three girls were seated facing me. All three were nice looking. There was one blond, one brown-haired lady, and one lady with red hair. In addition, two guys sat at the table with their backs to me. One man had sandy brown short-cut hair and appeared to be about 5'10". He was slender. The other man had dark brown hair and appeared to be a little shorter than the sandy haired man. As I took up my place at the head of the table, the sandy brown-haired man had his arm tightly around the brown-haired man's lower back. The dark brown-haired man in turn was giving the blond girl across from his seat a French kiss.

I was in position to wait on the five of them. I took out my menus, order slips, and pencil before looking up. I opened my mouth to speak as I did look up, and stopped speechless. The dark brown-haired man bore a striking resemblance to my Tyler! He wasn't as sculpted, shapely, or as handsome as my Tyler, but he looked like he could be Tyler's brother! I was so shocked, I just stood and stared.

I stood there staring in disbelief for what seemed like several minutes watching 'Tyler's brother'! Finally, one of the girls waved her hand in front of my face.

"Hello!?" She said politely, still waving in my face. "I believe you are our waiter?"

"What?" I snapped back to reality. "I mean… well yes… I'm sorry for staring, sir. You look like a friend of mine."

I quickly passed out menus, and then started over.

"Good afternoon ladies, gentlemen. I am Drew and I'll be your waiter until three. What can I get for you all to drink?"

"We'll start with cocktails." Remarked 'Tyler's brother'. "We are celebrating our mutual wedding anniversary!"

"Mutual wedding anniversary?" I asked, somewhat puzzled.

"Yes, the five of us. This is Meg." 'Tyler's brother' waved at the first woman, the blond he had been kissing. "The brown-haired gal is Patsy, and Alice is the redhead. They are my wives. This is my co-husband, Lee, and I am Gary. We have been married for two years today!"

"Well, congratulations!" I said, curiously. "I'll get your drinks and be right back. In the meantime you can peruse the food menus and decide what you want to order. I will take your orders when I bring the drinks back, okay!?"

"Sounds great!" Gary exclaimed as he smiled at me. He then turned to Lee and they shared a tender kiss.

'Weird situation!' I thought as I hustled to deliver the drink orders to tables five and six to Sylvia at the bar. How could all five of them get married legally? Gay marriage was only sporadically legal in like four states, and any marriage licenses would be in the nation-wide databases. Surely that would prevent them from being married to so many people!? I would have to be nosy and inquire of them how it was that they were all legally married.

As well I couldn't believe the uncanny resemblance of Gary to Tyler. They said that everyone had a 'double' almost identical twin somewhere. Well, here must be Tyler's. However, he still wasn't as hot as my Tyler!

Unfortunately now I needed to stop back to every table to take food orders from the patrons. I grabbed a pad of order forms, and my pen. I dreaded Jaba 'George' at table one. I would have to make sure I stayed far enough away from Ben and Jaba so they couldn't grab me again. Then there was the dark, mysterious, foreboding Jovan the Dominator at table three. Would I, should I agree to have a session with Jovan? I had an urge to ask Sylvia to get my food orders from those two tables, but I couldn't. This was my job and I had to do it.

"Let's get this over with!" I whispered to myself.

# BEING THE MAIN DISH

I reluctantly approached table one. I kept reminding myself to maintain a good distance from Ben and Jaba. I didn't want either one of them to assault and molest me again. I closed in on table one, staying a good five or six feet from the head of the table. As I did so, all three bikers, Jaba, Gus, and Ben were there in their seats talking about several of us working waiters. As I arrived in my safe position at table one their conversation switched over to me, my physical assets, and what the three of them wanted to do to me with or without my consent or approval. I felt threatened by their conversation! What I heard of it was vulgar, violent, and injurious to me and my body. However, my job was to serve them food and drink at least, so I had to serve them. I had no choice! I just decided that I would keep my distance from them, and I definitely wouldn't service them in a private sex session later.

I tried to stand at the table to take their food orders far enough away from Jaba the Hutt so that he couldn't grab me again. It was hard because I also had to avoid Ben, yet remain closely enough situated to them to take their orders. Jaba, however, traveled to the other side of his inside booth gasping and licking his lips as he leered at and pawed me, and grabbed my ass. Once he had me again he held on so powerfully that I felt pain! I gritted my teeth and struggled to get away. Things were going downhill!

"Someone looks good enough to eat!" Jaba gave a series of ecstatic orgasmic groans, and pulled me onto his lap. "Blondie, I should take your ass right here, you little male slut! I want my meat young and raw, Blondie, like you!"

Jaba's body odor made me gag as I struggled to get away. Jaba and Ben were again pawing, groping, and stroking me as I fought to get free. I felt dirty, abused, violated, and victimized! I realized I was receiving a taste of the fear, panic, and shame someone who is raped must feel. I knew right now I was at the bikers' mercy. I could feel Jaba's hands inside my pants. He was hurting me! Shaming me! Infuriating me!

Jaba then proceeded to imitate anal intercourse with me right there at the table. At the same time he began to attempt undoing my belt and pants. I was really scared and panicked now! Jaba might rape me right here in front of everyone! Yet with his weight, the table, and the way he was seated, Jaba's rape of me probably wouldn't be visible to anyone else! I started to really struggle and fight to get away, but it seemed the more I struggled the more that I was hurting myself. I also was not accomplishing my freedom and escape. What could I do to prevent being raped here at the table?! What the hell were these scum thinking?! Should I call for help?! I doubted Jaba would let me make a peep before covering my mouth as he continued his assault.

Ben and Gus snickered and felt me up under the table as Jaba did his thing. In the midst of his imitation of anal rape on me, Jaba managed to undo my pants, and was starting to push them down. I was becoming desperate. I struggled to hold my pants up now as well as trying to get away from Jaba. However, in no time at all Jaba, Ben, and Gus had my pants and briefs down around my knees. All three were now stroking and grabbing my genitals, and poking their fingers up my ass. I felt so cheap and filthy! I was almost to the point of begging them to stop. Would that work?! I didn't know.

Gus caught my eye and winked at me seductively, his eyes gleaming with animal passion. He put his hand on my penis and licked his lips. I closed my eyes briefly so I didn't have to see Gus or Ben leer at me, telling me how they were going to sadistically and hurtfully rape me, use me, abuse me, and then leave me harmed and bleeding in their body fluids and my own blood.

"Will you do two for one, sexy?" Gus's look became serious but without feeling and any sense of humanity or sympathy.

"Hey!" Ben protested in anger. "I want my turn on him!"

I fought to stand, and to get free from Jaba's meat hooks. Jaba held me in his lap, blew in my ear, and suddenly had my pants down to my ankles. He was licking my neck, face, and kissing my lips, blowing in my ears, and kissing me on my bare shoulders and chest where he could reach them. I felt so filthy...

I again had a strong urge to hurl. I gagged several times, becoming breathless and weakened. Things seemed to slow down to slow motion in my sense of time. My vision blurred as I tried to resist the rapists. In this state with time almost seeming to stop, I had a surge of clearer thought. It was obvious that all my struggling was doing for me was hurting me, and causing Jaba to hold on more tightly, which also hurt me even more. I realized that Jaba was so much stronger than I due to his sheer size. I also concluded that, even though I worked out, I would never be able to defeat someone as large as Jaba by physical means and fighting! But I had to get away!

The bikers had now stripped me naked from the waist down. They were fondling my genitals and had poked their dirty fingers in my anus such that I was bleeding. When I tried to fend off Ben, my now bare foot felt his pants down around his knees. I could feel Jaba's rolls of bare flesh on my ass and knew he had his pants opened and was trying to accomplish his cruel attack.

I was desperate to get away! Panic gripped my being as I knew that these sons-of-bitches were going to accomplish raping me if I continued as I was and did nothing to change my strategy. In my desperation I decided to pull out all the stops. I stopped struggling to build up my reserve energy and to hope that Jaba would relax his hold on me. I managed to relax my struggling for a couple of minutes and to tolerate the physical and oral assault on my body from Jaba, Ben, and Gus. Jaba did relax his hold, and relaxed his defenses while struggling to get himself out of his pants. Ben was obviously pleasuring himself as he pawed and stroked my genitals. After a few minutes my strength had increased and I could no longer stomach allowing this assault to continue.

At this point I did something that was against my employer's policies. No one was around to give me assistance, and I had to do something to protect myself! I knew I could be fired for what I was about to do, if the sons-of-bitches reported me, but I didn't care. I simultaneously punched Jaba's crotch as hard as I could with my elbow, and kicked straight into Ben's crotch with my bare foot. I repeated the attacks several times as quickly as I could, hoping it would be enough to get Jaba and Ben to release me!

At the instant I elbowed him, Jaba yelped, groaned, and literally pushed me off of him. Ben, quietly howling and moaning in pain, bent over so fast and involuntarily that he threw down his head cracking it hard on the table. He was now in pain from his crotch and his head/face, I didn't know for sure which. What I did know was that I was free!

I stood up quickly, retrieving my briefs and pants from under the table, and turned to face the three pervert scum. Jaba was holding himself, moaning and grimacing. Ben was also bent over, moaning and cursing me to hell and back. Gus was chuckling and clapping his hands in mirth over his friends' pain. 'What revolting pigs! They are a waste of a perfectly good manhole!' I thought to myself as I realized my nakedness and quickly shook out my briefs and pants. I whipped them back on and pulled them quickly up, reapplying my belt and fastening them around my waist. I quickly straightened my attire, regained my composure, and I picked up my order pad and pencil.

"I was not hired to be mauled by the patrons!" I hissed at the bikers, the sons-of-bitches, angrily and with embarrassment. "Further, my services are one-on-one, not package deals! Finally, I don't do any private sessions until six in the evening. As for you three?" I mustered my courage, flexed my arms, and made myself look as formidable as possible. "You couldn't possibly have enough money to afford my services! Now, what do you want to eat that is actual food!" I was soft spoken so as not to make a scene, but firm enough to let them know I meant business.

"I have a large enough tip in my pants, to afford you, you piece of shit, little queer 'ho'! I have 350.00 dollars!" Growled Jaba, still grimacing and moaning in pain. "Blondie, I will have you, voluntarily, or involuntarily for sure now… sometime tonight, somewhere… especially after this assault on my jewels! It doesn't matter to me if I have to rape you to get your cute, round, lily-white ass and plow it to hell!"

"I have $400.00! That should pay for a turn on you, Drew!" Gus exclaimed, winking at me wantonly.

"I can top both of you paupers!" Ben sneered, as he cursed me more and rocked, still in pain. "I'll give you $450.00, blond dude, for a private session! And after you kicked me in the 'nads like a cowardly son-of-a-bitch, I too, will plow your ass to hell! We'll all make you bleed!"

"Your ass is mine, Blondie!" Jaba snarled at me in pain and anger. "You owe me, Blondie! Especially after assaulting me! I will have you, do you, and make a whore out of you multiple times!"

"Sir, you or your two cohorts will never have any sex from me! I have standards for my sex partners and clients, and you three fail all of them miserably!" I stated flatly and vehemently. "I don't slut around with just any dead-beat pieces of unmitigated shit that slither in here! As I said, I have standards!"

"You blond male whore! So feisty! That turns me on, boy!" Jaba slurred as he finally sat back up straight. "I'll give you $500.00, Blondie, for your ass in back! Or else, I will rape your ass for nothing all night long!"

"No deal, George! I don't do gutter trash that assault me!" I put special emphasis and sincerity in my voice and tone.

"Why you male cocksucking slut! You little man-pussy whore! I'll take you here and now!" George lunged toward me as he struggled to get up, his fat girth moving the table over.

I stepped back, a surge of fear gripping me again as I could feel my face flushing hot and red. I had to regain my confidence. I also needed to shut up!

"I will report you to management, men, if you do not quit sexually harassing and assaulting me! Management doesn't take kindly to what you have just done to me, and they will throw you out of this establishment and ban your asses from ever leaving skid-marks anywhere in this business again!" I took a few more steps away.

Jaba stopped, and all three of the bikers were staring me down, assessing my sincerity and the veracity of my threat.

"Order your food, men, or I will call security and have you thrown out!" I spoke loudly and threateningly.

Jaba glared at me, his fat face waxing several shades of red as he slowly and fiercely pointed his fat finger in my direction.

"You may have won this round, Blondie, but your ass is mine! I will have you for my little whore, my bitch, soon!" Jaba slowly sat down, seething with rage.

"We shall see." I said coldly. "Now, what food can I get you to eat?" I faced what I realized might be a gang rape if I didn't get friendly with them. However, I found Jaba so repulsive that, even though the other two were clean cut and okay looking, I was revolted to even be civil to them. I had to get away from the table before Jaba and Ben became fully functional, and before I said some choice words that I would regret, and perhaps for which Mr. Richard might reprimand or fire me.

At this point I was able to get their food orders, and I moved on to table three hurriedly and with much relief.

I had only once, maybe twice a year experienced anything that dangerous, horrific, injurious, and threatening. However, this year I had had three or four such assaults, and the frequency, strength, and physically and sexually threatening nature of the attacks were intensifying. I didn't want to go through more such attacks any time soon! However, I knew that continuing to work here at The Flamingo Lounge doing what I did would further expose me to more such attempted rapes, assaults, and sexual attacks.

As I approached table three, I looked more closely at Jovan. He was a nice looking man, and his dominating personality intrigued and attracted me! I decided I couldn't pass up this mysterious man, and I would do his private session.

A flash of my life's love, my Tyler, came into my mind. I couldn't do Jovan! It wouldn't be loyal to Tyler! I would be breaking my 'diminishing sex' promise to Tyler…! I had to say no… I wanted to be a few-month virgin for my first time to make love to Tyler. I had to say no… but Jovan was dark, exciting, sinister, attractive, dominating, and a sexual mystery…

he was such a temptation! I couldn't pass him up! I had to know why I was attracted so much to him. I had to 'know' him!

"Drew! Drew!"

I turned to see Aaron approaching. He didn't look very happy. 'Shoot! What the hell did he want now!?' I thought. I was doing the best I could at my job considering the adversity posed by some of my patrons. I had just been sexually assaulted, sexually abused, injured, and harassed! What else was I supposed to do?!

"Drew! I just talked to Mr. Richard. He is really pissed right now! You have been off your normal number of clientele for private sessions and your income for him is down. You have been off your game, Drew! Then there was the whole fiasco with the women at table two. He told me to tell you that you better make your session quota tonight, or you may be retired! Are you going to get your two to three sessions in tonight?" Aaron was stern and in charge. He was older than I by two or three years. Aaron was new to his management position, and it was hard sometimes taking orders from him because he was so 'green'.

"Yes, Aaron!" I frowned as my face felt hot in anger. 'Tyler I tried! I'll keep trying to save myself sexually for you, lover!' "I have two coming up, one with multiple people involved. I'll make my quota, Aaron. Tell Mr. Richard to keep his pants on!"

"I'd try to get at least three sessions in tonight for good measure if I were you, Drew! Mr. Richard was so pissed about that whole thing with the table of women that just blew up in our faces because of you! Now that has brought him to question your lessening of private session income over the last month… You need some brownie points right now with him!" Aaron put a hand on my shoulder, and smiled a firm recommendation to do three sessions to me.

"I'll see what I can do, Aaron! I am not promising you anything! I have at least one private session so far, probably a second with multiple partners and a fat payroll. I am your best at what I do, Aaron! Trust me, I will do my best!" I shrugged toward Aaron as he squeezed my shoulder. I turned and went to Jovan the Dominator's table.

I took up my position at the head of the table, smiling at Jovan and Lynette.

"Have you decided what you want to eat, ma'am, sir?" I asked in a friendly, charming voice. My body and anus hurt.

The dominator gave me a quick, business-like grin, and then spoke to his wife.

"I'll order, honey…" Jovan handed Lynette his hat and coat. "Would you go and hang these up in the cloak room." Again it was more of a command than a question. Jovan was compelling Lynette verbally to obey him.

I looked at Lynette, expecting at least a disappointed look if not a frown!

However, Lynette, still wearing the demure, adoring smile and holding Jovan's hat and coat, nodded, rose, and promptly left toward the cloak room.

"Get another double of vodka and diet for my wife. I'll have a beer, and an order of cheese sticks as an appetizer. We'll both have the steak platter. What time are we on, Drew, for our session?"

"I can start at eight, Jovan. Our session will last a half-hour…"

Jovan waved me impatiently to silence.

"I'll set the agenda, pick the duration of the session, and decide what different sexual acts I want done to me and I want to do to you. I'll be in charge. In case you haven't noticed I like to take charge, and I like being a dominator in the bedroom. That is one of my many sexual fetishes." He looked at me as though I were a child. "Eight o'clock is fine, but I will dictate the duration of our activity! And, remember Drew, I am the customer! The customer is always right! In addition," Jovan looked sternly and attractively at me, "the happier you make me sexually, the more I will tip you when we finish!"

"Well, Jovan." I said, unsure now because I was used to being in charge. Being dominated sexually was new, alluring, and sexually intriguing. "You paid, and will pay, but for me to go for domination activity... well… I usually charge more for that… $500.00 just isn't cutting it anymore!" I wanted to see how much I could get from Jovan for our sex session. How much did Jovan really want to dominate me sexually? Would he pick someone cheaper?

"I'll up my tip to $625.00, but not a penny more!" Jovan gave me an angry but compelling look, reached in his pocket, and hauled out another roll of bills. He peeled off another $125.00 and pressed the whole $625.00 into my damp but eager palm.

"Thank you. Eight o'clock it is then, Drew! Now, go place our order. My wife is returning." He placed another fifty on my order pad and waved me on commandingly.

As I returned to the bar/kitchen area to place my orders and get my drinks, I was strangely and perhaps even perversely looking forward to my session with Jovan. I had never been the 'dominated one' in a session, and it might be fun?! I was already sexually aroused at the thought of my being dominated in lovemaking with Jovan. I wondered what kind of domination/submission Jovan did in his lovemaking. Did he introduce and use any toys in his sexual activities with those whom he dominated for sex? I guessed I would be finding that out later.

I quickly returned with new drinks to table one. Jaba must have gone to the bathroom, so I was home free for now, but I had their food coming up soon. 'I am not out of the woods yet', I thought as I hurried on. I delivered table three their drinks, and moved on to table four.

At table four I expected to find the four nicely dressed, conservative businessmen. They were in a booth table, and two of them were gone. My first reaction was that they, too, were in the bathroom with Jaba. However, I noticed the table was jiggling. Then I looked at the two businessmen whose faces I could see. They were slouched down in their seats with very happy, ecstatic, kind of drunk looks on their miens, and low gasps and groans occasionally escaped their lips. It didn't take a genius to put two and two together! I knew what was happening.

I lifted up the tablecloth on the businessmen's table. Sure enough! These four probably wouldn't need me tonight! The two missing businessmen were giving their partners blow jobs under the table. I quickly dropped the tablecloth to cover up reality and rolled my eyes in disbelief. What the hell was I going to do now!? I felt embarrassed for them. What I thought I was used to doing and seeing on the job was beginning to seem seedier, more perverse, more outrageous, more immoral, and more sinister. I just wanted a normal, non-sexual job, and sex forever with Tyler! Why was tonight turning out so shitty for this kind of activity?! Why were all the patrons trying my patience and pushing the envelope of normal sexual behavior and public non-sexual behavior?!

"Gentlemen." I had to say something; it was company policy that sexual activity took place only in the back bedrooms. "We have accommodations in the back, really nice rooms, for this kind of activity. It is against company policy, and state law for that matter, for this activity to be done by patrons at the eating tables. Pull in your sails, take your seats, and I will get you a room in which to have sex."

"It's all right." One businessman said, straightening in his seat. "We're done. Maybe we'll use the facilities later." He put it back in under the table, and zipped and buckled his trousers.

The other man followed suit. "This was just… this was… well you know, it was… it was part of our… it was part of our game of new and unusual sexual locations and stimuli! Kind of like the mile high club, a church, a bank, at work… you get the picture?"

"Yes sir, I get the picture!" I chuckled inside, but I knew I had to warn them. "However, sometime you guys are going to do it in the wrong place and you will all be arrested for at least indecent exposure. The arrest, prosecution, publicity, and public exposure will cost you all much more than just money and sexual titillation. I would find some other fetish with which you can get your jollies that won't perhaps cost you so much or land you in jail!"

At the same time I was speaking the two receivers under the table slipped out and sat down, straightening their ties and collars and wiping their chins. Then they rose and left for the restrooms.

"I am here, gentlemen, to take your new drink orders, and your food orders!" I explained. "So, what will it be? What do you wish to eat and drink?"

"Beers all around." One of the givers said, flushed red with a sheepish smile.

"We just want an appetizer sampler and a plate of hot wings." The other giver said, sighing. "We figured out our order before… well, before… well, you know!"

"Thank you, gentlemen!" I picked up their menus, and headed toward the kitchen/bar area to place the orders.

I pondered the balls, excuse my pun, of those four to do what they did in plain sight! They looked like the consummate conservative business men, yet they were on the down-low in public. They must be into exhibition, and to do it in public must be a part of their thrill-seeking. It all left a bad taste in my mouth, literally!

I couldn't imagine having a fetish of doing my thing in public, in all sorts of public and semi-public locations. What kinds of sexual tastes and fetishes I had witnessed over the years and not batted an eye! Now I was becoming more surprised and convicted where I never had before... before... before Tyler! What was it about young 21 year-old Tyler that had accelerated my questioning of my job and my duty to service so many men and women?! I shook my head in wonderment at the power of love. I loved Tyler passionately and completely, and I wanted to do whatever it took to be worthy of him as a lover!

I gathered my drinks and delivered them. Then I headed to table five.

# CHAPTER 19

# EVERY TABLE HAS ITS OWN STORY

As I approached table five I could see Eddie and Carl were quite friendly with each other, as were the girls. Carl had his arm around Eddie's neck, holding him close. Eddie sat with his head on Carl's shoulder. They all were talking animatedly. The gals, May and June were sitting closely, a hand on one another's legs. They clearly had very tight, close, loving, touchy-feely relationships and were obviously very committed to each other. They kissed one another tenderly and liberally on the cheeks and lips, put their arms around each other, and touched one another presumably intimately under the table. They had the type of relationships that allowed them to have their hands all over each other no matter where they were, as long as they were a little, but not very discreet. I smiled as I witnessed these two gay couples and their obvious love for one another. That was the kind of loving, verbally and physically expressive, and committed relationship I wanted with Tyler! I wanted Tyler and me to be able to touch each other intimately, hold hands, and kiss in public without being shy, fearful of who might see, and embarrassed about whom we were. I wanted to be Tyler's lover, and I cared not who knew it!

It was also abundantly clear who was the male and who was the female in both relationships. Eddie was clearly Carl's female, and it turned out that May, the tall, slender, blond-haired, comely woman was short, cute, petite brown-haired June's man. Carl and May were the two that talked about high paying jobs, their work life, income versus outgo, family budgets, and sports. Eddie and June were trading recipes and ideas on how to fix kitchen and bathroom appliances by themselves for their families. They all seemed happy, in love and content with their position and roles in their lives and relationships.

I thought about my relationship with Tyler based on this observation of the two gay couples. I did not want my relationship with Tyler to be such that we had one of us be the 'wife' and one of us be the 'husband'. I wanted us both to be husbands, men, equal, in love, together. If I wanted a wife, I would marry a woman!

Once again, though, I was flabbergasted as I marveled at the two couples.

I was gay because I loved, craved, and desired a hot, sexy, well-formed male body that wouldn't quit. Now, I didn't have the hots for all men. Far from it! I had my own tastes, standards, and criteria in the men that I liked on first blush, and if after a date or so the man fit most or all of those qualifications then he was fair game for me to pursue. But I daresay probably 75% of the male population fell outside of my parameters and standards of measuring good taste in male lovers. However, all of the men I chose to date as possible lovers I wanted to be buff, masculine men with a hot, male physique. I wanted all of my actual lovers to be male like I was, and I wanted them to be nicely muscled, hot, handsome, and manly! I couldn't imagine that a man, after having rejected effeminate, beautiful, sexy, and feminine women as possible mates, would go and find a person, a mate of his same male sex to cleave to, to live with, and to love who was more effeminate and more like a woman than some straight chicks! Likewise a woman, having rejected the machismo, ego, and masculinity of a male, why would she find a woman that was more like a guy than some guys?! It didn't make any clear sense or logic to me! As I had said, if I wanted to live with and love a girly man I would find a woman! However, I had to conclude that such were the tastes in mates of some homosexuals! 'To each his own!' I thought, shrugging.

"Hi ya, guys and gals!" I took up position at the head of their table. "I'm back to take your food order, and new drink orders if you are finished with your first drinks!" I smiled, marveling again at how each couple had definitely taken on their male/female roles in all aspects of their lives.

Eddie put a hand bag on the back of their booth-style seat that, although more masculine looking than a purse, was basically a male 'purse'. He rummaged and looked for a few seconds as I waited for them to be free to order. He finally proceeded to take a make-up kit out and blow in Carl's ear. Then he began applying blush to something on Carl's cheek, still blowing, nibbling, and nuzzling his ear and head. June was showing May some clothes from a Lane Bryant catalog.

I realized I couldn't wait for them any longer. I had work to do.

"Who wants to start?" I interrupted.

Eddie looked up at me.

"Say Carl, honey, and dear ladies!" Eddie spoke to Carl, May, and June. "I have to go and discuss Carl's birthday present with stud muffin Drew here." He stood up, one hand in the air with pinky extended. The other hand he planted on what little hip he had, and he copped even more girly. "I would like to get this 'present' planned and rolling before we eat. Now can you all be dears and just wait to order while I talk to hot stuff here?!" He looked around the table questioningly. No one objected as Eddie put a hand to his cheek.

"Thank you dears! Love you lots!" He prinked prissy and looked at me, licking his lips and appearing to undress me with his eyes.

"Can I speak to you, Drew, in private?" Eddie motioned toward the cloakroom and winked at me. He stood up and left his chair. "Follow me please, Drew?"

I paused, unsure of following Eddie. Silently I groaned. Now what?! What part did I play in a birthday present for Carl? Perhaps and hopefully Eddie wanted me for a session with Carl. But why would Eddie set me up with his lover to cheat on him with Carl?! Did Eddie intend to watch Carl and me? What the hell!? Once again, I was seeing it all today!

On top of it all, neither of these two men really appealed to me or turned me on physically or sexually. Both were cute and pleasant enough. However, they were not hotties either. I could still give either Eddie or Carl a good roll in the hay, but did I want to?!

Besides, I wanted to gradually stop doing private sessions for Tyler's sake! However, Eddie and Carl would help me meet my quota with Mr. Richard and Aaron that they had imposed on me tonight, a quota for private sessions I needed to have to keep my job.

At first thought I was relatively sure I wanted no part in this 'present' for Carl. Or did I?! As I thought about it more, I became fearful for my job, more circumspect, and more certain that I couldn't start seriously tonight keeping my commitment to Tyler.

I reluctantly followed Eddie to the cloakroom. At every chance he found, Eddie winked flirtatiously at me over his shoulder. We entered it, Eddie walking ahead of me, swinging his slender hips and little round ass in a feminine way. Once inside and out of sight of Carl and the ladies, Eddie turned, came up close to me, and draped his arm around my neck. His air was instantly different, more in charge, and definitely more masculine. Pulling a fat roll of bills out of his pocket, he smiled sleazily and winked at me.

"I don't need to keep up this effeminate gay veneer and girly act with you, studly! Drew, I can tell you are more attracted physically and sexually to manly men. Well, I can be a manly man, Stud. My girly act is one of the things that turns Carl on… it makes him wild with passion… you catch my drift, Drew?! I act like a chick, the female in our relationship, to keep Carl turned on to me, to keep him after me for steamy hot sex all the time! Don't let my act and choice of roles with Carl turn you off. It's all put on!"

"You mean Carl likes you more when you are acting like a prissy, air-headed, defenseless, senseless woman than a… than an intelligent, masculine, virile, logical man in his sexual prime…?" I interrupted incredulously.

"Shhh!" Eddie shushed and interrupted me. "Please listen to me, Drew, time is of the essence! I don't want Carl thinking strangely about the two of us here alone and out of his sight in the cloakroom. Carl can be quite jealous of me and other men when he is not there watching! And yes, my girly act is a fetish of Carl's that I can, and am happy to fulfill."

I nodded in assent, giving Eddie a 'what kind of nut are you' look.

"Is $700.00 enough to entice a session with you, stud muffin?" Eddie licked his lips. "I have to have you! I want to @ your cute, round ass!" He winked at me and smiled lustfully as he stepped back to look me up and down again. He nodded in approval of my physical body.

Now, I normally charged $200.00 - $300.00 for a session, although I often got $300.00 - $400.00 for a session. Once in a great while I was given

$500.00. $700.00 was the highest bid I had ever received, and although I didn't find Eddie very appealing, I couldn't turn it down. My heart skipped a beat. I could do a lot with Eddie's tip for his session!

"Well, hottie!?" Eddie draped his arm back around my neck, put his hand flat on my bare chest exposed by my leather vest, and stroked me. "How about it? Do you and I have a session… a deal?!"

I was becoming stimulated by Eddie despite myself, despite my desire to wean off of sessions with clients for Tyler's sake.

"I am not… well, I mean $700.00… I promised a lover…" I stammered in a sense of luck and greed, tempered by my mad and passionate feelings for Tyler and my desire to save myself sexually for him only. "I don't know if I'll be available, Eddie." I managed to lie.

"Drew, honey, I'm making it well worth your while!" Eddie took his other hand and slipped it up under my vest where he began stroking my bare abdomen above my belt as well as my chest. I gasped involuntarily at the hormonal and sensual rush! "Drew, hot, sexy stud muffin! I have to have you… your body naked next to mine… You making hot, explosive love and sex to me… and me, making you a man… deep inside you… all around you…"

Eddie was making orgasmic sounds of extreme pleasure as he continued stroking my chest and my abdomen with his left hand and slipped his fingers down my pants, briefly touching my genitals. I was about to lose my luggage as Eddie ejaculated and a wet spot appeared in his crotch.

"Well, Eddie…" I gasped in the throes of pleasure. "$700.00 is a great tip… I can service… I don't know… I have a lot of work to do!" I had to remain strong and refuse Eddie for Tyler! But I really had no choice… Mr. Richard… quota… Tyler would have to understand…! I lost my produce. Fortunately my pants were a material that would hide the fact.

Suddenly another obvious objection popped into my mind.

"Besides, Eddie… I mean you… Carl… how is this session supposed to be a gift for Carl… how does our session gift Carl? How does your cheating on him with me 'gift' him?!" I breathed heavily as Eddie continued stroking me.

"That's the kicker, Stud!" Eddie cooed. His voice was sounding more masculine. He continued to stroke my bare chest. Now he reached downward with his left hand and stroked my crotch and package from the outside of my tight leather pants. He needed to stop, I was feeling major reactions and hormones increase again! Eddie could bring me on for a second homerun if he didn't cease and desist. I was breathing heavily and continuing with, well... another woody which was coming on hard and uncomfortable in my underwear. I needed to remove my pants and undies, but I couldn't in the cloakroom!

"Carl will watch. He loves to watch me get laid!" Eddie was not sounding prissy any more, and his hands were doing me up fine! I was getting close to a second climax and ejaculation. A picture of Tyler came to mind; I could do Eddie easily while dreaming of Tyler! One day I would just have to tell Tyler that I did Eddie and many others for him, for us, for our savings and our income.

"Then, you will do my Carl as well." Eddie finished his desires as though he were ordering a pizza or a Happy Meal.

His last statement caused me actual disappointment even though I didn't want to do Eddie or Carl in a private session. I was going to do it and fake it for the money.

"That last demand changes things, Eddie." I stated apologetically. "I don't do two for one..." I took another breath to continue my message, but instead I gasped and shuddered. "I don't do two for one..."

I was interrupted by my climax and ejaculation. I went a little limp at my pleasured second orgasm.

"You had one hard and full, Drew! It is such a turn on!" Eddie purred seductively. "I love that in a man... a lover!"

Eddie released my crotch and took his arm from around my neck. He took the seven $100.00 bills in one hand.

"I want you, Drew!" Eddie now sounded almost manly. "Carl and I picked you out from all the other waiters. How about $800.00?" He took another hundred out of his pocket and waved it in front of my face.

"Eddie, I don't do two for one... that is not enough!" I protested again. I surreptitiously rearranged my package so it would fit in my wet underwear more comfortably.

"$1,000.00, Drew!" Eddie was almost pleading as he took $200.00 more out of his pocket.

"It's not just me, Eddie. My employer's policy forbids two for one..." I didn't get any further.

"$1,200.00, Drew?!" Eddie was sounding prissy again and a little desperate. His voice squeaked. He reached out and stuffed twelve hundred dollar bills into my pants, catching a feel of my package in the process.

"$1,400.00, Eddie, and I will be the one in charge." I smiled, but remained firm. Piss on company policy, $1,400.00 would be worth it! "I'll pick the maneuvers, session will last only an hour, and only you and Carl are in the room. I also will not do a threesome."

"Some anal and oral for both of us, and you do us a threesome. Here's another $400.00." Eddie had to push me a little further just for the hell of it.

"Make it another $700.00, and you have a deal." I smiled.

Eddie smiled and got all prissy again. He appeared very happy with our arrangement. He pulled out another 7 hundred dollar bills, gave them and me a kiss, stuck them in my pants, and shook my hand.

"I look so forward to our session stud muffin!" Eddie almost sang. "What time will we go?"

"Seven." I said as I emptied the bills out of my crotch, folded them, and placed them in a pocket. I turned, headed out the door, and then back toward table five. Eddie followed, oohing and aahing over the view of my backside.

"You have an awesome body and an amazing ass, Drew!" Eddie spoke softly and slapped my butt. "I look forward to having you!"

We arrived back at table five, and Eddie sat down, returning to his sickening prissy act. I took their food orders and moved on to table six.

As I arrived at table six the five married people talked and laughed. They looked very happy. That again was what I wanted with Tyler. That happiness together, and a good sex life is what I longed for for us!

"I am back for your food orders." I smiled around the table as Gary and Lee kissed. What a strange situation! A family of five married adults, all obviously bisexual!

They ordered cocktails again, and then their food. As I wrote it down I wanted to ask the five-some how they were able to become legally married. However, I was afraid to because I didn't want to offend them. Finally, hurt them or not, my curiosity won out. I couldn't help myself.

"I don't mean to offend any of you!" I began apologetically and curiously. "Forgive my curiosity, please?! But how did the five of you get married legally? It isn't exactly 'legal' is it?" I had gone this far, I might as well continue! "I mean you can say you are spouses with no wedding licenses... You would be married by common law..." I trailed off, my face feeling hot as I flushed. I did know some things about American and English Common Law.

"Well." Tyler's 'brother' Gary sighed and then chuckled. "No, it's not 'legal'. But we did it around the law, and we have all the licenses to prove we are married to each other!"

With that began a very strange, complicated, but effective marriage process that my five patrons had gone through to get married.

"I married Alice in Elgin, Illinois." Lee explained, smiling at her. "Then I married Meg in Des Moines, Iowa."

"Patsy and Meg married in Vermont." Gary continued. "I married Lee in Massachusetts. Meg married Alice in the Bahamas, and I married Meg in California. That's how five people get married around the law!"

"Several months later I married Patsy in California." Lee finished.

"How do you file your taxes?" I blurted before I could stop myself. "If I may be so nosy!? You don't have to answer if..." I trailed off sheepishly.

"Each year Alice and I file jointly claiming three dependent 'children'." Gary used his fingers to make air quote marks as he said 'children'.

"That is very interesting, you all!" I gathered my orders. "I'll bring your drinks right back!" I left the table for the bar/kitchen area.

'Man, Gary looks a lot like Tyler!' I thought to myself. However, Tyler was so much more handsome than Gary, his facial features so refined and sculpted, his body so manly in form. Oh! How I wanted Tyler! I had to stop torturing myself and focus on work.

I took tables four through six's orders to the kitchen. I prepared and gathered the drinks, delivering them to the respective patrons.

The food was beginning to come up. The night began to blur as I rushed around delivering food and keeping my patrons' drinks up. I also began to drink myself, preparing myself for my performance and sessions later.

I would be taking home a considerable sum of money tonight. $2,500.00 or so was no chunk change! I had locked all of it in my dressing room. I now could buy Tyler a cell phone of some kind, and other gifts. Tyler wouldn't be bringing home a pay check for at least a week, so the household bills were up to me. Tonight's income would help there, too!

Tonight was one of the first times I was beginning to feel my work was dirty, scary, dangerous, and perhaps not as desirable as I used to think it was. These doubts and feelings were not huge yet, just seeds with sprouts from the last few months of the exchanges. I pushed them out of my mind.

I had one more run in with the bikers. I turned them all down flatly for a private session.

They were not happy. I received several threats from them. They told me they were going to have me sometime, somewhere, whether I liked it or not! However, I was so busy I didn't have time to worry about it anymore.

I scheduled a session with two of the conservative businessmen for six o'clock, but things became a blur for a while due to business and my drinking. I don't remember my session with those two men. I do know it fixed me up with Mr. Richard quite well because the businessman paid me $1,200.00 for a half hour with each! I was out of Mr. Richard's dog house and into his good graces again since I had met and surpassed the quota!

# CHAPTER 20

# A PERFORMANCE WATERLOO

The evening wore on and actually did go quite quickly. My memories of those next few hours are blurred together as I rushed all over creation to wait on and serve my tables, and suppressed many new doubts and bad self-feelings with alcohol and Avatar.

I picked up table two again after Flo received her private session. The four women were replaced by two heterosexual couples. In the process of waiting on and simply table servicing them I discovered that they were swingers out to eat before another sexual liaison.

The bisexual, married penta-partners, including Tyler's 'brother', at table 6, ate, celebrated, and then left. They were replaced by three women and a young, cute man. This whole group turned out to be prostitutes preparing for an evening and night proffering themselves out to their 'johns' on 'prostitute pathway' in downtown Aurora. I remembered them because of the young man, cute and attractive in a rustic way, who wasn't a day over 18, if he was 18. Although he was cute, slender, and about my height, he was actually emaciated, had dark bags under sunken eyes, and one eye was black and blue. He looked ill. Someone like him in good health would appeal to me, but he did not appeal to me in his condition. He ordered vodka, and I carded him. Of course he had what must have been a fake ID showing him to be just 21. 'Green' 21 year-old drinkers don't start with vodka, but I served him. True to my suspicion, his first deep drink resulted in a coughing and throat clearing episode afflicting only new drinkers and their first hard liquor. He then requested a half hour private session with me for $300.00 which I contractually and legally had to refuse because I wasn't sure of his real age. He looked young enough to be jail-bait. I felt so sorry for him though, and because of this sympathy and some physical attraction to him, I really wished I could give him a private session just to provide him some respectful sexually comforting activity and talk to him about leaving the lifestyle in which he found himself.

Otherwise, I don't remember much about this time period. I was steadily imbibing vodka and had almost totally abandoned my work place refusal to use avatar. I was continuing to consume it as well. Don't ask me why I persisted to ingest alcohol and avatar. I do not know! I do know that these two substances made me happy, very high, efficient, confident, and quick. However, the side effect was a loss of most of my short-term memories. I could handle that! I didn't... did... didn't feel so dirty and... dirty and... and contaminated and... and guilty while I consumed alcohol and avatar and worked.

Finally it was time for me to pass on my patrons to another waiter. This little chore was hard because there were three new, young waiters that Melody and I were training. Patricia, the girl, was 22, and the two boys were Kirk, 21, and Kyle, 19. All three were working, meaning they were waiting tables, serving patrons, and observing private sessions, and learning the business this weekend, including today. Melody and I had been responsible for them and their training on The Flamingo Lounge rules, standards of service, and sexual provision and behavior. They were not doing so well in training, and neither Melody nor I figured things would go smoothly once they were alone. However, I had to hand them my tables, forcing them to spread their wings and try to fly in my business and work so I could do my strip acts on stage for three hours, 3 to 6 p.m. I did my passing of patrons to Kirk and Kyle. I then laid into the sound system my desired songs to which I wanted to perform. I decided to retire to my dressing room with a vodka tonic, shower, change my outfit, and then to relax while I awaited being called to the stage to begin my performance. I headed that way casually and reflectively.

Patricia, Kirk, and Kyle were all handsome, well-figured, and physically attractive trainees. They were hard workers, they had ambition, and they followed instruction well. They just lacked the experience that Melody and I wished they had! In addition, rumor had it that all three were going to be 'working waiters', although no one, including Patty, Kirk, and Kyle would either confirm or deny the veracity of the rumor. If the rumor were true, guess who would train them for this capacity as well!?

We senior 'working waiters', or 'working associates' as they were more innocuously calling us now, had trained waiters and waitresses every year to replace those who would burnout, quit, retire, or be retired. The senior staff at The Flamingo Lounge now consisted of me at almost 26, Melody at 28, Marcus at 25, and our bartender Sylvia at 30. If there were new 'working waiters' or 'working waitresses' to be fully trained in busing tables and dealing with customers, as well as the finer arts of sexually servicing patrons and clients, it was three of us (Sylvia did not sexually service patrons or clients) who did the job. We would train them on the floor for the high quality and level of restaurant service and experience we upheld. Then it was we who would also 'teach' them about sex, various positions, techniques, and acts, all aimed at heightening the patron's or client's sexual experience. Often times this teaching required us to actually physically show the student how to do the act to achieve the best orgasm. It was pleasant for me when I first started doing training of the guys four years ago. I continually was 'asked' to have sex with hot, sexy, lithe, and physically beautiful young learning male 'working waiters' aged 18 to 26! It had been a dream job!

However, now that I had Tyler and my plans and desires for him, I felt like a guinea pig! It seemed to me that sex had been degraded and cheapened to just another activity, chore, job, means of entertainment, or a man-made scientific or business endeavor rather than an act of love between committed lovers! With the adorable and pulchritudinous Tyler in my life, I wanted only to make passionate love to him so that sex for Tyler and me would return to its original purpose; true, monogamous, lovemaking. This original purpose was that sex was suppose to be a pleasurable act, a merger of one person to another, an act of sharing and commitment between spouses, and a contract between two persons of a forever relationship. My views were definitely changing about sex!

Based on my changing views on sex, I was now questioning a lot of the things I had to do at The Flamingo Lounge. My job wasn't nearly as fun, sexually appealing, orgasmic, and exhilarating a job here as it used to be. I wanted a normal, non-sex based job, a spouse like Tyler, and a house in the suburbs! Now, after meeting and falling in love with Tyler, I was madly desirous of marrying him, and I even was now considering and sometimes longing to adopt children. I had never expected, desired, or considered the idea that I may someday want to pursue adopting children. My dreams, goals, and ideas were changing to those of the average normal person, straight or gay. They were normal desires everyone had as they matured.

Arriving at my dressing room, I unlocked its door. My mind continued to wander. I entered and went back to my wet bar for a vodka tonic. I added some Avatar for good measure. I took a long dreg of it, feeling its warming rush down my esophagus into my stomach! I knew that in a few minutes I would feel very loose, and very adventurous to do my strip dance on stage. I needed and longed for the euphoria and relaxation that all of this would bring to me. Tonight at least my performances would be safe and incident free. And I would be 'high' as a kite, feeling no pain or emotional extremes over anything!

I went to my costume rack and secondary closet. I thumbed through until I found what I thought would work for the music I had picked. It was a typical 80's outfit that made me look like the main characters on "Miami Vice", Crockett and Tubbs. I took the hangers holding "Crockett's" outfit, crossed to my bed, and laid the outfit on the bed. Then I hot footed it to my bathroom. I began to strip to my birthday suit for a shower.

Performers had an informal schedule. For the first three hours I would strip tease, removing all of my clothing over the course of 15 to 20 minutes. Then I would gather my tips and clothes off the stage and return to my dressing room. There I would put all of my tips in the safe. I would change into a different outfit. Practice would come for my next dance, and then I did the whole dance thing all over again, only with a different song and routine. I would repeat this schedule for three hours, and then I would be done, able to start any private sessions I had scheduled.

To begin my private sessions I would once again shower well and clean myself. I would pick out an outfit, get dressed, and go out to do my first session. In between the private sessions I would shower and change costumes for the next session. After my private sessions I would shower and change again and then I would return to the restaurant and wait my tables for three more hours. Then I would go home.

I turned on the water and entered the shower. Cleansing waves of water washed over me, tickling and soothing my skin as I fancied that it was cleansing me of my job, my drinking, and my drug use. It certainly was cleansing me of Jaba and his goons! It felt wonderful!

It wasn't a rough schedule, my job that I worked and endured here at The Flamingo Lounge. It was stimulating… exciting… interesting… repetitive… disgusting… humiliating…

The major worry and work I had here was to: stay in tip top health; maintain my physical, sexual, emotional, and mental strength, stamina, and endurance; use protection; and maintain good personal hygiene all the time. Some work-days I would shower six or eight times. It was an extremely important aspect of this job to maintain my body in a clean condition and smelling good all the time. I went through a lot of deodorant and cologne. I used the stuff religiously like we were supposed to. I always worked and strove to maintain an odor all over my body that would appeal to my clients, partners, and lovers, an odor that would drive them into mad, passionate, sexual animals.

However, there were those who wouldn't, couldn't, or didn't maintain good personal hygiene and would draw complaints about their body odor from patrons and clients. They would start the lounge from out of college, a sweaty profession, a dirty job, or a street life, and they wouldn't make it more than two months because they did not address their body odor issues. In order to work here you had to stay appealing in every way while working. If you did not practice good personal hygiene, and any patron complained, you were out! Gone! Fired!

I remembered one guy that I had trained as a waiter, and then progressed to training him as a 'working waiter'. He was a 20 year old former gymnast and had competed at every level except the Olympics. This guy was handsome, and he was very buff. He and his body were so appealing and attractive! I could have had a thing for him and a fling with him at the time, if I would have allowed myself, because I was only 21 then.

At any rate, one day in pillow talk after a bedroom training session, the gymnast seemed to be troubled about something. I comforted him the best I could, and finally got him to talk. He shared enough of his past that I was able to piece together his story.

This young man had worked for four years in the gymnastic competitions, and had faced the dangers, the cut throat competitiveness, and the smelly fellow gymnasts. He had developed an attraction for and a lust over some of the handsome, physically fit fellow male gymnasts, and had grown so accustomed to their and his smells, that body odor did not turn him off sexually. In fact, he had become so acclimated to them, and he had mixed them so often with seducing and making mad love to fellow gymnasts, that he associated rank body odor with hot, buff men and awesomely pleasurable male sex therewith. Body odor actually stimulated him! He had had many hot, torrid, self indulgent, and narcissistic affairs with several fellow competitive male gymnasts. We did not know all of this when he started. We did know he was a homosexual, and very sexually active.

While I trained this former gymnast in the restaurant waiting tables, serving patrons, busing tables, and engaging patrons in friendly conversation, things seemed to go well. Being a new hire, aware immediately of The Flamingo Lounge's policy on body odor, he wore at least deodorant most of the time. Occasionally I would get a little whiff of underarm sweat from him, but it was nothing that turned me off or made me sick. I suggested a few times that he go back to the locker room and refresh his deodorant, or cologne, but it was no big deal.

The Flamingo Lounge hired its 'working waiters' for six weeks. If they learned enough and made enough progress in pleasing clients and patrons sexually, and as long as patron complaints had not established in the probationary hire a pattern of behavior or activity contrary to company policy during that time, they were given a full time job and benefits after that six weeks.

So this young gymnast stud maintained good hygiene through his first six weeks. He impressed the hell out of all of us because he had most all of the gay sex moves down before he even hired in! I had sex with him only like five times to show him a few moves and methods that he did not know or had never experienced before. Other than that he was a hit physically and sexually with clients during his probationary period.

The day after his six-week trial, having been fully hired, this gymnast stud started coming to work just letting any body odor he had hang out. He never really 'stunk' as in 'rank'. But it was not a turn on for most customers. He lost patrons and clientele, and Mr. Richard began losing the same. When confronted, this young man voiced his mistaken idea that there was a large population out there that wanted to have unclean, raw, odored animal sex, and body odor didn't matter! Needless to say, exactly one month after his full time permanent hiring, he was given one week to improve. During his probationary week this young, well-hung, gymnast stud made little or no effort to improve himself in the area of body odor. I don't know if he did not do so because of his ignorance, stupidity, stubbornness, arrogance, or laziness. However, at the end of one week Mr. Richard almost literally threw him out of the doors of the Flamingo.

Afterward the employees who were on staff on all shifts at the time were brought in for a big pow-wow where Mr. Richard laid down the law. All customers want pleasant experiences in their sex for all of the five senses, including smell! We employees were to stay clean at all times, well covered in deodorant and cologne, and liberal with the showers. Otherwise, we employees were history!

I left the shower, dried, applied deodorant and cologne, and put on my thong and muscle shirt. Running a comb through my curly blonds, I walked out of my bathroom to the bed in my under suit and dressed in my Miami Vice costume. I scurried to the wet bar and poured myself a vodka tonic. Then I crossed to my lounge area. I sat on the edge of my recliner, took a long drink, and I shaved my fast growing shadow. I put an 80s twist in my coiffure. My mind continued to wander as I combed and drank my vodka tonic.

The waiter's knock on the door broke my thought process and startled me. I jumped first, and then promptly landed too far out on the edge of my chair, which caused me to slide off. I sat down hard on my ass in the plush carpeting in front of my recliner.

"Drew, it's time! One minute!" The stage manager called.

"Thank you, Orin!" I called. "I'll be there!" I guzzled on my drink.

I heard Orin disappear down the hall. I rose, finished off my vodka tonic and avatar, grabbed my fake gun and tucked it in between my pants and right hip, and opened the door to the hallway. The beginning bars of "Miami Vice" theme song wafted in. I exited my room, locked my door, and I was off to the stage.

I had had a bit too much vodka tonic too quickly even for me as I had gulped down an 8 oz. glass in the short time before I took the stage for my first performance. All day I had been steadily imbibing, and then what I had drunk in the short time in my dressing room just now was finally catching up to me. As I walked toward the stage I began to feel light-headed and dizzy. My vision became slightly blurry and my eyes were hard to focus. All of my senses seemed hyper-responsive, yet it seemed I was experiencing life from under water. Consequently it, my first performance, was a bit of a blur to me. I did manage to time it just right, and earned much applause, all according to company policy. Before I knew it I was picking up my outfit and nice tips off the stage. Apparently I was not too drunk!

I returned to my dressing room and counted the bills I had gathered after my performance. My stage tips this time were $405.00, slightly lower than normal, but not disappointing. I was slowly drinking another 6 oz. vodka with Coke.

I decided to look up some more 80s dance steps to practice and perform. I needed to change my program. I spent a few minutes on the internet and gleaned some more 80s material and moves to which I could strip. I then used some of my old moves, and some of the new moves I had found and created three new dance/strip routines. Then I worked several minutes practicing one of the new routines, so I would be brasher, more brazen, and appealing on my second strip dance!

I spent ten minutes practicing a second routine, adding enough bar time, and clearing my head so I could dance new and innovative techniques on the spur of the moment like was expected of me by patrons and management.

After seven to fifteen minutes of practice and preparation and clearing my thinking a bit, I scurried to my costume racks and quickly decided on my next strip/dance outfit. I would be adorned with the accoutrements of a typical 80's teen in high school. As I opened, closed, and locked my dressing room door I was ready, I was hot, and I would wow the audience! I headed to the stage.

The music of "Take On Me" by Ah-Ha began as I burst out onto the open stage. The stage lights brightly dancing, and the loud roar and applause of the audience welcoming me back were intoxicating and invigorating! Did I ever REALLY want to give this up??

I began my new, daring dance and strip routine, straddling the poles, whirling, twirling, swinging my hips, performing mock sex on some stage props, and slowly disrobing. I was receiving all sorts of positive audience response and creating so much hormonal, sexual, and physical pleasure in myself and the audience that you could cut it with a knife. The air of the performance and I were so provocative, so rousing, and so electric, that I and most of the audience were completely absorbed and almost frantic with my new routine. Then, from out of nowhere, it happened!

As I danced into the first 'chorus' and removed my handkerchief from my neck, a dark, jumbled cloud of reality, negativity, and foreboding seemed to cascade from the ceiling upon me. Despair, guilt, hopelessness, loneliness, disappointment, doubt, self-loathing, fear, feelings of inferiority, anger, distrust, loss of confidence, and other feelings and emotions equally disturbing, debilitating, crushing, and self-damning filled my mind and my being. I suddenly felt like a sex toy, a victim that males and females in the audience were about to rape, beat, and abuse for various reasons of sexual immorality and perversion. I became unnerved and fearful, glancing around quickly and apprehensively for any signs of danger, or any threatening behavior from any patron.

Alternatively several of the dark emotions and feelings bubbled to the surface of my mind. What did the members of the audience think of me? I stumbled, but I recovered gracefully. I was nothing but a fag slut, that's what they thought! How the hell could I end up like this?! I was worse than a prostitute! Damn the foster care system! Damn the society in which I had grown up! Why was it that so many males looked at me and automatically thought I was gay, and believed I was a good roll in the hay?! I removed a tennis shoe and, as I dangled it over the audience, I slipped. I didn't fall and again quickly recovered. I was a scum, a reprobate! I couldn't dance! What the hell made me think people liked my performances?! I was uncoordinated and untalented! I slipped again and had to recover using a fall to my ass and a jump back up to my feet.

'If there be a God,' I thought with derision and shame, 'He must hate me!' What the hell, I hated myself! I was now becoming totally unnerved, uncertain, and unfocused. How the hell did I allow myself to get into such a repulsive business?! I began to take off my button shirt and lost my balance. I slid sickeningly close to falling off the stage. My mind was now becoming so incomprehensibly jumbled and unfocused that I was tempted to just leave the stage for my own safety.

Damn it! How did I get to this low point in my life!? No one except Tyler liked me as a person or friend! He wouldn't like me if he knew what I did for work! Did he really actually like or love me?! I was totally alone! I was a disposable condom, sewer fodder to everyone else! What was that man laughing about?! I was late on a move and had to abandon it. He was laughing at me and my pathetic life, duh! Damn Mr. Lyons! I loved him, gave him my body, my whole being, and he dumped me! I was trash to him! How could I have disobeyed Mr. Breen and brought what's-his-name into his foster care home for illicit sex at sixteen!? That's what started the shit hole my life had become!

I jumped up for a hump and then a slide down the pole and I lost my grip. I fell hard on my ass on the floor. The audience response was scattered tepid applause and some gasps. However, this did snap me back to reality.

'I have to overcome these negative feelings and emotions and focus on my performance, my job! I have to get over and rid of this distressing funk!' I chastised myself. I again managed to recover gracefully from the pole fall, resumed my dance, and determined to focus on continuing and finishing my routine with flair and panache. 'After all,' I told myself sternly, 'there are worse jobs than mine. Jobs that are far dirtier, more distasteful, less honest, less flattering, and more dangerous than mine!'

'On the one hand,' I continued my self talk as I strove to do my normal awesome best on my remaining routine, 'to some in the audience I was a gay prostitute, but to many others I was a means to achieve a sexual high. To others I was a sex idol, almost a god of sex, stimulation, and sensuality!' I smiled as bills continued to be thrown like snow on the stage. I began to regain my confidence, and I began the climb to a personal sexual frenzy.

But then I saw three women whisper and laugh heartily. I tried not to, but I commenced downward again. I became more nervous, anxious, and even paranoid as I continued my dance routine.

It was then that a whole host of new thoughts and realizations crossed my mind. I was developing an uncommon concern for my moral and physical health. This had to be Tyler's influence on my life already! The mention of the Bible, and what I remembered that it believed and taught about homosexuality was causing me to question my job, my lifestyle, everything about my life. Could I continue to perform like this? Where was my morality? Was there sin? Was I sinning? When would my luck run out and I would contract an STD? Maybe it was the alcohol and avatar talking, but I was pretty tolerant of the stuff. I tended to think my problem today was a combination of my guilt after meeting someone like Tyler who wouldn't approve of my lifestyle and job, mixed with my own guilt and depression, and a mix of the alcohol and avatar that I had tonight. I really didn't realize at the time what a mess I was in in my then current state.

I danced and pondered things a bit more. The talented and frenetic edge to my performance was gone. I had to face all of these negative emotions and feelings, face them, and eradicate them. But I couldn't do that now! 'Oops! Damn it I almost fell again!' I thought as I skidded after a step in my routine. I had to focus on my performance!

Finally, I managed to clear the doubts and fears out of my mind so I could dance well. I would not be intimidated! I never had before! I had never obsessed over these type of thoughts before, and I wasn't about to start now! Mentally I managed to drive a stake through the heart of my conscience for the short term.

I began to really get into my dance again. I swirled, I slowly continued taking my clothes off seductively and threw a couple of items into the crowd. I 'made love' to the bar, I 'made love' to the wall, and I 'made love' to the floor. I gyrated and danced all over the stage, and worked the crowd up into a lather! The stage and auditorium area was a roar with applause, catcalls, and clappings! I felt justified as a professional at what I did. I fed off the adulation, appreciation, desire, and abject lust coming from the patrons and clients. 'I have a talent that not many people have, a job or calling to do that which not many people would or could perform!' I told myself. I had the stuff! I was proud of myself and what I did for society! Wasn't I?! Yes, I had to keep myself certain?! I couldn't go through the hell again of the negative attack I had just endured from my own self doubt!

I was still kind of in a limbo room because of the vodka and avatar buzz, although I was now performing my new routine flawlessly and provocatively. My vision was a little monocular, like I was seeing The Flamingo Lounge and its patrons through a train tunnel, albeit still a large train tunnel!

I was still whipping the crowd into a stimulated frenzy, and I was down to my muscle shirt, briefs, and a thong. Suddenly, as I was approaching the removal of my muscle shirt, Jaba the Hut and the two bikers appeared before me in the audience. As I slowly lifted and lowered my muscle shirt in my routine, Jaba was on the floor leaning onto the stage grabbing at and trying to reach me. I had to add a couple of new steps in order to stay out of his reach. After I saw what Jaba was doing, I decided to leave my muscle shirt on until he either settled down, left the stage, or was kicked out of the lounge. I stayed robed and just danced slowly and seductively for the audience, rubbing myself all over with my three pieces of clothing still on.

At this point Jaba and the bikers began trying to climb on the stage. All three of them commenced telling me what physical and sexual acts they were going to do to me. They shouted what parts of my body they would rape and tear. Jaba and Ben managed to climb on to the stage, cursing and threatening me. They lunged for me. I tried to get away, but Jaba caught me. He wrapped one fat, flabby arm around my neck, my jaw and chin were covered by the girth of his arm. Jaba then ripped my briefs off of my body in one arm/hand movement. It hurt like hell as it felt like a high-grundy, squeezing and ripping at my balls and penis.

I continued to struggle to get away. Jaba and Ben began making a major scene, touching, groping, fondling, and mauling me in front of everyone in the place.

By this time I was down to my muscle shirt, a thong, and a smile. Jaba grabbed me and pulled me backwards toward him. I struggled, but to no avail. Jaba began to simulate anal sex on me again for the second time tonight! I felt humiliation, fear, and desperation overwhelm my mind and emotions!! The audience seemed to think it was part of the show. A few others charged the stage. What was I going to do?! I couldn't hit Jaba in the crotch in front of all of these people... these witnesses! I would surely lose my job!

Now, I worked out and kept my muscle tone and figure at an appealing level for my work and to my personal taste; but in that moment I realized again that I should fear Jaba. This time no matter what maneuver I tried of self defense or of physical resistance and escape, Jaba had a counter-response and had me under his control. My strength would never be a challenge to his muscle and size! Apparently earlier the table and the close proximity of other clients/patrons had restrained all of Jaba's ideas and strengths that he could muster to keep me under his power. Now, on stage, fighting these three scums, I could hardly wiggle, let alone get a good elbow, fist, knee, or foot into the action!

Then Ben was there and groped for my legs, grabbing one and pinning it stationary as I struggled. He went toward my crotch with his teeth barred. I struggled as hard as I could! Jaba continued simulating anal sex on me as he held my arms behind me. Meanwhile Ben literally growled and snarled threats to bite my privates off as he swore to perform oral sex on me. I now literally feared disfigurement as well as rape! I managed to hold Ben off with the one foot that I had free. I was, however, on the verge of panic, when Mr. Richard appeared in back, ordering house bouncers to surround the stage in force!

The biker, Gus, loomed in front of me and off to the side. He ripped my muscle shirt off as I continued to struggle. Gus then began to fondle my package. I managed to free my other leg. I used Jaba as leverage to lift my feet as high as I could to try and fend off Ben. I placed one foot up on Ben's right shoulder, and I planted the other foot on Ben's forehead. However, he too was one big muscle! He forced forward, ripping off my thong next. I was now nude, fighting three men who were going to rape me and disfigure me on stage in front of the entire audience! All the negative thoughts and doubts came rushing back as fear filled my heart and my entire being!

I had heard of people being raped. I had wondered what women felt like when they were raped by one attacker. I had contemplated all of the fear, the pain, the humiliation, and the emotional damage that would haunt the person who was raped for the rest of their life. I was facing three men who were determined to rape, molest, disfigure, and do as much damage to me as they could! I would carry this attack with me for life! Who knows if I could live with the humiliation, emotional pain, torture, and permanent damage these perverts wanted to do to me?!

I had heard of men and women being gang raped. Again I had wondered what each one would feel like while being raped by a group of attackers. Again I knew they would have terror, pain, a sense of fighting for their dignity and very life, humiliation, and traumatic emotional damage. I knew they would be changed forever. I had always felt secure that I would never have to face that kind of massive traumatic event in my life!

Now, here I was, the innocent man being gang raped by three men! I now knew exactly the fear, the panic, the terror, the pain, the struggling, the humiliation, and the emotional damage that these three rapists were doing to me, and causing me! I was going into shock, and I could feel it!

The house bouncers arrived on stage. Six burly male 'body guards' converged on us. Three tackled Jaba, two took Ben and Gus. One bouncer grabbed me and, as my bouncer and the three restraining Jaba ripped me from Jaba's grasp, I felt major pain. I crashed to the floor, nude, in pain, and afraid for my life. Then I saw the blood.

As I lay there in growing pain, searching for the source of the blood, trying to fend off my dizziness, shock, and fear, the bouncers were ushering the three bikers out the back way. I could hear them threatening me with every vile act imaginable during their promised rape of me! They declared again that they would have me sexually in every way but loose sometime! I should fear the day when I would see them someplace where I would be alone or vulnerable to their attack. I was totally scared, startled, confused, and discombobulated! My vision was blurring and my heart pounding 'out of my chest' as I glanced back to see Mr. Richard hurriedly approaching the stage. The audience apparently thought it was all part of an act or program, for they were applauding raucously, and giving me a standing ovation. I was not in normal or good shape, for I was in pain, major pain. I realized that it was I who was bleeding rather profusely. I was increasingly not with it, losing blood, and scared shitless!

I looked up, my mind swirling and my vision increasingly blurring from alcohol and blood loss, to see Marcus and Melody, our second best male and first female strippers rushing to my side with first aid supplies and concern. Light began to fade. I collapsed back flat on the stage. I passed out, welcoming blessed peace and rest through darkness!

# CHAPTER 21

# AURORA'S GRACE PENTECOSTAL CHURCH

I sat there feeling paralyzed, basking in the aftermath as Andrew abruptly left. He kissed me! He actually kissed me! As he closed the door I rejoiced. He did appear to have romantic feelings toward me. Any guy who would kiss another guy on the cheek in private must either be one who is not afraid to show affection, or he must harbor strong, romantic feelings for that guy! Was I right?! Or was I right? I knew I wouldn't kiss any guy, other than my dad or brother, anywhere on his face or body unless I had romantic feelings for him! I couldn't imagine Andrew being any different than I in that area. I therefore had to conclude… well, I could conclude… odds were that Andrew had… he had romantic feelings for me? Perhaps my mom was right about Andrew and he was pursuing me romantically, emotionally, physically, and sexually?! Yet I couldn't believe it! If mom were right, and Andrew did want a romance with me, I didn't care! I was developing strong feelings for, and an affinity with Andrew. I wanted him in my life, I wanted his love, and I was really beginning to want him in all aspects of my physical and sexual body.

I snapped back to reality in our kitchen, realizing I had a large, stupid grin on my face and I looked like a silly, infatuated teenager in love. Suddenly I felt guilty and chagrined at my immediate previous thoughts about Andrew and his kiss. I should be ashamed of myself, wanting the love of and lusting after another guy! 'Christians do not pine after people of the same-sex!' I told myself acrimoniously and in shame.

I shook my head in an attempt to rid my mind of the thoughts and desires I had and felt toward the beautifully figured, unbelievably handsome, and totally perfect man, Andrew. These romantic feelings I had toward and for Andrew were wrong! Everyone I had known throughout my childhood and growing up years had said that homosexuality and all of its manifestations were wrong whenever the issue of same-sex love had come up. Anyone who hadn't actually said these feelings and desires were wrong, had lived as though they believed it. Were they wrong? Were they right? No one had bothered to prove to me either way! Why?! An issue so important to one's soul, salvation, and eternal life, and no one bothers to show or prove why, from the perspectives of all the major aspects of life, including the Bible, that same-sex love is wrong, or a sin. No church and no individuals could show where in the Bible, in the law, in the knowledge of good health, or in the natural laws of science it is written, or gives reasons why having same-sex relations were bad, a sin. No one could seem to provide cogent proof or any reason that same-sex love was bad, wrong, and a sin. Everyone just said it was wrong, and treated the whole idea with such programmed revulsion that it was totally predictable.

Why did my church leaders leave me so ignorant on the whole issue of same-sex relationships?! Was I supposed to learn what the Bible says about, and how the Bible applied to today's issues through osmosis of unspoken words?! From whom? Pastors, preachers, laymen, parents, or friends? I had already tried to talk to them and they did not want to be bothered, or were apparently unable or unwilling to answer! Same-sex lovers? They would be biased toward the gay lifestyle and interpret the Bible their way, and/ or were unfamiliar with the Bible and what it had to say on the subject!

Whatever the correctness of the Christian opinion against same-sex relationships and love with which I had grown up, I still had these feelings, these desires, these… these… these lusts for some members of the same-sex. Had not God created me this way, with all the qualities, behaviors, feelings, emotions, desires, intelligence, health, opinions, beliefs, and physical attributes that make up me, a creation and Son of God? The Bible, God's Word, certainly teaches that God created all of us in His image, with all of our individual traits, looks, beliefs, etc. It then follows that God created me with these feelings, desires, and longings for some of the same-sex, in my case men! Did God make a mistake with me when he made Tyler Belmont? God had led me to Andrew, it didn't happen out of anything that I had done! Andrew was now the current focus of all of these feelings with which God had obviously created me! Was God wrong to bring Andrew into my life?! Was I wrong to move in with him and want a relationship with him?! Was God or I in error over same-sex relationships and love?! Did God make me incorrectly by giving me same-sex desires and love?! If same-sex relationships and love were wrong and a sin, then perhaps God did make me defectively, a sinner! He made me with interest in, desires, and lust for other men. That would mean God made a mistake and created sin! The Christian church, without much of any variation, taught that God does not make either. God does not make mistakes and He is incapable of creating sin!

I looked down at the table and continued my efforts to clear my head of any carnal desires concerning Andrew. I had to find a church to attend today! I was beginning to think I needed any and all good church teaching to fight and win this battle over my same-sex lust... lust?... lust, desires, and love... for Andrew.

At home I had always attended church with most of my family. Dad sometimes didn't go. We had been Nazarenes for a few years, and then had attended Harvest Life Church to the present. Now I was ready for a church with the same teachings as Harvest, the same modern praise and worship, and the same practices and Bible doctrine as Harvest. That is what I was used to after all! That is what I prayed for briefly as I sat reflectively at the table.

Like a ton of bricks falling on my head, I suddenly fully realized and knew that in order to have any hope of resisting any 'carnal', 'evil', same-sex desires toward Andrew and anyone else in the future I had to be attending church and getting into the Word! I would have to hope that the issue of same-sex relationships would be brought out and studied in detail by the church I chose. I had to pray it would be covered in a manner that would bring out fully, truthfully, finally, and non-judgmentally what the Bible had to say about the issue! I needed loving truth, proof, and guidance in my struggles with feelings for other men, especially and most immediately, Andrew! I did not need judgmentalism, disgust, and disdain.

I stood up, still struggling with beliefs, feelings, emotions, and thoughts warring with one another over my attraction to and desires for and over Andrew. I crossed to the phone. Instinctively I opened the drawer under the telephone where I knew the phone book should be for organized people like me and Andrew. I took out the phone book, sat on the bar stool next to the phone, and began looking at local churches.

I thought more about Andrew as I looked through the 'church' section of the yellow pages. I couldn't shake my thoughts about Andrew, my desires for him, and the temptations that he posed to me. Andrew was so hot! He was so exquisitely handsome and had a tempting and stunning, drop-dead figure that wouldn't quit! Andrew had and possessed so much of which I was… I mean… of which to be jealous! He had so many good qualities and characteristics, including his dazzling facial beauty and his enticingly superb body. I wanted his ability to make new friends, his ability to accept who he was, his acceptance of his sexuality, his self-confidence, his strength, his charming personality, his honesty, his kindness and gentleness, his determination, and his love. I wanted and desired all of this and more from Andrew. Fact was I wanted Andrew, period! Truly Andrew had so much to share with… with a lover! I wanted him to love me! I wanted to… I wanted to love… then I realized I did… I did love Andrew! A rush of adrenaline and pleasantly stimulating hormones coursed through every nerve of my body at my admission. I shivered and closed my eyes, more out of glee and ecstasy than anything else. At that moment my body was gripped with a fiercely potent desire, need, and hunger to be loved and held by Andrew in a physical and sexual way. The feelings quickly switched, and I was gripped by a strong desire, need, and hunger to express my love to Andrew in a physical and sexual way. I shivered again and winced as actual physical pain resulted. I was getting hard, and that didn't help. I found myself physically aching and longing for his body near mine. It scared me, titillated me, and stimulated me! I never knew one's physical body and spiritual being could really ache for someone like mine did for Andrew! I closed my eyes again, smiled sublimely, and nodded my head. What euphoria! What painful pleasure!

Opening my eyes again, I looked at an ad for a Pentecostal church just a few blocks away. Meanwhile thoughts of Christianity and guilt were also percolating and reminded me again that my homo… homo… homosex… same-sex love of Andrew was a sin. My feelings and desires for Andrew were wrong! I had to hold on to that fact, that belief of mine. I must stop these same-sex thoughts and feelings, bringing my mind and my thoughts under God's and my control. I had to put God in total control of my life. Had I maybe innocently already crossed a line into sin with Andrew?! I didn't know… did I care?! I wasn't sure!

The Pentecostal church in the ad I perused was just a few blocks away and within walking distance. It was perfect! I saw from the ad that they had a service starting in a half hour at noon. On a piece of paper I made note of the address and directions and stuffed it in my pocket. I put away the phone book. Grabbing my jacket and Bible, I left our apartment, locking our door behind me.

I exited down the elevator, passed through Candlestick's empty lobby and left the building.

As I walked to church on that beautiful early summer day, I couldn't help thinking more about my situation and temptations with Andrew. I already felt an attraction and longing for him. However, I had to admit I faced an ever increasingly powerful and deepening desire and craving for Andrew in his entire glorious person. My… My appetence, avidity, and… and… well my ero… eroticism for Andrew was not all purely physical attraction either. I was becoming emotionally, intellectually, and spiritually attracted to him. I wanted to know all about Andrew, to share my deepest thoughts with him, to be intimate with him emotionally and spiritually, and ultimately physically! But that was Biblically wrong! I had to put the brakes on things with Andrew before they grew out of control, before I… we did something that we… I'd regret!

I walked briskly around this block, down this street, and up this one; all streets leading toward the Pentecostal church that I had read about in the ad. I hoped that this church that I would try today would feel comfortable, would preach the word, was indeed charismatic, and would fit the bill for my needs! Especially my needs in the area of same-sex relationships and love! I walked the last block quickly and stood before the address I had written down.

The church was a beautiful, big, red brick building. It sat back off the road a ways, its expansive structure covering a huge area; I estimated it was at least a half a block in size. Its location, on a plot of maybe three acres, was like a park, with beautifully landscaped yards surrounding it.

A very large parking lot sat to the right of the church. It was full of cars, vans, and a church bus. People milled around outside and on the stairs to the door talking and laughing. Children played and frolicked in the yards and on the sidewalks. As I approached the front doors, praise and worship music called to anyone passing on the street. I noticed the sign advertised the church as it did in the phone book: Aurora's Grace Pentecostal Church. I felt at home already! However, I was also kind of giddy, scared, and apprehensive too. Would I be accepted, welcomed, or ignored?

I nodded and greeted a few people who bothered to respond so to me. I reached the doors, opened one, and held it open for some patrons I did not know. Then I entered myself.

As I stepped inside the church, I first noticed that the interior was beautifully designed. It had a large lobby with a vaulted ceiling, and was finished in a tasteful beige and gray interior. The carpet on the floor was a light green burbur.

Probably a hundred people milled around from group to group, hugging and greeting each other. As I gazed around the lobby I noticed an older couple who were standing at the doors to what must be the sanctuary. They were greeting everyone. Other people shook my hand, introduced themselves, and welcomed me. Soon I approached the greeters at what I ascertained was indeed the sanctuary.

The male greeter was shorter than she. She had bobbed hair of gray that had obviously been dyed blond. She was tastefully plump, pleasant looking, and somewhat reserved with a bubbly personality. He was slender, balding with a gray fringe. He had a wonderful smile that made you feel very comfortable, and an outgoing personality. Both made me feel like I was at home with my own grandparents, and I had not yet met them!

"Oh my! What a handsome young man, Ray! He is definitely a new face in church!" She extended her hand as I blushed. "You are so... so... blessed with good looks! We have many beautiful young ladies at this church that will, I am sure, line up to meet you... date you!"

"Thank you!" I blushed, smiled, and shook her hand.

"What's your name, young man?" She smiled and her eyes twinkled. For an older lady she was attractive and very merry!

"I am Tyler Aaron Belmont, ma'am." I responded shyly, but pleasantly.

"How are you, Tyler Aaron?" The woman asked. She squeezed my hand cordially.

"I'm fine!" I answered. "Thanks for asking. How are you?" We released our hand clasp.

"I, too, am fine, thank you!" She pointed at her male compatriot. "This is my husband, Ray Frome. I am Polly. Ray, this is Tyler!" I shook his hand, as he beamed at me.

"Hello, sir!" I smiled. "How are you?"

"I couldn't be better! After all, this is the day that the Lord has made! And I am rejoicing!" Ray firmly shook my hand. "How about yourself?"

"I can't complain! It is indeed the Lord's day!" I smiled. Ray released my hand but remained attentive to me.

"Welcome to our church!" Polly patted my shoulder. "Enjoy the service, and I hope you come again!"

"Thank you!" I turned to go into the sanctuary, but Polly wasn't done.

"Where in Aurora do you live, Tyler?" She looked inquisitively at me, still smiling broadly.

"I live with one of my brothers at Candlestick Apartments about five blocks away. Do you know of the place?" I answered and then countered. I felt a little guilty lying about my relationship with Andrew, especially in church, but I felt it best. I had this intuition I could tell them about Candlestick, but not anything about Andrew being my roommate instead of a brother.

Now, I have seen people who could change their countenance, mood, and facial expression very fast. However, Polly Frome was definitely the speedy expression and mood change winner! When she first asked me where I lived she had a big, bubbly smile on her face. However, as soon as I named the apartment building of my abode, her smile disappeared instantly, and a look of pity enveloped her face. Her mouth dropped open. The color in her skin drained away, and she looked like she had seen a ghost!

Further I saw that Ray was frowning, and several people close enough by us to overhear our conversation had stopped talking and were looking at me in surprise and disapproval. They were now obviously tuned in to my talk with the Fromes.

I looked from Polly to Ray and back again curiously and in great surprise at their change of emotion and countenance! I held out my arms and hands in a 'what gives?' look and shrugged.

"I'm so sorry, Tyler!" Polly spoke quietly. "Candlestick…well… is pretty… well …pretty seedy…. isn't it?"

Seedy?! The only meaning for this expression that I was aware of was run-down, old, and crime-ridden! 'Seedy' was definitely not a word with a good connotation! It definitely was not a word I would use to describe my new home and what I knew about it!

"No…" I looked puzzled and spoke slowly. "It's actually very nice… fine apartments… why do you?…. What do you mean 'seedy'?"

"Most of the people there… well… the tenants…they are… well…" Polly paused, clearly searching for tactful words. "The tenants are mostly employed in… in…. the sex industry… aren't they?" She was whispering by now, her head bent near mine.

I was stunned! If the tenants were involved in the sex industry, I had seen no signs of it so far! I hadn't seen a speck of pornography anywhere at Candlestick! I had seen no prostitutes, drug dealers, pimps….

"I don't think so!" I muttered slowly and deliberately. "Of course I have only lived there with my brother a few days. They could be, ah… in the… in the sex industry… I don't know! What makes you think that?"

Polly fidgeted and looked between her husband and me with quick glances. She clearly was not done, and she ignored my question.

"Honey, you or your brother, you're not… well… you aren't… employed in the sex industry in any way… are you?" She was so close to me, quietly talking so others couldn't hear her, that I could smell her perfume and breath mint. Her cologne was an awesome scent! However, the words and meaning of her question had quickly sunk in.

I was stunned again! Why would she think I… we… Andrew and I were employed in the sex industry (whatever exactly that was!)?! Just because I… we lived in a beautiful apartment complex with a purportedly bad reputation, we were somehow just as guilty as our fellow tenants!?

My mind then became very puzzled for several seconds. Andrew had never said anything about or warned me that Candlestick had a supposedly bad reputation in Aurora! Maybe he didn't know? In addition, I had seen no evidence so far of any kind of low-lifes or criminal type people in the apartment complex! She thought I worked in the sex industry? What the hell was that?! Would I come to church if I did work anywhere in that industry?!

I determined innocently that I couldn't truthfully answer Polly's question until I knew what exactly the 'sex industry' was!

"What the he… what… Mrs. Frome, what exactly do you mean by the 'sex industry'?" I asked naively, whispering myself by now.

"You know… Tyler…!" Polly winked and smiled weirdly at me. Her head twitched to the left, and she clicked her tongue. The only thing I could figure was that Polly was trying to flirt with me.

"Polly Marie!" Ray exclaimed in a hissing voice. "Not in church! That isn't appropriate!" He smiled at me.

"Well, how else can I explain this to Tyler here!?" Polly whispered back harshly.

I was flummoxed.

"No, Mrs. Frome, I am afraid I still don't know what you mean!" I hissed at Polly, painfully aware that some other people were still frowning, quiet and watching us. "What is the 'sex industry' and who works there?!"

"Tyler…" Polly took a cursory look around and grasped my arm gently with her left hand, cupping her right hand over her mouth, still whispering. "The sex industry includes people like… well… sports… johns…"

"What kind of sports are they in?! And everyone named John?!" I innocently exclaimed in a normal talking voice.

I heard a twitter of quiet laughter from the on-lookers.

Polly shushed me, frowning. I felt my face flush hot in some embarrassment as her face also became red.

"Tyler!" Polly bent in and forcefully whispered to me. "The 'sex industry' includes prostitutes, their pimps, gay people, sexual perverts of both sexes that sell their bodies for bad or immoral purposes… those in the porn industry, the strippers, exotic dancers, male escorts... do you understand now? That is the type of people that live at Candlestick!"

I looked at Polly in shock! I couldn't believe what she was saying to me! I was temporarily speechless!

"Tyler, you or your brother…" Polly looked around furtively, gulping. "You aren't employed in the sex industry… are you?" She looked back at me seriously and sadly.

"No!" I finally managed to croak. "Neither one of us is involved in a sex industry! I work for Computronix, and my brother works for Bear Stearns downtown!"

"You're not pornographers?" Polly whispered, a sad and questioning look moving on her face.

"No!" I was offended. "Mrs. Frome, I am a computer programmer, and my brother is a stock and securities trader at Bear Stearns!" I was taken aback by her questioning and irritated that all those who may stay at Candlestick would be painted with the same immoral brush! But Polly was not done.

"Tyler, do you or your brother… well… moonlight by working at any… well… strip joints, modeling agencies, full-service night clubs?" She looked worriedly into my eyes, whispering still.

I was aghast! Where in the hell was this coming from? What misconceptions did the greater Aurora community share about Candlestick and its tenants, or any other apartment complex in their town for that matter! I was becoming pissed!

I really had to set this woman straight! This was so ludicrous that it was laughable! People were really taken in by lies and gossip about the people who lived in Candlestick. They should walk a mile in our shoes, facing all the vicious lies, half-truths, and assumptions that developed from their un-Biblical, insensitive, and licentious gossip!

"Mrs. Frome." I began, firmly, and as politely as possible. "I assure you my brother and I have respectable jobs. We don't lead secret lives in the sex industry or moonlight in the sex industry! As for anybody else at Candlestick, I have not seen any evidence that they work in the sex industry. However, I really don't know! Maybe, since God has laid this concern on your heart, you should ask some of them! Come to the complex and save the wayward souls that live there!"

Mrs. Frome gasped, but otherwise maintained her composure at my challenge. I immediately regretted what I had said! I didn't mean to be nasty to any people I hoped would welcome me and help me discover the Biblical truths on same-sex love and relationships.

"Oh, but dear!" Mrs. Frome picked up quickly. "I have been to Candlestick! I have seen the rabble and the sinners that live there! I have tried to witness, to be an example, to help those in need at Candlestick! But it is such a bastion of… of… well… You see, Tyler, I am a social worker by trade. I work at Child Protective Services. I have been to Candlestick on business to check on children many, many times. I have had exposure to the element that lives there! I have reported people who live there for their activities as strippers, child pornographers, gay prostitutes… employees of the sex industry! Children have been removed from Candlestick on my word alone because their parents were really backward, sinful, horrible people, exposing their innocents to all sorts of sordid sin! I know of what I speak from personal witness!"

There was a brief, uncomfortable pause as I analyzed and assimilated what she had just shared. So Mrs. Frome was one of those better-than-you bitches who broke up families! I was sickened with that information. Mrs. Frome seemed so nice otherwise.

"I don't see that kind of element at Candlestick, Mrs. Frome!" I replied firmly. "Maybe I haven't been looking, maybe I have been blind and preoccupied, I don't know, but so far all is well there where I live with my brother!"

Polly shook her head sadly and then smiled wanly at me.

"What is your brother's name, Tyler?" Polly asked sadly, and with a look of resigned understanding clasped my hand.

I was so pissed and confused! Who the hell did this woman think she was!? In my anger I let my guard down!

"Andrew!" I blurted. "Andrew DiPree. Why?"

"Is his nickname Drew, Tyler honey?" She asked morosely in a concerned voice.

Now she looked and sounded like she knew Andrew, or knew something about him! Which and what was it?!

"I don't know!" I retorted a little too forcefully. I didn't know, I had never asked if he had a nickname! "It could be a nickname for him. I call him Andrew!"

An understanding, yet sympathetic look came over Polly's face.

"Why do you ask, Mrs. Frome?!" I queried rather urgently.

"No reason, Tyler." She smiled wanly again. "I just urge you to be on your guard, use the Holy Spirit to guard you and your spirit, watch out for the temptation to sin, and if you need anything, anything at all, call this number! We will pray for you and your 'brother'. Enjoy church, Honey."

She shook my hand again fervently and impressed a card into my hand, looking at me as though her emphasis on the word 'brother' meant she didn't believe me that Andrew was my brother. Then she turned and shook her head at her husband. She clearly knew, or thought she knew something about Andrew, but decided against any further questioning or sharing with me. I was very puzzled, angry, yet curious about our conversation! What did she know that I didn't know about Candlestick and Andrew! Why wouldn't she tell me what, if anything, she knew about Andrew?!

I looked at the card as I turned away from the Fromes. It was a business card for a home cleaning service, with the Frome's names on it, and two numbers to get a hold of them. I put the card into my back pocket.

I walked casually into the sanctuary. I greeted a few more church people, and took in my fill of the look of the church. It was a beautiful sanctuary! The carpeting was the same light green, like grass. The pews were cushioned in a rich green velour. The walls had tons of windows, and were painted in a pattern of the most heavenly shades of whites and tans. At the front of the building, where all the pews faced, was a wonderful stage area, with two keyboards, drums, and several people warming up with their various instruments. The lectern was a magnificent mahogany, beautifully carved and polished. It looked awesome!

I looked around in the back area for a seat. I found one, and sat down.

'Clearly where Andrew and I are living has a really bad reputation!' I puzzled to myself as I sat there looking around. I wondered why? I hadn't seen anything so far at Candlestick that was illegal, unseemly, or questionable! What would give people in the Aurora community the idea that the tenants of Candlestick were all involved in the sex industry?! They didn't know Mrs. Kurtz and her anti-immorality attitudes! Mrs. Kurtz would clearly not allow only sex industry employees to live in her building! What did Polly Frome know, or think she knew, about Andrew? If it was negative, or a belief that Andrew worked in the sex industry, she didn't know Andrew very well. Andrew wouldn't lie to me! I was so sure of that. Andrew loved me! He had kissed me! I refused to believe he would or could lie to me. I refused to believe that his kiss was a kiss of betrayal.

I shook my head in disbelief. I finally decided to just dismiss this curious and obviously nonsensical conversation. I told myself that Polly Frome and some others at the church were probably just busybody gossips. From where did they get their 'information' or gossip? Did it matter? Of course not! Who were they to help ruin people's reputations by spreading lies and propaganda about Andrew and the other tenants at Candlestick! Mrs. Frome might be a CPS social worker and a Christian, but she certainly wasn't shy about using one of the deadly sins, gossip, to destroy the reputations and lives of innocent people like those at Candlestick.

I dismissed the thoughts and questions placed in my mind by Polly. I would enjoy the service here today, and then go home.

Singing began. It was an awesome worship service! The music was an eclectic mix of modern praise and worship and older hymns revved up. We sang for about 20 minutes. People clapped, wailed, and the Lord blessed all in attendance. I was blessed! I knew God was thankful for the praise!

Announcements were given, and then it was message time.

The message topic was about standing up for God, for Jesus, and for whatever was righteous, right, and good. Scriptures were taken from Isaiah and Jeremiah. We were encouraged to stand up for what is right in Jesus' eyes in all areas of all issues. No issues were mentioned as right or wrong, and I again felt like I was not being guided. However, it was a good message. I struggled not to let my mind think about Andrew and to keep my mind on the message. I was in church; I needed to behave and keep my faculties under the power of God!

The sermon preached was summed up by our pastor in a quote from Thomas Jefferson.

"If you would have a happy life, remember two things: In matters of principle, stand like a rock; in matters of taste, swim with the current."

Soon enough church was over. We were dismissed. I shook some more hands, met some more people, exchanged some more goodbyes including to the Fromes, and I hurried to the door.

I walked briskly back to our apartment in Candlestick. I now could plan the rest of my day! What would I do?

# DANGEROUSLY NAIVE!

As I entered the doors of glazed glass at the Candlestick apartment building Polly's comments about the tenants living here came to mind and caused me to take notice of the few tenants milling around in the lobby. I decided to take a seat here and watch tenants and observe for a while. I walked to the far end of the lobby, opposite the doors through which I had just come, and sat on one of the padded faux park benches placed there.

I couldn't believe that Polly Frome and others thought that Candlestick was the home to sex industry employees, pornographers, sexual prostitutes, and sundry sexual perverts, druggies, and who knows what else! She had referred to the tenants as sinful rabble, basically scum. It seemed to me that people in general were so judgmental and off the wall that I was speechless! I had lived here for two days now and, granted I hadn't met any fellow tenants or even seen very many, but I had not been given any impression or reason to believe that only sex industry employees like pornographers and prostitutes lived here at Candlestick. It was rubbish! Cruel, mindless gossip!

I gazed around the large rectangular lobby and then down the main hall to the right and the left, shaking my head and chuckling at Polly Frome's misconceptions. I felt certain that she was so wrong. The few tenants that I had scanned in my gaze looked perfectly fine. It was time now for closer observations and analysis.

My eyes were drawn first to the main desk.

At the desk was a very beautiful, shapely, dolled-up, younger blond lady talking earnestly to Mrs. Kurtz, who was standing behind the desk. The blond lady's outfit was a bright red, strapless, skin-tight dress that stopped about midway between knee and crotch. It was a little short for general public wearing I guessed, but not anything I hadn't seen in Gurnee on 50th street. She wore very attractive, expensive looking, rainbow pearl-colored high-heeled shoes. She carried a matching colored hand purse, and wore a pearl-beaded necklace that hung down well below her waist. 'She looked okay!?' I shrugged. 'What could she be? A hooker? Nah! She was too sophisticated and respectable looking!' From my view she was very much upper-class, which would fit the reality that Candlestick Apartments were definitely upper-class housing facilities.

The younger lady in red, whom I estimated to be about 25, stood at the front desk, resting most of her weight on her right leg with her left leg relaxed. This allowed her shapely right hip to stick out. She rested her right hand on that hip. With her left hand she spun the necklace around in front of her. She chewed a cud of gum gracefully with an open pouty mouth as she talked and listened. The red-dressed lady was carrying on a long, animated conversation with Mrs. Kurtz, who, as usual, did not seem to be in a good mood. Both she and Mrs. Kurtz gesticulated angrily as they took turns talking, and Mrs. Kurtz pounded the desk occasionally, an ugly frown on her very plain face. The lady in red would return her desk-pounding with a finger in Mrs. Kurtz's face.

I wondered what they were arguing about as I quickly glanced around the lobby and back down the hallways. All that I could hear of their conversation was angrily hissed whispers and an occasional word or phrase spoken in a normal tone of voice. I crossed my legs as I fought the urge to get up and walk back to the doors just so I could overhear something of their conversation.

Suddenly the lady in red fiercely plopped her handbag down on the counter, roughly opened it, took out a wad of bills, and began counting out money. Now, this wad of bills that she had could choke a horse! It was at least an inch in diameter. I was shocked! From my vantage point the bills appeared to be mostly 50s. Where did she come across that kind of dough?! I could work a couple of years and still only come close to the amount of money in that tightly wound wad of cash from which she was counting. I gulped and blinked involuntarily in shock!

As I watched, the red-dressed lady offered a handful of bills to Mrs. Kurtz. She then took a key, what looked like a receipt, and a list of something from Mrs. Kurtz. She thanked her tersely, and turned toward me, her hair flowing around her head like a halo.

What the hell!? I looked up at the wall behind me just for reference as to why she was looking and heading straight for me. I realized too late that I had sat down at a park bench right between the elevators. 'What an idiot I am!' I thought to myself. 'Of all the park benches on the walls of the lobby, I chose this one!'

I looked back at the young lady in red. I did have to marvel at her, and react with some appreciation of her body, as she walked toward me. This blond bombshell gave new meaning to the phrase 'poetry in motion'! She was so graceful, her hips swinging sexily from side to side as she strutted toward me, yet she was dignified and high-class. She held her handbag in her left hand, which was swinging forward and backward with each step. With her right hand she had the necklace twirling in a circle off to here right side. She clicked toward me on five inch heels. She obviously and purposefully chewed her gum, blowing bubbles at intervals. If she were to wear an era-style woman's hat, she would look like a movie starlet from the 40s.

I looked away and scanned the lobby as the red-dressed lady approached me, hoping she would ignore me and just get on the elevator.

"Hi ya, gorgeous!" The lady in red spoke as she stopped just to my left. She madly chewed her gum with her mouth partially open and her pouty lips in a smile. She winked at me suggestively, as she assumed a sexy pose.

I was instantly uncomfortable. I didn't know her, and I didn't particularly want to get to know her! That was not my purpose here in the lobby, to pick up hot chicks. I ignored her for the time being, hoping she would take the hint and leave.

"Hi ya, gorgeous! Are you shy, handsome?" The young lady in red asked in a sexy, Betty-Boop style voice as she reached down and stroked my cheek.

I realized I would have to speak to get rid of her. Silence was obviously not working, and, for my part, silence was not golden in this instance.

"I… ah… I mean no… I mean yes… I am… a little shy!" I stammered and blushed as I looked up at her. She continued by cupping my chin in her hand and stroking my cheek. I felt strangely stimulated by her physical touch. If I were totally hetero... However, at the same time my stronger feeling was that I would rather have Andrew touch me like this! I wanted Andrew.

"You are sexy and hot, studly!" The lady in red continued. Her voice was a dead ringer for the woman who sang <u>Santa Baby</u> or Betty Boop. "Where do you live?"

"I wive... I mean live... I live here in SandleCick... I mean Candlestick. Floor 8." I felt like a fool! Why in the hell did she have this effect on me? I was nervous and anxious to distraction being in her company. I wished that she would just go!

"Do you... are you... are you involved with anyone, gorgeous?" The blond bombshell gently pulled my chin up to look me fully in the face. She then forced me to make eye contact with her, smiled, and winked again at me very seductively. She made it clear that she 'wanted' me.

"Yes... I mean... well... I am involved... I have a lover... I stay with my brother here at the apartments though!" I stammered. I knew I wasn't making a whole lot of sense as unnerved as I was!

"Well, handsome!" The lady in red opened her handbag and took out a card. "Here is my card. If you ever get a little lonely... if you ever want to let out... to share that animal lust inside you... just call me, and we can 'talk'!" She winked lustfully at me a third time. Her voice was soft and sexy like a lady from Brooklyn. She blew a bubble and then licked her lips slowly. I was stimulated some by her actions.

I noticed her nails were a brilliant red and her hand was smooth and beautiful. I blinked, blushed, and quickly took the card. Would she leave now?!

"Thanks..." I looked curiously at her wondering why she still held me by the chin.

"Fifi! Call me Fifi!" Fifi smiled lustfully and stroked my cheek again.

"Thanks, Fifi." I responded tentatively. "But I am happy now with my... my... my lover.. I mean brother, Andrew."

"Well, you centerfold stud... if things change, you now know how to get a hold of me. Just call me! I have no attachments or requirements for...

for my lovers. I just promise a good time to all!" Fifi winked at me, growled a compliment, and then pressed the button for the 'up' elevator. "I spend my best times and energies with lovers in more… shall we say… exhausting activities!" She took her hand away from my chin and put it on her hip.

I glanced at the card. She lived on floor four in apartment 4B. Her name was Stefanie Fanille Miles, or 'Fifi'. The card offered her services as a professional paid escort for lonely distinguished gentlemen in and around Aurora. Professional paid escort? Apparently she was paid by men to accompany them around town, like a paid date. It sounded respectable enough to me. But I did wonder exactly what 'exhausting activities' were that she could provide so that I could have a good time? I could take an educated guess! Oh, well, she was either a good conversationalist or a prostitute, and I chose to believe she liked to talk.

I swung my eyes back around the lobby. I looked closely to the right, where an older man, probably in his upper twenties or early thirties, well built, and dark complected, was getting a latte at the coffee kiosk. He wore very tight, fake leather pants that were so tight they showed off his package and every curve and detail about it. I blushed, yet was strangely stimulated and attracted to him because of it. The man also wore a tight, short-sleeved shirt, and a sexy vest. His hair was moussed. His phone rang.

"Yes! This is Finn! What do you want?!" The older man, probably eight or ten years my senior, answered impatiently.

I decided to listen in. I turned to look the other way briefly, but I focused my hearing and mental attention on the man to my right so I wouldn't miss a word. However, I couldn't resist looking toward the man often. His face and physique were pleasant viewing, and I wanted to see what his face registered during the conversation.

"Yeh! I am the lover of Liberace!" The man said quietly, his cute face flushing red briefly.

I waited, tense and nervous. I realized I was hardly breathing.

"I am Hobart!" The man hissed, fidgeting and looking around the lobby furtively. He was acting like he had something to hide.

I continued looking toward the doors at the far end of the lobby so I could see the man out of the corner of my eye.

"I have the product and the trade from Liberace!" The man spoke softly and insistently into his cell phone.

I glanced at him, staying as quiet and inconspicuous as possible.

"I will have the regular delivery service, and I am free Monday!"

There was a pause. I wondered what delivery of product was going down, but I didn't have time to contemplate for very long.

"Bring 5 year-old Alisameth and 4 year-old Cokie Roberts to me at the address as normal, and I will pick them up. I have your green salad all ready!" The man spoke in a subdued, but angry voice. "What?"

There was another pause as I continued gazing at the newspaper stand and its contents.

"What!?" The man was obviously upset. "What the @! You are trying to screw me! You are totally screwing me!" He listened for a few seconds. "I paid for those years! I paid dearly, damn it! Why don't you keep your word!?"

There was another pause during which I looked toward the man, and beyond toward the hallway to my right. There were two people passing through. They were a diversion for a few seconds and then disappeared.

"I said…!" The man I was focusing on spoke again in anger. "I live in Candlestick Apartments! I have told you that! Why in the hell do you insist on sending child support to other buildings! I am their father!"

I watched another patron or two enter the lobby.

"What the @ are you doing to me! I already paid their support! You owe me the prod… I mean kids!"

I thought to myself about how this man cursing into his phone was cute with a hot body. He was older than I, but he was still hot! However, he wasn't hot like Andrew! I had my eyes and attentions focused only on Andrew, and his awesome physical and facial attributes; attributes which would make even the Fonz take a second look.

I couldn't help puzzling over this guy in the lobby. Was he a porn star? A male prostitute? A pimp? A drug dealer? Ah! What was I thinking! I was letting the gossip of a busybody question perfectly normal people. He was going to pick up his kids, and was arguing over child support, probably with an ex-wife. It was logical and evidentiary that he had probably had an ugly divorce, and his ex-bitch was messing up his child support and parental visits. What did that have to do with the sex industry or drugs?!

"Yeh! That's fine!" The man to my right snarled into his cell phone. "I will deliver the money and the knave to you this Wednesday, even though it is dangerous! I will take him home also. You need to stop putting me in these dangerous situations, or I will dump you! I will dump you like yesterday's garbage! I have other people I can deliver to!" The tightly dressed hot man slammed his phone closed and put it in his pocket. He strode to the doors from the lobby to the street and exited to the outside.

I sat there, briefly reflecting on this man and his conversation. Maybe Polly Frome would have looked at him and seen a drug dealer, a pimp, or a male prostitute. He looked normal, or closely so to me. He was dressed and looked hot! Polly Frome was out to lunch on her assumptions!

Clearly by his conversation, this man was in the midst of either a divorce or a custody battle. He was picking up his four year-old and five year-old, and was giving his ex something green, maybe a dish to pass at a family gathering he was not attending. Then apparently his ex-wife added some new demands for years of child support that the man claimed he had paid. I didn't know what the man meant when he talked to his ex about the 'knave'. Maybe he was talking about a yard gnome or a new boyfriend? At any rate, this man was a normal citizen, not involved in criminal activity or the sex industry!

I scanned the lobby a little more. There was a woman dressed in a '60s retro mini-skirt with a bodice that approached the underarms, made in tiger hide print. She wore knee high fancy boots and sported poufy hair. She chewed a piece of gum purposefully, and her hips moved like a hula dancer's hips. She boarded the elevator and I lost sight of her. Polly's conversation made me question everyone, especially her. She definitely could be a hooker!

A highly made up, poufy haired woman wearing a long trench coat that exposed bare legs from her knees to her pumps entered the lobby from an elevator. She dragged a girl of about four behind her. The girl was almost running to keep up. All the while the girl was begging the woman to stay home and play games with her that day and night. The woman was barking at her daughter about the fact that Mommy had to work the night at the studio, and that the daughter would have to wait for Mommy on the set. She occasionally cussed at the child about different petty things. The woman dragged the child to the main desk, gave Mrs. Kurtz an envelope, and then exited the lobby to the sidewalk. She was still dragging a very unhappy little girl behind her as she disappeared out of the door and down the sidewalk.

Two cute guys entered the lobby together from the street. They were laughing and punching each other on the shoulders, and in general were very friendly and physical with one another. One was dressed as a policeman in a hot, tight uniform that showed off his manly shapes. The other looked like a construction worker. His outfit was also tight and displayed his physical attributes well. They were very boisterous. I was able to hear their conversation from the lobby entrance to the elevators.

I listened in. I knew it was naughty, but I had to know! Was Polly Frome right?! So far I concluded that she was probably delusional, but I had some suspicions about some of the people I had seen.

"So how many tricks did you turn, hot stuff!" One man, blond and cute, asked the other as he ribbed him in the chest.

My instant question was, what the hell is a 'trick'?! Could it be a sexual encounter? I was raised on a farm, I'm sorry I was not up to speed on all of the street talk!

"I had my share! The question is, which ones of yours and ones of mine left satisfied, and mine were all VERY satisfied when they left!" The brown-haired guy next to him answered, winking back as he laughed knowingly at the blond.

"Oh, mine were all satisfied! I did them up right!" The blond assured the brunette with nods as he lovingly gave him a 'nuggie'.

"I'm not talking about just helping them relieve themselves! I am talking about explosive positions and techniques! I am talking about which clients left feeling satisfied completely, body, soul, and spirit!" The brunette blew on his nails and rubbed them on his shirt.

"Oh, and like the one guy who ran shrieking from your vehicle claiming rape was satisfied! And the one who fled while he was bleeding?

You satisfied them alright!" The blond slapped the brunette's shoulder. The brunette rolled his eyes and shook his head.

This didn't sound good! Perhaps Polly was right about these two!

"Hey! I was giving them what they wanted!" The brunette exclaimed defensively. "They both said they wanted it rough! I gave it to them rough!"

"They wanted it rough! They didn't want to be put in the hospital!" The blond laughed as he gently hugged the brunette's neck.

At that point both saw me, and they started whispering. I didn't know who they were. I also didn't know where they lived in the building.

After checking in at the desk, where Mrs. Kurtz gave them their mail, and a key, they approached the elevators and I heard them again.

"I earned $750.00. What did you earn, Adonis?!" The blond asked the brunette.

"I earned $700.00. If I could have gone one more game, I could have beaten you!" The brunette combed his hair with his fingers. They pushed the elevator button 'up'.

"Losing that last inning was your fault, Clark!" The blond laughed and tousled the brunette's hair. "Your way of 'satisfying' clients scared him away!"

I stared straight ahead and ignored the two of them. I didn't know exactly what the hell they were talking about, but it didn't sound very good. I didn't want to get involved!

The elevator opened, and they disappeared into it, boisterously slapping each other's back and discussing their 'tricks'.

So far no one seemed way out of the normal from what I had heard about big cities, the big city culture, and their contained communities and suburbs. However, I was suspicious of a precious few of the tenants I had seen so far. Maybe Polly was just partially right?!

I scanned over to a man perusing the large selection of newspapers and magazines at the paper stand. He was dressed metrosexual as I believed I had seen in photographs and heard it called and described. He had hip-hugger jeans that rode low and tight on his butt cheeks, a skin tight neat, untucked button shirt, choppily cut longish hair, earrings, and he was kind of effeminate looking. When he turned so I could see his face, I could tell he was wearing a lot of make-up. Could he be in the gay sex industry? It hardly seemed likely based solely on his dress style, since a guy I had known in Gurnee and seen regularly in the local grocery store wore make-up and dressed similarly while still straight. Although the metro-man by the newsstand was pleasant looking, he was no hot looker, no stud muffin he!

Unfortunately Metro-man caught me gazing at him. I quickly turned away and gazed straight ahead. What if Mrs. Frome were right!? What would my gaze get me from Metro-man?!

Metro-man continued to gaze at me smiling as he paid for his paper. He was so focused on me he forgot his change. I gathered this by peeking at him out of the corner of my eye. Then he turned toward me. He approached quickly, winking and smiling at me and nodding knowingly. I tried to act uninterested.

"Hey, studly!" Metro-man called, pitching what I'm sure he thought was a sexy pose as he took up position in front of me and twinked his eyes. "What is up?! Are you lonely?"

Again I mistakenly thought that if I ignored him he would go away. I glanced back at the front desk, hoping for some activity to erupt that would distract both of us. However, even Mrs. Kurtz had left her post.

"Studly! Passion muffin! Hot stuff!" Metro-man cooed sexily in a tenor voice. I caught his obvious meaning immediately and I blanched. My heart sank! He was a homosexual metrosexual! "Are you lonely, honey? I can fix that! I can keep you company for a while!? Do you want to accompany me to my apartment or shall we get it on in yours?!"

I turned to him and tried to answer as coldly, quickly, dismissively, and with as much certainty and disinterest as I could.

"I have a lover, a significant other! I am committed!" I spoke solidly, firmly, and lied flat out. I didn't have any of the above, but I wanted to get rid of this… this… masher metrosexual, whoever he was!

"Oh, fox! Dude! Being or feeling committed in a relationship means nothing these days! In fact a little guilt adds to the pleasure! You can have anything you want on the side without harming anyone, including your lover, or anything, like your relationship. Whatever you and I do as adults can remain behind closed doors. Here take my card! I am available anytime day or night should your lover do you wrong, should you break up, or should you desire a relationship on the side!" He handed me a business card which I took discretely and shook his outstretched hand.

He was making my flesh crawl, and I shuddered at the thought of any kind of intimacy with him! I was not into effeminate men. If I wanted effeminate, I would date Fifi! I wanted him to leave so I did what I felt necessary to get rid of him.

He winked at me, touched my cheek, and then moved in front of the elevators. He punched the 'up' button.

"Remember floor seven is the party floor, hot stuff!" He winked at me.

"Good day, sir!" I responded tersely, as I turned quickly away.

At about that time a stout, yet shapely woman with huge jugs and six inch heels walked in from the sidewalk. She had a skin-tight leopard skin print outfit, lots of make-up, and bouffant hair. 'Now her,' I thought to myself, 'she's probably a hooker, or in the sex industry somehow!' The woman in leopard skin got on the elevator.

Maybe… just maybe Mrs. Frome had a point about Candlestick! There were a few 'different' people living here!? I shook my head, clearing her words from my mind. Mrs. Frome couldn't be right! Such a large concentration of sleaze and evil could not possibly inhabit one facility like she said. I felt stupid even believing Mrs. Frome partially! There were logical and innocent explanations for all the 'different' people here at Candlestick, 'different' people that I too might think, based on appearance and actions, worked in the sex industry. I knew better. I was sure they had normal, clean, moral jobs like Andrew and I did.

I gazed around the lobby one more time. There were four tenants around at different lobby concessions areas.

Purchasing a coffee was an older, graying, heavy set man dressed in a business suit. He looked repulsive because of his weight, which was an impression not mitigated by the fact that his suit was bright yellow. I chuckled with the realization that he resembled a huge bumble bee. On his shoulder was a material badge with a business name and logo on it. I strained to see what it represented. I saw the words "Swing Set" and two small couples swing dancing. He seemed harmless enough. It must be that he owned a dance studio. That was perfectly legal.

Perusing a newspaper entertainment section at the paper stand was a lady decked out in a medieval-looking outfit made up of black leather bra, short waist vest, mini-skirt, and high-topped high-heeled women's boots. Her hair was pitch black, almost bluish, and she sported black eye shadow, lipstick, eyebrows, and fingernails. I watched her a few minutes, because I thought it odd that someone might be going to a masquerade party when Halloween was months away. Perhaps she was in a movie? Oh well, either activity that this strange woman might be involved in were perfectly legal. As I moved on to tenants three and four, this black adorned woman turned and quickly left the lobby for the sidewalk.

My surveying eyes came to rest on tenants three and four in the lobby. They were clustered at a rack offering travel and attraction guides from all over the United States. Both were well-built, buff, tanned, bleached blond, and cute in the looks department. Each wore skin tight Speedos which left nothing to the imagination. They then had a fancy vest over their shoulders and torsos. Each vest had the same business logo on the back. The picture on the logo depicted four men in a hot tub. The wording of the logo read 'Guy's Tub Romping', and below the picture 'Aurora, Illinois'. Across each of their buttocks, imprinted on their Speedos, was the word 'Lifeguard'. It was clear to me at the time that, although their choice of swimsuits for their job as lifeguards left something to be desired, it was great that these two guys were actually lifeguards at some business swimming pool or hot tub place.

I rose to my feet, sighing. My viewing, in my mind, had been nothing but inconclusive. There may be some sex industry employees living in Candlestick, but no more than any other apartment complex, I concluded. Why did I put any credence in the words of a gossip? And wasn't gossip a sin too, in the Bible?! Of course it was, although that was another issue preachers didn't cover Biblically from the pulpits very often!

I decided I had watched enough! I had a life to live, things to do!

I walked over to the elevator, punched the 'up' button, and waited. As I did so I slowly scanned the lobby again with my back to the elevator door.

The elevator dinged, and I heard the door open. I turned and entered, barely noticing a young man in a trench coat. I still watched the lobby, and turned to the console. I punched the button for the eighth floor and then the 'close door' button. Thinking to myself and paying no particular attention to anything, I turned to take my usual place along the back wall. There, in front of me, blocking my path to the back wall, was the young man in a trench coat whom I had seen out of the corner of my eye as I entered the elevator.

"Would you mind kindly giving me my personal space, and letting me go to the back wall?" I asked, smiling at the young man. "I usually stand there. There is plenty of room for you there too, I'm sure!"

I waited. The young man stood his ground and fumbled with the belt around his waist on the trench coat. I began to get a little peeved until the young man spoke.

"Would you mind pleasuring me?" The young man asked as he threw open his trench coat. He was stark naked, and he exposed his full figure to me.

I couldn't help but look at his nakedness. He was in my way, he wanted me to see, and in order to continue my attention was drawn to him. I had no choice! Before I knew it, I was gawking.

Now, I had seen some male packages in my day, and some were quite large. But this young exhibitionist beat all I had seen before. This young man, probably nineteen, was HUGE. He was fully erect and ready to go, and he was HUGE. I was so shocked at his size that I'm afraid I was gaping, and I couldn't stop looking at him; Oh, and did I mention that he was HUGE?!

"Well?" The young man queried. "What do you think of what you see?!"

"I… well, I mean… I … you are…" I stammered as I marveled at his size. "I… you are… are… so huge!"

"So, what about it? Do you want it?" The guy jiggled his stuff when he talked.

"What… I mean… ah…" I gulped, as I forced my eyes to move up to the young man's questioning eyes. "What about what?" I shrugged.

This guy's size had me speechless!

"Will you pleasure me?!" He asked impatiently. "Would you like to touch?!"

"Yes… I mean… No! I'm not that way! Now shut the trench coat, or you'll catch pneumonia. Worse yet, someone might see you naked and arrest you!" I quickly looked away, realizing that what I had said sounded silly. I didn't know what else to say, though, so I just kept quiet. I turned and leaned my head against the door. I hoped the elevator would hurry!

The elevator dinged, the door opened, and I almost ran to my apartment!

I closed and locked our apartment door behind me. Then I faced the living room and leaned back against the door. I couldn't believe this happened to me, or that it happened in this apartment complex. Was this evidence that Polly Frome was right? Or was this just a coincidence? I didn't know, but it was disconcerting! I decided that I needed to more closely monitor my fellow tenants. I needed to pay attention at all times. I needed to know if I was living in a normal facility, or a den of iniquity and evil people.

I looked around thankfully at the beautiful apartment and the safety that I now shared with Andrew. Polly Frome's accusations about this beautiful apartment complex's tenants couldn't be entirely true. Such a gorgeous façade, building, and structure, and such awesome apartments couldn't possibly house only sex perverts and workers in various sex industries. Like bugs and insects that lived under rocks, or in other filth, sex perverts and sex industry people congregated mostly in truly seedy flats and buildings. That is what television, the media, former sinners, churches, and parents had told us all of our lives!

Now that I was home, what was I going to do the rest of the day? I remembered that I wanted to go to a gym to work out today. I needed to find a good gym. I crossed to the phone, and opened the drawer. I took out the phone book and, as I stood up, I noticed the tenant applications from Mrs. Kurtz that I needed to fill out. That should be done first, I realized. I found a pencil and sat down to fill out the forms.

An hour or so later the forms were filled out and ready to turn in. I decided to hand deliver them when next I left the apartment to go to the gym.

I then returned to the phone book. I wanted to know where the nearest public gym and body building center was. I felt like a good workout; I wanted to remain muscular and manly for… I'm sorry, Lord… for Andrew. Why, Lord, do you allow me to have these desires, when you say they are wrong?! You say that same-sex attractions and relationships are wrong, yet you made me to have both! How can this be for one who doesn't make mistakes!? Why don't you take them away from me?!

I found the gym listings. I looked at the ads. I finally found one three blocks east and five blocks south. Perfect! I'd call a taxi and go for a workout.

I called a taxi, and then quickly changed to my muscle shirt and sweats. I packed a complete change of clothes, deodorant, and cologne. I put on my tennis shoes, and my jacket. I closed the door of our apartment and locked it. I was on my way!

I delivered my forms to the main desk and Mrs. Kurtz, and caught the taxi to the gym with a few hours left of open time in the gym. I was doing well in my new life!

# CHAPTER 23

# TOURING THE 'TAJ MAHAL'

The exercise gymnasium that I chose was called "Tawny Bods Fitness Center". As I approached the gym in the taxi, I assessed the exterior of the business building. The gymnasium façade facing the street was beautiful architecturally and aesthetically! A brownstone exterior with red stone trim faced the street, and appeared to continue all around the exterior of the gym. Tall, gorgeous, black and white marble columns on the front of the building finished off its opulent and elegant appearance. The building looked to be three or four stories high, and I guessed the expense that must have gone into its construction betrayed what must be a pricey, high-class gymnasium.

The taxi stopped and dropped me off across the street from the gymnasium entrance. I paid my tab, which was also pricey.

As I crossed the street and approached the main entrance door, I was in awe of the pristine beauty of the frontal architecture and the spectacular form of the rest of the building's fine facade. The facility looked huge. I would be proud to work out here, if I could afford it!

I entered the door which opened into a spacious lobby with vaulted ceilings and candelabras. I went right to the front desk. Placing my elbow on the counter, crossing one foot over the other, I turned to survey the lobby.

I gazed around at the opulence and yet subdued beauty of this lobby area. It was gorgeous! Live potted ferns were growing every 10 feet around the walls. Green plush carpet caressed my feet through my shoes as I walked. Green velour couches and Lazy-boys were arranged neatly around a central pillar that went up to the ceiling. Televisions were running on all different channels at intervals around the pillar. A few patrons sat around on the chairs watching television. I stood there marveling at the beauty!

Finally, I turned and looked behind the counter at the help. A well-built, blond-haired, very handsome man of about thirty, and a cute, bubbly twenty year-old woman sat talking behind the desk. I waved at them.

The blond-haired, ripped Adonis jumped up and approached me at the counter. He had a wide, pleasant smile and a helpful demeanor as he looked me over. His visage was accented by Scandinavian features that molded his handsome face into a very bewitching and lovely countenance. His bodily physique was really too muscular for my liking, but I did enjoy gazing at it. His name tag gave his moniker as Neils Hanson. The cute blond-haired woman stopped her work and sat watching us from her desk. She looked very interested in what her counterpart and I were going to do. I was a bit nonplussed by the sly, questioning, and knowing smile she had on her face. She winked at me suggestively. I waved shyly at her and smiled.

"Hi!" The blond Adonis said. "My name is Neils Hanson. How can I help you, handsome?" He winked at me in a familiar, sexy air and held out his hand.

"I'm Tyler, Tyler Belmont!" I answered, shaking his hand. "I want to come in just today and use the facilities for a workout. Do you have an hourly or daily charge I can access? I'm kind of low on money and I am looking for a good deal."

"I'll tell you what Tyler, Tyler Belmont…" Neils lowered his voice and leaned toward me until his face was six inches from mine. I was going to back away at first, but Neils' beautiful blue eyes were mesmerizing. I looked deeply into them. Suddenly I either couldn't, or didn't want to move!

"I really appreciate a hot, buff, handsome guy like you, Tyler! We all have to do what we can to maintain and improve that awesome… sexy… delicious… buff ass… I mean body of yours!" Neils seemed to be almost drooling by now over his description of me as he spoke in a hushed voice. "I'll give you the day free! Pretend you are paying me for Jessica Mills's sake back there, but I really won't be taking any money!"

I couldn't believe he would do this for me! A free day! I was ecstatic. I smiled at Neils. He was really a nice… hot… handsome… buff… I shook the rest of my thoughts about Neils away. This was too good to be true!

"Thanks, Neils!" I blushed as I whispered back. "Are you serious? I… I mean… you will really give me a free day?!"

"Totally serious, Tyler!" Neils replied quickly and quietly. "On one condition!"

My heart sank. Naturally there was a condition! Good breaks and things in my life seemed to always come with conditions or strings attached. It was probably something I couldn't or shouldn't do!

"Condition?!" I gulped involuntarily. "Well… I don't know… What is the condition, Neils?"

"You get today free, stud, if you will meet me on some other day to talk about our membership packages! I know a buff hunk like you takes pride in his body and will want to work out at least every three days. We have many package options that I can offer you. We can fit you with a package that will perfectly suit you, your goals, and your physical needs. I can get you a really good deal, Tyler! We have really excellent and affordable package rates!" Neils smiled at me questioningly. "Is it a deal, studly… handsome, fine epitome of a perfect man?!" Neils wiped hair out of my eyes gently.

A day free, and in exchange all I had to do was meet with Neils to discuss membership packages?! Something I wanted to do and ultimately purchase anyway?! It was a no-brainer! Unfortunately I was too naive to realize that he was asking for a date.

"Sure, it's a deal, Neils!" I effused happily, perking up at Neils's comments about my physique. "It is definitely a deal!" I smiled broadly at him.

"Okay, hottie, make your fake pay here good for Jessica! I don't want her to know about our deal!" Neils whispered, winking at me. He licked his lips slowly and wantonly toward me, making sure that I was watching.

My heart skipped as he flattered and seemed to flirt with me! I blushed and smiled back. My 'shields' were dropping.

"Thank you, Neils!" I whispered breathlessly.

Neils backed off and stood up, hands on the counter. He looked seriously at me but winked flirtatiously again.

"Okay, Tyler, that will be $12.00 for the day!" Neils held out his hand and moved between me and Jessica, the cute blond behind him and the counter. He mouthed the words 'this way she won't see you give me nothing'.

"$12.00 it is then, Neils!" I took my wallet out and dramatically pretended to give him some money.

"Thank you, Tyler!" Neils pretended to take the 'money', fold it, and stuff it in his pocket. He made a good show of it for Jessica.

"Welcome to the Tawny Bods Fitness Center, young Tyler! If you will allow, I will give you a tour of the facilities, we can work out, and then later set up a time for a discussion of our membership packages. Is that suitable?" Neils spoke out loudly and in an uninhibited manner. I was surprised at his friendliness.

"Yes, that is fine!" I responded quickly, hoping to quiet him down by example.

I fancied that Jessica looked a wee bit jealous and disappointed over me.

"Go ahead to the stretch center straight down that way and entertain me, hot stuff! I will meet you there in a few minutes and give you a tour of the facilities." Neils pointed straight ahead to an area covered by gym mats.

I smiled at him and nodded my head.

"Okay, Neils!" I responded, turning and walking casually toward the mats. I wondered, as much as Neils was 'flirting' with me, was I being a bit uninformed… loose… naïve… or unknowledgeable about something?! Was he really flirting with me? Or was he just overly-friendly?

As I left, I heard Jessica say to Neils:

"He is so damn hot!" Out of the corner of my eye I saw her watching me intently, a seductive, lustful smile on her face.

"I know! I know!" I heard Neils say in a guttural voice lush with feeling as he groaned in pleasure. "But he is all mine, Jessica! I saw him first! You go get your own stud muffin with a body that won't quit!"

I slowed as some papers fell on the floor. I could still hear Neils.

"I will sign him up this week as a member. You can have your turn on the next hot guy who comes in to work out!" Neils's voice sounded like he had just had a workout. He panted and groaned slightly.

I don't know what else transpired between Neils and Jessica about me, because I was out of ear shot. I felt very flattered that they both liked the looks of me! I felt exhilarated and stimulated, despite my love and desire for Andrew, by Neils' claim on me, and his seeming crush on me! Then I shook my head, angrily reminding myself that I wanted only Andrew! I wanted Andrew to want me romantically, not Neils!

This gym I had chosen, "Tawny Bods Fitness Center", from the outside had appeared huge. From what I had seen of the gym so far, the lounge/lobby area and the stretching area, it was huge, and also very modern and very ritzy! The help was certainly… nice, eager to please, and encouraging.

I looked around the mat covered stretching area. Five patrons were going through their warm-up or cool-down routines. I noticed that the whole wall to my left consisted of glass from the waist up to the ceiling. Through this glass I could see all sorts of exercise equipment for all parts of the body, banks of televisions, and other weight lifting equipment. All of it looked very modern and complex. I was impressed!

I took another step to check out an odd looking machine half covered by the door on my left. I put my foot out and, when I thought it was planted, I found myself slipping! I caught my balance and looked down to see what had caused my near fall.

It was a colorful brochure. I picked it up and briefly perused it. It was an overview of all available machines, activities, and facilities at Tawny Bods. As I glanced through it casually, I could see that anything and everything one could want or need to tone up, maintain tone, or build up bulk was available here! There were basketball, racquetball, tennis, and volleyball courts, tanning beds, and every type of weight lifting equipment available for every muscle in the human body. Swimming pools, lap pools, a walking track, and walking/running machines in front of banks of televisions for distraction were also available. I was in body builder heaven! I smiled in approval and happiness.

"Does it look good, Tyler?!" Neils startled me as he approached me from behind. "Does it appear we here at Tawny Bods are complete and up-to-date?!"

I jumped, looking over my shoulder in alarm in the direction of Neils' voice. I quickly smiled at him.

"It looks awesome, Neils!" I exclaimed, as I turned to face him. "Based on what little I know of the power gyms, gymnasium equipment, and exercise gyms movement, I would say you folks here are complete and up-to-date."

"This matted area is the stretch room where you can limber up before starting your workout on the many machines, at the weight lifting station, in the courts, or at any of the facilities we provide." Neils waved his hand around. "Step this way, please!" He pointed to the large door opening at our immediate left. He waited patiently for me to go ahead of him.

I walked toward the door. As I came abreast of him, Neils put his right hand on the small of my back just above my buttocks, and pushed me gently toward the door at which he gestured. I tensed a bit in surprise because it was a very familiar thing for Neils to do to someone he had just met. Early on I had decided to let Andrew touch me like this, because I… well… knew Andrew more… better… longer… well, I knew him a little more than I had known Neils. But what to do about Neils? I looked with some alarm at him.

For his part Neils smiled back at me and spoke softly and tenderly.

"I'm a very 'hands-on' person, Tyler. I hope you don't mind! I don't mean anything bad by it." Neils looked straight ahead, left his hand in place, and guided me through the doorway. It was clear that his hand was staying almost on my ass unless I threw a fit.

"This area, Tyler, is the walking, running, stair climbing, exercise machine, and weightlifting area. We have the very latest, most elaborate, and best equipment for exercising all the muscles of your body of any of our competitors in Aurora. We serve you the best here at Tawny Bods!" Neils stopped, motioning toward the large expanse of area filled with all sorts of equipment. He looked like one of Drew Carey's exhibit babes on <u>The Price is Right</u> in his position as he displayed the area proudly.

I scanned the area filled with machines and weightlifting equipment. I noticed with some disappointment that there seemed to be only several slender, shapely, pretty girls working out at the various machines nearby. If there were no hot guys, today would be mentally and visually boring! Where were the buff guys… ? Then I saw several handsome, moderately built young men working out at various machines and stations deeper into the room. My heart skipped in anticipation of fine viewing! 'Yes, it would be a pleasant afternoon!' I thought to myself. I immediately felt ashamed that I would enjoy looking at and checking out the guys more than the girls as they exercised. Why did guys interest, attract, and thrill me so much more than a beautiful woman? I did appreciate beautiful, shapely women… but men… Oh so much better for viewing and… and… anything!

Neils put his hand back on the small of my back, a little lower than before, right at the point where my back ended and my buns and crack began. I tensed again, surprised that he was being so familiar! I looked at Neils again in some alarm. Neils smiled reassuringly at me.

"You could do with a massage, Tyler! You are so tense! Your muscles are all in knots!" Neils prescribed quietly as he gently pushed me to start walking again. As we walked he began massaging the spot where his hand rested with his fingers. I stayed tense. With his middle finger sliding ever so slightly into the beginning of my crack it felt good and stimulating, but I didn't know how Neils meant this physical touching! He was raising the ante and making me more nervous. I didn't know if I should rebuke him, or ignore his friendliness!?

"I am not tense, I am just surprised…" I didn't get very far in my objection.

"Let's walk this way toward the opening in that far wall over there!" Neils interrupted as he motioned me forward with his left hand, leaving his right hand on the small area between my very lower back, and my butt cheeks. He continued massaging my lower back down onto my buns as we took off for the doorway.

It did feel… well, good!

We walked slowly toward the opening as Neils launched into a vivid and detailed spiel explaining what some of the machines we were passing could do for me. It was interesting, and I forgot about where he had his hand massaging upon my body. It did feel good! I became lost in pleasure, listening, and contemplating what Neils was telling me.

Shortly we passed through the next large doorway which opened into a hallway with glass walls and doors about every 35 feet. I looked into the first two rooms just inside the hallway to my right and my left. They looked like tennis courts, but without nets. Painted lines and circles were patterned on the floors. In one room were two men with rackets, taking turns returning a ball to the back wall as it bounced and flew like it would in tennis.

"This hallway houses our racquetball courts first. We have six of them, three on each side of this hallway for the first 100 or so feet." Neils guided me briskly through the racquetball area, pressing gently on my extreme lower back where he had his hand resting, his middle finger now draped just inside my crack.

We passed the last two racquetball courts and came upon one double door on each side of the hall that opened into two huge areas.

"These are our tennis courts, Tyler. We can entertain 32 tennis players at a time! We have 16 courts, 8 on each side of this hallway, just inside these doors." Neils let go of me, and opened the door to our left.

"Shall we?" He asked, motioning toward the inside of the door.

I entered first, followed by Neils. I could almost feel him ogling and lusting after my body as I did so.

I gazed around in awe! Inside were indeed full, state-of-the-art tennis courts. They were lavishly laid out, one after another straight ahead. The nets were bright white, the floors immaculately clean, legal lines were newly painted, and the fluorescent lights brightly illuminated each court and every corner.

"Each of these eight courts, Tyler, is of regulation and full size. You can play singles, or doubles. We cater to beginners as well as more experienced players. Do you play tennis, Tyler, stud?" Neils asked as he smiled at me.

At the end of his question I looked back curiously at Neils. He was smiling at me in a very suggestive, lustful, familiar, and longing way as he looked me up and down and licked his lips. I blushed. As soon as he saw that I had caught him looking, he was all smarmy sweet and professional instantly.

"I've been known to play. I am not very good at it so my batting average is not very high. But I enjoy the game!" I knew instantly that I had just shown my ignorance of sports. Of what sport batting average concerned I did not know, but I knew it had nothing to do with tennis. I turned back and looked at the courts. Four were occupied, one with doubles who seemed be carrying on a very intense and active competition.

"Okay, Tyler, I'm sure you want to get to your workout. Let's go and finish the tour!" Neils quietly purred. He opened the door for me to exit. Out of the corner of my eye I saw him looking my backside up and down, and then he rested his gaze on my buttocks.

I left the courts first and passed back into the hallway, followed closely by Neils. He again took his place on my left side. As we began walking he gently but firmly placed his hand smack on my ass this time. Two fingers rested inside my crack under my gym shorts. I tensed again, and jumped to the side in alarm. I glared over at Neils, an angry expression on my face. Who was he to grab my ass and play under my clothing in my upper canyon!

"What the hell... What the hell are you doing!" I stuttered in angry confusion. "What gives you the... who do you think... what makes you think...! You act as though... You don't own me!"

"I'm sorry, Tyler!" Neils chuckled, smiling broadly at me. He seemed to be taking my rebuke professionally in stride. "I am a hands-on communicator. I am just so touchy-feely with potential lov...I missed your back. I didn't mean to grab your ass! Don't take it the wrong way! I'm sorry! It won't happen again!"

I dropped the angry countenance, looked at Neils curiously, and shrugged at him. I didn't seem to be able to remain angry with him... I didn't know what to think! Was he truly sorry? Did he really mean nothing by it? Or was he really hitting on me?! He was calling me some familiar pet names and liberally touching me everywhere but my crotch!? Was Neils after me for a same-sex relationship?! I know now that I was so inexperienced in 'courting' techniques that I was missing the true implications of what Neils was doing to me.

I shook my head. 'I am too paranoid and vain for my own good! I am not so gorgeous and hot looking that every guy and girl lusts after me!' I concluded, angry at myself. Neils was not hitting on me! That was my vanity speaking! He was just innocently giving me friendly touches and meant no harm. Neils was probably right, he was just a touchy-feely, hands-on communicator!

"Let's continue to our left here, Tyler. Our next stop is the basketball courts and then the swimming pools!" Neils motioned to the left.

I started off in the direction that Neils indicated. Neils was beside me on the left in no time, his right hand on the small of my back on the same spot he had put it when he was massaging my lower back and upper buttocks. This time he was gently squeezing my butt cheeks and running three fingers up and down into my crack as far as they would go. I rolled my eyes, realizing he was an incurable touchy-feely guy. I didn't let the thought cross my mind again that he might be lying about grabbing my ass, and he was really trying to feel me up! A fleeting nausea sullied my stomach as I realized that he might want me to do the same to him. Although a little titillating and tempting, I couldn't imagine stimulating any other guys' butt crack... unless it was Andrew.

We approached two more sets of double doors on each side of the hallway. Beyond these doors I could see the beginning of what looked like a staircase off to the left, and a wall straight ahead.

"We go through these doors, Tyler!" Neils removed his hand from my back and jumped around in front of me to hold the door open. He definitely was sensitive, demonstrative, chivalrous, and a gentleman!

I followed his inviting hand and walked into the next room. Inside I determined there was indeed a stairway rising in a circular fashion on the left. To our right was another set of double doors.

"The stairway here leads up one floor to the walking track that goes around the building." Neils smiled as he motioned toward the stairs. "The track is conveniently measured so you can determine your distance walking each session to the exact inch!"

Neils went to the double doors on our right. I followed.

"There are two full, regulation-size basketball courts in each of these great rooms just through these doors on each side of the hallway here." Neils explained. "We have a lot of leagues that play here on all days of the week. Let's continue forward, and I will show you one court."

Neils opened the door and gently pushed me forward with his hand again on the small of my back, and all of his fingers now under my pants and in and out of my canyon. We entered the next hallway. Inside the hallway I observed that on our end and on the far end large double doors allowed entrance and exit to what were clearly labeled basketball courts on our left and right hands. At the far end of the hallway was another set of double doors with a hallway beyond.

"Let's check out a basketball court and its facilities, Tyler!" Neils opened the door to the right hand court and motioned for me to enter.

I entered and Neils followed. He quickly took up his place on my left with his hand on and in familiar territory.

"The first door here is the men's lounge room, showers, and locker room area. The second door here is the same for the women." Neils then pointed to doors on his right. "These doors lead to the men's and women's restrooms."

Neils then propelled me forward through the large opening at the far end of the hallway. His hand was slipping lower onto the top of my crack and his middle finger was fishing further into my butt crack. I was getting angry again! What was he trying to do to me?! It couldn't help but cause him stinky fingers!

However, even more infuriating to me was that my body was responding to Neils's intimate touch. I was rising, and getting sexually excited! I was Andrew's! Only Andrew should sexually arouse me! I couldn't cheat on him with another man's physical and emotional attentions. This could not be happening! What the hell could I do to explain this to Neils and get him to stop touching me so intimately?!

Then my attention was seized elsewhere. Inside the arched opening was a huge basketball court, polished floor, brightly painted control lines, gleaming backboards, and a set of bleachers along the wall just inside the court.

I gasped in awe! Even though I cared nothing for the sport, this basketball court and facility were impressive. It was as impressive, if not more so, as pictures I had seen on television of the most modern courts. This basketball court appeared to me to be top-of-the-line.

Neils gently propelled me to the left down toward the doors at the other end. As we walked he explained all the amenities and possibilities their fully legal basketball courts offered. He was so excited as he expounded on the facilities that it was appealing. He was like a teenager. Soon we were through the court, the far hall and doorway, and back into the central hallway. Neils opened one of the set of double doors to our right.

"We have showers, locker rooms, and three swimming pools each to the left and the right of the hallway just through these doors!" Neils exclaimed, motioning for me to enter the next hallway.

I entered, followed closely by Neils. We walked about twenty feet to the first doors, one on the left and one on the right. The sign over the first doors read "Women's Locker/Shower Rooms".

"These are the entrances to the women's pool facilities. Let's go down to the men's pool facilities and I will show you the whole pool setup!" Neils again resumed our walk with his left hand on my lower back/upper buttock spot. With his fingers he kept playing between my cheeks.

We walked about sixty feet to the "Men's Locker/Shower Rooms". One door was situated on each side of the hallway directly across from one another.

"Here we are, Tyler! Entree!" Neils grabbed the door on the right and held it open for me.

I entered the door to the men's area and walked immediately to the left, and then right, and to the right again. I came to a stop in front of an arch and stood in awe as I looked around. Neils slipped up beside me on my right, placed his left hand on my ass, and smiled proudly as I gazed around the room we were about to enter. I had forgotten all objections to Neils's intimate touches as I whistled in appreciation.

Just inside the arch was a spacious, bright, and beautifully furnished small lobby. The deco was a tasteful combination of beige, brown, teal, and green. Two televisions played, one on each side of the lobby area.

"This is an area you can use for a snooze, or to wait to swim until your food settles. Isn't it… well… manly?" Neils rubbed and gently squeezed my backside, taking advantage of the fact that I was too awestruck and impressed by the lounge to notice.

"Yes… it is very… very manly!" I breathed out slowly with each word. I couldn't believe how ritzy everything was! This was more evidence that "Tawny Bods" was probably a gym that was too pricey for my budget.

"Come on, stud!" Neils exclaimed, excited like a child in a candy store. "Let me show you the rest!"

Neils walked me on further through the lounge. We next passed hall after hall of lockers, five in all. Neils pointed to the right at a doorway that disappeared around a wall.

"The showers are through that door." He explained. He pointed to another door on our left.

"That is a large restroom." He explained happily.

We continued on to the door at the far end of the large hallway/room in which we were walking. Neils opened it and guided me through with his hand on my ass.

I stopped and gasped. Inside were three large, placid, beautiful pools, and then two smaller pools off to the right, steam rising from them with their water bubbling like cauldrons. I whistled in pleasure.

"The first pool here, hot stuff, is the children's pool. The second one is the open swimming pool for adults and children, with a shallow end, and a deep end. The third pool is the competitive swimming pool for doing laps and holding swimming tournament events. These two steaming, bubbling, smaller pools are hot tubs for relaxation." Neils put his left hand from the small of my back to my left shoulder and draped his arm on my back.

I was impressed. This would be awesome! I definitely was interested in a package plan to this fitness center! However, I sadly realized I probably couldn't afford it.

"Do you like?!" Neils cooed seductively, his face so close to the right side of my head that, as he spoke, he blew in my ear. At first I jumped, but quickly realized it felt really, really good… and… and… and… well… stimulating!

"I love it, Neils!" I effused. I did love it! Not just the gym facilities, but, unfortunately and to my chagrin, I loved and enjoyed the attention I was getting from Neils.

"Great!" Neils guided me to turn around with his arm around my shoulder, and we started back into the locker/shower room. "Let's get this tour over so you can start your use of our facilities! I am sure you are anxious to get started."

Neils led as we retraced our steps back to the central hallway.

We reentered the great hall and I turned instinctively to the right toward what was obviously another corner of the building. A door opened shortly before the corner off to the right, and one opened straight ahead at the end of our current hall.

Neils stopped and was quickly beside me on my left, and yes, he placed his right hand half on my ass, half on my back. We walked toward the corner doors.

I decided it was high time that I set some boundaries for my interactions with Neils! I love… I mean… well, yes, I loved Andrew, and, although I somehow perversely enjoyed the attentions of Neils, I felt extremely guilty allowing him to touch me so intimately. I also did not want to possibly lead Neils on since it appeared that he was gay and was hitting on me for a relationship.

"Neils would you please…" I began firmly, turning my head to look at him.

"These two doors ahead, Tyler, will perhaps interest you!" Neils interrupted rather forcefully. "Each door leads to two regulation size volleyball courts. Parties and intramural leagues make use of the volleyball courts. However, they are more than suitable for one-on-one or pairs playing as well!"

At the corner Neils guided me to the right, and together we walked down that hallway.

I tried again to speak to Neils about his hand, considering he now squarely rested his open hand just above the waist of my shorts, partially on my ass, and gently stroked his fingers up and down inside my butt cheeks.

"Neils, please don't…" I got no further. Neils excitedly interrupted me.

"On either side of this hallway are large aerobics rooms, classrooms, a large bank of tanning machines, a laundry area, a restaurant, and a cafeteria." Neils motioned to doors as we passed them. "This rectangular main hallway system itself is two miles in length total, and serves as a track for patrons to walk or jog. As I pointed out earlier, though, we have the second story walk-around-path to walk, jog, or run as well."

I was opening my mouth again to speak to Neils about removing his hand when inexplicably Neils detached his hand from my ass and stepped away from me a step by himself. I closed my mouth.

We reached the final turn of the hallway, and followed it back to the right. We passed through an area where the smell of food permeated the air, and a large cafeteria opened to the left.

In no time at all we reentered the stretching area with the mats on the floor.

"That concludes our tour of Tawny Bods Fitness Center, Tyler! Are you impressed?!" Neils put his left arm around my neck and laid his left hand flat on my chest. He then squeezed my neck and rubbed my chest. I could smell the sweet, tantalizing, erotic, and provocative scent of Neils's deodorant mixed with a little sweat that enveloped my head and tickled my nose as he held me.

I turned to look at Neils as I answered. Neils was not even looking at me. I noticed he had what could only be described as a triumphant smile on his handsome face. He was looking at and motioning to Jessica Mills behind the front desk. I rolled my eyes upward and saw that Neils was pointing with his right hand at me and then his left arm, back and forth. He appeared to be gloating?!

I gazed back straight at Miss Mills behind the front desk. She was clearly not happy! She had a very disappointed frown on her pretty face. She mouthed what looked like 'You won' and shrugged.

What was going on?! I thought uncomfortably. I stepped a little away from Neils's arm and turned to face him.

Neils looked back at me, and then blushed slightly. He put his right arm down to his side, while he removed his left arm from my neck. He shrugged at me as he smiled innocently.

"I'm sorry, Tyler! I'm giving her hand signals of a repair we need to schedule in the swimming area! She's not happy about the expense!" He looked at me apologetically.

"I think I can start my workout now that I know my way around, Neils." I stated firmly but simply. "Thank you for your tour." I smiled at him and abruptly turned around to the doorway into the equipment area/workout bay.

I left Neils standing there, watching me. Neils made me a little uncomfortable, yet I found him attractive, enticing, strangely intriguing… even sexually stimulating. I didn't feel stimulated by him as much as I did by Andrew, however! 'Shame on me!' I chastised myself. 'I shouldn't be thinking this way about men! I shouldn't be having any of these thoughts about Neils, let alone Andrew! I am a Christian! I am a Christian!'

# CHAPTER 24

# THE NEW AGE HOTTIE

I knew my attraction for, and intrigue with and in Neils was wrong. Especially when I wanted Andrew only, and had determined to wait for Andrew until he either accepted me or left me. I began to chastise myself vehemently about Neils, about cheating Andrew, about Andrew, and about the feelings, desires, wants, and needs that I was quickly and steadily developing for and from other men. I began to denigrate the way distance from my past seemed to loosen my inhibitions and allow me to manifest more and more of 'me'.

I went quickly into the workout machines, treadmills, and equipment bay. I started toward the treadmill area and chose a machine, determined to forget Neils for good. I set the timer at five minutes, set the resistance, and began walking on it. I had no radio, or any modern means of listening to anything for distraction so I looked up at the bank of televisions in front of the treadmill area. Obama was on every television, every station, in some speech or appearance. It was like all the mass media stations had become an Obama propaganda machine much like Pravda and Isvestia had been for the former USSR. I wanted to hurl chunks! Obama pissed me off so badly! His communism made me sick!

My family had always been God-fearing, church-going, and conservative/libertarian in our lifestyle, political views, and voting for as long as I could remember. I ignored a strange, dark fog in my childhood memories. Anyway, as such we identified with and voted for the Republican party and its candidates most of the time. My dad had been in the local militia for years. My parents, Mom especially, had taught us kids a thorough knowledge of and respect for the precepts, beliefs, and wisdom codified in the Constitution of the United States of America. In addition, we kids had been taught the precepts and beliefs of the Founding Fathers and of the great American statesmen like George Washington, Abraham Lincoln, Thomas Jefferson, several early presidents, Thomas Paine, and, more recently, Ronald Reagan. This education about and on philosophy surrounding these topics had been taught, debated, and learned over the 21 years I had lived at home.

My parents were very proud that they had successfully raised three 'Rush babies'. We had listened to Rush all the time while growing up. I remembered Rush's coverage of Bill Clinton's administration and his verbal imitation of Clinton. Rush had been hysterical in his conservative coverage of every issue. We had learned much from Rush, much about the issues, and much about the opposition democrats. We had cheered Rush's philosophy and plain talk about the times and politics. Fun times were spent with our mother, with Father, or with both listening to Rush tell it like it is! Then as Sean Hannity, Michael Savage, and others came along we listened to them as well. All of my family shared similar conservative views with each other, and with the conservative talk show hosts. As a family we had many lively discussions on many, many issues we heard about on conservative talk radio.

It was because of this truthful, Biblical, Constitutional, and conservative upbringing that we knew the truth about Obama, his radical socialist regime, and his some 50 czars that were employed with no Constitutional authority and were totally unaccountable to the voters. We understood each individual American leader was either for or against freedom, for or against free markets, for or against God-given rights, for or against the rule of law, and for or against America and Americans.

We could plainly see Obama was against everything America and freedom: by his support and passage of nationalized health care; by his view that the power, size, and control of the federal government needed to grow; through his efforts to control and muzzle the new internet; by his refusal to follow the will of the people; and his efforts to take over private banks and industries through direct loans of fraudulent capital. Clearly Obama was furthering fascist goals by 'buying' U.S. businesses and then controlling them through finances and massive government regulation.

It was equally obvious that Obama was against free markets because he supported the takeover by the federal government of the healthcare industry, the car industry, the banking and insurance industries, the stocks and securities industries, and any other industry it could through 'loans', outright control, and more regulation.

Obama was even more clearly against God-given rights of the individual. You had to be a blithering idiot not to see that! He supported abortion on demand and public funding of abortions which denied the most basic of God-given rights, the right to life, to a whole class of citizens, the unborn. Through the death panels in his national health care bill he also supported denying life to the elderly and giving to the government the power to determine life and death for everyone. He denied us an excellent health care system by passing his Obama care. He wanted to impose his 'moral beliefs' on churches through the IRS. His beliefs on homosexuality, abortion, right to life, and other issues were appalling. He was in favor of controlling everyone's pursuit of happiness by seizing unconstitutional control of industries and companies. Not to mention his goal of raising taxes for all, which would destroy the middle class.

Through Obama's restrictions on free political speech, his efforts to shut down or limit the freedom of speech on the internet, and his efforts to limit the ability to donate to political campaigns showed he hated freedom of speech. His increase of the federal debt by several trillion Federal Reserve Notes, thus enslaving us and our descendants to foreign lenders, showed he hated freedom for all people. These were all evidence that Obama was against God-given rights, freedom, and capitalism.

Because Obama opposed life, freedom of speech and press, free markets and business, freedom of pursuing happiness through free business, freedom from slavery to debtors, and a myriad of other freedoms, it was clear to me and my entire family that President Obama was a radical left-wing liberal; and that was being kind. We also recognized his policies to be those of a hybrid communist, fascist, and socialist. During Obama's first two years he had so openly, arrogantly, and radically expanded the power and scope of the federal government and the unconstitutional fourth branch of our federal government, the administrative agencies, that he had almost formally dismantled our constitutional republic!

None of our family had voted for the scum, but millions of foolish, brainless, and mentally challenged liberal Americans and other hopeless and careless Americans had voted for Obama. Every person living in this country, and future people currently unborn, but to be born for generations, were paying for and would pay for these stupid liberals and their poor voting and spending habits.

Now, horror of all horrors, Obama had been President of the United States of America for two years, and still had two years to inflict his policies on our failing nation. It was a depressing, sobering, and devastating fact of which the colossally ignorant, liberal, rudderless, fawning media made us painfully aware on a daily basis! Heaven forbid that Obama might be elected to a second disastrous term!

Today Obama was babbling about our exit strategy from Iraq in one speech, and in the other he was trying to sell the implementation of his passed and signed Obama nationalized health care reform plan.

I hadn't paid a lot of attention to Iraq, although I believed we owed it to those Americans who had already died in the Iraq war to stay there until the job was done.

On the issue of Obama's national health care plan, however, I had followed it from Obama's first day in office. I was sick that his plan had passed. I didn't like the idea of the federal government running health care into the ground like it had our economy, currency, social security, banks, national defense, and everything else it had taken over. I also did not want the federal government setting national standards for diagnosis, treatment, and follow-up for any health problems I might have. I agreed with those who pointed out that any federal government efforts to reduce health care costs would only result in a growing list of conditions, treatments, and procedures that would no longer be paid for by insurance companies or government. It would thus result in rationing of healthcare. I did not want the government making health care decisions for me! I didn't want the government running healthcare and doling out treatments! I did not want any level of government able to decide when and how my parents should die based on the expense of their treatments in their old age!

I knew and had been taught that government at the federal level has constitutional limits on its powers, and healthcare was definitely not in the scope of the constitutional powers held by any branch or agency of the federal government. One only had to read the U.S. Constitution, specifically Article one Sections seven and eight to verify that!

As I walked on the treadmill I was facing the bank of televisions, so I had to listen and pay attention to one Obama or the other. I decided to listen to Obama on health care, and hope I didn't get too ill to work out!

Obama droned on and on, and one could plainly see he would be lost and speechless without a teleprompter. I chuckled as I thought about how he had stumbled and misspoke himself when his teleprompters had failed to work in a couple of speeches previous to this! Obama was such a poor speaker, lacking any ability to formulate or express an intelligent thought on his own. My chuckle changed to a frown. Our nation was in real trouble under the tyranny of such a bumbling, inexperienced buffoon!

I looked around. My eyes came to rest on a cute, shapely girl on a treadmill ahead and to the left. She had flowing blond hair and an hour-glass figure. She was probably 20, and weighed around 150 lbs. I watched her for a minute or two, admired her facial beauty when I was able to glimpse it, and even gawked and marveled at her almost perfect physique. I pondered the thought of asking her out. She was pretty, shapely, and female. She was definitely within the Biblical requirements for a male's significant other! I could date her while I waited to find out whether Andrew did, or did not want me. When Andrew made up his mind and potentially chose me, I would…

That wasn't very nice! Use this girl as entertainment dating until Andrew and I could get together, and then dump her! If I maybe wanted Andrew… If I really wanted… Since I really wanted Andrew, I should not date or lead-on anyone else of either sex!

I then realized, with much chagrin but a little relief, that I just didn't sense, feel, or have the hormonal and sexual drive, or sexual interest in a female relationship. Nor did I have the teeming desire to pursue any girl, let alone this girl. I didn't have the mental, emotional, hormonal, or physical strength, will, and desire to exert the energy to approach, meet, date, or marry any girl, let alone this girl!

'Why, God?! Why do I lack that drive, desire, or energy for women?!' I thought angrily. 'Why did you not provide that to me like you did to everyone else?!'

I thought about my future plans. I wanted a Christian life and a family. I really did! I just didn't know if I wanted to marry a woman, or a man like Andrew. Right now I had discovered that I preferred, in a sexual way, men... I preferred some... I preferred Andrew... the Andrew man! Did I say that!? I meant, I wanted to live like the Bible dictated! I wanted to live as Christ called us to live; man cleaving to woman, woman cleaving to man. I wanted to be attracted only to women, but unfortunately, I was not. I was attracted instead to certain men!

I felt ashamed of myself suddenly. Why did God allow me to be like this?!

'Once again, God!' I thought fervently and perhaps petulantly. 'If same-sex love is really wrong, why did you create me to prefer a man, Andrew, and implant in me the desire for same-sex love! Why?!'

I thought about Andrew DiPree. He seemed so right to me and for me! He was blond, drop-dead gorgeous, awesome figure, and so manly! He was the perfect man package! Andrew was buff and well-built, but not grotesquely muscular. I did not like the grotesque musculature of the body builder types. Andrew smelled manly, yet pleasantly and even tantalizingly all the time because of his use of appealing and stimulating deodorants and colognes. He appreciated the need to smell good all the time. I did too! He was so attractive and stimulating to look at, admire, adore, and desire. He was definitely 'eye candy'! I knew it was not Christian to keep lusting after Andrew, but I couldn't help it. I found I was really attracted to Andrew, and every day I was falling... falling more... well... falling more in love with Andrew. I hoped he was feeling the same for me!

I glanced in dismay toward the doorway to the stretching area. Where were the cute guy patrons...? At that moment I caught sight of two hot, handsome, buff men entering the gym/equipment bay. They were in their twenties, and dressed in short sweats and muscle shirts. One guy had jet black short hair, he was cute, and he was very shapely and muscular in a manly way. The other had light brown hair, he was also very cute, and well-built in all the right places. They qualified as 'eye candy' in my book!

I smiled in appreciation of the beauty of their figures! This time of exercise today was definitely looking much better and more interesting for me all of the time. I just needed... needed men to... ogle...

There were by now two more lovely, shapely, ladies on the treadmills, but I more preferred to watch the two male hotties that had just come in. The men were now on the treadmills straight ahead of me, and oh my gosh! What a couple of cute butts they had, what awesome physiques! They didn't threaten Andrew's attributes, but they were appealing! I enjoyed watching their bodies, their backsides, as they exercised and I thought of Andrew.

What was I thinking?! I shook my head in shame and disgust. I was embarrassed to stand this way before God, a man attracted to another man mentally, emotionally, physically... and... well, sexually. I felt so guilty before God to have and harbor these thoughts, feelings, and desires for any male. Why did I find some men so desirable, so sexy?! Why did I find these two guys so preferable to the cute, shapely women here?! Why was I attracted to any guys?! Why would God create my mind to work this way?! Why would God make my being and body to be attracted to and stimulated by men?! Why did I feel giddy and shudder slightly in pleasure as the first arousal coursed through my body when I saw or was around handsome, hot guys?! Why did I become fully aroused whenever thoughts of Andrew appeared, someone said his name, or when I was around him?! Why would God allow me to be this way?! God did declare same-sex relationships a sin didn't He?! Or did He?! 'God must hate me!' I concluded. 'God must hate me, thinking like a queer and a sinner! He must loathe me because I look at handsome, hot men with desire! He must truly despise me because I have the hots for Andrew!'

My treadmill timer went off and startled me! I glanced around at the jumble of machines and the cute guys. Quickly I grounded my reality and where I was currently. I grabbed my towel and bottle of water, and left the machine.

On my schedule for the next part of my workout were my arms and upper torso. I entered the area where the weight lifting and muscle building equipment were located. My machine for my arm crunches had to be strategically located, I decided. I picked an arm crunch machine from which I could see a television and the two hunks on the treadmills. I set the weight, and began working out with my arms.

I watched as the two hunks worked the treadmills, their gluteus maximi flexing… suddenly there was a loud bang. I glanced around to find the source of the noise. Four machines over a really cute, buff guy was preparing a machine. He was hot too! He saw me curiously checking him out. I looked away quickly.

"Sorry, buddy!" The hottie smiled apologetically and waved. "I just dropped a weight on this machine clear from the top!"

I gazed back at him.

"It's okay, pal!" I smiled and held up a hand in a 'stop' motion. "No harm, loss, or foul!"

I pumped vigorously. As I worked out I watched the two cute hunks. They seemed very friendly. They carried on an animated conversation as they walked on the treadmill. Their hot bodies flexed and worked, giving me enjoyment as I watched. I dismissed an urge to go over and introduce myself. I had Andrew! I wanted only Andrew!

I glanced back at the cutie down the machine row from me, enjoying the pleasant viewing of his nice physique. His pants were tight and you could see his perfectly formed bubble butt and his package. Nothing was left to the imagination! He was nicely handsome, with clean and clear facial skin, blond hair, and a body that was a bit over muscled for my taste. However, he was…

"My name is Ian… Ian Mock!" The blond cutie from four machines over was looking directly at me as I gazed at him. He had obviously caught me checking him out a second time! I blushed.

"What is your name?" Ian inquired, smiling broadly at me.

"I… ah… I mean… Are you talking to me?" I stammered, disbelieving that he indeed was talking to me.

"Yes, you, dude! What is your name?" Ian answered smoothly and soothingly.

"I'm sorry! I normally don't talk to strange…" I began apologetically.

"Dude!" Ian interrupted me. "Don't apologize to someone when you haven't wronged them! You're cool with me, dude! I just want to know your name so I don't have to call you 'dude'!"

Ian beamed at me as his calm yet corrective voice faded. Even though he reprimanded me, I felt an intense friendly wave from him. I sort of melted, my warnings from Mom about talking to strangers slipped away.

"Tyler, Tyler Belmont! I'm... I mean... that's my name..."

"Well, Tyler, I have seen you four times today so far..." Ian began.

Now it was my turn to interrupt.

"Why have you seen me four times today and I haven't seen you at all?! Have you been following me?!" I asked a bit peevishly. I paused my labor and looked suspiciously at Ian.

"I saw you here in the exercise machine area first. Then I ran into you when you visited the tennis courts and swimming pool, and I saw you pass as I ate in the café. No, I'm not following you!" Ian chuckled.

"Oh!" I exclaimed sheepishly. "What a strange string of coincidences then." I resumed my exercise.

There was a pause as we worked out and Ian stared at me as though he were intensely interested in me. I blushed a couple of times as I caught his gaze.

"Okay! Okay! Tyler, you've caught me!" Ian shook his head, frowned, and then laughed. "You've dragged it out of me!"

"Dragged what out of you?" I replied, stopping to up the weight on my machine for the hell of it.

"I was... well... not... not really following you!" Ian began again, smiling apologetically at me. "I was more like anticipating your next move. I more like kept strategically ahead of you so I could keep seeing you!"

I was a bit unnerved now! Most men did not trail or pre-trail another guy! What the hell?!

"You anticipated my next moves..." I pondered, a wee bit spooked. "Then made sure you were there to... you were at each location to... to see me?!"

I paused my arm crunches again and glanced at Ian suspiciously.

"In a manner of speaking… well… I guess…" Ian's countenance read as one for whom the wheels of thought were turning, and I imagined I could see smoke from overheating gears rising over his head. Ian's handsome face finally formed a determined, contented smile, and he looked at me.

I would have been thrilled at this man's attentions and blushed except things with him were becoming a little creepy! Instead, as he looked at me, I eyed him warily.

"What the hell were you shadowing me for, Ian?!" I demanded solicitously as I frowned.

"I didn't actually shadow you, Tyler!" Ian stopped, and upped the weight on his machine. "As I explained, I actually…"

"You actually predicted my next move and met me there, blah, blah, blah!" I interrupted impatiently, as I tensed up with unease. "What I want to know, Ian, is what the hell you were doing pre-following me, whatever you call it!"

"Tyler, you are a handsome, fine figured, and fine epitome of a man!" Ian continued to pump, but smiled at me lustfully, licked his lips, and winked at me.

"Surely you have a better excuse for doing your tracking of me than lusting after me!" I exclaimed in an irritated voice. "Damn it, Ian! Why were you shadowing me?!"

I realized I was becoming angry, and because of the adrenaline from that anger I was becoming more forward, demanding, and less refined. Did I give a shit? No! What the hell was his game, his motive, his plan?! I wanted to know, and while in Rome, I was beginning to act and talk like Romans for my own good!?

"I am not lusting after you, Tyler!" Ian chuckled as I began to pump my weights with angry force. However, his facial expressions betrayed those proclamations with more signals of his desires.

"Iiiaaaannnnn!" I growled, slamming my arms back and forth. "Come clean, damn it! I am sick of your games!"

"I'll level with you, Tyler!" Ian exclaimed, smiling in a serious manner. He winked at me again. "Your aura, Tyler, is all screwed up and very unique and intriguing! I was simply attempting to ascertain…"

I let him continue no more. I stopped my work out and swiveled my whole body to face him.

"What the hell are you talking about, Ian!?" I interrupted, shrugging. I gave him my condescendingly shocked and questioning gaze.

"Your aura, Tyler, is all… well,… it is all… well, all @ed up!" Ian continued to pump his arms as he now looked seriously at me. "Your aura is, because of this fact, very unique and intriguing. By pre-following you I was simply attempting to ascertain if your aura were really that @ed up. In the event that it was, I wanted to read your aura and tell you my findings!"

"What are you, Ian, an 'aura doctor'?!" I asked sarcastically, snorting in derision.

"No, Tyler!" Ian shook his head vigorously as his weights clanged. He didn't seem to be getting tired yet, and that pissed me off too! I had done thirty at two different weights and I was feeling the burn and panting some!

"No, actually I am a New Age shaman specializing in personal auras!" Ian winked at me.

"Okay! It's time you answered a few questions!" I exclaimed in a disdainful and commanding voice. "What the hell is a 'shaman'!?"

"Well, technically it is a… well… a doctor…" Ian purred hesitantly before rushing to clarify and also answer my next question. "However, Tyler, the only reason we use the moniker 'shaman' is because it is illegal for us to call ourselves 'doctor'! We do much the same thing. We diagnose and treat diseases, we offer treatments, guidance, and prescribe cures. The only difference between a doctor and a shaman is that doctors can provide surgery, but shamen will never operate on the physical body. We will operate only on the 'chi' and the 'aura'!"

"Okay then, shaman Ian!" I retorted combatively and in disbelief. "What is an aura?!"

As soon as I was finished with my question Ian stopped his workout and twisted to face me. He wore an earnest and loving smile.

I shivered. I felt somehow this man was gay, and was flirting with me!

"I thought you'd never ask!" Ian chortled happily as he took up sitting on the edge of his workout bench. "Tyler, let me explain!"

I snorted, hung my head for a few seconds, and then shook my head as I looked back at Ian.

"Your aura is the electromagnetic field that surrounds your human body. It is called the Human Energy Field, or HEF. Every human, organism, and object in the universe has one aura, or HEF. Your aura is an assemblage of electromagnetic energies. These energies penetrate through, into, and out of the physical body of every living person. These particles of energy stay around the body in an oval shaped field called the auric egg. The aura all around your body consists of seven layers called auric bodies. They are all interrelated. Each one affects the others and each affects the person's feelings, emotions, thinking, behavior, and health. Are you with me so far, Tyler?"

I nodded assent as I actually had no clue what the hell he was blubbering about! I must have had a brain fart and placed a dumb-founded look on my face while staring at Ian because he asked me again.

"Tyler, do you understand me so far?" Ian winked and gazed inquisitively and lovingly at me.

"Yes, yes!" I lied impatiently. My voice cracked, and I hung my head briefly. I looked back up and over at him seated on his machine. "Get on with this bunch of bunk!"

"It is a scientific and holistic fact, Tyler!" Ian cleared his throat. His expression changed again to kindness. I felt very uncomfortable.

"Let me explain, Tyler." Ian winked again at me and licked his lips. "The first auric body is our physical aspects. It includes your physical sensations, simple physical comforts, pleasure, and health feelings. The second auric body is our etheric aspects. This body holds the emotions dealing with self, self-acceptance , and self-love. The third auric body is our vital aspects auric. This rational mind is there representing rationality and logic. Number four auric body is the astral or emotional one. It covers our relations with others and loving interactions with friends and family. In auric body number five, the lower mental powers, we find the divine will section. Its job is to maintain alignment with you and your other auric bodies, and a firm commitment to speak and follow the truth. The sixth auric body is the higher mental faculties. In it are divine love and spiritual ecstasy, among other perhaps more ethereal things. Finally, auric body number seven includes the divine mind, serenity, and the universal understanding. Do you have any questions, Tyler?"

Ian held his palms open on his knees in a partial lotus position and gazed questioningly at me.

I was flabbergasted at his claptrap. This otherwise hot, buff, and handsome man to whom I had otherwise been attracted was a real crackpot once you came to know him a bit! I wanted to run away screaming to the hills, but curiosity about one thing caused me to extend another query.

"What are they?" I asked curtly, eyeing Ian in a slightly contemptuous manner.

"What are what?" Ian asked softly, almost sweetly as he eyed me questioningly.

"Your findings, Ian, your findings about my aura!" I exclaimed in frustration and suspense. "What things did you discover when you studied my aura?!"

"Oh, yes, your aura!" Ian nodded his head and looked at me with concern and compassion. "Well, Tyler, I am worried about you. Your aura told me much, and some of my readings are very disturbing. You are a troubled soul, Tyler. You are in conflict…"

"Specifics, Ian, specifics!" I demanded sardonically, waving my hands in front of me and fake smiling.

"Are you sure you want to hear this, Tyler?" Ian queried in a disturbing tone and manner. "It is not good news. Your aura and you need help. It might be better if…"

"You are not in a position to know WHAT is better for me, Ian!" I interrupted angrily, pointing at him. "You don't know me well enough!"

"Okay! Okay!" Ian smiled rather smugly and halted me with his hand. "First, I need to know your age. How old are you, Tyler?" Ian smiled broadly and looked quizzically at me. I sensed a distinct impression that he really did not need to know my age, but was taking advantage of the situation.

"Twenty-one." I responded.

"You and Neils are a couple, or you are involved with another lover?" Ian lowered his head and his eyes probed me. He seemed to be holding his breath in hopeful anticipation.

Neils and I a couple? Hell no! What did this have to do with my aura... whatever?!

"I am not a 'couple' with Neils! I am involved with another lover!" I blurted emphatically in self defense. I immediately regretted my answer... "Well... I mean... there... this is unfair... there should be a third choice, 'uninvolved'! I am..."

"Your lover is a male or female?" Ian interrupted with baited breath.

"Male!" I again blurted without thinking, inexplicably scared of the word 'female'. "I mean... I am not... I am not involved with anyone!"

Ian seemed confused yet excited at my answer.

# CHAPTER 25

# THE VAGUE INTERPRETATION

I had really made a blunder here! 'Now Ian thinks I am gay!' I mentally castigated myself for talking without thinking again and getting myself into trouble. What the hell was I doing?! I knew by now that no amount of clarification or backtracking would undo what I said, and I knew for sure that that rule applied 100 times over to this instance. Especially since Ian appeared happy that I had said I was involved in a same-sex relationship. He would not now believe otherwise! I looked shamefully at my hands and blushed.

"It is all right to be a homosexual, Tyler!" Ian said softly and sweetly. "There are much worse things to be! A thief, a killer, a traitor, a Christian…"

I popped my head up and eyed Ian furiously. His features bore a look of tenderness, comfort, and sincerity. Ian's attack on Christianity completely escaped me as I tried to correct the record and defend myself.

"I am neither homosexual nor gay at the moment!" I growled, no longer able to contain my defensive disgust for Ian and his 'aura' crap. "Now, Ian, get to your findings on my 'aura'! Otherwise run along... I have work to do!"

"Perhaps we could discuss my findings over supper today at the Caberfete?" Ian suggested seductively and tenderly.

By now I was truly not attracted to Ian in any way, shape, or form. Nor was I attracted to him at any level of intelligence or understanding. I had no intention of doing anything with him that he, or anyone else could misconstrue as a 'date'!

"We will discuss your findings here and now, Ian! I will not dignify you by doing anything with you that may be construed as a 'date' or an 'I like you' meeting! I do not date men!" I declared emphatically, frowned, and folded my arms across my chest.

"Tyler, that statement is false." Ian spoke with certainty, shaking his head. "You do date men. You are living with a male lover, and you have a date with a male on Wednesday."

I was floored. How in the hell did he know these things?! From whence did his information come?! How did he 'know' that Andrew was my 'lover' when I didn't even know this? I didn't have a date with any man on Wednesday. How did he 'know' this, when I had nothing scheduled? What the hell was he talking about!? It was a little spooky!

"The man with whom I live is my brother, and I assure you, Ian, I am not seeing any man on Wednesday!" I exclaimed emphatically. "Now produce your findings, or I am on with my work out!"

"Okay, Tyler." Ian smiled in a very loving and concerned manner. "I'll do the good news first, but be aware the portions of your aura that are still good are being infected by all of your bad aura. Soon all of your aura will be bad, infected, toxic, @ed up!"

Ian cleared his throat and motioned a circle in front of himself with a finger.

"Tyler, over your whole aura is a dirty gray overlay. This overlay partially obscures your other energies and auric bodies. This tells me you are very guarded, protective of certain thoughts, feelings, and parts of your life from some, or all, of the people with whom you associate. The danger here with the dirty gray overlay is that it could escalate, gradually trapping you in a lonely prison of obscurity which neither you, nor any other person will be able to penetrate. You would be totally unable to communicate, function, or anything else in your life and gradually your health will fail."

"Thus starts the 'positive' portions of your studies of my auric body?! I dread hearing the 'negative' portions of my aura!" I stated sarcastically.

"Bear with me, Tyler!" Ian firmly quieted me. "In your aura I see definite spots of gold concentrations. This tells me that you have a divine spirit guide protecting you. This gold 'layer', when present in one's aura, means that the person is being guided by THEIR highest good. The spirit guide along with your highest good should be allowed to guide you, Tyler, you need to surrender yourself to it. The gold also tells me you are wise, highly intelligent, spiritually minded, and intuitive. Now gold was positive! Would you not agree, Tyler?" Ian looked at me questioningly.

"Well… I… I mean maybe… I guess…" I stammered like one suffering from stage fright. I was beginning to feel a little insecure for some reason.

"Fine! Did you understand what I have shared so far?" Ian again paused for a response and smiled.

"Yes, I think… I mean… well… I think I did… I mean… Yes." I finished with certainty. Suddenly I wanted this whole conversation over! I must answer accordingly.

"Wonderful, Tyler!" Ian proclaimed. "The next most positive layer is colored violet. The violet in your aura tells me that you are sensitive, wise, and intuitive. In addition it means you are idealistic, striving for the best in every situation. You also have a visionary mind and being, working for what is right for all citizens of the world. You are also futuristic in that you dream of and work for a better, more cohesive, egalitarian, controlled world in the future. You are a developing 'world citizen'."

I was somewhat shocked by this insight. I did not seek a 'controlled' world! Nor did I ever want to be called a 'world citizen'! I was an American! However, I was sensitive, wise, and I strove for the best in every aspect of my life. I was developing a very egalitarian spirit as I realized what I was and whom I loved. I decided to listen carefully to the rest of Ian's words.

Ian counted off fingers with each new color and flashed me a sincere, serious, loving countenance with each important point.

I was becoming strangely intrigued in Ian's analysis of my aura. Part of me strongly believed this was a bunch of bunk, silly Pollyanna propaganda, and that I should tell Ian off and get back to my workout. However, the other part of me was captivated by the mystifying analysis, aberrantly desirous to hear more, and inexplicably unable to move away even when part of me tried desperately to leave.

"The next positive color in your aura, Tyler, is lavender. Lavender is an awesome color for you! In your aura, Tyler, lavender holds a prominent position." Ian was giddy, like a politician who can spend limitless taxpayer dollars. "Lavender tells me that you are primarily driven in your inner spirit being and highest good by your imagination. You are a daydreamer in planning, and a visionary in action."

"Next, Tyler, is indigo." Ian was really into his explanation. "Indigo in your aura means you are intuitive, you have strong, correct, and actionable instincts. It also means you have powerfully deep feelings, true feelings, and strong emotions that spring from your inner spirit being. They reflect and determine who you really are in this plane of existence."

Some of what he was sharing was making sense. I could identify with many of these readings! It seemed to me that he was hitting some nails on the head. I shuddered in fear and anticipation.

Ian swallowed hard and then leaned forward. His eyes twinkled.

"Your next aura color is bright, light pink. Tyler, bright, light pink tells me that you are loving, sensitive, sensual, and artistic. It also tells me you have stumbled into a new romantic relationship, not only in person, but in sex. The letters 'A' and 'D' are prominent in it, Tyler. You should pursue this new romantic relationship and consummate it. It is right for you! You and this 'AD' person will know each other the rest of your life."

Ian paused as he stood up and walked to the machine next to me, sat down on the bench, and took my right hand in both of his manly, strong hands. I felt an adrenaline and hormonal rush.

By this time I was completely mesmerized and ensnared by Ian as I listened to his words and contemplated how amazingly they did fit my life, of which I was certain Ian knew nothing.

Looking back now I understand the danger in which I was engaged allowing Ian to fill my mind with all that anti-Christian, New Age crap. I wish now I could go back and drag me out of that area and away from shaman Ian. However, no such technology exists, and I can only recall and share what really happened.

"Tyler, you have many small spots of green in your aura." Ian stroked my hand. "Green is a comforting, healthy color of nature. It tells me you are growing in knowledge, understanding, tolerance, and acceptance of new things and things you once rejected. Green means you are destined to accept and embrace change, change that may have once been rejected by you. It tells me you are slowly moving toward and will ultimately accept a new, healthy balance between your religion and your deepest desire, your deepest secret, your one true love. Green says you are a social person and a teacher. You will bring many to what your spirit guide shows you is true 'enlightenment'."

Ian paused, the blood veins in his forehead now visible and pumping blood vigorously. Ian was very sexy and appealing to me suddenly. He was passionate, enlightened, certain… I wanted him… Wait! I loved Andrew! Andrew was everything good Ian possessed and so much, much, much more! Andrew was a god, an absolutely gorgeous and perfectly manly man, possessor of so much to claim, to have, to hold, to love, to sleep with…

"The final good news I have for you concerns the orange in your aura." Ian patted my hand as he held it.

I was mystically and inexplicably beguiled. It was like Ian had some special power, some way to hold me, win me over, and make me fall in love with him. I watched him as he continued, smiling at me, stroking my hand, and licking his lips.

"Orange tells me that you are currently in good health. You are very energetic, creative, and productive. You are normally moderately adventurous in your personal life. However, orange also tells me you are experiencing stress in your life related to your addiction that is preventing you from acting on and living in pride with a natural appetite you possess." Ian paused to breathe. "Those are the good colors in your aura and what they mean. Do you understand all I have told you, Tyler?"

I was, at the moment, so charmed and now enamored with Ian and his soothing, loving, comforting message, that I answered late.

"Tyler?" Ian asked again.

"Yes, yes I understand!" I replied, in a daze. "Continue."

"Things get worrisome and bad here, Tyler." Ian had a warning expression on his handsome face. "Are you sure you don't want to hear the rest over dinner later?"

The question fortunately snapped me out of my bewitched state and back to reality. I was pissed that Ian kept pushing himself on me for a date!

"Ian!" I frowned at him. "I don't date men! Now, get on with the analysis, damn it!" I paused briefly. "And let the hell go of my hand!"

I snapped my hand down, escaping his grip.

Ian took my chin in his left hand and held my face to look him in the face. I was disgusted, yet entranced... It was like I suddenly became frozen... I couldn't move.

"Tyler, I'm sorry! I really am! I shall continue." Ian drew a deep breath, but held my face focused on his. For some unknown reason, because of some unknown power, I was putty in his hands.

"On the negative side, Tyler, your bright, light pink areas are surrounded by a dark, murky pink color. This tells me you have a dishonest nature in that you are lying about yourself to yourself and to others. You have a part of you that you are hiding, and about which you share falsehoods. You need to eradicate your fears and come clean before your mental health is compromised."

I was beginning to feel like many of Ian's findings were worded to direct me in my struggle with same-sex relationships and my love for Andrew! I didn't know whether to be impressed or pissed at Ian's interference and subterfuge!

"You also have black in your aura, Tyler." Ian laid a hand on my knee. "Black tells me that you have had severe abuse forced upon you by a man in your life. This abuse occurred during your childhood, and still strongly affects your life today. It prevents you from becoming close friends with any man in your life. It especially interferes with your developing a loving relationship with the one man in your life who loves you dearly and who will make you happy the rest of your life."

Ian removed his hand from my knee as I pondered his words. I suddenly felt that he was somehow right, but I had no memories of abuse... yet I felt pain and rejection from my father! I felt a tear trickle down my left cheek.

Ian reached up and wiped my face gently.

I became angry. My childhood had been superb! I had not been abused by any man in any way!

"I don't believe your malarkey about black, Ian!" I exclaimed resentfully. "I was never severely abused by anyone, let alone someone in my life!" I chuckled. Ian was such a quack!

"The meaning of these colors and their application to you are undeniable and easily interpreted, Tyler. All this has come true, or will come true soon! Or you will see and remember their veracity soon!" Ian nodded his head and looked at me confidently.

I was pissed at his smug belief in his own talents!

I chuckled and shook my head in skepticism.

"The next color present in your aura, Tyler, are blobs of muddied red." Ian continued after the next breath. "Muddied red tells me there is friction in your life. Anger over a personal issue in your life and how admitting it to family and friends would affect your relationship with them is one issue. You also need to forgive yourself over something in your life that defines who you are. Anxiety and nervousness over the same issues can accumulate to cause physical problems for you, Tyler!"

Ian sat back and put his hands behind his head.

"The next color prominent in your aura is a bright lemon yellow. This color tells me you are struggling to maintain power and control in your personal relationship between you and a significant other. You fear losing control and respect, even to the point of hurting others to keep it."

"Now we come to dark blue!" Ian smiled, winked, and licked his lips suggestively at me. "Dark blue in your aura means you have a fear of the future destined for you. You also feel afraid to express your true self to everyone. Finally, dark blue tells me you fear to face or to speak certain truths."

I was disturbed at all these negative messages. I wanted to get back to my work out! How the hell did he know all of this?! How was he so uncannily accurate?! I knew exactly what he was talking about! It was very deceptive!

I focused on the fact that I wanted to get back to my work out. What time was it? Oh, shit! I had been talking to Ian for fifteen minutes!

"Dark gray also is clustered in your aura." Ian patted my knee familiarly. I jerked it away. "Dark gray tells me that fear and negative energy are building up in your body. Health problems will develop, Tyler, if you do not deal with the fear and negative energy."

"Finally, Tyler, I saw an enveloping dark forest green aurical body. You are jealous of someone dear to you because they have something you can't easily and freely acquire due to your addiction. You also resent a group of people; freedom for you will come through self acceptance of your issue. You also are insecure in yourself, and suffer from low self-esteem. Finally, you are hyper-sensitive to perceived criticism. There, Tyler, are my findings in your aura!" Ian sat straight up and laid his hand back on my knee.

"Any questions?" Ian asked as he massaged my knee gently.

"No, Ian." I replied with certainty. "But I have a workout to finish so I will bid you adieu."

His words had hit home in certain areas of my current conflict. I didn't want to belabor my thoughtful concern and worry.

With that I stood up and left Ian who was stammering a protest. I went to the next machine, made sure I could still see the two cute dudes, and then sat down to work my arms differently. I began vigorously working out on the new machine.

I couldn't help pondering Ian's words. He had hit home in some areas! How?! Where did he get off with the bull that I had been abused by some important man in my life?! I felt a surge of fear come on with that question so I skipped it quickly. Then he had said I was insecure, that I needed to accept myself and forgive myself for who I am. What would that be about? Maybe my feelings of being... being... loving Andrew? And what addiction was he referring to? Did he mean same-sex love with Andrew, or my life-long Christian faith? He sounded like he was counseling me to accept my desires, my love for Andrew, and act on them. But why didn't he just say that was what he meant? I became angry at myself, Andrew, Ian, even God! Why must I deal with this issue, this personal part of myself! Why God!?

# IS THE GRASS GREENER?

My pecks, deltoids, biceps, and triceps began to burn as I exerted them. I was breathing heavier as I watched the two hunks. Their cute asses… their manly figures… their attractive muscles… the burn increased, and I pushed further. I closed my eyes as the burn in my arms intensified. I continued to pump. I groaned as I pushed out five more pumps, finishing my count at forty. I groaned out loud on the last one and went limp as I stopped. I hung my head with my eyes closed as I panted.

"Hey, stud, stop the orgasmic reaction to your workout! You are turning me on big time!" Neils purred right in front of me.

I jumped in complete surprise. I snapped my head up, opened my eyes, and jumped again! Neils was leaning in a suggestive and sexy pose against the machine directly in front of me, smiling wantonly. As he caught my eye he winked at me in a manner I could only characterize as sexually meaningful. He licked his lips provocatively at me.

He had to be flirting with me!? It was clear to me that I lacked any gay-dar… any ability to sense flirtations from anyone when they were directed at me.

"I didn't mean to startle you, Tyler! Sorry!" Neils's blond curls were too long for my liking, but they did a good job of framing his handsome face. I looked Neils up and down. He was well built, muscular, and definitely physically attractive. He was now wearing a skin tight pair of exercise shorts and a muscle shirt. His clothing showed all of his body and curves. It also betrayed the fact that Neils had a woody. I had to admit he had a hot body!

For his part, Neils was checking me out and smiling with a greedy, lustful look on his face. His eyes darted up and down my body as he rubbed his crotch slowly and sensually. I felt uncomfortable and very much over exposed as Neils seemed to be sizing me and my body up for some nefarious purpose. I sat waiting awkwardly for him to speak and share the reason for his visit. His gaze came to rest on my crotch and I knew he was assessing my package. I blushed, my face becoming hot. I knew it was wrong, but I mostly liked and only slightly disliked Neils checking me out.

Suddenly I became angry. I didn't need to be the one to be intimidated by other men checking me out! Why not turn the tables and put the gawkers at unease?! And Neils was the perfect first one on which to try this new strategy!

"What do you think, Neils?" I asked, giving him an innocent but questioning look.

"Excuse me?!" Neils asked, glancing up from my crotch and meeting my gaze.

"You were looking at my package! What do you think?" I shrugged as I pointed to my genitals where he had been staring. "Is it appealing or what?" I looked up and stared into his eyes.

Now, I expected Neils to be surprised, embarrassed, and off his game at my unexpected personal, straight forward, and inferential question. However, was I in for a curve ball!

"You are looking really hot and delicious, Tyler!" Neils didn't miss a beat. "I'll eat your toy any time, any place!" He had a big, boorish grin on his face.

I almost fell off of my bench. Instead of putting Neils on the defensive, he had masterfully punted and put me in an even more compromising position. I blushed and looked at my feet. I did not have a comeback.

"I definitely dig what I see!" Neils enthused in a sensual voice. I could tell through some strange insight I received that he was being perfectly honest with his feelings and findings.

Could I conclude definitively and authoritatively that Neils was gay?! I didn't feel I had ample enough evidence to believe that yet. His only action that had to show he was gay was running his fingers in my cheeks. Was he just being friendly? Was this how he complimented all his patrons?! Did the management allow employees to be this sexually blunt and familiar with the patrons? Did the management realize Neils hit on his patrons so persistently? Did they know that he massaged patrons' buttocks while he gave them tours? I decided to pursue this by again attempting to knock Neils off his pinnacle of confidence and threaten him.

"Neils, does management know that you are so sexually suggestive, familiar, and touch-feely with patrons? Or should I report you to them for unwanted and unsolicited sexual harassment?" I felt a surge of empowerment as I exercised a right of all patrons; complain to the management.

Neils blanched as he gaped at me.

"Pardon me, Tyler?" He asked timorously.

"Neils." I began slowly so even an ass could understand. "Does management know that you are so sexually suggestive, familiar, and touchy-feely with their patrons?" I decided to ask one question at a time for simplicity, and to make Neils feel and look stupid.

"Yes!" Neils matched the tone, tenor, and speed of my voice.

I was a bit surprised at this first answer. In the same voice I plunged forward.

"Neils, does management know that you sexually harass patrons?"

"Yes." Neils answered again in the same voice as I.

Now I was a bit deflated. What the hell?!

"Neils." I tried again. "Does Tawny Bods management know that you, a trainer, fondle and massage the privates and buttocks of patrons?"

"Yes!" Neils answered in the same condescending voice.

At this point I was really deflating. Was it hopeless to pursue this line of questioning? I decided to play my last tactic.

"Neils." I used the same confident, condescending voice as thrice before. "I don't believe you! Should I report you to management for unwanted, unsolicited sexual harassment?"

Neils smiled broadly, confidently, and victoriously.

"You just have!" He chortled. "I am the manager of Tawny Bods!"

Now it was my turn to at first blanch white and gape at Neils as he played judge, lawyer, and jury, verbally discharging all claims and complaints of sexual harassment against him, the defendant. Then he granted himself full pay and a small raise.

Meanwhile I blushed beet red in anger and embarrassment. What the hell were my recourses to stop Neils from sexually harassing me again?!

Suddenly Neils composed himself and focused apologetically in my gaze.

"I'm sorry, Tyler." Neils hung his head contritely. "I only flirt with and hit on patrons for their flattery and amusement and the ambiance of this facility. If you want me to quit flirting with you just say so and I will stop."

During the last sentence, Neils's proposition to quit was drowned out by an accident in the canteen. A shelving unit tipped over sending a cascading roar of water bottles over the seating area.

After I peeled myself off of the ceiling and Neils had regained his composure, I continued eyeing him. I was getting impatient with Neils. He had some request to make and I wondered what it was about.

"So what about it Tyler? Do you agree or disagree with my question?" Neils asked, a curious smile on his face.

Although I now know I should have waited, back then I was nothing if not a man on a mission! Rather than ask Neils to repeat and clarify his statement of which he wanted my opinion, I brushed all concerns aside and plunged forward. I had interpreted his last statement, delivered during the shelving unit falling over, as:

"If you want me flirting with you just say yes and I will."

Obviously I had to say 'no' to stop Neils's sexual harassment of me. Little did I know what Neils had actually said. I should have asked him to repeat his statement before answering it.

"No, Neils, that is not necessary." I frowned and shrugged as I placed a hand on Neils's shoulder. "I am perfectly happy with the way things are. Remember, Neils, flirting should be reserved by an individual for the person with whom he/she would like to date, and dating saved for the one with whom he/she wishes to spend the rest of their life. Sometime I will like and you will like being the objects of another's flirtations and romantic attentions." I winked at Neils, not realizing what it meant in the gay community.

Neils beamed excitedly, breathlessly, and gleefully at my final statement. He acted as though he had received an all expense paid trip to Hawaii.

Why in the hell was he so happy!? I had told him to stop flirting with me and to stop sexually harassing me. Neils should be irate with me! If he were not gay my demands of Neils would basically accuse him of being so. This allegation would insult and infuriate any straight man!

Neils calmed down to a low simmer of ecstasy. I continued to wait for Neils to show me his hand. What did he want?!

"Tyler, I apologize for being so flippant about the issues of my touchy-feely ways." Neils looked sincerely at me. "I realize it is a major issue for you…"

"Hold on!" I interrupted, waving my hands to cross in front of me. "I don't mind friendly touching, Neils! As I already affirmed, I approve of the way things have been and are. I just do not want you to sexually touch me! Okay?!"

At that point what I said and meant and what Neils heard and understood from his question were two totally different things. However, I did not know about this vast difference in our communication.

Neils smiled broadly at my assurances that I wanted things to stay as is. I didn't mind joke, false, or even true flirting. I didn't mind being touched by men in friendship. I just didn't want my private areas groped or massaged, or fingers running in my crack!

"Neils!" I exclaimed as an afterthought. "Just don't ever touch my package or my crotch." I forgot about my ass for some reason.

"I guess I can… maybe I can… I guess I'll try and control… I think I can control myself around you, Tyler." Neils stammered uncertainly. "I'll do my best! It will be really hard, though, Tyler. You are so damn hot and handsome, so physically perfect and beautiful, so sexy and tempting!" Neils ogled my body again, and surveyed me with a happy, contented countenance. After all, in his mind I had given him approval to touch my merchandise!

I blushed. I had very seldom heard such complimentary words and flattery from anyone other than Mother, Andrew, and now, Neils. I didn't know yet how to act when men complimented me so.

"Anyway, Tyler," Neils continued, "things are slow today, as you can see. I was wondering if you'd need or want any training, advice, or direction for your workout today. You see, I am also a trained coaching and personal training professional. Part of my job here is to serve as a personal trainer for any and all members. Would you like me to help you work out, to develop a well-balanced routine, and learn more about how to exercise?"

Neils looked at me hopefully and smiled expectantly. He patted my knee gently.

"Does it cost me more for your advice, help, and training on top of my daily fee, or membership fee when I join?" I asked cautiously, although his offer sounded very appealing.

At that moment Neils's eyes twinkled and a shy grin slinked over his visage. He looked so cute... so handsome at that moment that my heart and mind melted. Neils was very alluring and attractive.

"For you, stud, because you are you and since I caused undue misunderstanding with my flirtations, I work today for free!" Neils winked sexily at me. "When you become a member, Tyler, I can do your ass... I mean... I can do your assignment and service you... I mean provide my services of advice, help, and training..." Neils stammered and gulped uncharacteristically. "All of it, Tyler, I will provide for free to you only!"

I sensed, and thought I heard, some double entendre in Neils's statement, but I ignored it. I wouldn't discern or apprehend exactly what Neils had meant to say until much later.

I thought about Neils's proposal. It wouldn't hurt if he worked with me off and on throughout the afternoon. I'd see him probably five or ten minutes per hour max. Besides he was hot, and obviously physically attracted to me! If he trained me for the day I could check him out too when he appeared every hour or so. From his frontal view, Neils's tight gym outfit showed off his mid-sized genitalia and his awesome chest. I knew it would be revealing of his cute ass too!

'Shame on you!' My conscience pricked me suddenly and ferociously. 'Tell him NO!'

"Awesome! Sure thing, Neils." I heard myself say, against my better judgment. "That sounds great! I'll work out with you, Neils! I accept your free tutelage."

"Great!" Neils exhaled, as though he had been holding his breath the whole time I was pondering. "Let's get started!"

Neils grabbed my hand and I stood up. A wave of pleasure washed over me. He let go of my hand and then wrapped an arm around my shoulders, open right hand gently rubbing back and forth on my chest as we walked. I was feeling very stimulated!

It felt good to have Neils that close, rubbing my chest with one hand and arm draped over my shoulders. Then it occurred to me; my chest and the rubbing thereof were the domain and property of Andrew alone! What was I to do now about Neils?! His touch, although no way near measuring up to Andrew's touch, still felt so good. Andrew's touch, his body, his gorgeous face, luxurious hair, manly scents, character… every quality and standard by which I judged men were met and, in most cases, surpassed by Andrew. Neils couldn't compete with Andrew in most of my areas of critique. Should I just ignore Neils's touch?

I smiled, and it almost seemed that Neils was Andrew. The chest massage I was receiving from Neils was being administered by Andrew as foreplay… Andrew and I were playing with each other… we were pleasing each other physically through massage and oral stimulation of the correct spots, and we were preparing each other for lovemaking… I wanted Andrew! My body ached for him…

"I think we will alternate exercises; we shall do arms, legs, arms, legs, etc." Neils announced as he led me to another machine.

We arrived at an odd looking piece of equipment. Neils motioned me toward the weight bench and beamed lovingly at me. I blushed again, feeling the intense spirit of flirtation and desire coming from Neils. He was so charming, acceptably handsome, admirably buff and well muscled…

manly… he smelled good… he had an awesome package that made me wish to pull his pants down for a better viewing…

I sat down and Neils began talking as he leaned over me to begin adjusting the weight and settings of the weight machine. His face and right arm pit were right in my face, and I could smell his awesome body, deodorant, and cologne.

Neils continued to talk as he set the weight and other parameters on the equipment upon which I was preparing to exercise. All the while he stayed with his face and arm pit a mere two inches from my face. I had backed away from him as far as I could, but he had followed, keeping the same body parts in my face. He punched buttons, put three pins into a series of weights, all the while explaining how this weight equipment worked to improve muscles and the body.

I couldn't focus. In amongst Neils's cologne and deodorant, in his arm pit that was two inches from my face I could smell the smallest hint of manly sweat. His sweat secretions smelled sharp and sweet. The odor of his cologne, deodorant, and small scent of sweat made him extremely alluring and stimulating to me, both physically and sexually. I longed to see him naked…

I could feel my body beginning to be aroused. The rush of hormones prickled through my body. I breathed in quickly and shivered in ecstasy as my soldier began to rise. I wanted Andrew now, to pleasure me… but Andrew wasn't here! Neils was here! Perhaps a little dalliance with Neils so close wouldn't…

No! I couldn't… I wouldn't allow myself to be attracted to anyone but Andrew! I would be true blue to and for Andrew. He was my… he was… he was mine!

Neils was here, in my face. I knew he was attracted to me. He smelled so damn awesomely good today, manly, virile, strong, captivating, and sexually tempting. Neils's aroma, the visually pleasing effect of his body, his closeness, and his fine and chiseled musculature… all had me hard and ready to go in no time. How I would like to commence going physically and sexually all the way with Andrew! I trembled as another stimulating wave of hormones coursed through my body. I could do with a workout with Neils until I saw Andrew again! But to do so I would definitely have to focus my attention off from Neils.

Andrew… his name alone was beguiling to me. I actually… I was to the point… I mean I liked… loved… I loved Andrew, damn it! I admitted it! I romantically loved Andrew as a lover, not as a brother! Andrew had every quality and characteristic possessed by Neils and so much more! I began mentally rejecting Neils as I swore in my heart to be faithful, loyal, and exclusive to Andrew should he seek me for his lover.

Then it occurred to me. There was someone else for whom I should be faithful, loyal, and exclusive; it was the man from Galilee, one Jesus Christ and Father God. How displeased He must be with me right now! It was a wonder He didn't just crush me like the worm I was being under temptation!

Neils was efficient, helpful, and all over me throughout the afternoon like butter on bread. As I worked out he did too, and he asked me all sorts of questions about my past and present. He was so inquisitive that at one point I asked him acerbically if he were writing a book.

Neils asked me questions concerning my family. He commented after I had finished that he felt like he had known my family forever. Neils asked me about my childhood, my schooling, and my work history. These questions disquieted me and caused a sense of fear for some unknown reason, but I told him my truth as I remembered it that I had had a wonderful life.

Finally, we had a lively discussion/debate over politics. I won the debate most of the time, boxing Neils into various corners with the facts.

Neils, as it turned out, was a dyed in the wool, card carrying, certified mentally ill liberal. He was so 'tolerant' that he was intolerant, so 'egalitarian' that he was discriminatory, so 'non-judgmental' that he was a mealy-mouthed wimp, and so ignorant of the true news behind the news that he was of no earthly good to any political party. I chuckled to myself.

Neils then returned to inquiries about me. He bombarded me with questions. I did my best to answer each and every one, but I suspicioned that I botched a few. At one point I was so frustrated by his interview technique that I curtly asked him again if he were writing a book. He responded in the negative, but continued to question me as we worked out on the new machines.

Finally Neils got around to the opposite sex. When he asked me about girls and found I had no girl friend, he was happy, excited even! He also seemed more excited, confident, and flirtatious when I told him I lived with my 'brother' Andrew in Candlestick.

The workout for me and my needs was designed and directed by Neils Hanson. As he explained each machine and what part of the body it would strengthen, he punched the machine, resistance, weight, and number of repetitions into a computer. His computer was actually a cell phone, but I knew what he was doing. This schedule, Neils announced as proudly as a peacock, would serve as a baseline and a road map for each of 'our workouts together'. I noticed that he included himself in my future exercise workouts. I wasn't too thrilled about that because continued work with Neils would only further increase my interest in and crush on him. However, he had offered his services to me for free. I wasn't going to look a gift horse in the mouth!

Little did I know how this philosophy was to backfire on me! I had no clue about the danger in which my naivete would place me!

We were both wet with sweat by the time Neils announced that the workout was almost complete. He did some more data entry into my computer file while I finished the last exercise.

I was panting, and that seemed to 'turn' Neils 'on'. I could hear a faint moan coming from Neils at regular intervals as we finished our work out. Suddenly Neils went stiff, grimaced, and whispered my name in a lascivious delirium.

At that point I scooted forward on my bench and looked in concern and curiosity at Neils. It was clear that he was after me, I just didn't know how seriously he was pursuing me. Then there were his actions; moaning, his body going stiff, and then calling my name… If I didn't know better I would have to guess he was ejaculating to thoughts of me!

As I sat there pondering the exercise workout I was undertaking and otherwise lost in thought, I did not realize that Neils had risen from the machine he had chosen. He walked up close to me at my bench and leaned in over me, pretending to read the screen behind my head. His crotch was in my face. A growing wet spot was there coming through his tight shorts, and he was clearly hard. I knew now that he had indeed pleasured himself to thoughts of me. The thought made me begin rising, and yet his crotch in my face made me a little nauseous.

It was then I realized we were both wearing the kind of deodorant that was reactivated by perspiration. I knew I could still smell my own deodorant clearly and lusciously. While Neils leaned in toward me, smiling coyly, I noticed with pleasure he smelled almost as good as he had when we had started, maybe a little more manly sweat smell mixed in. His odor was provocative and attractive, and I felt ashamed of myself again as I wanted to touch Neils's package. I became flustered, confused, and angry!

"Well, stud." Neils exclaimed, smiling lustfully at me. "We… ah… we could… what are you going to do now?"

"Oh, I'm going to shower." In my confusion over my feelings and guilt I spoke without thinking of the obvious outcome of my destination. "Then I will go home and watch television. What… Why do you…" I stopped, the stupidity of my response hitting me like a ton of bricks. I looked at Neils, whose countenance was filled with excitement, exhilaration, expectation, and greed. He was going to take advantage of my response and my plans! I didn't have to wait to find out how.

"Oh, studly!" Neils purred happily. "I'm taking a shower too! I can't continue to work looking, and probably smelling like this."

"Neils, honey…" I copped a fake sexy voice and smiled at him. "You look and smell so hot and desirable!" I immediately knew this was a mistake.

Neils smiled and began to pant in pleasure. He looked my body up and down, licking his lips, and rubbing his crotch. I could see he was fully aroused and ready for sex again. I realized by his reaction that I was so close to making him lose control of his inhibitions and attack me that I had to stop it! I wouldn't 'flirt' with Neils again!

"Let's go to the shower room now, together! I want to continue our conversation. We need to set up a time to meet and discuss membership packages available here at Tawny Bods!" Neils motioned to me coaxingly, then came quickly back and slipped his left hand on my ass again. He gently and slowly guided me off toward the showers in the swimming hall utilizing a hand pressure on my ass as he made sure I was staying with him. To my surprise he again began massaging me as we walked.

Hadn't I told him NOT to touch my private areas?! Damn! Neils had his hand on my ass against my wishes. Apparently we had miscommunicated when I had thought I told him to stop touching me intimately.

I paused mentally as we walked. Now I was in a pickle! Clearly Neils was very interested in me, and now it was obvious he wanted to see my naked body. However flattering this situation was, and regardless of how handsome Neils was, he was no Andrew, nor was he as gorgeous and attractive to me as Andrew was! I wanted this kind of attention from Andrew! I wanted Andrew to be the first one in Aurora to see me naked. But unfortunately if I backed out of a shower here and now after saying I was going to take one, Neils would know I was shy, scared, a prude, or rejecting him. I would look immature, stupid, like a shy, naïve, and overly modest child from the past. Hence the pickle. I didn't want to seem like a backward hick, a frightened little boy, or a stuck-up prick! I needed to start thinking before I spoke! My honest, quick answers could get me in big trouble some time!

'Well, Neils might be the first in Aurora to look at and lust for my naked body, but Andrew would be the second!' I swore to myself. 'Andrew also will be the only one in Aurora to have the privilege or right of fulfilling his sexual fantasies with me, if he so desires.' I also vowed that Andrew would be the only man I would ever consider making love to, or to whom I would ever consent to have sex and consummate our love. With these plans established, I reluctantly followed Neils to the men's locker and shower room, not knowing what he might do, try, or say, and not certain I wanted to find out.

Once inside the shower facilities, I picked a shower away from Neils. I turned toward a wooden bench running the full length of the showers to start slowly taking my clean clothes out of my back pack. I laid them down neatly on the bench. I entered the shower to turn the water on so it could warm up. I exited back to the aisle way. I looked up and jumped first. Neils was right next to me, slowly undressing. I was cornered now. He had his clean underwear in a neat pile on the bench, a clean outfit hanging above, and a towel, wash cloth, soap, and shampoo ready to go. I slowly took my shower things out and put them down on the bench, hoping Neils would finish undressing first and get in the shower. However, he managed to undress from his work-out clothes more slowly than I unloaded my back pack. He chatted about himself and sneaked longing looks at my progress. I neatly lined my things up on my bench to the right. I put my towel on a hook, the soap, shampoo, and a wash cloth in the shower, and came back out. Neils shadowed my every move, and was now standing in front of me, taking off his socks. I had nothing more to do to delay this. I was kind of committed now, so I began to undress. I started with my shoes first, however, then my socks, etc.

Finally we both were undressed down to our briefs, whereupon I paused and looked at Neils. I hoped he would enter the shower to undress from his briefs, but no such luck. It didn't occur to me to take my own briefs off in the shower away from roving eyes! Neils continued talking, turned away from me, and removed his briefs. His backside was attractive and my hormones began surging. Then he turned back to face me as he finished his thought. I got a full frontal view of his naked body, and it was nice! He wasn't at all shy, modest, or embarrassed, and he had no reason to be. He was indeed well-built, shapely in a manly way, attractive naked, and was of average size. 'Nice!' I thought, 'but not impressive!' I looked forward to… and… and… and longed to… to see Andrew naked instead! Suddenly my body ached to see all of Andrew like I was viewing Neils here. I became fully aroused sexually. I had to stop thinking about Andrew or I would have to relieve myself. I couldn't let Neils think it was he by whom I was aroused.

Neils just stood there, expectantly, suddenly silent, and gazed at me. I had to finish undressing and get in the shower, allowing him as little view as possible. I gulped involuntarily and blinked. 'Let's get this over with!' I thought to myself. I was a bit angry with myself that the thought of Neils seeing me naked embarrassed me so. But I was also angry with Neils that he was intimidating and harassing me like this!

I quickly took my briefs off and, without a pause, smiled at Neils and scurried into the shower. I drew the curtain in place behind me so no one could see me shower. As I adjusted the water temperature, I could hear Neils doing the same next door.

We were quiet for a few minutes as we washed. I always shampooed my hair first.

"Tyler?" Neils called over the sound of the water from both of our showers.

"Yes?" I returned cautiously and coolly.

"I enjoyed our workout today immensely!" He sputtered back to me. I could hear water splash and soap fall on the floor.

I did pause in thought briefly before I spoke.

"Yes. So did I, Neils." I decided to be honest, perhaps to my detriment. I had enjoyed the day, our day of exercising together, even though somewhat perversely. Neils had to be all right. He was cool! He might be gay, but he wasn't a predator or a rapist!? I had nothing to worry about from Neils.

"I think you could gain a lot with my training of you and guiding your workouts, Tyler, and I enjoyed working out with you. I'd like to continue?"

I was thrilled, excited, yet struck with hesitation and trepidation at the prospect of hooking up with Neils as my trainer. My heart skipped and I blushed at the flattery! He was putting out feelers as to what I thought, and he was serious. I felt myself kind of surrender to him. However, I had reservations about the invitation and prospect, I just couldn't put them into words or wrap my mind around them. I knew I should say 'no', but I couldn't for some reason.

Seriously though, I had enjoyed the workout! And Neils was cute and very attentive! I repudiated an errant wave of desire for Neils, his nicely muscled body, and his cute ass.

"Well..." I thought quickly of the negatives and, although I could come up with no specific negatives, I was not so agreeable here. "We'll have to talk about that and see..." I finished tentatively.

"Tyler?" Neils called inquisitively right back.

"Yes?" I answered, a bit irritated by now at receiving a bit of a bum's rush from Neils. Couldn't he give me some space… a little time… a period to take a decision?!

"I thought maybe we could… ah could ah… maybe we could… ah… get together later this week. I could bring you… ah… bring you our brochures about our membership options and offerings and we could discuss membership packages?" His voice was hopeful and inviting. I could tell he was still waiting for my response; the water was now the only sound from his side of the wall.

By now I did want to join and use this gym. Neils's timing was perfect. I figured we'd meet and talk at the gym… I would settle on a package… and he would train me for free as he had offered.

"That was a part of our deal today, Neils, as was free training from you." I responded, biting my tongue from responding 'no duh!'

"Sure!" Neils reassured me. "Over dinner?"

It was a request that I found a little strange, and a time and event I hadn't expected, but okay. We'd be discussing business anyway. It wasn't like it would be a date!?

"Sure." I called back.

"Wednesday at five in the afternoon?" Neils continued.

"Okay!" I said. "But I don't have a car, or any private transportation."

"That's fine!" Neils exclaimed. "I'll pick you up at 4:40. I'll pick the restaurant."

"Don't make it too steep!" I broke in. "I won't have much money."

"This meal is on me!" Neils spoke happily. "I can claim it as a business expense. Tax deductible, you know. I offer this to you because I want you as a pais… patron. This will be awesome!"

I chuckled to myself, turned the water off, and exited the shower stall. There I found Neils drying off. 'Damn… I mean dang it!' I thought as I turned my back to Neils. 'Why was I suddenly swearing so much?' I asked myself. It never had been a problem before Aurora!

I grabbed my towel to begin drying myself off, dangling it strategically to protect my private areas against Neils' roving, lustful gaze. I could see Neils was making every effort trying to peek at me naked. Although I was very flattered by his obvious desire to see me naked, and I was interested to know what he thought and felt about my body, I wanted to save myself and my nakedness as much as possible for Andrew's beautiful blue eyes if that be possible! I roughed up my head and hair as I dried them, and then I lowered the towel to do the rest of my body. I jumped. Neils stood fully naked, face to face with me, a wanton smile on his mien. I was in shock and paralyzed momentarily. He was partly aroused as he gently took my arms.

"Let me see the slate that I have to work with, mold, improve… Tyler!" Neils's voice trailed slowly off as he took my arms, pulled them up into a "t", and extended them straight out from my shoulders to the sides. My towel fell to the floor and I stood buck naked facing him.

I was so surprised that I didn't have time to resist and, as he gazed up and down my naked body, I wasn't sure I wanted to resist whatever Neils had in mind! I did want… I kind of… I wanted Neils to see me… see me… naked. Neils was clearly pleased with what he saw!

"Yes… perfect…!" He cooed as he became fully erect. He had a grin from ear to ear. "You are already well-built… but… I can help you do more…!" Neils smiled as though he were in Heaven. He released my arms and stepped back, admiring my body.

We both stood there, admiring each other's naked body. For some reason I was transfixed. Neils was hot! Again, not as hot as Andrew, nor as physically beautiful. However, he was definitely gifted physically! I could… I could get into his pants and… and thoroughly enjoy myself!

I dropped my arms slowly to my sides, but I stood gazing longingly at naked Neils and his manly, buff, beautiful body as he gazed lasciviously back at me. I was feeling stimulated too, slowly rising. I blushed at the effect of this stimulation on my physical anatomy. Neils was ecstatic, however! He reached out and turned me around. He looked appreciatively at my back side as I checked out his expression over my shoulder.

"Like a Greek god…!" Neils panted happily.

A warning bell went off in my spirit, then my mind… but I ignored it.

Suddenly the door to the shower room burst open and three early-teen boys came raucously into the showers. They stopped dead in their tracks and stared quizzically at the two of us ogling each other's naked bodies. I was instantly embarrassed by how we must look to other uninvolved or uninformed people!

I blushed. Quickly I picked up and stretched the towel back over my body to finish drying. Neils just casually grabbed his underwear and began to dress. He continued to discreetly watch me dress as he progressed.

The boys went past us to showers down the line, whispering and watching us. They had curious, questioning, and sarcastic looks on their faces. I knew what they were thinking about Neils and me! I was humiliated! They began to undress, and I turned and looked away.

I put on deodorant and finished dressing in my clean clothes. Neils had put on his deodorant, dressed, combed his hair, applied an intoxicating cologne, and was waiting for me. I splashed on 'Mambo' and headed for the door with my backpack. Neils followed me out of the shower room. In the locker room I turned to face him.

"If you don't mind me asking," I started tentatively, "how old are you, Neils?"

"Not at all!" Neils smiled. "I'm 31. Do I look it?"

He certainly didn't look 31! He was in excellent shape!

"No, you don't." I smiled, and continued out of the locker room.

"Tyler!" Neils reached out and gently caught my arm, spinning me around to face him.

"Yes?" I responded, a quizzical look on my face. A creepy feeling ran down my spine and I shuddered at his grip.

"How old are you?" He had a slightly worried look on his face. I didn't know why he would be worried, concerned, or that interested about my age.

"I am 21 years old." I responded with certainty. "My birthday was May 8."

A look of relief came over Neils' face, and he smiled happily. Again, it didn't occur to me why he was so relieved!

"Well then, our supper on Wednesday will also be my birthday gift to you, Tyler! That is hot! Much like you, hottie!" Neils exclaimed.

We continued on from the showers to the lobby. Neils chattered all the way about the gym and his job there. He told me what seemed like everything about the place; how old the business was, how much the building cost to construct, who owned it, how much he was paid, what he did here at the gym, and on and on. He was quite the chatterbox when he wanted to be!

I stopped at the front desk as Neils went behind it and gave the bubbly Jessica Mills a thumbs-up. She frowned and looked my way. Neils turned to me. Jessica smiled then, winked, and licked her lips appealingly.

"So, I'll see you Wednesday at 4:40." Neils grinned and patted my hand on the counter. "I drive a Gran Prix. Red!"

"Okay!" I smiled, and didn't think again. "It's a date!"

I left the gym and was in the street before I realized what I had just said. It's a date?! I had just confirmed a date with a man!? I felt guilty, sinful. Nah! I was sure Neils didn't view it as a date! Or did he? Was I cheating on Andrew? Sinning against God? Nah! We were just discussing membership packages at a restaurant over dinner, not love! It was business, nothing more. Although Neils was handsome, he was no competition for Andrew in the 'looks' department, or in any other way!

I reached the taxi stop, still mentally kicking myself for calling my meeting with Neils a 'date' to his face. I tried logically to assure myself it was no big deal. However, the verbal slip and Neils's flirtations, touching, stroking, and viewing my nakedness had me spooked. A date! What the hell was I thinking... again!?

"We will discuss your findings here and now, Ian! I do not date men!" I remembered informing Ian in no uncertain terms.

Then Ian's next words caused me to stop trying to hail a cab and look at my hands in shock, awe, and some fear.

"Tyler, that statement is false! You do date men. You are living with a male lover, and you have a date with a male on Wednesday!" Ian's prophetic voice echoed in my head.

How in the hell did he know I was going on a 'date' with another man on Wednesday when I didn't know it and it hadn't been set up yet?! Did Ian have some gift as a shaman of truly reading auras and foretelling the future? What else that he shared in his analysis was true or would come true?! He had accurately pegged many things about my current difficulties, moral questions, and relationship with Andrew!

"… you have stumbled into a new romantic relationship. The letters 'A' and 'D' are prominent in it, Tyler. You should pursue this new romantic relationship and consummate it. It is right for you!"

I gulped involuntarily and my hands became wet with sweat. Clearly Ian referred to Andrew DiPree! Ian was telling me to nurture, pursue, and accept a romantic relationship with Andrew. I was exhilarated, ashamed, amazed, and shaking in fear. What power did Ian have?

From where or whom did it come?!

Ian's concerned and loving face suddenly appeared in my mind. His voice was kind and imploring, commanding and convincing.

"… orange also tells me you are experiencing stress in your life related to your addiction that is preventing you from acting on and living in pride with a natural appetite you possess."

In my mind's eye Ian focused like a laser on me.

"Green is a comforting, healthy color of nature. It tells me you are growing in knowledge, understanding, tolerance, and acceptance of new things and things you once rejected. Green means you are destined to accept and embrace change, change that may have once been rejected by you. It tells me you are slowly moving toward and will ultimately accept a new, healthy balance between your religion and your deepest desire, your deepest secret, your one true love."

My addiction? Clearly religion?! Preventing me from living in pride with my natural appetite? My love for… for a man?! I will ultimately adopt and embrace a healthy balance between my faith and my love for Andrew?!

I shook my head in shame and fear… and hope. I couldn't face this now! I was busy. I hailed a cab and headed home to Candlestick.

# CHAPTER 27

# RECOVERY AND 'COMFORT'

I was becoming conscious enough to realize and sense things, and register, recognize, and distinguish feelings. I was sore, pained, and hurt all over. I felt like I had been beaten over my entire body. My right shoulder especially burned like hell.

My mind began to bring focus to feelings and sensations which originated outside of me and affected the exterior of my body. I also began to sense external concrete things.

From my growing sensations that were officially recognized and distinguished by my brain I determined two things immediately. First, I realized that the air climate of my current location was warm, yet frightening. There was, or had been, a foreboding spirit that felt like it was attempting to suffocate me. I felt like I weighed a ton. Secondly, when I opened my eyes, the room was pitch dark. I panicked for a minute as I struggled to see. I finally saw a pin point of light at the far end of a tunnel, and from there I heard voices calling my name. The voices were hollow and distant and I recognized none of them at first.

However, I realized I must struggle toward the distant light. In my mind I fought to stand up, and I began walking toward it, but my feet felt heavy as if I were wearing cement shoes. I was only able to slowly approach the light, and I realized the voices talking to me and calling me were beginning to sound more familiar. However, the voices were also oddly slapping me. Someone was slapping my face, and someone my left hand. What the hell were they doing!? It was annoying, and damn! They were hurting me! I mustered my strength and grabbed the hand that was slapping my face and stopped it. Suddenly I burst out into the light at the end of the tunnel. I blinked, trying to focus my eyes. The light was blinding, and everything I could see was a blurry haze.

"Drew!" Marcus called as I realized he gently held my head cradled in his lap. This brought back memories of our lovemaking. My vision began to slowly clear. What I could see of Marcus above and around me looked sexy in his skin tight cowpoke outfit. I had another brief flashback of making mad passionate love to Marcus, a flashback that threatened immediately to pull me back into unconsciousness.

"Drew, wake up!" Marcus pleaded urgently. He wiped my shoulder with a wet, stinging clothe. I grimaced with the pain.

I fought the pull to unconsciousness and clung to the light. My vision slowly began to clear.

I gazed around, confused and alarmed. Where was I?! At least I recognized Marcus, but what or who were the other blobs I could vaguely see?! I began gulping air, which made me dizzy, but which I could not control. I began to panic as I commenced struggling to sit up.

However, I was pushed down to the floor and held there by four strong arms around me.

I discovered I was restraining Marcus's right hand, holding it tightly with my left hand. I was really fighting a battle to hold him off from slapping me.

I fought desperately, but to no avail.

Marcus began slapping me again with his left hand. Damn it! I grabbed his left hand, holding it at bay. I looked up at Marcus's face and blinked again, frowning and giving him an angry look.

"Damn it, Marcus! You are hurting me! I… I am awake! Stop it!" I assured him. I looked tentatively around me as Marcus put his hands down and began stroking my cheeks and neck. It felt good, comforting. It helped me to begin focusing my faculties on my surroundings.

I had to get it together. I was… I was Andrew. Andrew… ah… what the hell? I was Andrew DiPree! I was Andrew DiPree. I was… I was… how old was I?! I was… ah… I was 25… I would be… I'd be 26 on… on June 20th. Okay! I could do this! My muddled mind began to come to order and my jumbled thoughts began to come together.

For the moment I still wasn't exactly sure where I was and I freaked out inside. I still recognized Marcus, but none of the other blobs. What or who were these blurred blobs around me?! Where in the hell was I?! Was I in danger?! I gazed around in a panicked fashion trying to discover the answers to these questions and continued to attempt to orient myself. I knew I could answer my own questions if I could just totally focus! My fear and panic told me that running seemed the only option to get away. No! I could do this! I had to calm down!

Did I recognize my surroundings at all? Could I remember anything I saw?! What building was I in? Who was Tyler?! Why did the name 'Tyler' keep coming to mind?! Was he one of the blobs I didn't recognize? Was he the other person next to me and Marcus?!

I gazed anxiously around the room again and began to refresh my memory. I had a strong feeling that I had been here before. I could smell food and booze.

One wall a few feet to my left was all soft, beautiful lavender velour material hung floor to ceiling in beautiful arcs. The floor I was on felt like a soft, slightly sticky, solid rubber. The wall directly in front of me had a large opening, and then a slanting wall away from me that disappeared into darkness. On my right was a solid wooden wall, beautifully polished and brightly cleaned. Ornate 'cement' looking pillars every few feet went from floor to a ceiling that was currently so dark it was out of sight to me. I had no damn clue where I was!?

Suddenly I had a brilliant idea, hoping to clear my mind and vision. I closed my eyes again and shook my head, hoping to clear the fog. That was a mistake! I had instant pain in my head and my neck. I groaned as I opened my eyes and rested my head back in Marcus's crotch. The thought crossed my mind that I just loved Marcus's cologne, and it was mixed with a slightly manly, maybe sweet sweaty smell that would have turned me on if I were myself right now. His crotch was no longer like a cushion, but harder as he grew. I dismissed the thoughts as I was too out of it yet to care.

I realized then that the lavender hanging material on my left side appeared to be stage curtains which had been drawn closed. I strained my eyes to focus on the room in which I lay and noticed as I gazed wearily around the space that the many vague blobs had merged together and clarified in my sight. They were actually several people that looked slightly familiar, but whom I could not name. Who the hell were these slowly emerging people?! Where was I?! What was I doing here?! Why did I hurt so much all over?! What had happened to me?!

"Where am I?" I asked one of the blobs next to me apprehensively. My mind began to bring focus and feelings together, and I struggled and slowly sat up, a wave of dizziness and nausea washing violently over me. I noticed casually that I was still naked, but I was too busy trying to answer all my questions to be modest. There was a puddle of blood on the floor under my back, shoulders, and head. I realized I had quite a bit of blood on my body. The sight of it unnerved me, and my heart began to pound with worry. I felt blackness closing in again. I fought it with all my being. I couldn't pass out again!!

"Tyler!" A voice exclaimed.

"What happened?" I was getting desperate to have someone tell me what the hell was going on!? "What am I doing here?! Where am I?!"

"Drew, honey, you were assaulted while performing your strip act here on stage. This is where you work! The Flamingo." A girl loomed in front of me, whom I now remembered was Melody, explained. Melody was pretty, a welcome sight for clueless, desperate eyes!

"Three disgruntled, angry, and violent patrons were trying to gang rape you during your act, Drew. One of them stabbed your shoulder pretty badly trying to get out a switchblade. We've bandaged you up as best we can!" Melody finished as she motioned to a small woman beside her.

"Drew!" A man several years my senior stepped forward and interrupted Melody. "You should go to the hospital to be checked out. I'll call emergency services…"

"No! No!" I stated emphatically, shaking my head as vigorously as the pain allowed me. "No trip to the damn hospital! I am fine! I'll be fine! I don't want to have a bunch of goody-goody two-shoed, expensive doctors and nurses poking and prodding me. I don't want any blood tests or intravenous connections, and I definitely don't want to hear the hospital staff's medical song and dance about the dangers of my work and my drinking. Besides, I cannot afford it. No, just forget the hospital! I am fine!"

I put my head in my hands and briefly closed my eyes, wishing that this were all just a nightmare. The pain in my head and neck was subsiding some, but not the muscle pain I felt throughout my body. I felt like my memory and reality were somewhere in my mental grasp, but they were very elusive. I peeked back up pleadingly at Melody.

"Melody, I just want to know where in the hell I am!? Do you know?!" I exclaimed.

"You're on stage at work, Drew!" Melody responded in a concerned voice. "Don't you… can't you remember, Drew…? Oh my God! He has… he has… Dawn?! Is this normal?!"

"This is The Flamingo Lounge, Drew." Marcus added hopefully, reaching my lower back and massaging me lovingly and provocatively. "Do you know where that is?"

I looked furtively and thoughtfully around my 'stage' surroundings, for indeed I was not sure where I was. I felt like I were fighting to think and I was wandering mentally through a fog. I closed my eyes and willed for the fog to clear, straining to remember where I worked. I forced myself to calm down. The pain was still lessening. I was going to be fine! I could do this! I could remember! If I didn't get this memory back, these people would send me to the hospital. I couldn't let that happen.

"Drew!" The man who was older than I and wanted me to go to the hospital spoke. He sounded stern and concerned. "Drew, son, look at me now! Focus on me!"

I opened my eyes and looked at him. Suddenly, like a ton of bricks it hit me who he was!  It was my boss from work, Mr. Richard. I smiled wanly, my head hurting more again from the strain. At least something was coming back to me!

I tried to respond to Mr. Richard's call to me, but my lips and tongue wouldn't move for some reason.

"Drew, son!" Mr. Richard demanded again urgently and commandingly. "Do you know who I am, son?!"

I tried to respond, but at first only managed to mouth the words. I pinched my mouth gently with my hands.

"Who am I, Drew?!" Mr. Richard stepped a little closer.

I attempted a response again.

"You… you are… my… you are my boss, Mr… Mr. Richard." I finally succeeded. My head hurt like hell and I blinked.

"Drew!" Mr. Richard gazed at me sternly. "Do you know where you are, son?!"

I put my head down and looked between my spread eagle legs briefly. Marcus was massaging my entire lower back gently and tenderly. It felt so calming, so good, so stimulating. I was thankful to and for Marcus.

I concentrated as hard as I could. I knew I could remember everything if I just focused! My mind was becoming clearer. I could do this! Then it all came rushing back to me. I raised my head and looked back at Mr. Richard with certainty and clarity.

"I am at The Flamingo Lounge. I work here." I stated simply, licking my dry lips. "I am at work. I am a waiter and a working stripper."

I paused. By now my vision had completely returned. I was so focused on rediscovering my memory and self knowledge that I took leave of my senses.

"I was performing a new strip dance… was strip dancing… and… and… and I was… I remember now… I remember! I was attacked… violently attacked…" I paused again, because very debilitating flashbacks threatened to reduce me to a stuttering, speech restrained, yellow belly puddle of fear.

"I remember… now! It was Ben…" I stalled as the other two assholes temporarily escaped me. "Ben and… and… Gus! And… and… and one I called Jaba the Hut. His real name was… was… his real name was… George. He was a fat… gross pig! He was one of those who… who… who wanted… who tried to rape me."

I paused again, fighting against the memories, the terror, the reality of my assault. My body hurt, my head hurt, and my emotions and mental stability were in shambles.

"Those three assholes had sexually harassed, verbally threatened, and physically assaulted me all afternoon and evening. They threatened to… to violently… they threatened to violently rape me… They were gross… scary!" I shuddered and gagged involuntarily as I inadvertently opened a real can of fish, a pet peeve for Mr. Richard. "I've never… never… I've never experienced anything so… so bad… so… humiliating as this attack here at work!" I muttered in anger.

"You mean, Drew, you have been sexually harassed and physically assaulted here at work before tonight?!" Mr. Richard sounded incredulous and pissed. His face flushed red and he trembled.

'Damn it!' I thought angrily. 'I said too much! Why in the hell hadn't I shut my mouth! The last thing I needed, but the first thing I would now get, was a lecture from Mr. Richard!'

"Drew!" Mr. Richard sounded like an angry father. "Drew! Answer me honestly, son!"

I hung my head and frowned.

"I have been sexually harassed before here at work." I couldn't look at Mr. Richard while I admitted this because I knew what the next question was going to be. "I have been physically touched and harassed, threatened, verbally assaulted…" I trailed off.

"Damn it, son!" Mr. Richard's eyes sparked, his face twitched, and his color assumed a light maroon and purple. "Why did you never… ever… report any of it!?"

I kept my head down in some fear and shame, and shrugged.

"I appreciate my job, Mr. Richard. I didn't want to complain as long as they were just isolated incidences." I answered simply, looking seriously at Mr. Richard. "Besides, I handled them all in my own way, sir."

Mr. Richard looked around at all of our workers and trembled as though he would explode.

"Have the rest of you working associates put up with harassment or physical and verbal abuse that you all have not reported!?" Mr. Richard looked around at my co-workers. One by one they all nodded their heads in agreement and flushed red with embarrassment. I was not alone. Mr. Richard appeared enraged.

"You all listen up, now!" Mr. Richard gazed at each of us as he spoke. He was clearly irritated. "If you are ever, in any way, sexually assaulted, sexually harassed, physically assaulted or harassed, mauled or touched without invitation, or verbally assaulted or harassed by a patron, or patrons here at work, I want it reported! These patrons who do this will be escorted out of my establishment! Do you all understand me!? Your safety is a top priority here!"

Mr. Richard glared around at each of us again for good measure, disgust showing in his features. We all nodded our heads in assent.

"People!" Mr. Richard seethed. "I have rules to control patron/client behavior and your behavior for a reason! For your protection! But if you don't invoke, enforce, and use the rules to your advantage, you put yourself in danger! Do you all understand?!"

We all nodded affirmation sheepishly, checking each other out for reactions.

Mr. Richard stepped back, muttering angrily to himself.

There was an awkward pause as we all thought about what Mr. Richard had said.

"Drew, do you know who we are?!" Marcus broke the silence. He moved in front of me and motioned to those assembled in a semi-circle behind him. He put his hands on my legs and massaged them gently.

I was amazed at how tender, loving, caring, and helpful Marcus was being. He was normally so narcissistic. He had been an animal whenever making love to me during our cross country dalliance!

I was still sitting up spread eagle as I looked around at those assembled before me. I looked back down when Marcus questioned me and noticed, to my chagrin, that I had forgotten I was fully naked still. No wonder Marcus had stayed close to me, caring for me, touching me, with his eyes glued to me. Now, out of some shame, I drew my legs up and hugged my knees. This way I wasn't quite so exposed.

One of our burly, almost grotesquely muscled bouncers entered the stage from the large opening ahead of me and handed a blanket to Mr. Richard.

"You asked for this, sir?" The man gruffly asked. I recognized him as Roger. I didn't recall his last name.

"Thank you, Roger!" Mr. Richard said, smiling at him.

"Drew, son, here is a blanket!" Mr. Richard spoke kindly as he gave it to Melody. "Are you sure that you are going to be all right, son?"

"Yes, I'm going to be all right, I think." I looked around at the people surrounding me.

"Do you know who we are?" Marcus asked me again, motioning to all those assembled.

Melody walked around behind me, careful not to step in the blood.

"Yeh." I rubbed my face, and touched the bandage on my right shoulder. It was wet. I was still bleeding. Melody wrapped the blanket around me.

"Your shoulder is still bleeding, Drew!" Melody explained. "You'll have to change the bandage again, soon."

I nodded and smiled at Melody. I briefly wondered if I could reach and change the bandage by myself as I felt for it. I could reach it all, I discovered, so it should be all right.

"Thanks, Mel, for all of your help!" I shivered under the blanket. "I appreciate it!"

Then I turned to Marcus. I had to answer him.

"You are Marcus." I looked him in the eyes and smiled. He and I had had enjoyable, pleasurable, and stimulating times for three years prior to Tyler. He had been a good roll, sexually pleasing and fun, but he was extremely rough and an animal making love. Therefore toward the end of our two year tour I had decided I didn't want him sexually any more. Now I believed even more that I was done with Marcus because I had Tyler whom I loved and on whom I was focusing all of my attentions.

"You are Melody." I gazed at her affectionately and smiled. She and I had had a couple of sexual trysts while on the road touring during the last two years, but I really didn't enjoy sex with women that much.

I then surveyed the people standing around in front of me. They were mostly employees of Mr. Richard, fellow waiters, waitresses, and strippers.

"Thanks for the blanket, Mr. Richard!" I glanced at him and nodded, smiling. Then I decided I had better finish my identification of everyone, because all regarded me expectantly and anxiously.

"That is Holly, Dante, Destiny, TJ, and Ricky." As I spoke their names I nodded at them. "The bouncer there is Roger. I don't know her!" I pointed at the very pretty, short, slender brunette by Melody.

"That's no surprise, Drew." Mr. Richard chimed in. "None of us knew her until she came forward to help you a while ago."

"She's Dawn, Drew. Drew, Dawn." Melody said with a smile as everyone seemed to breathe a sigh of relief or show signs of ease. "Dawn is a registered nurse who came forward to help us help you, Drew. She checked you out, and other than your cut, she believes you are okay! Good to go!"

"Just a quick check though, Drew!" Dawn spoke up, smiling sweetly at me. "What year is it?"

"2010." I responded, wrapping the blanket more tightly around me and shivering.

"Do you know what day it is today?" Dawn asked.

"Sunday." I smiled at her. I was damn cold! I continued to puzzle as to why?!

"Who is the current president of the United States, Drew?" Dawn queried with a look of hope and firmness.

"Shit!" I sneered with every ounce of disgust and dislike I could muster. "Everybody knows what scum is President! Barack Obama! He is destroying this country! Don't even get me started!" I shook my head gently as I frowned.

"He's fine mentally!" Dawn laughed. "He certainly has strong opinions now doesn't he?" She continued eyeing me as she felt my face gently.

"Yeh!" Marcus remarked as he chuckled. "There is no love lost between Drew and Obama! He makes that known whenever politics come up in a conversation!"

I wasn't feeling so well again. I was nauseous and dizzy. I sat there with my arms hugging my knees to my chest, shivering and rocking back and forth. I shuddered and grimaced as unwelcome flashbacks to the bikers' sexual attack on me came flooding back, despite my best resistance to them.

I closed my eyes briefly again as I heard Mr. Richard whispering to some of the assembled employees. Marcus remained in front of me, his left hand on my knee, and Melody stayed standing on my left side, her hand on my shoulder.

"Drew." Mr. Richard again sounded like a nurturing father, something I had experienced very seldom while growing up.

I opened my eyes and peered at him wearily. I realized I was now seeing things in duplicate or in blurry form again. I blinked, trying to straighten out my vision. I could stop it and see normally, but only for a few seconds. I sighed, anxious that something was seriously wrong!

"You are done stripping and dancing today. You have obviously been through enough because of the attack. You can wait tables again for a while." Mr. Richard folded his arms across his chest. "Do you have any sessions after six this evening?"

"Yes, sir," I ran my fingers through my hair, "I do."

"You can cancel them, or pass them off to someone else, without any repercussions to your pay or your job, son." Mr. Richard offered. "I think that might be best. Maybe you would be better off to take it easy the rest of your shift today."

"No!" I blurted. "No, I can't… I won't… I mean… I… I'll be fine!"

I didn't want to lose almost $2,500.00 I had coming in client tips, let alone give them to someone else! I was already losing the rest of my performance tips for the evening! I couldn't give away my $2,500.00 I had already taken for my sessions tonight! However, I couldn't tell Mr. Richard that, or else he would want a portion of my increased fees. I only wanted to give him his percent off the usual normal fees we earned, then I would pocket the excess.

"Mr. Richard…" I began, gulping involuntarily, a bit self-conscious over my deceit in this matter, "I just need a drink and a rest for a few moments. I need time to collect my thoughts and prepare myself, clear my head and calm down. Then I will wait tables until my sessions. I can do my sessions myself, Mr. Richard! I promise you, I will be fine."

I smiled as confidently as I could at Mr. Richard, or both of the two Mr. Richards who currently stood before me. He shook his head and frowned.

"You are one stubborn son-of-a-bitch, son! I do admire your tenacity and pluck, and I hate your occasional stupid stubbornness! This is one of those times when I hate your determination, but… ?" Mr. Richard quietly exclaimed. "But it's your work… if you think you are able…"

"I'm able…" I replied.

I blinked three times in quick succession and managed to correct my vision. I didn't know how long it might last, so I figured I should hurry and stand up. I knew I would need help with that task though, and probably I would need help walking to my suite.

I reached my left hand up to Melody motioning for her to help me rise. I held my injured right arm up to Marcus.

"I'll be in my dressing suite, Mr. Richard." I said quietly. Marcus grabbed my hand and Melody held the blanket around me as they helped me to rise. I almost fell because at first I was shaking so badly and my low-grade headache seemed to throw off my balance. I managed to keep my feet, however, as I clung to Marcus and Melody grabbed my waist.

"Are you sure you want to do your sessions?" Mr. Richard asked with uncertainty and concern as he watched me stand and wobble.

"Yes, sir…" I smiled at him and nodded. "I will be fine! Honestly! I'll rest for a few minutes and then get back to work. I'll be back to normal in no time!"

"Drew, take your time and rest!" Mr. Richard assured me. "Technically I don't need you back to work now for at least 45 minutes. Your performances are covered as are your tables. Rest, son! That's an order!"

Fortunately my vision seemed to be remaining normal. I looked around me.

Marcus and Melody were partially holding me up. I found I was quite sore and, to my surprise, I was still trembling with fear and anxiety from the attack. They helped me across the stage.

"Where are the three bikers who tried to rape me?!" I asked in some fear as I gulped involuntarily and gagged again, my legs feeling and shaking like jelly.

"It took all six, but our house bouncers threw them out on their asses through the back way!" Marcus said as he sneered. "Sons-of-bitches thought they had a right to rape you and treat you that way! It serves them right! They should have their dicks cut off and fed to them! Why I'd legally castrate them, throw them in jail, and throw the key away! If I had my way…"

"Okay, Marcus!" Melody interrupted. "We get the picture already! You can stop bloviating now!"

I chuckled and breathed a sigh of relief. My balance was totally back to normal, my dizziness had subsided, and my heart rate was returning to normal. I was feeling marginally better.

"Drew, I'm going to have to leave you in Marcus's capable hands." Melody sighed apologetically. "I… I have to get back to work or Mr. Richard will have my hide. Are you going to be all right, Drew?"

"Yes, thanks for everything, Mel! I'll be fine after a short rest and a drink." I nodded assurance to her.

"Marcus, are you staying with him for a while?" Melody asked in a tone that let both Marcus and me know she wouldn't take 'no' for an answer.

"Yes, Mel." Marcus nodded and smiled. "I will stay with Drew for a while."

Marcus helped me toward the doorway and stairs to the hallway. As we left the actual stage area I saw that Mr. Richard was directing the janitors in stage clean up of my blood and any other fluids thereon. I also noticed Dante getting ready to finish my performances. He was a good stripper, but I fancied I was better than he. Mr. Richard had confirmed it when he chose me for the tour.

Marcus put his left arm around my waist, helping to hold me up since my legs were still so weak, and held my right elbow to steady me. Together we descended the seven steps from the stage to the hallway as I clung to Marcus and the railing. I was surprised to find I was still trembling involuntarily, and unable to walk on my own.

Marcus helped me carefully through the hallways to my dressing suite as I grew stronger and calmer. At my suite door I used my secret password to unlock it. Marcus and I went into my dressing room. By now I could walk on my own so Marcus let me go and went directly to the wet bar.

"I'll fix you and me a good stiff drink, Drew." Marcus smiled at me as he opened the refrigerator and retrieved four bottles of strong liquor. "I have a new, delicious, but powerful concoction I want you to try that is guaranteed to give you a buzz after two good swigs. Are you game?" He looked at me as he set the bottles on the bar and then lined up two large long stemmed glasses next to them.

"Sure… that sounds great, Marcus! I need a good stiff drink." I responded and smiled back as I went into my bathroom.

I quickly grabbed a wash cloth, put it in the shower, and then laid out a towel on the counter-top next to the sink. I took the bandage gently off my right shoulder blade. Pain still jabbed from the wound where I had been cut by Jaba's switchblade. I observed the cut in my surround body mirrors. It was more of a slash, a rough looking, clean cut that was about four inches long and hurt like hell. I wondered how deep it was?! Had Jaba's thrust severed any muscles or tendons in my shoulder? Or had I missed the bullet this time and come out with just a flesh wound? I gently moved my arm from the shoulder, rolling my arm back and forth. I seemed to be able to move my arm well, although the cut made my shoulder feel stiff and restrained in movement as I also feared I would rip the wound open again. The movement also caused sharp pain. Was that a sign of muscle damage? I shuddered and began trembling slightly again. I felt woozy.

Should I go to the hospital and get stitches? Was it worth having the police harass me, Mr. Richard, and my family here at the Flamingo just to get this cut checked out and treated? Was it worth hearing warnings about my lifestyle and generally being berated and put down by hospital staff? I decided no. I didn't want to mess with it.

I moved my arm in a circular motion. It was painful. I felt faint. I realized I had to forget about the cut and quit obsessing over it, or I might faint again. I forced myself to get back to the business of a shower.

I turned on the water to a temperature just warm enough to cleanse myself, but not hot like I liked my showers normally. I jumped in and quickly began washing myself.

Unfortunately as my mind acquired this 'down' time, the horrific flashbacks of my sexual assault by the bikers came flooding unnervingly back. I couldn't stop them or get rid of them. I could see fat, slovenly Jaba simulating anal sex on me, touching every inch of my naked body with his filthy hands and clothing… Ben trying to hold my legs open to perform oral sex on me… I shuddered and closed my eyes. Other images of the assault and the three bikers crowded my mind. I started gagging, shaking, and weakening. I scrubbed my body hard a second time!

I felt filthy, violated, contaminated, ashamed, and grossly abused even though I knew and kept telling myself I had not actually been raped. Just the thought that raping me was the final goal of the biker assault made me feel all those feelings and more with acute emotional pain and anguish. As devastated and poorly as my attempted rape was making me feel while I lived through the event over and over again, I couldn't imagine living with actually having been raped! I scrubbed my private areas over several times compulsively. I was trying to cleanse my body and, symbolically, my mind from the vile memories, disgusting physical contact, and horrifying thoughts of what the bikers had done to my body, had wanted to do to my body, and had tried to do to me. Why couldn't I get clean?!

Suddenly I noticed a blood red color mixing in with the water washing over my body and cascading onto the shower floor. I realized my wound was beginning to bleed again. I had washed too much already. I had to get out before I washed the entire scab off my wound and started it bleeding in earnest again.

I turned off the water, remembering with horror the sweaty, almost slimy hands of Jaba clutching my arms behind my back and holding me prisoner as he 'humped' my naked body. I shuddered and gagged as I grabbed the towel to dry. Jaba had smelled so badly of body odor and a cheap deodorant. His bearded face had kissed my naked neck, face, back and chest. I was becoming nauseated! I wanted to shower again, to get clean from these memories! I had to stop thinking about it and reliving it. But I didn't know if I could?!

I quickly dried off, then wrapped and secured the towel around my waist. I clasped a dry wash cloth over my bleeding cut. I found some bandaging material and managed, in between gagging and retching, to replace the bandage and secured it over the cut on my shoulder. I then left the bathroom and hurried to my wardrobe and closet.

Marcus was still fussing over the drinks. He looked at me in my towel longingly as I grabbed my backpack for work. I blushed a little, remembering our sex life during the first year and a half of our nationwide tour. I felt a wave of lust and desire for Marcus course through my body from head to foot. No! I would not betray Tyler! I would not cheat on Tyler with Marcus! Never!

I gathered a new thong, underwear, muscle shirt, and skin-tight button shirt and pants out of my backpack. I renewed my deodorant and cologne. I carefully checked the bandage on my shoulder and added some more tape. Having finished that task, I crossed to a chair near an overstuffed chaise lounge on the other side of my dressing room suite with my clothes and towel.

I dropped the towel onto the chair, piled my clothing on the cocktail table next to the chair, and sat down to get dressed.

Marcus came over softly and quietly with our drinks. He set them down on the coffee table in front of me, sat down on the chaise lounge next to me, and cleared his throat. He was so close that I could feel his body… his heat… I was excited again!

I picked up my thong to begin dressing. Marcus, however, had other thoughts and things to say apparently. He smoothly and tenderly grasped my right hand, removed my thong from it, and put the thong back on my pile of clothing.

I was really becoming stimulated now and hormones began doing their thing to my body.

"Drew, I… well I… I wanted to say a few things…" Marcus swallowed in a gulp, but recovered. "Drew, I was… we were… I mean… I… I was really feeling for you up there on stage. Being assaulted, I mean, by those three scum. I felt your pain… your pain as those three scum… touching you… stripping you… groping you… kissing and licking your body… It was like it were… was like it were happening… happening to any or all of us! It was…" Marcus shuddered and gagged. "It was scary!"

Marcus had spoken so softly and tenderly. I was surprised! Now he began stroking my hand that he held.

"Tell me about it!" I replied. "I was the one being assaulted! I never dreamed I… well… I never thought… dreamed attempted rape could ever happen to me!"

"We all learned… realized it… discovered the same could happen to anyone of us as we… when we strip on stage. It was very disconcerting!" Marcus shook his head and looked down for a minute.

'Marcus is surprising me!' I thought, moved and impressed.

Marcus was being uncharacteristically attentive, kind, caring, and giving tonight! I decided he must have been really affected by my assault, affected for the better. I also concluded he must really still have feelings for me romantically, despite his repeated statements to the contrary. That fact was actually quite flattering, irritating, and yet a sexual turn on.

Marcus was taller than I by about two or three inches, 28 years of age, pleasantly and appealingly handsome, and attractively well-built at about 185 pounds. He had beautiful black eyes and hair, with a very light and mostly unblemished skin complexion. I had been very attracted to him when, upon changing employers, he had come to work at The Flamingo Lounge as an experienced waiter/working stripper. Four years ago he and I had begun a passionate and torrid sexual affair that had lasted about three years.

However, after the three year relationship of sexual liaisons and affairs, and tolerating Marcus's modus of operandi of sexual needs, desires, and practices, I had realized that I wasn't in love with Marcus. I was now very much over him, and very much in love with Tyler! Marcus did not know any of this though. I knew he had taken it hard when I cut him off, but he had seemed to have dealt well with it since.

Now, tonight, as sweet, loving, and caring as he was being with me, I felt the old feelings of love and desire coming again from Marcus. As uncomfortable as he appeared sitting next to me in the chaise lounge and holding my hand, I knew something was up!

Marcus cleared his throat nervously, and then moved forward to the edge of his seat. He settled in face to face with me.

"Drew." Marcus paused and cupped his hand under my chin, holding me to face him. "It has… well, it has been a while… since you… and I… supported… comforted one another…" His voice was soft, sexy, slightly raspy like a pan-flute, only in the base cleft.

I was suddenly so attracted to Marcus again that hormones gushed through my body and every fiber of my being wanted sex from him right now!

"You need comforting… I need it too… I can provide the comfort you need… I need… the comfort we both… we both know we want!" He was now just a couple of inches from my face. His tone was so tender, convincing, and longing. He was breathing a little heavy already, his breath hot and smelling very good. His deodorant and cologne were really turning me on, intoxicating my senses, invigorating me with memories of being with Marcus intimately.

I liked Marcus, don't get me wrong! As I said, Marcus and I had begun a sexual relationship four years ago. Then, during our nation-wide tour of exotic dancing talent, Marcus and I indeed had a full-fledged on-going affair and had 'comforted' one another quite regularly. He was good at physically pleasing his male partner, then sexually pleasing him, and bringing on a mutual orgasm that drove men, including me, crazy! When you had sex with Marcus, you both always left in a euphoric state with a smile on your face!

Like I said, however, I found I didn't love Marcus, not like I now loved, needed, and wanted Tyler! I mean, Marcus was likable, pleasant, sexy, handsome, and at the time very handy, and so I had become involved with him even before the tour, within the boundaries of our mutual work place.

Marcus and I had a sexual attraction and chemistry, two things that I now longed to develop with Tyler. However, Marcus and I differed majorly in the area of sexual desires, methods, practices, preferences, and in general how we liked to make love to another man. I preferred tenderness, passion, gentleness, and a wholesome, all around relationship with the man with whom I slept for the rest of my life. I hoped and dreamed of this kind of relationship, love, and sex life with Tyler; one of gentleness, respect, pleasure, and fulfillment for both of us!

Marcus, however, liked the wild, extremely passionate, rough abandonment to sheer sexual pleasure, and dangerous relations achieved through pure, unadulterated animal sex. His sexual preferences were often as painful as they were pleasurable. He was rough, uncontrolled, and often self-absorbed in his sexual activities with other men. Because of his narcissism, lack of consideration for lovers, and concern only for his wild and rough sexual needs to be fulfilled, Marcus and I were most often animals with each other in our affair. I did not like this kind of sex all the time! This helped me to grow dissatisfied with Marcus as a potential lifelong lover and lustful, meaningless, and rough sex.

Marcus had also turned me off from considering him for an actual romantic and long term lover because of his character with respect to recreational activities. On our two year tour circuit Marcus had begun using steroids to bulk up. While under the influence of steroids, Marcus was mean, a real bear. He would cuss and swear at everyone, threaten bodily harm, and take swings at innocent people. He had even hit a couple of the help we had along on our trips. To counter the effects of the steroids on his personality, Marcus had shortly thereafter begun smoking marijuana or eating marijuana laced foods. That made him loopy and happy, but often somewhat out to lunch. I didn't agree with taking any kind of drugs other than my avatar, which I consumed mainly at home, and the occasional vicodin buzz, and of course alcohol. After the first year of the tour with Marcus on drugs, I began to lessen my liaisons with him, slowly moving away from him sexually and romantically.

As I said, a month or so before I met Tyler, which hadn't been long ago, I had determined to drop Marcus. Even before that it had been a while since we, Marcus and I, had been together and 'comforted' one another.

"Drew, I want to comfort… to comfort you." Marcus closed the gap and kissed my lips tenderly. "I… I need you… I want to wrap my… wrap my naked writhing body…" He kissed me again for a few seconds. "My ripped… hot body around yours… and hold you…" This time he and I locked in a French kiss. He ran his hands up my naked legs and torso. I cupped his head in my hands and ran my fingers through his hair. We paused for a moment and looked at each other. Then we passionately grabbed each other, devouring each other's faces.

As I said, I didn't love Marcus in the romantic, lover way. However, the assault and stress of the day had left in me a strong desire to be intimate with someone with whom I had a relationship, a 'love' if you will. 'Perhaps a quick one now, which I did desire from one for whom I did care somewhat, would be okay!' I thought to myself. I was releasing myself for a quickie even as I was mentally justifying it. I was surrendering to an intimate time with Marcus.

# CHAPTER 28

# 'NO' MEANS "NO!"

Marcus slipped his shirt off in between our kisses as we both began panting and hormones kicked in big time. I was grabbing for his belt buckle, when suddenly there was Tyler. He was sad, looking like a lost puppy dog. Tyler's awesome physique, gorgeously handsome face, and obvious distress at what I was about to do with Marcus broke my concentration on making love to Marcus. I remembered my goal of weaning off and ceasing my sexual services, leaving me in a period of sexual chastity for Tyler. I stopped kissing Marcus, pulled my head back, and shook it to dislodge Tyler from my mind's eye. At the moment I wanted this right now, this sexual attention and activity from a former or current lover, and Tyler wasn't here. Marcus was here, and I did care some for him. To him, I knew now, I was still his lover. Tyler's image melted into the air, and Marcus and I resumed kissing passionately. I unbuckled his belt and undid his pants as we shared our tongues. Marcus was feeling me up. I was fully stimulated and erect. Yes, a quickie with Marcus would be okay! It was just what the doctor ordered!

Marcus continued to feel and stroke me all over as he began kissing down my neck. I was alternately opening and closing my eyes as I caressed Marcus's chest and abdomen and began slipping a hand in his loosened pants to stroke his package. At some point I opened my eyes to look into Marcus's face. Instead there was Tyler! He was beside Marcus watching him and me going at it. His face showed the hurt, anger, and humiliation that he felt because I was breaking my own goal, my own 'promise' to him! Maybe I needed to rethink having this roll in the hay with Marcus? Maybe it was wrong?! I mentally began fighting my hormones and desires, trying to stop the activity with Marcus, although physically I continued going through the motions with him. Physically and hormonally I wanted to do Marcus again. I wanted to feel his body on, around, and in me. Emotionally, morally, and because of my true love with Tyler I did not want to make love with Marcus! Why was it that that which I did not want to do (have sex with a man) was so tempting, while the one man I wanted 'to do' (Tyler) was currently off-limits!

I closed my eyes to Tyler as Marcus hurriedly stood up and resolutely pulled me to my feet. Marcus pushed his pants down below his buttocks as he pulled and pushed me toward the bed. I slipped both hands under Marcus's briefs and pulled them and his pants below his knees. Marcus continued forcefully guiding me to my bed. I wanted this with Tyler passionately!

Once we were at the bed, Marcus firmly tried to force me to sit down towards the headboard. My hormones and senses were so stimulated and I felt such a sexual rush that I just obeyed him and sat down on the bed. Marcus sat down beside me. We continued our make out session as we moved toward our quickie. I opened my eyes and tensed. Instead of witnessing Marcus and his reaction to our sexual encounter, there was Tyler again, gazing sadly and reproachfully at me, tears running down his cheeks!

This view of Tyler's apparition woke me up, broke the hormonal and sexual rush I was experiencing, and shook me to my very soul. My heart melted and I felt awful seeing Tyler cry! His tears were my fault! I had to fix this!

I forced myself then to remember and face my commitment to Tyler, that I would begin saving myself sexually, physically, and emotionally for him. To abide by my decision and commitment it only made sense to slowly or immediately end my selfish personal sexual encounters with men with whom I voluntarily desired to sleep. After I ended that portion of my sex life and could deny myself the voluntary sexual encounters in the hay, then I would begin refusing to service patrons in private sessions at work in pursuit of my goal to be a secondary 'virgin' for Tyler. Ultimately, I would abstain from sex and become chaste until Tyler and I were one and made love in our monogamous relationship.

My heart sank as I felt so guilty, ashamed, unworthy, and traitorous over what I had almost done with Marcus against Tyler. I had almost cheated on Tyler! I had almost betrayed my love for and commitment to Tyler! I had almost broken my promise to Tyler! Would I ever succeed in denying my voluntary sex drives?! Could I ever achieve chastity and maintain it for Tyler for a month, two months, or however long it took to seduce him into a committed monogamous spousal and sexual relationship? I had to say 'no' right now to Marcus, for Tyler's sake, and my sake, and for Tyler and me as a couple. I stopped, pulled away from Marcus, and gently pushed him away. I was so aroused that it hurt, and I wanted to continue to climax with Marcus for relief, but I knew I couldn't morally or in any other way.

"I… I can't…" I was kind of breathless, panting, and I was becoming sweaty. "I can't and… won't do this anymore!" I stated firmly, waving and then dropping my hands in front of me. "I don't want this… this… this illicit, uncommitted, and meaningless unbridled sex from you anymore, Marcus!"

Marcus, however, was persistent, determined, and cunning. He acted quickly before I could rally a resistance. He began fondling my package vigorously with his right hand. Then he forcefully pushed me back onto the bed before I could arch my back to prevent it. When I was flat on my back on the bed, naked as a jaybird, Marcus pinned my arms down. He kissed and licked my face, neck, and torso. Marcus's actions in having sex with me were becoming increasingly rough, forceful, and uncomfortable. I began to realize that Marcus hadn't changed. His narcissism, selfish nature, and lack of concern for his lovers were rearing their ugly heads. He truly always let his sexual needs, desires, sensations, and feelings control all of his sexual encounters. For Marcus every sexual encounter was all about him and his pleasure. He mounted me, straddling his legs over my waist and resting his lily white ass on my legs heavily enough so I couldn't move them. This all happened so fast I had no time to prevent them or to launch counter measures.

I was really being stimulated now, with Marcus pumping and grinding his privates against mine in a frottage frenzy. The hormones created and released caused me to briefly stop my protestations. By the time Tyler popped into my head for the fourth time, Marcus was totally naked and going wild on top of me.

"Marcus!" I asserted loudly and firmly, struggling against him. "Stop! I don't want to do this anymore! I don't want to have sex with you anymore! You are hurting my injured areas!"

I fought hard and freed my arms. In a burst of power meant to catch Marcus off guard, I quickly pushed him back up into a sitting position. I grabbed his hands to remove them from my body.

At the sound of my demand Marcus tensed, and his wild body language stopped me from doing anything more. He stopped his oral stimulations and sexual activities on me. Marcus positioned his head to look me in the eyes. The animalistic and wild passion, uncontrolled lust, anger, sexual determination, and narcissism I saw there was worse, stronger, and wilder than I had ever seen in Marcus's eyes before. It startled, alarmed, and yes, it frightened me! I flashbacked to every sexual rendezvous with Marcus, and yes, I had never seen him like this before! Marcus was like one possessed by the demon libido and sexual abandonment. He was so focused on our sex that he appeared to be unable to control his faculties.

"Whatever your problem is right now, DiPree, is too damn bad! You were on-board when we started this thing, and I'll be damned but you'll be on-board to finish it!" Marcus's eyes were wild, flashing, and sparking like fireworks with every word. He was in the throes of passion and lust as he breathlessly began licking me and trying to push me back on the bed again. He freed his hands from me, and grabbed my hands, struggling to hold my wrists behind my back with one hand. His strength was marginally more than mine, and after the attack I now hurt all over, and I was limited in the resistance I could rally.

It was now clear Marcus planned to go all the way to his sexual orgasm with me, even if he had to rape me in the process. This whole thing was no longer an act of love between Marcus and me, that was the thing for which I had signed on. It was now all about Marcus, his lust, his desires, his pleasure, and to hell with me!

I suddenly lost all desire for a quickie now or ever with Marcus. I realized I genuinely and definitely wanted Marcus to stop now and leave me alone. Marcus had shown me though, that he was not going to stop voluntarily. I was going to have to show him I meant it. I hurt all over still and I didn't know if I had the strength to force Marcus to stop!

"Marcus!" I struggled as he continued to attack me again, licking and kissing my face, chest, abdomen, and crotch. He was struggling to hug and caress me. "Marcus! I said stop!" I cried out again, grimacing from the pain of his affections.

I tried to push Marcus off me with my hands, arms, and legs in a coordinated attack. Marcus responded like a caged lion, countering my every move and each time gaining a little more power over me. I quickly realized that in the hormone and adrenaline induced sexual craze in which he found himself, Marcus was much stronger and more clever than I. Marcus made fast work of neutralizing my legs. He pinned my upper legs again by sitting on them, and my lower legs he incapacitated by wrapping his legs around them.

I was able to hold Marcus at arms' length at first. However, Marcus grabbed both arms, bent them until I yelped in pain and relaxed, and then he swept them both above my head and powerfully clamped my wrists in a crossed position. He held both hands above my head with his right hand. I struggled to get free, but it was like Marcus suddenly was the possessor of unknown strength and power! Marcus was like an animal.

With his torso and left arm, Marcus was now in control of my body. He immediately went about using my body to pleasure himself sexually. Fortunately as he became more pleasured and approached orgasm, he became weaker. I was able to free my arms and hands again.

However, Marcus was already safe within my embrace, his naked body wrapped around my naked body. I could not get my hands on his body sufficiently to exert the force necessary to push him away.

I pounded on his back, but that seemed to accomplish more sexual pleasure for Marcus. His animalistic sex attack became rougher and more violent with every blow I landed. He was really hurting me and my body! My only break was that I was still in a sitting position. Now things really became jeopardous for me.

Marcus suddenly lunged at me to push me back on the bed once and for all. I really struggled now, trying to stay in a sitting position. I had to stop using my arms and hands as a defense against Marcus and use them to prop me up and maintain my sitting position. I began to panic with the certainty that not only did Marcus weigh more than I, but, under the influence of his sex drive and sex 'demons', he definitely was stronger than I!

"Marcus!" I raised my voice and demanded emphatically. "If you do this, I will report you to Mr. Richard for rape! I said 'no' and I mean 'no!'"

Suddenly a sharp pain caused my right elbow to give out. Marcus threw me backward flat onto the bed. I groaned in pain as Marcus's full weight lay on top of me and he went physically and sexually wild.

He did not let up. I fought to push him off of me or at least to get him to support some of his own weight. With his hands now free and me incapacitated by his weight, Marcus fondled, caressed, felt, and poked his hands and fingers all over and in my body orifices. I couldn't help feeling intense stimulation as I fought Marcus and my desires to just surrender to him. I wanted Tyler! Tyler was there cheering me on to stop! Why did I want to give in to Marcus?!

"Marcus!" I exclaimed angrily, mustering all my strength to push him back so I could sit upright again. "I will report you to Mr. Richard if you do not stop! He will fire you!"

Marcus was humping me furiously. When his body arrived at the next 'up' position I pushed upward and thrust with my body to dislodge him and to get his face out of mine. Marcus out-maneuvered me again. When my strength to struggle gave out, Marcus not only still straddled my waist with his legs pinning mine, but he had managed to pin my arms again above my head.

Marcus stopped and menaced me with a crazed, piercing, and lascivious stare. His face was only three inches from mine. His nostrils flared, his breath came in short hot gasps, and his eyes sparked with anger and danced with darts of hormonal pleasure. Once again the sexual passion, adrenaline, anger, narcissism, and physical determination in his eyes were even wilder, stronger, and more frightening than ever before. As I lay there on the bed pinned under Marcus, I was scared of him, fearful of what was going to befall me, and desperate to overcome him.

"Drew!" Marcus's tone was deeper, meaner, and more guttural suddenly. I almost didn't recognize his voice.

I gulped and blinked in surprise and alarm into Marcus's eyes.

"Drew! I want you… now!" Marcus growled in this disturbing new voice. "I need you… I know you want me! I desire you… I lust after you almost every day at work! But you… now you think… you cut me off… you act like you are too good for me! Well, Drew, that is tough shit now! I will… I will have you… I will have you for sex now, and from now on, one way or the other! I will @ you raw and by so doing, I will cure you of your feelings of superiority and your condescending attitudes toward us all!"

For the first time since I had known Marcus and during our now ended affair he seemed entirely possessed by the demons of his own sexual desires. His whole character, behavior, attitude, actions, and physical strength had completely morphed. The change in his voice and his words further startled and alarmed me such that I wasn't paying attention to anything else. I didn't recognize this Marcus! I detested this Marcus!

Almost immediately after he finished threatening that he would have me one way or the other, Marcus lost all control and became totally sexually maniacal. Now, throughout our relationship for the last few years I had found that Marcus and I were almost of equal strength, physical ability, and fighting ability. However, it was now clear that Marcus was actually overpowering me. He was stronger than I! His hands were all over me and he was mouthing me all over. He suddenly grabbed me, lifted me up, and physically thrust me back on the bed flat. He was all over me like an animal, and again he was hurting me. I cried out a few times in pain as I desperately struggled against him. I shuddered as I felt him come close to penetrating me several times. If he did decide to go anal and all the way, there was nothing I could do to stop him. I was too weakened from the ordeals of the day to resist. In addition, he still had me pinned to the bed. However, I knew I must still resist Marcus to the bitter end.

As I fought to get Marcus off the top of me I realized that sex with him no longer was even remotely pleasant sounding or desirable to me. I wanted out not only for Tyler, but for myself! I fought with all my strength against him, but Marcus was possessed of a hormone induced strength that was actually fed by my resistance.

"Marcus!..." I managed to grab his arms and pushed up. No effect. "Marcus! Stop!"

I again pounded on Marcus's back and shoulders, hoping to distract him and to get him to back up so I could have a clearing to hit him in the face and chest. Nothing worked. Marcus was fully involved in frottage and attempted penetration with me. I knew, though, that he would want more than that! Much more! I had to stop this somehow!

# CHAPTER 29

# A PRECARIOUS PEACE

"Marcus! I don't want to do this with you!" I was really scared! I couldn't stop someone from having sex with me and it petrified me. 'This is the second time today someone has tried to rape me!' I thought angrily and fearfully. "Marcus! Stop!" I yelled.

I stopped struggling briefly. Flashbacks of the bikers' assault on me came tumbling back as I felt the helplessness and abject desperation of a rape victim again. The difference was that both Marcus and I were naked now. I had to stop this soon or… I remembered how smelly and gross Jaba had been. I shuddered in fear and disgust as I remembered his assault at the table where he had begun undressing me. I remembered elbowing him hard in the crotch to get him to stop sexually assaulting me…

The feelings of terror and despair tend to cause one to accept and use anything to solve the circumstances causing them. So it was with me as flashbacks of the assaults earlier in the day provided me with a last ditch idea to dissuade and end Marcus's attempt to rape me. I knew what I could try; I knew what I had to do.

Quickly I reached down between my body and Marcus's with my right hand and grabbed a certain pair of body parts between Marcus's legs. I cupped my hand firmly around them. As I did so, I felt wetness develop on my wrist. I knew what that was. Marcus had emptied one on me.

With my right hand I squeezed those delicate body parts of Marcus's that I held. Marcus yowled and stopped his attack. He lay motionless and still on top of me, his breathing slow and his body tense. For my part, Marcus's full weight resting on me again hurt like hell, and I was finding it hard to breathe.

"Drew…" Marcus spoke slowly and carefully as he gently breathed my name out. "Drew… you wouldn't… hurt me this… way now… would you,… Drew?!"

"Marcus!" I said slowly, firmly, and businesslike. "I said I did not want to have sex with you did I not?" I ever so slightly squeezed Marcus a little tighter. Marcus cried out in anticipated and actual pain.

There was a pause. Marcus was ever so still on top of me. I wanted to wipe myself up from him and his fluids, but I knew I couldn't release my grip on his parts.

"Drew…" Marcus carefully and deliberately breathed. "You… you started out… as much into me… as much interested in… a roll in the hay… in sex with me as I was… interested in the same from you…"

"I changed my mind though, Marcus. Besides that was not my question. I told you I did not want to have sex with you did I not?!" I squeezed Marcus again.

"Yes, Drew, you did! Please let go of me!?" Marcus stiffened, grunting in pain.

I groaned too because any movement from Marcus caused great discomfort to my poor, sore body.

"Then, Marcus." I continued, maintaining my grip on him. "What were you about to force me to do?"

"I was about… about to…" Marcus talked slowly again as he lay still on top of me, hands resting on my bare chest and head on my shoulder. "I was about to force… you to have… sex with me… anyway. Now Drew… you know I… was just joking… trying to… 'comfort' you…!?"

I squeezed his gonads tightly for a brief second just to cause exquisite pain and to stop the lie I knew Marcus was telling. Marcus howled and began moaning.

"I was lying…" He gasped slowly like before, so as not to cause more pain. "I was lying, Drew… I was trying… to force you… to have sex… with me period…Drew… let me go please…!?"

I interrupted.

"What is it called, Marcus?" I had one point to force him to admit. I squeezed secondarily again. "What is it called when someone forces another uninterested and/or unwilling person to have sex with them?" I maintained a solid grip on Marcus's pair of crotch parts.

"Drew...?" Marcus whimpered. "Drew... you know I... wouldn't hurt you...Why force me to lie?"

I again squeezed tightly for a brief second. Marcus howled again, and when he spoke he was almost crying.

"It is called..." Marcus drew a quick breath. "It is called... rape... Drew... it is called... rape... " He paused. "Drew...!" Marcus pleaded. "Please let... go...!"

"Marcus!" I spoke in the same businesslike tone. "Will you ever do this to me or anyone ever again?!"

"No, Drew... no! I won't!" Marcus exclaimed cautiously.

"Okay, Marcus." I released my grip a little on his proper delicate parts. "You will get up and off me now... carefully! You have caused me enough pain already!"

"Okay, Drew!" Marcus agreed. He slowly raised his head and pushed his torso up with his hands, groaning in pain. As he moved I followed, still holding his gonads securely in my right hand.

Marcus slowly and carefully executed the movements necessary to sit up. I shadowed his every movement until we both were sitting up side by side.

"You promise, Marcus, never to sexually assault me again?" I asked. Gently I squeezed him again for special emphasis.

Marcus cried out in pain as tears came to his eyes and I could officially see them.

"Drew!" Marcus called out. "I promise... I will never... sexually or... otherwise... assault you again!"

I released Marcus's gonads, smiling to myself over my victory. If I had done this earlier I would have saved myself considerable physical and emotional pain.

Marcus lay on the bed clutching himself, tears flowing down his cheeks, moaning, groaning, and wincing in pain. I busied myself wiping my body off with a towel and put on my underwear. Marcus glared at me reproachfully as he writhed and rolled around on my bed.

I got up and went quickly to my bathroom. There I washed Marcus's fluids off me. With my cut shoulder hurting like hell and bleeding again, I also changed the bandage. I then reentered my outer suite room. Marcus was still doubled up, holding himself and writhing on my bed.

In the main area of my suite I began to finish dressing. Presently Marcus sat up and glared at me again.

"What do you mean, Drew, 'I don't want to do this anymore!'?! You have wanted to have sex with me for the last three or four years. We have had sex, good hot sex for the last three years! Tonight I know you wanted to have sex with me at first. That wasn't my imagination!" Marcus briefly extended his arms and shrugged. "What do you mean, Drew?! What has changed in you as regards us?!"

"First, Marcus, there is no 'us'! You and I are over, history! Secondly, I'm not having voluntary promiscuous sex, one night stands, or selfish sexual affairs anymore." I informed him firmly. Marcus groaned loudly. "Now, will you quiet down?! It's not like I hurt you or anything!" I wanted to rub it in.

Marcus stood up, all bent over, and retrieved his clothing.

"I still don't get it!" Marcus came closer and began dressing. "You are not having promiscuous sex anymore! I'm 'promiscuous sex' to you!? A one night stand?! I thought we meant more to each other, that our lovemaking was more than just 'promiscuous sex' or a 'one night stand'! I thought 'we' meant something to one another?!"

"Marcus, as I told you a couple of months ago when I cut you off and officially broke up with you, I was not, am not, and will not ever be in love with you." I calmly put on my pants and drank a long dreg from Marcus's secret cocktail. It was delicious! "You were then and would be now just a selfish promiscuous affair to me." I put on my muscle shirt and began combing my hair. "Now, after what you just pulled on me you'll be lucky to ever be anything more than just a co-worker to me. Anyway,

I'm turning over a new leaf. I am gradually ending all of my formerly self-desired promiscuous sexual encounters."

Marcus placed both feet in through his underwear and pulled them up to his waist. He then reached for his pants and pulled them up while I grabbed an outer button shirt and began to put it on.

I crossed the room to the refreshment bar and began perusing more new dance moves for the hell of it. I had to stay here until Marcus was dressed and I could kick him out of my suite. I didn't want him alone in my chambers lest he hunt for and find my cash money, vicodin, or avatar and steal it.

"Drew, you know and I know you enjoy having sex with me! Besides, I don't know how you can give me up as 'promiscuous sex' when you are still turning tricks in private sessions!" Marcus blurted angrily.

"The correct tense, Marcus, is that 'I enjoyed' having sex with you at one time. I don't enjoy it anymore! I will get to surrendering my private sessions. If I give you up, Marcus, I'm one person closer to abstaining from any sexual encounters until I make mad, passionate love to my Ty..." I stopped and gulped involuntarily. I had said way too much! I didn't want anyone at work to know about Tyler! Had Marcus caught my verbal faux pas revealing my reason for giving up voluntary sexual activities?!

"Who is Ty, Drew!" Marcus demanded petulantly. "Do you have someone in your life other than me?! Do you have a significant other!? I know! You're seducing a new hunk with whom you want to be monogamous?! Are you @ing him?!" Marcus stared at me with a mixture of anger, and incredulity. He spoke loudly and jealously.

By this point in the interrogation I was pissed! I was pissed at myself for what I had almost done with Marcus. I was pissed at Marcus for trying to take advantage of me in my time of need and weakness. I was pissed at Marcus for being such a sex-crazed jerk. Finally, I was pissed at Marcus for being so nosy and prying into my personal affairs! They were none of his business! However, instead of keeping my mouth shut, I spoke again without thinking.

"Yes, I have a significant other, Marcus!" I raised my volume slightly. "I won't be able to work here at The Flamingo forever, and I want a lover with whom to live, love, and grow old. In pursuit of that goal I have found this hot, facially, and physically gorgeous, awesome guy! He is the perfect man package, brilliant, buff, kind, down to earth… and he is mine! I am romancing him presently, lobbying for a relationship. I am honoring him and our future together by reducing all sexual liaisons with any other men, personal lovers, clients, former clients, and fellow employees. You fall into that latter category, Marcus, in case you didn't know!"

Marcus's eyes flashed in fury and jealousy as he was putting his shirt on. His beautifully and attractively muscled arms and hands trembled as he buttoned his shirt. He glowered at me, and yet his countenance still showed lack of understanding or belief in what I was telling him.

"What about your job, Drew!" Marcus's nostrils flared as he impudently continued to challenge me and my plans with respect to Tyler. "Your whole job here at the Flamingo revolves around @ing patrons and clients and sexually pleasing them! What about these obligatory sex sessions you must do to remain employed here?! You can't do your job without giving it up to whomever wants it! What about the private sessions you must do to work and get paid, Drew!? Any private sessions you do now, Drew, will constitute cheating on this… this Ty of yours! Are you @ing him yet?!"

"They are my job, Marcus. That is arguably different than the relationship you seek with me!" I retorted as I continued to peruse new dance movements and stripping techniques.

"Again I ask, Drew, what about private sessions?" Marcus lowered his voice, and taunted me. "They are 'promiscuous sex' then too. As I said, you are cheating on Ty by continuing to work here! If you can continue your private sessions here at work and your job here at the Flamingo, why can't you and I still hook up for sex once in a while?!"

"Yes, Marcus, my private sessions here at work do constitute promiscuous sex. My job here, however, is essential to our financial survival and my relationship with Ty. We have to be able to pay our bills. I believe my job is just that, a job. It means nothing in the grand scheme of things when I have to perform sexually at work." I stopped studying and eyed Marcus with certainty. "Sex with clients here at work is meaningless, loveless, just simple lustful physical pleasure and exercise. Now, Marcus, are you finished?!" I was struggling now to control my anger and not blurt anything out unwisely, while I knew I had already blown my secret plans.

"Ah, well!" Marcus had almost fully recovered from his pain now. He was developing a point that seemed to be making him very happy. I was becoming fearful again of what was happening.

"You'll have to stop doing private sessions too! This by your own admission! They are promiscuous sex, and you are giving up promiscuous sex for Ty! Yet I saw you setting up a session with the fairy at table five!" Marcus smiled cunningly. "Isn't that cheating on your Ty?"

Marcus tied his shoes, then gazed challengingly at me. He stood with that smug, victorious look on his face, hands on hips, looking defiantly at me. I was tiring of this conversation, and I was tiring of Marcus.

"Marcus, Marcus!" I forced a fake, nervous chuckle. "I can't do everything to achieve my goals all at once. As I explained, I need to continue to draw pay to make my bills and support Tyler and me! Marcus, I have three private sessions tonight. Don't even go there!"

"But you and I are…" Marcus began.

"Look, Marcus!" I interrupted. "I have my reasons for still doing some tricks, and they are none of your business. Besides, I'll quit private sessions soon as Tyler and I become an item, and I can afford it. Now, let's chalk this little event here up as a mistake and a misconception and then forget it. Marcus, you and I have work to do!" I headed for the door. I heard no one follow me. Marcus stayed where he was when I finished talking.

"Drew!" Marcus almost chortled. "Drew, stop! I have something to say to you!"

I halted wearily and reluctantly and turned to face Marcus. The expression on his face had turned to that of one who had just turned the tables on another person. My heart sank. It was obvious that Marcus figured he had me over a barrel. And why not?! I had shared much too much information and details of my plans and goals. I knew I was in trouble, I just didn't know how much or what kind of trouble!

"Oh boy, Drew!" Marcus folded his arms across his chest and strutted around me in my own dressing room. "Oh boy! It looks like I will be @ing you now after all! You think you are so smart, don't you, Drew?! You think you are smarter and better than Marcus, eh?! And, oh! By the way, Marcus, you are so history, old hat, yesterday's garbage! I don't want you anymore!"

Marcus copped a snotty, mocking voice and attitude. He continued pacing around me smugly, smiling victoriously.

I sighed, looked upward, and folded my arms across my chest. I didn't answer. I failed to see that Marcus was worth my attention or concern any more.

"Hot damn! Drew, you are a 'working' waiter or 'associate' here at the Flamingo Lounge. You can't stop @ing patrons and doing private sessions for clients and still work here at the lounge." Marcus paused. "If you stop doing private sessions with patrons and clients for this Ty, Drew, then you'll be in breach of contract and fired immediately!" Marcus stopped, faced me, and planted his feet. "Mr. Richard has done a lot for you, Drew! He has saved your ass many times! He brought you off the streets... gave you a job... provided you an apartment at reduced rent... all he asks of you is loyalty... loyalty to him... loyalty to the lounge and your job. How do you think he will take it if he finds that you are secretly planning to break your contract, quit your job, and leave him short a valued and excellent employee?!"

I realized at this point that Marcus may have me over a barrel. I flushed in anger. Marcus was again circling around me triumphantly. He was gaining his ground to force me into sex.

"I don't expect he will be very pleased..." I muttered in response.

The other shoe was now dropped by Marcus.

"I think I'll give Mr. Richard a heads up that you plan to stop servicing patrons on the sly and soon!" Marcus smiled in an evil manner. "He will fire you tomorrow! Can you say 'unemployed', Drew?" Marcus mocked me triumphantly. "I can give you the address where you need to go to file for unemployment tomorrow!"

I didn't remember if what he said about contract contents was true, but as I stood there, anxiety and concern were causing a deep fear of what Marcus might be planning. Marcus was not finished.

"Drew!" Marcus hissed in his menacingly deeper, guttural voice. It was clear he had just surrendered to his sexual demons. "I want you emotionally, sensually, physically, and sexually right now! I don't care about you as a person, I just lust after your... hot... gorgeous body. I want to @ you up one side and down the other. I have to have your body! I have to be inside you, I want to be all over you. I want a roll in the hay, a quickie, and I shall have it, NOW! I will have you from now on whenever I want, or Mr. Richard shall know of your plans!" He paused, smiling like a Cheshire cat. "We will rock 'n roll like we used to for the past three years, just for old time's sake!" He began seductively and purposefully undressing again.

"I'm not having sex with you, Marcus!" I stated flatly and angrily. I could now put two and two together and figure out where he was going with these points, questions, and threats. If I refused him, he was going to get me fired. I shuddered and gulped in dread.

Clearly Marcus's sole focus right now was on packing my fudge. There was a wanton, lustful, and carnal scintillation forming in Marcus's eyes. I sensed from this gleam in his eyes even more trouble and bad news. Marcus approached to within a foot of me and stuck a finger in my face.

"I will have you, Drew, right here, right now, and any way I LIKE IT!" He emphasized those last words loudly. "If you don't have sex with me, Drew, on my demand, I will tell Mr. Richard your plans and get you fired immediately!"

There it was! His dastardly, narcissistic plan! My heart began to flutter and sink. I became very apprehensive. Marcus was now holding all the cards. I felt weak, dizzy, and suddenly nauseated.

"So, DiPree, how does it feel?!" Marcus taunted. "Who holds your balls in his hands, able to squeeze or crush them at will?! Huh?... What?... Oh yeah! That is I!"

As he continued to dance and undress, I thought quickly for an out.

"What's wrong, DiPree?! Cat got your tongue?!" Marcus chortled. Then he gazed lasciviously at me and purred. "Don't let the cat take your tongue, Drew. I have so much I want you to use it for on me!"

There had to be a way to deflect this rape again. I decided delaying tactics were in order while I looked for my out.

"What could you or Mr. Richard possibly use to get me fired out of my plans I have shared or what I have said, Marcus?" I asked, planting my feet and folding my arms over my chest in defiance.

"As I said, Drew, it is our company policy for strippers to do any private sessions that guests demand, upon demand!" Marcus was down to his underwear. He stopped undressing at this point to explain how he had me. "If you're going to stop private sessions, or if you refuse too many private sessions, you will be fired! Remember the old saying 'the customer is always right'? That reality is according to company policy and it is also in the business policies book and our performer contracts. I had it written in all those sources, Drew! Most importantly I had it put in the agreement and understanding that all of us signed when we came to work here!" Marcus's face was lit up with a grin. His expression made him very attractive, but his current attitude and his narcissism were sickening. I shuddered!

The sources of the rule he was citing to have me fired had slipped my mind. All employees, upon their hiring, were given a company policy book, business policy book, and were told to read certain parts. I remembered that the situation and conditions of my plans were indeed addressed just as Marcus had said. I now felt my job was not only threatened, but my future was at stake! Tyler and I were on thin ice as well. I was scared shitless now!

As for the other sources Marcus cited I now realized he was correct there as well. I looked at the floor. Of course in my forgetfulness I had blurted out too much truth to a potential enemy. Marcus now had my gonads in his hand, and he could squeeze at any time. I had told him much too much about Tyler and my plans for my work here! What could I do?!

It wasn't that Marcus's ultimatum left me with no options. I could think of at least three options, but each brought with them uncomfortable and unacceptable consequences.

One option would be to surrender to Marcus. I could give him his animal sex, and satisfy his sexual needs right now. Then I could hope this was over and continue working as before, as if nothing had, or would happen. Unfortunately, I knew Marcus! I knew if I gave in this once, he would hold my plans over my head from now on. Any time he wanted sex from me he would threaten to go to Mr. Richard and get me fired. I'd be his sex slave from now on until I could quit The Flamingo Lounge!

Another option would be to threaten again to file a rape charge with management, law enforcement, and Mr. Richard against Marcus if he insisted on us having sex. However, the most that would accomplish would be to get both of us fired. Either that or my allegations would go nowhere because it would be my word against Marcus's. In that case Marcus would probably still hold his truth over my head in lieu of sexual favors until I could afford to quit.

The final option I could see would be to quit The Flamingo Lounge now preemptively. I could then continue to pursue Tyler, and go about finding another, better, more respectable job. However, this option brought with it two devastating and more pressing problems. I couldn't bear either one!

First and obviously the worst of the consequences of this final option was that, as per the agreement between me, my former pimp, and Mr. Richard, if I stopped working for Mr. Richard before my ten year contract was up, I would have to work the remaining years of the contract for my pimp on the streets again. In other words, I had signed an agreement to work exclusively for Mr. Richard for ten years. Only three years remained of my ten year commitment to Mr. Richard. If I quit certainly, or possibly if I were fired, I would have to go back to my former pimp and prostitution on the street for the remaining three years. Again, this would mean losing my apartment, my belongings and 'toys', and certainly Tyler! I could bear losing my apartment and things at this point. What I could not bear would be to lose my love, Tyler!

At the least the consequences of quitting The Flamingo Lounge preemptively would still be very hard to live with. Assuming I could somehow avoid going back into prostitution and working for my former pimp for three years, I would still face severe consequences. If I didn't work for Mr. Richard in The Flamingo Lounge I would have to move out of Candlestick Apartments. I would lose my home and most likely Tyler, and I would be forced to look for another apartment. I would also have to look for other employment. I would have to sell the bulk of my belongings as would Tyler if he stayed with me. I would probably lose my Tyler under this scenario.

At this point if Tyler didn't take his belongings and go back home or get a tiny one person flat, leaving me alone and heartbroken, there might be one or two positive outcomes. I would be free to pursue Tyler as my lifelong lover. I also could pursue a more respectable, less dangerous, and healthier job. However, under this option, how I would have time to find an apartment for Tyler and me, pursue Tyler romantically, and look for a good, respectable job all at once I did not know. I believed I couldn't swing all those things at once. It could be months in the Obama Depression before I found a good-paying job and a housing setup for Tyler and me like we enjoyed now. I therefore needed my strip club job until at least a few months after I won Tyler's heart and became his exclusive lifelong lover.

Marcus certainly had me over a barrel! It appeared to me that he had me cornered. This strip club rule mandating that I do all client service sessions as a condition of continued employment, and my big mouth telling Marcus the damning evidence against me, could well be my undoing in this current confrontation with him. It was clear that the only option that came with the least consequences to my personal life, my relationship with Tyler, Tyler, and our lifestyle and living standard was to just surrender to sex with Marcus now and any time he demanded it. In return for providing a willing sex slave and fulfilling his every sexual fantasy, I could only hope Marcus would keep my secrets.

Clearly my contractual obligations were now going to force me to forget my goal and desires to become and then be celibate until I could make love to Tyler forever. I clearly had to have sex with Marcus now and indefinitely unless I could think of something quickly!

Marcus leered at me. He danced over to me in his underwear and began to unbutton my shirt. Simultaneously he began feeling me up roughly. I knew that, after what I had just done to Marcus by squeezing his gonads, he would make sex with me as painful for me as he could and wanted to for his own narcissistic gratification. I realized with chagrin and trepidation that it definitely would not be at all pleasurable for me to have sex with Marcus from now on until I could stop the affair permanently and leave The Flamingo Lounge. I knew Marcus held grudges and remembered 'wrongs' or things done to him forever!

Marcus took off his underwear. He smiled lubriciously at me, gloated over me, and lusted after me. He danced around me, roughly feeling, grabbing, and pawing me sexually. His demeanor and visage was that of personal want, desire, and self-gratification, not mutual love and concern. Having sex with Marcus now and from here on out would be like having sex with a piranha, painful, humiliating, psychologically draining, and even bloody. Marcus would rape me, have his sick and perverse way with me, and in the process 'eat me' alive. The only purpose in our relations would be Marcus's pleasure, not an act or expression of any love between two people. I hated Marcus at this moment! I would have initiated a physical altercation with him here and now except for the weaknesses caused by the injuries I had sustained from the bikers.

Marcus stopped dancing and approached me calmly with a countenance of tender passion. He began French kissing me, and his hands were all over me. Marcus ripped off my button shirt, tearing a sleeve off and pulling my underwear over my leather belt in back. He lifted my arms and put them straight up in the air. I knew where this was going, and I didn't dare resist for fear of Marcus exposing me to Mr. Richard. I wanted to spit in Marcus's face! He began to lift my muscle shirt off of me. I also knew I had better cooperate, or he would make our sex the most painful for me of his career.

Marcus had never shown this ugly side of his character before, or I would have dumped him long ago! It was like Marcus was... well, like he was... was possessed or something! I had heard about people being possessed by demons, but had never witnessed it. Now, in Marcus, I believed I had an example of a demon possessed person.

I continued to tire my brain trying to come up with a way to reverse the power struggle and overcome Marcus.

Suddenly, as he was removing my muscle shirt over my arms, it came to me! By now Marcus was writhing in place, brushing up against me naked as he was. He began to undo my belt and pants.

"You report me for refusing any tricks, Marcus, and I'll tell Mr. Richard about your 'special deliveries' that are spirited in every few days with the new food. I'll also report that you are taking illegal drugs, namely steroids, crack, and marijuana while on the job!" I knew this would give me something to hold over Marcus's head. I wasn't stupid! I knew Marcus was taking and distributing steroids and crack out of The Flamingo Lounge and had been since he had started taking both within the last three years. I knew he supplied many of his clients. I had just forgotten about it because of our good relationship. Now that our relationship had taken a quick bad turn and I was desperate not to become Marcus's sex slave, it was good information to use against and hold over Marcus's head to protect my Tyler and my plans for my future.

"If I report to Mr. Richard your consumption of illegal drugs at work and selling them to clients from out of the lounge, you'll be fired too, Marcus, as well as lose your drugs to use and sell! You'll certainly also go to jail!" I chortled victoriously.

I now had Marcus by the gonads again!

Marcus stopped undressing me and stepped back a bit. I stood with my pants down to my knees. The look on his face turned a little cloudy. He looked like a storm was coming. Color began draining from his face.

"What 'special deliveries'? What the hell are you talking about?!" Marcus's face turned to a countenance of innocence, lying, and desperation. He began to become less erect as his chance for sex with me appeared threatened again.

"Come on, Marcus! Do you think all of us here at work are so blind, drunk, strung out, or sex-crazed that we are stupid?!" I asked sarcastically. "Do you really think that all of us are oblivious to your use of steroids and drug use of marijuana and crack, that we do not know that you sell them and launder the money through The Flamingo Lounge here behind Mr. Richard's back!" I decided to prove it. "Come here, Marcus." I pulled up my pants and secured them.

Then I motioned for Marcus to follow me.

Marcus grabbed a bathrobe and put it on, then he followed me through several hallways to a back store room. I had seen a delivery specially placed just yesterday after the food and drink had been unloaded. I walked to the boxes marked 'special product' for which I had seen Marcus sign. Before Marcus could stop me, I opened one box. Inside were bottles of steroid pills. I showed one to Marcus. I then proceeded to open the other two, proving to Marcus that I knew of what I spoke. One box held baggies of marijuana, and the other held baggies of white powder. For an added benefit, and of surprise even to me, in the crack box there were many drug supplies and some other prescription narcotics.

"So you see, Marcus, I am not going to have sex with you anymore! I will gradually stop servicing patrons after hours. You will keep your mouth shut! In return, I forget about your drug consumption, drug laundering, and drug selling business here!" I closed the boxes and shoved them back on the top shelf. "You can go on taking, buying, and selling whatever you like, and I will look the other way! The key is keeping your mouth shut about my plans! If Mr. Richard finds out the faintest clue that I am planning my escape from this slavery, you, Marcus, will pay big time! Do we have an understanding?!"

Marcus hung his head briefly, wiped his brow, and looked up. He gulped involuntarily.

"Yes, Drew, we have an understanding!" He responded in a cracking voice.

I started for the door.

"How do you know those are mine?" Marcus declared, impudently blocking my egress.

"Because the shipping label reads 'Attn: Mark Dever', which I believe is short for 'Marcus Devereaux', is it not?! Besides, one innocent of my charges would not act as guilty as you are doing right now."

Marcus fidgeted nervously as he looked off into the distance on his right. He was breathing erratically, and I could tell I had him between cement and a rock.

"I also saw you sign for it, Marcus! Most really smart people would not sign for their own drugs! So you see, 'Mark Dever', if you report anything against me to Mr. Richard, ANYTHING, I will go to Mr. Richard and the police about your drug use and dealing! Kapiche?!" I gently pushed Marcus aside and turned to face him.

There was a pause as Marcus drooped his head.

"Do you understand, 'Mark Dever'!?" I demanded firmly and seriously.

"Yes… I do, Drew…" Marcus stood fidgeting and refused to look at me.

"You will keep your mouth shut and not try to get me fired! Correct, Marcus?!" I verified angrily.

"Yes… Drew, I… I will!" Marcus looked at his feet.

I turned and made tracks out of the store room and down the hallways to my dressing suite to put on my shirts for work.

Marcus stayed in the storeroom. I don't know what he did, but I could imagine he was trying to cool down from trying to have sex with me.

❖

# CHAPTER 30

# WORK LIKE AN AUTOMATON

It was about 4:45 pm. that Sunday when I resumed my table waiting, busing food and dishes. I was still sore, painful, and kind of stiff physically from the sexual assaults I endured at the hands of Jaba and the bikers and then Marcus. I hoped I would get over it by six when my private sessions were set to commence. If the soreness, pain, and stiffness did not lessen considerably by six I would be performing my private sessions of sexual service to clients with the hindrance of lacking flexibility, suffering physical discomfort, and the resulting lack of focus and concentration. In short, I would not be as pleasurable, resourceful, intense, or pleasing to the clients. I wouldn't enjoy the sex sessions either.

Unfortunately I realized too that, as busy as I was waiting tables, probably my remaining ailments from the assaults would not go away. They might even get worse as much walking, lifting, balancing, and cleaning as I usually had to execute or was called on to do while working the floor.

My options were to grit my teeth and bear my ailments while I did my private sessions, or surrender my sessions to another working associate, lose those fees, and go home early. I knew I would love to see Tyler some more this evening, especially since my shift until midnight meant I would not see Tyler until tomorrow morning. I certainly didn't feel like performing my sessions this evening. However, I could not afford to lose the fees for the private sessions I had scheduled! Not only were they a necessity for me to pay the bills until Tyler could help, but I had some items I wanted to buy Tyler soon. That would not happen if I made it a habit of frivolously giving up sessions over some pain and stiffness. I would just have to endure and keep taking my vicodin for pain, Flexeril to relax my muscles, and I would step up the avatar and double Long Island Teas. They all seemed to be my best bet for pain control and muscle relaxation! That way I would do fine in my private sessions.

As I rushed hither, thither, and yon delivering tableware, taking orders, delivering drinks and food, and busing tables, I had a chance to ponder and analyze my developing relationship with Tyler. He and I had already climbed and experienced a few rungs on the ladder to a lovers' relationship. We had wrestled together on Tyler's bed in nothing but our briefs Sunday morning. That had been so stimulating for me that I had had to restrain myself from pressuring Tyler to make love to me. He had grabbed my crotch and felt me up! That act had been even harder to take any other way than a request for sex. I had kissed him on the cheek and he had been nothing but smiles about it. I had felt the electricity and the chemistry between us when I had straddled him crotch to crotch Saturday evening. To me that had been a moment of realization and understanding that the two of us were meant for one another. Finally, he had already told me that he loved me without even knowing me much longer than a day and a half. These facts gave me a certainty that Tyler did have more romantic feelings for me than just the love and feelings that a guy would have for a brother! These actions that Tyler had participated in and performed with me betrayed deeper ideas and feelings that Tyler had toward me. From that perspective I knew that our relationship was progressing nicely. I smiled and my heart skipped a beat!

I began busing table one on auto-pilot.

However, I was nothing if not impatient! On the other hand there were my lusts, desires, and hormone drives pushing me to boost my relationship with Tyler into the sexual realm. I longed to be emotionally, intellectually, physically, and sexually intimate with him. I wanted not only to be physically close to Tyler, but I wanted to be with him, on him, and in him. To make love to him was now my only obsession. I longed for these intimacies with Tyler and the first time we could have sex so badly that my body ached and the feelings were so intense they were almost uncontrollable!

I felt a giddy, euphoric feeling and I just coveted and ached for Tyler every time I saw him or heard his name. My yearnings for Tyler, to see him naked, to feel his naked body next to me, to make mad, passionate love to him were so strong in my being that I believed if I didn't get satisfied soon I could spend all day aroused 24-7-365! I felt like I would just die if I didn't make love to Tyler soon.

Perhaps fortunately for me I was still governed by some nagging self doubts as to Tyler's intentions toward me. Even though I was quite certain that he had romantic feelings for me, I was not 100% sure if he were gay. To tell the truth, my self doubt and fear of rejection told me I was not even 50% sure that Tyler was gay! I also knew that with his Christian upbringing, he probably had been indoctrinated and scared shitless about homosexuals and homosexuality. Religion and doctrine were most often homophobic, not gay-friendly. Therefore I knew I couldn't yet lay all of my cards on the table and tell Tyler straight up how I felt about him, how I loved him, and how hot I was for his love and his awesome body. I had to be patient! I had to take it easy with Tyler and his Christian upbringing, and bring him to my side cunningly and lovingly. I had to go slowly enough so I wouldn't chase Tyler away, yet I had to push it quickly enough so that he and I would soon be a couple. I could hardly wait to be an official lover for and of Tyler, for him to consent to a full emotional, spiritual, physical, and sexual relationship with me, and agree to be my spouse!

Somebody, God if you're there, give me patience, please, so I don't ruin this relationship with Tyler!? Did I say that?! Damn! Tyler, without saying a word about his Christian beliefs or trying to proselytize me, was already influencing me in the area of my religious beliefs. He was having a 'good' effect on me!?

I realized as I delivered food to table two that I had to change the subject. I was still so hard and had been for the last I didn't know how long. My erection had embarrassingly begun during the first assault by Jaba, had continued going strongly as I was assaulted by Marcus, and was even worse as I thought about Tyler and my times so far with him. I didn't want to spend frivolously all my hormones and hard-ons over Tyler and then not be able to perform during my sessions!

I thought about the day today. As I did, I experienced a small sense of pride in myself. I had done something that I had never even done over the period of a week, let alone one day. I had refused to have sex with four guys today. That was unprecedented in my sexual history! The most I had ever refused sexual service in my nine years of using my good looks and beautiful body to earn money was one person a day. Anyway, the four I had refused were Marcus and the three bikers. None of them were happy that I had refused them sex and rejected them. I shuddered again as I experienced a vivid flashback to the assault by the dirty bikers and the vile threats that they had hurled at me as they were carried out of the lounge by the rough treatment by the bouncers. I also flushed with anger as the biker flashback became mixed with and changed to Marcus assaulting me. Marcus had some 'balls' to take advantage of me, to sexually assault me, and to try to bribe me for sex! Especially after what had happened already to me today!

At any rate, I was still proud of having had the courage and will power to refuse these sexual liaisons. I had refused them for Tyler and our future together! These refusals represented my first small steps toward my new goal of becoming a secondary virgin by having gone a few months without sex with any man; this for my Tyler, before he and I were intimate.

I slipped back into stimulating and glowing thoughts about Tyler as I served drinks to table one.

Tyler had so many good qualities! He was drop-dead gorgeous, brainy, yet well-built and athletic, kind, naïve, trim, and clean cut. His deeply tanned skin and beautiful deep brown hair were so sexy. I was blond and light-skinned, but I was especially attracted to brown-haired, brown-skinned American men. Where, other than the country, range, or farm, did you find decent, properly tanned men?! Men that were as perfect as Tyler?!

I was so smitten with him that I… I lusted after him all the time. I could think of nothing or no one else all day! So here I was, thinking about Tyler again! I needed to stop thinking about him or I seriously was going to lose some of my luggage before I boarded planes at six.

I was still determined to slowly stop servicing patrons. I wanted to be good enough and chaste for Tyler when we finally would commit to each other and begin consummating our love and commitment. It would be hard because I would have to keep my gradual separation from that part of the job a secret. No one else could know! Additionally, the pleasure and stimulation I experienced by doing multiple different men each shift that I "worked" was intoxicating! However, even though variety in men had in the past been the main bait drawing me to this job, it had, in the last year, been losing its luster and appeal. I now believed I could resist and overcome what little temptation this aspect of work posed to me. I knew I could do it for Tyler!

I had to do it for Tyler and me, but especially Tyler! He deserved it!

The biggest worry that I had right now was having someone else find out about Tyler and my plans and then instigate my dismissal from employment. That was why my thoughtless and stupid slips of the lips to Marcus were such a big deal and angered me so! What if I got pressured and angry and slipped with someone else?! I still had to keep this plan a secret from Mr. Richard especially. If he knew I was going to stop servicing patrons for Tyler, yet still work at the lounge, he would fire me! How could I keep it from him though, when my tips and stuff started falling precipitously as I implemented the plan?! He would know something was up based on his lack of income from me.

I feared Marcus, his mouth, and his sense of and desire for retribution for being scorned by me. However, I believed with the drug thing I now held over his head that I had him safely in my pocket. He would keep silent about me for a while at least.

The realization crossed my mind that I was almost going about my job in a robotic state. I was so lost in thought that I had kicked into automatic mode in performing my job. Each task that was my responsibility, and some that were not, I executed with very little thought or directions from my brain. I was exerting so little attention to my job, and was so lost in thought about my plans for Tyler and me, that disaster struck unexpectedly.

Having just bused two tables and leaving them clean and ready for new customers, I was carrying a tray of dirty plates and tableware from the restaurant area to the bar/kitchen. As I approached the end of the tables and the Berber carpet in the restaurant area to the beginning of the hard laminate flooring of the bar/kitchen area, I glanced at the last booth in the row of tables. In that booth were seated three young ladies and a young man. They were talking, laughing, eating, and drinking, generally enjoying themselves.

I focused back ahead of me to my destination; the bar where Sylvia was tending patrons' drinking needs. I had begun pondering ways to begin a dating relationship with Tyler without him knowing we were officially 'dating', so I was very much preoccupied again and was on dangerous automatic mode tending to my duties. The drugs and alcohol that I consumed only added to my lack of concentration on my work.

Just as I arrived abreast of the second to the last table in the row, the young lady who sat with her back to me suddenly decided to go to the restroom or something. She stood up right in front of me and turned to walk toward me.

Now, under normal circumstances where I would have been focused on what I was doing and not zoned out, I could have stepped out and around her. It still would have been a close call, and I might have lost the tray in avoiding her, but the fact is I could have avoided her. However, these were not normal circumstances and I was zoned out. In addition, I had a really good 'buzz' going on from the combination of vicodin, Flexeril, alcohol, and avatar. This combination of factors merged to put me in a relatively pain free, happy, and efficient 'high'. However, this 'high' had also deadened my mental speed and slowed my reaction time. I was operating in a trance-like, robotic state.

By the time I mentally registered that the young lady had stood up in front of me, I couldn't stop. Because of my wandering mind, the three drugs, and the alcohol, my reflexes were shot to hell! I plowed into her and my tray full of dishes flew over her head. The young lady stumbled backward and fell, and I came down on top of her. There was a loud clatter and sounds of shattering dishes as the tray reached the hard laminate floor of the bar. I snapped to reality! I gaped down from my vantage point on my hands and knees into the face of the woman I had knocked over. Fortunately I had landed safely and was now bridging the young lady under me nicely. She was on her back on the floor glaring up at me. I shook my head and then peeked furtively at the surrounding tables.

I was stunned! What the hell had happened!?

Reality sank in quickly and I flushed in embarrassment. I looked down apologetically into the young woman's face. Her countenance betrayed her feelings. She was clearly livid!

I shook my head again in disbelief as I rose up to my knees, grabbed the edge of the nearest table, and stood up. I teetered as my sense of balance slowly readjusted. Again I looked down at the young lady whom I had mowed over. She rolled over to her stomach and sat up quickly. She caught my gawking eyes and continued shooting me dirty looks, her eyes sparking angrily, and her cute, pouty lips curled in an icy frown. I stopped thinking about anything else then and stared at her. I couldn't help it! I blinked in awe!

This young lady was on the short side and very petite. Her countenance and appearance were exquisitely beautiful. She had evenly set hazel eyes, slightly tear-drop shaped, perfect red lips, even cheekbones, and precision teeth. Her light brown skin was unblemished and her dimples were slightly pink. She looked to be in her early twenties. She was of mixed race, namely white and Oriental or Asian races. She was very slender, and sported an hour glass figure. As she sat there looking angrily and expectantly at me, I forgot my manners and just stared at her. I was stunned at what had happened, but now I had to add astonishment over her beauty.

"Are you all right, Olivia?!" The young man at her table exclaimed anxiously as he scooted to the outside of the booth chair.

"Livie! Are you okay?" Another young lady at the booth cried as she looked at the young lady named Olivia, who was sitting on the floor still glowering at me.

"Hey, doofus!" The young man slapped my arm angrily, waking me from my trance. "Are you going to be a gentleman and move so I can stand up and help Livie!?"

I flashed the man, probably two years older than Tyler, an eye briefly. He frowned at me contemptuously.

"Ah... I... you stay... I mean..." I gulped involuntarily and took a breath. "You stay seated, sir, this is my fault. I will help her up!" I extended my hand to the young lady they called Olivia.

Olivia stayed seated, not attempting to grab my hand, and glared at me. Her beauty was not inhibited or dwindled by her unhappy countenance.

"You make it habit not watch where you go?!" Olivia said in a soft, mellifluous voice that dripped with outrage.

I shook my head vigorously 'no'.

"No! Honestly, no!" I assured Olivia. "I no make hab… I mean, I do not make it a habit, Miss Olivia! I am so sorry! I am afraid that due to extenuating circumstances I was unable to avoid you!"

I fidgeted as I held Olivia's gaze and left my hand extended to help her.

"Miss Olivia." I spoke sincerely and softly. "I am so very sorry! I did not mean…"

"Blah, blah, blah!" Olivia replied sharply as she grasped my outreached hand. "I know you sorry! Ngu people like yourself be inconsiderate, no watch where you go! No care who you hurt!"

Olivia jumped to her feet as I pulled on her hand.

"Miss Olivia…" I began again in my defense.

Olivia stuck a finger in my face, interrupting me.

"You no call me 'Miss Olivia'!" She exclaimed in a lowered voice as she glared at me. "You call me ma'am! Friends call me 'Olivia'! I no sure I like you, Ngu!"

I felt awful. How I now wished I had been focused on my job instead of enraptured with Tyler! Olivia had called me ngu, and whatever that meant was probably mild compared to the names I deserved for this mishap.

"Ma'am." I respected her wishes. I continued as apologetically and sincerely as I could muster. "I am so sorry I ran into you! I am even more ashamed that I knocked you down and fell on you! Are you hurt? We have a fully stocked first aid room. Do you need anything from it?"

Olivia began looking herself over.

"Are you all right, Livie?" The other woman in the booth asked urgently.

Olivia nodded, brushed her stunning dress skirt and blouse off and looked crossly at me. She straitened her hair and exhaled quickly.

"Yes, I okay!" She responded in her melodic voice. "No thanks to Ngu!" She thrust her pointer in my direction again.

"Again, ma'am!" I exclaimed in abject shame and apology. "I am so sorry for this!"

Then an idea struck me as Olivia sat down. I turned and stood at the head of the table.

"May I order each of you at this table a drink on me?" I peered inquisitively and hopefully at each of them in successive order. "It will be my way of making up for my clumsiness and lack of focus on my work!"

They heartily agreed and gave me their orders. As I left to make their drinks, Olivia rose from her seat and left for the restroom.

I hurried to the bar and personally mixed the drinks. Then I poured a pitcher of my favorite beer as well. I brought it all out to Olivia's table. Olivia had returned. I placed the drinks on their placemats to cool appreciation. Leaving the pitcher at the head of the table, I turned and left them to their party.

My next chore was to clean up my mess. Fortunately a custodian had arrived behind my back and was already hard at work cleaning up the glass, silverware, and food/drink mess on the tiled laminate floor where my tray had fallen. I quickly thanked him and returned to my tables to resume work.

Things were busy the rest of the afternoon, but not impossible. I still had time to think. However, I managed to consider my life and focus as well for the rest of the afternoon. I had no more accidents. Of course ceasing the alcohol and drugs until my private sessions may have helped.

It was necessary this morning to give Tyler a reasonable excuse for the fact that I had to work at the lounge on a Sunday/Sunday night. I couldn't give Bear Stearns, my 'employer', and a Sunday shift as the excuse. I knew Bear Stearns was closed Sundays and I could not take the chance that Tyler might call there to talk to me about something, anything that might come up that he did not know how to handle. In such a situation, Tyler would discover the truth that I didn't really work there. I couldn't take that chance!

Instead I had told Tyler today that I was going to mentor young people at Westchester schools in Westchester, Illinois. I wished now that that were true! If I had been mentoring I wouldn't have been at work, I wouldn't have run into or been assaulted by Jaba the Hut and his biker friends, I would not have been cut, and I wouldn't be working today having a shitty day.

Thinking of the cut that I had suffered, a few other issues came to mind. My injury now required medical care on my part. I would have to change the dressing periodically until it was pretty much healed. How was I going to do this at home without Tyler knowing…? Then it hit me!

How in the hell was I going to keep all of my injuries a secret from Tyler?! If I couldn't, what was I going to tell him to explain away the black and blue marks on my torso and the cut on my right shoulder?! Tyler would be bright enough to know you don't get bruises and a stab wound from mentoring kids in high school in Westchester, Illinois! Or… could I?

I could think of ways I could get stabbed and bruised while mentoring kids in a public school. I could be attacked by a mugger in the dark parking lots. I could go to a local bar for supper and get caught up in a brawl while there. I could have been cut while breaking up two of my mentoring students. I could have become caught up in a student brawl. Maybe a gang attack.

I quickly dismissed all of these excuses.

If I went with the mugger excuse Tyler would insist I go to the police. This excuse would lead to lie after lie, which, although I wouldn't hesitate to deliver to just anyone, I had no stomach for feeding so many lies to my love, Tyler. Three other excuses, a bar room brawl, mugging, or a student brawl would ultimately end up in the local news. When Tyler didn't see whichever excuse I had used on the internet, in our local or regional newspapers, or on the evening news, which he and I watched avidly every evening, he would certainly question me. This would force me to spin another web of lies to Tyler, and I couldn't tell Tyler that many lies and still feel good about myself. I loved Tyler! I felt and unilaterally had made a pact of honesty with him. I could tell him little white lies or distort the truth to him if it meant protecting him, me, or us as a couple. However, I could not so blatantly and continuously engage in falsehoods and subterfuge with Tyler!

I also realized that any of those reasons for my injuries could spread as rumor, and spark police investigations. I could ultimately go to jail for my lies, for filing a false report, or damaging the school or children's reputations by lying.

The only other possibility of keeping Tyler in the dark about the existence of my cut and bruises was… I stopped in front of a mirror used as a decoration in the eating area… I buttoned my shirt up higher so I didn't show so much beautiful hairy chest. Sure enough, my shirt hid the bandage. The bruises would be covered by my sleeves if I wore a solid, long-sleeved shirt. So, I could hide all my injuries from Tyler quite easily. 'Excellent!' I thought, relieved. 'I like to have viable options in any situation.'

It was settled! I would simply wear solid, long-sleeved shirts for a while and hide everything with my clothing. I would do so until I healed. Then I would resume normal apparel for summer. Tyler effectively would not be able to see any of my injuries that might cause him concern and prompt him to ask me questions. In this case, what Tyler did not know would not hurt him, me, or us!

I waited, served, bused and served, waited, and bused. It was tiring, but worth it. My patrons this afternoon were very generous in their tips. During the hour and twenty minutes that I waited tables I was given tips of \$205!

Time flew by as I worked my six tables to which I had been assigned. Soon it was a quarter to six and I had to get ready for my private sessions. I passed my tables off to a regular non-working waitress (one who did not do any sexual services) named Phoebe. Then I hurried to my dressing room to get ready for my three evening sessions.

I unlocked my door, slipped into my dressing suite, and locked the door behind me. I immediately went to my bathroom and took out three vicodin. I hurt still. I had pulled several muscles, my cut shoulder was burning, and I had a throbbing headache.

Vicodin in hand, I left the bathroom and entered my dressing room with my bed. I went straight to the wet bar. There I mixed myself a Long Island Tea. After adding some avatar, I popped the three vicodin in my mouth and took a long, refreshing drink, swallowing the vicodin. I would finish the LIT plus avatar while I dressed.

I crossed to the bathroom. After removing my clothes and the bandage, I jumped into the tub and turned on the water. I showered quickly, turned the water off, and exited the tub. Once on the floor I replaced the bandage and brushed my blond haystack. I shaved in the mirror while brushing my teeth.

As soon as I finished my morning ablutions evening style, I reentered my dressing room. I went over to my costume racks, and selected all the clothes I would need to do my first session. I crossed to the dresser to get out my under things. I drank another long slug. Then I went to the chaise lounge and sat down.

I put on a brand new, latest style thong, a pair of brief style underwear (to extend the stripping time), a pink muscle shirt, and some tight, gray, fake leather suit pants and vest similar to what I had worn to wait tables earlier this shift. Around my neck I tied a lavender dickey and tucked it inside the sport-style, skin-tight vest. Finally, I put on a pink bow tie and fastened it securely.

Guzzling the last of my drink, I put on some Curves cologne and my deodorant. Then I grabbed my keys, exited my dressing suite, and closed and locked the door behind me. As I walked down several hallways to the bedroom assigned to conservative businessman, Reece Morgan and me, I went over in my head some wild, new, and sexually pleasing moves and techniques that Morgan probably had never known or experienced.

I had high hopes that Morgan's session would go well and signal a change in my luck with patrons on this shift. I hoped and… and… and prayed for a pleasurable and uneventful session with Morgan.

As I stated earlier the blur of all the action that day, (we were always VERY busy on the weekends!), the assaults from the bikers and Marcus, and all the drugs and drinking I had done had shot my short-term memory to hell. I don't remember everything about my session with Reece.

Memory is a complex and strange function of our brains. What I do remember of Reece Morgan's session is distinct, very clear, and different. What I don't remember well is just a blur. I know I did many sexual acts to Reece and he to me. I remember he told me about his wife and three kids while he drilled me a new one. Most clearly of all I remember he had a birthmark resembling the whole male sex organ on his right cheek that was pointing right to his anus. Reece also clearly liked his gay sex on the rough side. From that standpoint his session was difficult for me as I was still painful, despite all the nerve center depressants I had consumed.

At any rate my session with Reece was full, full service, and he was well-pleased! He asked if he could be a biweekly regular with me, and I acceded. He was so pleased that he paid me $1,000.00 for the half hour. When I gave Mr. Richard his usual cut of 10% he was tickled pink. I was out of the doghouse with him!

I didn't have much time to think about or try and remember what I had done with Reece. I simply paid Mr. Richard his take, and then hot-footed it back to my dressing room. I had to hurry and get ready for Eddie and Carl.

# JOVAN THE DOMINATOR

How would Eddie and Carl like me to dress? About what type of man or what career man did they fantasize? Should I do them up with all the sexual acts, positions, and tricks this session, or just tickle their sexual appetites and tempt them to return? How would it feel and what would it be like to service both members of a committed gay relationship, basically two men married? Believe me, it didn't happen like this very often oddly enough! I couldn't remember the last time I had done a married gay couple!

I poured myself a diet soda with some vodka and headed toward my bathroom. Inside I turned on the shower water to warm up. While it did so, I removed my shoulder bandage.

I stripped, showered, and washed my entire body, paying special cleaning attention to any part of my body upon which Reece's body fluids had fallen. I scrubbed my face, my package, and crotch, chest, and stomach an extra time or two. I exited the shower, dragged long and hard on the spiked diet soda, popped two more vicodin, and dried off using my towel from earlier. I quickly replaced the bandage over my shoulder cut again, brushed my teeth and rinsed with mouthwash, applied a new fragrance of deodorant and new cologne, and exited the bathroom for my wardrobe.

I needed to hurry so I wouldn't be late. I went to the wardrobe racks to pick out my under things and outfit for Eddie and Carl.

I chose a hot new thong and a muscle shirt. I grabbed a pair of boxers that was hanging to dry. Then came the quandary as to how to dress for Eddie and Carl. What were their interests, or what kind of men really turned them on? How would they want me to dress? In what profession or career did they like their men to work?

I thumbed through the outfits at my disposal. There was the baseball player outfit. That was an awesome one! It really displayed and accented all of my physical beauty and attributes. Football player, basketball player, horse racer jockey, transvestite, fire fighter, miner, doctor… They were all there and more. I decided on the doctor outfit. For some reason I could see Eddie and Carl having a doctor's appointment and managing to seduce the unsuspecting handsome straight male doctor into some gay sex in a lab room! Eddie struck me as a very charismatic and convincing homosexual, one who could talk a straight, impotent man into stripping and sex.

I retrieved the tight doctor's outfit and lab coat, designed to accent all of my well-built and masculine body. Gathering all my clothes in a bundle I crossed the room to the chaise lounge chair and sat down. I quickly dressed in my underclothes. Then I put on all of the doctor's outfit, which had several accoutrements and was designed for a good strip show. There were of course the pants, smock, lab coat, booties, breathing mask, cap, and stethoscope. The pants were tight to my body though, instead of baggy, and revealed my manly form, sexy legs, enticing package, and cute ass. The smock was likewise tight to my body, enhancing the size, shape, and contours of my nicely buffed deltoids, pectoralis major, latissimus dorsi, and abdominal muscles, all the muscles of the torso. It was low cut and showed a nice portion of my upper hairy chest, sternum area, and all of my collar bone. The lab coat was loose as normal, but then again it never stayed on very long in a show. I smiled knowingly to myself!

I put on the final accoutrements of my doctor's outfit and sprayed the new cologne on my lab coat, smock, and pants. Basking in the intoxicating and erotic scents of my deodorant and cologne, I grabbed my doctor's bag of sex toys and lubricants, and left my dressing room, locking the door behind me.

I almost envied Eddie and Carl! They would enjoy great sexual pleasure with someone who smelled so good you wanted to do them all night; me. Smelling myself, my cologne and deodorant… Hell! I wanted to have sex with me!

As I went down the hallway to the playrooms where we serviced patrons, I marveled at the creativity of the differently themed rooms. Hawaii, Caribbean, athletics, Victorian parlor, cruise ship, kitchen, dirty dungeon, bedroom, classroom; people had strange sexual tastes and even stranger sexual fetishes!

When I approached the room themed as a doctor's office, I was pleasantly surprised. Eddie and Carl's names were on the door with my name as the 'doctor'. I had unknowingly picked the right suit for our session!

I quickly entered the 'doctor's office', placed the 'occupied' sign outside on the door knob, and closed the door. It locked automatically. I turned toward room center, expecting to see Eddie and Carl fully dressed and waiting for me. What I saw surprised me!

Eddie and Carl had decided to start without me. Eddie had donned a doctor's smock and lab coat, but was buck naked otherwise. He was examining Carl, who was standing bent over the foot of the examining table with his pants and underwear down at his ankles. Both were erect and at attention. Needless to say they were doing some entertaining of their own!

"Ah…gentlemen!" I cleared my throat to get their attention.

Both Eddie and Carl stopped their play and looked toward me with looks of annoyance. When they saw it was me, they both smiled. Eddie came right over and began dancing provocatively around me. He started to take my stethoscope off.

"Ooh! A sex toy, doctor!?" He cooed as he continued his erotic dance, bumping and grinding around me.

"Eddie!" I grabbed his shoulders and squeezed him enough to hurt him into stopping.

"Oh!! That hurts but it feels so good!" Eddie groaned in pleasure and became all the wilder. I released him immediately, not wishing to start the session just yet without an understanding.

"Guys! I have an announcement before we start!" I exclaimed impatiently in a raised voice.

"What is it, Drew!" Carl asked in his gruffer, manly voice. He stood up, pulled up his briefs and pants, and secured them again around his waist.

"We need to have an understanding, an agreement if you will, on safe sex." I replied authoritatively and seriously. "We will all be wearing condoms for every act we do to each other, or this session is off! Company policy! Is that understood?"

"Oh! Drew you are so sexy when you take charge!" Eddie stopped dancing, but still caressed my chest and neck. His voice, actions, and mannerisms were as girly and effeminate as ever, and belied the fact that he could act and speak as manly as Carl or I. "Drew, baby, we wouldn't have sex any other way! Carl and I are very particular about condoms. We wear them all the time too. We don't want any of those nasty little sexually transmitted diseases, either do we, Carl?!"

Carl cleared his throat and shook his head vigorously.

"Damn straight, Eddie! We don't need any STDs! We don't want to die at a young age." Carl gazed at me assuredly. "We always wear condoms when we swing, Drew!"

I heaved a sigh of relief and smiled broadly at Eddie and Carl. I prepared to perform and enjoy our session.

I decided to provide Eddie and Carl with a basic package that would satisfy them, but at the same time leave them wanting more. The package was designed to titillate, sexually please, and draw the clients back for even more sex and pleasure at another time. I had deduced early on that Eddie and Carl would make good returning clients. They paid well, and struck me as very loyal and easy to please. So it was that I decided on a pleasing, alluring, and eminently tempting basic package. True to my conjecture based on my first impression, Eddie and Carl loved their session, and promised they would return when next they chose to swing.

An hour later I walked toward my dressing room breathing heavily, sweating, and relishing the aftershocks of physical and hormonal pleasure. I walked briskly with a smile on my face. Eddie and Carl had been quite pleasant to service and play with, and nothing out of the ordinary had happened. I awaited their return with some anticipation.

Counting my tips in my head, I approached my dressing room door. I stopped in front of it, took out my electronic key, and glanced up as I swiped my card through the door lock. My eyes caught the presence of a note, written in old English script on onion skin paper and burned ragged along the margins, taped to the sash. Copping a speculative Spock mien, no smile with one eyebrow normal and one raised and pointing up toward the temple, I took down the note. I opened my door, entered, and closed and locked it behind me.

Once inside I crossed to the loveseat where I had occasionally entertained men that I was dating at the time. I sat down for a brief rest and to read the note.

It read as follows:

"Drew, Jovan desires your attendance at a private party in the medieval room. He requests you dress as yourself, a serf. Thank you, Jovan."

I raised my eyebrows and smiled. A serf eh?! I chuckled to myself. This sounded… well it sounded… mysterious… ah interesting… kinky…!

I went to look on my costume racks. I did have a serf outfit, and it was amazingly and uniquely tight and sexy. Very revealing even!

I looked back at the note that I held in my 'trembling hand.' What a strange request! The medieval room had only been open a year. I had used it with clients three times in that year, and the clients had wanted to be the serf. I had been a lord, or duke, or knight, things like that. I had never been a serf before. The prickles of sexual anticipation coursed through my body at the prospect of being a serf in Jovan's sexual role playing plan. What part would Jovan portray in his role playing sexual fantasy? A fellow serf? A king? A duke? I shivered in sexual excitement!

Wide-eyed and lost in thought I went to the wet bar. Methodically I took out the ingredients for a double Long Island Tea including avatar. I mixed the LIT while pondering what it would be like to be dominated in a client session instead of being the dominant one. I had never actually been dominated in a sex session before, whether it was at work, or in my own private dating life.

I added avatar to my drink and glanced at my watch. 'Holy crap!' I jumped in surprise. 'I only have ten minutes left! Get the lead out DiPree!'

I strode quickly to the bathroom. There I jumped into the shower. I scrubbed and cleaned myself off from Eddie and Carl's session, once again paying special cleaning attention to those surfaces of my body upon which fluids and contacts from the couple had been made. I finished quickly and then jumped out. Drying myself off, I applied new deodorant and new cologne. Hastily I replaced the bandage on my right shoulder, steri-stripped the cut, applied drawing salve, and covered it all with a soft gauze that I secured with Medical tape. I then popped two more vicodin and two more Flexeril. At the last minute I remembered that I needed to brush my teeth. I did so, and then exited my bathroom to my 'living area'.

I gathered the clothes that I would wear under the serf outfit, and the outfit itself, and hurriedly dressed. I contemplated in the mirror how hot and sexy I looked in typical serf's attire, modified of course for a stripper's purposes by manufacturing the garments to be skin tight. The outfit left no part of my anatomy to the imagination, yet it was stretchy and as comfortable as an old glove. 'Jovan should be pleased!' I fancied as I appraised the costume that he had requested.

I smiled seductively into the mirror at myself and copped a strident, muscleman pose, assessing my appearance in the reflection.

"Have mercy, stud!" I exclaimed as I winked at myself.

I whipped out a comb and coiffed my beautiful blond curls. I took another pose in the mirror and clicked my tongue, winking at myself again.

"You… look… mahvelous, baby!" I mimicked again.

I paused, making various sexy, suggestive, and sly faces at myself in the mirror. 'I am damn fine!' I smirked and pointed at myself. 'A really delicious and aromatic piece of male meat! I am an irresistible temptation to any self-respecting, intelligent man! Even straight men would find it hard to resist me!' I laughed at myself as I vainly adjusted and admired my blond curls.

I smiled in the mirror as I 'sobered' up. Seriously, I was so thankful to whom or whatever was responsible for my hot and sexy body, my awesome physique, my beautiful, soft, blond, curly hair, and my handsome and inimitable features. They had brought me a long ways and earned me a lot of money in the sex industry!

I guzzled my Long Island Tea with avatar until it was gone. I felt pressure for a few seconds in my gut, and then I belched. It was time to go to Jovan! I hurried to the wet bar and threw together a carafe of vodka tonic and avatar. I drank three mouthfuls of it before capping it. This would get me through my session with Jovan. I felt a head rush from the guzzled alcohol and was dizzy for a minute or two.

Waiting out the head rush and dizziness, I wondered what pleasures Jovan had planned for me. What kind of sex games or sexual role playing would he show me this evening? Perhaps he would wind up teaching me some new sexual tricks in our session that I could put to immediate and future use!?

'At any rate,' I thought, 'he is going to be in charge. It is all up to him!'

Hesitant and disquieted as I was, surprisingly I was also becoming very intrigued and stimulated. However, even knowing that Jovan was the one I had to please, I found all of my sexual lusts, desires, longings, and energy focused not on Jovan and my work, but upon Tyler. I wanted him as a lover, an equal in all ways, but one with me through our sexual intimacy.

I guzzled some more of my vodka tonic. I had to keep my buzz up. It made the sex so much better and pleasurable! It also masked any pain, or any mental and emotional scarring from the slowly growing shame and doubt I was beginning to feel over my job and my servicing of clients.

My thermos of vodka tonic in tow, I crossed my dressing room to the door. I opened it and entered the hallway. As I locked my door I looked up and down the hallway both ways. A few clients were coming and going, and I saw Melody enter and Dante exit their respective dressing rooms.

Turning to my right in the direction of several themed pleasure rooms, I walked briskly toward the Medieval room. It was located in a wing of The Flamingo Lounge that had been constructed a year and a half ago. It was one of six new themed rooms, two bathrooms, and two viewing chambers therein. All had finally been finished and the wing opened a year ago. I hadn't even been in four of the themed pleasure rooms in that wing. I had serviced clients in the medieval room before, however.

I arrived at my destination and noted with approval that the door had a sign on it that read "Jovan and Drew". I opened the door with my electronic ID card and slipped discretely inside. From the hook by the door frame I took the "Do not Disturb" sign and hung it on the door knob outside. I took a deep breath, fought my anticipatory jitters, and assured myself this would be a pleasurable and excellent session. I closed and locked the door. I flicked the lights on, turned around, and stepped a few feet into the room. I was not in any way, shape, or form prepared for what happened next.

I opened my mouth to explain to Jovan our policy concerning the use of protection as I ran my vision around the room searching for him. Jovan came into view, perched on the wooden great table in the middle of the room. However, I did not have time to see, register, or prepare for anything else. I heard a loud crack like a tree limb snapping from the trunk in a storm, or a lightning strike. The crack was so sharp, loud, and sudden that I was instantaneously surprised and startled.

The sound waves of the loud crack had not even begun to fade when I was suddenly struck with a long, stinging pain that started on my right butt cheek, ran up the right side of my back, and onto my right shoulder. Instantaneously with that line of pain came a strong force like a ton of bricks on my back and shoulder along with an even more severe pain. The combination of the force and the severe pain brought me down onto my right knee with such force that my knee joint cracked loudly.

The pain was unbearable and I issued a primeval scream. I grabbed for my right shoulder and the bandaged stab wound. I feared the bandage may have been compromised and I had to check it out. Tears came to my eyes and I screamed again as another wave of pain rolled up from my buttock to my shoulder. As I felt of my right shoulder I discovered that my serf coat and top was split down my back on the right side. My bandage appeared to be intact, but it was wet indicating that my stab wound was bleeding again.

A new wave of pain started on my right butt cheek and coursed rapidly up my back to my shoulder. This time the pain did not lessen or abate, it stayed the same. In addition, my cut also began throbbing with every heart beat. My head hurt.

What the hell had happened?! What had hit me?! Why did Jovan do this?! I looked up and glared reproachfully at Jovan. To my shock it appeared he was brandishing a long, long bull whip. I screamed in pain and rage, closed my eyes briefly, and bowed my head. When I could I raised my head and glowered at Jovan again.

"What the hell was that?! Why did you strike me?! What do you think you...?!" I began, my voice cracking as I struggled not to cry.

I didn't get any further. Jovan's next action interrupted me.

"Silence, peasant! As a serf, your only job is to shut your trap and do as I tell you!" Jovan commanded in a cruel and detached voice and manner.

The silence and the air was again split by another louder crack of noise like a lightning strike or the detonation of an M-80. I ducked and flinched, but it was too little, too late! The sharp crack, which I now came to realize was the crack of the bullwhip, was immediately followed by another long, stinging, and fiery pain commencing on my left butt cheek, running up the left side of my back, and onto my left shoulder. Again I felt like a ton of bricks had been placed on my back and shoulders as the powerfully strong force that resulted from the impact of the whip and the corresponding severe pain that followed brought me down to both knees.

I doubled over until my head bumped the floor as I screamed in pain, agony, and outrage. Waves of burning, stinging, throbbing pain ran up and down the wounds from my shoulders to my ass. I didn't know where to nurse first, my ass, my back, or my shoulders! All three were alive with pain and sensations of prickly burning. I howled another primeval scream as my wounds felt like they were on fire. I grabbed my left shoulder, hoping the pain would subside. I still held my right shoulder. Nothing worked and, sure enough, the top to my suit was smoothly split down my back on both sides now.

I was crying now. I bellowed again in abject and unmitigated pain. I was on my knees, my head touching the floor, resembling a Muslim worshiping Mecca and Medina.

I frowned as I looked up again, trying to focus my blurry eyes and scrambled attention through my tears, severe pain, confusion, and outrage. Jovan stood handsomely and powerfully on the wooden great table, wearing only tight black, spandex pants like British royalty might have worn under their pantaloons and robes. He had a hot, black leather vest on his upper torso through which his attractive, bare, hairy chest was partially visible. He wielded a long, thin, bloodied, bull whip. He had obviously donned a wig to mimic British royalty. He was really quite attractive physically and facially… but apparently looks were very deceiving. This man was cruel, a sexual sadist, and probably a lunatic!

"Damn it, Jovan! What the hell are you whipping me for?!" I yelled in rage. "This was not part of our agreement…!"

I didn't get any further. Jovan interrupted me in a loud, domineering voice.

"Silence, peasant! You do not speak to Jovan in that manner. Jovan is obeyed, not questioned! Further, from now on you will refer to me as 'the Dominator'!"

There was another loud, frightening crack. Before I could react to escape, another long, stinging pain came up the center of my back, from my buttocks to my neck. The tip of the bull whip roughed the hair up on the back of my head. It now felt like my entire back was on fire! I shrieked another primeval scream of agony and bowed again from the force of the strike.

Despite my pained and agonized condition and all of the blood, Jovan was suddenly all over me like an animal. He was rough and hurtful in his actions. He ripped my clothes off, pawing, molesting, and raping my body. Alternately he would strike the backs of my legs, my back, and my buttocks with the butt of the bull whip. He threw me down on the floor on my face and stomach and had his way with me over and over again. I don't even know whether he used a condom or not, it didn't feel like it. I was in such pain and displeasure that at the time I didn't even think or worry about it. I was more concerned with surviving this 'session'.

Jovan performed many varieties of sexual acts upon me, many perverse and disgusting. He then forced me at the end of the bull whip to perform the same acts on him. I was brutalized, traumatized, physically harmed and in pain, bleeding, and an emotional basket case shortly into our hour. I spent much time fighting the urge and need to pass out.

Such went my private sex session with Jovan the Dominator. His perverse sexual tastes and pleasures were fulfilled by totally dominating his partner emotionally, physically, and sexually. He also seemed to reap kinky and perverse pleasures from inflicting intense and agonizing pain on his partner and, to a lesser extent, himself. He was personally and sexually overpowering, intimidating, and humiliating, and he loved every minute of his mega-power trips. I did not enjoy this at all! Abject pain, rough and masochistic sex, and pleasure derived from beatings, intimidation, and humiliation did not mix in my book. I was not into S&M activities. They did not result in pleasurable sex for me in any way, shape, or form! By the end of the session I determined that I would never again service anyone who, like Jovan the Dominator, wanted to be in charge. I would not service them whether voluntarily, for management, or for pay!

By the time Jovan dismissed me about 8:45 I was 'raped', humiliated, ashamed, naked, in major pain, bleeding, and furious! I had welts on my back, buttocks, and on my legs; several of the welts had bled and now had scabs on them, and some were still bleeding. My suit had been shredded by Jovan's bull whip and his ripping and tearing at my clothing during sex. I reflected in shame, anger, and fear that I had been whipped and beaten to bloodshed, 'raped' for pay, forced to perform innumerable perverse and disgusting sexual acts on and with Jovan, threatened, and generally made to feel lower than a common whore. I was outraged that Jovan had done this to me, since it was not part of our verbal deal, nor was it allowed by any policy of my employer. I knew that I should report this to Mr. Richard. I also knew that I should tell Jovan that I was going to report him to management and that he would be banned from The Flamingo Lounge. However, I knew better than to stay after our session and argue this out with and threaten someone who had a bull whip and knew how to use it to a "t"! Jovan the Dominator was just too damn dangerous! I just wanted to get the hell out of there and back to my dressing suite. Then I wanted to go home to my Tyler!

I scurried around gathering up what was left of my ruined outfit, mentally doing the same for my shattered ego, pride, and emotional well-being. I used the shreds of cloth as some cover over my nakedness as I hurriedly left the room and Jovan the Dominator behind me. I moved as quickly as I could down the hallway toward my dressing room. I hoped I didn't run into anyone who would ask questions and want to call the ambulance, and I winced and cried out in the pain that any movement caused my welts and my anus. I felt like I had diarrhea and some was leaking out and down my leg. I looked at the location on the inside of my leg where it felt like liquid leaking from my anus. It was blood.

I quickly reached my dressing room. No one had seen or heard me. I was fortunate and happy that no one had. I painfully unlocked and opened the door and slipped inside. Hobbling over to my dresser, I took out a towel. I put the towel down on the nearest chair, and I carefully sat down. My body hurt all over! I put my head in my hands to rest. I still could feel blood seeping out of some of the welts and my anus. All were so agonizingly painful I almost couldn't stand it! Without a doubt this session had to have been the worst, the most painful and physically damaging, and the most humiliating one that I had EVER had here at The Flamingo Lounge.

I couldn't believe all of what I had been through on this work shift, in my 'home' away from home, The Flamingo Lounge! Tears came to my eyes as I seriously faced and contemplated the truth that my life had come down to this hell on earth. I was a voluntary sex slave to the sexually perverse, the sexually starved, the sex addicts, and the sexually abusive scum of society. But as evil, bad, misguided, and pathetic as these sex fiends were, I felt like I was far worse! I was the one who used, enabled, facilitated, and submitted to them! I was the idiot, the pervert who satisfied their sexual depravity and perversions for their filthy lucre! I was lower than the scum of society! I wiped the tears from my eyes and blew my nose as I gagged a few times. I felt overwhelmed with grief as I realized I may have reached rock bottom in my life. There had to be something better in and for my life than this existence!?

Surely I was better than this! I was a handsome and physically beautiful young man with my whole life ahead of me! Was it all going to be like this?! Was I to spend my whole life serving as the mattress pad, the boy toy, the tool, the slave, the condom to the sex maniacs of society?! Once I was too old, or no longer pleasing to the sex perverts, I knew they would discard me like used toilet paper! Were all workplaces like this? Discard employees when they became no longer useful, no longer money makers, or too highly paid?! Why did I stay here and submit myself to this kind of abuse? Was it true that only those who loathed themselves tolerated and stayed in this and similar employment abuse? Did I loathe myself? I didn't think so, but right now I didn't know!?

I knew that for anyone to endure this kind of treatment in the performance of their work was wrong and should not be tolerated. I knew I should just quit after what I had been through today. However, as much as I hurt physically, sexually, mentally, emotionally, and spiritually, the thought of looking for other employment immediately without having sufficient monies for me to support Tyler and me was a scarier proposition! If I quit The Flamingo Lounge now, Tyler and I would be homeless. I knew I could survive by going back to my male prostitution. However, Tyler wouldn't survive, and I couldn't support both him and me on my prostitute pay. I absolutely couldn't lose Tyler now, nor could I ask Tyler to become a male prostitute or live with me in a dumpy apartment or on the street! I knew he would just go home. I couldn't mentally, emotionally, and physically bear to lose Tyler now! I already loved him too passionately, and mentally and emotionally depended on him.

I pondered going to Mr. Richard, showing him my injuries, explaining what had happened, and filing a complaint and a police report. After all, it was Mr. Richard who had reprimanded all of us to report abuse to him and probably the police. However, as I thought about it I remembered that Mr. Richard's record of supporting his working waiters in their accusations of verbal, physical, and sexual abuse during the first years of my employment had been abysmal at best, and I realized I really would probably lose my job. I could think of several other instances and reasons I could not, or would not report this to management.

First of all, before Jovan had removed his body off my back the last time, let me up, and had pronounced our session over, he had hissed in my ear a threat on my life if I breathed a word of our session to anyone. He proclaimed he would search me down, whip me, rape me, torture me, and finally kill me. Based on how he had dominated me, debased me, hurt me, and over-powered me in our session, I believed him! I knew he was capable of anything, including my murder.

Secondly, I knew Mr. Richard probably would summon the police, and insist I go to the hospital. I didn't want to do either! I didn't want the attention of the authorities on me and my work. Ultimately Mr. Richard didn't either, and I knew that is why he would fire me if he knew of my injuries during this 'session'.

I concluded that I would just have to deal with this alone, keeping it secret from everyone, including Tyler, if that were possible. I knew now I would have to wear full body clothing home to be with Tyler so he wouldn't see my injuries.

I carefully rose because I needed a very stiff drink!

I crossed carefully to the wet bar, still grunting and groaning from pain on almost every step. I decided on a quadruple Long Island tea (if there were such a drink!?), which would be one of the strongest drinks I could make. I felt a glimmer of shame over my alcohol abuse, but I needed the alcohol to dull the pain I felt inside and outside of my body and psyche.

Still naked and bleeding some, I stood behind the wet bar and mixed my LIT. When I finished, I took a long, delicious, and relaxing dreg of it. I felt its warmth and relaxation sting my mouth and then wash down my throat, taking away my breath briefly. I soon would experience some relief from my physical pain, and the buzz would help me to deal with my feelings and emotions.

I slowly and deliberately crossed back over to my towel-covered chair and sat back down. I decided I needed a little more rest before I attempted a shower so I could go home… Oh shit! I remembered I had three more hours of waiting and busing tables before I could go home! How in the hell was I supposed to do my final three hours of work in this condition, in this pain! I wasn't sure, but I knew Mr. Richard would not let me leave early for no reason, not after refusing service to the ladies earlier in the forenoon, and then running over Olivia and breaking that tray and all those dishes.

I began psyching myself up to shower and then return to my work. I would stay liquored up to help with the pain, and then otherwise grin and bear it. It would be hard, but I knew I could do it. I had to do it! I remembered too that I had more left over vicodin in the cupboard in my dressing suite bathroom, and avatar in the refrigerator. That would help with the pain as well!

In no time at all I would be going home to my beautiful, desirable Tyler!

I arose carefully, painfully, and hobbled into the bathroom. Lord, I felt weak, in agony, and like shit! I wanted to get home now for some interaction with and comfort from Tyler! With all the pain I was suffering and how much I was missing Tyler I felt like crying, curling up in a pathetic, wounded, blubbering ball, and dying. My ability to deal with my current life situation was wearing thin.

In my restroom I glanced at my backside from my feet to my head in the surround sides mirror on the wall. I about blew chunks!

My back was red, angry, bloody, scabby, and in general looked almost like raw hamburger in some spots and strips. My buttocks were bloodied in streaks from the whipping. Scabs had formed on some welts. I felt like I had some hemorrhoids in my anus and, as I spread my cheeks, I could see scabs there too.

I twisted around and down so I could see the backs of my legs. They too were riddled with welts, some just red and angry, others bleeding and/or scabby.

I felt dizzy and faint, and my vision began to go. I realized I would go into shock and faint if I didn't resist it. I began to fight the darkness that threatened to swallow me.

Tears came to my eyes again. How could a homosexual do this to another homosexual or human being?! Homosexuals had enough hate, mistreatment, and prejudice focused on us from heterosexuals, let alone facing worse from fellow homosexuals. I didn't understand it! I detested it! I detested Jovan the Dominator for inflicting this on me! I would never agree to be dominated like I had been by Jovan, in a session again.

I opened the medicine cabinet and found the vicodin. They were 750-10s. I took out three and took them with a long dreg of LIT. I then took the vicodin out into my dressing room and put them in my knapsack that I would be taking home. I would need them there tonight!

I reentered the bathroom and guzzled the rest of the double LIT. I then drew a deep breath and prepared myself for my shower. I started the water running as my injuries prickled and burned.

It took me a while to shower, but presently and after a considerable amount of pain I was finished. I left the shower and gently dried myself off. I applied my deodorant and cologne again. I left the bathroom and took out an outfit of clean civilian underwear from my dresser. I retrieved a faux leather rather tight outfit that would show off my body, muscles and physique, hide my injuries, and wouldn't hurt too much. It also would not let the blood soak through.

My body felt like it was on fire as I carefully got dressed. Fortunately, I told myself, after private sessions shifts were always laid back and much more relaxing. It should be a breeze from now until midnight when I could go home and see my Tyler! I just had to have the stamina to endure. After the shower my backside looked better at least.

# CHAPTER 32

# ENTERTAINING ANGELS?

The cab ride home that Sunday from Tawny Bods was almost the cause of my demise. The cabbie seemed nice enough, but he sailed through two stop lights, jumped five curbs, and narrowly missed two pedestrians, a sign, a fire hydrant, and a large blue postal box. I clutched the car, bracing myself in place because it felt like the seat belt would not be sufficient to keep me safely in the back seat. I was so happy and thankful when he turned onto Wax Figure Lane and began to slow down for the approach to my building!

As we approached Candlestick Apartments building it was obvious something was going down there. I noticed there were fifteen or twenty people marching out front on the sidewalk with large signs and Illinois State and American flags. To distract myself from the cabbie's pathetic driving I strained to see what the signs said as we were still a few hundred feet away.

'Close this house of perversion!' read one sign that I could decipher first.

'This den of sin must go!' came into view.

'Candlestick houses sinners!'

'The tenants here give Aurora a bad name!'

'Close this brothel!'

'Close this sexual sewer!'

My immediate reaction and feeling was humiliation that my place of residence was being so attacked as a 'brothel' and 'sexual sewer'. Oh my God… gosh! Andrew never told me this might happen, and that our apartment complex had such a sullied reputation!

But humiliation didn't last very long. Next I became pissed and puzzled at the same time. I was pissed again at the mistaken rumors about Candlestick and the fact that the sentiments voiced on the signs so closely matched the gossip I had heard earlier at church from Polly Frome. I was pissed because of all the 'good Christian' people here spreading and perpetuating untrue gossip about Candlestick and its residents despite the fact that gossip was a cardinal sin. I was pissed that these brainwashed fools embarrassed me, and were judging me on where I lived rather than on the content of my character. I was pissed because they had the audacity to demand the destruction of my new home.

Were there any people I had seen at Grace Pentecostal Church this morning in this tiny demonstration? I couldn't tell because I didn't know anyone from the church, nor had I even remembered any faces to match with these demonstrators. Besides I had just had a very titillating and memory replacing experience with Neils at the Tawny Bods Fitness Center.

I was still angry, however, because it seemed these people who believed Candlestick housed sexual reprobates were wrongly judging me and my fellow tenants. In addition, assuming that Candlestick did house sex industry employees, these demonstrators were picketing the symptom of the problem not the source! They would make far better use of their time, and be far more effective were they searching out and picketing actual sex industry business establishments.

I was puzzled again, just as I had been all morning, over this issue of what type of people or employee predominated amongst the tenants of Candlestick. I had just this day, perused in the lobby some of the tenants. With a few exceptions, I had deemed the tenants I had seen as 'normal' people. I didn't recognize any obvious prostitutes, porn stars, or flaming gay men or women. I wondered where and how these 'concerned' citizen demonstrators had acquired the 'facts' upon which they were picketing?! Upon what evidence or information were these picketers judging all tenants at Candlestick to be sex industry employees?! Why did they think that 'all' residents of Candlestick like myself were perverts? How dare they judge me, let alone everyone else! How dare they paint us all with one untrue brush! It took a lot of gall on their part to judge all of us residents here without first getting to know us!

This whole issue was infuriating, frustrating, and puzzling! And it was still humiliating, embarrassing, and instigating doubts and fears.

My taxi pulled up in front of the beautiful Candlestick Apartments building and stopped. The demonstrators were now right outside the vehicle between me and the door. I had seen many news clips of demonstrations where the demonstrators were abusive, ugly, and cruel to people who lived or worked in the buildings they were picketing or stalking. I worried a bit about what to expect. Would they be verbally and/or physically abusive to me? Would they prevent me from entering the building in which I made my home? Would they mob me? Would they just ignore me? I certainly hoped the latter! I steeled myself, however, for the worst, and with my mind being occupied over dealing with the danger and potential ugliness, I didn't concentrate any attention on the taxi driver.

The seemingly nice driver was a large, malodorous, gruff man in his fifties who spoke with a Brooklyn accent. He turned, looked in his rear-view mirror at me, and barked:

"The fayer is ten dahllars and fifty-seven cents, son!"

I was shocked. Was he kidding?! I realized my mouth had dropped open in surprise. I closed it.

"P… par… pardon m… me?!" I stuttered incredulously, intimidated also by the man's domineering aura, self assurance, voice tone, and size. His arms above the elbow were the diameter of small pumpkins, and his chest was barrel-shaped.

"The fayer is ten dahllars and fifty-seven cents, son!" The taxi driver repeated impatiently.

"Don't you think that is a little steep for eight blocks of travel?! That seems a bit much, especially when you traversed it at such a high rate of speed!" I croaked in a quiet, perplexed, and bewildered voice.

"The fayer is ten dahllars and fifty-seven cents!" The driver growled firmly.

"But a taxi from your same company took me from Candlestick here, to the Tawny Bods Fitness Center where you picked me up, for five dollars and twenty-one cents not three hours ago! What is the deal with you charging me so much more for the same trip and exact same distance?!" I demanded reproachfully.

"The deal is, chump, that you owe me the fayer. The fayer is ten dahllars and fifty-seven cents!" The driver was getting visibly angry. He was acting now with condescension toward me.

I, too, was becoming angry and was waxing defensive and rebellious!

"I can't believe this, sir! This is highway robbery! Fares couldn't have risen over five dollars in the last three or four hours! What gives?!" I exclaimed angrily. I was jealous of what money I had! I just didn't want to throw it around on over priced goods and services. If I would have known this, that this cabby would charge me so much, I would have hailed a cab from a different company.

"What gives is you youts don't like to pay your bills! The fayer is..." The driver repeated, teeth clenched as he glared at me in seething rage.

"I know! I know!" I interrupted. "The fayer is ten dahllars and fifty-seven cents!" I mocked his accent out of rebellion and a growing disrespect for him.

I could not believe he was gouging me in cost for my trip home versus the other taxi!

With betrayed reluctance, anger, and muttering to myself, I reached in my pocket and took out my wallet and change purse. I counted out the change and took out a five and five ones. I counted it into the driver's hand, and then scooted toward the door. I wanted to get home! I wished Andrew were waiting for me!

From the front seat the driver cleared his throat loudly. Warily and somewhat petulantly I turned to see if he were all right, or were in need of assistance. The burly driver sat there looking at me sternly and expectantly while holding his hand out palm up. I gave him a fake smile.

"Thank you, sir, for your ride!" I spoke as positively as I could muster and smiled wanly again. I opened the door and swung one foot out onto the sidewalk.

Again the driver cleared his throat loudly. I stopped, looked down and bit my lip angrily. Slowly I turned to look at him. Somewhat to my surprise, he still sat there looking at me expectantly with his hand held out palm up. The only difference was that he was now frowning intimidatingly at me.

I puzzled over what he wanted?! We never had this situation in Gurnee. In Gurnee we would never sell a product or service to someone and then hold out a hand for… for… for what?! In Gurnee we paid our fare for service to the one taxi cab company in the county and left.

Suddenly I realized I had forgotten my back pack. Maybe that was what the cabbie was trying to tell me?!

"Oh! My back pack. Thank you, sir, for telling me I was forgetting something!" I grabbed the bag, shook the driver's out-stretched hand, and threw my other foot out onto the sidewalk. I grabbed the taxi cab roof to hoist myself out of the car.

Again the disgruntled driver cleared his throat, the sound coming out almost in a roar like a lion. His outburst scared the hell out of me since I considered our business relationship terminated. I was getting pissed, as well as perplexed. What the hell did he want! I turned angrily and in irritation to look at him.

"What now?!" I held both hands up and shrugged. Under the circumstances, with this baboon making demands of me which I did not understand, I was now frowning and glaring at the cabbie.

"Are you gonna grease the palm, or what, son!?" The cabbie asked rudely.

He wanted me to put lotion on his hands? I thought a moment before I remembered I did carry some lotion around in my back pack to use on any rash or jock itch I may develop during exercise. It might assuage the cabbie's dry hands. I opened my pack and found the lotion. I took off the cap, reached up to the cabbie's hand, and squeezed out a generous portion onto his palm.

The cabbie's face bore at first a look of surprise, but it quickly changed to a countenance of ferocious anger. He violently shook the lotion off of his hand onto the floor of the front passenger side seat. Angrily he turned on me.

"What are you some kind of wisenheimer!? A moron?!" He was basically spitting his words out. I was totally taken aback and confused. "The tip, you idiot! The tip! I want my tip!" The cabbie yelled at me.

"Tip about what?!" I wasn't thinking clearly now in any way, shape, or form because of some fear of this guy, and it did not dawn on me he might want money for himself. We never asked for extra money in Gurnee.

"The tip! Money you give me as a bonus for driving your stupid ass home, you idiot!" The cabbie snarled and glowered at me.

"Oh!" I began to feel hot as I blushed. I felt stupid! Tips were almost unheard of in Gurnee. Maybe we would tip a waitress, but not a cabbie.

However, I was also instantly pissed! This money grubber had already charged me over five dollars more than the other cabbie had charged for the same distance, and now he wanted a tip?! 'No way in hell!' I thought angrily. 'I'll give him a non-monetary tip!'

"Take your tip out of the more than five dollars that you overcharged me on the cab fare, sir!" I exclaimed coldly and firmly. I turned quickly to the door.

I jumped out to the sidewalk, turned, and slammed the door. The cabbie swore, flipped me the bird, put the taxi in drive, and pealed tires showing his anger and displeasure as he was driving off in front of me. I whirled around and started to walk toward the door of Candlestick, pissed at the cabbie's rudeness and nerve!

I had taken three steps to cross the wide sidewalk parallel to the building when I heard a dog yip and carry on like it was in severe pain. At that moment through my shoe I felt the unevenness of the 'ground' I was on, and I immediately stumbled, looking down as I struggled to stay on my feet. I had stepped on a little toy poodle.

I was so shocked that I completely lost my footing. I fell forward onto the grass just off the sidewalk toward the building. As I was falling, I heard a haughty female voice with a British accent cry:

"Oh, Lulu, you poor, poor dear! Did the 'blind', mean, thoughtless, and naughty lad step on my little poopsie!?"

I rolled as I fell and landed, and came to rest in a sitting position. I quickly glanced up at the lady who had spoken, and then did a double take.

Before me stood a stout, pudgy, white-haired, yet dignified lady in a ritzy, dazzling green dress, a white mink fur wrap, with spectacles perched on her nose. She held a yelping toy poodle close to her generous bosom. The poodle yipped as it also licked the woman's chin and mouth. For her part, the woman looked reproachfully down her nose at me. She was definitely well-to-do, and apparently dressed to rub it in the face of everyone she encountered wherever she went. She was gaudy, obviously prideful and vain, and probably a busy-body checking up on this demonstration outside my apartment building.

"I… I am so… I… I mean I am so clumsy… I mean… Ma'am I am so sorry!" I stammered in embarrassment. "I didn't see your dog, Ma'am, and I am… I was… I am afraid I stepped on her! Is she all right?"

The lady looked at her toy poodle and assumed a pouty sympathetic countenance as she addressed her dog.

"Is poopsie all right!? Did bad boy hurt her too much?!" She frowned at me. If looks could kill, I would have been dead on the spot. "I think you'll survive, Lulu!" She cooed.

She looked at me again with anger and contempt glinting in her eyes.

"Young man, you are an ogre! A cad!" The lady huffed condescendingly. Her eyes sparked and she gave me a very dirty look. "I am an icon in this neighborhood! I am Mrs. Arnold Pompadora, and you have just stepped on the heir to my estate, Lulu Pompadora!" She scoffed at me then, and continued. "What pathetic excuse do you have to say in your defense that might make any sense or excuse your uncouth and careless behavior!?"

I blinked and gave her a look of surprise and disbelief. I sat there a minute marveling at this haughty, self-absorbed woman accosting me. Who in the hell was she to make those judgments about me, someone she didn't even know!? What made her think she was better than I?!

"I am so sorry, Ma'am, again! I wasn't… I mean… well… I wasn't looking when I exited the taxi!" I stood up. "I didn't mean to step on your dog!" I looked at her apologetically as I stood up, brushed myself off, and straightened my clothing.

"Dog?!" Mrs. Pompadora gasped and bristled. "Dog!? You dare call my Lulu a 'dog'?!" She stuck her nose up in the air and huffed again, looking down her nose at me as if I were rancid meat.

I shrugged and looked at her questioningly.

"Well, it is a dog, is it not?" I asked matter-of-factly.

"Well, I never! Now you call my little girl, Lulu, an 'it'?! First you call her a 'dog', and then you refer to her as an 'it'!" Mrs. Pompadora approached me and stuck a finger in my face. "You, young man, are an impudent, ill-mannered, uncaring narcissist! All you can think about is yourself! I am shocked by your treatment of my Poopsie! I ought to report you to the authorities!" She hugged Lulu to her bosom, glaring at me.

"I am sorry, Mrs. Pompadora! I didn't mean to insult you or Lulu!" I exclaimed out of a feeling of civility and training in the obligation to be patient and nice to difficult people. At this point I actually was sorely tempted to flip her the bird and tell her off, but I restrained myself.

It was by now abundantly clear that I could do no more to satisfy the bitch Pompadora, so I decided it was time to go. I apologized again to her as she sneered at me and then I turned to go back toward the Candlestick doors, noticing that the demonstrators up and down the sidewalk had begun to chant in their protest. I paused a minute to hear what they were saying.

"Hey, Hey! Ho, Ho! The tenants here have got to go!" They repeated over and over again.

I frowned angrily. Their chant pissed me off totally! These misinformed, idiot gossips, and busy-body 'Christians' (and I used the name loosely!) were ruining the reputation of all residents who lived here at Candlestick! The bad attention, lies, and media scrutiny that these malcontent, 'better than thou' demonstrators were bringing to us good people and our homes were devastating and despicable. They were making spectacles of us tenants, labeling us perverts, and themselves as uneducated protesters.

I took one furious step to resume my trek to the door.

"Young man!?" Mrs. Pompadora called contemptuously.

I turned back around to face her warily and with trepidation. She was still standing where I had left her. She glared at me down her nose, which I noted sardonically could not possible go any higher into the air.

"Yes, Mrs. Pompadora?" I asked with complete false respect and politeness. She was a bitch and I was already sick of her! I managed to smile at her. It took all I could do to be nice to her.

"Do you... do you... live here!?" Mrs. Pompadora pointed at Candlestick, acting and speaking like she were trying to avoid contact with something so vile that it was toxic.

"Yes, I live here!" I exclaimed a little defensively. "What's it to you?!" I couldn't restrain myself any longer and I became a bit lippy.

Mrs. Pompadora huffed and stiffened as she looked at me with the greatest of disdain. There was no love lost or squandered between us! I felt the same about her as she did me.

"Don't you see these demonstrators, young man?!" Mrs. Pompadora motioned toward the now probably 40 to 50 people marching up and down the sidewalk along the way in front of Candlestick. "They do not want your kind in our neighborhood, or our city for that matter! This... This..." Mrs. Pompadora looked the façade of Candlestick up and down briefly with utter contempt. "This... this place is a den of iniquity! It houses the scum of society! It is housing for those involved in the sex industry and sundry sex related endeavors including pornography, prostitution, and drugs that the tenants here brought with them when this building was built and they moved in! If you are living here, young man, you must be a sexual deviant and/or a sinner as well! I wouldn't be caught dead living here!"

"Mrs. Pompadora." I began as quietly and calmly as I could muster, biting my tongue so I wouldn't sound as mad and lippy as I felt like speaking to her. "If you were dead you would be baking painfully in Hades because of your gossip, pride, un-Christian attitude, vanity, and judgmentalism. Candlestick would then be a step up for you and your sins!"

"Well, I never!" Mrs. Pompadora huffed, sticking her nose up in the air again. "You are so uncouth, so uncivilized, so... so... so rude, young man! With your savage behavior, disrespect for your elders, and pathetic untrained attitude I'm sure that you fit in well with the unwashed, unrepentant, anti-Christ filth and pond scum that lives here in Candlestick!"

With that last insult Mrs. Pompadora stalked off down the sidewalk, carrying her Lulu with her. I sneered at her, shook my head in disgust, and turned to walk toward the Candlestick doors.

I managed two more feet into the grass.

I did not realize that, in my anger at Mrs. Pompadora, I was not registering that which my eyes were seeing. Likewise I did not realize the force with which I whirled around and tried to begin walking. Consequently I did not see him when I turned around to head toward the Candlestick doors. I walked full bore into a man carrying a Christian flag, who stood directly behind me. I felt the collision and a millisecond after it realized I had walked into someone. I jumped in surprise and embarrassment and fell back, propelled by my forward momentum that had been forced now to focus in the opposite direction. I lost my balance, falling hard on my ass in the grass again. I looked up and gulped involuntarily.

I had run into a man. His Christian flag fluttered and flowed often to full length open despite the fact that there wasn't currently a wind strong enough to cause it to act so. The man was a blond, his hair curly and shoulder length. He was probably 35 years old, handsome, and his face bore a countenance of complete love and compassion. The weird thing was that from his entire body there seemed to emanate a bright glow. He was surrounded by enough glow so as its light was visible in the clear light of the sunny day! I was dumbfounded for a few moments. Where did his glow come from?! He was, or at least appeared to be, human. Humans do not glow! This man, however, glowed brightly, shading my sun glasses more than the sun.

I sat there in the yard in front of Candlestick and stared at this... this... beautiful glowing man for a few seconds. I was speechless. I gulped involuntarily. For his part, the glowing man smiled at me, transmitting clearly to me feelings of love, compassion, kindness, and security.

"I am... sir, I am... I wasn't... I didn't mean..." I gulped again involuntarily as I searched for my voice. "I am sorry I... I am sorry I ran into you! I wasn't..."

The glowing man smiled even more meaningfully and interrupted by waving me to silence. His flag continued flying and unfurling in the non-existent wind. He looked directly into my eyes, seemed to look into my very soul, nodded in affirmation, and spoke.

"Tyler Aaron Belmont, Dion, God loves you!" His voice was mellifluous, comforting, firm, and loving. He oozed all the Christ-like qualities that man strives to develop over years of spiritual growth. I felt instantly at peace! I was speechless as I gazed at him, transfixed and unable to move.

The glowing man held out a smooth, clear-skinned, and physically beautiful helping hand to me. His broad smile faded, but he still gazed kindly and encouragingly at me.

"Tyler Aaron Belmont, Dion, let me help you!?" He spoke again. His beautiful voice washed over me like a wave of peace, reassuring me of God's love.

In a daze, I grabbed his hand, and he easily and smoothly pulled me up to stand in front of him. He was a couple of inches taller than I. His beautiful brown eyes seemed to penetrate and search my soul. He smiled sweetly at me again, still holding my hand tenderly.

I was still staring at him, speechlessly. He was so… so… so strange, yet he was so… so… so normal! It was hard to explain. He frightened me with his glowing body… yet everything about him, including his glow, comforted and reassured me. Who was he? What did he want? Why wouldn't he let me go once I was standing? How did he know my full name and my parents' nickname for me?! Was I wearing it on a sign? On my forehead? Did he read my mind?! Did he have ESP?

"I don't know you from Adam, sir! How do you know my full name and nickname?!" I finally was able to exclaim in disbelief and incredulity.

"Tyler Aaron Belmont, Dion, God knows all! He is all knowing and omniscient. Everyone who is God's child will know much that will mystify those who are not His children!" The man smiled, and I felt like I was looking directly into Heaven, into pure love. This man was… he was… well, he was lovely! Heavenly! God forgive me, but he was hot!

However, it did sound somewhat to me like he were speaking to me in riddles.

"I don't understand?!" I managed to utter, as I looked curiously at the... well, the man who stood gazing back at me. He reminded me of an angel. Was he an angel?! He glowed! He appeared surreal! He seemed to appear out of nowhere?! I knew, however, that he was just a gifted Christian man... wasn't he?! Angels did not appear in visible form in real life, did they?!

"Tyler, God knows all. He is All. He was, He is, and He is to come." Glowing Man spoke patiently as he took my right hand in both of his. "Do you believe that, Tyler?"

"Well... yes... I do! Of course!" I was still struggling a bit to speak in this man's presence. I was still disoriented, conflicted... in fear of this... this 'man', and yet comforted and at peace in his presence.

"God shares knowledge with His children, knowledge that those who are not His children do not know, or understand." Glowing Man squeezed my hand. "Do you believe that too, Tyler?"

"Y... yes. Christians do tend to be prescient." I was beginning to maybe understand.

"I am a child of God, like you, Dion." Glowing man let go of me and held his flag pole again with both hands. The wind still blew only on his Christian flag, and I could see no signs of it in his hair, clothing, the bushes, or other environmental accoutrements nearby. I myself was now hot and sweating. "Unlike you, Tyler, the Holy Spirit is in residence in me, and it is through the Holy Spirit that God shares special knowledge with me and others like me."

"Oh!" I exclaimed breathlessly and thoughtfully. "I think I understand..." I actually did slightly understand, but I was strangely puzzled in that understanding. What exactly did he mean when he said that the Holy Spirit was in residence inside him?

"Tyler, I have come from 'I Am' with a special and urgent message for you. God wants you to know that you are in great spiritual danger." The man's expression was one of great concern, but still his heavenly looks beamed from the love of God and love infused his words. "Your spiritual life is in danger here in Aurora! You must focus on God, through His Word, the Bible, and a strong prayer life! You must continue to go to the church you attended this morning, regularly. You must seek out Christian fellowship there. You must get your life grounded completely in God again. You must nurture Godly relationships."

All of the questions and disorientation in my emotions, mind, and spirit kind of blocked me from quite accepting his message immediately. Who was this... messenger?!

"Who are you?!" I asked in a cracking, somewhat fearful voice.

"Who I am is of no real consequence. My message from God is of utmost importance for you to focus on, know, and remember! However, I will tell you my name if it will impress my message upon and into your tripartite being more solidly, to emphasize upon you the urgency and validity of my message. I am, when I am present here in the flesh, called Landon Whitmore, child of The Most High God." The handsome blond glowed even more strongly as if God himself were affirming his words. "You must heed the Word of God, read the Word of God, pray to Him, and follow His precepts, or you will fall into sins here at Candlestick, Tyler, Dion!"

His words hit home for some reason and disquieted me considerably. Unfortunately they also instigated a tremendous amount of questions on my part so that I might fully understand the message.

"What sins?! What are you talking about? Who the hell are you, Landon? From where do you come?!" I responded, bewildered and frustrated that he was speaking in what seemed to me to be such ethereal and ambiguous words.

"Exactly who or what I am and where from which I come are not important. As for sins, I am talking about the sins of relationships, associations, and activities, Tyler! God has determined what relationships, associations, and activities are acceptable and Biblical to Him and for His children. There are some of those things that are not acceptable or Biblical, they are an abomination to God, and a threat to your eternal soul. You are close, Tyler, to embarking upon some relationships, associations, and activities here in Aurora that are sinful. You need to avoid these things! You need to get back to church, Dion! You need to renew your devotional and prayer life." Landon glowed strongly for a moment, and then waned a bit.

It was clear that Landon was very wise, much wiser than I, and I appreciated that fact… However, it was also frustrating, coming as it did out of nowhere. I felt broadsided… confused… Why in the hell didn't Landon speak in plain terms and lay his message out simply for me to see and understand?! I didn't know what Landon meant!?

I closed my eyes. I didn't want to be angry and rude like I felt like being when next I spoke.

"What the hell are you talking about, Mr. Whitmore!? What sinful relationships, associations, and activities are they upon which I am about to embark?! Will you please tell me what the hell you are exactly, from where do you come, and please clearly explain your message?!" I asked angrily as I opened my eyes.

"Well, if that is your attitude, I don't want to talk to or get to know you either!" A young man responded in anger, glaring at me reproachfully.

Before me was a young man about my age, with brown hair and cute features. He was slender, but had a nice manly figure. His voice was a bit high pitched, but he was sincere. His hand was extended to me but, when he finished rebuking me, he withdrew his hand and frowned at me.

I was chagrined and embarrassed.

"I am so… I am so sorry… ah… who… whoever you are!" I stuttered, looking around curiously for Landon. "I am a… I am confused over recent events. I am afraid I may have been ill-mannered and hasty in my responses because I was talking to… I thought you were… there was another man here… a blond, handsome, 35 year old… I was talking to him. I am so sorry I took after you… ah…. I thought you were… Sorry!"

"You thought I were who?" My new compatriot gazed curiously at me.

For my part I looked up and down the street and around the yard for Landon.

"I thought you were… you were Landon Whitmore…" My voice trailed off as I saw how confused my new friend was. "The glowing man… a bit taller than I… blond…? The man I was talking to when… when you… must have… walked up?"

I gave the guy a hopeful, pleading look as I trailed off again. He shook his head vigorously and looked at me as though I were crazy.

"You were alone gazing at Candlestick here when I walked up to meet you. You were muttering to yourself, but no one was near you or talking to you. I thought you were thinking out loud about the apartments here or the demonstration." The brown-haired young man explained, shaking his head and giving me a strange look.

"He had a Christian flag flapping in the wind? He held my hand?" I stopped as I again saw some alarm, confusion, and curiosity fill the guy's face.

"No, you were definitely alone! And, dude, there is no wind today!" My new friend replied, shaking his head again in apparent wonderment.

"Well, I am sorry I bit your head off! I thought you were… I was talking to… well, I thought I was talking to a very… very frustrating man…" I stammered, completely mystified and very embarrassed. 'I must look and sound really stupid!' I thought, blushing in my self-consciousness. I peered up and down the street one more time for Landon Whitmore, but he was gone. He had like disappeared! How could he vanish amongst the demonstrators so quickly?! And how come this nice looking guy in front of me hadn't seen him?!

"Again, I am sorry…" I focused on the guy in front of me. He was very cute and buff. He carried a sign that read 'We don't want these sexual perverts in Aurora!'

"Apology accepted!" The young man held out his hand again and smiled broadly at me.

I focused on my new conversationalist.

"My name is Austin Baker. What is yours?" He asked.

"Tyler, Tyler Belmont." I smiled back as I shook his hand. "No hard feelings?" I asked tentatively.

"No!" Austin chuckled and shook his head. "I forgive others as Christ forgave me! No hard feelings. Friendships are hard to make, let alone keep. Life is far too short and precious to hold grudges and bad feelings against our fellow man. God did not want us to judge others in that way!"

There was a brief pause as we both watched the demonstrators. Then Austin turned to me, bearing a countenance of concern and a desire to help me on his visage.

"In response to your question, 'What sinful relationships, associations, and activities are they upon which I am about to embark' I have a response, Tyler. Care to hear it?" Austin focused questioningly and honestly on my face. He was like an open book. He was a Christian. For some strange reason I did want to 'read' him.

"Sure, Austin." I responded blandly, smiling at him. "What is your theory? Take your best shot!"

I couldn't see his response having anything to do about what Landon was talking! How could Austin give me any insight on a conversation to which he was not a party?!

"If you live here, Tyler…" Austin rejoined, frowning at me seriously, "you may be about to embark on any one of several kinds of sinful relationships, associations, or activities. Heterosexual, prostitution, homosexual, sex industry, pornography, drugs, dealing, pimping, sex masseuse, escort service, drinking, gambling, etcetera, etcetera. All kinds of sexual perverts and sinful souls live here at Candlestick and other apartments like it!" Austin shook his head, and waved at the demonstrators. "That is why we are here today demonstrating, Tyler. We are sick of having these sexual perverts define our community, culture, and societal mores as evil or non-existent. We are tired of the residents of these apartments blackballing us for prospective residents and tourists. We have to draw the line somewhere!"

I was shocked! 'His response could very well be the correct response! That could well be what Landon was trying to tell me!' I thought. At least it may be correct if I actually believed all these people who claimed that sexual perverts, sex industry employees, and sundry law-breakers were the only tenants of Candlestick.

However, I still didn't buy that gossip about my fellow tenants. What denigrating, destructive bunk!

"Austin…" I said somewhat condescendingly. "Honestly… how do you people know that all, or the majority of tenants here at Candlestick are sexual perverts, deviants, sex industry employees, and those who break the law? Do you have any proof? Can you prove it to me? I know I am clean of those charges! I am not in any of those groups of deplorables, my brother isn't, and I know of no one in Candlestick that is in one of those groups. Really! I think this is all just idle and sinful gossip and a violation of the commandment not to bear false witness against thy neighbor."

"Proof?!" Austin exclaimed, snickering a bit. He stopped snickering quickly when I frowned at him. "How long have you lived here in Candlestick Apartments, Tyler?" Austin queried kindly.

"Two days and two nights." I responded honestly. "Why? What does that have to do with who lives here?"

"With whom are you living here at Candlestick, Tyler?" Austin questioned, turning to watch someone leaving the apartment building.

I followed his eyes. I recognized instantly the shapely young lady in a tight red dress leaving the building. She was Stefanie Fanille Miles, the one who had introduced herself to me earlier and then proceeded to hit on me.

"My brother, Andrew Di..." I began.

"You see that blond woman in the tight red dress, Tyler?" Austin interrupted. "Do you know who that is?"

I scrutinized her again, wondering why her awesome figure did little or nothing for me emotionally, physically, or sexually. Curious, I looked back at Austin.

"Yes, actually I do." I replied. "I met her just this morning. She is Stefanie Fanille Miles. Why?"

Austin turned to fully face me again. He stared seriously into my eyes. I found him very believable and trustworthy.

"Stefanie Fanille Miles is a current star of hard core heterosexual and lesbian pornography videos. She works at a studio called 'Wet Dreams' in Naperville, Illinois." Austin looked at me like a lawyer cinching a case.

"Are you sure?!" I asked him doubtfully. "She is so classy and obviously rich! How do you know this?"

"Her videos are currently the biggest sellers in adult bookstores in surrounding communities. Some of us," he motioned to the demonstrators, "have done actual visits to these adult bookstores. We picket them, too! Anyway, yes Miss Miles is classy. That is her shtick in her videos. And yes, she is very rich. She makes a lot of money doing her evil work!" Austin studied me as I looked at him in surprise.

"I didn't mean to interrupt you, Tyler! I'm sorry. Now with whom did you say you lived, Tyler, here at Candlestick?" Austin requested again.

"My brother, Andrew DiPree..." I answered slowly, lost in thought.

"Is he in the phone book, Tyler?" Austin asked.

"Yes..." I replied, turning to meet his gaze. "Why?"

"Could we get together sometime?" Austin asked. "I would like to discuss this further with you, give you more proof. But I have to get back now to the demonstration. Can we have dinner or something soon?"

"Sure!" I smiled. "I'd like that! I need more good friends here in Aurora! Good Christian friends that is!"

"Great, Tyler!" Austin thrust out his hand. "I'm glad we met, and I will be in touch soon."

I shook his hand heartily.

He released my hand, smiled and waved, and then ran to the sidewalk, waving his sign and chanting.

I smiled and waved back. How odd it was that I had struck up a friendship with the 'enemy' here in Aurora! Oh well! He was now my friend... my Christian friend.

I gazed around now at the demonstration. The 45 to 50 people assembled carried more Biblical signs condemning the residents of Candlestick and their professions as sexual freaks, perverts, scum, and reprobates. I was sure they were all screwed up! I felt insulted and disgusted at their myopic, parochial, and purist thoughts and opinions. However, having met Austin who seemed level-headed and normal, I did wonder more about the veracity of these people's claims. I shook my head now in wonderment and confusion.

I looked around again for the curly-haired, blond cutie, Landon Whitmore, who had talked to me initially. He was not to be found among the demonstrators. I was flabbergasted! Maybe I had imagined him?! To where in hell could he disappear so quickly?! I had only closed my eyes for a few seconds or so at the most!

I headed toward the entrance doors to Candlestick. What had this Landon meant? I was about to embark on various 'sins' here where I lived? Sins of what?! With whom!? He hadn't told me. What a jerk! I shook my head. He had not given me word one on who and what to avoid! His advice had been vague but simple; Get back to church, read the Bible, start up my daily devotions, and get back right with God. I felt fine with God already. I knew these other things were all goals that I needed to do, and I would do them in time. When I had the time I would start up daily devotions, continue attending church, and improve my prayer life. Right now I was busy settling in with Andrew and trying to establish my life here in Aurora. God would understand?!

# CHAPTER 33

# DOCTOR BELMONT

I quickly passed through Candlestick's large lobby and went directly to the elevators. All the while I pondered Landon's words: I was in spiritual danger here at Candlestick, that I would potentially fall into a variety of sins here at Candlestick, and that I was 'close to embarking upon several things' that were sins. Then, when Austin had 'answered' my question about what was meant by Landon that I was about to embark upon sinful relationships, associations, and activities, Austin had included among the possible sexual sins present here at Candlestick homosexuality. That was no coincidence, I was sure! Was God trying to tell me to refuse to commit to anything more with Andrew?! Was He trying to slap me in the face with His truth that same-sex love was a sin?! Was same-sex love indeed a sin?! I realized that I needed to do much study and perhaps counseling about these subjects!

I pressed the 'up' button for the elevator.

The only conclusion that I could draw from Landon's message, juxtaposed with Austin's words, was that Landon was warning me against further developing and entering into a deeper and an intimate relationship with Andrew. Nothing toward that end had actually been said by either, but clearly Landon and Austin were two guys who believed that relationships between two men or two women were sinful. With my insecurity about God's view of my sexual orientation I automatically jumped to an anti-gay twist to the events. I was sure that they believed such relationships were, as the Bible did say somewhere in the Old Testament, an abomination to God. They called it 'homosexuality', as I would have perhaps when I was younger and less exposed to the world; certainly I used to call it 'homosexuality' before I really started looking at and being attracted to guys. With my shoes perhaps on the correct feet, I was now, I realized with surprise and some chagrin, rejecting that word for the phrase 'committed, monogamous same-sex relationship.' The 'H' word didn't apply to Andrew and me!?

The elevator dinged again and the door opened. I stepped to the door and scanned quickly inside it searching for the young exhibitionist. I really did not want to see him again! Discovering he wasn't in this elevator, I entered, pressed the eighth floor button, closed the door, and stepped to the back wall to continue studying Landon's words.

I didn't want to hear or believe that Landon's warning had anything to do about my potential to enter a 'relationship' with Andrew and that it would be a 'sin'. I knew Landon had spoken only of 'sinful relationships, associations, and activities', but my uncertainty, fear, and insecurity told me that in my case he meant 'same-sex relationships'; he meant Andrew and me. I was torn between Landon, God, Austin, and my strongly and steadily growing feelings for Andrew. Was 'same-sex love' a sin? Why did I have these feelings for Andrew? Why did I take more pleasure in checking out and watching men than women? Why did I want to be Andrew's lover? Did God make me a pervert? Why was I more attracted to some men than to most women?

I now questioned and didn't believe a committed, life-long, monogamous relationship between two members of the same-sex like Andrew and me was 'homosexuality'. I believed 'homosexuality' and 'homosexual' referred to a person who engaged in same-sex relations multiple times a night, week, or month with multiple different partners. I pictured and believed a homosexual to be basically a same-sex prostitute or tramp.

In my own desires, longings, and plans for Andrew and me as a couple, I believed we were building a monogamous heterosexual-like relationship. I supposed you could call it a… ah… well… how about a hetero… I thought for several seconds before my name for my hoped and longed for relationship with Andrew came to my mind. What Andrew and I were hopefully developing and building was a monogamous spousal relationship. Lord willing maybe one day we would be each other's spouse. We were not gay, or homosexuals, we were monogamous spouses!

The fact of the matter was I did have feelings for, desires for, and longings for handsome men much more than I did beautiful women. Now Andrew had come into my life, and I was falling... falling hard and fast... for him. I already only had eyes for... and pretty much only thoughts about Andrew. I didn't look much at any other men any more, to ogle their physique and think about... think about being alone... being naked... with them.

I couldn't help it. I was attracted to gorgeous men with beautifully masculine physiques, especially Andrew! I wanted him... I longed for him! I wanted him inside and outside of me! God had obviously made me this way; He was the only Creator after all! I refused to consider or believe that God made me this way on purpose knowing I would have a lifelong struggle with a sin that He implanted. If He did, it was a cruel joke! I knew too, that God didn't make mistakes. He was perfect. So I couldn't be a mistake! Therefore my hoped for and planned monogamous spousal relationship with Andrew couldn't be a sin, for if it were, then God was either a cruel Creator, or capable of making mistakes!

The elevator dinged and the door opened. I exited quickly to the hallway, brushing past two women in tube tops, miniskirts, and high heels who were carrying classy clutch purses and wearing long strings of pearls. I mumbled an apology to them and scurried to our apartment.

As I unlocked our apartment door, I longed for Andrew to be waiting inside. I could see his soft, tousled blond curls, gorgeously sculpted and handsome face, and buff, shapely male body seated in front of the entertainment center. He would look up at me and smile one of his lusty, melting smiles, and say 'Hi, Tyler'. Then he would stand up, quickly cross the floor to stand in front of me, grab my buttocks, and press my crotch into his crotch. Then he would... he... he would begin kissing me. Ahhh! My body ached for Andrew and I was developing a woody. I had to stop!

What?! What the hell was I thinking! Here I was, a Christian, sinfully fantasizing about Andrew. It was wrong! At least what precious little my church and Christian upbringing had contributed to the subject claimed that my lust and desires for a love relationship with Andrew were wrong. They never offered much proof. However, I had to stand on what little I knew the Word of God said about same-sex love, and God said that

Andrew and I would be in sin if we acted on our love, our lust, despite my opinions to the contrary. Therefore it, our potential romantic relationship, and we were wrong, and moving toward a sin.

Sodom and Gomorrah of the Bible were destroyed by God because the men of the city practiced sex with other men. The men of the city even tried to rape two men of God visiting the cities and would have succeeded were it not for Lot hiding them in his home. The men of the two cities wanted to 'know' the two visitors sexually. God punished both cities by destroying them with fire and brimstone! At least that is how this event was preached by 'religion'.

Why didn't this episode that I remembered from the Bible concerning same-sex intimacy 'scare me straight'? Why did I still love Andrew so?! If this were indeed a 'relationship, association, or activity' of sin about which Landon spoke, I was in trouble! Was my developing relationship with Andrew really and truly what Landon meant when he talked about me being close to 'embarking on... sins'? I hoped and believed not!? I didn't consider my feelings and desires for Andrew as homosexual. I was not a homosexual!

I swung the door open and entered our apartment. I turned expectantly, but not too excitedly, to the couch in front of the entertainment center. No Andrew, I noticed sadly, but not with surprise. I hung my head in loneliness and longing for Andrew. I didn't care what Landon and Austin thought or believed. I love... I was... I longed for... I loved... Andrew! Yes, I loved him romantically! 'Lord, make me right?! Andrew and I are Biblically okay?!' I thought with desire and passion... with concern and fear.

I had such an internal Biblical and moral battle going on inside. I realized I had a big time love crush on Andrew, and yet I knew any romantic relationship between us would be a sin according to what little I knew about and had been taught on the subject from my church, the Bible, and my parents. Now I had Landon and Austin potentially telling me the same thing! I knew I had to stand on what I believed, or had believed growing up. But I didn't want to! I wanted to believe a new interpretation of the issue. However, I remembered there was a scripture in the Old Testament that said something like:

"Mankind shall not lie with mankind as with womankind. It is an abomination."

I didn't know where to find the scripture in the Bible, thanks again to so little teaching on 'same-sex love' from my parents and my church teachers. I just knew it was there. Further I remembered a New Testament verse where the Bible made clear that the 'effeminate' are not going to heaven. 'Effeminate' meaning the men who 'liked' and 'knew' other men, if I had read the track I had found correctly. There again I couldn't cite book, chapter, and verse, but I knew these scriptures were in the Bible somewhere.

Or were they?! No preacher or condemner of the 'homosexual' lifestyle had ever really proven their existence to me. In fact, any preacher, youth leader, or other authority from whom I had asked direct questions on the subject had never responded. Could they not prove their anti-same-sex love positions? Could they not justify their bigotry? I wondered!

Yet, here I found myself in love with a man, Andrew. He was so physically attractive, so emotionally and so mentally in tune with me, that he was the first person I had met that I would ever consider taking, marrying as a 'spouse'! It sounded really weird, even to me sometimes, but Andrew and I were so very compatible in all of the ways that we had interacted so far. We were compatible in all ways…

I wandered to the kitchen to get a diet. I felt so conflicted and confused still! What was I going to do?! Where was the education and support of church teaching on the issue?! It obviously was not there while I was growing up. Did any church ever teach on the issue, or prove to their congregants the sin and evil of same-sex love? Or was it now not taught because it was okay to love one of the same-sex?

Then it occurred to me. We, Andrew and I, must be total opposites politically, in sports, and in hunting, or something! That is how we could stake out positions that the other could not and would not tolerate, and it would drive us apart! Should I try it? I was beginning to believe that I had to find something that would split us up and end our relationship since it was a sin. Then I would not be into men anymore, or at least I would have a good reason to give them up and go modernly defined 'heterosexual'.

At first I felt sure that a plan to split me and Andrew on sports could work because I could not stand sports nuts as anything more than friends or siblings. While growing up I had hated it when my dad and brother had forced the family to listen to or later, watch sports on the holidays and for the bigger games. I had better things to do than watch over-paid baboons chase balls and each other around a field, arena, or stadium. The only positive I gleaned from watching sports was ogling the hot men on the field! Anyway, from what I had witnessed with Andrew so far, he did not seem to care for sports any more than I did. Unless one counted the playing of Wii as sports, which, now that I had played it, I did not. However, I still was not sure if he might actually be a sports nut or not! This could be a possible issue of division for us.

I also didn't like hunting, nor did I care to listen to a guy blubber about his hunting experiences and conquests. I couldn't possibly care less about a sports team's latest win/loss stats or another guy's tale of bagging a ten-point buck. Andrew had shown no signs of being a hunting nut either, but again I couldn't be sure. If hunting were an issue, again I could use it as my divisive issue with Andrew.

There were other things, other differences that I could bring up and use to divide Andrew and me and split us up. For example, I couldn't stand, let alone love or deal with, domineering men, men who insisted on making all the decisions and who felt they were right all of the time. In this area it appeared so far that Andrew and I were a perfect fit. Andrew had shown no signs of being domineering or desirous of a dominant role in our relationship. In fact, based on our relationship so far, I would have to say that Andrew was very egalitarian, treating me as a complete equal.

I could not stand hair on my own face. Nor did I like guys with hair on their faces, and I would not even consider a guy with a beard on his face as anything more than a friend. On this issue at the current time Andrew was more than qualifying as my lover (did I say that!). Andrew was always clean-shaven, and his facial skin was smooth and soft as a baby's bottom! However, this could change in the future. Andrew might try and grow facial hair. Then this would be a divisive issue for us.

I also did not like guys covered with tattoos and piercings. Here again Andrew fit my bill perfectly. I had seen briefly almost his entire magnificently naked body and he had no tattoos or piercings. However, that could change too. If it did I could take issue with it.

I had definite positions and opinions on various religious, economic, moral, and political issues, and they were all conservative. Many of my positions and beliefs were not flexible, or up for compromise. I felt sure that Andrew would probably disagree with me on a few of them. I could use these differences on my strongly held ideals as a divisive tool to split us up. I decided first to try and break Andrew and me up by searching out and exploiting our differences in beliefs and positions on these controversial religious, economic, moral, and political issues. I had to do this, according to 'religion', to avoid any 'sin' with Andrew and to 'save' my immortal soul!

Odd as it may seem, at this point in my developing relationship with Andrew, my guilt and shame, my Christian beliefs and upbringing, and my encounters with Landon and Austin had brought me to take a momentous decision. Since everything and everyone in my life, except Andrew, was condemning me and telling me my love for and potential relationship with Andrew was and would be a sin, I would put God, me, and Andrew to the ultimate test! My goal was to show Andrew and myself why we were not compatible to be lovers. I would attempt to drive a wedge between me and Andrew using any differences I could find in our religious, economic, moral, and political views. Ultimately I would use them to split Andrew and me up! If same-sex love were a sin, God would ensure that I would be successful in breaking Andrew and me up...

If I broke up with Andrew I was sure this would break and destroy my same-sex feelings for any man. After all, Andrew was the perfect man, his beautiful body the perfect male specimen and meat, and he was so seemingly compatible with and complementary to me that if we couldn't make it as a couple, I'd never find another man who would! I would no longer be interested in any other same-sex relationship with another man. I would be a heterosexual. God could show me the sinfulness of same-sex love by aiding me and bringing me to victory in this endeavor. God and I could use my success in this test to show Andrew that same-sex love was indeed sinful. Maybe our experiences in failing to build a strong relationship would help Andrew reject any more same-sex relationships and help him to become heterosexual as well!?

If I were not successful in breaking Andrew and me up, I would take that as God's approval for Andrew and me to develop, have, and continue a lovers' relationship and all that that entailed mentally, spiritually, physically, and sexually. Andrew and I would have a stronger bond by my testing of us, and our relationship would be deeper and stronger. I realized that I longed to fail at splitting us up, and I so wanted God's clear, tacit, and spiritual 'approval' of our relationship through said failure!

Looking back now, I realize just how mixed up I was in my developing love for and relationship with Andrew versus my Christianity and what was, is, and always will be right and wrong according to God. Because I did not want to face the emotional, mental, and spiritual reasons for my homosexual feelings and desires, I told myself that Andrew and my love for him were the causes of my homosexual tendencies. I mistakenly convinced myself that getting rid of Andrew would 'cure' my homosexuality. I didn't realize then that discrediting my legitimate love for, and compatibility and relationship with another man was not going to change my sexuality or whether I was attracted to men. It would simply potentially begin to cause problems between Andrew and me in our relationship that were unnecessary and detrimental to 'us'. Problems that I could focus the light of God on in an effort to break us up would never 'cure' me or Andrew of anything. These problems could be quickly resolved by us once we realized what fools we were being. Now, I realize too that Andrew and I could have simply ignored any differences or disagreements and just loved one another!

I now know I should have dealt with my homosexual feelings in some other way. I should have faced them straight on, not picked around the edges at the symptoms. I should have begun counseling, talks with a sympathetic Christian friend or mentor... something! I should have done as Landon Whitmore, whoever he was, had warned me to do, and buried myself in God, the Bible, and prayer. Those actions would have gone a long way toward sparing me the emotional, physical, and spiritual pain rushing my way in those coming months! At any rate, I now realize that the action I took was actually one of the easy ways out. They also were undertaken to test the rightness or wrongness of my same-sex relationship with Andrew, an issue not needing to be tested if I had spent more time studying it and arrived at an educated approval or rejection of same-sex love from God in the Bible.

Oh, well! Hindsight is always 20/20. I had no real way of knowing at that moment what I now know. My mind was clouded by love for Andrew, desires and lusts to be his lover, a temporary setting aside of my religious practices and beliefs, and the fact that church teaching on the issue of homosexuality was almost entirely absent from my education while I was growing up.

I had to change the subject and engage in some fluff if I were ever to relax. I also wanted to busy my mind so I could stop pining after Andrew.

I sat down on the floor and set up Andrew's... our Wii System. I decided playing Wii would help me to think about and to remember my special time playing with Andrew and what I had to look forward to. I picked up the Mario races and began racing. I had a blast, but I still missed Andrew, my heart and body longing... desiring... actually aching... for him to be with me. However, my head began to bob, and before I knew it, before I could stop it, I was asleep.

I don't know how long I slept, but time must have flown. I awakened in an alarmed and confused state as I heard a key slip into our lock, the lock click open, and our door open. I panicked! I whirled around and looked up anxiously, ready to throw my Wii control, or get up and defend myself. I know my eyes were probably wide in terror, and fear must have covered my mien along with confusion and alarm.

My eyes flashed to the door and came to rest on Andrew's beaming beautiful face. I relaxed and sighed in relief.

"Tyler!" Andrew's expression changed to one of concern as he stopped and looked at me. "It is Andrew! I am your Andrew! I am home! Are you all right?!"

"Yes, Andrew." I breathed deeply and smiled happily at him. "I see it is you! I was sleeping and... well... I am still not used to being here. Your arrival petrified... scared... startled me... that's all!"

"I'm sorry, Tyler!" Andrew exclaimed apologetically. "I didn't mean to startle you! I feel like... well... you and I have... well been together... been with each other for a month... at least!" Andrew glanced at his hands, then looked back at me. "I forget you have only been here two days... we get along so well... I feel I know you... you know what I mean?" He gave me a hopeful and questioning gaze like a beautiful... gorgeous man...

"It's all fine, Andrew!" I assured him, smiling. "I do know what you mean! I too feel...like... I feel like I have... known you... been with you for... for longer than two days."

There was a pause as Andrew took off his shoes, hat and jacket. He was moving very stiffly and deliberately, and he had some funny, unpleasant looks on his face. I became concerned as I watched him. When he finished, Andrew gazed back at me and managed a loving smile.

"Are you... Are you all right, Andrew?" I inquired worriedly. "You are moving stiffly, and appear like you might be... like you are... well... in pain?!"

"I... I am fine... Tyler!" Andrew waved me off, dismissing my concern. "Really, I'm fine!"

Another pause ensued as Andrew went to the kitchen, mixed himself a stiff drink, and popped a couple of pills. He was still moving carefully, even painfully... oh well! He had said he was fine. Of all people, he should know how he was physically.

"How did your mentoring go, Andrew?" I changed the subject as I stretched and yawned.

"Well, actually, Tyler..." Andrew began, a little sheepishly. "On my way out of Aurora I was called to work on an emergency at Bear Stearns. I have been there all day fixing some portfolios and trades. I called the school and canceled my mentoring sessions. It was a profitable day rather than a charitable day."

"Well then." I tried again. "How did your work go? Was it actually profitable?"

"Hell, Yeh! It was awesome! Very profitable!" Andrew answered enthusiastically. "I cleared over $3,700 at work today! It was very profitable!"

"Is that $3,700 for the week, or $3,700 for each trader for today?" I queried, as I sat in a state of shock. "How could it be $3,700 per trader for the day?! How could a person clear that in prospective tips and pay in one day?!"

"That, my dear, is at least $3,700 in tips for me, and each trader who showed up today individually for the whole day of wheeling and dealing!" Andrew beamed. "I worked hard for this, we worked hard for this, but it was worth it! We work with large sums of money and some huge accounts of millions, dear Tyler. It isn't hard to make that kind of money in a day. The wealthy are very thankful and appreciative when we make them more wealthy."

I was incredulous! How did he make that much money on trading stocks and securities on a Sunday?! I had never made that much money on any job in a month, let alone a night. Maybe I had the wrong career! (I didn't know the half of it!)

I had to marvel at Andrew's obvious skills in buying and selling stocks, bonds, and securities for Bear Stearns. For him to make over $3,700.00 in one day, and on a Sunday yet, he must be one hell of a seller and wheeler-dealer! It was clear Andrew must bring a lot of good clients to Bear Stearns, and he must have an excellent way of trading on the markets. He must be bringing Bear many good deals with high yields and dividends. I was impressed with Andrew! His knowledge of and savvy for the market had given him a good reputation for making money, and obviously he did a fine job lining up new trades and accounts to get clients a good return.

"How did you do it? How did you make that much money in one day?" I demanded excitedly. "I mean…It's none of my business but, I'm really curious… I'm really impressed… I think that's awesome… I think you are awesome… Andrew!" I stood up and approached Andrew, holding my arms out for a hug. I was so thankful for him!

"Well now." Andrew smiled coyly, taking me in his arms but strangely tensing and groaning when I touched his back. "I had double time because of the weekend, and I had an extended work period. I received a bonus from my employer because it was Sunday. I had $1,700 in income in several of my investments, and another additional $1,000 in dividends deposited in my account! Really cool, huh?"

Andrew gently pulled away a bit and winked enticingly at me as he kissed the air in my direction. My heart skipped a beat as I blushed. I smiled and briefly looked down between our very close bodies. Andrew was clearly hard through his tight pants. I was glad that I had that effect on him, because he did the same for me!

"Yeh, it is cool!" I exclaimed, again hugging him tightly. Andrew softly hugged me too, but winced and groaned. It felt so good, so right, so stimulating for me to be in his arms! I was becoming so hard that it almost hurt. "What are you going to do with it? The money... I mean?!"

"Well, Tyler." Andrew said mysteriously and slowly. He held me at arms' length and studied me intently and tenderly as he spoke. "I hope it isn't too... well... too early... for you... me... and I hope it wasn't.... wasn't too presumptuous of me... but... well... I bought you and me a weekend out at 'The Hot Springs Restaurant and Resort' in Deer Grove, Illinois. I thought... well... I thought you and I... well... could get away... get away alone together. I thought you and I could sight-see, and walk the streets shopping. I also thought we could get to know one another better and spend some quality time alone, together. I hope... I'm not too... it isn't too early... in our relation... relationship, dear Tyler...? Are we... are you game to... to go with me?" His voice was suggestive, enticing, seductive, and very hard to resist!

I was thrilled! My heart rate increased, I emotionally melted into Andrew's putty, and my mind went apoplectic as I nodded that yes, I'd go on the trip.

"It's not too early, Andrew! It... it is... an awesome, thrilling idea!" I gushed as I warmed to the thought that Andrew might consider it a 'date'. He also considered us in a 'relationship'... and he called me 'dear'! I now knew he had some romantic feelings for me!

Andrew gently stepped back a bit and gave me a questioning look.

"So... exactly what are you saying? Is it... is that a... is that a 'yes' then?"

"It is a definite yes! I will go with you! When is it?" I asked excitedly.

"Good! I was worried that you might... that I might scare you... that it was too soon. Anyway, it's a month or so away." Andrew licked his lips, exhaled in relief, and smiled. He put down the tickets. "We'll have a blast!" Andrew carefully and softly hugged me again. He groaned softly as I returned his hug energetically.

"Andrew! Take me away!" I joked as Andrew stepped back and opened his back pack.

Suddenly I felt a wave of sinfulness wash over me. My joy was spoiled by a nagging regret like I had let God down, like I was letting Landon down, like I was even letting my parents down. I had made a mistake because of my sinful desires. I had just planned a weekend date with Andrew! However, if I refused to go now I would let Andrew down!

Why did I do this to myself?! Since I had fallen for Andrew, I kept putting myself in places and situations where my temptation to 'sin', make love to him, would be there, and sooner or later my weakness was going to get me in bed with Andrew. I knew that! That, as God said, would be an abomination!? I wanted to correct myself with Andrew and refuse the trip, but my interest in and love for Andrew kept me mum. I could withstand the temptation. If I couldn't, did it really matter?! At the moment sleeping with and being intimate with Andrew sexually sounded really great! I felt ashamed of myself immediately, but it was the truth.

Andrew pulled two smaller boxes out of his back pack and set them both on the island counter. He smiled proudly and lovingly at me.

"Tyler, I also bought you and me new cell phones under one package deal. They are the newest phones out, complete with all of the bells and whistles. Now we can talk, text, send pictures, get on the internet, use GPS directional services, and a variety of other useful tools all on our cell phones! We can download any useful app we want. We have the power of a computer almost, right in these little Palm Pres." Andrew sounded like an excited child at Christmas opening presents.

At that moment I was so… so amazed… so completely speechless, shocked… and I knew that I was so blessed! Tears came to my eyes. I gazed into Andrew's beautiful eyes and gorgeous face as he handed me a cool, streamlined, small cell phone in a belt carrying case. It was all so surreal, so sweet, and so like the Andrew with whom I was falling in love!

"I don't deserve this, Andrew. You shouldn't have…"

"Tyler!" Andrew implored softly and tenderly. As he spoke he approached me closely. "You deserve this and… and… and so much more!

I just hope I… we… can give each other… everything… together! I… I am the one who doesn't deserve you!"

Andrew's face was so close to mine that I could not only hear his love, I could feel him breathing against my lips.

I realized something life changing as I shook my head and stammered, fighting back tears. I realized at that moment that I loved Andrew more than I had ever loved any man or woman before in my 21 years of life! Whether my love for him was a 'sin' or not I would still be conflicted and debate in my soul, but I LOVED Andrew DiPree!

"I don't know how to pay you back, Andrew… I… I mean I won't get paid for… for a… couple of weeks yet… and then there's rent… utilities…" I stammered since I didn't know what to say. I blushed as I looked down at the shiny new cell in my hand and flipped it open.

Andrew gently gripped my arm and guided me to a position in front of the front window. He seemed so firm, secure, and in charge. I felt comfortable and safe with him. I was excited and I felt weak! What was he going to do for… to me?!

Andrew cupped my chin in his left hand and lifted my face gently to gaze into my eyes. His blue pools sparkled happily. He was only a few inches from my face, and his closeness to not only my face, but my body too sent chills of pleasure through my being.

"Look, Tyler Belmont!" Andrew whispered excitedly. "We have a chance here to be a family. A couple of people who do for one another, care for each other, and long for one another just as a heterosexual family would. Let's take a leap of faith and do it!" Andrew was smiling, pleading… expectantly and hopefully studying my face. "Tyler Belmont! You and I… we met in… we were destined to meet… to be together… I know it! I feel it!" He touched my face and neck with his open hand and caressed me.

I was melting! My heart felt like it were going to jump right out of my chest and my head was swimming with excitement, feelings of love, and hormones.

"You're not… not prop… proposing we get married, Andrew?" I asked softly and breathlessly, my heart jumping for joy and hope. "I don't think we are really ready for… for that… I mean… we did just meet. We hardly know one another." I didn't know what Andrew was saying, and I still was not certain that Andrew was coming on to me. Besides, I still was not ready for that kind of a commitment to Andrew; I didn't yet know him well enough. However, I wondered...

Andrew grabbed my hand that I was using to accentuate my points. He held it tenderly.

"So, what if I were proposing marriage? Would your answer be anything other than 'yes'?" His eyes twinkled and he smiled lovingly at me. He squeezed my hand.

He turned then and crossed into the kitchen to the refrigerator, watching me over his shoulder as he moved. He was still stiffly walking and wincing. However, he still looked so hot, so sexy from the front and the back... I was still hard.

He took out the vodka, the diet Coke, and the avatar again. He began mixing himself a vodka drink as he watched me for my reaction. I smiled at him as I wiped my eyes and sniffled. Andrew was right! If he were proposing marriage I would say 'yes'. A million times 'yes'!

I decided not to answer or pursue this topic with Andrew anymore. My sinful feelings toward him were clouding my better judgment and my decision-taking ability, and I still didn't know if he were actually serious. Was Andrew really gay? Why would he make this kind of proposition and word it as he did if he weren't gay? No guy I knew would venture anywhere near this type of verbiage with another guy unless he were gay. Then again, I knew no one who was gay... The mere thought that Andrew was gay and interested in me made my heart flutter! I felt light-headed and elated at the prospect.

"I'm just proposing some options for us!" Andrew winked at me. "Nothing we have to take decisions on any time soon. But trust me, Tyler, those are things I am considering for the two of us, and I hope you are too! As far as the bills, I'm not concerned about when you are able to start paying your agreed to bills. The phones? Pay me back by using it and enjoying it. That will be payment enough." Andrew took a long dreg of his drink he had newly mixed.

I gazed over toward the refrigerator and Andrew in time to see him remove his button shirt, exposing his bare, hot Andrew skin and his muscle shirt. I inadvertently looked down his back and onto his butt, smiling with pleasure at Andrew's awesome, buff, manly body and bubble butt.

I stopped and gulped when I saw bright red, angry sores, some bloody and scabbed over, protruding above and below his muscle shirt, one above each shoulder, and one along his spinal column. I gasped! They were very nasty looking!

"Oh, dear God! Andrew!" I hurried to Andrew where he stood by the refrigerator.

Andrew hurriedly tried to put his long sleeved button shirt back on, but I ripped it away from him and threw it on the floor. He wasn't going to hide those nasty injuries from me!

I turned Andrew so that he faced away from me, and I lifted up his muscle shirt to his shoulders. I was speechless as I stared at his back in horror.

Andrew quickly turned to face the living room and me. He then brushed my hands away gently and pulled his muscle shirt back down to his waist. He was flush red, and seemed a bit mad.

I walked around him and firmly lifted his shirt back up, gently forcing his hands away from my hands and preventing his interference. I gasped in horror again as I saw the backs of his arms. They were bruised and scratched, blood oozing from several cuts on his upper arms.

"What?!" Andrew said immediately, twisting his head around to look at me, and smiling at first. Then, when he saw how pale I was and what I was looking at, he seemed to give up, hung his head, and spoke in shame.

"What is it, Tyler?! Damn it, what is it?! What the hell are you so shaken and upset about?"

"Your back... It's been... I mean the... these welts!" I gulped again involuntarily. Some were beginning to blister, and the inner parts of others were turning deep purple! "No wonder you have been moving stiffly and strangely, making weird, unpleasant, and pained faces... groaning and wincing... you said you were fine... like hell! You are hurt badly!"

"Oh!" Andrew decided then it was time to play like nothing was wrong. His voice had the 'oh that's nothing' sound as he continued. "They're nothing! I have matching ones on my legs and ass. Ha! Ha!" He attempted a chuckle.

I wasn't laughing! I could tell now that the strange looks he had playing around in the background on his face since he had been home were from pain! He must be in constant pain! And there were more matching welts and injuries on his legs and ass? Andrew's beautiful fair, manly, soft… awesome… touchable… caressable… gorgeous skin! All of it riddled like hamburger… my heart was breaking! I had to do something for Andrew.

Adrenaline took over and I did something that later would make me blush. I reached around Andrew's waist from behind, my face in his lower back, and with the dexterity and speed of a lock picker I had Andrew's pants unbuckled, unbuttoned, and unzipped. Because they were so tight, I pulled them down hard below his ass as he yelled in pain. I knelt down on my knees as tears came to my eyes.

I could clearly see through his white briefs the welts and cuts on his cheeks. Blood oozed from his anus into Kleenex he had in his shorts and had soaked through.

I stood up, adrenaline and fear pumping me up and empowering me. I took Andrew firmly by the arm with my right hand and pushed gently with my left hand squarely on his ass. I was fighting back tears again. I didn't want Andrew to see how distressed I was! I stayed behind him so he couldn't see the occasional tear run down my cheeks. I led him into the dining room where the light was brighter. Andrew grumbled all the way, but I was insistent yet gentle. I directed him right to the dining room table, which was directly under the large, bright ceiling light. I crossed to the wall and I turned the light on higher. I closed my eyes as I mentally prepared to look at all of Andrew's injuries and braced for the worst!

"Lie down on the table, belly first." I calmly ordered Andrew as I opened my eyes. "I'll get the medical supplies from the bathroom."

I hurried down the hallway to the bathroom. Once there I blew my nose and wiped my eyes in secret. I had to be strong for Andrew! I quickly looked in each cupboard in the bathroom until I found the one holding medical supplies, bandaging, antiseptics, tapes, wraps, etc. I gathered what I thought I might need to treat Andrew onto the counter. I blew my nose again for good measure. I gathered all the items into my arms, and when I had all secured, I carefully walked back to the kitchen, my arms precariously full of the supplies.

I dumped everything on the kitchen counter and then organized everything neatly on the kitchen island. When I was finished I turned to Andrew, who had done as I told him, and was lying flat on the dining room table, belly down first. His pants were still below his ass as I had left them when I pulled them down. I briefly looked at his hot… sexy ass and bubble buns… his slender waist rising up to his well muscled… manly back, shoulders, and arms… I wanted to touch… I suddenly felt a surge of love and emotion. I wanted to hold him, to caress him, to comfort him, but I restrained myself as I began an investigation of the extent of his injuries. I realized now that his whole back, ass, legs, and arms were all in need of care… I sighed and picked up some sani-wipes.

Andrew was softly moaning, but struggling to show as little response to the pain as possible.

After a short effort at perusal of his injuries, I quickly realized I was in over my head. I began to think that really I should take Andrew to the hospital!

It was obvious that, for me to do anything for Andrew, his pants and clothes had to go, and I had to have him naked in order to adequately doctor his injuries as best I could. I felt uncomfortable telling Andrew to strip. I wanted to do so… to see him… to see him naked again… to touch his… naked ass… legs… I had to stop thinking like this! With those thoughts I was never going to get relief from my hard-on!

However, I also should probably tell Andrew he was going to the hospital. How could I tell him that he must go to the hospital because I was not capable of medicinally caring for him?! I knew that he was the type to refuse hospitalization.

"I'm sorry Andrew, but stand up again." I realized too that I needed to be strong for Andrew and just take charge. Andrew would respect me more for my strength and my ability to take charge in a crisis. I needed Andrew naked, so naked he must be. If Andrew truly had romantic feelings toward me, what I had to do to him would be painful, yet as stimulating, erotic, and pleasurable for him as it would be for me.

By now Andrew was grumbling, as well as moaning and yelping at the pain as he struggled to sit up. I helped him to a sitting position. He scared the hell out of me by wilting onto my chest for a minute or two. Then he did as I told him and stood up. He was no longer hiding his pain, and had begun to break down into the injured man that he truly and obviously was. He seemed to really have dropped the façade of strong, uninjured, and grin and bear it.

I turned Andrew so his back was facing me. He was putty in my hands. I wanted to take advantage of this and feel him up…

I took his arms and put them straight up into the air. I was struggling with raging hormones, a hard-on, and desires I had never experienced before toward any woman or man. God, I loved Andrew!

I started at his shoulders, took his muscle shirt, and lifted it off of him over his head. I bit my own lip as Andrew yelped in pain. Then I paused. I looked at his pants just below his hot bubble butt. It stood to reason that parts of his pants material had dried into the welts. It would be extremely painful to take Andrew's tight pants off the rest of his legs and feet. It might be easier… I decided to plunge to the next logical step.

"Andrew, I need to take your pants off." I paused.

"So! What's the problem?!" Andrew grunted as he twisted his head around and looked at me questioningly.

"It is obvious to me that part of your pants material has dried into the scab tissue of your welts. Do you think it would be easier and much less painful for me to just cut your pants and underwear off, or take them off down your legs and off of your feet?" I paused again, hoping he would allow me to cut his clothing off.

"Cut them off." Andrew was sullen but decided. "I have plenty of these pants. The loss of one pair is no big deal."

I was so hot for him right now, having an opportunity and necessity to help him, touch him, care for him like he cared for me! I wanted him so badly it hurt…!

"Tyler, would you please get me more vodka straight and two more of the vicodin from the refrigerator, please?" Andrew leaned against the table.

I let go of Andrew's shirt and let it fall to the floor. I hurried to the refrigerator and retrieved the things for which he had asked. While he swilled the vodka and pills, I grabbed a pair of scissors and began to slowly, carefully cut his pants and underwear in pieces. I cut each pants leg from the waist to the ankle, enjoying the erotic smell of his deodorant mixed with just a slight hint of sweet sweat… and blood. I cut the material in his crotch between his legs. I now had pieces of pants that I could lift off of his legs and feet, rather than ripping scabs all of the way to his feet. I knew it was still going to hurt, although hopefully not as much.

I bit my lip and gulped, swallowing back more tears. How could I spare Andrew some pain here!? How could I tell him I would still be hurting him tremendously?! I manned up and plunged ahead.

"Andrew, it is still going to hurt when I remove these pieces. Are you ready?!" I asked firmly yet lovingly.

"Go for it!" Andrew answered, sighing, grimacing, and managing a pained yet tender smile at me. "I trust you! I love you, Tyler Belmont! You won't hurt me more than is necessary."

I was thrilled, touched, and turned on big time that he had pledged his love for me several times this evening! However, the adrenaline was flowing and I was preparing to do Andrew… I was preparing to care for Andrew to the best of my ability. I just hoped I didn't hurt him too much! In the hospital he could have intravenous pain medication. I decided to broach the hospital idea first.

"I think, Andrew, that these injuries are really over my head as far as treatment. Are you sure that you don't want to go to the hospital and get trained medical treatment?!" Using my left hand I somewhat desperately turned his head lovingly to face me.

"No, Tyler!!" Andrew's response startled me in its intensity and emotion. "I cannot and will not go to the hospital or a doctor! I do not want any inquiries or bothersome questioning and publicity about how I acquired these injuries. I'll get fired and possibly killed if there is anything of my injuries recorded or investigated by the hospital or the police. Tyler, you can do this! If you love me you will honor my wishes! Please, fix me up!? I am so NOT ready to talk about how this happened! Please, just do your best to help me?!"

I sighed, resigned to treat Andrew as best I could. I had to reign in my hormones and desires to sexually touch and fondle him, yet I had to do some 'fondling' to treat his shoulders, back, buttocks, legs, and heels. I wanted to take my clothes off too, but I was still a bit modest and embarrassed, and unknowing of Andrew's total feelings toward me.

I steeled myself to Andrew's coming cries of pain as I ripped off the pieces of pants and underwear. I really didn't know if emotionally and physically I could cause him this kind of pain without losing it!? I loved Andrew so much by now that this was going to be hell on earth!

"Get to it, Tyler! Take off the rest of my clothing." Andrew muttered firmly again. "I will be fine!" He braced himself and grabbed the table edges.

I went to it. Andrew cried in pain, and it was sheer hell as I took off the four pieces of pants and underwear knowing that I was hurting him so. My heart broke, and I almost threw up! How could I be expected to cause this kind of pain to one I loved so desperately and 'sinfully'?!

It was then that I discovered a deep cut on his right shoulder. It was a jagged, ugly wound that really worried me. It should have stitches. What should I do?!

"Andrew, I believe you said you have welts on your ass, legs, and feet, and you do have them in spades." I paused and began to gently wash the cut on Andrew's right shoulder with cotton and warm water alcohol.

There was a pause. I slowly and carefully began washing the right hand welt down to his bubble butt. I did it as sensually as I knew how to tempt him rather than hurt him. He waited a minute or two and then spoke in resigned pain.

"Yes, Tyler, I have welts all over my body. They are numerous and I cannot see them all.  I just hurt like hell all over! I am in so much pain that I can't stand it! Can you get me some more vodka and avatar right now?" Andrew exhaled painfully and wilted a little more. I wanted to wrap my naked body around his to comfort him…

"Andrew, I'll get your drink." I finished washing the right hand welt and put down the cotton. "Caring for these injuries is going to hurt like hell! I don't know what happened to you, or how you came about these welts, but they are damn bad! I don't understand why in the hell you did not go to the hospital to get these injuries treated!"

I moved to the refrigerator and took out the vodka and Canada Dry. I mixed them, and then took out the white powder that Andrew called avatar and poured some into the glass, stirring it strongly.

I looked at Andrew as I turned toward him carrying the drink. He was heaving and tensing with pain as he stood next to the dining room table. His hot and handsome manly body tantalized me! I wanted Andrew now! I knew it was wrong?! I also knew it would cause him additional pain to be physical with me. I couldn't do that to him! I had to restrain myself.

I placed the drink in Andrew's hand. He took a long and deep dreg, and then placed the drink on the table beside him.

I positioned myself behind Andrew as he put his arms down. I knelt down and checked out his soft, muscular thighs. Then I continued to clean his welts. I was getting so hot and bothered. Andrew yelped and groaned as I cleansed each wound.

"I'm sorry, Andrew, I didn't mean…" I started to apologize for causing him the pain on his body.

"Don't fret it!" Andrew interrupted. He was gritting his teeth, and I could tell he was drawing from his endurance and ego to sound as manly as possible. "It doesn't hurt that bad." He lied.

Andrew clenched his teeth.

"Andrew, you're doing fine!" I replied as I moved around so that if he fell I could hopefully get away from him quickly.

I surveyed Andrew's entire backside. It looked like he had been whipped with a cat of nine tails! I was so shocked I almost threw up again. Further perusal showed that some of the whip marks went around the legs to the front of Andrew's body. I managed to turn him around enough on one side to survey any damage to the front of his body. The fronts of his legs and bottoms of his feet were also injured. His penis looked like someone had taken sand paper to it. Blood oozed from his anus down onto his scrotum. I marveled how he had even made it home!

Andrew cranked his neck to look at me. He smiled painfully. I could tell by his facial expressions that he was still in major pain despite the alcohol, avatar, and whatever the hell the pills were that he was taking.

"Oh, Tyler, you do want me!" Andrew tried to joke, as I ran my hands gently over his body. I wished my touch would restore his beautiful, hot, sensuous skin, but I knew only time and care would do that.

"I do want you!" I retorted truthfully, checking out the injuries on Andrew's back. "But don't say it so loudly! Now what happened!? What or who the hell caused this!? You owe me at least an explanation since I am caring for you against my better judgment that you should be in the hospital!"

I was expecting an answer, but instead as I knelt to look at his lower legs, Andrew suddenly dropped. He folded like he were trying to sit down, and his naked butt came down on my head and forced me to the floor where he collapsed. His head and fully naked torso and body flopped backward. I was still for a moment, with my head trapped between his butt and feet. I couldn't believe what had just happened! Andrew was badly injured, and I was his only nurse! How could I help him while trapped like this?! What had caused Andrew to faint?! Was he hurt more than I or he thought?!

# CHAPTER 34

# THE DAMAGED TEMPLE

I sat there, my head trapped between Andrew's naked ass and his feet, in shock for a minute or two. I could smell his cologne, his deodorant, a little blood, and some of his manly sweat. They melded together to form a scent that I found quite an aphrodisiac. I felt trapped in this entanglement with Andrew, yet thoroughly stimulated to have the closeness between the two of us. I wanted more of this closeness to go on between Andrew and me! However, now was not the time to become hot and bothered over my desires for him. I had to focus on Andrew!

I felt two trickles of liquid dripping on my head and one upon my ear. I touched one trickle with my fingers, peered at it, and sniffed it. It was rich, red blood. I kind of panicked! I had to get free so I could care for Andrew before he bled to death. He was heavy from his well-muscled body and I struggled to wrest my head free of his limp, folded form. I could feel the dribbles of bodily fluids from him flowing slowly to my face. Finally, doing my best to lift Andrew's heavy torso, I grimaced and pulled my head out quickly and roughly from between his legs and his ass.

As I gazed lovingly and worriedly at Andrew's beautiful, battered, and bleeding naked body I realized that he was badly hurt in order to pass out here. He might even go into shock! I prayed to God that that did not happen; I couldn't remember first aid for shock. I wiped Andrew's blood off my head as I looked longingly at him lying there.

Andrew's broad shoulders moved slightly as he breathed shallowly. They were so well sculpted and masculine, gorgeous examples of God's creative and artistic abilities. Andrew's chest was bare, a little hairy, but also very beautiful. I stroked his chest gently, inhaling quickly in pleasure!

He lay there naked where he had fallen, his privates partially excited and splayed out nicely from his crotch, tantalizing me. I was tempted to stroke his crotch and his awesome package. However, I restrained myself. His gorgeously muscled legs were bent backward at the knee, but still perfectly sculpted. I wanted to feel him up again big time… but no! I would not sin in that manner! I could not violate Andrew like that! Andrew was my friend, and he needed medical help, not a friend/lover feeling him up while he was unconscious and ill. I asked God to forgive me as I realized that I only wanted Andrew physically when he could enjoy it and reciprocate on me!

I took note that Andrew was still breathing, albeit in a labored manner. I moved around and sat briefly at Andrew's knees, adjusting his body into a more comfortable position by unfolding and spreading his legs straight. Then I went to his crown and I cupped his head back lovingly into my crotch and ran smelling spices under his nose twice. I hoped to revive him, to wake him up. Andrew couldn't die or go into some kind of arrest now! I didn't want to make a run to the hospital with him; especially since he had made it clear he didn't want to go there.

Piercing all of the worries and fears that now tormented me was another thought. What would my folks say if they heard about Andrew's accident or beating, whatever the hell it was!? If I went to either the police or the ER with Andrew, my folks would find out. They would be scared for my safety. Mom would insist that I move back home. Andrew would be alone to heal, and I… I couldn't imagine my life without him right now! I realized I couldn't risk a hospital visit and police report either. I had to treat him myself!

I looked down as Andrew suddenly inhaled deeply; the second time he awakened, coughing and hacking. I breathed a big sigh of relief! I began interrogating him about any injuries he might have sustained in his fall. He insisted there were none, that he was fine, and that he wanted to get the hell up. I put the salts on the table and carefully and tenderly helped Andrew up from the floor. He was weak and tipsy, but still managed to smile wanly at me and pat my shoulder reassuringly. I held him up and helped him to stand.

Once established and stabile on his feet, Andrew paused. I held him with his right arm over my shoulders and my left arm firmly wrapped around his waist.

"What happened?" Andrew asked in a broken voice, blinking, and shaking his head.

"You passed out." I stated softly. "You went down like a rock. You are really hurt, Andrew, and I need to get busy caring for you now! I'll help you to the table and I want you to lie down on it, belly first."

Andrew nodded wearily and took a step toward the kitchen table, almost falling forward in the process.

I helped him to the table, where he did lie down belly first. Andrew was totally naked, back and bubble butt up, in a position from which I could treat all his wounds.

I could hardly take my eyes off his gorgeous, manly body as I hurried to the sink, and drew out a bowl of nicely warm water. Bringing it back to the table I almost cried again.

Andrew's back side was in bad shape! I shook my head and gulped to stifle a sob.

"Andrew." I tenderly stated. "This is bad! This is really bad!"

I lined up the warm water, wash cloths, hydrogen peroxide, alcohol, iodine, antiseptic cream, cotton swabs, and bandaging material on the table next to Andrew. Then I prepared myself to begin the lengthy process of cleaning, disinfecting, and bandaging his wounds.

The shoulders seemed to be the logical place on Andrew's body to begin my work. I washed and disinfected the right welt on his shoulder. I decided it would be good to finish the right welt with salve and bandage, and then move across the back to do the other welts. I stood beside Andrew as he lay on the table and I administered my health-care, carefully and tenderly washing a wound with the warm water, wash cloths, and an anti-microbial wash. Then I softly and lovingly caressed the medicines one by one into the wound. Andrew was now, by his choice, my patient, and I had to be the best nurse I could be to him! Slowly I moved from wound to wound, following the same procedure with each. Some were so bad I began applying thin bandages to them.

For each wound I first gently washed it with warm alcohol water. This caused any level of pain for Andrew depending on the severity of the wound. Then I gently dabbed hydrogen peroxide into it. I knew it would smart and pain, and he did groan and flinch a lot. Next I swabbed some iodine on each welt. Andrew cried out in pain with each application. With every cry, groan, jerk, or sign of pain from him I wanted to hurl or cry. I already loved Andrew so much that I couldn't bear to see him suffer in any way!

On the welts that were not bleeding I applied antiseptic cream or salve. On those welts that were or had been bleeding I applied antiseptic cream and a little drawing salve. I then applied small bandages as they were needed.

As I worked on the welts on his back, Andrew continued to wince, groan, and cry out in pain, all the while cursing someone named 'Jovan'. I was suffering so much from Andrew's trauma that at first I ignored his rantings against 'Jovan the Dominator'. I cleaned, disinfected, and bandaged my way down his back, while simply salving some welts and leaving them exposed.

I was shocked at the wounds! How could this happen to Andrew at or in the vicinity of a business like Bear Stearns?! Where in the hell could he come up with and receive such massive injuries in or near a stock brokerage?! Especially at a blue collar position of employment!? I knew I wanted to and needed to ask… but Andrew had given no sign he wanted to talk about it. I pondered the situation for a bit as I worked, building up my courage.

Finally, I could not resist the elephant in the china shop and my inquisitive nature any more.

"Andrew, how did this happen to you at Bear Stearns? Who did this to you?! Where did it happen?!" I kind of guessed from Andrew's cursings of 'Jovan the Dominator' that Jovan had done this to him. But who was he, and why had he done this to Andrew? "You keep cursing this 'Jovan the Dominator'! Who or what is he? Did he do this to you? Please tell me, Andrew?!"

Andrew didn't respond, but continued groaning expressions of pain and discomfort. I continued working as I awaited Andrew's response.

After a few minutes with nothing forthcoming from Andrew, I was a little frustrated.

"Andrew, how did this happen?!" I insisted. "Andrew! I am your… your roommate… I… well… I… I love you, damn it! I deserve an explanation!" I pressed into his soft flesh seriously and yet tenderly to cause him just enough pain to make him answer, but not enough to further injure him.

"Tyler…" Andrew began, yelping in pain, "the other Bear Stearns employees and I went out to supper at a local bar in a rough neighborhood a few blocks from work. We knew we shouldn't be in that neighborhood, but we figured we would have a deterrent strength in numbers." Andrew continued, gritting his teeth, and groaning. "We planned to eat, have a drink, and discuss some of our business, trades, stocks, and such. The fellows wanted to hear about my big deals. Then we were going home." He moaned as I applied more iodine on an open wound.

"Go on, Andrew…" I urged as I worked.

"All the parking spaces were taken near the restaurant and I had to park in a ramp down the street from the establishment. The ramp is a little remote, out of the way, and has a reputation of muggings and physical/sexual assaults, but I thought I would be fine. I wouldn't be a target." Andrew's face was red and contorted in pain. I was down to the wounds just above his cute but injured bubble butt by now. His masculine, gorgeously nude body was such physical poetry and a masterpiece!

"And?" I prompted when Andrew didn't continue right away. Reassuringly I stroked his soft blond curls on the top and back of his head. I wanted to kiss him so badly, but…

"After we ate and talked it was dusk. I walked back to the parking ramp where I had left my Intrepid. I had parked my car on the middle level of the five level parking ramp. Everyone else with whom I went to supper had found parking closer to the restaurant. I was alone, had just arrived on the third level, when I was attacked by a brute calling himself 'Jovan the Dominator'! 'Jovan' must be obeyed! 'Jovan' demands this… and you do that!" Andrew closed his eyes tightly and cried out as I worked on an open wound very low on the small of his back. I could see that tears were in his eyes. I gulped involuntarily, and hot tears came to my eyes. I wanted to wrap my naked body around Andrew and comfort him… hold him… caress him…

Andrew's groans and cries, and shouts of pain and discomfort were getting to me, and I fought to steel myself to his obvious anguish so I could treat his buttocks, legs, and feet without throwing up or burning out. I gently and lovingly finished medicating the welts on his lower back. I bandaged two of them.

"Go on, Andrew…" I paused again as I stroked his hair, hoping to show more comfort and reassurance. "I am starting on your buttocks, Andrew, prepare yourself!" I warned. I grabbed the warm water bowl which was now bloody, and took it to the sink. I emptied it and put warm water back into it. I carried it to Andrew on the table, grabbed a wash cloth, and prepared to work on his cute ass.

I briefly glanced down his cheeks. He was still bleeding from the anus, a steady trickle. It scared the hell out of me! What was the source of this bleed?!

"Andrew… honey… you are… your anus… you are bleeding from your… your anus! Are you sure that you don't want me to take you to ER?!" I exclaimed with concern and uncertainty about my skills as a nurse.

"No!" Andrew raised his head to look at me. He spoke so forcefully and emphatically that I was startled. "I don't want to go to the damn hospital! I don't need their crap right now!"

I glanced at Andrew. His gorgeous face was firm and almost angry. I gulped involuntarily.

"I give you, Tyler, permission to deal with it. Do what you have to do… what you have learned on the farm to do for these injuries…" Andrew smiled as well as he could muster and put his head back down.

At Andrew's permission to be that intimate with him my heart skipped in happiness! I would have to inspect his anus. However, I was also scared at what I would find when I spread his cheeks. I decided to deal with his anus in a bit later.

"Go for it!" croaked Andrew, smiling wearily. "Anyway, as I said before, I was alone. This Jovan guy was waiting on the middle level for someone like me. He had a bullwhip and a billy-club. He used both on me! He attacked me mercilessly and quickly whipped and pummeled me into submission. When I finally passed out from the pain and bleeding, Jovan left me for dead I guess. He disappeared anyway…" Andrew paused to wince, flinch, and groan as I finished gently washing two of the wounds high on his gorgeous buttocks.

I stopped again to stroke Andrew's curls and head.

I winced because I knew I had to ask the next questions, and I knew they would be uncomfortable for Andrew, and me.

"Andrew… did he… this Jovan…" I began softly and firmly. "Did he steal… did he steal anything… from you? Wallet, keys?"

"He didn't take anything of mine from my pockets that I know of, he just whipped the hell out of me. I came to consciousness naked from the waist down and my shirt ripped and tattered. Jovan was on a power trip in my opinion. When I regained my strength I walked and crawled to my car, put on some clothes, and I managed to drive myself home here to you."

Andrew raised his head briefly and gazed lovingly at me.

"Andrew… this next question… it is… well, uncomfortable… I have to ask though…" Cautiously I stroked his head as I cleared my throat and looked at him somberly, not sure I wanted to hear the answer.

"What is it?!" Andrew sounded a little alarmed as he looked back at me.

"Did he… this Jovan… did he… well… were you… well, did he… rape you?!" I stammered as I gazed lovingly into his blue pools. Andrew was so hot! I could understand any guy wanting to get in his pants and be intimate with him…!

"What?!" Andrew's face showed what I interpreted as fake shock, but his answer was instantaneous. "Hell no! He didn't rape me!"

Andrew put his head back down on the table in finality.

I paused with my right hand on his head gently. Then I bent over him, stopping with my face a foot and a half from his blond curls. Andrew was facing away from me, but I could smell his manly shampoo… so stimulating!

"Andrew…" I whispered firmly, "I want the truth… your injury… your anal bleeding… are you positive… positive he didn't rape you?! It is okay if he did… it is not your fault… we can deal with it! I will still love you!"

Andrew lifted his head suddenly and forcefully, and as he turned to meet my gaze, his eyes sparked with anger and sincerity. He drew a deep breath.

"Tyler Aaron Belmont, I told you! I was not raped!" He replied through clenched teeth. "I woke up bloodied and naked from my waist down, and my shirt and 'tee' ripped and tattered like I said. If I were raped, I would have known it and felt it. Don't you think I would know if I had been raped?!"

"But you passed out…" I protested. "How would you know whether or not you had been raped if you were unconscious?"

Andrew paused and frowned at me. He was, however, stumped by my point.

"I was not raped!" He sputtered. "Don't you think I would recognize signs of rape if I had been raped? If I had been raped I would have found used condoms around. I did not."

With an angry finality Andrew gave me a questioning, challenging gaze, and then laid his head back down facing away from me.

"Andrew…" I returned cautiously, "where are your tattered bloody clothes then?"

"I threw them away." Andrew replied flatly. "Why should I keep them? To remind me of my humiliation and pain?"

There was a brief pause before Andrew spoke rather curtly.

"Now get on with the doctoring, Tyler! Please?! I am tired and I want to go to bed."

Slowly, deliberately, and thoughtfully I straightened up my posture. I deftly moved to Andrew's cute ass. I knew things were not adding up in his story. His injuries were too great. Too extensive!

Taking a deep breath myself, I knew I had to visually look at Andrew's anus and the injuries therein. Carefully I put two fingers inside his crack on each butt cheek. I quickly closed my eyes, breathed deeply, opened my eyes, and gently opened Andrew's cheeks.

"Oh my dear God!" I blurted in shock before I could determine to remain calm and not upset Andrew. "Oh my dear God, Andrew!?"

I was not prepared for the injuries Andrew had suffered in his anus and between his cheeks. Someone definitely had somehow caused some trauma there!

There were scratches and bruising on the insides of both cheeks. At least two lacerations on the edges of Andrew's anus still were bleeding quite steadily. His anus itself looked as though it had been stretched out of shape. Everything between his cheeks was red and angry.

I closed my eyes, gulping so as to prevent throwing up. Hot tears welled up in my eyes. I realized in that moment that Andrew was lying to me. He was dangerously injured, had indeed been raped, and was lying to me out of fear and shame! I released his cheeks and pulled up a chair upon which to sit before I fell down.

Andrew lay still when I turned to sit and faced him. However, as I lowered myself to the seat I felt faint and lost it. I flopped down heavily on the chair and it skidded a bit on the tile. Andrew quickly raised his head, twisted so his field of vision included over his shoulder, and looked at me in alarm.

"Tyler?!" Andrew exclaimed anxiously. "What is wrong?! What did you see?!"

"I... I... And... Andrew, you... you're..." I didn't know how to say what I was feeling as I stifled a gag. "I can't finish doctoring you, Andrew! You need to go to the hospital!" I managed to blurt out. The danger of my parents' discovery of Andrew's assault was small compared to the danger that he might be very seriously injured!

Andrew's face darkened as he became angry, defiant, and firm. His teeth clenched again. Even in anger and negative emotions he was gorgeous! Lord, I wanted to kiss his perfectly red, pouty lips and...

"I told you, Tyler... honey!" Andrew seethed. "I am not going to any DAMN hospital... anytime... anywhere! Any trip to a hospital would require a thorough hospital report, including a reason and cause for my injuries. Because I was assaulted, the police would be contacted. Publicity would follow. Any negative publicity on Bear Stearns and they will can my ass! I need my job… for us… to pay our bills!"

Andrew gave me a firm and angrily compelling look.

I gazed tenderly at him. However, I couldn't help becoming a little pissed myself.

"Andrew!" I pleaded firmly. "Your… your… the injuries inside your cheeks are more… more superficial… scratches… some bleeding… much bruising… But, Andrew, around your… your… your…"

"Yes?! Around my what… what?!" He prompted impatiently.

"Andrew, around your… near your… around your misshapen…" I gulped and then gagged. I felt as though I were going to violently throw up.

"Tyler! Get a grip!" Andrew blinked and smiled wanly at me. He grimaced as he rose up on his elbows. "Around my what are what? What the hell are you trying to say?!"

"This is… you… Andrew… this is hard!" I put my head down briefly, gathered my gumption and mental fortitude, and then looked up, meeting Andrew's questioning gaze.

"Andrew, around… around your… your… anus are at least two, maybe more, lacerations that are bleeding. I don't know how deep they are… I don't know if they severed the sphincter muscles there, but I think they may require stitches! Then… then… then your…" I paused to catch my breath from my outburst.

Andrew had a kind of dumbfounded look on his face, and his eyes were wide like those of a child caught with his hand in the proverbial cookie jar. These expressions on his countenance struck me as genuine, totally natural, and not faked. He was clearly concerned.

"That's why it hurts like… Is there more?" Andrew queried, his voice a little shaky. "Tyler, whatever it is, tell me, honey!"

"Andrew, your anus is… is… is angry red and misshapen!" I exhaled, feeling like I had been holding my breath for the last five minutes or so. "Andrew! You have been lying to me. The injuries on the whole backside of your body are too severe to have occurred through clothing. Your attacker stripped you almost naked and then beat you. He then… he then… raped you… or stuck things up your ass or something to cause such injuries as are there in your cheeks and anus. Why are you lying to me?!"

I lost it, sobbed, and buried my face in my hands. I loved Andrew so much already that I felt betrayed and broken by his subterfuge over what he had endured.

I became limp and light headed. My hearing began to fill with the sound of static. I couldn't control my sobbing now that it had started. My Andrew was hurt badly and in pain, yet he was lying to me about some of the details, if not the whole cause. It felt like my heart were breaking!

Suddenly I felt a hand on my head, stroking me gently and reassuringly. I tried to look up, but the hand firmly kept me in place, the fingers still stroking my head.

I heard Andrew groan, but the tender stroking continued.

"Tyler…" Andrew spoke quietly and calmly, "you are a good man, an excellent roommate, a beloved companion and brother!" His voice cracked and he paused briefly. His petting of me continued.

"Tyler…" Andrew's voice was soft, pleading, yet compelling as he continued to stroke my head and hair. "Tyler, please stop crying?!"

"Why!" I exclaimed between sobs. "You don't trust me enough to be honest and tell me the truth! You have been assaulted and raped, yet you lie to me and deny the obvious?! What the hell?! I thought we were lovers… friends that had an understanding of emotional and mental honesty and intimacy!?"

I realized too late that I had made a revealing slip of the tongue, but right now I didn't care. Andrew was lying to me! He was betraying our relationship.

I heard Andrew take a deep breath. With many groans and grunts Andrew's feet hit the floor in front of me as he struggled to stand up. He then gently put his hands under my arms and signaled me to stand by pulling tenderly up on me. I rose to face him. Andrew grasped my face lovingly with both hands and directed me to look him in the eyes. As I did so I noted they were filled with tears.

"Tyler, honey…" Andrew breathed quietly, "we do have an understanding…" He gazed sincerely at me. "I… I… I have been lying… I… I'm sorry!"

He briefly hung his head before reengaging my gazing attention.

I had managed to stop crying. Andrew wiped my face with his thumbs.

"Jovan did… when he… when I… upon reaching the third level of the parking ramp…" Andrew choked up briefly, "Jovan attacked me like I said. He did beat me with the bull whip, which shredded my clothing. You are right though… he then… he then…"

Andrew paused, gulped, bit his lip, and wiped tears from his eyes. He then cupped my face back in his hands before continuing.

"The first whipping shredded my clothing. Then Jovan stripped me naked from the waist down…" Andrew paused again, this time wiping a tear from my cheek. "I'm okay, Tyler!" He assured me. "Then Jovan whipped me some more with the bull whip and beat me with the billy-club…"

He bowed his head briefly as he gagged twice. I could feel a few hot tears run down my cheeks as I sucked back stuff from my nose.

"Just when I thought… as I felt I… I thought I would pass out, Jovan… he attacked… he…" Andrew lifted his head and caught my eyes again as I realized I was holding my breath.

Andrew put his hands on my shoulders. I was transfixed. Lord! I loved Andrew so! He was almost hypnotic as he continued.

"Jovan sodomized me with the handle of the bull whip and the billy-club…" Andrew gulped and moved toward me, his face within three inches of mine. I could feel his breath on my face. "It was… was very… very painful and humiliating!"

He hung his head, dropped his arms, and began to wilt. I grabbed him quickly and helped him stay on his feet.

"Then I passed out. I don't remember anything else… I swear that is the truth!" Andrew breathed while leaning heavily on my shoulder.

My heart melted. I steered Andrew around to face the table. As I helped him to lie back down on the table belly first I felt a little guilty.

"Andrew, I'm sorry I… well… I am sorry if I… offended you in any way… I didn't mean to!" I managed. "You have done so much for me… you… you mean so much… so much to me… I…"

Andrew lay down and placed his head on its side so he was facing me.

"Apology accepted, Tyler, honey." He interrupted as he raised his head again. "Will you finish treating my wounds now?"

I would stand by Andrew as long as he told me the gospel truth. He had leveled with me, and wild horses couldn't force me to abandon him now!

"Andrew, I will do my best!" I replied, patting his leg. "I will do the best that I know how from the farm where I grew up."

"That's all I ask, honey!" Andrew laid his head back on the table facing me and smiled. "Thank you!"

I began gently washing the wounds on his lower butt cheeks and prepared myself mentally to doctor his anus. Andrew groaned and winced.

"I have never been so beaten, so abused, so hurt, or so humiliated in my life of working the street… ah, I mean working in public at Bear Stearns!" Andrew finished, having changed his tune, tone, and verbal import suddenly.

My eyebrows went up again as I caught his change of words describing something like maybe his career?! However, I was so angry and furious that someone would so brutally hurt Andrew that I ignored it and plunged on in outrage.

"Did you call the police and file a police report?!" I demanded furiously. I couldn't believe he had just come home after this kind of attack without filing any kind of complaint and/or going to the hospital.

"No, I did not. That part of my assault is still true." Andrew answered simply. "I already told you the main reason I refused to involve the police or go to the hospital; I could lose my job and our income. But in addition, guys out alone in that parking ramp have a bad rep to start with, and anybody frequenting the place after eight o'clock is especially a suspect for either being a car-jacker, pimp, male prostitute, or a mugger. If I would have thought about it and been smart, I would not have parked there to begin with, but I ignored the stats, it was late, and this is what I get."

Andrew winced as he shrugged. "Besides, it was Sunday. Nothing bad usually happens there on Sundays!"

I was still not satisfied, nor did I fully comprehend or believe the danger and risk Andrew faced of retribution or losing his job were he to wind up receiving publicity over his attack. To me this was a no-brainer, simple, and easy; go to the police and the hospital.

"Do you know what this 'Jovan' looks like?" I asked. "We could still fill out a description, an incident report, a complaint, and file them with the police. Did you see his face?" I wasn't sure I wanted to know the answer, but it just came out automatically. What if he came after Andrew?! I didn't need that worry either, but the question just came out.

Andrew breathed in deeply and then sighed. I could tell he was becoming impatient with me, but he seemed to think long and hard about that one. I worked, not realizing at the time why he took so long to answer, but I waited for him impatiently. I now know his answer was mandatory. Above all he had to sweep this situation under the rug, especially with Mr. Richard. I didn't realize at the time that he was really... truly protecting his job, me, and our relationship! At that contemporaneous moment it seemed to me to be only the very prudent thing to do; to be completely honest! But in fact Andrew was trying to cover up brushes with the law by any means possible. Had I known that and been thinking more clearly, I would have thanked him for doing so.

Andrew was groaning and writhing in pain and didn't respond.

"Do you know what Jovan looks like?!" I pressed. "Could you help a police artist draw a picture of Jovan for a report?!"

Andrew again sighed in irritation and bit his lip as I leaned over him to look into his face questioningly.

"Yes, Tyler,... I know what he looks like... He wore a mask that covered his eyes... kind of like Zorro... that was it!" Andrew seemed deep in thought. "I could describe him for the fuzz... It wouldn't be a complete description though..." He snapped his fingers and seemed to come back to reality. "But I won't do it!" He flapped his arms to punctuate his statement.

"I won't risk the publicity, a police investigation, trial, and ultimately the loss of my job, honey!" Andrew laid his head down facing me.

# CHAPTER 35

# THE BATTLE CONTINUES

"You won't do it!?" I exclaimed angrily, incredulously, and naively. "Andrew, this man violated you! He sodomized you with foreign objects that left external injuries and may have caused internal injuries. He messed up your asshole. He whipped you and left you unconscious, injured, and dead or dying! Doesn't that make you mad?!" I was pissed! I paused and threw my hands in the air in frustration.

"It makes me mad as hell." Andrew stated without much feeling. He clenched his teeth. "The issue is not moot, it is closed. Please finish me up? My ass, anus, legs, and feet?"

I was so angry, curious, and emotionally distraught over Andrew's assault, but I knew I had to reason with and question him piecemeal or he would completely shut down and possibly completely shut me out.

I continued to seductively massage the medicine into his wounds, carefully watching out for bleeding and trying to comfort him at the same time. I finished his butt cheeks and moved on to his crack and anus with trepidation. I knew this was going to hurt Andrew the most due to the lacerations and injuries therein. I also had major doubts as to the positive or negative benefits and efficacy toward healing that any treatment I could administer might have for Andrew, especially given the biological function and reality of the area.

Perversely and surprisingly to me was that I was getting such a physical and sexual charge out of this intimacy with Andrew that I was purposefully dragging it out. I had to just plunge into doing what I could for the inside of Andrew's butt cheeks and his anus. My best was all I could do at this point.

"Andrew, I still disagree with you. I think you should go to the police. I don't understand why you won't go to the police? I think it would be worth the risk." I stated firmly.

"Tyler, honey, it would be a potential breach of business-client privilege. The publicity it would bring…" Andrew stopped, crying out loudly and in anguish as he cursed. I felt awful as I knew my work was really causing him great pain. I gagged.

"The publicity it would bring… to Bear Stearns and the restaurant with whom… I and my coworkers… do business would be of a negative nature and would be incalculable… I would lose my investment contract… with the restaurant at the very least! I'd probably lose my mentoring job at Westchester. Bear Stearns could lose accounts to any of our more lucrative but more controversial companies. I might even lose my job at Bear Stearns trading stocks, securities, and investments because of clients leaving so as not to be tainted by my publicity. I can't afford to jeopardize any of those jobs! I cannot jeopardize my job!" Andrew said it all so matter-of-factly, like he had memorized it from a book. However, his explanation was interrupted by cries of pain and curses as I worked between his cheeks.

"Do you really think that your investment account with the restaurant would be in danger and Bear Stearns would fire you for doing the right thing? I mean, Andrew, you were attacked! Wouldn't they want you to do the right thing and seek justice?!" I queried.

Andrew again sighed impatiently as he carefully laid his head back down and faced me.

"Tyler, don't take me the wrong way, God knows I already love you and need you so much that I can't imagine life without you!" Andrew looked up at me and smiled, and then frowned mildly. "However, Tyler, you are a bit naïve of the world outside a smallish town like Gurnee. Things are 'dog eat dog' out here. Things out here are not wrapped all in pretty wrapping paper with bows and salutations of love and concern. People are not as friendly, forgiving, and concerned with their fellow man. Out in the big world it is not a bed of roses! Absolutely they would fire me for bringing disrepute on their businesses." Andrew answered firmly. "They would not want any negative press brought on their companies, and anyone who would bring negative light on the restaurant and Bear Stearns would be eliminated. They have no particular true allegiance to me as a good employee, investment manager, and volunteer. I am as sure of that as I am sure that I have been injured!"

I felt a little offended, however I knew Andrew believed that he was right, and hell, he probably was right. I finished his crack and anus as quickly and the best I could. I then began on his upper thighs.

There was a long silence. I finally decided to clarify and verify a couple of things in Andrew's story.

"So this Jovan." I began, gently. "What all did he do to you?"

"Jovan was into dominance." Andrew groaned as I worked. "He whipped me with the billy-club and the bull whip. He made me kneel to him, to massage his back, massage his front, and rub his body. He whipped me some more. He forced the handles up my ass repeatedly. He beat me some more." I figured Andrew was done; that's all he had said Jovan had done before.

"Jovan then made me give him oral sex. I was humiliated. It was gross." Andrew's voice trailed off. Then he perked up briefly. "There is one person to whom I would gladly give oral sex…" He had a forced smile on his face, and he turned his head to show it to me. "That person is, with great talent, knowledge, and love, treating and fixing my injuries. It is you, Tyler, hottie!" He finished quietly and coyly, winking at me.

I didn't know exactly what 'oral sex' entailed, but I was flattered, and the thought thrilled me. However, it was sin and I had to wipe the thought out of my mind. I focused on my work on Andrew's thighs.

"Did Jovan take anything?" I asked Andrew again.

"Damn it! Yes, he did!" Andrew groaned and cried out again. "He took my pride, my will, and my security. He took my anal virginity. He took my wallet. Now I have to go through the bull shit of replacing my license and cards and stuff! Fortunately he didn't get my tips… I mean my money I made. He didn't get my earnings for the day!"

This was different from Andrew's story before. Was he lying again to me?! Or was this now the rest of the truth he was giving me to come clean from his previous lies?!

I decided to push further before I informed Andrew I knew his story had lies in it. I was again confused and hurt.

"Why didn't Jovan take your money you had made today?" I queried, innocently.

"I don't know!" Andrew seemed peeved. "I guess because it was in my shoes, and not in my clothing, pockets, or wallet. Yeh, that's it! It was in my shoes!" He groaned again and turned his head away from me.

I was really sure now that Andrew was still lying to me about some things. He was stripped naked from the waist down by Jovan while his shoes were left on? Jovan didn't remove his shoes?! If Jovan did remove his shoes the money would have fallen out, and Jovan certainly would have taken it!?

"How is it that after being beaten senseless you still managed to go with the money, buy our trip package, cell phones with package while in all the pain you are obviously suffering?" I gently continued to press.

"I got paid before the atta... I mean... well, I am just so damn infatuated with you, Tyler, so in love with you... The trip package I did over the computer at work... I just gritted my teeth and did the cell phone thing despite my pain!" Andrew turned to me again and managed to give me his majorly charming, disarming, loving smile that I couldn't resist. "Are you done writing your book!?" Andrew winked at me seductively and rubbed my stomach gently while I worked.

"You have awesome abs, Tyler!" Andrew said softly through clenched teeth and a grunt of pain. He continued to stroke my stomach.

"Thanks, Andrew." I managed as I blushed.

I waited a few moments, disappointed that I had encountered some lies, or at least inconsistencies in Andrew's story. What was he hiding? I brushed the doubts aside.

"Andrew, honey." I said softly. "I know you have still lied to me about some small parts of this whole horrible assault you have endured. You said first that Jovan did not take anything. But now you say that Jovan took your wallet. Where would you keep your earnings other than your wallet, which you then said were in your shoes! Then you say Jovan forced you to give him oral sex, whatever the hell that is! If it is some sex, you were raped! Yet you didn't go to the police or the hospital?! These kinds of differences in stories only occur when one is lying and forgets details from one lie to another. What the hell!? He either took your earnings and wallet or not, as a robber, and he at least partially raped you or he didn't as a rapist!"

"Tyler, honey. I lied at first… but now… now I'm not lying! I swear!" Andrew protested, giving me his hurt look that just melted me with guilt.

Insecurity, fear, and shock washed over me concerning Andrew and this whole situation. Hot tears again filled my eyes as I almost romantically and emotionally lost it with Andrew. I looked quickly away because if I didn't I knew I would cry.

I struggled valiantly and managed to compose myself. Only then did I gaze back into Andrew's handsome face and beautiful eyes.

"You just badgered more detail out of me, Tyler, than I wanted to share initially!" Andrew gave me a puppy dog look. "I wouldn't lie to you unless it were absolutely necessary, Tyler! Life and death, peace or anarchy."

Andrew reached back out and stroked my abdomen. I gulped involuntarily. At that moment I so wanted to kiss Andrew and tell him it was okay…! Instead…

"I know you are lying about parts of your story, Andrew, if not all of it." I interrupted. "But I am not going to ask you why or any more questions, because I trust you have a good reason for lying to me. Maybe I don't need or want to hear the truth. I trust you, Andrew, I love you, and I guess I don't want to know any more."

There it was again! I had slipped and said the 'I love you' thing again to Andrew. How many times had I said it this evening to him?! How many times… had Andrew… said it to me?! He had said it to me now that I thought about it! Was I being too presumptuous, too compulsive?

Although I meant it, I didn't want to actually say it until I knew for sure if Andrew were gay. Oh well! I was almost 80% certain Andrew was gay… That wasn't the reason I was upset about saying 'I love you'. After all Andrew had said 'I love you' and other longed for platitudes tonight that gave me even more confidence that he was gay. I was upset because again I had sinned! I had let God, Landon, my family, Austin, and Andrew down.

I was pursuing a same-sex relationship with Andrew, and it was sin! I felt ashamed and dirty morally.

"I'm not lying. I'm sorry my… my first… lies have… have made you distrust me!" Andrew weakly and gently protested again. "But thanks. I love you too, Tyler!" He smiled again at me, before wincing and groaning loudly.

When he composed himself, Andrew continued speaking.

"Tyler, I love you so much! I do want all of you, but I know that you are Biblically hesitant. I will wait. I will save myself for you. Will you wait for me?!"

I was thrilled at Andrew's pledge! It appeared all doubts as to Andrew's sexual preference were gone. Andrew must be gay to say those things to me. Wasn't he? Mustn't he be? Why did I find Andrew as a gay man so hard to believe and accept?!

At the same time, however, I blushed in shame. Maybe I was embarking on a sinful relationship… with Andrew… the exact thing Landon may have been warning me against?! How had Landon known? Where had he disappeared to so quickly? Was he right? Who or what was he? Exactly what all had he meant in his warning against 'relationships, associations, and activities' that were sinful?!

I felt so tenderly toward Andrew right now, that I nodded in approval.

"Andrew! Lord help me… but… but… I have such feelings…" I knew I shouldn't continue, but my feelings and emotions were on my sleeve and would not be contained right now. "I have such feelings for you that I have… I have to say… I have to say I love you! You stay… You stay in love with me… I love you too! I will wait for you." I stammered ahead even though I felt condemned saying it. God surely hated me now! Would He abandon me?!

Each of Andrew's legs had one or two welts from his buttocks all the way to his ankles. Some were bleeding or weeping. I had only his legs from just below the thighs down to his feet to finish.

As I rubbed in the antiseptic on Andrew's left lower thigh and lower leg, feeling and massaging his skin and muscle tissue, I couldn't help but feel turned on! Andrew, for his part, laid there muttering and cursing Jovan and some other guy. I heard an occasional hateful word for Jaba the Hut and some bikers. As I applied the salve to take away the burn and redness, Andrew started cooing to me about the good job I was doing, and what a good masseuse I was. He wanted me to massage his entire body, and he emphasized 'entire'. I blushed as I realized I longed to massage his 'entire' body... Andrew was sore and very tender though he hid it quite well behind a stony expression. He was no longer crying out and only groaned intermittently.

I was still worried about the severity of Andrew's injuries. I really didn't want to take any chances by having to take Andrew to the hospital, but what if he became hopelessly infected? What if his anus wouldn't heal? What if he said something to my parents when they next called? If my parents found out about Andrew's assault, I would simply refuse to go back home to live! But I knew Mom would not rest until she knew that I was safe!

"You should go to the hospital, follow procedure, get medical care, and file a police report, Andrew." I chided again. "I don't know how to treat these welts so they don't leave scarring on your flawless...perfect... sexy skin and... body." I had to stop myself and quickly say 'body'. I was wandering in my speech because I felt so turned on. I wanted to take Andrew now, although I didn't necessarily know how. I wanted to get naked... to wrap my body around his... to...

"I appreciate your concern, Tyler, but I'll be fine. I've had cuts and scrapes before and they healed just fine. I will not go to the hospital! I will not jeopardize everything over this!" He had said his word, and it was final. "Now, Tyler, no offense please... but drop it! I'm done with the subject."

I paused.

"Andrew, I am serious! These injuries are bad! I would hate for you to have some disfiguring scaring from these welts. Your skin... your body... is so... your skin and body are so perfect, so... so flawless... so sexy." I stopped and closed my eyes briefly. I had to stop! I was giving even more of my secret feelings... my prurient desires... away. "Your body is so much to be proud of that I think you would want to get professional help to heal it!" I blurted instead of the lustful things I wanted to say.

I wasn't finished treating Andrew yet, but I took my hands off Andrew, stepped back, and waited.

I was so attracted to Andrew at this point that I couldn't stand it. I wanted him! I wanted to hold him! I wanted to comfort him! I wanted to force him to go to the hospital to preserve his beauty! I wanted to force him to pursue justice for his assault! I just couldn't believe his refusal to do any of these things.

"Tyler, I understand your position!" Andrew sounded a bit pissed. He lifted his head, turned, and faced me. His face was flush in obvious anger and his teeth were clenched. "I know you do in fact admire the beauty of my body, as do I, and as do I yours, but believe me… I have greater things to preserve for us than my body! I do not… I cannot… I will not lose my job over something this small! I will not lose both of my jobs over something this small." Andrew grimaced, and then smiled wanly at me. "I could lose everything if I go to the hospital and the police. I'm telling you, Tyler! I could also lose you too! I cannot bear that! I have to stay away from that reality. You have to help me. Now, you are doing a fine job. Just keep doctoring me. I heal quickly, and well! I will be fine! I always have! Even as a kid I healed well and quickly without going to the hospital with every injury I sustained. Please, Tyler, help me keep this quiet, and doctor me!?" Andrew looked pleadingly at me.

I shrugged, frowned, and reached for the pair of scissors. I loved Andrew enough already that if he felt that strongly about this situation, I would trust him to know what was best with his body. I cut off some excess bandaging on his back, ass, and legs, and then gazed at how he now lay naked, belly down in front of me. Man, I got hot! I prayed for my feelings to get clean and Christ-like.

As I picked up the medical supplies, loaded them in my arms, and went to put them away I pondered why Andrew, a normally strong, self defensive, jealous, and independent guy from my observations, would try to sweep this whole event under the rug!? I knew what his excuses were, but I wasn't sure I believed them. What was wrong? What was his game?! Was I being a sucker? I did know I loved Andrew, and I again whitewashed any doubtful thoughts. After all he did say he figured and feared he might lose me if he became involved with the police or if he went to the hospital.

I didn't know really how or why he feared he might lose me?! However, whatever his game was and if he were still lying, he was partially doing it for me.

Finally I was done! I was tired and weary as I sat down at the table next to Andrew, who breathed deeply in front of me. Andrew had an uncomfortable but pleased look on his face. I gazed over the beautiful, albeit marred naked body of Andrew lying on the dining room table, tempting every nerve and fiber of my body for some hot sex. I wiped my hands on some paper towels and picked up the medical debris off of the table and the floor. When I had picked it all up, I stood up, gathered all the refuse medical supplies and soiled towels and linens and took them to the trash. I then returned to the table where Andrew lay breathing heavily.

"It hurts, Tyler!" Andrew moaned, grabbing my hand. "Would you get me some vodka straight and avatar from the fridge, and vicodin from the bathroom?"

"That sounds harsh, Andrew!" I exclaimed in surprise. "Are you sure that isn't too much… that those are… are you sure you are not taking too many… drugs and… and alcohol?!"

"Tyler, trust me!" Andrew smiled reassuringly and nodded. "Please get it for me!? I'm in a lot of pain here… I can handle my drugs and alcohol just fine!"

I hurried to the bathroom and searched through the long mirrored medicine/cologne cabinet. I found the vicodin and opened the bottle.

"Get me three of those please, Tyler?" Andrew called.

I grabbed three, cupped them, and hurried back to the kitchen.

I retrieved the vodka and avatar from the refrigerator, mixed an eight ounce drink, and then took it over to Andrew. He smiled weakly at me.

"Thank you, Tyler!" He made a kissing motion and winked at me. He lifted up his head and rested on his elbows. He guzzled down the drink.

I walked to Andrew's left side and began gently massaging his neck and parts of his shoulders that were not injured or bandaged. I realized then that I wanted to touch Andrew over every inch of his naked body. I wanted the surface of my naked body touching, rubbing, and holding

Andrew's naked body. He appealed to me so much I was almost sick with longing and desire for him! I again had sparked an internal battle between my knowledge and 'training' in Christian Biblical heterosexuality and my love, feelings, and desires for Andrew. What should I do? How would I resolve this battle? I wanted to surrender to Andrew and an intimate relationship with him, but I was terrified for my immortal soul. I did not want to go to hell!

"Ooohhh!" Andrew cooed contentedly. "That feels so good, so natural, Tyler! I want things like this from you for the rest of my life!" He smiled happily. "Aaaaahhh! That's how I want you, Tyler! You have hit the right spot!"

"Andrew?" I queried thoughtfully, still gently massaging the healthy spots on his back. I enjoyed the thrill and stimulation of his gratitude and compliments.

"Yes? What is it, Tyler?" Andrew asked, gazing directly at me.

"Were you really telling me the truth?... about Jovan and your assault, I mean?" I met Andrew's gaze and looked seriously at him.

"Tyler, I was!" Andrew lifted his head and studied me firmly. "I would only tell you what is right, needful, and best for you to know. It is best you know the truth. I owe you only the truth, Tyler. You deserve it, and so much more!"

"Thank you, Andrew." I responded softly, blushing. "I hope you are always honest with me."

I watched Andrew's beautiful naked, partially bandaged body as I massaged him for another minute or two. Then I stopped and held out both arms.

"Andrew, let me help you to sit up." I spoke tenderly.

Andrew grabbed one of my hands with his left hand and pushed up with his right. I grabbed his legs and pulled them over the edge of the table as he sat up. Andrew, immediately upon sitting up , began shaking and wobbling. He closed his eyes and dropped his head. I grabbed his shoulders to steady him.

"Andrew!" I was alarmed. "Are you all right?!"

"Tyler!" Andrew rasped, as he was visually exhausted and weakened. "I'm more exhausted than I thought. Pour me another vodka, mix in a teaspoon of the avatar, and put it on my bed stand please? I need it desperately again right now. The pain... I may pass out!"

"Okay." I said slowly, crossing to the refrigerator. I kept an eye on Andrew as I pulled out the vodka and poured half a glass. The other half I filled with Canada Dry. I measured a teaspoon of the avatar, whatever that was, and put it in Andrew's drink. I mixed it vigorously, and then quickly carried it in to Andrew's nightstand.

As I returned to the dining room, Andrew was standing, leaning against the table and wobbling. I could see his whole, glorious, naked body... his ample package... and it did not disappoint! I wanted him now, again, and I fought a physical/spiritual battle right there in the dining room as I hurried to his side.

Andrew was oblivious to this, or so it seemed. He stood there, looking desperately and needfully at me. His eyes and countenance seemed to beg me physically for help.

"Tyler!" Andrew bowed his head briefly and I thought he would fall. I picked up speed to reach him more quickly, but Andrew lifted his head again.

"Tyler, honey, would you help... would you... help me... to my bedroom and help me... help me to get into bed?" Andrew was breathless and obviously in pain and physical distress.

I was worried about Andrew. He didn't look well and he clearly didn't feel well. He had been whipped and beaten senseless, had lost a lot of blood, and he was exhausted. Without my concern over all these issues I would have refused Andrew's request. But because of these concerns I let my guard down and agreed to help Andrew to his room. I wanted to do whatever I could to help him in his time of need.

I got on Andrew's right side and grabbed his right arm. He and I draped his right arm over my shoulders with my right hand. I put my left arm around his naked waist, grasping his hip bone with my left hand. We hobbled that way to Andrew's bedroom.

I fought all sorts of sordid love scenes with Andrew against the little I knew of the Biblical mandate against same-sex love and behavior. I was so pissed that the church and my parents had so pathetically prepared me to battle against this temptation! Was I the only one fighting this battle? Why did God make me to fight this battle inside myself largely alone? How was I supposed to stop my gay feelings and become a 'natural' heterosexual?

Inside Andrew's bedroom I sat him down on the edge of his bed. I quickly released Andrew and went back to the dining room table. I brought back his bloody pants and shirt into the bedroom to put them in the dirty clothes. I wanted to lie with Andrew and hold him, but I knew it was wrong! I must leave! I must flee the temptations that he presented to me! I must rebuke the devil in the name of Jesus and banish all of these thoughts and desires. I turned toward the door, but Andrew stopped me.

"Help me into bed, Tyler?" He asked plaintively. "I don't need to wear pjs in my condition. I'll just… just sleep naked with my bandages. I just… I just… I need your strength right now!? Please help me? I feel very weak!?"

I turned around and smiled. He needed me! He wanted me… my help! I tenderly put my left arm under Andrew's legs, and my right arm around his shoulders and under his right underarm. My alarm bells began going off! I was becoming hot touching this intimately a man for whom I carried such a huge torch. Andrew, smelling of tantalizing odors of masculine cologne and deodorant, and even medical supplies, basked in my attentions and was becoming hard as well.

I picked Andrew up and turned him to a horizontal angle with the bed. As I lowered him to the bed, I lost my balance, and dropped him into bed, upon which I promptly fell on top of him. I was so embarrassed! However, we were now in his bed, his whole bed was available… and I wanted to stay with him so dearly… I stopped myself again. I started fighting my desires with whatever scriptures would come to mind. Unfortunately none of the few I knew would come to mind. I did need to seek more Scripture ammunition. I needed to do daily devotions!

"Oh!… I… Andrew… I mean… I am so sorry!" I hurriedly struggled to lift myself off of him. I was up on my hands, trying to get my knees and legs under me when Andrew spoke in a soft, sensuous voice.

"I'm not sorry, Tyler." He reached up and touched my cheek gently. I nuzzled his hand. We looked deeply into each other's eyes. Time, doubts, space, and life seemed to melt away for me as Andrew and I touched each other spiritually and emotionally through our gaze and his stroking of my cheek.

The mixture of our colognes, a smidgen of Andrew's underarm sweat, and the obvious chemistry between us that I suddenly felt, the electricity in the air, the scent of our deodorants, and the sweetness of the moment intoxicated me. I had only been drunk that once with Andrew, but I now felt drunk, yet acutely and wonderfully alive at the same time. Suddenly I became caught up in the hormones, desires, and the moment. I leaned forward toward Andrew, and he rose a bit and stopped. We gazed at each other again, and then I slowly moved in, cupping Andrew's face in one hand and giving him a lingering kiss on the lips.

I suddenly felt dirty and ashamed, and I backed away.

"No, Andrew… I shouldn't have done that. I am sorry, I didn't mean it!" I blurted in embarrassment as I shook my head in shame.

I couldn't look Andrew in the eyes. Hanging my head, I castigated myself for really blowing it with Andrew this time!

"Tyler." Andrew whispered. "I'm not sorry! And I do mean this!"

Andrew ran the fingers of his right hand through the hair on the back of my head, sending chills of ecstasy that I had never felt before coursing through me. Then he pulled me toward him. All of my senses and hormones began pumping and racing. He locked me in a kiss to end all kisses. It felt so right! So natural! It felt like I had lived all of my life for this moment, this reality, this man. Andrew continued to run his hands through my hair. How could feelings… and… love like this… be wrong?!

Suddenly, after what seemed like several minutes, I came to my senses. This was wrong! I pulled away forcefully.

"Good night, Andrew." I said firmly as I rose and left his room.

I was so torn. I now knew Andrew was gay, or else was pretending to be. I also knew I had gay tendencies, I, a Child of Christ! How could this be?! I kissed Andrew, and enjoyed it! I wanted Andrew to kiss me, and I enjoyed it too! But as a Christian I was supposed to abhor sin in all its many manifestations. Why did I not abhor the thought of a same-sex intimate relationship with Andrew?! God said he would not allow his children to enter into a position of temptation from which he/she could not escape. What about my situation? Why did not God help me to escape?! Maybe I didn't want to escape?! Maybe I wanted this with Andrew in my life, for my life time!

I couldn't do this thing with Andrew! I had to stop it!

I also had to go to bed. Tomorrow was my first day of work. I quickly undressed, and put on my pjs. Then I crawled into bed.

Was I about to enter into a relationship of sin of which Landon Whitmore had spoken?! 'Who the hell was he?!' I thought again. 'Why hadn't he been more specific in his 'warning'?!' I no longer believed that a monogamous spousal relationship with another man was universally wrong or sinful. Landon and Austin most likely did believe it was wrong.

I fell asleep to thoughts of Andrew and of being with with him... in life... in bed...

# CHAPTER 36

# MY STRATEGIC ASSESSMENT

A warm summer breeze wafted through the large open bay window, gently blowing my blond curls around my face. I looked over at Tyler who was sitting next to me on the living room floor. The breeze also ruffled the longer brown hair on the top of his head. He turned to me, a smile adorning his gorgeous face. I smiled in return, and then looked back at the TV where we were playing Wii.

Suddenly I felt a hand, fingers extended, run tenderly through my hair. I turned carefully to see Tyler right next to me, smiling at me as he played with my hair and stroked my head. His expression was one of pleasure, desire, and lust.

"Andrew…" Tyler purred as I reached up and began stroking his luscious cheek, neck, and head. "I love you madly! I… I… I want you… now!"

I lovingly continued stroking Tyler's face with my left hand and wrapped my right arm around his waist.

"I love you too, Tyler!" I softly assured him as I neared his face. "I want you so badly it hurts!"

I locked lips with Tyler in a sweet, passionate French kiss as he wrapped both of his arms around me. He was massaging my back as we kissed.

I wrapped my arms around Tyler. His buff body rubbed mine, causing my hormones to go crazy and my flag to rise. I began taking his t-shirt from his pants, lifting it up to his head for removal. I put Tyler's arms straight up in the air. Kissing his bare chest and abdomen I lifted his t-shirt up and licked his underarm…

There was a racket right next to my head. It wasn't strange to my internal synchronous clock, but it shook me awake and out of my wonderful dream. Damn! I was just going to make mad, passionate, sweet, erotic love to Tyler and the damn racket awakened me! That always happened to me when my dreams were that spectacular and I wanted them to continue to the end!

The dream, however, caused me to remember Tyler and his new, hot, stimulating presence in my apartment. I continued to feel hot and to become fully aroused from the prospect of making love to Tyler, even if only in my dreams.

It took a minute for me to realize it was my alarm going off, and when I did I flopped over and hit the alarm clock until it turned off. I felt euphoric but exhausted, and I wanted to snooze a little more. However, I also remembered with joy that I wanted to help Tyler get up for work. I wanted to encourage him and give him my support for his first day at work. I had to get up now.

The movement required to get out of bed caused me to yell and fall back on the bed in pain. I hurt all over. My back, the backs of my arms and legs, my buttocks, my anus, my feet, and my neck still pained, stung, and smarted. Although Tyler's expert first aid had done wonders, everything still hurt. As I lay there waiting for the pain to subside, I briefly pondered seriously if I should still go to the hospital and seek professional aid. What if some of my welts became seriously infected? What if I needed some stitches, steri-strips, or attention to prevent permanent, disfiguring scarring? What if my injuries, without professional medical attention, permanently scarred my unblemished, baby soft, beautiful, light complected skin? What if I did have some internal anal or rectal injuries from my session with Jovan that Tyler couldn't see or discern? What if I had some complications with any of these injuries? Could I continue to work this way? Should I continue to work like this, or wait until I healed? How long would I take to heal without professional medical assistance? I couldn't afford to take any more than a day or two off work for this situation.

On the one hand my concern and fear over infections, further complications, disfigurement, and missing work were serving together to herd me bitching and pleading to the hospital and the police. On the other hand, when I managed to calm my fears and anxieties, logic counseled me that the consequences of hospital and police involvement would be catastrophic.

First of all, if I went to the police and the hospital with the explanation of my attack as I had told Tyler I would be committing a crime. In their investigation of my assault, the police would most certainly discover that this story was all lies. I would be guilty of filing a false police report and complaint. I would have to come clean about the actual way and means of receiving the wounds I had endured, and hope that the police didn't prosecute me and send me to jail. I would also have to drag The Flamingo Lounge into the mess. Mr. Richard would find out about my beating and blow his stack.

Obviously Tyler would find out about my deceit too. As my roomie I could not keep him oblivious to and of all the surprise visits and investigations by police and lawyers. He would definitely find out about my true 'attack', my true job, my true life, and I had no doubt that he would be appalled. In his disgust and revulsion at my true job and his anger and feelings of betrayal over the lies I had told him to establish and protect 'us', I knew he would leave. I would lose my true love forever!

At this point, my dishonesty in my police and hospital reports and their prosecution of me would generate court action and sanctions. This would further cause publicity and a media 'anal exam' of me, my lifestyle, and my job. In the zoo that the media would cause The Flamingo Lounge and Mr. Richard would most assuredly fire me. I would lose my job, my Flamingo-subsidized home, my income/investments, and Tyler in one or two weeks, max.

Finally, if I went to the police and hospital and were totally honest with the way, reason, and means of how I received my wounds, I would be up shit creek without the proverbial paddle as well. The same consequences would certainly develop as in the first scenario, except I would not be guilty of a crime. Both ways would take Tyler away from me.

I didn't want to do or say anything to screw up my potential developing future with Tyler. I would move heaven and earth... and hell to preserve 'us'! The facts were I could not risk 'us' by going to the hospital and police. I would have to trust Tyler's Christ-inspired and farm-learned expert medical care and my uncanny healing abilities to see me through this crisis. I had to have faith in Tyler, me, and God. What!? Had I said that…? Tyler was definitely having an effect on me, helping me to begin thinking and talking about God and religion.

As I thought back, I was very thankful for the intimate experience that Tyler and I had had while he cared for the welts and injuries that I had sustained from Jovan. I remembered the thrill of having Tyler stroke my head and run his hand through my hair; the sensual, loving massage and touch that Tyler had given me in applying the medication and bandages. He had touched every inch of my naked backside. His fingers, his hands had felt my flesh, some of it intimate flesh! Despite the pain and discomfort, I had a major hormone rush and pleasure time when Tyler's fingers worked their medical wonders between my butt cheeks and on my anus. I was so totally aroused, stimulated, thrilled, and ready for action with Tyler during his treatment of me that it was all I could do to stay on my belly on the table. I knew now the hormonal and sexual thrill of having Tyler in complete control of my body… touching, massaging, petting, prodding me… The gentleness and comfort of his loving touch, the sexual stimulation of his hands all over me! I had been and was in gay heaven!

For a minute I couldn't believe it! Had Tyler and I actually been that close… that intimate last night? Had Tyler actually undressed me? Had he really seen me naked?! Had we actually shared passionate kisses in this condition, me naked and Tyler in a t-shirt and house pants? Had Tyler really massaged medicine into and cared for my wounds?! Had he really touched me all over my body? Had he really worked in my ass?! Or had I dreamt it all?!

I looked under the covers. I was nude, had some visible bandages, and suffered from pain. It hadn't been a dream. Tyler had undressed me, massaged medicine into my naked body, had touched me all over, helped me to bed, fallen spread eagle on me, and then he had initiated the kiss. The kiss that told me he was gay, or at least had gay tendencies. Then I had kissed Tyler. It had been the best, most sensually explosive, chemically active, stimulating, and meaningful kiss I had ever shared with a guy! I knew I owed it all to my hopefully 'life-long lover', Tyler. I couldn't wait to kiss him passionately again!

I had for so short a time, but what seemed like such a long time, hoped for a life-long lover who would accept me for whom I was, a gay man, a lover who would never leave his lover, his spouse, and never forsake him. For me, I longed for my lover, my spouse, to be Tyler! I longed for him to feel about me as I did about him! I wanted Tyler ever so much, and I felt he was the one for me. I had now a pretty good set of evidences that he was gay, and I knew he could meet my needs. However, I was not so sure that Tyler was the 'one' for me until after last night. I was almost certain now that he was gay. In addition, the proverbial dies were cast. I now knew without a doubt that Tyler was perfect for my life-long lover. He was the one for me, he was perfect for me, and he equaled or surpassed me in every way. He was a perfect helpmate and he was the right sex. He was the most facially and physically gorgeous man I had encountered in all my sexual liaisons with men and he turned me on in all the right physical and sexual ways. I was so emotionally, physically, and sexually turned on by Tyler that it was all I could do to restrain myself from jumping his bones.

I lay there a minute or two basking in the afterglow of the previous night's advancements with Tyler. The memories of last night would comfort me for a while, at which point I planned on having more to add to it. If I played my cards right I knew I could fully win Tyler's heart, his lust, his desire, and his life-long loyalty despite his Biblical and religious hang-ups. I just had to play the game right! I had to convince him on his own familial, familiar, moral, and religious background that being in love with another man was not a sin. I had to convince him that our love, our relationship, and our intimate sex would be all right Biblically. I had to convince him that we could be lovers and spouses and still be Christians, go to church, be heaven bound, be respected, and be solid, proud citizens.

The snooze alarm kind of jolted me back to reality. I turned it off.

I remembered again that I had the day off, but I was taking Tyler back and forth to his first day of work. If I had my way I would take Tyler to work and back to our home every day, but I knew that would be impossible because of my job. I got up and threw on a bathrobe, the bandages and welts felt prickly and made me feel pained and uncomfortable. I smiled as I remembered I had my love for Tyler to make me feel fine! However, I also needed and had plenty of vodka, avatar, and vicodin to ease my pain.

I turned on the lights as I made my way to Tyler's bedroom. I expected to awaken him, but I found him up and already in the shower. I slipped in to go to the bathroom.

"Andrew?!" Tyler worriedly called. "Is that you?"

I smirked in pleasure and a little amusement at Tyler's alarm and seeming fear in an apartment as secure as mine.

"Yes, Tyler!" I answered reassuringly. "It is I! Who else would I be?"

There were a few seconds of pause as Tyler resumed washing hesitantly.

"Well…" Tyler mumbled and sputtered. "You could be an intruder,… burglar… voyeur… rapist… or anyone who broke into our apartment! I didn't know you were going to get up this early too!"

"Tyler! Tyler!" I smiled to myself and spoke in a reassuring voice. "I can safely say I have the strongest door and locks on our apartment doorway that are on the market. No one is going to easily break in to our apartment! You need not worry about that!"

While I did my thing I admired the blurry image of what I could see of Tyler's naked body through the shower door. I smiled again and nodded in total approval of his hot body… his manly physique… his blurry package. I finished and washed my hands. I then turned my attentions to breakfast. Omelets sounded good. I hoped Tyler liked omelets!

I scurried to the kitchen, poured a vodka tonic with avatar, took two vicodin, and set about the business of breakfast. Soon I would be feeling no pain, but I would be very happy! While I went about preparing two ham, cheese, mushroom, and sweet pepper omelets, I contemplated and considered my plan and efforts to fully seduce Tyler to fall in love with me and be my life-long lover, and the roadblocks and bumps in the path to that goal.

Last night had been a revealing night to both of us that we had a relationship deeper than familial ties. The fact that Tyler had cared for me so willingly even though that care required him to touch me so intimately and the fact that he had kissed me, and allowed me to kiss him told me that we both felt our relationship was more that of human love, as in heterosexual love. At least it should have told Tyler so. I didn't know how Tyler took it, but I took our making out seriously; I took it as a sign we were falling in love or were already in love. I took it as a sign that Tyler did have gay feelings for me, and I was thrilled! I knew I was already head-over-heels in love with Tyler.

I knew that truly, strictly heterosexual guys would not and do not kiss another guy on the lips. Hell! Truly, positively, and self-assuredly straight guys would not come anywhere near to kissing another guy on the cheek, let alone on the lips! Most guys, insecure in their own sexuality and as homophobic as that made them, would not tolerate more than a handshake from another guy. Any heterosexual or homosexual guy knew that. Yet Tyler had initiated our first passionate lips-to-lips kiss, even though he seemed to have scared himself in so doing. My second kiss to Tyler, our most passionate of the two, was open-mouthed. It wasn't a French kiss, a sexual kiss, but it had been open mouth. Ignore their self-imposed homophobia and insecurity, it just wouldn't have happened between straight men. Tyler had to be gay to initiate a lip kiss! I flushed and felt a wave of ecstasy at the thought.

However, my rapture, joy, and sexual thrill at these events and my final conclusion that Tyler was gay were tempered by one big honking roadblock. I knew that Tyler was conflicted about developing and deepening our love and relationship because of his upbringing in the Christian faith. I knew about the 'poison' (at least I considered it poison!) that Christians injected into the issue of homosexuality. Also I knew that that Christian 'poison' caused young Christian people struggling with their true sexual identity to feel extreme guilt, shame, self-abasement, and low self esteem if they felt anything but heterosexual desires and tendencies. It was cruel, heartless, unchristian, and disgusting to so vilify a sexual orientation created by God that the Church risked driving away hurting people!

I felt, however, that my plans to acquire Tyler as my life-long lover and convince him it was Biblically okay were progressing quite well and on target. My mission was to overcome any moral, ethical, Biblical doubts or misconceptions, and hang-ups that he had about 'us' and convince him that we were meant to be, our relationship was Biblically okay, and we could be Christian and still be homosexual lovers and spouses. I just had to overcome and lay to rest any doubts that he had from his Christian 'poisoning', and convince him that we were meant to be! I had to convince him that homosexuals were created by God to be homosexual and love their same-sex as others loved the opposite sex. That's what I knew and believed after all!

Tyler's Biblical hang-ups with our deepening relationship were particularly irksome and frustrating to me! It wasn't that I didn't believe in God, because I did... I did... believe... in God?! It was just that I did not believe in a God as preached by most churches... or TV preachers. I could count on my two hands the number of times I had been in a church over my lifetime, so my knowledge of church doctrine was from the media. Anyway, I didn't believe in a God that excluded and condemned certain groups of people based on how they were created by Him, whether black or white, heterosexual or homosexual. I believed that I was created gay, and that God would not make a mistake, a delinquent, a sinner, or a weirdo. Therefore, in the eyes of God I was just as equal as a heterosexual, deserving all of the same rights and privileges due to heterosexuals. I believed God loved all of His creation and His children equally, regardless of race, religion, sex, or sexual orientation. I believed all of our genetic characteristics with which we were created were okay in the eyes of God!

Even assuming it were true that homosexuality was a sin, and that same-sex love and relations were Biblically wrong, the Bible documented how God loved and sent Jesus to die for the sinner. Biblically I understood all of us were Christians, unless you were an adherent to a non-Bible based faith. All we had to do to earn the title 'Christian', as I understood it, was to accept Jesus' shed blood as a propitiation for our sins, and then live a good life as we were created. We were to be ourselves, yet be separate from the world. We were to do unto others as we would have them... was this it? ...as we would have them do unto us.

I had repented of my 'sins' and accepted Jesus as my Lord and Savior at least twice as a child. It was between the time when I was maybe five or six. I kept praying for a better life, better foster parents, and no abuse. However, God did not answer my prayers, and I just gave up on Him. I determined to survive my life as best I could and not worry about God, the Bible, and 'sin'.

As I grew up I didn't consider my homosexuality a sin, so of what did I have to 'repent' in that area?! Rather I viewed my life as created by God, and my being, characteristics, and sexual orientation as created by God. I was living my life as God created me to live it! Therefore I was a good person… a Christian too!?

These beliefs and more I would use as ammo to take down Tyler's Church and Christian induced prejudices against our sexual orientations, his Biblical opposition to our homosexual relationship, and his Biblical prejudice against 'us'.

I realized now I had to begin engaging Tyler in the spirituality of our relationship. He was clearly developing homosexual feelings and a strong love for me. I had to tackle him on and in his basic Christian beliefs about our relationship and love. I needed to face the issue of religion and homosexuality head on, counter it, and reform it in Tyler's ethics and mind. I needed to reform his beliefs in his Christian faith to include an approval of and for homosexual Christianity. What's more, I needed to do it now. The sooner, the better!

I paused as the omelets fried merrily away. I took several long dregs of my drink, basking in the feeling of the alcohol warming my body, relaxing and modifying my mood and tension! I smiled contentedly again over my progress with Tyler. I just needed to relax and play Tyler and my plan out! All was in control and going well.

I could hear my Tyler finish his shower. I felt happy inside as I surveyed our breakfast. The omelets were almost done and the coffee was percolating in the maker. I set the table and put the condiments onto it. Then I set about making toast. I retrieved butter, peanut butter, and jelly from the refrigerator and took my seat next to the appliance to finish the toast. As I waited for Tyler, I continued thinking about him.

Whistling happily I listened to Tyler shaving, applying deodorant and cologne, and dressing… Dear God! I wanted to watch him… clothe his hot… naked body!

Tyler was shortly preceded into the kitchen by the wonderful and hormonally intoxicating fragrance of Axe deodorant and Avatar cologne. He appeared from his room spic and span, combing his hair, and dressed casual/nice for his first day of work. He was so hot, suave, and debonair that I wanted to take him right there in the kitchen! I fought the urge to attack him, kiss him, take off his... No! I won't go there yet in thought or deed... I decided. I had to restrain my passions for Tyler.

"Good morning." Tyler greeted me, smiling. "Great spread! Everything looks delicious! How are you feeling?"

"Good morning to you, Tyler. I feel fine, and thank you for your excellent medical care!" I replied, smiling back. "Have you ever had omelets?"

"Is that what you are preparing?" Tyler's face showed pleasure as he winked at me. "No, I can't say I have ever had this breakfast food. They look delicious though, as I said. What all is in them?"

I took the omelets out of the skillets and put them on our plates.

Tyler took a bite as he looked questioningly at me.

"Well, omelets have eggs as a base." I winked back at him. "Then these omelets have a little milk, ham, cheese, mushrooms, and sweet green peppers in them."

I took a bite as Tyler loaded a rather large bite in his sexy mouth.

"Do you really like them?" I inquired.

"Yes... yes!" Tyler chewed and swallowed. "They are... they are scrumptious!"

He smiled warmly at me.

We ate in silence a minute.

"Did you sleep well, honey?" I inquired then.

Tyler stopped and put the napkin in his shirt collar like a bib. I smiled and chuckled inside. Tyler was so cute and predictable!

"Aww! Okay, I guess." Tyler was unsure of anything as it sounded. "I was thinking a lot about my new job, and... well... things..." Tyler's voice trailed off. I knew what he meant immediately! I found it comforting and exciting that Tyler and I were so much on the same wave length that I could finish his sentences. I also found it thrilling and stimulating to know that Tyler had spent some of the night thinking about me and our relationship! I knew at that point that I wasn't the only one considering the developing and growing relationship between us.

"How about you, Andrew?" Tyler gazed at me with questioning concern. "Did you sleep well? I mean with the welts and all, you must have been so uncomfortable!"

"I slept fine, Tyler!" I lied seductively. "I thought about you... about us, all night!" I winked lustfully at him. I tried to convey as much true love as I could through my expression.

Tyler seemed unaffected by my efforts and continued eating heartily.

I quickly changed the subject. My food was so good! Besides I had to plan my conversation with Tyler carefully step by step.

"What would you like to drink?" I asked. "I have milk, oj, vodka, coffee, rum, scotch...?" I arose to comply with Tyler's request.

"I'll have oj." Tyler replied. "I'll also have a cup of Joe if you don't mind."

I poured Tyler his oj, both of us coffee, and me a shot of rum and vodka.

I sat down again. We ate in awkward silence for a few minutes. I began to wonder if I had been too forward. However, when I perused his gorgeous face I knew immediately Tyler had something on his mind about which to talk to me, but he was unsure how to broach the subject. I waited patiently. Happily I peered at him. He was so hot when his beautiful mind was hard at work!

"Look, Andrew, about last night..." Tyler began. He was visibly uncomfortable, and was almost mumbling. He stopped and took another bite of his omelet. "Was that... your giving me a kiss... our kiss... the kissing we shared... did last night... was it... were they... our kissing... real kisses from you...? I mean... did you... do you... did you kiss me because you... really... well... love me... or were you just joking with me... trying to weird me out?" Tyler gazed up at me firmly and seriously.

I could tell by his expression he wanted to know the truth, now! Not that I would automatically lie about my feelings to and for Tyler at this point.

However, then I did question whether to be honest or not. What if my senses… my 'gaydar' was slipping… were faulty? What if it were too early for Tyler for me to be honest? What if the time was right for me to be completely honest?! Would I scare Tyler off? Had I misread him last night?! Maybe he was feeling gross, guilty, or evil even about our making out!? Should I just laugh it off, make light of it?! Or should I affirm it, endorse it, and assure Tyler that I had been completely honest with my feelings when I kissed and made out with him!? My desire to be honest won out, and I just plunged ahead into the truth.

I reached across the table, took his right hand, gently cradled it in both of mine, and looked at him firmly and passionately eye-to-eye. He didn't resist me. I saw a look of love, desire, longing, and hope in Tyler's eyes that encouraged me on.

"Tyler, I meant that kiss and the feelings that went along with it more than any promise I've ever made! You are my one and only love, Tyler! I want you forever!" I murmured intensely. Suddenly I gleeped, and choked on the saliva; I became slave to a violent coughing spell.

Tyler jumped up, rounded the table behind me, and carefully swatted my lower neck, just over the beginnings of the welts. As I calmed down and began to regain my composure, Tyler returned to his chair, sat down, and watched me in concern. However, I also couldn't help but detect sadness and disappointment in his beautiful brown eyes and handsome face.

My eyes watered so badly that Tyler was blurry. I struggled to clear my eyes and to get the liquid out of my pipes.

"Are you all right, Andrew, honey?!" Tyler asked me when I was finally able to stop and down my shot of rum to clear the tickle in my throat.

"Yeh! I think so!" I cleared my throat. "Anyway, the answer to your question, hon, is that yes, I very much meant the kiss. I love you, Tyler! I don't regret anything, any act, words, or expressions of love that have transpired or will transpire between us!"

There was an uncomfortable pause as a deep sadness, anger, and disappointment passed over Tyler's countenance. He curled one side of his lips up in a sarcastic half smile and shook his head in anger and disbelief.

"I knew it!" Tyler exclaimed angrily and sarcastically. "Ha! Ha! I really meant it, Tyler! Ha! Ha! So funny it was! So funny you thought I meant it!" Tyler fake laughed and looked at me in disappointment, curiosity, and reproach.

# CHAPTER 37

# GUIDING MY LOVE TO THE 'WATER TROUGH'

He sounded genuinely hurt and certain that it all had been a joke to me… that I had kissed him passionately… opened mouth as a lark! I had opened up totally to Tyler, and he… his insecurity… I was flabbergasted and nonplussed that he would have this reaction to my honesty and true feelings. It must be because of my ill-timed and unexpected coughing spell.

"Tyler!" I was a little peeved that he didn't take me seriously. I was wearing my heart, my emotions, and my very soul on my sleeve! "Look at me… Look at me very closely! Do I really appear as though I am telling you a joke?! Do I really look like I am someone who could… who would kiss you like I did and not have it mean anything seriously… just do it to humiliate you?! Didn't you feel the electricity, the intensity, the chemistry, and the passion we shared in our kisses?! Didn't you feel my raw emotion… desire… longing for you, my love for you, and my love for us in our intimate kissing?!"

Tyler's face had become serious as he did look at me straight, boring his beautiful brown pools deep into my soul. Tears came to his eyes when I finished. I could tell that they were tears of joy and understanding. He nodded quietly and gently as he looked down at his plate briefly. When he again raised his head and gazed into my eyes his face was flushed and he looked happy and relieved.

"Lord forgive me!" Tyler said as he frowned and then nodded positively again. He smiled at me, appearing a bit proud, and then ate a little more. His countenance was thoughtful but serious as he looked down at his plate. "Lord forgive me, but yes, Andrew, I… I… I did feel… I felt all those things… and so much more… so much more truth… in our kissing…"

He didn't attempt to make eye contact yet.

I again picked up his right hand and cradled it in mine, gently stroking his forearm.

"Tyler…" I gulped, a little doubtful about the timing and appropriateness of what I was about to say, "Tyler… honey… I don't… I don't want to scare you… but I feel you need to know. This will impress upon you the truth of what I feel. I wanted to… when we were making out… intensely kissing… I was fighting the lust to… I wanted to make moves on you sexually so badly… I was hard… I had to fight to leave… to keep my hands off of you! You almost lost your virginity!"

Tyler flushed and looked up at me. He gazed into my eyes, a grin playing across his beautiful lips.

"How about… how about you, Tyler? What did… what effect… what did our making out do to you… how did it make you feel?"

Tyler blushed again, and looked away from me. I could tell his Christian bias against same-sex love was causing him great difficulty in admitting the truth of his reaction and feelings.

"Tyler?! Look at me… come on… I want to know! How did our kissing make you feel?" I prompted gently.

He gazed back at me, his face scarlet red.

"Well?"

Tyler squirmed, and the muscles in his hand clenched briefly. He held my gaze, but was obviously uncomfortable as he kept opening and closing his mouth. Lord, I wanted to kiss him! I wanted to kiss every inch of his naked…

"I… well, I… my mind… my body… I…" Tyler stammered, looking down at his plate again.

"Tyler. Look me in the eyes, honey." I spoke softly.

He looked back up at me, and gazed steadily into my eyes.

"I… well… I had a major… a major hormone rush… I felt… I felt euphoric… turned on… I too, was… well… I was… I had a woody." Tyler hung his head briefly. His Christian beliefs obviously made him feel ashamed and guilty. These exact feelings that religion heaped on those in the LGBTQ community were one of the precise reasons I stayed away from all churches!

Despite my brief anger, I smiled and nodded. I knew it! I knew he had felt sexual and physical lust, desire, and urges from our kisses in a major way! I patted his hand.

"So, you did really mean our kisses?" Tyler stared timidly and hopefully at me. "You really meant them to signify your love for me? You really... do... you really do... love me?"

"Tyler, I meant those kisses more than anything I have ever said or done! I meant them to signify my growing love and desire for you." I gazed seriously and lovingly into Tyler's face. "I don't joke about love! When I speak about my love for you, Tyler, I mean it more than almost any oath I could say!"

We both ate in silence for a minute or two again. I watched with joy, lust, and love as Tyler's pulchritudinous face exhibited signs of majorly serious thoughts still taking place in his beautiful, brilliant, enviable brain. He wasn't finished talking to me about 'us' I easily concluded.

"Andrew..." Tyler began quietly. "As for me... the kiss... well... it was meant to... it was meant to... to show that I... I too love you, Andrew." Tyler looked up in little peeps, as though he felt very guilty and desperately ashamed about what he was saying. "We... ah... we have a... well, we have a problem... well, more problems than one, but... ah... well one of the... two of the major, all encompassing problems forbid our relationship. I can... I can't... I cannot continue to ignore them!"

Tyler looked up at me with a disappointed, pained, and yet firm countenance. My heart sank, but I knew what one of the issues he would bring up was, and I had already begun preparing for it.

"What are these two 'all-encompassing problems' that we have in our deepening relationship, Tyler?" I asked quietly and respectfully. At first I wanted to swear at him, chastise him a bit for leading me on to this point and then springing 'new' problems on me! However, I knew it wasn't his fault entirely. It takes two to tango. Tyler didn't know before this how much I truly, fervently, and completely loved him. I also knew what he was struggling with and confused about; Christianity vs. his growing homosexual reality. Besides, I craved him and respected him too much to chastise him!

"Well," Tyler began, moving his sliced omelet from one side of the plate to the other nervously, "I may have… well, I may have… occasionally I… well, I fell half off… well, off the heterosexual wagon by… falling in love… by having crushes on… well, other guys… by falling in love with you now, but I still… I still date girls. I like… well… I think I like... I should like... I do... I think I like... girls…" Tyler looked up fully at me and our eyes met again. His pause before 'girls', the expression on his face throughout, and the fact that he mumbled off told me that he was not mentally and emotionally enthusiastic, certain, or honest in his claim to like girls. He almost begged me to dissuade him in his claim.

This was not the first problem interfering with our relationship that I expected him to bring up! I was fully expecting the religious/Christian issue would be number one for us to overcome. I paused briefly in surprise.

"Is that right!?" I asked Tyler disbelievingly, a plot slowly coming to mind as I ate my omelet. I looked him in the eyes before speaking again. "You think that you also or really like girls? I…"

"No!" Tyler interrupted. "I know that I like… I do like… well, yes, I think I also… really… also like girls!?"

That was it. I had to squash this doubt of his immediately!

"Tyler, you must now answer me totally honestly. No messing around, no lying! I want you to be totally and boldly forthright and truthful. Do you understand, honey?!"

I gave Tyler a firm, serious, but questioning gaze. I took a long swig of a new vodka tonic I had poured while he had vacillated in his response to my pledge of love and sincerity. Then I sat back, holding Tyler's eyes. He was getting very nervous again and began fidgeting in his chair. He was clearly growing in fear, insecurity, and reticence as I pushed forward in our discussion of his sexuality. He also seemed to be, as the band Toto had said in their song <u>Africa</u>, "frightened of this thing I have become."

"Okay." Tyler answered coolly and with great trepidation. "I will answer you truthfully. What do you… What's your first question?" He buried his view and attention in his plate and continued eating.

Now I was the one thinking and planning how to show him he had always been more comfortable with, attracted to, and preferential to guys rather than girls. He did not 'date' or 'want' girls! His making out with me last night told me that.

Tyler dabbed his mouth with a napkin and glanced up at me.

"How many girls have you dated in your life?" I asked, continuing to eat breakfast and draw on my drink.

"Oh, I don't know!?" Tyler pondered, still not making total eye contact.

"Truth, Tyler!" I affirmed, watching him closely as I ate. "I want the truth!"

He thought hard for a few moments. He was very uncomfortable as he chewed his food and frowned.

"Tyler, look up at me as we are talking." I exclaimed firmly. I wanted to ascertain if he were telling the truth, and part of that was the necessity to see his face and eyes.

I waited until he did make eye contact before continuing.

"Now, Tyler, I want the truth! How many girls have you dated in your life?" I gave him a serious eye.

"I guess maybe 50. My mom set me up all through my high school years. I didn't have much choice!" Tyler looked back down at his plate, slowly playing and eating. I knew he was lying.

"Cut the crap, Tyler Aaron Belmont!" I commanded involuntarily, hoping my intensity and sincerity would elicit more truth and not fear. As with last night I didn't know where his middle name came from, but I used it. I apparently was right, for Tyler looked up in startled surprise and stared at me in amazement.

"How… how… I mean… where… how did you know my real middle name!?" He exclaimed incredulously, confirming I was right. "I mean…

well… I've never told you what my middle name is…?" His voice trailed off, and I interrupted.

"I don't know, it just came to me. However, tell me the truth, Tyler Aaron Belmont! How many girls have you ever socially dated in your life? And I mean dated for four or five times, maybe even just two or three times." I looked at him firmly, sternly, yet lovingly, demanding the truth.

Tyler gazed at me shyly in the face. He blushed.

"Okay, maybe 35! Mom was really persistent you know!" Tyler shrugged. He was almost pleading me to accept his answer as the truth.

"Tyler Aaron! I cannot help you if you do not tell the truth! How many girls have you socially dated in your high school and early years of 19, 20, and 21? With how many girls have you actually gone out more than once?!" I asked again, as I stopped eating and looked seriously at Tyler.

"I… well… I dated… my mom set up… she had me always… well… I mean… okay, Andrew! If you must know the actual number of girls that I ever dated more than once was probably 9 or 10! There! Are you happy?!" Tyler was clearly angered as he glared at me, his beautiful brown eyes sparking. "I didn't actually socially date very many girls for more than one date! I never found a girl that attractive physically or sexually, or they never found me that attractive, one or the other. I don't know which!? I was never that interested in very many girls.  I was never… I was… I was never that interested… in any girls. Are you happy? You are making me miserable already! I don't like feeling this way!"

Tyler briefly buried his face in his hands before looking back at me reproachfully.

I felt badly, but I knew at this point this line of questioning was necessary to force him over his heterosexual rut into new consideration, recognition, and acceptance of his true sexual orientation and our relationship.

"Really!?" I asked Tyler, winking at him seductively. "You were never that interested in any girl?!" I paused.

Tyler squirmed and fussed in his seat, visibly struggling to maintain eye contact with me.

"No." He said softly and with a sense of finality.

"What is the longest period of time you have dated any one girl more seriously and how many dates did you actually have with her?!" I asked.

"Five to six weeks. We probably had eight dates." Tyler answered promptly. He sounded quite certain in his lie. He fidgeted in his seat as he scratched his head and sniffed.

"Tyler...!" I looked at him firmly, boring my blue eyes into his soul. I could tell he was lying again.

Tyler buried his face in his plate and took a couple more bites.

"Okay... Andrew! This isn't fair!" Tyler glanced briefly, embarrassedly at me. "I can't... I am not able... I can't hide... You are employing... You have me at a disadvantage! I love you, you love me... How the hell can I hide anything from you?! How can I lie to you? You're so damn gorgeous... and hot. You disarm me!" He whined, glancing at me in almost fear. "The longest was three weeks and probably four dates! Are you happy!?"

"Thank you for the compliment, Tyler. You are damn gorgeous and hot too!" I blushed briefly.

I had to plunge forward in my argument of points with Tyler. Especially since all the evidence so far was falling into place to prove to Tyler that he had preferred guys, not girls, for most of his life.

"How old are you, Tyler?" I fired back. I felt that a little heartlessness was called for here.

"21." Tyler was getting sucked into the 'gay quiz' I was making up as I went along.

"When did you first have a 'crush' on, or a deep desire for another boy?" I inquired of him, peering over the rim of my vodka glass.

"I can't remember... I didn't know... I don't know what is a crush and what is not...!" Tyler took a long drink of his orange juice.

"Tyler, honey..." I began patiently, ignoring his obfuscations, "when did you first feel attracted to or interested in another guy... like you feel toward me?! In other words, when did you first have romantic feelings for another guy like you feel for me?!" I demanded, pressing further.

There was a pause as Tyler pissed around with the tiny piece of his omelet he had left on his plate, and sipped his coffee. I could tell he was thinking hard as to whether to be truthful or not. I guessed he would try to lie first.

"I never have… well… I mean… I have… I had never been… I had romantic feelings… like I feel toward you, Andrew… for another guy beginning when I was in the sixth grade. Since then I… since then I have… well… I have been romantically attracted to several guys… I have admired them… admired their facial beauty… enjoyed their hot bodies… wanted them… their brains… Will you shut up now, Andrew, and leave me alone!?" Tyler was definitely sweating as he looked reproachfully at me.

"I will shut up, Tyler, when I am finished with my questions of you! I am trying to show you the fallacy of your first major problem with our deepening relationship." I winked lovingly at him, placing my hands gently over his across the table. "Now, do you remember the first time you had those same admirations and romantic feelings for a girl that you have always had for boys, Tyler?!" I inquired.

"When I was in kindergarten I harbored an attraction to a female schoolmate!" Tyler answered confidently, yet unhappily. He looked at me with his beautiful brown pools and tried to assume a certain and serious visage. He didn't succeed. I could see the uncertainty and fear in his eyes.

"You never loved her or had any feelings toward her, Tyler! Your parents and hers were just using you two for their own laughs about your 'relationship'. They were to blame for your early admiration and supposed infatuation were they not, Tyler?!" I asked, finishing my coffee and gazing at him knowingly over the rim of my cup.

Tyler dodged my eyes and finished his omelet. He paused, and then looked at me in anguish.

"Okay, Andrew! You're right!" Tears began to run down Tyler's cheeks. "I have never had any romantic feelings for any girl like I have had for guys… or anything like I have now, for you! Are you happy?! Are you quite finished ruining my self-esteem?! You are denigrating my dignity and… and… and attacking my faith!"

He looked down at his plate as he sniffled and wiped his nose with a napkin.

I reached over the table, cupped his chin in my hands, lifted his head to look at me again, and gently wiped the tears off his cheeks and out of his eyes. I gazed tenderly into his eyes.

"Tyler, honey, you are wrong about those things…" I purred soothingly.

"Oh yeah?" Tyler's eyes lit up as he blew his nose. "What is that?"

"Admitting who you are… what you are… should make you happy!" I encouraged him as I ran my thumbs over his luscious lips. "Being honest with yourself about… about who you are… being honest with others about your sexuality… definitely it should not ruin your self-esteem… It should help it! It should make you proud, Tyler! As for denigrating your dignity, you should be proud of who you are, no matter your sexual orientation! Your sense of dignity should not in any way depend on how society or religion feel about you and your sexuality. Your dignity is defined by the quality and sincerity of your character and life, not your sexual orientation. And no, I am not attacking your Christian faith."

I put my hands back gently over his and we smiled at each other.

Tyler hung his head as his countenance became sullen and determined. I could tell he was going back into denial and self-protective mode.

"I am not admitting anything to anyone." Tyler muttered defiantly. "I may be in love with you, Andrew. I may have tendencies toward and attractions to same-sex people and relations, but I am NOT gay or homosexual!"

Tyler looked back up at me, the sullen, defiant countenance set in stone on his gorgeous features. He pulled his hands away. 'God! He is so beautiful!' I thought.

"What is next, Andrew?" Tyler inquired, his voice cracking. He smiled wanly at me. He was becoming resigned to my 'findings'?!

I gazed at him and smiled. I mapped out my next set of points.

"Tyler, when did you first have a crush on, or a strong liking of and a strong attraction to another guy? When did you first look at another fella and think 'I would like to touch him!' or 'I would like to see his penis!'"

I asked as I stared sternly and lovingly at Tyler. I knew he had lied when he had answered this question before. I thought asking it again right now might trick him into telling the truth. Besides, since he was slipping back into denial I needed the true answer to hammer home my point to Tyler that he was and always had been gay.

"In the sixth grade!" Tyler blurted, and instantly blanched embarrassedly at me. "I already answered that, Andrew."

I knew he was still lying.

"You are lying, Tyler. I don't believe you. I know it was earlier than that for you, honey!" I pressed comfortingly and reassuringly. "At what age were you when you FIRST actually had a strong attraction to another boy?! The truth, Tyler!"

"Damn you, Andrew! Please stop?! Can't we be finished already?!" Tyler put his elbows on the table and crossed his arms. He glared angrily at me. "I'm sick of… sick of being… I'm sick of being challenged… challenged about my sexuality… and faith!" Tyler put his head down on his arms, burying his face.

"What is the answer, Tyler!" I pressed.

"Andrew!" Tyler raised his head and returned my gaze. He bore a pained, pleading countenance. "Andrew, damn it! Please? Enough is enough!"

"Tyler, I know the truth may be hard to face, but…" I picked his hands up again in mine and squeezed them lovingly. "Honey, answer the question truthfully!"

"I… well, I have… in the sixth grade…" Then Tyler's face assumed a mien of defeat, and tears came to his eyes again. "Damn you, Andrew! Okay! You win! I had a crush at the age of eight on a little boy in… in…. in church youth group! Are you happy now, Andrew!? You are totally destroying my 'normal' past! You are making me feel like a real scum! A real creep… a predator! Do you want to continue, Andrew?! Are you going to continue muck raking through my childhood and youth to make me feel like… realize I could be… a sexual deviant?! Do you want me to feel any more worthless and dirty than I already do?! What the hell do you want?!"

By the time he finished, Tyler was crying again and almost hysterical. I stood up, reached across the table, grabbed both of his shoulders, and gently shook him.

"Tyler!" I commanded worriedly. "Get a grip! Get a hold of yourself! Everything is all right!"

At my touch and efforts at solace Tyler stopped, raised his tear-streamed face, and gazed at me. He was in such pain, conflict, and anguish and it all showed in his face. Before I could organize my thoughts and feelings, Tyler stood up and thrust his face into my chest.

"Hold me a minute, Andrew?" He pleaded as a sob caused his shoulders to heave.

I thrilled that he was asking this of me and I more than willingly complied. Tenderly and lovingly I wrapped my arms around his head and rested my cheek on his crown. Tyler grabbed my arms. I held him until all his sobs were gone. It was so stimulating that again I struggled to keep from initiating intimate behavior with him.

Gently I took Tyler's head in my hands and pushed him back so we were looking into each other's eyes. I drank him in! I wanted his kisses… his body so badly!

"Tyler, do you think I am 'abnormal' as a gay man?" I asked seriously, looking questioningly into his hot, lovely face.

Tyler jerked out of my hands and stood erect. He then frowned and pounded a fist on the table.

"I am NOT gay, Andrew!" He exclaimed angrily.

There were other ways to make my points. I could humor Tyler!

"Okay, Tyler, do you think I am 'abnormal' as a man who prefers men?" I responded patiently.

I reached out and gently grasped Tyler's head, pulling him back toward me over the table. I pulled his head so his face was six inches from mine. Tyler held my inquisitive gaze. Finally he smiled and looked down. I even detected a chuckle.

"No, Andrew." Tyler spoke softly. "You are the most normal person in my life right now! I don't see you or consider you abnormal as a... a gay man."

I cupped Tyler's chin with one hand again, raising his head and face back even with mine. Then I returned to gently holding his head and gaze. Tyler was now at least smiling.

"Do you think I am a scum because I prefer same-sex relationships, Tyler?" I inquired.

There was no pause.

"No, Andrew!" Tyler smiled. "You are a fine, kind... loving... hot... gorgeous... man!"

"Tyler, honey, do you think I am a creep... or a predator... just because I like guys... and love you?" I asked, giving him a loving, questioning gaze.

"No, Andrew!" Tyler did actually chuckle. "You are mentoring kids, not stalking them. And you love others. You'd never..."

"Do you think I am a sexual deviant, or are you really one, just because you and I love each other and are of the same-sex?" I interrupted firmly.

Tyler paused and his smile faded to a sad look.

"Andrew... all my life I... I've been told the few times it came up.... that same-sex relationships... well... are a sexual deviancy..."

"Tyler!" I said gently. "You know me now... you love me now. I love you! Do you think I am a sexual deviant?"

"No! No, Andrew! Of course not!" Tyler assured me.

"Then you should never... EVER think of yourself as any of those things just because you and I love each other! Do you understand, Tyler, honey?!"

Tyler gazed into my eyes, and a loving and grateful smile took over his face.

"Yes, Andrew. I do... understand." He murmured.

I released Tyler and, still maintaining our loving visual embrace, we both sat down.

"Now, Tyler, I have a few more points to make!" I continued gently. "I am laying the groundwork for them with these questions."

"Andrew, this whole line of questioning is unfair!" Tyler exclaimed immediately after I finished. His facial expression had returned to one of anger, pain, and protestation.

"How, Tyler, is it unfair?" I asked coyly and curiously.

"You are taking advantage of my feelings for you, my love for you… my desires… my attraction to you, the fact that I cannot say 'no' to you… to get me to interpret my past as that of a homosexual! I am not a homosexual! I am a man who has a heterosexual-style and monogamous love for another man!"

"Tyler, hottie, whatever you want to call same-sex relationships, or our relationship, is fine with me! That is not my point. I am just striving to prove to you that at some level you have always known you are g… hom… into men more than women. I have to ask these questions of you to prove my points." I reassured Tyler. "Are you ready to continue, Tyler?"

"I guess." Tyler shrugged and frowned at me. He was so damn gorgeous even when he was angry! I wanted to jump his bones right here… right now!

"How old were you when you had your first date with a girl?" I continued, changing the subject.

"Ah… about 15." Tyler responded. He fidgeted in his chair, ran his hand through his hair, and itched himself in the crotch.

How I wanted to do that for him! However, there would be plenty of time in the future to do that. Someday I would be able to be intimate with Tyler…

I was also giddy because I just had a feeling I had Tyler trapped in the truth again.

"Tyler, you are not a good liar! Lying doesn't come easily for you, or become you. Just stop trying, eh?!" I implored as I ran my right hand through his enticing brown hair. "Now, how old were you when you had your first date with a girl?"

Tyler squirmed, and at first would not meet my eyes. I gently grasped his chin and held his face looking at mine.

"I… my parents… well… they had rules…" Tyler gulped, and then looked me directly in the eyes. "My parents said I could date at 15, but I actually never officially dated a girl until mom set me up for the first time when I was 16 ½ ."

"Okay!" I stated. "First dated a girl at 16 ½ … When did you get your first urge to go out with another guy, to a movie, to a dinner, to an outing of any kind?!" I asked Tyler, a bit cockily.

"Okay! Andrew, since…" Tyler was sputtering and looking between his hands at me. "Since you seem determined to… since I think…. Since you seem… Since I think you want to destroy me!" Tyler gulped and I knew he was close to the truth. He was definitely ill at ease. "I will tell you I… well, I wanted… I planned to… I had desires to go out with guys to the movies or anywhere, from the age of eight! I cannot understand your desire to destroy me today! Why are you forcing this?"

"Tyler, I wasn't born yesterday! I have good motives for asking you these questions. Trust me!" It was obvious now that, despite being a Christian, Tyler would lie, obfuscate, deceive, or almost anything to protect his deepest secret; his sexual preference and identity.

"Did you ever go out on a date with a guy? A date that was unofficial, but still a date?!" I continued to press an obviously oppressed Tyler.

"Well, I started… I mean… I went to…. I started going to… I went…" Tyler stopped now and almost fell into his coffee.

"When was the earliest time you were comfortable going ALONE to the movies, dinner, or local dive with a male!?" I asked again, becoming stern, but loving to Tyler.

"Damn it! Andrew!" Tyler put his head down, before looking at me pleadingly and lovingly. "I went to movies with guy friends since I was nine! I have been alone with guys to all sorts of places! I suppose you could call all of them dates! What the hell does that have to do with the price of tea in China?!"

"How about a girl?" I asked, smilingly in a way I knew was bratty. "When did you feel comfortable actually going on a date alone with a girl?!" I took another long drag. I looked at him forcefully and questioningly.

Tyler again turned his gaze from me and looked to the side.

"I told you, Andrew!" Tyler exclaimed. "I was 15 years of age when I went out with girls and... well... continued with guys to movies and restaurants... I..."

I could tell he was not going to answer honestly. Boy, he was learning to lie like a rug!

"Tyler Aaron, you tell me the truth!" I cajoled, looking at him like a parent to a child. "I am talking about a date, not chaperoned, one on one with a girl. I'm not talking about a group date."

"Shut the hell up, Andrew!" Tyler burst out as he doubled up his fists. Then he looked at me and covered his mouth, his face flushing red as a beet. "I'm sorry, Andrew..." He muttered. "I didn't mean it... I'm sorry!"

I ignored his outburst and apology.

"When, Tyler, did you actually have a serious first date with a girl? A date where you were alone, with no one to chaperon, and no group?!" I had now put every utensil down except my drinks. I was ready to take this home.

"I went to dates alone with girls to movies and lunch at the age of 16 ½ ! There! Are you happy!?" Tyler again was exasperated as he looked desperately at me for help, love, and forgiveness. "What do you want Andrew! Just spill it! I can't take much more of this! I feel so... so... so... so gay!"

# CHAPTER 38

# 'THE QUIZ' AND OUR FIRST FLAP

I smiled to myself as I finished my vodka. I had him going my way now!

"Which did you enjoy more? Your dates from the age of nine and on with guys, or your beginning dates with girls at 16 ½ ?" I asked, looking at him kindly, but slyly as well.

Tyler frowned at me and covered his face with his napkin. He looked so cute, so hot. I wanted him again, now! On the breakfast table, on the floor, or in the living room did not matter. I wanted to rip his clothes off and…

"The guys." Tyler interrupted my lust fest and gazed up at me wearily. "I preferred going out with the guys. I never felt comfortable or… or compatible with… girls in a romantic way. I didn't feel any attraction to… any chemistry with… any real physical attraction to… any desire to kiss… any girl. All those things I did feel for… for certain guys… while I was growing up… Where are you going with this, Andrew?!"

"Are you a virgin? That is, a virgin with respect to women?" I queried, changing the subject.

"Yes." Tyler spoke, and smiled proudly. "I have never had any level of sex with a girl! Hell, I have never kissed a girl like I have you!" He stopped abruptly and looked up at me self-consciously.

"Are you a virgin as far as males are concerned? I mean, Tyler, have you ever been sexually intimate with, or had intercourse with a guy?" I pried even further, knowing if he weren't a virgin and had had sex of any kind with a guy or guys he wouldn't be able to lie at this point. I could almost feel the vibes, the power I had over him. I was like a truth serum to Tyler.

Tyler gave me a puzzled, surprised look. Then he looked down and kind of surveyed his body before answering.

"Does it answer your question, Andrew, when I say that I have no clue as to how two guys would have sex?! I mean… well… I believe I am… must be… a virgin with respect to men!" Tyler looked at me. "To my knowledge no guy has ever had sex with me. I know I have never had sex with a guy consciously."

"Has any guy ever touched you… your genitals… has any guy touched you there… caused you to ejaculate?"

"Hell no! Only in my dreams!" Tyler blurted defensively. Then he went beet red as he apparently realized what he had said. "I mean no… never! I am… I am not that way…!"

Tyler peered at me self consciously, yet questioningly. He appeared to be almost asking me if he were 'that way', and praying that he wasn't.

"Tyler, clearly you prefer men… males for love interests. You always have. You have never had a successful relationship with a girl. You have never been very interested in any one girl. Yet you have had interests in, attractions to, desires for, and crushes on certain guys since you were around eight. Tyler, you prefer same-sex relationships!"

"I don't know… I mean yes… NO! I can't… I… I am a Christian… it is wrong!" Tyler buried his face in his hands.

Tyler was clearly overloading on the truth… the realization that what I had said, what he had felt and known all his life was true. He preferred men… wanted and longed for a male love interest… a lover. I felt sorry for him suddenly, gulped, and waited for him to speak… to do something. I could see he was suffering, so I paused.

"This can not be… I can't… I love God… I've liked a couple of girls…!" Tyler muttered amid renewed sobs. "I… why did… how could God make me like this? Loving those of… being attracted to the… the… the same-sex is… is a sin!? Why… God!?"

I reached out gently and lovingly to stroke Tyler's bowed head, feeling the sobs wracking his body. His brown hair running through my fingers…

his vulnerability... love... it was all such a turn on... my woody wanted to burst out of my pants and it hurt...

Tyler lurched up and gazed at me suddenly. I moved my hand to stroke his cheek and wipe away the tears thereon.

"Andrew." Tyler exclaimed with surprising strength and determination. "I may have... I think I was... I was too hasty with... I have misrepresented my past! I can name two hot girls I would have dated... if... if they would have... if Mom would have... If my parents wouldn't have interfered."

I was surprised briefly. I would have to investigate this argument more... However, before I could speak, Tyler continued.

"There was Alicia Silvers when I was 17. She was so damn gorgeous. I was... I was attracted to her... enough so that I determined to go out with her and her gorg... I mean hot... with her and her brother. I was going to ask her on a Tuesday for a double date with her brother and his date. But my parents kept me so busy at home... then my mom had her over for supper and introduced Alicia to a neighbor boy... they eloped a week later... my mom said Alicia was a tramp and not good enough for me..." Tyler paused.

I jumped in.

"You said you wanted to go out with Alicia and her 'gorg... hot... brother and his date...'" I had heard it. "Tyler, you were attracted to and liked Alicia for her gorgeous, hot brother and his characteristics and attributes. You were not particularly attracted to or liking her for her attributes and character, right?"

"No... I mean yes!... I mean no!" Tyler pounded the table in obvious frustration. I had hit on the truth. "I liked Alicia for Alicia... I did... My dad... and my mom screwed it up!" His face flushed and he spoke through clenched teeth.

"Tyler!" I spoke firmly. "You're lying again! You wanted and desired Alicia's brother, not her!"

Tyler was visibly very angry as he peeked at me periodically amid his fidgeting and uncomfortable movements.

"Dakota Silvers had a hot, muscled... gorgeous body that wouldn't quit..." Tyler stopped and turned a shade of red that, when combined with his tan, made him look like an Indian. He was splendiferous! He peered at me sheepishly. When he spoke again he was contrite. "Okay, yes... I wanted to be with... to be close to Dakota! Damn it, Andrew... I have to go to work! Would you stop it with the forty questions?"

I had more questions, however, that were coming to my mind to prove to Tyler that he was gay, had been, and always would be. I smiled coyly at Tyler and grasp his free hand, holding it firmly but tenderly.

"Just a few more questions, Tyler?!" I said slyly. "These questions were developed by sex therapists to discover if guys were gay or not. It was in the <u>American Psychiatric Association Journal</u>. It is a sure-fire way to tell us if you are gay or not."

I almost laughed at the line of bull I had just given Tyler. But maybe it would work... maybe it would fool him... I mean convince him!

"Whatever, Andrew. I am not gay or a homosexual! I just admire God's handiwork in the male form, figure, and physique more than in the female." Tyler spoke resignedly and definitely.

"Okay, Tyler, dear..." I began with dramatic pause. "Question one: You have a choice on TV of watching 'A. WWE wrestling', 'B. basketball', or 'C. professional figure skating'. Which would you select to watch?"

"Professional figure skating." Tyler answered without hesitation. "I hate sports like basketball, and watching bulgy, huge, muscle bound men fight... like animals..." Tyler shook his head and grimaced. "It is inhuman and denigrating to the human race. Gross!"

Just as I expected.

"Okay, Tyler." I returned. "Question two: You have a choice of watching on TV 'A. <u>Will and Grace</u>', 'B. <u>Welcome Back Kotter</u>', or 'C. <u>Everybody Loves Raymond</u>'. Which would you choose?"

"<u>Will and Grace</u>." Tyler replied quickly. "<u>Welcome Back Kotter</u> portrays way too much testosterone, manly bull, and women-chasing in the characters. <u>Everybody Loves Raymond</u> portrays males as weak, simpering asses or total jerks. It is disgusting!"

This was going very well! I smiled to myself. Tyler was answering these questions and commenting exactly how I would!

"You have an opportunity to go to a music concert. Your choices are 'A. Dixie Chicks', 'B. Backstreet Boys', or 'C. The Cults'. Which would you attend and watch?"

"Backstreet Boys." Tyler looked at me as he responded. "They are good looking and have hot bod… hot songs that I like."

'Right on, Tyler! Correct answer!' I thought happily.

"Who would you say was a better actor of the past in Hollywood? 'A. Rock Hudson', 'B. John Wayne', or 'C. Clark Gable'?" I inquired of Tyler, who was clearly… more gay than straight.

"Rock Hudson." Tyler set his jaw firmly, and showed no doubt. "John Wayne was too big and a horrible actor, and Clark Gable was too fond of and dependent on the ladies. It makes me sick how he threw himself at everyone in a skirt or dress!"

"Which of these three songs do you like the best? 'A. Lay, Lady, Lay', 'B. Where Is The Love', 'C. YMCA'?" I prodded.

"YMCA." Tyler smiled. "I don't know 'Where Is The Love'."

"You have a choice of three colored shirts. Which would you choose? 'A. black', 'B. paisley', 'C. lavender'?" I asked Tyler, giving him a knowing gaze.

"Lavender." Tyler stated flatly.

"Which event would you rather attend if you had to attend one? 'A. a performance by Chippendales', 'B. the opera <u>Les Miserables</u>', or 'C. a concert by Insane Clown Posse'?"

Tyler covered his face with his hands and hung his head. By his reaction and his answers so far I knew what his true answer would be, but I also knew he might try to lie first. I would not let him get away with it!

"Honesty, Tyler!" I prompted.

Tyler looked up and faced me.

"Oh well!" He shook his head and frowned as he glanced at his hands. "I am clearly in trouble anyway! The performance by Chippendales." He shrugged.

I was ecstatic! So far Tyler was one hundred percent for 'gay' answers.

"Which Hollywood star do you admire and desire more for their physical beauty? 'A. Jennifer Aniston', 'B. Brad Pitt', or 'C. Colin Farrel'?"

"Ah… I… I guess… I would say Colin Farrel…" Tyler wasn't so happy now.

"What figure would you rather look at and admire naked for its physical beauty?" I began, slowly moving in for the kill. "Would it be 'A. Jennifer Lopez', 'B. anyone of the Backstreet Boys circa 1998', or 'C. Courtney Cox'?"

Tyler squirmed some more and frowned. I knew he wanted to lie again. However, I had struck a chord, and I knew he couldn't lie anymore.

"I… well… I guess… I would say any… I would say…" Tyler gulped involuntarily as he thought about how to lie. "I guess… I think… I would have to say… J… J…" Tyler covered his face as it blushed red and shook his head. "I would have to say anyone… anyone of the Backstreet Boys circa about 1998!"

"You have a choice of careers. Which of the following would you choose if these were your ONLY choices? 'A. car mechanic', 'B. hair dresser', or 'C. pro-ball player of some kind'?"

Tyler paused, looked up, and gave me a strange facial expression.

"Those are my only choices?" He queried.

"Yes, Tyler, your only choices!" I replied.

He threw his head to one side in frustration and rolled his eyes.

"Hair dresser… I don't like to get greasy, and sports are a bore."

"What character do you like the best and would enjoy having as a friend? Your choices are the following: 'A. Jack McFarland from <u>Will and Grace</u>', 'B. Bulldog Briscoe from <u>Frasier</u>', or 'C. Robert Barone from <u>Everybody Loves Raymond</u>'?" I watched Tyler's expression as I spoke.

"Of those choices I would have to pick Jack McFarland. However, I don't like girly men normally… Bulldog is a sports nut and a rude, lewd pig, and Robert Barone… he gives me the creeps!" Tyler explained thoughtfully.

I drank some more vodka. I smiled tenderly at Tyler, who was now gazing at me again.

"Which genre of music do you prefer, 'A. classical', 'B. heavy metal', or 'C. country'?" I proffered.

"None of the above." Tyler said flatly and quickly. "Next question?"

"You can't take a pass on a question in this quiz, honey! In order for the results to be accurate you have to pick one of the choices given." I admonished Tyler.

Tyler sighed in frustration and lowered his head to look into his crotch. Then he focused back on my face.

"Classical." Tyler was adamant. "Country is too depressing and repetitious… heavy metal?" Tyler grimaced. "It is just noise! A lot of it is satanic too!"

"Which hobby do you prefer if given the chance to choose one? 'A. stamp collecting', 'B. collecting baseball cards', or 'C. crocheting'?"

Tyler though a few moments. Then he mustered himself, faced me, stared intently at me, and answered.

"Of those I would choose crocheting, definitely. I'm not into collecting… especially anything to do with sports! Crocheting is creative… I would be making something…"

"What type of movies do you prefer? 'A. horror', 'B. chick flicks', or 'C. war movies'?" I asked him matter-of-factly, smiling to myself. I already knew the truthful answer Tyler should give to this question.

I swallowed some more of my new vodka I had poured, and looked knowingly at Tyler. He was squirming and I could tell he was uncomfortable and unhappy still.

"Well?!" I prodded again, a bit self-righteously. We would be getting the truth soon.

"I… well of those choices… I mean… well…" Tyler stammered and was so uncomfortable he couldn't sit still. He looked furtively at his hands before turning his gaze back to me again. "I hate war… and war movies…

horror movies are sick… evil… too awful for my mind and emotions… so… I guess I would have to say chick flicks."

Tyler scowled.

I smiled broadly and took Tyler's hands firmly in mine. It was time to finish this 'quiz' up and announce the 'results'.

"Would you prefer to listen to 'A. Backstreet Boys', 'B. Madonna', or 'C. Bette Midler', Tyler?" I asked, struggling to keep from laughing. I knew the answer!

"The Backstreet Boys, of course!" Tyler pronounced in a no-brainer way.

I was briefly taken aback! It wasn't the response I had expected. However, I guess at this point it wasn't out of pattern for homosexuals. I preferred the Backstreet Boys too. Besides I guess it followed. After all he would rather see the Backstreet Boys naked than JLo!

I paused a moment to guzzle the rest of my large vodka tonic and avatar. I wondered at what to say next? This last answer had thrown the gay quiz that I had created on the spot somewhat on its 'head'.

As I guzzled I figured 'what the hell?!' Tyler had answered every other question as I, a gay man, would have! Why not press him and make him think he tested gay?! I finished my drink and smiled at Tyler as I set the glass down.

"You are gay, Tyler. You have always preferred other guys for love interests. You have never had a successful relationship with any girls and you admit you are not attracted physically to females." I chuckled as I summed up my findings from the 'gay quiz'. "Whatever you believe, or think you believe, I hate to burst your 'denial bubble', but you are gay!"

I finished eating while I watched Tyler's expression. He was quiet and frowned.

"This quiz I have just given you as I explained was developed by some top sex therapists to identify gay men. It came from the <u>APA Journal</u>. Tyler, honey, join the club of us men who love men, and who love sex with other men!" I pushed my plate away and folded my arms on the table.

Had my quiz scam worked? Had I successfully bluffed Tyler into admitting and believing he was gay or not? Had I gone too far?! I was suddenly pissed at my own insensitivity, realizing that I was walking on such thin ice with Tyler, his Christian beliefs and conflicts, and his fragile psyche and ego. Had I scared him with what had just been revealed and learned by him? Would he retreat from me and our relationship? I truly did not know what would hold Tyler and what wouldn't, or what would convince Tyler and what wouldn't.

For his part Tyler was scowling, sheepish, shame-faced, but thoughtful. He looked at his plate and poked around at the crumbs. He had one piece of toast left, and some of his coffee and orange juice. Finally he spoke quietly, but with determination.

"I don't believe any stupid quiz will tell someone's sexuality with any degree of accuracy, now, or at any time!" Tyler exclaimed, frowning as he took a bite of the toast. "I think that this has been a bunch of bunk, and I am not gay! I may be attracted to… to other guys, I may have better luck going out with guys, I may be more… more comfortable with… with other men, I may prefer male company to female, and I now am in love with you, Andrew. However, I am not now, nor ever will be gay or a homosexual!"

Damn! I had struck out! Tyler was on the retrograde again and in denial mode. Had I pushed him too far? Would he reject me now that I had forced him to face his true sexuality? Would he push me away to prove his 'heterosexuality'? Based on some of his reactions to my 'gay quiz' I knew that our blossoming relationship, the stress of his move to Aurora and his new job, and all the changes in his life had triggered a rebellion to his perceived 'reality'. What could I do?! Should I back track and lie? I couldn't bear it if I were to lose Tyler now! I was so totally in love with him that life would be pointless without him! Should I continue being honest?!

"Tyler," I began cautiously and sincerely, "the quiz was real, but I did lie about from whence it came. The quiz was based on one from <u>Playgirl</u> magazine and it was not written by any particular authority or specialist in sexuality or sexual orientation. I was only trying to make and then help you face your sexual orientation, your reality, the feelings and emotions over your attraction and love for men and me in particular. I only wanted us to be closer, to deepen our relationship."

I smiled apologetically and grasped Tyler's left hand, stroking it tenderly.

"You are right though, Tyler, honey!" I continued softly as Tyler looked at our hands. "You may or may not be gay, but a quiz is not going to determine that fact. Only you can recognize that fact in your life and then admit to yourself and the world that you are or aren't gay."

We finished the crumbs of our breakfast in silence. I was now wondering whether he had been offended by my questions, behavior, and goals? Especially if he didn't believe it! Was he planning to flee from me? We cleared the table, and did the dishes, again in silence. I chugged my vodka tonic and avatar at this point, wishing to drown out the painful feelings I had that I had gone too far and offended or scared Tyler. Did he hate me? Did he feel I was a threat? I was becoming more worried the longer he didn't speak!

Afterward Tyler finished gathering his things for work, and I threw clothes and shoes on to drive him to work. I couldn't stand the silent ignoring of what had happened anymore! What could I say? What could I do? I had to break this ice of silence, for it was scaring the crap out of me!

I could tell Tyler was deep in thought and uneasy. I could also feel that he was strengthening his own denial and rebellion against the truth… the truth that he was gay.

We grabbed our last necessities and headed for the door.

We left the apartment together, and I locked the door behind us. Tyler was clearly disturbed, as he took off without waiting for me. I had to jog to catch back up to him. He had been too silent since I had apologized for trying to trick him with a 'gay quiz'. What was he thinking? Was he doubting us Biblically again?! Damn it, I had been a fool! I had rushed in where only wise men fear to tread. Piss on society's myopic, bigoted, and paranoid 'morals', and piss on his religious convictions! I knew he was gay, and I was going to bring him around if it took a miracle! (Did I say that! I didn't believe in miracles!)

"Tyler!" I spoke with some command as I came to a walk by his side. "I am gay. I love certain men I find attractive, and I only have sex with men with whom I have a serious relationship. I am not attracted physically or sexually to women. For those truths I will not apologize. I meant to tell you all of this when we first met, but I was afraid you'd bail out of our rooming agreement if you knew that I was gay." I touched his arm gently.

"Andrew." Tyler stopped, took my hand to stop me, and turned to face me in front of the elevator. "I hoped from day one that you were gay! That's not the problem. The problem is me. I… I… I love you, Andrew. God forgive me, I… I want only… I desire only you! But, Andrew, as God is my witness, it is sin, homosexuality is a sin. Our relationship is a sin. I cannot be a part of that scene as a Christian! Homosexuals go to hell!"

Tyler had tears in his eyes as he glanced at his feet.

"Continue, Tyler." I urged, my heart wrenching and my stomach churning. We could address homosexuality, Christianity, and hell later. I wanted to hear Tyler out and hope we were still together!

"In addition, you have put on quite an act here in the last 24 hours. I am not sure what is true and what is false. I love you! However, I cannot live with this drama. I need stability in my life. Not… not… maybe now… maybe later… I need to know you are here for me forever! Not just when it is convenient. I need to know that you understand that I am not familiar with this type of… type of relationship. I need to know you will encourage… you will encourage it, nurture it. I need to know when you hurt… and why you were hurt… I need to know that you… you kiss me… because you mean it. I need to know you regard our relationship with the same sincerity and seriousness that I do… not make… not make… a mockery of it with a 'gay' quiz or dishonesty for your own selfish interests!"

Tyler turned again, and pressed the 'down' button near the elevator. I was devastated! I had only attempted to learn more about Tyler, and through that more about us. Yes, I lied a little, but what the hell?! My goal was to bring Tyler to a realization and admission of his sexual orientation. I did not mean to mock him, or hurt him! I was completely perplexed as we waited for an elevator to ding and open. We both were deep in thought. I was considering ways to try and reason Tyler's Bible hang-up away, and assuage his confusion. Who the hell knew what all he was thinking!? I realized that I had a lot of work to do to bring Tyler into our relationship comfortably and with a knowledge of spiritual acceptance and God's approval!

The elevator sounded and opened. We walked in. I did not even look around at the people already ensconced therein.

"Tyler…" I reached out and took both of his hands in mine and held them. I gazed lovingly into his handsome, awesome face. "Tyler… I'm sorry for… for…. for everything that has happened the last 24 hours, but getting assaulted was not my fault…"

"I know that, Andrew!" Tyler interrupted. "It just scares me for you, for me, for us! Are we in danger? Can we walk the streets… go out safely? Besides, Andrew, you lied about a few things in your explanation of the assault! Then this… gay quiz thing this morning…" Tyler shook his head, rolled his eyes, and looked at me reproachfully.

Tyler's reaction at this point was not making total sense… one could see that it didn't to even him. However, I knew this whole thing was clouded by and twisted in with his internal conflict between his sexual orientation and his Christian faith. If we could fix that 'conflict with God' I knew that a lot of the other problems would work themselves out.

"Tyler! Tyler!" I squeezed his hands. "I have lived here seven years and the assault I received yesterday was the first time anything like that ever happened! Honestly!" I smiled at him. "And I'm sorry I lied. 'Jovan the Dominator' took from me what I told you in my final explanation. He did force me to have oral sex with him, and he did sodomize me. Obviously I was ashamed, in pain, I don't know what I was thinking! It's not an excuse, but my embarrassment was why I lied at first. I was so emotional and confused that I took leave of my senses and common sense. I am so sorry, Tyler."

I paused and gently took Tyler's chin in my right hand.

"As far as stability, being with you forever, and encouraging and nurturing our relationship; I promise you all of it! I would never mock you and/or our relationship. I love you, Tyler! I will provide as much stability as I can for you forever, or as long as you still love me and will have me. I will encourage and nurture 'us', and we will learn about our relationship and each other together. I love you, man!" I looked seriously into his eyes. "Are we clear and in agreement?"

Tyler smiled wanly, but less than convincingly, and hung his head, gently holding my hands still.

"Thank you, Andrew, but 'us' is still a sin! Any loving relationship between us is a sin! How do I overcome that… that belief?!" He looked back into my eyes, his brown pools pained and pleading to me.

"Sin?!" I hissed so others wouldn't hear. "Tyler, follow these questions and points, and I think I can assuage your feelings of guilt over who you are!"

Tyler looked forlornly into my eyes and nodded his assent.

"Tyler, who created love?" I asked firmly, a line of reasoning quickly forming in my mind. I touched his arm gently and seriously.

"God." Tyler responded. We both watched as the elevator stopped and three people from the fourth floor joined us. I hardly noticed the other two people we had joined inside. Tyler punched the floor '1' button, and I continued with my line of thinking.

"For whom did God create love, Tyler?" I loudly whispered.

"For the crown on the relationship between God the Father and his sons, us Christians." Tyler answered promptly and sincerely.

"And…?" I prompted.

"And speaking of love, would someone please love me?" a young male voice interrupted. "I am cocked and loaded and ready to go!"

I turned to see the speaker, a black-haired, cute young man in a trench coat. As soon as all eyes were on him for his curious personal question and declaration, he threw open his trench coat. Everyone except Tyler and me gasped and/or looked away. The young man was totally nude except for sandals, and he had a well-endowed… and I do mean 'well-endowed'… package! I knew it was Phil Fleets, the building flasher, and evidently Tyler had seen him before as well, because he was not disconcerted or obviously offended by the flashing either.

Tyler and I ignored the distraction.

"And God also created love for…?" I prompted Tyler.

"God also created love for… two people to share in a relationship…" Tyler sighed. I knew that he knew that he was losing this round of the argument as well. "Where are you going with this, Andrew?!"

The elevator door opened on the first floor. The other occupants exited quickly, followed by a now covered Phil.

"All I am saying, Tyler, is that God created love." While speaking we entered the lobby. "Love therefore is good. Love is a special gift for relationships between…" we passed through the spin doors to the sidewalk, "people, humans. God's creations. Two guys, two girls, a guy and a girl, it doesn't matter. We are people, humans. Aren't gay couples entitled by God to share the same gift of love between them as heterosexual couples are entitled to share? If love between anyone is a sin, then God created sin, and He can't do that because He is perfect!"

By now we were approaching my car in the parking ramp. Tyler's face showed an intense level of thinking going on inside. He hadn't spoken, but I could tell my words were having an impact, though which way I couldn't tell.

I unlocked my car remotely and started the engine. Tyler and I got in, buckled up, settled ourselves, and I had shifted into reverse before anyone spoke.

"I suppose you have a sound line of reasoning there, Andrew." Tyler mused out loud. "That is certainly a line of logic in this whole issue of same-sex love that I want to believe with every fiber of my being. But why do I feel that I can't be in love with you because it's so dirty, so unnatural, so queer, such an aberration! How can I prove to you that 'us' in a relationship as a couple is wrong? How can I prove to me that it isn't wrong?! How is it that, try as I might, I cannot whitewash our relationship into a heterosexual one?! Given the obvious argument you make, one with which I agree, why do I still doubt whether our relationship is right?! How do I overcome this doubt?! Why cannot I trust and believe that you and I are all right with God?!"

"Well, you feel that it is wrong because organized religion has convinced society that homosexuality is so wrong, so evil. Organized religion and society then force same-sex love into the proverbial 'closet' and ostracize the LGBTQ community members therein. Society then teaches these biases, misinterpretations, and lies to our youth and so on to perpetuate the demonizing and denigrating of a valid, God-created, lifestyle. The discriminating lie is passed from generation to generation, and here we are!" I used my arms and hands on Tyler as much as I could to emphasize certain points.

"But the Bible preaches against homosexuality specifically. What do you say to that?" Tyler had a look on his face like he was the victor and the victim.

We pulled into the street, and I came up with the comeback that I was sure even Tyler wasn't expecting.

"The Old Testament condemns homosexuality in violence and idol worship. Jesus died on the cross and the New Testament was written to create a new way to heaven that didn't emphasize works, but emphasizes grace instead. Isn't that right?" I spoke from the memories that I had from what little church I had had throughout my life. "Isn't grace such that you live your life the way you know, the way you have been born and trained, and you are forgiven? You are grafted into heaven anyway?"

"Well, yeh." Tyler shrugged. "That's right."

There was a period of silence. I watched Tyler. He was deep in thought.

"I'll think about it." Tyler responded presently.

Several minutes or so passed in silence.

We pulled into his workplace, Computronix Inc. Tyler opened our car door to exit.

"I'll think about it… Andrew… my… my love… thanks for the ride! I think I feel better." With that he got out, shut the door, and hurried toward the entrance of his employer.

I didn't know what exactly to think. Oh well, at least he showed no signs of moving out, or rejecting me! It appeared, and I had to believe, that our love for each other was still on and growing toward a serious lifetime lover relationship.

# FIRST EXPOSURE

As I entered the door of Computronix Computer and Information Technologies, Inc., the thought occurred to me that I had left Andrew rather rudely and abruptly. I was chagrined! I had not said a proper goodbye to the love of my life. How could I be so stupid, insensitive, and self-absorbed?! He probably needed some reassurance from me, and I was so focused on my hang-ups that I had just... left. I hoped he understood?!

I gazed around the lobby in which I found myself. I realized I must find a way to put my current relationship with Andrew and my feelings of guilt and worries about the morality of our love behind me for the day. It was going to be hard, because I already felt such a strong and growing love for Andrew, and a growing sense of Christian guilt and shame over that love. However, I had to do it. I had to focus on and prove myself at my new job.

In my conflict and guilt over my sexuality and my love for Andrew I realized something too. Now I had the elation and thrill of having so passionately kissed him and finding out I was his lover. It was very tantalizing and stimulating! Several question marks about Andrew and about 'us' had been cleared up this morning.

All doubts I had felt and harbored about whether Andrew was gay and over how he felt about me I could now realistically lay to rest. I did, at this moment, know that Andrew was gay. We now knew that the other was in love with us. Andrew knew I loved him and I knew he loved me. I was giddy and excited! A chill of pleasure, happiness, and anticipation ran down through my body from my head to my feet.

Then, through my overwhelming feelings of love for Andrew, my hormonal desires for him, and my strong attraction to him, some sobering thoughts began to needle and worry me. Was I living in sin already?! Was God totally displeased with me at this point?! Did He hate me?! Was Landon right and I was now embarking on and into a relationship of sin with my love, Andrew?! Is that what Landon's message meant... and which he sought to circumvent?! Could our love for each other and relationship really be such a sin... so wrong?! Did God create me to be attracted to and into men and same-sex love only to condemn me to hell when I acted on what He had given me and how He had created me?!

Then I became angry and resentful. Lord, why won't or don't you just put up a sign for all mankind!? Same-sex love and relationships were a sin, are a sin, and always will be a sin!? Where were the churches in teaching anything that would guide us about God's rules for living Christ-like in relationships, about Christian responses to sin, and about our Christian response to same-sex love?! What a bunch of wimpy preachers we have created! They don't teach squat about how the Bible applies to modern cultural issues. Why? Because they must be scared of losing parishioners, money, and God only knows what else!

'Stop!' I ordered myself. 'You must focus today on your work. It is your first day and you want to make a good impression. You cannot keep obsessing over Andrew, your relationship with him, whether it is a sin, or what the churches do or do not teach!'

I snapped back to reality and moved forward across the nicely furnished lobby.

At the front counter I was given some paperwork to fill out, a pen, and I was directed to a nice corner lounge chair. I read and filled out the employment and IRS forms and signed them as quickly and efficiently as possible. Upon returning the forms to the front desk I was given a name-tag with my name and position displayed on a company logo. I was directed first to the packing and shipping department, where I would spend a few days learning that department and its aspects of the business. 'This part will be a breeze!' I thought to myself after the lady behind the counter gave me the directions. I left the front counter and took off for that first department about which I would learn.

I went up and down hallways for a few minutes before arriving at my destination.

In the packing and shipping department I was told to look for the boss, a Lou Ryan. I assumed anyone with that name would be male. Lou Ryan would assign me to my first job and get me started. As I entered I immediately began looking for a guy who appeared like he was in charge. I stopped and scanned the shop looking for such an in-charge male, or a management office of some kind in which I might find Mr. Ryan. As I swiveled from left to right, I saw nothing for a few minutes until I moved back to my left. My eyes fell on a very cute, shapely, and feisty looking thirty-something young blond woman in a pony tail approaching me at a good clip from the left. She looked knowledgeable, determined, and competent. I decided to ask her where Mr. Ryan was.

"Miss?" I stepped in front of her. "Excuse me, I do not mean to interrupt you. However, do you know the supervisor, Lou Ryan?"

"I do!" She said perkily. "Intimately, in fact!"

"Well…" I blushed as I groped at ways to back pedal. "Your personal life with Mr. Ryan is…" I nervously chuckled, "your business. Just direct me to Lou Ryan, and I won't bother you anymore, please?"

"You are speaking to her!" The blond lady replied as she smiled brightly and glanced up and down my body, gave me a lustful look, and winked.

"Oh, well ma'am, I need your husband." I smiled back apologetically.

"You do?" She asked sadly and in a concerned manner. "So sorry to hear that! Are you sick?"

"No…" I was bewildered! This was not going well. I looked at her quizzically. "Why do you ask that?"

"Mr. Trey Ryan is a doctor/surgeon." She explained with a grin. "He and I do quite well together, but he doesn't work here! He works at the hospital."

I was now totally flustered and my face flushed. As the realization that this woman was Lou Ryan set in, I didn't know what to say and/or do next. I hoped I had not come across as a back-water hick or a sexist pig!

"Perhaps we should start over." I muttered in embarrassment. "I need to see a Lou Ryan. I am the new hire, Tyler Belmont."

"Lou Ryan is the name!" She shook my hand. "I am the supervisor here in this packing and shipping department. I have been expecting you."

I must have been as red as a tomato as I smiled and released her hand.

"I'm… I'm… I'm so sorry Miss… Ms… Mrs. Ryan…" I stammered.

"Call me Lou." She corrected me. "No harm done! With a name like 'Lou' your mistake in my gender is made more often than I would care to admit!" She reached back and undid her pony tail, shaking her blond curly hair out over her shoulders and again winking at me. I had to admit that she was beautiful, but not in any way a threat to my gorgeous Andrew.

"I… I mean… Lou… I am so… so sorry, Lou!" I gazed at my hands in shame. "I… I just… I mean, I'm not… nor did I mean to come across… across as a male… chauvinist. I mean, women can manage a department! They manage households for goodness' sake. Women are even company CEOs!" 'Shit!' I thought angrily, 'I am coming across even worse than before!'

Before anyone could save me from further verbal blunders I plunged ahead.

"Of course you're the supervisor. You appear very capable! I mean… I am sure you are very… well…" 'Shut the hell up, Tyler!' I thought to myself, 'or you will dig yourself in more deeply!' I hung my head quickly, hoping to hide my embarrassment.

"Tyler…" Lou spoke in a sensuous and lewd voice, "has anyone told you that you have a hot and sexy body… a gorgeous physique… you are extremely handsome and beautiful… and you have the cutest, shapely, hard ass…!?" As emphasis Lou briefly grabbed my buttock and squeezed.

I jerked my head up to look at Lou in surprise. I am afraid my mouth dropped open.

Lou Ryan had a sexy, lewd, hungry, and longing expression on her countenance. Her wavy, blond-haired head bobbed as she moved her gaze slowly and obviously appreciatively up and down my body from head to foot. As she eagerly checked me out she was licking her lips. It was almost like she were shopping for a prize piece of meat, and I were in the display!

I blushed red again and quickly closed my mouth as she finished undressing me mentally and returned my gaze. She winked seductively at me and ran her hand through her blond curls.

"Th... Thanks... I... I guess..." I replied uncertainly, holding Lou's gaze.

There was a weighty, uncomfortable pause as I looked further down at my feet. I was still embarrassed and my face had again turned a nice scarlet red I was sure. My skin was becoming afflicted with like a prickly heat. The whole situation was becoming so awkward.

I peered back up meekly, but firmly.

"Well, where do I begin, Lou?" I asked.

"Naked with me in my office...!" Mrs. Ryan began, clearly thinking out loud. "I mean..." she quickly regained her composure, "follow me to the box cutting department, Tyler."

I followed her down a confusing tunnel of hallways that finally culminated in a large assembly room. There Mrs. Ryan pawned me off on the packaging manager. She said her formalities, promised to come back and check on me, winked at me, gazed longingly up and down my body again, and then she left. 'Man! She made me feel uncomfortable!' I thought.

My body language and facial expression obviously betrayed the fact that I had been embarrassed by Mrs. Ryan.

"That's typical Lou." A rough, deep voice came from directly behind me.

I jumped and whirled around.

The speaker was a short, stout, plain looking, fiftyish man.

"I didn't mean to startle you." The man stuck out his stubby hand. "Bert, packaging manager. Who are you, again?"

"Tyler, Tyler Belmont." I answered as I regained my composure.

"Don't mind Lou... the behavior you witnessed is typical of her." Bert smiled.

"What do you mean?" I asked curiously.

"Her flirting with and come-ons to you... She flirts with all and sleeps with some of the hot young studs like you who work under her. Any of them who appeals to her and will give her the time of day she will seduce. If you are not interested in her just be informed and wary." Bert led me down a hallway between machines.

"Oh." I definitely was not interested! "Why hasn't someone reported her to management for sexual harassment?"

"We all value our jobs, our advancement potential, and our rate of pay, all of which Mrs. Ryan threatens if anyone reports any of her negative characteristics in the workplace to management."

Bert instructed me in working on a machine folding and pre-cutting boxes. He informed me I'd be on this machine for a day or two. He taught me how to run it, adjust it for different size boxes, and how to stack the finished products on skids to be taken elsewhere in the department. Then he disappeared.

'Lou must be a real piece of work!' I pondered. 'A married woman, sleeping around with willing and unwilling underlings, and cheating on her husband!' I wondered if he knew what his trampy wife was up to?!

I did my job that day. The first half was rough learning the ropes, how to run the machine, and how to program the folds and perforations for each size box. By afternoon I was making rate and helping kick out plenty of skids of boxes. It gave me plenty of time to analyze my workmates for the next few days. There were five others in the department; four boxers, and a machine repairman.

The machine repairman was a tall, lanky, kind of a scary and clumsy looking guy. What was weird was that he dressed in women's clothing! He apparently wanted to be a woman. Truthfully he did make a scary, ugly looking man. However, he made an even more hideous looking woman! He reminded me of Olive Oyl in drag. He wore way too much makeup to cover up his manly features and his age. He sported an obviously fake wig. Seeing him was creepy! The others called him Roberta. I just tried to avoid him, and hoped I could do so until I finally left this department.

Boxer one was an average looking shorter, 40 year old balding man, slender, and clean cut. He was, by character, what I would call mousy. He was shy, and corresponded in quickly delivered short answers or sentences. He wore glasses, carried a New Testament in one front pocket, and a box guide in the other. The others called him the 'church mouse'. His actual name, I was told, was Thurgood Vasieu.

Boxer two was a young bombshell brunette, bubbly, pretty, and apparently unmarried. She had no ring, and she flirted shamelessly with most of the men under 40. I noticed from personal experience that she flirted big time. She was almost as bad as Mrs. Ryan! She was very smart, witty, and good at her job. She was known as Brandy.

Boxer three was a short, stout, bib-over-all wearing, bottle blond. Her face was so covered with jewelry ensconced in various piercings in her face that she could have been a jewelry rack at Niemen Markus. She was cute otherwise, although all of the jewelry turned me off. She also had a huge chip on her shoulder, and turned me off as far as her personality. She chewed a cud of gum that could choke a fire eater. The others called her 'CC'.

Boxer number four, who introduced himself and latched on to me shortly after the manager left me alone, was a young, really cute, 20s something, sandy brown-haired, blue-eyed guy with another beautiful male figure. He didn't match Andrew's hot, awesome figure, but I found myself admiring him quite often. His name was Thaddeus 'Thad' Chrysler, and he and I became friends almost instantly.

Thad helped me quite a bit that morning. I was thankful for this as I learned the work and machines. He was kind, patient, and very attentive. He was also so eager to help and seemed to thoroughly enjoy hovering around me, and looking over my shoulders. With normal guys this might have been a turn-off, but I didn't have time to even think about it, let alone react anything but positively to it.

In no time at all the lunch bell rang. Our group cleaned up and retrieved our lunches. Then I followed them to a picnic table outside to eat.

The business provided a beautiful park-like area for its employees to enjoy during lunch and breaks, and I was impressed. The park area boasted nicely paved pathways weaving in and out of groves of various trees indigenous to our area. Picnic tables and ornate park benches were nestled here and there throughout the park and its pathways. It was beautiful, relaxing, and very enticing! I gazed back at the windows of the two story company facing this beautiful park, and the parking lot area beyond. The windows were professionally well-kept, and I realized that probably the company executives had offices there, with windows looking out on the park.

We all sat down and began eating. I carefully emptied the lunch sack Andrew had so thoughtfully packed for me this morning and arranged it in front of me. There was a pressed ham, cheese, and lettuce sandwich with Miracle Whip and mustard, a pudding cup, cheese stick, and a huge, juicy navel orange. For liquid enjoyment there was a diet Pepsi. Andrew was such a sweetheart, and an excellent lunch-maker!

During lunch I was the subject of the conversation as everyone asked about me and my life. I answered their questions and tried to tell them as much as I was comfortable revealing about myself, while avoiding any of the touchy issues I was coming to face with Andrew as a lover. Thad pried some, questioning me several times about my 'girlfriends' or whether I was 'dating'. A few times he had me on the run to conceal my relationship to and with Andrew. Several times I had to avoid the honest truth, or change the subject gently to avoid any uncomfortable revelations. I felt a little guilty, but chalked them up to necessary avoidance, dodging the subjects, and white lies. Besides, I reasoned, I didn't know these people, and I owed them nothing... especially not all of the truth.

By the end of lunch four of them could have written a partial biography of me sans actual specific details, and I was mentally exhausted, as well as almost suffering from clench-mouth. I wanted to stop talking for a little while as we returned to work.

After we finished our lunch, we all rose and broke up to return to our departments and machines. When I arrived at my station, I was surprised that Thad had somehow switched his station next to mine. I realized he must have some kind of pull with someone in management. Must be with Mrs. Ryan? Thad was a looker like me. Maybe they had an affair going on?! Mrs. Robinson… I mean Mrs. Ryan was clearly interested in cute, younger men! I pondered again if Mr. Ryan knew what his wife did and what he might think about his wife's philandering ways!?

I tried to start my machine up. I began to wonder about Thad again, as the machine booted up. How did he switch his assigned station to the machine at my side?! What was going on?

My computer screen showed a menu briefly and then the screen switched to a blank. That had never happened before! Then a message flashed on the screen. I had it turned on, but it wouldn't do anything that it was supposed to do. I didn't understand it! It had worked fine before lunch. What the hell was wrong?! I was becoming pissed! I tried everything I knew, but to no effect. I was on the verge of losing it, when Thad spoke softly and tenderly to me.

"Tyler? Is everything all right? Is there a problem with your machine?"

"No!" I exclaimed, punching buttons through flashing screens trying to fix the problem by answering questions. "I will be fine!"

"Tyler, Tyler!" Thad spoke calmly and I could swear, were I paying more attention, lovingly, as he approached me. "Pounding on the machine won't help! Tell me what is wrong? What won't it do? I will help you work through it."

"This da… I mean… it turned on, but…" I was spitting and sputtering as I punched buttons angrily. "this da… I mean… the machine will not begin its functions!" I finally was so pissed, that I pulled back my fist and prepared to pound the computer screen. I had no idea from where my intense anger came. I had never become this angry before over something so simple or silly!

Thad calmly and tenderly grabbed my fist with his right hand and then firmly held me from my swing. I felt a strange and scintillating chemistry flow from him to me. His touch and strength were almost as sexually stimulating as Andrew's touch and strength.

I stopped at his touch and restraint, and turned to look at him face-to-face. Thad was no more than six inches from me, and his face close enough to mine so I could feel the tickle of his breath on my cheek.

Thad looked me deeply in the eyes and gave me such a heavenly and calming smile that I melted! He was so attractive. Judging by how close he was to me, he acted like he found me attractive too. I blushed deeply but could not look away and break our gaze. The distinct impression that he wanted to kiss me enveloped me… I would not have resisted…

"Tyler," Thad stated softly, "calm down! Let me help?!" He looked questioningly at me.

We seemed to drink deeply of each other's feelings and souls. I became uncomfortable, blushed deeply again, and managed to look back at the screen of the uncooperative machine. 'How dare I react like this to anyone but Andrew!' I thought angrily!

"Go ahead, Thad! Knock yourself out!" I replied, somewhat snippily as I struggled with my emotions and attraction to Thad, versus my obviously stronger attraction and commitment to Andrew. I lowered my hand out of his grasp, and he removed his hand.

To my surprise and pleasure, Thad gently grabbed my waist with both hands, his fingers plying my flesh in a massaging motion as he softly pulled me back from the computer. I felt like putty in his hands and I didn't resist. At his touch a massive rush coursed through my body...

Thad faced the computer and began to explain to me how to find out what was wrong. He punched buttons as he talked, and looked back at me, his handsome face inquiring if I understood. I watched, nodded, and watched some more. Thad stepped me patiently through several self tests and procedures to determine what was wrong. Suddenly the machine whirred to life, and Thad explained what I had done wrong, showing me a page of explanation, and reading it with me.

Throughout his time of helping me I kept glancing at Thad's cute, round ass. Thad wore a nice pink button shirt neatly tucked down into hip-hugger, black jeans which hung low enough on his hips that it was sexy. No underwear showed, but I could see the indention for the beginning of his crack.

When Thad finished I was greatly relieved, simply because I had been so frustrated both with the machine and with my conflicted feelings toward Andrew and now Thad. I didn't know why I should entertain a crush on Thad when I now knew I had Andrew as a lover. Besides, I had no overwhelming indication or evidence that Thad was gay, or truly interested in me.

"Do you understand now, Tyler, how to do a trouble-shooting check on this machine?" Thad gazed kindly and lovingly at me. I felt my heart skip in enjoyment of Thad's attentions. I knew I had to guard against Thad and a full-fledged crush on him. I could love this man, this friend. But I loved, admired, and knew Andrew more! Andrew was much hotter, handsomer, and much more physically attractive than Thad, and I knew that too.

"Yes, Thad." I answered, as my voice cracked from my emotion toward him. "I think I do!" I recovered quickly. I did not want Thad to think, I should say realize, that I could have… had a crush on him.

Thad turned to me and grabbed me softly by both shoulders, turning me to face him fully. As I gazed into his face and he slowly leaned in to me, I thought surely he might kiss me. I became very embarrassed and I blushed red. I looked down at my hands in nervousness.

What the hell was Thad's intent looking at me like this?! What the hell was I doing suddenly swearing so easily?! I was so confused because I loved Andrew and I was attracted strongly physically to him, yet now I had this attraction to Thad, too. I was a Christian! I should have no such attraction to any man, let alone Thad… I mean Andrew and Thad! What the hell was going on!? How could this dual crush and love go on!? How could it be normal?! Was I sick?! Why was God allowing this to go on?! Where was God when I needed Him?!

I felt so abandoned, misinformed, hurt, and distant from organized religion at this moment. I felt so estranged from the church in which I had been raised, for that matter. They both had taught absolutely nothing, or if anything, a very slight bit about same-sex love and the correct Biblical Christian response to it. I had little idea of any Biblical reason in particular to oppose same-sex relationships, love, and sexual activity. All I had received from organized religion was the pastor's or laymen's opinions against it, not the position of the scriptures. Nothing was ever taught about the case against same-sex relationships from the perspective of history or science. There was never anything of any substantive matter taught about same-sex love! Nothing I could hold as the solid rock against same-sex love and 'intimacy' or its temptation. I felt so cheated and so 'alone' in my current dilemma!

On the other hand I had heard and seen a lot in the secular media, on television, and from the left on the issue of same-sex couples and marriage. I had seen and read the same-sex propaganda in national news magazines about how same-sex love was a naturally occurring phenomenon of genetic pre-destination. People were born to be either drawn to the opposite sex, or the same-sex, these articles argued, citing some report or study to that effect. Therefore same-sex lovers and couples were a naturally occurring minority and deserving of acceptance by and equality with recipients of all of the rights of heterosexuals.

I had viewed <u>Will and Grace</u> a few times late at night after everyone of my family had gone to bed. The show had desensitized me to the open same-sex love and relations promoted there. I had even found much of the show's content, script, and situations hysterically funny!

Now I wasn't sure it was so funny! I loved Andrew desperately and I so wanted to… to be… to be his lover, but I questioned our relationship versus my faith in God and what He said in the Bible.

Here I also had the impression Thad was coming on to me. What had I done to have two male suitors in one week?! Was I wearing an advertisement to that effect?! Was I that hot physically, or were my suitors just over-sexed and hot-to-trot with anyone? I couldn't believe that I was physically hot, so it had to be that the men who had shown interest in me just wanted to have sex with anything in pants and sans boobs.

"Tyler!" Thad gently moved my shoulders as he demanded my attention. I snapped back and focused on him with what I could only guess was a look of confusion. "Are you sure you understand what I have just explained to you?! Are you sure you know and understand what just happened here… what is… what is happening here?!" Thad looked longingly and questioningly into my eyes, burrowing deeply. I looked away again in discomfort and confusion as I blushed nervously.

"Ah… I guess… I ah…" I was suddenly confused, "ah… I… yes, I understand what you have just explained to me." I shook my head. 'I must focus!' I told myself angrily. 'These confusing personal thoughts must end and leave!'

What the hell did he mean though when he asked if I knew 'what is happening here'?! Was he really 'coming on' to me?!

"I may need help in the future though, Thad?" I ended with caution as I gazed questioningly and pleadingly into his face, melting all over again at the love and understanding clearly present there.

Thad released me, stepped back, and turned to face the main aisle. He motioned expansively to the machines in our row.

"I know how to run all the machines here, Tyler, and in the whole department. I will be more than happy to show you how to run all of them, or help you run any of them."

Thad turned around and approached me again. He put one hand just above my hip, and the other on my cheek and chin, gently forcing me to look him full in the face. I couldn't really resist him! He was so persuasive, charming… and hot… and cute. I was so vulnerable and unknowledgeable of this new environment in which I found myself. I was also confused by the worldly stimuli and characteristics of society outside of Gurnee. Things were so different here, so tempting…

"All you have to do, Tyler, is ask me!" Thad looked into my eyes with his blue pools, pleading with me to come hither! "I will help you anytime, anywhere, over anything in this shop." Thad stroked my sideburn. "I will help you with anything outside this shop. I want to make your work and your life here easier, I want to help you fit in, and I want to help you to learn your jobs. Just let me know?!"

I didn't know what to say. Thad continued to stroke my face. I didn't know if my vibes from Thad were right or not. Was he really… really into… was he really… gay? It surely seemed like it. He seemed to be all over me and he was touching me in rather intimate ways.

I looked furtively back into Thad's face, mainly his eyes. He had a hungry, longing expression on his visage. Yet his eyes also contained a firm and impressing quality as well. Was I reading too much into this?!

"Tyler?!" Thad squeezed my upper thigh and my cheek. "Do you understand?!" His face was again so close to mine that I could feel his breath hot on my nose and forehead. All he had to do was bend just a bissel into me and he could kiss my lips.

I gulped involuntarily. 'Straight guys would not do this!' I realized suddenly and with guilt. I was cheating on Andrew!? How could I just sit here and allow Thad to touch me like this? What the hell was I thinking? I didn't want to be the 'choice' or the 'prey' of any gay guys! Let alone Thad! Or Andrew! Or did I?! I fought the urge to wretch. I again looked at my hands.

It was at that moment that I realized that I enjoyed Andrew… Thad… and other gorgeous men touching me. 'Why God?! You made me this way?! If my feelings are sinful, then you made sin, God!?'

"Thad, I don't mean to be so bogue, but…" I sought out the correct, polite words with which to tell Thad to back off. "Please don't touch me like this!" I trembled in anger and ecstasy in his grip.

He released me.

"I'm sorry, Tyler!" Thad spoke quickly, his look changing to an apologetic and knowing expression. "I didn't mean to make you uncomfortable! But did you understand my instruction?"

"Yes… I think… I mean… yes, I did, Thad, thank you!" I blurted as I tried to recover from my embarrassment and confusion.

Thad patted me on the shoulder.

"Tyler, if you need help this afternoon, just ask! I have been here a few years and can, as I explained, help you big time. I will be right here next to you!" He smiled, clutched my shoulder briefly, and then turned to what had quickly become his station, right next to mine.

I was totally confused. What was going on?!

# CHAPTER 40

# HOW TO OPEN A BOOK

"So, Tyler!" Thad began, smiling pleasantly at me. "You are new to Aurora?"

"Yes, I am." I responded, as I purposefully buried myself in my work. "I have been here since last Friday. It is really a large, busy, bustling suburb here. The ethics, mores, and society here are so different from Gurnee!"

"Yes, they are, Tyler." Thad stated tentatively, looking secretly back and forth at me and his work. "Where are you living?" I could see him studying up and down my body. I was cautiously pondering whether Thad was checking me out like I had checked him out all day.

I didn't know how exactly I should respond to Thad, vaguely or specifically? Especially since I hardly knew him, and knew nothing but impressions of his interest and attraction to me. I quickly chose to go the vague pathway and answered Thad accordingly.

"I have an apartment here in Aurora in a large apartment complex. It is a few miles from here… on… on Wax Figure Lane…" I paused as I contemplated whether I had said too much already.

"Oh, yeah!" Thad's cute face lit up with a broad smile. "I know Wax Figure Lane! The street is lined with apartment complexes!"

Thad paused as the two of us worked.

"Where do you live, Thad?" I asked, hoping to keep him from asking me any more personal questions requiring me to dodge, avoid, and lie about me and Andrew.

"I live west of here, on another long street of apartments called Barclay Avenue. It is an excellent apartment complex in which I live, and a higher class part of town. It is similar to most of those apartment complexes on Wax Figure Lane." Thad smiled at me. "There are a few of the apartment complexes on Wax Figure Lane that are pretty full of bad people! It is rumored that drug dealers, prostitutes both male and female, porn movie actors and producers, full service escorts, homosexual escorts, drug runners, pimps, and other sex industry workers, owners, and advocates make up the bulk of their tenancy. I don't know that for a fact, and I can't remember which buildings they are. I have heard it through the grapevine. The buildings are gorgeous, but the tenants are trouble. They bring down the reputation of the whole street!"

I gulped involuntarily at this last part of his comment. If I told him I lived at Candlestick, I might hear more crap about its tenants! I also was sure it might jog Thad's memory that Candlestick was indeed one of the rogue apartment complexes with bad tenants that he had heard about from the rumor mill. I guessed I would keep my mouth shut about the exact complex on Wax Figure Lane in which I lived. But what would I do or say if Thad asked me directly which complex it was in which I lived?

"My apartment is in the Carter Apartment complex on Barclay!" Thad volunteered, moving forward in our conversation. "It boasts a small library, a fitness center, two pools, meeting and convention rooms, two restaurants, and a large shopping center. It is awesome! I can almost do everything at home, over the internet locally, or in the complex, and not leave Carter's or appear in public!" Thad chuckled and nodded his head in approval, winking at me.

"My apartment complex boasts much of that, either in the building, or right next door such that we have easy access to them!" I poked back, a little defensively. "I love the complex where we live... It is comfy, large, beautifully decorated, kept well, and he has it extravagantly furnished and packed with all the latest technology! It is... our haven... home... It is the Cand..." Then I caught myself! I had said 'we have easy access', 'we live', 'he has it', and 'it is our haven', when at lunch I had led them all to believe that I mostly lived alone! Would Thad notice? If he did, what would I say?!

I also was almost ready to name my complex when I had decided not to do so!

There was a long, uncomfortable silence. I worked feverishly, hoping to distract Thad from our conversation and my faux pas. I noticed that Thad seemed a bit displeased with something I had said, nervous about what to say next, but clearly he had something he knew would be difficult to ask of me. I longed for him to be quiet and work so that he could forget about whatever over which he was cogitating.

I was dreading any more conversation, because I realized I was being a bit defensive and impulsive with my answers, not thinking before speaking. I did that too often and it was a compulsion with which I was working very hard to overcome. I had to slow down and think before I did or spoke anything!

"Tyler," Thad began carefully, but inquisitively, "I… you… when we were… at lunch, I… you kind of… well, you really led… you led us to believe more that you lived alone. I don't mean to accuse you of lying or anything." Thad pushed several buttons and grabbed a clipboard without looking at me. "I know we have just met, but I want… I would like… I hope you feel you can tell me. Are you… do you… are you living with someone?"

I dropped my head and turned it slightly away from Thad so he could not see my face. I was in a pickle now! He had caught it! Damn! I decided to still play it vaguely and calmly, releasing the bare minimum of truth.

I turned my head to look over at Thad at his machine, and jumped back a bit. Thad was right next to me on my left side, writing down figures on a clipboard as he looked lovingly and firmly at me.

I paused as I searched for a vague, defensive response. I looked at him with a stone-faced gaze.

"Well, Tyler?" Thad prompted reassuringly. "Do you live alone… or do you have a roommate?"

Oh, what to say to get out of this one?! I mentally kicked myself and my big mouth! I had a feeling I was about to learn that desperation did not breed wise or good responses.

"Yeh… I mean no… well… I need… all of us need help… help paying bills…" I stammered in uncertainty and anger. "I mean… yes, I do! I have a room… I live with someone!"

I studied my machine and tried to kind of offer him a cold shoulder. I wanted him to take the hint that I didn't want to talk about this line of conversation anymore.

"Who is your roommate?" Thad pressed gently and innocently, going back to his machine and continuing to write on his clipboard.

"He is my lov… He is my brother! From Florida!" I blurted out of nervousness and frustration. Again I had spoken without fully thinking this through. 'What an ass I can be!' I thought angrily.

"You denied having any other siblings at lunch… you claimed only two siblings in Gurnee. Albeit you were completely unconvincing!" Thad continued cajolingly, staring at me inquisitively again.

I resented the anal exam from Thad. Especially since I hardly knew him! I took a deep breath before speaking again.

"Well… I… You all… I mean, I guess… well, I was caught off guard!" I defended myself lamely. "I forgot about my elder brother who lived in Florida, but recently found a job in Aurora and moved back here to Illinois."

"So you lied?!" Thad asked reproachfully, now standing at his station, leaning on his bench with his arms folded, and giving me a critical look.

"Thad!" I exclaimed exasperatedly, an idea of rebuke coming to mind. "How dare you judge me and my motivations for being 'forgetful', vague, and a liar!? I am totally new to Aurora. I know no one here except my Andrew… I mean Andrew… I mean, my brother, Andrew!" I felt myself take on a look of apprehension and fear. "I don't know you… my fellow employees… or anyone in this city from Adam! Let alone do I know if… I have no way of… I don't know if you or any of the other workers at that table, or anyone in this town is, or is not an axe murderer. Thad, I have to be careful, to lie when it is necessary to protect myself here, since I am all alone. I didn't say anything about my lov… my brother as a roommate because frankly I was busy figuring out how to vaguely respond to each question. Can you blame me for not mentioning my roommate to you or anything too personal to you all?!" I looked desperately and pleadingly at him for understanding.

I no more than finished when it occurred to me that if I were truly scared of a murderer or a thief finding out where I lived, that I was alone and vulnerable, and they began stalking me, it would make more sense to reveal my Andrew as my roommate and a real protector and friend of mine. 'Damn!' I mentally exploded. 'I have done it again! I have spoken before realizing the absurdities of my statements. Will Thad take me to task for it? Will he catch me?'

"I know how you feel, Tyler!" Thad chuckled and came from his station to face me. "I felt the same way when I first moved here from West Michigan. I was alone… no friends… scared shitless, with a secret I knew would further complicate and endanger my life. It will pass though, Tyler. It takes getting to know others in town… to make friends with different people… get to know as many people… get to know as many people intimately as you can. We can then, as a group… as a class…, as a community we can protect you!" Thad had come near me and was standing closely in front of me again. Again his words seemed pregnant with a double meaning somewhere.

I almost fell over! Thad reached up and ran his right hand through my hair. He ended by rubbing my bangs through his fingers. I backed away, disturbed, and a little guilt ridden. I liked his touch… I loved his touch…, but I wanted Andrew to be the one to do this to me! I knew I was in trouble with God! He must hate me for feeling so stimulated by and thankful for the touching of a handsome perfect stranger!? God must hate me for all of my attractions to and desires for some of the really handsome and physically hot men with whom I interacted!?

In addition, what the hell was he saying 'to make friends with different people, get to know as many people intimately as you can.' Intimately?! To me that meant sexually! Why would I want to have sex with numerous people for friendship and protection?

Then 'we can then as a group, as a class, as a community we can protect you'!? What did that mean? What did Thad mean in that statement? What 'group' or 'community'? Was Thad… gay?! Did he mean other same-sex lovers in the community could… could… could protect me?

"Tyler…" Thad smiled that heavenly, calming smile at me, melting my resistance to his approach and flirting again. "I don't quite… I don't know whether to say this… I don't know how to say it… I don't want to scare you… But… I…" Thad looked at me as a serious but gentle countenance descended over his face. He again stroked my head and cheek. I didn't resist because he was just so damn hot!

I had a small idea of what was coming, but I wasn't sure. Therefore I was dreading it.

"Tyler, I operate under the theory that one lays his cards out on the table in a new relationship so no one has much of anything to hide. I don't want to scare you… I value the friendship we have right now." Thad looked over into my eyes, a serious and pleading countenance in them. Like a laser his eyes bored right into my soul. "If you aren't… well, if you don't like… I mean if the answer is no, then I am content to… I can stay just friends…"

"Thad." I exclaimed as I gulped. "What the hell are you trying to say, Thad? I don't know what to respond if you don't spit it out! What are you getting at? And why are you… are you fondling me…? I like the touching… but Andrew is…" I quickly stopped.

"Tyler!" Thad sighed as he blurted out his mind. "Tyler, I am gay. I am really attracted to you! You match all of my criteria for the best masculine man that I can imagine marrying. I want to know if you would go out with me to lunch or dinner sometime?!"

I was floored as I felt my jaw drop in surprise! Even though I had felt this was what he had on his mind, I was still shocked. I was struggling to find the strength to be this honest with Andrew whom I had not even known for five days, let alone to Thad whom I had only known eight hours!

"I understand, Tyler, if you aren't gay that you would reject me!" Thad grabbed my shoulders gently. "Don't be afraid to say no. I would rather you and I stay friends than let my impatience and spontaneity cause us to divide. I understand if you are gay, too, and I am being too forward. I can wait for you to be more comfortable. Either way, Tyler, just be honest with me! I really… really… I REALLY dig you and I am… I am so attracted to you, Tyler! I want to get to know you better through a dating status between us."

I was still speechless and I glanced at my hands as I gulped again. I couldn't believe this! I was attracted to Thad, but not nearly as much as I longed for, wanted, and was attracted to Andrew! At this point I didn't want to, nor could I think about being with Thad sexually, but I wanted Andrew sexually every which way but loose. I couldn't do this thing! I would be cheating on Andrew! Sure, I didn't know for 100 percent that Andrew was gay despite his confession to me, or that as he professed he did really love only me, but I was 99 percent certain… or so I thought. He had claimed to have been serious when he said all those things about how he loved me and he was gay. Additionally guys didn't go around willy nilly handing out open mouth-to-mouth passionate kisses like Andrew and I had shared to other guys unless they were gay.

"Ah… Thad… I am flattered!" I looked at him fully in his beautiful blue eyes and shrugged, struggling to resist his offer, confession, honesty, charm, and my attraction to him.   "But Thad… I have another… I am involved with… there is someone else… Someone with whom I am involved… Someone with whom I want something more serious. Someone with whom I am madly in love and… who is madly in love with me. I cannot lead you on. I cannot go out with you."

Thad's countenance dropped and he was clearly disappointed. He smiled sadly, stroked my cheek briefly and held my other hand. Then he let go of me and looked at his feet.

"Tyler, I am sorry, but I had to try! I had to try and win your heart." Thad gazed back up at me and smiled wanly. "You are too much a catch to not give 'us' a try! I am sorry! Can we still work together and be friends?"

"I think so… I mean… yes." I stammered. "I think we need to just forget this ever happened, and move on!"

"Good! I… well… we can do that!" Thad went back to his station and resumed work.

I turned back to my machine and continued working. I tried to push most of our conversation out of my mind, but it was hard. The thought of Thad and his plea to date me… I had Andrew, damn it!

Presently Thad spoke in a soft, inquisitive, and cautious voice.

"Tell me, Tyler… are you… is your… is your lover a… a woman… or a man?"

"She is a woman of course!" I exclaimed a little defensively. "She is a gorgeous, slender woman!"

"Of course she is…" Thad responded. "Of course…"

It was quiet for a few minutes. Then Thad spoke up again.

"How long have you dated this bodacious woman, Tyler?"

"Six weeks today…" I spoke up, again not really thinking about what might come next.

"Do you have a picture of her? I'd like to see what taste you have in women." Thad gazed at me in interest.

Again I had walked into a really tough spot! How to tell Thad I have dated a woman for six weeks and I do not have her picture in my wallet! I could feel myself flushing in embarrassment. What should I do? What could I tell Thad as an excuse for having no picture of her?!

"Tyler? Do you have a picture of your babe?" Thad quietly pursued his question.

"I have all of my pictures of my woman and me at my apartment, Thad. Sometime I'll bring some in and show you." I lied.

The afternoon flew by. Thad and I worked comfortably, congenially, and closely with one another on the various machines in our department. Nothing more was said of Thad's proposal to me or our dating lives outside the shop. Making quotas for computer boxes, packing skids with unassembled boxes, and chatting with each other made the time go quickly.

Suddenly a big buzzer blew, and the day was over.

Thad and I rushed to the time clock computer. We said our formalities for parting, and I punched out and made tracks to the parking lot where I knew Andrew would be waiting.

Andrew would make me forget about Thad! His love was all I needed to take me away to a blissful evening of being together, Andrew and me.

Sure enough, Andrew was there in his plum Intrepid, one hand on the wheel and one hand on the outside of the door. He was partially turned to face the doors at which he had dropped me off this morning. He was so handsome and hot that way that I shuddered in ecstasy!

When he saw me his face lit up in the most handsome and beautiful smile I had ever seen. I smiled and waved as I increased to a trot to his car. I had to be near him now!

I hopped in the passenger side, closed the door, and snapped my seat-belt closed. As I turned to speak to Andrew, I bumped right into his face. Before I could protest, he had me lip-locked in a kiss, a passionate kiss that gave me an instant hormonal high, an erection, and curled my toes. I cooperated briefly, and then gently pushed him off. What if other employees had seen Andrew and me making out?!

"Mmf… Andrew mmf… stop!" I pushed back again. "What if my fellow employees were to see this?! I don't want to start fighting over my sexuality with other workers. Or, worse yet, management… they may try firing me for it. I don't want anyone at work here to know about me… about us!"

"Relax, Tyler!" Andrew said softly as he stroked my cheek and head and kissed my neck. "The windows, all except the back one, are tinted so darkly that no one can see inside. Anyway, you are so new to the company that it would not be remembered that we kissed today by the time all of the employees get to know you. In addition it is not legal for a business to fire a same-sex gay person. If they did we would sue their asses! Besides, Ty, why not just come out?"

"Come out?! Come out of what?" I asked curiously, giving Andrew a strange gaze.

"Come out of the closet." Andrew replied, smiling and looking expectantly at me.

"I'm not in a closet!" I exclaimed, confused. What the hell was he talking about?! "What closet? You aren't in a closet. Neither am I in a closet. We are in a car!"

Andrew laid his head back on the headrest and chuckled. Then he raised his head and looked at me with great mirth.

I must have scowled at him, because the mirth melted on his face and was replaced with a grin.

"I love you, Tyler, and you are so special and cute because you are so naïve to current words and phrases, and code words in the gay community." Andrew smiled and stroked the back of my head lovingly as he guided our car down street after street toward home. "I have to guard you well, Tyler, against your own naïveté to the people, predators, bad things, code words, actions, culture, sexual mores, and social relationships prevalent in our city here in Aurora. As you are, Tyler, you could really get hurt, taken advantage of, or mixed up in crimes about which you know nothing nor understand. This isn't Gurnee anymore! We will get you up to speed though!"

I almost interrupted Andrew to defend myself. I felt like he were being condescending and 'better than though' and it pissed me off! But Andrew continued before I could organize my thoughts, formulate my words, and spout off.

"There is nothing wrong with being naïve and somewhat unconnected with or unaware of some things in society, but some things are evil, dangerous, ugly, illegal, disturbing, and harmful to you. You are unique, Tyler, a virgin, untouched by the bad things in society. You are a gem and good as gold because of your naïveté, and I love you, Tyler!" Andrew grabbed my hand and held it as he continued. "'Come out of the closet' means that you admit to your community and family that you are gay, a homosexual. I know you want to keep it secret from your family for the time being, but Tyler, why don't you just tell your work mates and managers that you are gay, and that you and I are an item? That way you face your sexuality head on and clear the air. Then let the chips fall where they may?!" Andrew's voice was loving, corrective, soft, and comforting.

In one instant I wanted the whole world to know I was gay and Andrew was my lover! I remembered at that moment with pride, that I had just turned down a date with Thad because I believed Andrew and I loved one another. I hadn't wanted to cheat on Andrew, and I had refused to do so. Andrew was now telling me and demonstrating to me that I had made the right decision!

But then a little Biblical truth came back and I remembered the scripture something to the effect: "Thou shalt not sleep with mankind as with womankind; it is an abomination."

Once again, because of gross church neglect in teaching the Bible and applying it to today's issues, I had no idea of where to find the scripture, let alone any other scriptures I could use to ward off the 'flaming arrows of the enemy'. 'Thank you, church!' I thought angrily. 'You are completely guilty of not preparing the flock to fight the devil!'

However, as I considered this one precious little remembered verse, I realized that the scripture was quite clear. The act of being in love with and having sex with a member of your same-sex was a sin to God. Was having a relationship like I had with Andrew equally sinful?! I did not know, and I didn't know where really to find the truth! The number of scriptures dealing with same-sex love were so few in the Bible that to find them would be like looking for needles in a hay stack. The churches were too busy with bowling leagues, softball contests, hunting contests, and movies to really answer those questions, apparently. In addition, it seemed they were running scared of offending parishioners and losing their tax exempt status through the IRS to really preach the truth. 'What a fallen world I am in!' I thought sadly.

"I'm not going to tell my fellow workers that I'm gay, Andrew, even if I were. I just started working there and I want to win their trust and make friends, not alienate people because they are afraid of, or despise me and my 'sexuality'." I responded logically. I thought it was an intelligent answer.

"Oh, so you build your coworkers' trust by lying to them about your sexuality?" Andrew ask in a let-down and mildly sarcastic tone of voice. "Bear with me, Tyler, I am simply playing devil's advocate and forcing you to think through your life, morals, religion, and sexuality."

He pulled his Intrepid around another corner into traffic.

"They aren't being lied to, Andrew, because I am not gay." I shook my head vigorously 'no' and scowled as I gazed out of my window. "That is why I need not 'come out of the closet', because I am not gay!" I had to hang on to my claim that I was not gay for my own mental and emotional stability!

"If you are not gay, Tyler, I need to know where I stand with you? What do you call our relationship, or how do you define it?" Andrew spoke a bit defensively. He placed his hand almost in my crotch. His pinky he rested on my scrotum. It felt so good!

He had me! I didn't want to lie, and I didn't want to tell the truth. I didn't want to deny my intense love for and overwhelming attraction to Andrew, but I didn't want to ever admit openly to the world I had these feelings for him. I didn't want the public classifying me as a member of the 'gay community'. I was on thin ice now! I felt my face blush red in anger and embarrassment. Maybe Andrew would forget his question.

"Tyler, I want to know!" Andrew gently, yet firmly resubmitted his question. "I need to know. If you are not gay, where do I stand with you? I mean we both have expressed our love for one another several times… we have passionately kissed several times… Considering our love activities, what do you call our relationship?"

"I… ah… we…" I didn't know what to say. "I… I love… you, Andrew, but I like girls too. I…"

Andrew rolled his eyes and briefly hung his head. He took a deep breath and raised his head, boring into my very soul with his intense blue pools.

"Tyler, does your love for me transcend a brotherly love? Is your love and desire for me more equal to the love your mom and dad have for one another?" Andrew clearly was going to try to pin me and the truth down.

I wanted to curse! I wanted to curse me, Andrew, the church, and society! I wanted to… I was so angry! Why?!

"Well… I guess… I mean… I have never thought… never thought about it that way. I guess… I think… yes, Andrew, it does." I looked at my hands. "I… I love you like… like… like a husband loves a… a wife…" I grasped Andrew's hand and kissed it. "God forgive me!"

"Do you feel all tingly and excitedly when we are together?" Andrew continued.

"Y… yes. I feel… feel like a school boy… I feel like a school boy on his first date." I admitted, my face flushing. I was so ashamed! Yet Andrew, his love, and his loyalty wouldn't let me lie to him.

"When faced with hot, sexy, hunks you'd like to get to know, do thoughts and images of me interrupt your lusting after or thoughts about these other men and make you feel guilty for cheating on me?" Andrew glanced at my face.

"Yes! Yes, they do! Are you happy now, Andrew!" I willed him to stop. I felt so guilty before God! Tears came to my eyes as I turned my red, hot face to the window and scowled. It was raining now.

"Damn it, Andrew! I love you! God forgive me! Please no more quiz questions?!" I turned my head back to gaze angrily at Andrew.

Andrew picked up my left hand again and caressed it with his thumb.

"Do you find women physically and sexually attractive?" Andrew asked.

I was so frustrated! I closed my eyes and plopped my head back on the head rest. I sighed.

"I find hot girls attractive physically, sometimes sexually attractive." I answered, relieved that this was a question that I could answer honestly without feeling guilty. "But generally I find most women physically repulsive and a big turn off sexually… I mean… the whole period thing… big, pendulous melons… the smell… " I shuddered as I let my voice trail off.

Andrew was driving me nuts and making me very uncomfortable with his questions and the obvious point he was pursuing. I knew that if I could get in the upper hand of this conversation by asking Andrew questions, I could perhaps get control of this situation and not be at Andrew's mercy. 'I had to try!' I decided.

"Do you find men attractive physically and sexually?" Andrew queried, a sly grin playing on his face.

He beat me to the punch. Could I ever get control of this conversation?!

"Some men…" I quickly replied, but not totally honestly. "Well, most cute men of average weight, manly figures, and above." I hung my head in shame.

"Which turns you on more, pictures of men in their underwear, or pictures of women in their bras and panties?" Andrew was closing in on his point; I could tell by the expression on his face.

"Mostly pictures of men in their underwear…" I quietly admitted.

"If you had to pick now whether to have sex with me, or that bikini clad beauty there on the beach, whom would you pick?" Andrew turned into Pepper Avenue.

"I'd… I… I'd choose… choose…" I muttered, "I'd choose… you." I was becoming exasperated. "What is your point, Andrew!? You are making me feel like dirt! Sinful dirt!" As if I didn't know his point! I looked pleadingly at him to stop.

"My point is that you are bisexual at least, and probably gay, Tyler." Andrew purred. "There is no shame in being in love with me, a member of the same-sex. There is no shame in accepting that you are gay, calling yourself gay, being in love with a member of the same-sex, or coming out to the world about your sexual orientation."

"In my world it is different! Andrew, I keep telling you, same-sex love is one of the 'worst' sins in the Bible. For us to even allow our minds to become vessels for the thoughts and lusts of same-sex relationships and lovemaking is also a sin." I ended by adding. "Despite this I know from the Bible, I still love and want you, Andrew!"

There was silence for a moment.

"What do you consider…" Andrew began.

"You missed our corner, Andrew!" I interrupted him. "Where are we going?"

"I missed it on purpose." Andrew said warmly. "We are going on a date for supper. After that, well… who knows? Anyway, Tyler, what do you call our relationship? Are we like just chumming around, or are we dating?"

I was trapped again! I didn't consider our relationship just chummy, I felt like I was getting to know Andrew in a dating type way. But again, I didn't want to lie, nor did I want to tell the truth! I decided to plead duress with God, and answer truthfully.

"I… I'd say… I'd say we are… we are… we are dating, Andrew." I smiled and held Andrew's free hand again.

"I hoped you would say that, Tyler!" Andrew beamed happily.

I felt like gutter trash! And yet, I was thrilled! Andrew and I were dating!? Andrew was cool with it! He did love me as I loved him back!

Additionally Andrew was such a catch! So handsome, such a gorgeous body… nicely muscled… sexy… I wanted to brag about my man to the whole world! I ran my fingers through Andrew's soft, beautiful, blond curls as he continued to guide us to our destination.

# CHAPTER 41

# IGNORANCE IS THE ENEMY

The next day, on Tuesday, June 5, 2010, I again took my Tyler to work. We had had a delicious breakfast, a wonderful morning, and a lively conversation on our drive to work. As Tyler hurried away from our Intrepid to the entrance of Computronix, I felt great elation that I was moving my relationship with him forward toward that of my spouse. Tyler and I had expressed our love for one another. Now we were openly talking about our growing relationship and we had kissed passionately. We had pushed the envelope big time with nudity. I was the only one who had not seen Tyler's beautiful brown body clearly while naked. He had, however, seen my full, glorious body naked two or three times up close and personal. The memories of his massage with his bare hands on and in my naked ass and all over my body as he put medicine on my injuries made me hot just thinking about it!

Now I could begin planning for the time Tyler and I would first make love and become one, a couple. I so longed for that time Tyler would consent to a sexual relationship and we would enter our sex life. The thought of Tyler and me making love was like a drug-induced high… I was so hard!

I also could continue to map out the path to get Tyler as my 'official' spouse. I could now move and manipulate Tyler and me into a solid and growing marriage-like relationship. I longed for him sexually, spiritually, and emotionally so badly my body ached for him!

I drove home to Candlestick. It was my day off again, and it was my day to exercise at the local gym in which I was a member. The gym, "Tawny Bods", was eight blocks away. I parked my car in Candlestick's ramp, exited, and then crossed the street. I entered the building, took the elevator to my floor, and let myself into our apartment.

I scurried around gathering what I needed for a workout at the gym and afterwards. I packed a set of clean underwear, a casual suit including shirt and cargo pants, deodorant, cologne, swim suit, and my sweat pants and muscle shirt.

I wasn't quite finished. I popped a couple of vicodin, poured a 20 ounce flask of water with about 33% vodka and two teaspoons of avatar, and I neatly packed them into my duffle bag. Looking one last time around the room for anything I might have missed, I threw my duffle bag over my shoulder and left, closing and locking my apartment door. I was ready to exercise. I took great pride in keeping my body buff, muscular, lithe, and beautiful in all masculine ways.

I reached the elevator and pushed the 'down' button. I fluffed my blond curls in the glossy covering of the elevator door until the 'ding' announced the arrival of an elevator.

The door opened, but my mind was on my life with Tyler. I didn't check to see if anyone was inside first before I entered. I jumped in the elevator to go from floor 8 to floor 1. As I turned to go to the back wall, there was Phil Fleets standing in my way in his trench coat. He whipped it open, and although I didn't want to see anything I knew it wouldn't be possible to not look. His sexual organ was huge, erect, and ready to go. I quickly focused on Phil's face and didn't glance down again.

"Phil, I am… I mean, I really…" I couldn't help but be a bit flustered and I stammered as I held up my hand in a halt position. "I am not in the mood for you to flash me and beg me for sex! I have someplace to go, and some things to do!" I shook my head.

"I can meet that and any other request from you, you blond stud!" Phillip said slyly. "I didn't expect to see you here. I certainly didn't target you today! I am just exposing myself to all of the hotel clientele. It has been a busy day. But now you are here… You and I can make some beautiful music together!" Phillip stepped aside as I went to the back wall.

When I turned back to the front of the elevator, Phil had closed his coat and was watching me with a wanton, lascivious facial expression. I blushed as I also became pissed.

"What the hell do you want, Phil?! What the hell do you want from any of us who live here and face your visual assaults on a daily basis?!" I inquired roughly.

"Sex, Sex, Sex!!!" Phil hissed as he approached me. "You may be interested to know that I have had sex with every man living here in Candlestick except you and your roommate. Someday, Drew, I know you'll give in and I'll get my roll in the hay from you. I know you like big cock, and as you have seen I have probably one of the biggest! I'm gonna plow your ass, suck your cock…" He licked his lips and smiled knowingly and cunningly at me.

I was almost sick! Phillip was big and I knew he would tear me injuriously during any anal sex. It would be too painful for and disfiguring of my fine manhole. I wasn't interested in someone like Phillip, whose life purpose and morals were as vacuous and evil as Jezebel's, and whose penis was the size of a small tree.

"I'll never give you any piece of me, Phillip. I am not interested in your huge genitalia. Besides I already have a lover…" I trailed off, knowing I had said too much.

Phillip stood staring at me with his insipidly stupid, lustful grin. He copped a macho and certain voice tone as he continued to smile slyly.

"That's what all the macho gay men tell me!" Phillip slurred seductively. "But they always end up giving in to me and boy, the sex is awesome!"

I could tell by Phillip's slurred and seductive speech, and his overly brazen, pushy, and sexually aggressive behavior that he was pretty well soused with alcohol or drugs. Briefly I shuddered in fear. To my knowledge I had never dealt with a drunken or stoned Phillip. Did he have a knife or a gun? Should I reject, antagonize, and threaten him more? Or should I treat him with kid gloves, humor him? Should I take him down physically in a preemptive first strike? Should I pretend to give in, schedule a rendezvous, just to get the hell out of here?

My temporary fear, however, pissed me off. The hair on my neck prickled up and adrenaline rushed through my veins. Who the hell did Phil think he was!?

"Forget it, Phillip!" I shook my head and frowned at him. "This is one hottie mountain you will never climb! Now what the hell do you want from me?! Tell me now, or quit staring at me and leave me the hell alone!"

"I know you have a hot, beautiful, physically buff, and brown Adonis living with you now!" Phillip purred, licked his lips, and winked at me. "He is sexy and gorgeous, and I want to make him into a man as only a man can do. I thought though I would ask you about him first. I just want to know what his relationship is to you! Lover, brother, cousin, whatever?! Or, is he available?"

I was now between a rock and a hard place. I had three choices here as I saw things and quickly I sorted and thought through my options.

If I went with the lie and insisted that Tyler were just my brother, it was obvious that Phillip was interested in and wanted MY Tyler. Phillip was ballsy enough to begin pursuing my Tyler right under my nose! I didn't like that option and its consequences at all. I didn't want to 'free' up Tyler to be the prey of Phillip. I knew Phillip would really hit him up for sex until Tyler gave in. If Tyler were to remain tough and reject Phillip still, I had heard and believed that Phil was not against using deceit, drugs, alcohol, ecstasy, bribes, and rape to get his way with prey!

However, I knew if I spilled the beans that Tyler was not my brother but was actually my lover, there would result equally distasteful consequences. First, my admission would give Phillip ammunition to hold over my head for his sex demands. He could use the threat of turning Tyler and me in to Mrs. Kurtz as a means of extracting sex, drugs, alcohol, and money from both Tyler and me. I already knew Phillip wanted me and Tyler both for sex toys; he had propositioned me several times including today. Now I knew he wanted to have sex with MY Tyler specifically! With the knowledge that Tyler and I were lovers we would forever be at the mercy of Phillip's sick, painful, morbid, and demanding sexual desires.

The final option I could see was for me to admit that Tyler was not my brother but was my lover, and hope Mrs. Kurtz didn't find out, and that

Phillip did not know I was getting the family discount in rent. However, if Mrs. Kurtz did find out, I would lose my rent discount! I couldn't withstand that! We needed that discount to allow us to afford to live at Candlestick. I also needed it to save a nest egg for Tyler and me. I needed to more quickly save for us to escape my job at The Flamingo Lounge, and for us to look for equal housing other than Candlestick Apartments. If I admitted my true relationship with Tyler to Phillip it would only be a matter of time before Mrs. Kurtz would find out from someone about my deception.

What the hell should I, or could I do?! My mind was a whirl of conflicting thoughts, decisions, and their consequences. I was paralyzed in my confusion and conflict.

I had to focus!

"Well, what exactly is the relationship between you and the gorgeous brown hunk you have living with you, Andrew?!" Phillip pressed further like the devil himself taunting me for information.

Suddenly I was able to clear my mind. I thought quickly and then it came to me.

"Phillip Fleets!" I hissed in anger and contempt, with a threatening tone in my voice. "You leave my brother, Tyler, alone! He is not gay, he is not a drinker, he is not into drugs, or anything negative! He is my brother, and I will protect him from predators like you! I'll beat the shit out of you if I have to! Do you understand me?!" I doubled up my fists and took three threatening steps toward Phillip, glaring at him.

Phillip stepped back, looking wide-eyed in shock at me. Apparently chagrined and somewhat scared at my ferocity, he spoke in a regretful, trembling voice.

"I'm sorry, Drew!" Phil said quickly, frowning at me. "I didn't know! Calm yourself!"

I exited the elevator firmly and with finality. I stalked toward the lobby exit doors. As I left Candlestick through the front doors I turned toward the elevator where Phillip stood puzzled and flipped him the bird.

I stalked outside. I continued down the sidewalk to the street, fuming over Phillip's audacious, flamboyant, promiscuous, inconsiderate, and invasive homosexual style. How dare he!? He gave all of us in the normal and legitimate gay community a terrible reputation with the rest of cultured, civilized society. How could we ever gain equality and normalcy with our heterocentric society if the Phillips of our community continued their degeneracy?! Why didn't he tone it down and keep it to the gay bars and night clubs that existed here in Aurora and all over the country?!

I didn't watch where I was going, and when I reached the horizontal sidewalk with Candlestick Apartments building, I almost ran into a plump, ritzy Mrs. Pompadora on the sidewalk. I saw her at the last minute out of the corner of my eye and managed to jerk to a stop.

"Sick, pervert, Candlestick trash!" She sneered at me with a huff as she stuck her nose in the air. Her bright, red sequined dress shone in the almost blinding sunlight of day and her fur boa was wrapped loosely around her neck. She led her 'Poopsie' toy poodle, and, as I stared at her, she pushed her spectacles up on her nose and looked me up and down with obvious complete and utter contempt and disdain.

"Stuck-up prick!" I sneered back, scowling at her. I raised my nose and gave her the same contemptuous up and down with my eyes. I had to chuckle inside!

"Oh! How uncouth!" She huffed again loudly, and with that Mrs. Pompadora hurried on her way.

I went directly to my car on the first floor of the ramp. I turned it over and started it. As I allowed it to warm up, I picked up trash and generally cleaned the interior. Then I backed out of my space and took off for "Tawny Bods".

"Tawny Bods Fitness Center", the gym in which I had membership, was well-known in Aurora. I enjoyed it because it was so beautiful, large, and contained top-notch equipment and facilities that I used to the best of my abilities. They also offered a lot of price breaks and perks for people like me, those who were employed in the sex industry. We actually were given individual training and counseling upon demand when we went to work out. It wasn't a guaranteed thing that any time we went we would be able to access a personal trainer, however, I had only been refused once in a blue moon over the last seven years.

At the gym I parked in a gym-provided parking space in the ramp. I grabbed my duffle bag and locked my car doors. I turned and hurried toward the exit to the street, pondering "Tawny Bods" and the fact that I was so thankful for the treatment we received here from management. We in the sex industry were the primary customers, and 'Tawny Bods' recognized that. They treated us well.

I crossed the street and headed quickly inside the gym. Just inside the gym door I stopped. Neils was tending the front counter with a young lady I knew named Jessica Mills.

I reflected on the fact that I had carried on some relationships with a few employees here. I had only dated male personnel here, but there had been several over the last seven years. None had worked out, and I had abandoned them for various reasons. These reasons, I was beginning to realize, were not the actual reasons for breakup that I had thought, but were just excuses because of something else that wasn't yet clear. Now it was clear. I was waiting for Tyler!

I thought specifically of one of the clerks/personal trainers, Neils Jeremy Hanson. I had been hot into him at one point a few months ago. We had dated, we had loved one another, we had… well… we had been intimate in every Biblical sense. But during our dating time I had discovered what an ass he was, and I had dumped him after a relatively short period of time. He did not take it well, especially after I told him I was looking for someone who was not such an ass, and who brought more to our relationship table than he!

Naturally, after now having met my soul mate, Tyler, whom would I see in 'Tawny' first? Neils, my former love interest. I bucked up, pulled together my patience for idiots, lifted up my composure, and went toward the counter to face him.

Neils was now a major competitor and nemesis to me. He did not hesitate to give me glaring invitations to a second chance at a relationship. He now did anything he could do to get me back for my dumping of him and the fact that I refused to give him a second chance. He was civil, even friendly to my face, but would stab me in the back at every chance he encountered. I knew he was a constant threat.

"Well, 'Andrew'… hello!" Neils snidely commented as I came to the desk to sign 'in'.

"Don't speak my name that way, you bastard!" I responded, smiling insincerely at him.

"Well, well, DiPree." Neils said icily as a gaze of disgust slipped over his face. "I see your head is still up your ass! Fortunately the gym awaits. Maybe then you can manage to stand up straight, with your parts in the right place, and smell the coffee?!" He took the clipboard I had just filled out and handed it to Jessica Mills, the bubbly blond clerk at the computer.

"Thank you, Neils!" I replied as I passed my membership card through the reader. "Apparently you realize there is hope for me to free my head from my ass. What is your excuse for failing to do the same? After all, you work here!"

Neils fake laughed, sneered, and gave me a longing, yet contemptuous look.

"I look forward to the day you come crawling back to me, Drew! I will enjoy and relish your humiliation as I take my sexual angst out on you, ravage and rape you, have my way with you over and over, and then dump your battered, bleeding body somewhere where you will have to walk home naked!" Neils was being surprisingly civil today.

"Thanks for warning me of your plans for me, Neils!" I exclaimed, smiling snidely at him again. "But you have no chance of fulfilling that fantasy. I would never come crawling back to you, even if you were the last man on earth!"

"I'll be seeing a lot more of you!" Neils said in a knowing, superior manner that made my flesh crawl. "I am involved with someone you know very well. I will be dating him soon!"

"I doubt that!" I called as I walked on into the warm-up exercise area. "You and I are over remember, Neils?" 'Anyone whom I knew who would say anything about starting, having, or continuing a relationship with you,

you scum, I would quickly tell them not to bother!' I thought sarcastically to myself.

As I quickly and strenuously went through my warm-up routine I pondered whom Neils could mean that was close to me and whom he would be dating soon. I also thought about my own dating relationship with Neils. Neils and I had had fun, and he was an excellent lover. However, his character and personality left much to be desired! I finished warming up and headed to the exercise area.

I headed to the bank of treadmills and chose one giving me prime view of a TV, Neils, and a really cute guy to my right. I set the timer and speed to a brisk walk, and stepped on board.

As I walked I watched Neils at the check-in desk weed out the homosexual men from the heterosexual men. The latter he treated normally and got them on their way. Those whom he surmised were gay he schmoozed and lavished with attention and compliments. He ultimately acquired a few phone numbers for his efforts. 'Man!' I thought 'You'd have to be very naïve, or very... very desperate to fall for Neils and his lines!' Then I realized ruefully and in shame that I was judging my own intelligence and self-control! 'However, I fell for them at one time!' I frowned.

Then it hit me! Neils had said he would see a lot more of me in the future. How could that be since we had broken all ties? He then bragged that it would be because he was involved with someone I knew. Further he had said he would be dating him soon!? Tyler had said he had spent Sunday afternoon at a gym! I pondered the possibilities briefly. What if Neils were talking about Tyler... had schmoozed Tyler... had charmed him into a date?! Tyler was so sexually and culturally naive, and oblivious of and to the dangers in the LBGTQ lifestyle. I started to panic, and chills ran up and down my body. I gulped and my skin became clammy. The treadmill kept its pace but, in my concern, I was unaware of the fact that I hadn't kept mine. As I was sick with worry that Tyler may have been sucked in and fooled by Neils, I almost fell off of the machine.

However, as I regained my balance and position back on the front of the treadmill, common sense about the character of Tyler versus the bull crap of Neils began to set me straight. My fears seemed to be outrageous. Nah! Tyler would never fall for any gay man so obvious with his orientation and blatant in his pursuit of fresh, new man-meat to bang. He'd never agree to go out with a pig like Neils! Tyler had taste... good taste in men... After all, he was falling for me, was he not?!

As the day wore on I managed to forget about Neils and his possible designs on Tyler. I went through exercise machine after exercise machine. I was on the weight table benching 200 pounds when Neils was suddenly spotting me.

"What do you want, Neils?!" I asked wearily as I placed the barbells safely on the rack. I didn't trust Neils at this point any more than I would trust a pimp and a jon to protect the virginity of runaways and street youths.

"Oh, I just thought I'd comment on how your physical appear... I mean performance has improved over the past month. You're looking really buff, Drew!" Neils seemed genuinely sincere. However, I knew he was up to something!

"Drew, I'd like to give you some ass..." Neils winked at me. "I mean give you these passes for free visits. Keep them, use them, or pass them on to a friend or friends. Maybe your hot, bronze Adonis living with you would like to have some so he can use them to come and work me over... I mean work out with me!"

"Thank you, Neils, I appreciate it." I was oh, so leery of this scum! "I'll take the passes, but I am not interested in your ass anymore!" I ignored his comment about Tyler.

"By the way, nice piece of virgin meat you have living with you, Drew! 'Brother' wasn't it?" Neils now was speaking like a shopper, a critic of fine male flesh. He had a leering, lustful grin on his face, like he had me by the gonads. I almost puked I was so pissed and sickened!

What was Neils' angle? Was this a veiled threat to pay me back by pursuing and using my Tyler? How did he know about Tyler? Was Neils trying to scare me back into a relationship with him by threatening Tyler?

"How do you know about my Tyler, my bronze Adonis!?" I exclaimed angrily.

"He was here Sunday and worked out. I talked with him quite extensively during his four hours here. He is one hot hunk of male flesh! He is so… so… so scrumptiously virgin, handsome, and adorably naïve!" Neils leered and almost drooled at the thought of my Tyler. "He has one gorgeous… awesome… desirable… sexy body! By the way, I saw every muscle and hair on his perfect body; I saw him naked. Have you?!"

I was really pissed now! Neils clearly did have some kind of angle in this exchange. But which of the possibilities was it?

He also was infuriating me by rubbing my face in his obvious desires for and designs on my Tyler, and by informing me that he had seen Tyler naked. I wanted to be the only one to whom Tyler would display his masculine, sculpted, naked body! Neils had beaten me to it. He was really getting under my skin!

"Neils, why would I want to see my brother naked! Yes, he's a brother, if that's any of your business! And you leave your meat cleavers off of him! He is straight, not gay!" I snarled a reply as I stood up.

"Well!" Neils was now being the stupid ass that he was, only interested in his own sexual self-gratification and bolstering his own ego. "Brother or not, he is one fine piece of virgin meat whom I intend to make into a man! Whether he is gay or straight, only another man can make him into a man; that is where you are lacking, Drew. Using sex to make real men out of the heterocentric weenies peopling the majority. I'll show him real sex… real sexual pleasure! I'll find out for you if he likes it slow and gentle, or fast and rough. I will know every glorious inch of his beautiful naked body by the time I am done!" Neils puffed out his chest, rippled his impressive musculature, and smiled broadly and gloatingly at me. "While I take his virginity, I will remember our sexual liaisons, DiPree! And I will think about how I am stabbing you in the back!"

I couldn't take it anymore! Rage came on me like a tsunami, and a hormonal rush of adrenaline too. I had put up with so much of his shit during our dating and since our break-up a while back. Involuntarily I charged Neils. I hauled off and slugged him hard across his face. I drew my fist back and there was blood on my hand and my arm. Neils went down like a sack of potatoes, despite the fact that he was much larger than I, and he was also stronger than I.

I looked quickly again at the blood on my hands and arm. He was clearly bleeding badly from somewhere.

I stood ready to fight, fists doubled, as Neils sat up and shook his head. He massaged his jaw as he covered his bleeding nose with his towel. He glared angrily and hatefully at me.

"I will have Tyler's virginity, his tight manhole, regardless of whether you like it or not, Drew." Neils sneered at me as he brought both knees up toward his face. "I have already seen him naked, and Wednesday I will have a date and sex with him! Virgins have such a nice, tight ass and make so much sexually stimulating noise during their first sexual experiences, Drew, don't you agree! It will be so fun and stimulating to deflower him just to spite you, Drew!"

The statement about Neils already seeing Tyler naked now sank in and caused me to do a double take. Neils gloated and gave me a victorious smile.

In my growing anger Neils' revelation about his plans for a date with and deflowering of my Tyler on Wednesday totally escaped me the first time. I was stuck on Neils' claim to have seen Tyler naked. Tyler was mine! His love… his affections… his attention… his being… his body and nakedness… All were mine alone! I was the only one to whom I wanted Tyler to share his gorgeous… awesome… naked body. I wanted me to be the only one to feast on and be with Tyler's glorious body. I wanted Tyler to feel the same way about me. I didn't need the bastard Neils screwing up me and Tyler!

"Yeh, Drew! It's true! I have actually seen every inch of Tyler's naked body before you! He was so stunned and turned-on by my lust for his body that I could have played with his dick, his cheeks… maybe even penetrated him with my fingers. Now I intend to have my way with Tyler and make mad, passionate love to him Wednesday evening!" Neils smiled and nodded triumphantly, rubbing his jaw and dabbing blood. "We have a date Wednesday to go over membership plans to the gym."

Now Neils' statements about dating and raping Tyler on Wednesday evening totally sank in and hit me like a ton of bricks. My first reaction was fear and concern for my Tyler. I shuddered involuntarily. Tyler was book smart, but not street smart or big city gay culture smart. He was so naïve in those areas. In addition he was too trusting, too kind, and too sexually inexperienced for his own good. He was a virgin after all! He needed advice and protection. I'd have to do something about Neils dating Tyler Wednesday.

Then my reaction changed radically. I seethed with a rage I had never felt before over a lover!

"You take one more sexual step toward my Tyler, Neils, and I will beat you senseless!" I hissed. "Tyler is mine, and, when the time comes, I will take his virginity, not you, or anyone else! Tyler is too good for you, and I'll be damned if you take what is mine by raping Tyler!" I wanted to kick Neils right in the face to wipe that stupid grin off of his countenance.

I was furious! So angry was I that I forgot to be discreet about my relationship to Tyler. I didn't even realize I had spilled the beans until Neils visibly perked up and spoke.

"Ah…!" Neils grinned knowingly and nodded. "So he is not a brother, but your new boy toy eh!? I thought so, Drew! You are such a liar, such a transparent fool! I could tell when you cast me aside that your reason you gave for the break-up was not the real reason. You still loved me, but thought I just wasn't your 'type'. You felt I wasn't 'up to your caliber'. A male slut at a night club like you are, who flaunts his body for any pervert in the public is not worthy of a personal fitness trainer that has picked and chosen the best of the male fleet for their pleasure?! You do anyone, Drew, for money! I do only those who are the best, the healthiest, and clean of diseases! What the @ is your problem with me?!"

I then fully realized what I had said. I had given Tyler and me away to Neils! Did he know Mrs. Kurtz? Did he know enough about our apartments and Mrs. Kurtz's policies to tell her about us, about Tyler and me?! I decided to continue being honest. What the hell!

Tyler was mine and would stay undefiled until he and I were one together in lovemaking. The thought of him giving and rewarding me with his virginity and all his sexual firsts made me very hot and horny. Now and in the future I must focus on protecting Tyler, my territory, from predators, mostly sexual predators. With Neils knowing that Tyler and I were lovers it would hopefully turn him off from his interest in both of us. I was one step forward in protecting my Tyler and all of his physical and sexual attributes.

"Tyler is my lover… my desire… my future mate, yes!" I responded angrily. "As for you and me, Neils? You are a narcissistic, amoral ass! I want nothing more to do with you. I didn't lie to you in order to break 'us' off, I was just too stupid a few months ago to know what the hell I wanted. Once I realized what I wanted, it was clear that it didn't include you. I dumped your ass because you are a piece of… you are a slovenly dick! An uncouth, predatory, sexual pig! I may lay certain people for money, but I don't use my job as an opportunity and excuse to lay everyone like you do." I was pissed and on a roll! "Neils, you are worse than a slut because you pursue anyone and anything to assuage your personal sexual needs. I look for those I care to service, and I get paid by them because I cater to their fetishes and sexual tastes and make them happy. There is still a major difference between you and me, and you still rest at the bottom of the pond. Now you stay away from me and MY Tyler, or so help me I will beat you to a pulp!"

"Oh, shove it, Drew!" Neils wiped a little more blood away as he frowned harshly again at me. He then got a gloating look on his face. "Well, you'd better make your move soon, Drew." Neils stood up. "I have a date with Tyler for Wednesday at 5:00. And I won't be wasting any time to get in his pants and make a man out of him! Your boy toy, Drew, is about to become my man slam homerun!"

"If you keep that date, Neils, I'll put you in the hospital!" I yelled as he stalked away.

I glanced around. We had gathered quite an audience. Some had countenances of disgust and they quickly turned and stalked away. Others had guises of surprise, curiosity, and skepticism. However, to my pleased wonderment, several bystanders clapped and smiled at me as Neils stalked away. I blushed in some embarrassment!

"The show is over, people!" I smiled as I waved for them to disperse. "Go back to your workouts."

I looked briefly for Neils again. He was making a hot path to the front counter, using a hanky to wipe the rest of the blood from his face. I frowned and shook my head.

I turned back to the thinning crowd around me, some leaving, and some still gazing from me to Neils and back again.

I walked into the remaining crowd as they separated for me. Continuing on toward my next machine, I was painfully aware of the stares, the looks, the glares. Several faces registered looks of 'queer', 'pervert', and 'damn fag'. I was becoming angry again! So many people were so self-righteous, morally judgmental, brain-washed, prejudiced, myopic, and conservative that they made me ill!

As I sat down and adjusted my next workout machine I reflected on my past when I had viewed sex as a tool for income, a 'commodity' to sell and bargain with, and a working talent. In the last year that had gradually changed, and now I wanted sex to be between two lovers who were monogamous partners. I wanted sex to be precious, an expression of a love between two people that transcended tradition, culture, history and my lover and I. Then came Tyler – my man, my future lover.

I didn't like speaking of Tyler and his virginity as though it were a commodity for which to be bargained. I, unlike Neils, respected Tyler and I wanted him to want me, to want to give his virginity up to me when we finally made love. I was not like Neils, take the fortress at all costs!

I finished my workout. As I worked I knew that I must talk to Tyler about the whole Neils and Wednesday situation. Perhaps I could make him understand what danger he was in with Neils, and that he and I were a number and he would be cheating on me if he were taken by Neils. I felt like I had to protect Tyler not only as a brother, but now as a lover! He was a snow-white lily in a field of florists, waiting to be plucked and sold to the highest bidder. Neils had plans to pluck him, and sell him as such! I almost hurled because my fear, concern, and apprehension were so great!

To finish my workout I walked a mile on the track around the outside walls of the building. I could see Neils still trolling for dates amongst the males coming to work out. As I began my laps I could see Neils acquire several phone numbers. I cringed. I couldn't let Tyler go out with that… that… slut rat bastard!

I was so busy worrying about Tyler that I did not realize I was being followed. I had glanced back a couple of times at the two muscular, cute, well built young men, but had heretofore ignored them. In fact, I first became fully aware of them when I overheard one say to the other:

"This is a straight persons' gym, not a gym for fags and dykes! This faggot ahead of us needs to leave and go to his fruits at home!" One of the two behind me said loudly enough to ensure I would hear.

I could safely assume they were not interested in me sexually! At first there was a sense of relief. However, I began another low simmer. How dare they assume I was gay! How did they know?! Had they seen my altercation with Neils and heard our fight? I didn't remember seeing them in the crowd around us at the time. Did they know, or was I being too sensitive?

"Yeh!" The second guy added. "Strange things happen to the likes of him around here. Neils will see to that!"

"Neils caught a fag in here the other day fondling a kid in the shower!" One man exclaimed with a sneer. "Imagine a man molesting a boy in a public gym! Only a faggot pervert would molest a child! Especially a boy! Faggots are the perpetrators of a large majority of the molestation of male children and teens."

"Who told you about that situation?!" The other asked, incredulously.

"Neils! He said that queers are more likely to molest boys of all ages. It's a part of being queer. You are attracted to whatever male flesh you see, regardless of age. And when you think about it, it makes sense."

I bristled at that! I was an adult gay male, and had no attraction to, or desire to be with boys under the age of 19. I fought the urge to turn around and challenge the two idiots behind me. The mere thought that logical humans would assume that gays would automatically be child molesters put a bee under my saddle!

"Did Neils call the police and report the fag?" The other guy asked.

"Naw! He knew that by the time the police came the whole situation wouldn't exist, and it would be his word against the queer that did the fondling! He didn't think it was worth it!" The other replied.

"Yeh. I agree with Neils though, now that you mention it. Queers would be more likely to molest young boys than their heterosexual counterparts because, like you said, they are attracted to male flesh regardless of age." The one guy spoke up again.

"I think probably most molesters, male or female, are queer." The other guy added, sneering. "If you think about it it makes perfect sense! If you are attracted to those of the same-sex, what would age matter? You'd do it with any sex, any age, that moved!"

I was pissed! These baboons were so biased and wrong! I picked up my pace to get out ahead of them before I did, or said something that would get me into trouble. I knew one-on-one with either of them would be a fair fight. However, the two of them against me would result in them kicking my ass.

They trailed me through my final walk, making disparaging remarks about homosexuals, males in particular. Clearly they thought gays and lesbians were second or third class citizens not deserving of using their gym or oxygen.

They seemed to think Neils was on the level as a 'straight' man. I knew differently, but I was really curious as to what game Neils was playing; gays vs. straights, or straights vs. gays, or some other plan?! One of the two guys, a Benjamin Strong, was especially obnoxious to gays, and since Neils was gay, neither plan made sense for Neils. What was his agenda? Why was he hiding behind a front of anti-gay behavior?

As I showered after my walk and workout, I further pondered Neils and his possible motivations for being a sexual chameleon. Was he 'under cover' to find a pedophile among the gay clients? Was he playing the 'straight' guys a trick by exposing them to homosexuals? Was he targeting gay guys for the straights to victimize? All of this made me all the more certain that Tyler couldn't keep his date with Neils. Neils was far too dangerous for me to allow that!

I stepped out of the shower, grabbed my towel, wiped my face, and opened my eyes as I dropped the towel to my chest. There, standing in his bikini swim trunks with his soldier almost erect, no more than six inches between our noses, was Neils. He sported a frown, and glared at me.

"Stay out of my personal sex life, DiPree, and do not interfere with me and Tyler!" He hissed menacingly. "What you and I had a few months ago is over! Quit pining for me!" Neils stood his ground. I could feel his hot breath on my face.

"Pining!?" I spit out with a chuckle. "Pining after you, Neils?!" I laughed. "I am so not pining for you! You are an ass! I told you to stay away from Tyler because he is mine!" I was incredulous at Neils' arrogance!

The next thing I knew Neils had his right hand clasp on my left buttock. I felt very uncomfortable and humiliated. Neils squeezed tightly, and I could not free myself because he grabbed my right shoulder with his left hand.

"The early bird gets the worm, DiPree!" Neils said in a well-known metaphor, leaving his hands clutching my body.

"But fools rush in where wise men fear to tread, Neils!" I added with a warning in my voice. "And get your hands off my ass and my shoulder or I'll be giving them back to you in a bag!"

Neils kept his right meat hook on my left buttock, squeezed hard, and stuck his left pointer in my face.

"And by the way, 'better than me, DiPree'..." he hissed, "no one embarrasses me like you did out there and gets away with it! You won't know when it's coming, where it's coming from, but I am going to kick your ass for assaulting me!"

"You and what army, Neils?!" I smirked and snorted. Then I glared at him. "Neils! I said 'get your hands off me! Now!'"

Neils and I shared a brief stare down during which he released me. Then he whirled around and walked away.

I finished drying and dressing, and headed for the door. My last look at Neils was a mutual warning look. Neils added to his by flipping me the bird.

# CHAPTER 42

# CLIMBING THE WALL TOGETHER

I hurried to the counter to check out of the gym and get away from Neils as quickly as possible. Where Neils once turned me on sexually because I didn't know him personally, he now made my flesh crawl; he was such a self-absorbed, promiscuous, male gutter slut. While dating him I had also concluded that Neils was a horrible and nasty poster child for the homosexual community to have parading in public and flaunting his behavior in the faces of the everyone in the nation. He was the epitome of almost everything negative about homosexuals that the Church used to suppress those in the LGBT community.

Puzzling to me, though, was that he was somehow passing himself off as 'straight' to the straight members of the fitness center and simultaneously he was building hatred for and friction between gays and straights there. I did not know toward what ends he was doing this, but I decided I had better find out!

I knew I wasn't much better in my employment than Neils was as far as his job and activities. However, I knew I intended to leave the lifestyle and get different, more respectable work. I had plans for a better life after my many years in the sex industry. I also hoped and planned then to be physically and sexually monogamous with Tyler, my spouse, the rest of my life. In those respects I knew I was much better than Neils. I had goals and I had drive and determination to accomplish them. He was comfortable to just piss around and troll for quick rolls in the hay and other sundry slutty activity with those who could make him feel sexually and personally superior and desirable. He was a narcissist, a sexual scum. He made me sick!

I had never felt this way before. I had never believed that or considered whether my sexually pleasing clients at The Flamingo Lounge made me a slut. I had never, to my knowledge, felt like a terrible, filthy... almost sinful person for doing this work. However, seeing Neils at work, his promiscuity, and his sexual purposes and goals on display reflected back at me made me feel exactly that... terrible, filthy, and 'sinful'. I felt better than Neils on the one hand, and I felt worse than he was on the other. It was a confusing balance... or imbalance.

After quickly signing out at the counter and glaring menacingly at Neils, I grabbed my duffle bag and belongings and exited the entrance door to the street.

I crossed the sidewalk and almost tripped and fell when the sidewalk dropped to the street. It was obvious I was still high from the vodka and avatar I had consumed while working out. I felt fine, but I knew I was high and drunk to some extent. The thought crossed my mind that I really shouldn't... well, I shouldn't... I probably shouldn't drive back to Candlestick. However, I would be damned if I were to leave my plum Dodge Intrepid where it might get vandalized! Who knew what damage Neils might do to my second baby if he realized I had left it in the parking structure and had taken a taxi home? I had no doubt he would vandalize it if he found out it was sitting unprotected across the street. I couldn't take that chance! The decision was easily made. I would drive home despite my 'high' and slightly drunk feelings. I was young and stupid back then I know.

I crossed the street and entered the parking ramp. As I walked out into the parking lot toward my precious plum 2009 Dodge Intrepid I reflected on what an awesome and intelligent investment it had been. I loved my car! It was dependable, well-crafted, and a smooth ride. It was also beautiful and snazzy.

I opened the back passenger door and threw my duffle bag and belongings onto the backseat. Then I jumped behind the steering wheel and started the car.

I had to get moving in order to pick up Tyler from work. Then it was quickly home and I would be fine. We both would be fine. We could fall into each other's arms and hold each other all evening. I longed for Tyler's touch all over, around, and in my body. I ached for it!

I merged from the Tawny Bods parking structure into traffic. I pondered the incidents at the gym with Neils and what I had learned of his plans for Tyler on Wednesday.

I had to talk to Tyler tonight about Neils, sexual predators, and big town seductions and scams. Tyler was so naïve! That was a small part of what I loved about him, because I knew I was 'cracking a nut' that was completely fresh, 'uneaten', not violated, and newly ripened into a gorgeous young man. However, Tyler's naïveté, drop-dead good looks, and awesome physique could prove to be his downfall if someone like me did not take him under his wing and watch out for him. There were those out in the world like Neils who would just use and abuse Tyler, not caring about his virginity and his health, emotional, and physical weaknesses and needs. They would take their pleasures out on him somehow, and leave him raped, bleeding, and harmed physically, sexually, and emotionally beyond repair. I didn't know if anyone could pick up the pieces if these types of perverse homosexual experiences befell Tyler at any time.

I knew, however, I could help Tyler by easing him into life here in Aurora amongst all of the vicious, wicked, and downright evil elements in the underbelly of our community. I could help him identify sexual predators gay and straight, killers, the drug dealers, mobsters, sexual exploiters, and male and female prostitutes. I could teach him self preservation techniques and street fighting. It would probably be good to arm him with a street gun and teach him how to use it. I hoped he would be a willing student!

I also knew I needed to help Tyler by easing him into our deepening emotional and physical relationship and our sexual relationship safely and painlessly when Tyler was ready. That is what I longed for and wanted between Tyler and me. I desired a monogamous, tender, loving, painless, respectable, physically and sexually fulfilling relationship, and all of this experience over a lifetime or longer.

I knew that Tyler needed me to explain some basic come-ons, flirts, and signs of danger in the gay community and in the neighborhood in which he had come to live with me. I hadn't exactly been up front with him that the façade of wealth and opulence in this area hid the dark and vicious underground of the sex and drug industry from which it had come. I knew that I lived in one of the thriving hearts of sex and perversion, drugs, illegal alcohol, money laundering, male and female prostitution, and other crimes in this part of Illinois. In fact, Tyler had no clue; and I intended to keep it that way as much and as long as possible, while still providing him with the knowledge of how to stay out of trouble here. Maybe I even still had no clue how bad it was here myself!?

However, for Tyler's safety I still had to 'educate' him and mete out some of the most dangerous things Tyler needed to watch for in Aurora. I had to educate him to gay come-ons, gay solicitations, gay sexual practices, Phillip Fleets, Neils Hansen, female prostitutes, and what openings some drug pimps would use to put him in danger. He had to know some of the threats he would face, but I had to do it in such a way so as not to make him feel that I was belittling his intelligence, or that I was trying to scare him.

I thought about Neils's date with Tyler tomorrow night, Wednesday evening. This prospect scared the shit out of me! I knew what Neils had in mind for Tyler after dinner. I had to speak now with Tyler, or pick up his pieces, as scattered, shattered and as damaged as they may be, afterward. It was the same old story with Neils. I had fallen for it, as had many young men before and after me. And now, he was after my Tyler. Well, I wouldn't let him do it! Tyler just couldn't go out with Neils, that's all there was to it.

As I drove to Tyler's work, however, I happened to think that I couldn't make Tyler's choices for him in the big city all the time. I could educate him, but then he must learn to make wise, street savvy choices for himself when faced with probable danger. I couldn't be like an over-protective parent and smother him. He had just left home after all! I was sure he had had enough of parents telling him what he could and couldn't do. What the hell was I thinking?! I didn't want to become Tyler's parent! Damn it!

I wanted to be his lover for life, his significant other, his spouse... not a parent! I had to educate him as my lover or spouse. I had already educated Tyler first into a friend relationship. Next we would learn together a dating relationship. Then I would teach Tyler what it meant to be a 'steady', a relationship in which we promised to date each other exclusively and not date anyone else. Following would be teaching Tyler about what gays considered and meant in an engaged attachment. Finally, we would learn all of the various aspects of the married life, including gay sex. It was an intoxicating and tantalizing plan and purpose.

My thoughts skipped from my plans for Tyler and me to my dilemma over Neils' designs on Tyler for a one night stand just to spite me. Suddenly my protective nature came back. But this was Neils! He was like the worst predator of young men that I knew in the area. I didn't know of anyone so predatory and out for the conquest of young, virgin 'meat' than Neils. Even Marcus Devereaux at work was not as mean, forceful, and possessive of young male prey as Neils was! I had to stop him from having a chance at Tyler. This one time I had to somewhat take Tyler's decision for him. I had to tell him he shouldn't see Neils and go on what I knew Neils considered a date. I had to tell Tyler that 'discussing membership packages' was just an excuse, a reason for Neils to be alone with Tyler where he could rape him. I had to warn Tyler about Neils! I had to forbid Tyler to see Neils on Wednesday and tell him that he and I would pick a package for him together.

Then the flip-side of my conscience, my logic, kicked in again. I knew that Tyler might not take kindly to me telling him or suggesting to him what to do. After all, he was 21. He had his own ideals, standards, warning system, and beliefs based on his upbringing. I was sure that, since he was raised in the church, he had a good sense of right and wrong, and also had a Christian-based early warning system to things that might prove to be dangerous to him. At least he should have such an early warning system built in if the churches were doing their job! I didn't know, because I hadn't attended any church in a long, long time. I just realized, sadly in this case, that I had to treat him like a man, not a child. And oh, what a man he was…! Just thinking of him turned me on…! I felt a strong need to relieve myself behind the wheel before I picked Tyler up… but I resisted successfully…

Another thought then crowded my mind. The ease so far with which I was building my relationship with Tyler and breaking down his defenses to our gay bond, interconnection, and dependency with and on each other pleasantly surprised me. However, the speed of these positive developments perhaps betrayed the fact that the church was not nurturing in children a Christian defense mechanism against predators and bad influences! So far during my time with Tyler I had witnessed his naïveté, innocence, trusting and honest nature, and lack of street wisdom. It was obvious to me that Tyler had no clue about what was out there in the actual worldly society, and therefore had no clue as to how to morally, emotionally, socially, physically, and Biblically deal with them.

Another thought crossed my mind causing my brain activities to lose focus and veer off my main dilemma to a different branch temporarily. I knew that what I wanted the churches to teach included the fact that a monogamous homosexual spousal relationship was equal to that of a heterosexual married couple. However, I knew that this would be called a heresy, or 'abomination' by the modern Churches. But why then were the churches not teaching and instilling in every child and teen that it was an anathema to fall into prostitution, fornication, masturbation, sexual sin, 'homosexuality', fetishes, narcissism, and all the current issues and things that they, the Church, condemned?! Why were they not teaching the Biblical standards and precepts against these immoral and sinful behaviors!? Did they even exist?! I didn't understand! Maybe much of the moral, ethical, and Christian moorings that the Bible supposedly established had been misinterpreted over the ages of translation after translation and did not exist in the Bible at all?!

'Get off your soap box, Andrew!' I commanded myself. 'Back to the issues at hand!'

I couldn't just forbid Tyler to see Neils. I would warn him, and see what his reaction was. Then I would help him decide what was best to do in this circumstance. That's what a counselor of a patient should do in this instance, and that is what I must do with a fellow adult. Especially one as unfamiliar with the 'professional' and 'predatory' gay community that existed in Chicago and its suburbs like Aurora.

I admit I went well over the speed limit to Tyler's workplace. I worried about the police stopping me, especially in my condition. I still felt enlightened, kind of disconnected, and high. I felt pretty confident though, that I was tolerant enough of alcohol and avatar that I could drive fine in my condition. Nothing was blurry, distorted, or moving dangerously in my vision. Only the cars were moving.. maybe that tree... the park bench... I closed my eyes and shook my head. Then I reopened them and continued to ponder.

My sense of danger for Tyler made me irrationally think he would be safest around me as quickly as possible. In no time at all I pulled into

Computronix. I actually, for the first time in years, said to the air 'God, thank you! Thank you that I made it to Tyler's workplace so quickly!' I didn't even necessarily believe in God. I wondered later from where that utterance had come?! Tyler's presence in my life and his beliefs were definitely affecting me!

Tyler was just walking out of the main doors as I drove up. He put his satchel in the back seat and climbed into the passenger side front seat. I instantly wanted him, and I gently but firmly cupped my left hand around his right cheek, pulling his face toward mine. I leaned in and we passionately kissed for what seemed an eternity.

"Andrew… mmf." Tyler tried to speak and break the kiss. "mmf… What's the meaning… mmf… of this?" He pushed me back and looked me straight in the face and eyes. Shades of surprise, pleasure, and annoyance took turns dancing across his visage as he gazed intently at me.

"Hot damn! Tyler you… you are… you are so gorgeous… so handsome… so sexy…" I smiled blissfully at Tyler as I let my voice trail off.

Tyler hung his head briefly as he sat back and buckled up. Once finished, Tyler returned to gazing intently at me.

"What is wrong?! Why did you meet me with such a hot… such an erotic… a kiss?" He queried.

"Why does anything have to be wrong for me to kiss my Tyler?!" I asked petulantly.

"Oh, I don't suppose anything has to be wrong, but there is, isn't there?" Tyler responded.

"Tyler! Dear, sweet Tyler!" I beamed at him as I shook my head. "I assure you! There is nothing wrong! I simply wished to kiss my hot, tanned, and sexy Adonis!"

I glanced from the road ahead back to Tyler, and continued to do so. Tyler blushed and smiled self consciously as he looked at his hands.

"Thank you, Andrew, for the… for the compliment…" His voice trailed off.

An awkward minute or two ensued before the silence was broken.

"Let's stop and get fries and subs, then go home and talk." I exclaimed softly but firmly.

We commenced through McDonald's for French fries, and then it was time for subs. Finally, we would head back to Candlestick and home.

I guided my vehicle toward the best sub joint around. It was further away, but well worth the trip! I wasn't feeling so drugged; in fact I now felt fine. Was I really coming off my last drink? I didn't know, but I felt fine, and was performing well behind the wheel.

I decided to engage Tyler in idle chit-chat to keep me as alert as possible, and more importantly to guide our conversation toward discussing his 'date' with Neils. I had to warn him.

"It is a beautiful day!" I exclaimed, patting Tyler on the knee.

"Yes. It is so sunny and warm." Tyler responded in a somewhat distracted voice as he gazed out of the side window.

"Did you have any dealings or encounters with Mrs. Ryan today?" I stroked Tyler's left leg from his knee almost to his crotch.

I glanced at Tyler to check on his reaction to my hand being so… so… so close to his family jewels. Tyler had his head back against the headrest. His eyes were closed, a cute, almost unidentifiable grin flickered through his finely shaped lips, and he tensed and gasped a little every time my hand neared his crotch.

"Well…?!" I asked excitedly, thrilled that Tyler was obviously receiving pleasure from my touch near his package.

Tyler didn't move a muscle, but remained basking in the ecstasy of my touch.

"Well what?!" Tyler responded in a voice that made him sound like one spaced out on drugs.

I chuckled inside as Tyler continued to take such pleasure from my stroking and touching. Truly Tyler's positive reaction to the simple stroking which I was performing proved to me that he definitely was a virgin. I was on cloud nine!

"Tyler, listen to me!" I spoke firmly but in a gentle voice. I removed my hand from his leg.

Tyler lifted his head, shook it, and blinked before turning toward me and our eyes made contact.

"Tyler, did you have any dealings or encounters with Mrs. Ryan today?" I repeated patiently.

Tyler frowned and turned to look out of his side window.

"Yes." He muttered. "I cannot seem to get rid of her!"

Tyler dropped his gaze to his hands. His face was clouded and flushed.

"What happened?" I asked innocently.

Tyler looked back up and locked his eyes to mine. I shivered at the thrill…

"Well…" Tyler began hesitantly, "Mrs. Ryan cornered me twice. Once in the den, a confluence of shelves that form a 'separate' room-like enclosure out on the floor. Mrs. Ryan ultimately had me backed against a shelf, trapped with one of her arms on each side of my head. I ducked and squirmed, and I managed to escape. The second time I was bringing Mrs. Ryan machine settings for her approval. In her office she repeated her strategy from the den. She had me handcuffed to the book case and had begun unbuttoning my shirt and pants when her secretary burst in. Mrs. Ryan let me go."

"Are you the only guy Mrs. Ryan sexually harasses?" I queried in an angry voice.

"Currently Thad and I are the objects of Mrs. Ryan's affections and advances. However, she…"

I didn't let Tyler finish.

"Who is Thad?" I inquired curiously.

"He… ah… he and I… I mean he…" Tyler was clearly suddenly very uncomfortable, embarrassed, and worried as he stammered to find an answer. "Thad is… is… is my co… co-worker. He is a friend I met yesterday."

"Oh!" I returned, sneaking a smile at Tyler.

Though he was still red with embarrassment, he managed a wan smile back. It melted my heart! Lord I loved Tyler so!

"Anyway…" I broke the painfully awkward silence, "go on with your thought, Tyler. You and Thad are currently the objects of Mrs. Ryan's sexual desires and plans. However, she what?"

"Well…" Tyler began cautiously, "she apparently has chosen me to pursue at the expense of her marriage, her husband, you and me… at all costs. She is truly, absolutely, and unapologetically hot to trot!"

Tyler flushed and looked at his hands.

"It was so embarrassing being handcuffed to Mrs. Ryan's desk bookcase… unable to… to defend myself… being mauled and stripped by the office octopus…" Tyler shuddered. "Then to have her office manager burst in… seeing my briefs… my pants pulled down below my butt cheeks!"

"How did you… how did you manage to allow… How did Mrs. Ryan manage to get you…" I stumbled around and glanced uncertainly at Tyler. "You are stronger than she, Tyler… How did she manage to handcuff you to the office furniture?"

Tyler grunted and closed his eyes briefly.

"I feel so stupid! So foolish… so taken advantage of!" Tyler scowled and shook his head. Before I could react, Tyler slapped himself hard across the face. Then again he struck himself.

Tyler was preparing to hit himself with his left fist, but I grabbed his hand and pulled it away from him and down to the seat.

By this time I knew I was driving dangerously. I was probably still legally intoxicated, and now I was trying to subdue Tyler and prevent him from hurting himself too. I quickly pulled into a parking lot one-handed while holding Tyler's left hand firmly to the seat.

However, before I could get our car into park and stop him, Tyler punched his face twice with his right fist. His slugs were hard, because each one caused a loud cracking sound. He was doubling up his fist to hit himself more.

I whipped my seat belt off and jumped on top of Tyler. I grabbed his right fist and struggled both his hands down to the seat as I straddled him.

I looked at his gorgeously handsome face, and blood began to flow from his nose. One eye was becoming colored and swollen.

"What the hell are you doing, Tyler!?" I hissed at him sternly and with concern.

Tyler struggled with me some more as he bled. Then he spoke.

"Andrew! Get the hell off me! Let me go! I deserve this for my stupidity!"

"There is nothing you have done, Tyler, to deserve beating the hell out of yourself! What the hell is going on that you would pound on yourself?!"

"I was stupid, Andrew! I brought dishonor to my... to my... to my dad!" Tyler suddenly rammed me back against the dashboard and managed to free his left hand. With it he promptly punched himself hard in the face again.

There ensued a struggle. Fortunately as I had already surmised, I was stronger than Tyler. I gained the upper hand quickly, and pinned his hands back down to the seat.

"How in God's name did you dishonor your father today?!" I spoke loudly and firmly.

"Andrew! Let me go! I need to stop the bleeding from my nose!" Tyler struggled again, but I held him down.

"I will only let you go, Tyler, if you promise to stop beating yourself!" I looked questioningly into his brown pools.

"Andrew! Damn it! Let me go!" Tyler cried plaintively.

"You will promise first!" I demanded, maintaining my grip.

"Okay! I promise not to hit myself anymore!" Tyler went limp.

"Now, Tyler, let me clean you up!" I let go of his left hand and grabbed some Kleenex. I began cleaning his face of blood.

"What the hell do you think you did, Tyler, to dishonor your father?!" I demanded as I worked tenderly.

"I was dumb enough... naive to let... let a woman get advantage... control over me..." Tyler was still limp as he replied. "Dad would... dad would kick..."

Tyler let his voice and thought trail off into a reflective, ponderous silence.

"Dad would do what to you, Tyler?!" I asked urgently as I finished up.

"I don't know! I don't remember!" Tyler exclaimed petulantly.

I took my seat behind the steering wheel again.

"You must remember something your dad would feel and do to you in this instance, Tyler. Especially the way you were beating yourself!"

"No! I don't remember!" Tyler set his visage in a pouty, firm expression.

I paused and watched Tyler as he stared straight ahead. Then I gently prodded Tyler again.

"Okay, Tyler," I began, "How… how did Mrs. Ryan… how did she manage to get you handcuffed to her desk?"

"Andrew!" Tyler turned to me angrily. "I fell for Mrs. Ryan's flattery! She told me how gorgeous, masculine, strong, appealing, sexy, hot… strong… that I was in her opinion. She asked me to help her move her desk… When I grasped it to comply, she whipped out handcuffs and… and… locked me to the desk!"

I smiled.

"Tyler, that's the oldest trick in the world of sexual seduction!"

"What is?" Tyler glanced at me in alarm.

"Flattery… Tyler, flattery is… is the oldest… trick to sexual seduction…" I stopped as I could see Tyler was still angry.

"May we change the subject, please?!" Tyler muttered in a frustrated, angry tone. "I feel stupid and ashamed enough! I don't want to talk about this anymore!"

I patted Tyler's inner, upper thigh reassuringly and nodded, smiling. I didn't want to ruin the evening dwelling on Tyler's experience with Mrs. Ryan as proof of his naïveté and need to learn to avoid danger and protect himself against predators. The experiences Tyler had today spoke volumes themselves about the proof of that point to me, and hopefully to him too.

"Now, Tyler. I can reenter traffic to finish our trip without you beating yourself again, right?!" I asked firmly.

"Yes! Yes! I am fine now." Tyler looked out his side window.

In my right rear view window I could see that Tyler's eye that he had hit was a bit swollen and discolored.

I started our car and drove on out into the street.

When I felt like I had waited a respectable time for Tyler to cool down, I broke the silence.

"So you went to the gym on Sunday last, eh?" I smiled at Tyler and patted his thigh as close to his package as I could without feeling him up.

"Yes, I did." Tyler sighed. "It's called Tawny Bods…"

"Tawny Bods Fitness Center." I interrupted him and finished the name so he'd know I was a client when I said I was. "I know the place, Tyler. That's where my gym membership is. I know the employees there like family. I have worked out there for several years. I love it! The equipment is so modern and is updated regularly. Additionally the staff is so knowledgeable and helpful."

"Cool!" Tyler smiled coyly. "Then we can start exercising together!?" He then changed his voice to sound seductive and suggestive. "Then we can shower together…" I glanced at him in surprise, and his gorgeous face held a look of lust and anticipation.

I copped a very lewd and seductive voice and demeanor briefly.

"Oh yes, big boy toy! That sounds very… very… pleasurable and… and sexually appealing!" I responded while looking lasciviously at Tyler.

I paused a minute to let both of us get serious again. Then I turned to Tyler and gave him a firmly worried and important gaze.

"Tyler, there are more important things we need to discuss about some of the people that frequent and work at Tawny Bods. In a wider scenario of our neighborhood, community, and Chicago area we need to talk seriously to get you up to speed on our reality. But first we will focus on Tawny Bods." I felt like I was walking on egg shells. I so hoped I wouldn't offend or scare him!

"What do you mean?" Tyler exclaimed in a puzzled voice as he looked at me in some alarm.

A quick second thought registered again causing me to reconsider briefly discussing the Neils situation with Tyler, but I knew I had to. If I didn't I would lose my Tyler because of lack of knowledge about Neils' plans to rape and traumatize him.

"Now, Tyler, please hear me out! I am talking about this not to interfere in or run your life. You need to know this info to stay safe and stay as you are; protected, healthy, and a virgin. Do you understand, Tyler?" I put my hand on his inner thigh near his crotch and gently squeezed.

"No, I don't completely understand! Get on with it, Andrew, you are scaring the hell out of me!" Tyler's face clouded with concern.

"Well, for instance, Tyler, you have a date with Neils tomorrow evening, correct?" I asked softly.

"I wouldn't really call it a date… exactly… really… I mean… we are… you and I are… well… dating, Andrew! I would never cheat on you!" Tyler objected. "I am just meeting with him to discuss membership plans… I don't think that is a date. Neils said it was only a business meeting."

I could see disbelief and denial creeping into Tyler's brown eyes and gorgeous face. I was losing him! I had to bring out the big guns of the gritty, distasteful, and sleazy truth present in parts of Aurora and many of the people who lived here.

"I just came from the gym and a workout, Tyler. I talked to Neils there. You see, Tyler, this is hard for me to admit, but here it goes." I cleared my throat and glanced sheepishly at him, then back at the road. "I have gone to Tawny Bods for several years now. During that time I have gotten to know most of their employees. Neils is one of those employees that I got to know quite, ah… well, quite… ah… intimately. Neils is gay, in case you hadn't noticed, and he and I dated several times over a period of a few months. Our first date was to meet and discuss membership packages, which we did. But then Neils expected more for his date; much… much more! He was all over me! Ripping my clothes off, mauling and pawing me… penetrating me… I gave in because I wanted a membership so badly." This wasn't completely true. I had found Neils somewhat attractive, and being older than I was he had intrigued me. I had more than membership wishes to help me give in! "Neils raped me! He took advantage of me many times over those months in exchange for cut rate membership that was actually against company policy. He took advantage of me!"

"You gave in to what exactly?" Tyler asked, a look of concern settling over his handsome features.

"I gave into... well... let's say that he and I were very intimate. We became acquainted in the Biblical sense. Let's put it this way, Tyler. Mostly against my better judgment... and will... Neils and I know the surfaces, curves, parts, and pleasure points all over each other's naked body..." I didn't want to be too descriptive, but I wanted to be honest and graphic enough to get the point across. "First thing to remember with Neils, Tyler, is that any after-hours 'meeting' to do anything with a subordinate or younger person is to Neils 'a date'. He considers your dinner tomorrow to discuss membership plans a date. He will expect more than just supper. He will expect a nice roll in the hay with you, Tyler. I am talking male-on-male sex!" I gave Tyler a 'sorry, but it's true' gaze.

"I find that hard to believe!" Tyler, visibly shaken and unsure, shook his head in the negative. "Neils was a perfect... he was a... perfect... gentleman who...? Well... he said nothing... well, he did... maybe he..." He trailed off as he frowned, gazing out of the front window.

"Who! What?! What did Neils say to you, honey?! Did he do anything to or toward you?!" I demanded, startling myself with my forcefulness and instant outrage. I was alarmed at the way Tyler had trailed off with something obviously on his mind. He knew something bad that he was hesitating to tell me!

"Well," Tyler mused thoughtfully, "Neils did... refer to it... as a date. He did insist... on paying... for the meal, and he was very... friendly and flirtatious. Maybe he does expect more!" He looked at me with his gorgeous, innocent pools of brown filling with a growing alarm and belief, and I melted in love and fear for his safety, health, and my chances as his spouse! I also selfishly and presumptuously coveted Tyler's virginity for my own.

Suddenly another sure-fire evidence of Neils' prurient and dangerous intentions toward Tyler popped into my head.

"Did he workout with you, shower with you, and then check you out naked at some point using the excuse of seeing what he could sculpt out of your physique?" I queried, although I already knew the answer.

"Yes…" Tyler's face lit up. "That is exactly what he did… I take it… he did the same… to you…?" Tyler's face clouded up, as quickly as it had lightened up. I knew he was beginning to understand the connection between our two experiences with Neils.

"Yes… and many other former male prey of Neils to whom I have talked." I interrupted Tyler's sentence. We were now on the same page. I could tell I was making some progress in my warning to Tyler. "Tyler, he is playing his same trick again. I saw him trolling for phone numbers among the males who came for membership or a day's workout just today. He did the same to me that he has done to you and planned for you!"

"On the other hand," Tyler shrugged, "he seemed sincerely interested in me and my body building plan. He has probably changed!? He didn't seem to be exclusively assessing me for a conquest or a piece of meat, Andrew. I think you may be misjudging Neils!"

I was becoming alarmed and impatient with how trusting Tyler was being and how he refused to see the bad in people! However, I took a deep breath and plunged ahead, hauling out my big guns.

"Does this sound like he could have changed? He approached me about you today and said, and I quote: 'He is one virgin piece of meat I intend to make into a man! I'll show him real sex.' And 'I will have Tyler's virginity regardless…'" I put special emphasis where it would make the most impact.

I could see that Tyler was shaken, shocked, and angry. Then he became suddenly aware of my warning and scared about his Wednesday meeting with Neils.

"Andrew… I am up shit creek! Now that I know what a perverted letch Neils is, Andrew, what should I do? Should I not go? Cancel? Fall ill? What?" Tyler asked me plaintively. His brown eyes searched my mind, experience, soul, and emotions for advice.

"No." I spoke calmly and with confidence. "You are an adult, Tyler. You have a life, a free will, and I am not going to tell you what to do.

You are warned about and knowledgeable of Neils and his intentions toward you. I'd go Tyler. As a protection for you I will shadow you to the restaurant, stay in my car, and, if anything starts going badly for you, you call me on your cell phone. I will come in and make a scene, whereupon you can slip away and find my car. I'll get out of the fracas I cause and drive you home. Okay?"

"Okay, Andrew, I hope this works! I'm still worried… I don't know how to deal with any situation like this! What do I do?! What do I say?!" Tyler put his hand on my knee and dragged it up almost to my waist, where his fingertips were resting on my crotch. It was so stimulating! I wanted to tell Tyler to feel me up more!

"The key is to not become one notch of sexual conquest on Neils's bedposts." I continued. "He has been such a son of a bitch, having been known to fire those whom he likes for a lover, yet who reject him." My voice contained venom that had built up over the years. "If we get our signals mixed up or not timely, then drag out any excuse or situation requiring you to leave when Neils begins to get horny. Fake illness. Sneak out of the back. Anything to get away from him, Tyler."

I stopped and gazed firmly at Tyler. He looked plaintively and sincerely at me.

Tyler paused in thought. When he did speak his voice was tinged with hope and shame.

"So, Andrew… you are serious… you do consider… you definitely consider you and I a couple? All of our physical interactions… our kissing and stuff… you do mean it for true… true love, right?" Tyler looked quizzically at me.

At first I was devastated again! For several moments I felt I had wasted quite a bit of time getting Tyler to love me, and understand that I loved him! We had been over this before. How the hell could he not now believe me that I was his, that I loved him dearly, and I would not joke about my love for him! I had professed my love, I had initiated physical interaction and activity between us, and reassured him numerous times that I loved him!

However, then the memories and explanations for Tyler's doubt welled up in my mind. Among them was the fact that Tyler's mental and emotional conflict over his feelings for me, our love relationship, and whether they were right or Biblical was bound to make him very insecure, confused, and torn. Additionally, his flip out over Mrs. Ryan's advances and the resulting self-abuse showed that he was definitely very modest, moral, and rigid ethically. More interestingly, he had slipped and let it be known it had something to do with his dad! If his relationship with his dad was really and secretly bad, then it would stand to reason that those issues may also contribute to his conflicting realities, insecurities, and low self-esteem.

I looked hard at Tyler before I spoke. I didn't want to say the wrong thing. He now looked like he was fearful of my response.

"Yes, Tyler, I mean it as true love." I began carefully. "Everything you and I do together... hugging... kissing... being close together... Tyler, I assure you that I mean it! I don't want to scare you, or freak you out, or offend any religious... beliefs you may have, but Tyler I was in love with you at first sight on that bus from Gurnee, and nothing but the strength and intensity in my love for you has changed... for the better! My love for you grows every day, that would be the only change!"

I squeezed his hand and smiled at him with maximum reassurance.

"Do you believe me now, Tyler?!"

"Well," Tyler replied uncertainly, "You said you dated Neils, and went all the way with him sexually. I worry about you going back to him, or finding someone else whom you love more than me... I am just... I become doubtful... I worry. I know you have professed your love for me a few times now without taking it back or leaving me. I still worry... wonder... doubt that I will always be yours... be lover enough... be appealing enough to hold you forever. Thing is, Andrew... I love you so much! I could not bear to be... to be... to be without you!"

Tyler smiled at me, a more confident countenance setting up in his features.

"First of all, Tyler... I was stupid when I gave in to Neils sexually!" I chuckled. "For the life of me, I don't know why I was drawn to him in any way. I don't know what I saw in Neils, or the other guy I dated for a year, Andre! It was a time of rebellion and experimentation for me. I didn't know it at the time, Tyler, but you, my one true love, was for whom I longed, needed, and was searching! Neither of my previous boyfriends match up or hold a candle to you in anyway, hot stuff!" I looked at him quickly and saw that he smiled and blushed at my compliment.

"Tyler, being gay is an inherited, unlearned, non-religion violating, not embarrassing, or shameful condition. It is not a choice like deciding between a blue or green shirt. You wear blue, your choice, for a while, and then change your mind and pick another color to wear for a while. Being gay is who you are, Tyler, who I am, and this gay man loves you helplessly and hopelessly forever! Wild horses could never drag me away from you!" There! I had said it, and I meant it! For Tyler I hoped it allayed his fears and concerns and that he believed me once and for all. However, deep down I knew there would be more conversations with my lover like this to comfort, support, and convince him.

I waited and sneaked looks to see what wheels were turning in Tyler's mind by his expressions. I first looked to see if he had bought my words of love and commitment that I had told him.

Tyler was thinking, analyzing, and recording what I had said, I could tell. He had a serious, yet calculating look that switched back and forth two or three times. He looked so hot with those looks, I thought, and then I smiled to myself. He looked hot with most any look on his handsome, foxy face! Oh how I wanted him for my life-long, monogamous lover! I realized then that I would marry him in a heartbeat if I could!

I was still concerned that I may have scared Tyler by being so honest with him. Even though he voiced sentiments to me that he agreed with me and loved me, I knew that there were still influences from the Christian 'poison' on homosexuality and the Bible's supposed condemnation of loving monogamous same-sex relationships that were still bothering him. I didn't know how long it would take to wrest Tyler free from the Church and Christian inculcated propaganda that prevented him from fully trusting me and dedicating himself to me.

Taking my eyes off the road, I peeked again. Tyler looked contented, set on a decision and the facts. I turned into the sub-joint where we would begin purchasing our evening meal.

I took a space, put the car in park, and disengaged the engine. I was so exhilarated that Tyler and I had talked seriously about us, that he should know exactly how I felt about him, how I loved him, and what I wanted with him and from him. He might like what I had said about us and yet still fear the terms 'homosexuality' and 'gay' due to his Church poisoned mind, but my true feelings were out! His true feelings were out! I was thrilled and felt a weight had been lifted from me by being honest. I also saw a new door opening in our relationship.

Tyler interrupted me.

"Andrew?" Tyler gazed over at me, kind of like a child might look at a parent. His limpid brown eyes were questioning, sad, yet hopeful, and sparkled like a starry midnight sky. I again melted to a puddle of love! He had such a profound effect on me!

I wanted to take Tyler sexually right now, to physically express my love and loyalty to him right here in the parking lot! I didn't give a damn who saw us! I struggled to control myself.

I returned his gaze, and I could not help smiling lovingly at him as I responded to his inquiry.

"What honey?"

"If I were… well if I weren't so conflicted… if I were ready… if I asked you…" Tyler appeared obviously uncomfortable with his question. "Do you love me enough… if I were ready… and if I asked… would you… do you love me enough… would you… would you make love to me?" He finally spit his question out with great trepidation. As he did so he almost gagged and flinched.

I am afraid that at his question my mouth dropped open, I ogled him, and my heart leapt in joy. As the import of Tyler's question topic sank in, my stomach filled with butterflies and my mind and emotions overwhelmed my resistance to touching him more.

Tyler had not looked over at me since asking his question. I almost lunged at him as I adjusted my steering wheel to its highest position and ripped off my seat belt. I leaned way over into his seat. Rather roughly I clasped his face in my hands and brought his eyes and face in line with mine. I had tears in my eyes as I lovingly gazed into Tyler's eyes and answered.

"Tyler, honey!" I choked up and swallowed hard. "Love of my life! When you are ready… when you want me as much as I want you physically and sexually… When you have approved it with your faith… I will be here! I will make mad, passionate love to you… anytime… anywhere… anyhow… because I love you! Making love is like… well… it is the consummation of any lovers' relationship! It will be even more so for us! When you are ready… no one will stop me from making love to you!"

Tears came to Tyler's eyes now, and his face flushed scarlet red. I suddenly felt self-conscious and realized with chagrin that I might be coming on too strongly for him and he might be uncomfortable.

I quickly sat back up and turned toward my door. I grabbed the door handle and opened it.

"Andrew?!" Tyler urgently called again, causing me to actually jump as he placed his left hand in my crotch and grabbed my package gently but firmly.

His action was instantly so stimulating to me that it stopped me dead! Would Tyler feel me up?! Was he ready to make love to me?! The thoughts jumbled in my mind over and over causing a hormone rush that felt like a good dose of avatar. My heart and stomach jumped and skipped at the prospects of Tyler's grab for my crotch!

I turned slowly back to face Tyler, smiled, and looked down at his hand on my junk. Then I gazed straight into his eyes, smiled again, and winked at him.

Tyler hadn't moved, and his countenance also hadn't changed much, except I could detect some confidence building there. He then blushed and smiled in embarrassment.

"I… I am sorry… so sorry, Andrew! I didn't mean to… didn't mean to grab your privates! So sorry…" Tyler was flustered and slowly removed his hand.

"I am not sorry, Tyler! You can do it anytime!" I cooed as I winked at him again. "What can I do for you, honey?!"

Tyler looked back at his hands as he folded them in his crotch.

"Andrew… if you love me… really love me… enough to have… to make… to make love with and to me…" Tyler gulped and swallowed. "Would… I mean would… could… am I a guy… I mean…" he stammered, looking over into my eyes. He was pleading in that gaze and I could read it as plain as the nose on his face.

There was only one other question to clear up.

"Yes, Tyler?" I prompted him.

"Am I a guy you could… would… could consider your… ah… consider me your…," I could tell he was looking for the right and personally acceptable word or words to continue or finish his thought. "Am I a guy you could consider your only… your permanent… your lifetime, monogamous… lover… and your only lover and sex partner for life?" Tyler stifled a sigh when he finished. He briefly looked at his hands, and then looked hopefully, and I mean hopefully, and questioningly at me.

I realized I was breaking down those barriers! Tyler was really in love with me and was coming around to accept our love and relationship… now and… must be forever?!

With the tips of my fingers on my right hand I gently and playfully caressed Tyler's temple and cheek. I looked back at him, eye-to-eye. I had to touch Tyler some more lovingly and reassuringly. I wanted to hold him… wrap my naked body around his… become one with him in the passions of lovemaking… I snapped to and smiled. Then I firmly and lovingly replied.

"Tyler," I began with tenderness and certainty, "I have told you I am in love with you, how when you are ready we will make love to each other, how I want to have and to hold you forever. You are an Adonis, Tyler! A gorgeous, hot, sexy hunk of man!" I breathed in before continuing. "You are so handsome, your physique is like candy to my eyes, your body is so beautiful, and your skin and complexion is tan and alluring sexually!" I paused.

"Most importantly though, Tyler, you are a really excellent catch and match for me! My desires for you are not all physical and selfish. You are my type of man, my perfect help mate, my perfect idea of a man and a match for me! You are one I will date until you can accept us and agree to be my lifelong lover! Do you understand, honey?!"

Tyler smiled at me, and looked much more confident and happy. I didn't know if I had allayed all of his concerns, self doubts, or religious conflicts over us, but I had done my best for now.

There was a pause.

"Let's get our favorite subs!" I broke the silence and swung my legs out to place my feet on the tarvia of the parking lot.

# PREJUDICE ON PARADE

Tyler and I exited our Intrepid and I locked the doors. I glanced at Tyler as he rounded the back of our car. I had to resist the temptation to chuckle and then hug and kiss him. He was positively glowing. His face was lit up like a Christmas tree. Tyler almost skipped as I took my place at his side a little behind him.

As we entered the sub-joint I held the door open for Tyler and lovingly guided him inside with my left hand on his hot bubble butt. Tyler turned his head and smiled happily at me. I swatted his ass suggestively, smiled back, and winked at him.

In the subway shop we each took a side of the buffet style sub-making tables and made our favorite foot-long sub sandwich. I constructed a four meat Italian sub with pickles, lettuce, peppers, black olives, two kinds of cheese, mustard and Miracle Whip. Tyler neatly and happily formed a chicken and turkey sub with lettuce, tomato, cheese, pickles, and Miracle Whip. We each grabbed a 16 oz. diet Coke, picked up our food and drink, and carried them to the counter to pay. On the way I did an ass bump with Tyler and winked suggestively at him. Tyler smiled back and winked at me. I was thrilled! We were young, and we were obviously falling in love!

I was still smiling as we approached the cash register and I glanced up. However, the man behind the counter serving as clerk was a thunder cloud of obvious distaste, disdain, and displeasure. He was a burly, homely looking man, with much weight that he could lose. He wasn't obese, but he was definitely overweight. He was surly and obviously unhappy. I dare say he looked as though he hated us!

Tyler and I plopped our subs and pops down on the counter in front of the angry, fat clerk. I looked back up and opened my mouth to ask for a bag for it all, but the big cur who should have been at least polite, taken our money, and serviced us stood there like a brick wall and cut me off.

"Yous, pretty boy faggot and yur boy toy here is not welcome in this here stablishment!" He spoke and spit as he did so. It was disgusting, and I was taken aback. "We don't soive no damn ass jacks here! Get the hell out!"

I frowned, flushed in instant embarrassment and anger, and stepped up to the counter. I turned, glanced at Tyler, and shrugged, looking determinedly at him. He frowned, pointed at the counter and then the door, and gave a quick nod and a gesture to leave.

"I says, yous little sissy pretty boy ass licker, we's don't serve no damn queers like yous and yous pretty boy mitten queen there!" The fat, stupid clerk leaned forward on the counter and glared in my face. His breath was stifling and raunchy, and I stepped back once so I could breathe fresh air.

I pointed angrily at the clerk.

"The term, for me and all of civilization, is 'homosexual' sir!" I spoke angrily as I stood my ground, struggling against the desire to gag. "What the hell makes you think that my friend here and I are homosexual?"

The big prejudiced clerk snorted, shook his head and closed his eyes briefly in total rejection of us. When he had finished his show of utter condescension and hatred toward us, he resumed leaning forward over the counter as close to getting in my face as he possibly could. I had to step back once again because his breath was stifling.

"Straight guys doesn't grup each others asses, and bump and grind theys asses like yous and yous little twink here did as yous come in here, got yous food, and poached the counter here!" The clerk gave me a contemptuous sneer as he slaughtered the King's English in ignorant arrogance. "Straight guys doesn's slap nothers guys ass less theys in a sport like bucketball! You savvy? Now get the hell out of here and leave this here food; yous is not taking it with yous!"

"You, sir, are a sexual bigot, an ignorant, prejudiced cad! I am surprised you were even hired!" I sneered back. The clerk's body odor was now wafting over the counter as well as his breath, and I stifled the desire to gag, wretch, and plug my nose. "However, I will admit that you are right on one thing! I am a proud homosexual! My friend here, however, is not a homosexual! I believe that this kind of treatment of two patrons of your ESTABLISHMENT is ILLEGAL! Do you, sir, know what that means?!"

"Of curse, yous twat, I knows what the law estates! I knows what illeagle means!" The rude cur sneered again and shook his head. "What parts of the laws makes me serve faggots like yous two fairies?!"

I was becoming irate and impatient with this insipidly prejudiced, misinformed, unlearned, unwashed scum with clearly refutable, stereotypical, mythical, foolish attitudes and beliefs! However, I had faced this kind of bigotry, hate, and prejudice before and I was prepared now.

I glanced back at Tyler to see what condition he was in and how he appeared to feel. He was standing red faced and clearly uncomfortable leaning against the half-wall between the food and check out area and the dining area. He looked very hurt. I quickly smiled, winked, and flashed him the 'thumbs-up' in reassurance. However, he didn't appear to be convinced.

I turned back to the red-neck, prejudiced fool who refused to take my money. No one would make my Tyler feel this way, nor would they try to shame us in public like this! I actually began to tremble in rage as I stood my ground with the clerk bigot.

"The parts of the law to which I refer are called the anti-discrimination laws that forbid discrimination in business, public, housing, speech, hiring, firing, employment, treatment, service, and activities. The laws flesh out the prohibition of discrimination on the basis of race, color, creed, sex, sexual orientation, and class. Sir, you are legally bound and legally required to service me and my friend here! Now pull your head out of your ass, smell the fresh air, and get with reality in this, the year 2010. We want to buy this food, although I shudder when I realize some of my money might go to pay the wages of a bigot like yourself! Take my money and we will leave your establishment!" I was pissed! I crossed my arms in defiance.

"Pretty pansy boy stands here preachin' the 'law' to me, a zane, normal, straight pillow of the communities!" The fat clerk stood up straight and laughed.

Before I could speak in reaction or move to protect our food, the clerk acted. He leaned forward on the counter again, brushing our subs and pops forward off the counter and onto the floor. The pops burst and spilled all over, and the subs, since they were not yet wrapped, fell apart in heaps. I had to jump back to avoid being soiled by the splash of our meals.

"Take yous fancy nancy words, yous cock suckin' ways, and yous faggot asses and leave this stablishment! Now!" The clerk stuck his finger in the direction of the door. "And minds yous don't touches anythin' while leaving sos not to taminate this clean stablishment with your 'seased bodies or hands!"

Inside, my emotions and inhibitions were now in control only by a stitch. I almost jumped the counter to attack the worthless pig, but Tyler grabbed my right arm and restrained me. I only achieved two steps before I had to see what he wanted.

"Andrew!" Tyler whispered pleadingly. "It is okay! I… I will… I will fix supper… Let's… let's… We can… We can go home! He is making a scene and we… we are becoming… we are becoming a spectacle in front of the other patrons! This isn't worth it! Let's leave and get the hell out of here!"

I was not finished! This sub-joint had the best and freshest supplies, the best food, usually the best service, and the best facilities of any I knew of in the area. I would be damned if I would let this stupid, incompetent troll whom I had never seen working here before, run me off like this!

"No, Tyler!" I put my arm around his neck as I whispered harshly, but reassuringly in his ear. "There is a principle here, a basic issue of humanity, freedom, equality, and respect by all, for all! We cannot allow stupid, prudish, backwater, white trash like this fool intimidate us, discriminate against us, and deny us food service, because it won't stop there! I am not done with this prick!"

I stepped forward into the space of the clerk in front of the counter, straightened my back, stood my ground, and put my finger in the ugly, brutish face of the white trash worker.

"You, sir, and I use that term very loosely and hesitantly in your case, must serve my friend and me here! You cannot, under the rulings of every constitutionally reputable court in the land or under the laws of this state and nation, discriminate against us like this based solely on the fact that I am a homosexual and this is my friend!"

"Oh yeh!?" The clerk sneered like Archie Bunker. "And what the hell are yous two fudge packers going to dos about it, you cum gumming gutter slit?!"

I took a deep breath, and stepped right up to the counter. I furiously faced him eye-to-eye.

"I demand to see your manager, sir! I have a complaint to register!" I yelled as I stared him down with a fury that arose from years of discrimination that I had faced in so many places from so many people. A few battles I had won, but to date I had mostly lost any homosexual scrimmages and struggles for rights from a religiously defined heterocentric society. However, I had learned to face every instance head on and stand my ground, hoping that character, fairness, humanity, the law, and common decency would reward my fight against this kind of blatant prejudice, discrimination, and poor treatment based solely on my sexual orientation!

"I am here, Andrew!" I heard a familiar booming, deep voice respond. "What the hell is going on out here, Pete?!" The sub-joint owner came walking out from the back and approached the stupid bigot clerk.

I knew this man well, since I had frequented his sub-joint often over the last four or five years. I put my hands down on my hips and looked expectantly at the owner, Mr. Melnick, smiling.

Pete stood up straight, pointed an accusing finger at me, and began defending his position.

"Mr. Melnick, sir! We have a restitution to uproll in this fine eatin' stablishment yous own! This… this…" Pete, the fat repulsive clerk, stammered and paused.

"Yes, Pete?!" Mr. Melnick stood, his countenance that of authority, fairness, and curiosity. "We have a REPUTATION to UPHOLD in this fine eating ESTABLISHMENT and…?"

"This… This… This here faggot and his boy toy slut over there…" Pete motioned first to me, and then to Tyler. He looked defiantly at Mr. Melnick. "They be… well, they be… they be *homosexuals* and…"

Mr. Melnick's countenance took on a look of anger and he held up his hand in a 'halt' motion.

"Andrew is a homosexual, yes!" Mr. Melnick looked like a tiger, plotting how to destroy his prey. "So this homosexual and his consort are here for food and service! What is the problem?!"

Pete was visibly sweating it! He was beginning to wilt with insecurity.

"We's can'ts continue to be a reparable stablishment and allow this... this... these... these... kinds of... these types of... peeples to pepperize us!" Pete was kind of begging Mr. Melnick to understand his position.

I began to worry a little. Would Pete's ploy work?

"Pete, what is this food and drink doing on the floor!?" Mr. Melnick exclaimed as he peered over the counter to the floor in front of me.

"I am exempting to... tempted to... accepting to... trying to clean the clientmales of this stablishment! I am... I am..." Pete stopped a second, clearly flustered. His fat, stupid, and homely countenance was no longer gilded with power, authority, and strength. "I simply wept the counter of these twos... these twos faggots' food so theys would leave and not comes back! We's have to upbrade ours clientmale like we's have ours food venue, Mr. Melnick!"

I could not believe how this boob could have been hired by Mr. Melnick's sub-joint! I could not believe that society would tolerate in public the likes of Pete, his obvious lack of an education, and his prejudices and bigotry. I was thankful that most of those with whom I had interacted that did not agree with my sexual orientation were not as ignorant, mean, uneducated, and philosophically embarrassing as this cur.

"Who was the manager that hired you, Pete?!" Mr. Melnick demanded.

I couldn't read Mr. Melnick's philosophical position very well at this point. I was entranced at what would happen next! I glanced at Tyler. He approached me again, and I put my arm around his neck, resting my hand open flat on his chest. It was such a turn on!

We stood there that way watching the scene unfold.

"Well, sir... I ... it was... she... it been Dixie Chandrea, sir!" Pete looked fearfully at Mr. Melnick.

"Well, Pete, you are right in some things." Mr. Melnick gazed probingly at him. "We have improved our food menu and the quality of our foods that we provide to the public to make their subs and plates!"

Pete straightened into an arrow stance and smiled. He clearly thought he would be vindicated!

A shudder coursed down my body from head to toe as I looked back to Mr. Melnick. I felt like I was on the edge of a cliff! Would Mr. Melnick take Pete's side?! I did not think that was possible. Was it?! I thought I knew Mr. Melnick better than that!?

"Pete, you are also right that we need to upgrade and improve the quality and character of our clientele. However, you left out improving the quality and character of our staff!" Mr. Melnick took out his PalmPre and punched some keys. Then he put the phone to his ear.

Pete blossomed like a preening rooster. He clearly thought he had been right in this situation. I felt more like I was perhaps being pushed into the abyss!

"Hello?!" Mr. Melnick spoke into his PalmPre. "Hello?! Yes! May I speak to Dixie please? This is her boss, Mr. Melnick!"

There was a pause, and I had a sinking feeling. Would he congratulate her or criticize her?

For Tyler's sake, however, I kept a smile on my face, held my head high, and squeezed Tyler's neck. Out of the corner of my eye I could see him look into my face for reassurance, but I kept focused on Mr. Melnick.

"Dixie?" Mr. Melnick asked in a business-like tone. "I understand you are to work a ten hour shift tomorrow?"

There was another pause. I was on pins and needles.

"I understand you hired a Peter Basco a couple of weeks ago?!" Mr. Melnick asked firmly.

"Well, Dixie, Mr. Peter Basco is an embarrassing, racist, prejudiced, uneducated, sexist, slovenly piece of work! The fact that you hired him shows an incredible lack of good judgment in employees and management. Don't you bother to report tomorrow! You are fired!" Mr. Melnick closed his PalmPre and looked back at Pete.

"Mr. Melnick...!" Pete held out his hands. "Please! I needs this yob! My whole fam damily..."

"Pete, you are a joke!" Mr. Melnick exclaimed as he pointed a finger in his face. "You are all the negative words I ascribed to you and more! You will never hold anything other than a pathetic, menial job as long as you retain your out-dated, racist, sexist, and prejudiced views. I am cleaning up my staff now, and you too, are fired! Get your stuff and get the hell out of my fine food ESTABLISHMENT!" Mr. Melnick pointed to the door.

Pete exited toward the back room where the employee lockers were located.

The staff and clientele that had stopped working and eating to watch the drama unfold began to clap. Tyler and I clapped. I breathed a sigh of relief!

I glanced at Tyler. He was smiling, but also his countenance was convoluted with uncertainty, confusion, and surprise. I smiled reassuringly at him and winked. He winked back, shrugging.

"Andrew!" Mr. Melnick exclaimed, smiled, and walked briskly around the counter to shake my hand. "Who is your gorgeous young boyfriend?" He asked quietly over the shake as he winked at Tyler.

I smiled, blushed, but beamed proudly at Tyler as I put my arm back tightly around his neck and pulled him close to my side.

"This is Tyler Belmont! He is living with me!" I replied gratefully.

Tyler and I smiled at one another.

"Well, Andrew... Tyler... you two make yourselves two new subs each, take two drinks each, and they are on the house! I value your continued loyal patronage of my establishment more than I do the standards of narrow-minded bigots who would cut off their nose to spite their face! Understand? Vonnie here will help you!"

Mr. Melnick motioned for a pretty young woman to come forward. She did. Mr. Melnick smiled at me, nodded, and then whirled around and went back to his office.

Tyler and I had our two subs made the same way as those which Pete had destroyed, picked up two different pops, and then Vonnie wrapped our subs, bagged everything, and gave them to us.

We left the sub-joint. Both of us were pondering what had just transpired. I again held the door for Tyler who carried our food and drink. I again put my hand on his ass. He glanced back and smiled at me as he seemed to gain pleasure and confidence from my gesture. I smiled and winked at him seductively. As long as he enjoyed it, I couldn't care less how it appeared to the public! For his part, Tyler, mouthed 'Thank you' to me.

We crossed the parking lot and driveway to my Intrepid. I walked behind Tyler so I could enjoy the view of his backside as we walked.

We sat down in our car and prepared for travel. We buckled our belts and I helped Tyler by taking the food and drinks and placing them safely in the car holders. We had to drive home to Candlestick Apartments. I was looking forward to a close, tender, and loving evening with Tyler the rest of the time before bed.

Tyler was quiet and a peek at his face revealed to me that he had a contemplative and thoughtful expression on his face. I could tell he was troubled and thinking deeply about something. I almost asked him what he was thinking, but I knew if I were patient, Tyler would speak when he had organized his challenging thoughts.

I put the Intrepid key in the ignition and started the car. I gazed at Tyler's handsome face which was clouded with concern and trepidation. Exactly according to my assumption and patient wait, Tyler broke the silence.

"Andrew… I… ah… you…" Tyler flushed and looked out his window. "I… were you… I was…"

"Tyler." I exclaimed softly. "Spit it out! I want to hear any and all you have to say!"

"Andrew… in there… the restaurant…" Tyler gulped. "You don't think… based on my… on me…" Tyler paused, but then appeared to decide to just get it off his chest.

"Andrew, you don't think I am not a man, or that I am a…" Tyler gazed pleadingly at me, "a yellow wussy?!"

I was stunned, surprised, and puzzled!

"Tyler! I… you…" I was so confused I didn't know what to say. "What the hell do you mean?! Why do you think I might believe those things about you so suddenly?!"

Tyler stayed locked to my gaze, again begging me for forgiveness and validation over what I did not know.

"Well... in... back there..." Tyler begged. "I am so embarrassed!"

"Back where?! And what did you do to deserve my... disbelief... my scorn?!" I was flabbergasted.

"Back in the restaurant, Andrew!" Tyler stated flatly, as he hung his head in shame.

"Okay, Tyler, honey, back in the restaurant... what?!"

Tyler turned to me, tears visible in his eyes, fear, love, and desperation all over his scarlet face. He put both hands out to me palms up flat.

"You were so brave, Andrew! I was... I was... I was... I was scared... shitless!" Tyler exclaimed in bursts.

My heart fractured. I wanted an explanation, but I also wanted to comfort Tyler... physically... sexually... I reached out to Tyler's hopelessly pulchritudinous face with both hands and wiped the tears off both of his cheeks...

"What do you mean you were scared shitless? Tyler, you were fine..." I began.

"I was trembling like... like a poplar leaf in the breeze and I begged you to give up the good fight so we could leave!" Tyler interrupted, his voice full of apprehension and embarrassment. "I was a chicken... a pussy... a yeller sheep! Andrew, I am so... so... so... sorry! You are with a scared... idiotic..."

"Tyler! Stop! I will not tolerate you continuing to question and denigrate everything about awesome you that I love just because you were afraid there and question your love for and relationship with me!" I spoke with a love and conviction that I had never before had as I grabbed one of Tyler's hands and stroked the back of his neck.

"Andrew! You don't understand!" Tyler raised his voice. "I was willing to forget some feelings... values... and principles that you and I obviously believe and share... all in the name of safety... avoiding confrontation... to leave an awkward situation... public pressure..."

I reached up again, firmly yet lovingly grasped Tyler's face, cupped him in both of my hands, and made him look me in the eyes.

"Tyler! Hush!" I gazed tenderly into his brown pools. "Answer me this?"

Tyler dropped his hands into his lap as he surrendered.

"What?" He managed as his facial countenance softened.

"Have you ever lived in a large city like Aurora?"

Tyler didn't pause.

"No, Andrew... I have not."

"And Tyler?!" I continued. "Have you ever lived with and loved someone male?"

"Andrew!" Tyler briefly bristled. "I have not had sex with a female or a male! I am a bona fide virgin in all ways. Additionally, we are not having sex until I am okay with it versus my faith!"

"Tyler! You have my point all wrong!" I reassured him as I grabbed his hands. "Have you ever been so emotionally and spiritually in love with a man, and been so physically attracted to him that you would admit to and desire a relationship with him like you do me?!"

"No, I haven't..." Tyler trailed off.

"Now, Tyler!" I drew his face so close to mine I could have kissed him. Damn it! I wanted to! "Tyler! Have you ever been in a situation of hate-induced crime?! Criminal behavior based solely on hatred like you faced with me in this restaurant this evening?!"

"No, Andrew! I lived in Gurnee! I was raised in a farm family... a... a 'normal' family!?" Then Tyler realized what he had said could be interpreted elitist. "I mean a family... a dad... mom... you know what I mean, Andrew. I thought of my family life... mostly as being like 'Leave it to Beaver' or something like that?!"

I was shocked by his questioning tone on the end of that statement, but I ignored it and plunged on.

"Tyler, love! Your response of fear was perfectly normal! You had never experienced a scene like we were just forced to face. I have. Time and time again!"

Through my grip on his face I could feel that he was calming down. I gave into desire and gave him a lingering kiss on the lips.

"You still believe I am a man worthy of your love and devotion?" Tyler asked quietly.

"Tyler, you are a gorgeous, buff, hot, beautiful man that I want desperately! I want to make mad..."

"I am not ready for that, Andrew. I still need time to justify it with my beliefs from the Bible." Tyler pulled away and faced front.

I turned to the front and grabbed the gear shift lever.

Tyler interrupted me again.

"If Neils starts pressuring me for sex, Andrew... either tomorrow... or after I am a member of the gym, I'm going to tell him that you... I will tell him that I... me..." Tyler looked at his hands. He was clearly nervous again. "I'll tell him that you and I... that us... I mean we..." Tyler glanced nervously at me as I gazed expectantly at him. His expression betrayed fear of my reaction, and a loss of words for his statement and request.

"Tyler!" I said softly, lovingly, but firmly. "Continue. You can tell me anything, ask me anything, and discuss anything with me! I am your companion and I love you very much!"

He gained some confidence from that because in a strong, firm voice he continued.

"If Neils pressures me for sexual activity I am going to tell him that you and I are exclusive with each other, that we are steady dating lovers. Is that all right, Andrew?" Tyler looked hopefully and expectantly at me. "That won't offend or upset you will it?"

Tyler's question was such sweet music to my ears. It was kind of like the song said, when Tyler asked me that long desired and awaited question, 'I heard a symphony'! A veritable fireworks show went off in my mind, and hormones flowed freely. I was ecstatic! It was so heartening to me! I was thrilled and I gave him a look that betrayed my feelings toward him and what he had proposed completely.

"That's fine, Tyler! It is... It is awesome! I am so flattered and grateful for your desire to claim me as your lover!" I was so happy at what he had asked that my voice rose a few octaves. "I will be proud and thankful for you to say that! I think that would shut Neils down. I already told him if he sexually assaults you, if he sexually harasses you, or otherwise bothers you I will kick his ass right into the hospital! Go ahead and tell Neils that, Tyler! And thank you! I am thrilled that you feel this way toward me!"

"I will definitely need someone to pick me up and drive me home after I turn Neils down tomorrow evening. I doubt he will be in any mood to do a favor for a male that rejects him sexually and is off limits to him." Tyler hinted in a questioning tone. "Are you... would you... can I depend... will you... Are you still going to spot for me with Neils?" Tyler sighed nervously and then rushed forward. "Will you promise to pick me up after I meet with Neils?!"

"Absolutely! As I agreed earlier, I promise to pick you up, Tyler. I'll be watching things from a distance to keep you safe and I'll pick you up. Tyler, you can count on me! As long as I am living and have any strength you can always count on me!" I assured him. I patted his knee, and then gently rested my hand over his package briefly. It felt so good!

Tyler and I looked at one another as I finished. His face was flushed with a visage of love, admiration, and gratitude toward me. It was such a sweet look, a loving look, that I melted! I returned the gaze adding my own feelings of sincerity, seriousness, and assurance. I wanted him so much right now, that I struggled with the urge to kiss him and initiate intimate behavior. I knew it was way too early, so I mentally took a cold shower.

"Thank you, Andrew!" Tyler gazed at me lovingly. "I feel better now that I have you to help me adjust to... to Aurora... my new home... society and culture here... and help with Neils, facing whatever he wants." Tyler spoke softly. "I'm glad I met you, Andrew."

I knew the moment was ripe for some special expression of love and honesty about my feelings. I reached over and ran my hand, fingers open, through his hair, and then rested it on the back of his neck. Tyler seemed to relax at the stimulation, his smile changing to contentment and approval. He did not reject my action in any way. I was thrilled! Tyler was ready and showed by body language he would not reject my honesty and free expression of my feelings. Things were a go!

"Tyler, you couldn't... you can't begin to comprehend..." my voice choked, "I don't have the words to... to convey... to convey to you how thrilled… elated… joyful… and happy I am that I met you! You are the light of my life…" I had to stop talking to regain my composure. Tears welled in my eyes as I reflected on years of searching for 'Mr. Right'. "Tyler, you are the light of my life!" I pushed forward, now that honesty was in the air.

Tyler and I enmeshed our bodies, as well as one can do in the front seat of a car. We rubbed each other's back and head, gazing into each other's eyes.

"I love you… I love you so much!" I whispered, smiling at Tyler. "I love you and I want you so much!"

I wanted to seal this new stage in our relationship through some new physical expression of my love for Tyler. But what did I dare do? Feel him up? Go down on him? Those actions would be too much, too aggressive, and too fast! For someone like Tyler, a Christian who was afraid to be identified as 'gay', and who had never experienced gay sex, either of those expressions of my love for him would scare the hell out of him! It would fracture, probably break, and perhaps destroy all the progress that Tyler and I had made in our relationship.

Out of the corner of my eye I saw several teens of varying ages passing behind our car. I knew the dark tint that would prevent outside view into my car was not on my back window. Suddenly my next physical expression of the new stage in my love to and for Tyler was clear.

I have to admit a little mischievous intent and rebellion in my desire and decision. It seemed so delicious to flaunt my relationship with Tyler publicly! However, I decided to go for it primarily to show my honest and true love to Tyler, to prove it to him, to prove I wasn't ashamed of my love for and relationship with him, to clinch my promise to him, and to make my claim on him forever.

I kept facing Tyler while I reached over and beeped the horn with my left elbow. Then I cupped his hot, handsome, but surprised face in both hands and I French kissed Tyler for the first time. Tyler did not resist, and only jumped and gently recoiled briefly when I introduced my tongue into his open mouth during our kiss. I made out passionately with him in the French.

As soon as the kids heard the horn they looked at us and the car. As I said, I knew they could see through my back windshield. I was not disappointed! They saw us kissing passionately. I could see them over Tyler's shoulder and it was clear they could see we were both guys. There was a lot of shock, laughter, disgust, and watching. I managed to get a couple minutes of making out with Tyler before he stopped it.

"Andrew… mmf…" Tyler began shaking his head. I retracted my tongue. "Andrew… mmf… there are kids nearby! Are they… did they… did they see us… kissing?!" Tyler looked around and saw the kids leaving.

"Andrew! Did they see us?!" Tyler sounded worried, yet interested. He gazed questioningly at me and smiled.

"Of course they saw us, you goof!" I answered, stroking Tyler's cheek and hair, and smiling back.

"I didn't see their response. What did they do when we kissed?" Tyler chuckled and looked back again at the kids as they disappeared.

"Oh, we pulled off an awesome joke on those kids!" I exclaimed, smiling and chuckling at the memory. "Those kids will never forget the day they were in a sub joint parking lot and saw two guys kissing and making out in a nearby car!"

"Well," Tyler asked breathlessly again, "what were some of the looks we got? Tell me, Andrew! Please?!" Tyler was excited.

"I allowed you to switch during our kiss to a position from which you should have been able to see, Tyler. Why didn't you look, instead of waiting and asking me?" I was a little frustrated. Why was Tyler asking me when we both had had our eyes open? What the hell had Tyler done?!

Tyler sat back and looked out the side window. He looked at his hands as his face flushed bright red. He breathed in nervously.

"Tyler?" I said gently. "I'm sorry for nipping at you! What's wrong?!" I stroked the back of his head.

"I didn't look at or watch the kids because…" Tyler ran his fingers through his hair, grasped my hand and held it as he got the bravery to finish. "I had my eyes closed while we kissed. I… I… it seemed the right thing to do." He finished quietly and lovingly. He looked at me, and I melted at the love in his eyes!

I knew now that Tyler did love me, passionately! We had just made out and French kissed for the first time! Now Tyler admitted to closing his eyes during our kiss. Everyone I knew, including myself, only closed their eyes during making out when we became intoxicated in the passion of the moment. Tyler had applied more meaning to our kiss than just a normal gesture of friendly love. He had applied a much higher meaning; Tyler was in love with me for sure! No 'straight' male would let a gay man French kiss him in the matter like we had just shared!

Tears came to my eyes, but I had to act normal. I did not want to lose control and attack Tyler, ravage him, and make love to him… take off his… I had to stop! I shook my head, and plunged into a narrative for Tyler.

"Well…" I began, "all of them stared for a few seconds. Then some got righteously indignant looks on their faces, which quickly turned to disgust. They began leaving then. Others were just laughing and pointing." I saw the mixed lies and truths I was telling Tyler were being believed completely. "Some were shocked, and left right away. They were so shocked their jaws almost hit the ground!" I laughed.

Tyler smiled at the thought, and a contented look crossed his face and stayed there.

"Andrew?" Tyler looked at me as he put his left hand on my upper, inner thigh. I felt a prickly feeling of hormonal pleasure ripple through my body at the application of his touch! I wanted him to cop a feel of my package so badly I ached for it!

"Yes, Tyler?" I looked at him questioningly. What did he have in mind?! I had felt his package a bit, and he was now touching me so close to mine. Was he now ready to go further physically… or… or sexually?!

"Let's pretend there are more people to shock." Tyler said quietly, unbuckling his seat belt. Before I could respond, he somewhat clumsily crossed car center, and, leaving his left hand on my leg and running his right hand through my hair to the back of my head, he pressed his lips to mine. We shared a passionate French kiss, initiated by Tyler, much to my surprise and pleasure!

After about five minutes Tyler pulled back to a distance of about 10 inches from my face. He looked at me and smiled. I drank in his attentions.

His hand still rested on my upper thigh, but had slipped very close to my package. I wanted him to feel me up further… to touch me more… to unbuckle and open my pants… I wanted to kiss him more… to go down on him… 'Stop, Andrew!' I commanded myself. I was becoming so sexually aroused I was losing control…!

"Tyler!" I said, breathlessly. "I… I mean… we… you and I… we… we can make some beautiful music together! I… I really dig kissing you! However… I… we… I can't control… trust me! We need to stop kissing! Now!"

I grasped Tyler's shoulders a little roughly and moved him back over car center to his seat. However, I held onto him as we gazed longingly at each other.

The air was electric and I could feel more chemistry with Tyler, much more, than I had ever felt with any man before him. I smiled at him and stroked a cheek on his face as we looked into each other's eyes.

As suddenly as Tyler had become amorous, he quickly sat back and buckled up. A wave of fear washed over me! Had I gone too far? Had I revealed too much? Tyler hung his head and spoke.

"I'm so sorry, Andrew!" He was contrite, regretful. "I shouldn't have done that. It was so evil… I tempted you… I gave into temptation… I was wro…"

"Tyler." I interrupted. Tyler looked up at me. "Tyler, enough. I am glad you gave in to your desire to kiss me. I desire to kiss you. And it is not evil! It is an example of the gift of love from a loving God. We should be thankful, not full of self-condemnation!"

I smiled at him, and then I put the car in reverse. It was time to go home.

I began to plan an evening's entertainment for Tyler and me. An evening of closeness and more expressions of love in this the first evening of this new stage in our relationship.

# CHAPTER 44

# BATTLE A DAY IN MY SHOES

As Andrew drove I sat back and considered his affirmation that our kissing and making out was genuine and he meant it to express his love for me. I stared at Andrew contemplatively but happily. I loved what he had said and wanted to believe it. I wanted to accept it as gospel truth. I loved this man, Andrew! I had never felt this much attraction to, emotions for, and love of anyone, male or female, before Andrew. He also made me feel safer and more secure than had anyone in my life other than my folks. I also had come to realize that my powerful love and feelings for Andrew grew stronger every hour of every day. I knew I was in a blossoming and growing romantic type love relationship with Andrew, a love that only spouses shared. At this point it occurred to me that I already loved him more than I did any member of my family except maybe my mother.

Despite my strong love, feelings, and attraction toward Andrew I still struggled over whether our relationship was in any way Biblical and Godly, or was it wrong? Was I going to be in sin and doomed to eternal damnation by loving and dating Andrew? Would God simply abandon me if I made love to Andrew, or would He strike me dead?! Did God hate me already?! Had He already abandoned me to my 'flesh'?! Would He allow me to get STDs... or AIDS... as punishment for my relationship with Andrew?! Some would argue that these fears were valid, legitimate, and necessary... but I was growing to view them as a constant derogatory influence in many areas of my life.

I was afraid of not being the ambassador of Christ necessary to get into Heaven. I was afraid of a vengeful God who some claimed would punish us on earth as well as in hell for any sin we committed. I was scared shitless of breaking any laws God had outlined in the Bible. At times these concerns almost paralyzed me spiritually, emotionally, and physically.

I didn't want to believe any of my doubts, and I didn't want to entertain them for long lest they grow stronger. Just as I had begun the eradication process I heard Landon Whitmore's lilting voice warning me to be careful. Had Landon been prescient and speaking about Andrew and me? Did he instead refer to my danger from other sins in Candlestick? I didn't believe in ESP or clairvoyance or such claptrap that had become so popular these last few years, so how did Landon know those things?! Was he an… an… an angel? From whence had he come?

Andrew caught my gaze; we smiled at each other and he winked at me very provocatively. He lovingly took my left hand, squeezed it, and held it while he drove.

I leaned my head back gently on the headrest and smiled to myself. I was content and thrilled with my life as it was now constituted and established. I believed I was yet a heterosexual man in some kind of a monogamous relationship with another man; a hot… sexy… gorgeous… attractive… desirable hunk of a man! The thought pricked my mind, however, that I had sinfully justified away a 'gay' side of myself with which I really needed God's help to deal. I told myself and now believed my 'gay' feelings and attractions were normal and a trait of all or most straight males. I also told myself that 'gay' or 'homosexual' excluded two men in a monogamous relationship like Andrew and me. 'Gay' or 'homosexual' only referred to those men who had multiple male sex partners a day, or a week, or a month.

Part of my religious upbringing was counteracting my Church inculcated precepts negative to same-sex love. I was coming to believe that the love Andrew and I shared could not be a sin. God did not create sin. If our love were a sin then God was not sinless and perfect! I knew and believed God was sinless and perfect. Therefore Andrew and I shared a love that wasn't a sin. Didn't we?!

Had I learned with much certainty and assurance about Andrew's sexual orientation and his seriousness about our relationship in my long conversation and activities with Andrew?! Yes, a thousand times yes! In the last 20 to 30 minutes Andrew had professed that he was serious about our love when he kissed me and we made out. He had also assured me that he deeply and seriously loved me. He had honestly and firmly proved his feelings by intensely and passionately French kissing me. No 'straight' guy would French kiss another guy, let alone do any of the other stuff that Andrew had done to and with me unless love was involved.

Happily reflecting about Andrew, the realization came to me that he had never French kissed me before. This was our first French kiss! This act by Andrew represented a strong sign of the seriousness and escalation of our relationship. I had to believe he loved me as much as I loved him!

Our conversation had helped solidify my love for Andrew, and my feeling that we were indeed exclusive. It also had shown me how compatible and alike Andrew and I were. We were perfect for each other.

Not that I didn't have any feelings of Christian guilt or doubt still. I still had spiritual reason to deal with them. Although I now knew better, I assuaged any Christian objection and guilt I had over our kissing, touching, and same-sex activity with the belief that it was just a part of God's creation of love between humans. I was still a Christian and bound for Heaven.

I look back now and realize how mixed up and convoluted I was about several issues. I was messed up about my sexual orientation at that point, and my life, my actions, and my relationship with Andrew. Also confused in my mind were Andrew's sexual orientation and his intentions toward me, my spiritual life, my faith, and my sense of right and wrong. However, back then it was a totally different picture I had of my confusion! My spirit was telling me one thing, hormones and emotions other things, my heart had other messages, and my mind was even different in its ideas. I was actually lovingly confused and ecstatically happy that I had worked it around in my mind to the position and belief that 'gay' did not include two men in a monogamous relationship. I had also decided that Andrew did love me, and I would pursue a relationship of some more intimacy with him. However, I knew in my heart that I was not ready for anything sexual, although my body longed for it. I longed for physically and sexually intimate activity with Andrew so badly my body ached! It was all so new, strange, stimulating, exciting, and sensual that I was overwhelmed with the emotions, hormones, and desires. I was really not able at that time to make factual, logical, or rational decisions.

The whir of the wheels as we drove home almost lulled me to sleep in my love-induced intoxicated stupor. Then my conscience hit me. I should be alarmed and repentant about my life right now! Biblically, gay still included any man being with a man as with a woman, didn't it? Biblically I was on the verge of, or had already committed some minor sins. I was shaken by a huge wave of guilt! I had almost accepted a definition of 'gay' that would allow me to pursue a serious relationship with Andrew, or any other guy, monogamously. I ruefully realized that, not only did I not have a problem feeling, kissing, and making out with Andrew, I really loved it! I craved the physical activity in our relationship. Had I already sinned with Andrew by my physical expressions of love so far? I had to sort it out, and then set things straight with Andrew. I needed to seriously evaluate and analyze what had been said and done between Andrew and me just now and seek God's will and His face.

I was confused, confounded, ashamed, excited, exhilarated, anticipating, shying away, scheming, happy, sad, angry, and certain all at the same time about my deepening and strengthening relationship with Andrew. I wanted him so badly! Lord, where are you when I need you?! Why had no one better prepared and taught me Biblically about same-sex relationships and my current situation?! Why did the Church leave us blindly fumbling around in the moral fog of earth teaching a vengeful God who could strike the sinner dead at any moment?!

"Are you all right, Dion?" Andrew startled me back to reality. "You're not ill are you?"

His voice, query, and the name he used in his request did not register at first. I was becoming angry at the churches of today again, at society in general, and even my parents a little! None of them had prepared me to resist the temptations to be in this relationship with Andrew. No one had given me any real Biblical reasons to resist loving, being with, and expressing my love to another man in a monogamous relationship. No one had given me spiritual and scientific reasons to resist having sex with another man. No one had done shit to prepare me to face life's temptations and tests as they now stood for me in this matter. Why in the hell was I talking like this?! I hadn't... well I didn't think I had been raised to talk like this, whether out loud or in my thoughts!

Where was God when I needed him?! We had not really been taught how to access God, His power, and His teachings by the churches either. Sermons and lessons had been out of the Old Testament primarily, and had centered on the Bible being applied by God to the people of that time. Who gives a shit! I want and wanted to know how God's Word applied to today and its issues! How was I going to live in today's society if I didn't know how to apply the Bible and my faith to the challenges and temptations of today's society and…!

"Dion!" Andrew spoke fervently and firmly from the driver's seat. "Dion, are you all right?!" His voice was sweet, yet demanded a response.

I glanced at Andrew. 'Oh Lord!' I confessed, 'he is so hot! I want him naked next to me… I wanted to hold him naked to my naked body and…' I stopped the prurient thoughts. 'Lord forgive me! Lord help me? Where are you?! Your church has failed me! What the hell do I do?!' I pleaded silently.

"Dion!" Andrew called worriedly. "What is wrong?!"

Then it occurred to me. He called me 'Dion'! I was nonplussed! No one but my mother and father called me 'Dion'. It was a nickname they had come up with when I was old enough to talk, a nickname after their favorite group from the 1950's. The group, the Belmonts (our last name, incidentally), had a handsome male leader and lead singer named 'Dion'. My parents nicknamed me Dion to commemorate him. That name I had cherished as a nickname filled with a special love from only those who called me that; my parents. My mother especially!

Later when I was in my pre-teen years, they switched from 'Dion' and 'Tyler' mixed as first names they used to address me, to only calling me 'Dion'. They said it was because, just like Dion in the rock group, I was a handsome male from that age on, and from then on I looked more handsome than Dion, himself. I was flattered! Mother's opinion and viewpoint of me helped my self-esteem. But then Dad… I moved on not wanting to face the darkness associated with thoughts of Dad.

The name 'Dion' was then picked up by my grandparents too, and it became a name indicative of a deep and special love between my parents, grandparents and me. My brother and sister, and cousins never called me Dion. We weren't in that close of a relationship, a parent-child relationship.

So, how was it that, at this point in our relationship, Andrew apparently discovered and used my special name of love and endearment reserved for those in a deep love relationship with me? I was thrilled, but alarmed and deeply bewildered. I had not said anything to Andrew about that nickname, nor had either of my parents called me that when we had gone to pick up my things. How did Andrew know of this name?!

"Dion?! Are you okay?!" Andrew asked again, this time with serious urgency and concern in his voice.

I'm afraid I was looking quite oddly and ill-settled at Andrew at this moment, and it was because of my puzzlement as to how he knew, or had come up with my love nickname 'Dion'. The feelings of surprise, ponderings, and thoughts of wonderment were racing over my synapses and banging around in my brain like bumper cars. They were also betrayed in my facial expression. Andrew, who had only met my parents once and had never met my grandparents, had still come up with the deep-meaning nickname for me of 'Dion'! Andrew, who, because he was only almost 26, had as little chance of knowing of the existence of Dion and the Belmonts, their appearances, and the correlation of the name 'Dion' when used in relationship with me, had still just called me Dion!

"Dion?!" Andrew woke me up again with the urgency and concern in his voice. "Answer me, please!? You are scaring the hell out of me!" He squeezed my hand gently.

"I'm fine!" I said quickly and a mite emphatically. "I'm fine!" I smiled at Andrew and squeezed his hand back.

There was silence for a minute or two during which my mind continued to race with questions. I finally gave up. I had to ask the question that was haunting me right now!

"How or where did you come up with the name 'Dion' for me?" I asked quizzically.

Andrew chuckled. He looked at me briefly and his blue pools sparkled in delight. The baby-soft and blemish-clear complexion of his face glistened appealingly in the evening sun, and I wanted to stroke him. His five o'clock shadow, though blond too, gave him a young, hot, masculine look. I wanted him so badly!

Andrew looked back at the road, smiling broadly.

"I've been trying to think of a special name I could call you, a name that would be a secret that would signify to each of us our mutual love, and specifically let you know of my deep, passionate, and everlasting love for you." Andrew drew a deep breath as he beamed at me.

"There used to be a rock group in the 1950s and 1960s, and yes they had rock and roll way back then! They were called 'Dion and the Belmonts'." Andrew began his explanation.

I was shocked that Andrew knew of them! That was something else we shared in common, a knowledge of music from the 50s and 60s. 50s and 60s music were two of my favorite genres!

"I am… I know keenly of them!" I interrupted in happy spontaneity. I beamed at Andrew.

"Stay with me, Dion!" Andrew held up his hand in a 'halt' signal. "One of my favorite genres of music is 50s and 60s rock and roll, so I have listened to the music from those decades. The men in the group were quite handsome, according to pictures of the group I have seen on the internet, and Dion? The band leader? He was fine! However, not as gorgeous and hot as you are, Dion! Additionally your last name is 'Belmont', the same as in the name of the group 'Dion and the Belmonts'! So, I have decided my special nickname of love from me to you will be 'Dion'. Do you mind?" Andrew glanced at me and the road, me and the road, waiting for an answer. His face bore an expectant and hopeful countenance.

I looked at Andrew. God! I loved this man! I would love nothing more than to have him call me 'Dion' because it represented our special love! Biblically I knew that I was exhorted not to do anything to encourage sin. From Andrew's lips, my special nickname just turned me on! It made me want him to take me sexually right now! My knowledge of the Bible told me it would be better if I didn't let him call me 'Dion'. However, my decision-taking process right now was not good, let alone Bible-based. Under the thought and request for this kind of an established love name and relationship with Andrew I melted. I couldn't think of anything better, or worse, than Andrew calling me a love name always and forever more!

"No, Andrew, I don't mind." I spoke softly and gently, and stroked the back of Andrew's head with my left hand, running his blond curls through my fingers. "I don't mind at all! In fact it sounds... it sounds... awesome... flattering... loving! Please do!"

I had no more than closed my mouth when my mind was pricked again with guilt and shame! Why in the hell did I approve of and allow Andrew to call me a name that made me want to get into his pants!? I quit stroking Andrew's head and hair and quietly brought my hand down to my lap. I was so mad at myself! I needed to think before I spoke, and I needed more commitment to my morals and values... to my God. I needed more determination to fight and win my internal battle against... against my... against my own... same-sex... same-sex desires and feelings?! At this thought I exclaimed inside defensively, 'They aren't homosexual! They are monogamous love, attraction, and feelings, something that God created! I needn't feel regret, shame, or guilt over being what God created me to be!'

I thought back to the beginning of my conversation with Andrew. I did realize that Neils was likely gay, but I was so sure Neils was cool, sincere to help, not promiscuous or a sexual predator. I was shocked I had pegged Neils so wrong! I believed Andrew when he said he had been told by Neils how he was going to have sex with me. Neils thought he was going to get my virgin meat (whatever that meant?). Then Neils expressed the belief that his having sex with me would make a man out of me?! What prideful arrogance and stupidity! Here I let that man give me a workout, get to know me, see and lust after me naked, and set a date with me. I felt so stupid! I felt so used, so abused! But most of all I just felt stupid! How in the hell was I to know what other 'gay' guys were thinking, thought, or were planning? How was I to know who was and who wasn't gay?! It wasn't like every gay gave consistent clues of their sexuality! How was I to know who was and who wasn't a 'good gay' guy like Andrew was?!

I realized from the bigot in the restaurant and the parking lot attacker on Andrew that the hatred for and fear of same-sex lovers that I may have experienced in Gurnee reached an entirely different level here. In Aurora, and probably other large cities and metropolises this bigotry and hatred took on active and dangerous physical levels for same-sex lovers. It was unnerving and downright frightening for me, even though I was of average musculature and strength. I had defended myself from bullies, competitors, wild farm animals, and other sundry hooligans quite effectively in Gurnee, but I had never… NEVER experienced such prejudice, hatred, and willingness to do bodily harm just because of whom I loved! It was scary, and I realized I had a lot to learn from Andrew about living here in Aurora and those things to look out for and to avoid. I also must continue working out to strengthen myself even more to defend myself!

I wondered what else I might face as Andrew's companion here in Aurora or elsewhere? I knew only Andrew could catch me up on the dangers and pitfalls I would confront here; only he could save me from myself and my naivete. I decided that at the earliest moment I would talk to Andrew and start learning from his experiences and knowledge.

Neils crossed my mind and I both flushed in anger and shivered in apprehension. I found it hard to believe that Neils was as bad as Andrew described. It was sad that he, a gay man, would stalk and rape another same-sex man! However, Andrew swore it was true… I had to believe him over Neils or my impressions of him. I was just thankful that Andrew had my back in my meeting with him! I knew he would keep me from harm by Neils.

Ah! Andrew! He had finally officially admitted he was a same-sex lover and he loved me dearly. I was thrilled and elated at this news! I had hoped he was. Now there was definitely an 'us' with Andrew!

Andrew had repeatedly professed his love for me to me. Then he had French kissed me, and from the moment his tongue entered my mouth the chemistry between us was nuclear and my hormonal rush had become a deluge that had been almost impossible to control. Most of my confusion and doubt about Andrew's sexual orientation, love for me, and desire for a relationship with me were swept away in the tsunami of emotion, feelings, hormones, desires, and animal sexual attractions and reactions that came with our French make out session at the sub-joint. It was a sign of our growing intimate relationship.

As I pondered all of the miscellaneous events of the day, questions came up. The most important was the hesitation that Andrew had exhibited before answering some of my more pointed questions, especially where I demanded to know if he were joking when he professed loving me and when he kissed me. The thought occurred to me that if Andrew loved me so, why did he not try more often to get me into bed with him? Suddenly I had some doubts again of our relationship?! However, a realization came to me, reflections from conversations Andrew and I had had. Andrew was in a quandary.

Had Andrew been overly serious in pursuing me into bed, he probably feared scaring me into leaving him!? Was he trying to keep me on his side, and not scare me away?! I concluded in spite of myself that Andrew was right. If he really came on strongly to me as he may have wanted to do, it would be and would have been really easy for me to flee to the hills. I happily realized Andrew was wise beyond his years. I had a soul searching journey to go through about our relationship and it was wise of Andrew to give me space. He was moving slowly, pushing me where and when I was comfortable, and giving me time in the area of sex.

Early in my life, before I moved to Aurora, I realized I had 'known' and believed a relationship between me and a man would certainly be a 'sin'. But I now felt, after my current conversation and activities with Andrew, that I believed differently about a relationship with Andrew, and I was in love with him! Now I had to work this out for myself personally, Biblically, and spiritually. I was lost in the woods of confusion!

I gazed back at Andrew. Andrew caught my eyes and smiled, winking at me. I smiled back. Andrew took my left hand in his beautiful, strong right hand and held me as he looked back at the road. I continued to look at Andrew, marveling at how gorgeous and beautiful he was while pondering his thoughts.

Andrew seemed completely unfettered of and unbothered by any questions, beliefs, confusion, and conflicts over his sexuality, over his feelings and love for me, and our relationship such as were harassing the hell out of me. Of course he had no such conflicts as I had because his pronouncement to the stupid clerk who harassed us at the sub-joint was an unequivocal affirmation that he was a same-sex lover. Andrew was obviously blessed with a clear understanding and acceptance of who he was, how he felt, whom he preferred sexually, what sex to which he preferred to make love, and what he wanted in life. As I gazed lovingly at Andrew I envied him for his freedom from self doubts and recriminations over his sexuality. I actually envied his lack of religious teachings and convictions over same-sex love that gave him such peace… a peace that still eluded me.

Through my swirling confusions, conflicts, hormones, and feelings at this moment I had to remember and cling to one thing in order to stay somewhat grounded in my evolving life. That one thing was a new belief I held that, although in its infancy, was developing more clearly and strongly in my mind. I had to remember and cling to this new belief that Biblically a committed, monogamous, and life-long love and expressions of that love sexually between two people regardless of their sex were not 'sins'. Especially in this the so-called Age of Grace in which every church pastor I knew taught that we currently lived! It was their very teachings on this subject that insisted we were not saved or condemned by works anymore, but by God and His grace through Jesus Christ. All that was required by us to be Christians in this Age was to accept Jesus' shed blood for our sins and that He was our Lord and Savior. That was what saved us. Would the Bible, God, or church elders lie on this subject?! Besides, the Bible did not, in its teachings on love, distinguish what sex the two people in a spousal, monogamous love relationship could or could not be. Therefore, monogamous love between persons of the opposite sex, between two males, or two females must be Biblically okay. If love between two persons of the same-sex were a sin, then love between opposite sex couples must also be a sin. In addition, God would have to be imperfect for creating that sin! I didn't believe that for a minute. God was perfect, inerrant, and true. The same went for Jesus.

Such was my developing belief and philosophy in regards to the tacit Biblical approval of my monogamous, same-sex, spousal relationship to and with Andrew. I had to tell Andrew! I wanted to tell Andrew! I wanted to assure him that my beliefs were evolving, becoming more open and enlightened. However, I believed that before I did, more study of the Bible and gathering of evidence in this area were necessary. I had to wait!

All that thought and musing reminded me, good grief! My daily devotions! I hadn't had them in almost four weeks! Even before that I had been a little sporadic in my spiritual ablutions. Was I suffering spiritually from it? Would a solid prayer and Bible study life have prevented my current conflict over Biblical sexual orientations?! I didn't see how, since the church, my parents, or society hadn't provided any scriptures and guidance in where to find the proper ammunition against a myriad of sins that I would face in the big wide world. I was only now realizing how inadequately I had been prepared to live a life for Christ in our world of sin.

Then through the emotional, hormonal, mental, and contented haze that roiled in my being, Landon's mellifluous voice came to mind, and it was actually haunting! It caused me to gulp involuntarily from guilt, doubt, and shame.

"… God has determined what relationships, associations, and activities are acceptable and Biblical to Him and for His children. There are some of those things that are not acceptable or Biblical, and they are an abomination to God and a threat to your eternal soul. You are close, Tyler, to embarking upon some relationships, associations, and activities here in Aurora that are sinful! You need to avoid these things…"

Had Landon referred to me and Andrew in his warning to me?! Was this the relationship to which he referred? I looked back at Andrew. I did not want to even contemplate that Landon was condemning the love and relationship Andrew and I shared, let alone believe it! I brushed that thought from the forefront and switched gears. My mind continued to analyze things having to do with Andrew, however.

Things with Andrew seemed to be moving quickly forward. Our relationship and love for one another was growing rapidly. I was thrilled to be moving so fast, yet I was apprehensive… and yes… scared. I knew that at some point soon in our loving and relationship Andrew would expect to move into a sexual level with me. As much as I wanted that too, I didn't know what to expect. I had no idea really how two men could make love… have sex. What all did it entail? Would it hurt? Would Andrew teach me and be gentle? Was he into rough stuff? Would he wait for me until…

I knew I was not ready… spiritually or mentally… for making love to Andrew. I needed to end my Biblical doubts, concerns, and determine the Biblical position on same-sex love by a thorough study of God's Word. Prayer, much soul searching, deep thought, and seeking God's Will would follow. I had to be certain my love of and relationship with Andrew was Biblically acceptable and okay, and that my Christianity and eternity in

Heaven would not be jeopardized or sacrificed by our lovemaking. I prayed and hoped Andrew would be patient and wait for me in this area before having sex with me?!

Secondly, I had very little idea of how to have sex with a man. I did not want to make love to Andrew blindly! I was a virgin in all ways and had never slept with anyone, male or female. I had a healthy sex life of masturbation and self-pleasuring, but that was the extent of my sexual experiences. In order to please Andrew the first time we made love I needed to be at least halfway competent on how two men pleased each other in bed. I decided I would have to seek help on the internet. I would troll there for porn videos.

Then there was my family. I really believed I should not have sex with Andrew until I was ready to tell my family about 'us' and our same-sex relationship. At this point I was NOT ready to go there, and I did not know when I would be!

If Tristan knew about me and Andrew he would freak out and feign outrage, revulsion, and anger! He would NOT understand my decisions, relationship, and love for Andrew at all. I dreaded seeing what the long term ramifications of my revelation about Andrew and me might be on our relationship as brothers.

Soenya was a puzzle. I really did not know what she would say or how she would react to my revelations about Andrew and me. She had never said or done anything that I could remember that gave me an idea about her feelings in regards to same-sex love.

I knew how Mom would react. She would be horrified and totally without understanding of Andrew and me. That would morph into a lecture of denial. Next would come disappointment in me and anger and rejection toward Andrew. Finally I would get a sermon on God's plans for men and women, a sermon that would come in installments, one delivered every time I saw her. Andrew would be regularly criticized, and banned from visiting home with me. I did not know if I could bear or tolerate any stage of Mom's reaction to my sharing about Andrew and me!

Then there was Dad! I shuddered. Dad would go ballistic and probably... probably... As I sat there a cold and clammy feeling coursed over my body causing me to shiver. A dark, blurry, and barely discernible image flashed in my mind. Dad was standing over me. He was shaking his fist and yelling at me as I lay on my back. My nose was bleeding. Then it was gone. I shuddered again. However, I knew the answer to what Dad would do when he found out that Andrew and I were lovers; he would knock me on my ass and... and... beat me to a pulp... Then he would beat the hell out of Andrew by any means necessary! He might even... he might even... I shook the thought from my mind!

No, I was NOT ready to tell my family yet that Andrew and I were lovers! Additionally, to make a long story short, I was still not ready to make love to Andrew, anyway... Therefore, facing my family with the truth was not an imminent issue...

As I thought about it I remembered that Andrew had purchased us a weekend for two in Deer Grove, Illinois. He just hadn't yet told me when. Remembering that reminded me also that he had bought us special cell phones, and had basically proposed to me. Didn't much sound like someone who was anything but a same-sex lover! Nor did it sound like things Andrew would do if he were not absolutely serious that he was in love with me. And all that was just in the last couple of days... Any sane person had to take Andrew at his word each time I could remember, including the passionate kiss in private, and our conversations where he said he was gay and loved me truly, and conclude that Andrew was truthful and serious. I had to study it a little more, and share with Andrew that he and I, as a couple, were a monogamous, same-sex couple; not 'gay' or 'homosexual'.

How would I hold Andrew's loyalty, attraction to me, and our true love relationship for a lifetime?! I did not know for sure, but I sure as hell would discover the ways and means of doing so and work at it!

I looked back at Andrew. As he drove the breeze coming in the window blew his medium length blond curls handsomely around on his head. I admired his exquisitely fine and sexy facial features, and I just wanted to feel, see, and kiss Andrew's face for a long, long time. I focally browsed down what I could see in the car seat of his masculine, muscular, erotic body, envisioning undressing him, and my body ached for his body to be next to me. I felt like grabbing Andrew, going to the back seat, disrobing and…

I stopped myself. The Bible condemned same-sex relations like those between a man and a woman!? Sodom and Gomorrah were destroyed by God with fire and brimstone because their men were lovers of each other. I had to study this episode of Biblical history completely. Then I would talk to Andrew about it and get his input. If nothing else it was ammunition to convince him too that same-sex love was a sin.

Then it occurred to me. My relationship with Andrew would survive that Bible history. Sodom and Gomorrah were in the Old Testament. The Bible's New Testament was all about love, and the whole New Testament approved of monogamous love… I had already established in my mind that monogamous relationships between two people of any sex were okay by the Bible's New Testament; this just gave me more to look up and study, mostly in the New Testament. I felt much better though, because Andrew and I were two people. We were okay Biblically to have a monogamous relationship between two people based on love and Biblical sexual intimacy, as long as we stayed within the bounds of marriage as laid out in the New and Old Testaments and as covered by the grace of the New Covenant laid out in the New Testament. Or were we?! I wanted to believe so!

I further considered the church teachings that the New Testament and the death of Jesus established a New Covenant between God and man. The New Covenant was based on grace, not works. One could do whatever the hell one wanted and be heaven bound through grace! At least that was the import of the teachings on the New Covenant and the Age of Grace as taught by all mainline Christian churches. Who was I, who was Andrew, who were the preachers to deny such a basic tenet and its imports?! So, again I was getting an okay message for Andrew and me to be a couple!

At first I almost spoke up to tell Andrew about what I was remembering of the Bible, and what I had learned in church that supported our moral right to share our love as long as we were monogamous. However, I still felt sinful, ashamed, and suffered from so many doubts about loving him, about wanting him, and lusting after him. Additionally my better sense kicked in and I knew I needed to do my study, prayer, and proving first before telling Andrew. I decided quickly and in time to keep my mouth shut and not tell him now. It, the Bible and monogamy, would be my secret to continue verifying and working out. Then I would tell Andrew.

"What are you thinking, Dion?" Andrew asked softly.

"Oh," I looked at Andrew, caught his eye and smiled, "about you… and… well… you and me… and you some more." I winked at Andrew.

"I'm thinking about you and me, subs, fries, pop, and an evening with a good movie, <u>Brokeback Mountain</u>!" Andrew had a big, cute, sexy… grin on his face. He looked so excited, it was almost funny!

I, on the other hand, was puzzled.

"What is this <u>Brokeback Mountain</u>?" I asked, reaching up to stroke Andrew's enticing blond curls a bit again.

Andrew looked at me quizzically, and then returned to the road, a full-fledged pleasured smile on his face. I wondered what was so pleasing so suddenly, but I didn't have to wait long to find out.

"Oh, Dion!" Andrew chuckled, turning our Intrepid onto Wax Figure Lane. "I love you, man! And one thing amongst many that I love about you is your naiveté! Your innocence! Your freshness! Dion, you are like an author's plans for a book in outline form. You have all of the flesh and detail of the actual book for the author to fill in from day one and then publish. I want to help you fill in the flesh and detail of your life, Dion! You are like everything good about a child, coupled with all the good, desirable, and sexy things about a fully matured, hot, adult male!"

"I am not a child!" I was a little annoyed. I frowned at Andrew.

"Oh, you aren't, Dion, and don't I know it just by looking at you! You, Dion, are all beautiful, sexy, tasty, erotic, and incredibly attractive adult male. Any fool would be jealous of me because I have you! No, Dion, <u>Brokeback Mountain</u>? It's a movie that I want you to see."

I felt myself blush at the compliments.

"What's it about?" I asked curiously.

"You'll have to wait. It's a surprise!" Andrew smiled at me, grasped my left hand, and gently squeezed it.

At that moment, Andrew pulled into his parking place in the Candlestick ramp. We both unbuckled and grabbed our food. We exited the car and headed for the ramp exit to the street.

Andrew looked across the street at the entrance of the apartment complex. I didn't recognize anyone off-hand, but he did. He got an impish expression on his face.

"Dion!" Andrew whispered excitedly. "Let's hold hands as we cross the street! I want to freak someone out!"

Before I could put my two cents in, Andrew grabbed my empty hand and propelled us into the street. We walked a clipped pace to the sidewalk in front of Candlestick.

As we turned to walk toward the doors, a ritzy, plump woman approached us. I recognized her as the woman who had accosted me on Sunday and made a spectacle of both of us.

"Hello, Mrs. Pompadora!" Andrew exclaimed happily. He swung our clasped hands forward in her plain view.

For her part, Mrs. Pompadora looked at Andrew, and then our clasped hands, and she gasped.

"Well!" She huffed. "They said fags live in Candlestick!" She stuck her nose in the air and tried to push past us. "They were obviously right! Candlestick is a den of iniquity!"

Andrew stopped and turned slightly to address Mrs. Pompadora, to whom he refused to yield. I was caught off guard and couldn't stop. I bumped gently into Andrew, who still tightly gripped my hand.

"Remove your carcass from my path, you... you... you wretched queer!" Mrs. Pompadora hissed at Andrew.

"'Den of iniquity' is it, Mrs. P?" Andrew gave Mrs. Pompadora a probingly serious stare. "That is quite a nasty, yet nebulous accusation!"

I shuddered a bit at this confrontation that Andrew was initiating, still very gun shy from the bigot at the sub joint. I tried to let go of Andrew's hand so I could escape to Candlestick's lobby, but Andrew held on tightly, hurting my hand.

Andrew quickly looked at me, winked, and mouthed the words 'It will be fun! Watch and listen!' to me.

Reluctantly I stayed and returned my eyes to Mrs. Pompadora.

"The name, you… you cur, is Mrs. Pompadora! NOT Mrs. P!" Mrs. P spoke disdainfully and coldly. "And yes! This structure with the grotesque… hideous façade is a den of iniquity! 'Iniquity', you ignorant fag, means ungodly, evil, and sinful. You engage in an evil, sinful, repulsive, and deviant lifestyle with your naïve young boy toy here…"

I became angry and I felt blood and skin flush rising up my neck to my face.

"… and you both live together in sin here at Candlestick. Drug dealers, pimps, johns, bisexuals, male and female sluts and prostitutes, transvestites, male and female porn stars and producers, homosexuals, and sundry other perverts and criminals also live here as your neighbors. Why! I hear that there are sex offenders living here! Pedophiles…"

"Oh!? Do you live here, Mrs. P?!" Andrew interrupted and asked innocently.

I jerked my head right and gazed briefly at Andrew in surprise and alarm. Andrew's stunningly exquisite features were poised in an angelic, inquisitive expression that reminded me of Eddie Haskell. However, I had only a few seconds to ponder Andrew's meaning and intent when it began.

There was a gurgling, semi-choking sound. I focused back on Mrs. P. from whence the sounds emanated.

Mrs. Pompadora's face was a rosy pink and she appeared to be spitting and almost growling. I fancied I saw a bit of froth in one corner of her mouth. I expected drool to appear any time!

Suddenly she coughed and cleared her throat.

"You bastard sodomite!" She sputtered, her eyes flashing and sparking. "You deviant scum are all the same! You scurry around in the shadows spreading and purveying your poison…"

"That is interesting, Mrs. P." Andrew interrupted again. "One cannot see what lurks in the shadows when one is in the light. One must submerge oneself entirely in the shadows and move about therein to see and identify what life or dangers exist there. What is your vice, your sin, Mrs. P, that brings you to live with us in the shadows?"

I again glanced at Andrew. The breeze bounced his beautiful blond curls around his face. He still had the innocent, yet impish countenance and, although I wanted to giggle at him, the whole confrontation made me uncomfortable. I fidgeted on my feet and tried to release his hand again. He squeezed my hand securely.

I looked back at Mrs. P again. She was getting more scarlet, and visibly angrier. Her visage was becoming humorous as it reminded me of a gradually overheating pressure cooker.

"I… I… Well! I have no sin, no vice!" Mrs. P. sputtered through clenched teeth. "I am a member of the silent majority! Those who lead and live good, moral, and normal lives whereas…"

"Ah, Mrs. P…" Andrew calmly interrupted Mrs. Pompadora, "the Bible states 'only the fool says he is without sin.' Are you a fool, Mrs. P.?"

I felt like one of the bobble decorations in a car. At Andrew's quotation from the Bible I swung my head to gape at Andrew. He didn't believe, or hadn't he said he didn't believe in God!? How did he know anything from the Bible?! With my mouth hanging open and a look of consternation on my face, I stared at Andrew, puzzling over his obvious knowledge of some Bible verses and his seeming disbelief in God.

Andrew glanced at me, winked, and mouthed 'Look at her!'

I focused quickly back on Mrs. Pompadora.

Mrs. P. appeared apoplectic. Her face was so beet red now and I swear she was beginning to smolder. She was now spitting and sputtering and there was definite froth at the corners of her mouth. Three veins stood out in her neck and two in her forehead, and her eyes bugged out a little. I feared she might collapse right there in front of us!

"I am no fool!" Mrs. P. finally managed, her voice a few pitches higher in her anger. "I am NO FOOL! Why, I never! I, Mrs. Minerva Ilene Pompadora, am a better, more Christ-like person than you and your cocksucking boy toy here will ever be! Mr. DiPree, your type is not welcome here in this neighborhood… or anywhere in Aurora for that matter!"

I felt my temperature rising in anger again as I looked at the hateful, judgmental old witch!

"I am no one's cocksucker, you bat!" I hissed through clenched teeth.

"Oh really?!" Mrs. P. managed to sneer. A couple puffs of foam accompanied her as she continued. "I know how you queer men have… have… have your deviant sexual pleasures!"

"How is it that you know how we have sex, Mrs. P.?" Andrew asked. "Was your husband a homosexual? Did he sleep with men because you didn't please him in bed?! Maybe you like watching gay porn on the internet, Mrs. P.? I bet those things are your vices! There are apartments open here for you and your hubby, if he is still alive, here in Candlestick! We would love to have you and your kind join us, Mrs. P.!"

This time the fireworks began before I even had a chance to look at Andrew.

Mrs. Pompadora went into full fledged gasping and trembling spells. Her face was now deep red and her eyes looked as though they would fully pop out of their sockets. She flailed her arms around from her head to her mouth and out to the sides resembling a whirling dervish. I had NEVER seen anyone so angry, so out of control, so intensely hateful. I almost laughed!

"Why, I NEVER!" Mrs. P. fairly screamed. "I have NEVER been so insulted! Why you… you…!"

"Born yesterday, eh, Mrs. P.?!" Andrew impishly interrupted. He smiled victoriously at me.

Mrs. P. threw her nose in the air and huffed. She turned and began strutting the opposite way down the sidewalk. Andrew politely waved at her back as she stumbled a couple of times because she was not watching the sidewalk.

"Cum guzzling gutter sluts!" Mrs. Pompadora called haughtily over her shoulder.

"Pompous, self-righteous bitch!" Andrew laughed heartily and let go of my hand.

We reached the door to Candlestick, and Andrew opened it for me. We both entered the lobby and headed toward the elevators.

We were both silent until we were alone in the elevator.

"Wasn't that hysterical!" Andrew chuckled. "She is so wound up that her stockings attach to her bra!"

"Who was she?" I asked, a little concerned of my reputation. "I mean I know she is Mrs. Pompadora, but what kind of clout does she pull in the community?"

"Just the neighborhood judge, jury, and gossip. She's creating waves whenever and wherever she can!" Andrew looked at me jovially. "She's mostly harmless!"

As we rode the elevator upward, I felt so comfortable with Andrew. I felt at home, away from my childhood home in Gurnee. I hoped that this bliss would last forever! Andrew was a real catch! A real peach in a world of pits! He would help me, watch out for me, and together we would face the world. I could live on my own now.

# CHAPTER 45

# NO BROKEBACK HERE

We arrived at our floor and exited the elevator. I let Andrew lead to our apartment door as I was tired and he had his key out… well, who was I fooling?! I really just wanted a good view of my lover's perfect and attractive bubble butt! It was a pleasure to behold… so perfectly well-formed and taut… so enticing, tantalizing… sexy…

Andrew placed his key in the slot, punched in our security code, and unlocked our door. He stood aside while I entered first.

Like twins or copycats, together we entered the living room and put our food on the coffee table. Then we took off our shoes and put them by the door. Finally, we hung our jackets in the closet.

My mind was full of plans for a wonderful evening in a tee and house pants, eating supper with Andrew, and then the two of us holding each other while we watched the movie. To be comfortable I needed to change into my house clothes.

I turned to head to my bedroom, but Andrew gently grabbed my arm. I swung around with momentum, surprise, and a desire to see what he wanted.

Andrew stood there in all of his resplendent masculinity looking admiringly at me. His beautiful face bore a glowing smile and his eyes twinkled. The muscles in his left arm rippled as he pulled me close, face to face, our bodies touching waist to waist. He proceeded to passionately French kiss me. It was so stimulating and beautiful, heavenly; my heart beat faster and the hormones began flowing. Suddenly I could feel Andrew hard through his pants. A wave of ecstasy coursed through my body from my head to my feet. I quickly began to get woody too.

Andrew pulled back and proceeded to put one hand on my ass and the other on the side of my face. He caressed my right temple and cheek with his left hand and gently squeezed my butt cheek with his right hand. After a minute or two he wrapped his arms around me. We hugged each other tightly.

"Dion!" Andrew exclaimed tenderly, blissfully, and seriously. "Dion you are... I think you... you are such an Adonis... such a gorgeous Adonis... so manly... masculine... appealing! Your farm life and the sun has toned your skin and musculature... I... I mean I... I cannot help but love you dearly and forever!" He continued to brush the right side of my face gently with his open left hand.

I'll be damn... I mean I was alarmed at first, but a tear ran down Andrew's cheek as he finished his statement. Alarm was quickly replaced with euphoria and gleeful intoxication from Andrew's flattering announcement of his love of and for me. I felt tears of joy and thankfulness come to my eyes as well. I mentally hardened my countenance and emotions to prevent myself from crying.

"Thank you, Andrew!" I mumbled nervously. "Andrew, I am so... I am so... thankful... thankful that I met you... thankful for you... thankful that you are mine... and I am yours! Andrew, you... you are a... a gorgeous hunk of man... you are a gorgeous, hot, sexy, lovely, desirable man yourself. I love you, Andrew!"

Andrew smiled with happiness, his eyes moist.

It was such a tender moment. Andrew hugged me tightly again, and I reciprocated. Then he went to the kitchen to mix himself a drink, and I went to my bedroom to get on house clothes. As I was returning to the kitchen to get a glass and some ice, Andrew went to his room. I took my glass with ice into the living room and sat on the sofa in front of our food, drink, and the television.

Andrew returned, clad in house pants and a muscle shirt. He grabbed his mixed alcoholic drink from the kitchen bar and joined me on the couch. He positioned himself closely to me so that our bodies touched at the shoulder and leg. He kind of cuddled close to me. It was very cozy and comfortable. Lord, I loved Andrew!

"Are we ready for the movie?" Andrew asked me softly.

"Yep!" I poured some pop from the bottle into my glass and took a long swig.

"Okay!" Andrew seemed excited as he picked up the remote, turned the television on, and flicked the station to a screen that said 'On Demand'. "I'll order the movie." He informed me.

"Order the movie?" I had never heard of that before. I began eating my sub sandwich.

"Yeh!" Andrew smiled at me. "You can watch any one of hundreds of movies at your leisure on your own television in your own home. You order it 'On Demand' and pay for it in your monthly bill! It is handy and has been around for a while. I am surprised that you have never heard of it!?"

"Is is very expensive?" I asked, worriedly. I didn't know exactly how much Andrew was paid on a regular basis, but I was not yet drawing a paycheck yet. I didn't want him to have to pay a lot to 'support' me until my paychecks started coming in.

"Nah!" Andrew was punching buttons on the remote. "I can afford it! Remember Sunday?! I cleared that $3,700.00?! I can definitely afford $15.00 for the movie tonight so we can watch it!"

He punched more buttons on the remote until he apparently finished the transaction. Then he hit 'enter'. We chowed down on our food while the movie began.

It didn't take long for me to realize the movie was about the relationship between one gay man, his intimate relationship with another 'closeted' gay man playing it 'straight', and their interactions with family and friends. The first scene of the movie where the tent moved and pitched, was puzzling at first until it became clear that the men were having passionate sex. With that understanding it made me quite uncomfortable for its duration, but I settled in and became very interested in the rest of the movie. I didn't quite know or understand all the time what was going on, but I was still interested.

We finished eating in about 20 minutes and then lolled back on the couch to watch the movie. I basked in the fact that I was in the loving embrace of a 'family', Andrew, and enjoying a comfortable, large apartment where I could relax and be myself. Never mind the fact that 'myself' was an insecure, confused, and guilt-ridden young man. I was in the presence of the one I loved, respected, and admired, and I now knew he felt the same way about me. I was truly blessed!

After about 20 more minutes, Andrew moved discreetly closer next to me and put his arm around my neck, resting his left hand open upon my chest. This was so comforting! Andrew was confident... my love, and my rock. He was a go-getter, and certain of himself. He and I cared for ourselves and each other, and went so well together. For the rest of the movie we sat like that, closely. It was assuring and oh... so pleasant!

I watched the movie with intrigue and some sympathy. I had never heard of or seen it before. Andrew had seen it before, and explained a few of the more obscure facts and situations as we watched. I discovered that I identified with both of the main characters. They had a true romantic love and attraction to one another beyond anything, and I thought of Andrew. I loved him already! I had those same feelings toward Andrew that the protagonists in <u>Brokeback Mountain</u> had toward each other.

Andrew squeezed my neck gently and kissed my cheek.

I nestled my head next to his and smiled happily. Andrew was so warm, and although he was muscular, he was still soft.

I watched the obvious struggle of the main characters as they dealt with their attractions to, feelings for, and love of one another. I could imagine the one man was conflicted with many of the issues about his sexual orientation that plagued my mind and beliefs. As the movie unfolded I identified more with the Heath Ledger character because he was the most confused, conflicted, and in denial of himself, his feelings, and his sexuality. After all, he was married and had children as his very strained cover of being 'straight'.

I was tickled at the awkward yet tender scenes of affection between the main characters. It was almost as if they were not comfortable or knowledgeable about kissing, hugging, and touching a woman, let alone another man. I contemplated Andrew and me. Although I was awkward in the expression of love area, we were… well, I hoped in my flesh… were much more comfortable about showing affection to each other, interacting together, and expressing our love for one another than were the two lovers in the movie. I realized Andrew was also more knowledgeable about how to touch and where to touch me to stimulate the most feeling, emotion, and love than were the main characters.

I puzzled some over another series of situations in the movie. The main characters kept separating and going back to their 'straight' lives and families every year. I knew already I could never do that with Andrew! I was already tied intimately enough to him emotionally and physically that I couldn't imagine leaving him for much more than my work shift.

When the two ultimately split because of the opposition they would face from society as a gay couple, I had tears in my eyes. The thought of splitting up with Andrew was so painful and devastating. I knew that, at this current time, I had no intention of ever abandoning Andrew unless he himself sent me away!

At that point I glanced at Andrew. His eyes were moist, and there was a tear track on his right cheek. I realized at that moment that Andrew and I shared many emotions with each other and were both sentimental. We were kindred spirits, soul mates. I gazed back at the movie and smiled to myself.

The movie ended quite sadly, but I liked it. As the credits scrolled, there was a comforting silence between us, and I blew my nose to clear the few tears that had flowed.

"So?" Andrew sat forward and looked back at me. His face bore a look of contentment and inquiry. "What did you think of the movie?"

"I liked it." I smiled, and shrugged. "The first part where the two were lovemaking in the tent made me a bit uncomfortable. However, overall I liked the honest portrayal of two men struggling with their desires and sexuality, and dealing with society's learned and set moral judgment of their love and lifestyle. It showed me how… it portrayed how… I mean… I guess it showed… well, it showed me how…" I knew what I wanted to say, but I felt a little guilty saying it. "It showed me how jealous, prejudiced, myopic, scared, discriminating, and parochial some people can be in dealing with the issue of same-sex love and intimacy."

"Wow!" Andrew smiled and put his hand on my knee, squeezing lovingly. "That was a movie critic's answer if I ever heard one!" Andrew chuckled, and then looked at me seriously. "I liked the movie a lot. That's why I wanted you to see it, Dion. I identify most with Heath Ledger's character. From his character I learned I don't want to grow old alone, yearning for my one true love. I know what I want and love; manly, buff men. I know whom I want and love desperately and forever; you, Tyler Aaron Belmont! Dion, I will hold on to you for the rest of our lives, unless you decide you don't want or love me anymore!" Andrew squeezed my knee lovingly again. I knew by his look and actions that he meant it.

"Yeh." I looked at Andrew challengingly. "That is one of the major lessons to be learned from the movie. However, I saw another lesson to be learned as well. The movie clearly showed me that if something must be hidden from friends, family, and the public, and/or if it is deemed wrong legally or according to society's norms, then you avoid it and refrain from doing that activity."

At this point I didn't myself necessarily agree with my statement, but I was out to challenge Andrew, and try to disrupt our rapidly growing and deepening lover's relationship. This was a part of my decision to test God and give Him a chance to show me that Andrew and I were wrong.

Andrew's smile disappeared. He stood and strode to the kitchen. I worried that I had made him angry. However, that was the purpose of my plan; give God a chance to divide Andrew and me to show us our relationship was a sin.

I watched as he poured himself an extra strong vodka tonic and I admired his hot body. He turned back facing the living room and strode to his seat beside me. He sat down very close to me again and took a long drink. He offered his glass silently to me for a drink, and I shook my head 'no'.

Andrew set his drink down on the coffee table and sat back with one arm triangle to his head off the couch back. He was as close to me as he had been the entire movie, and I liked it. Andrew proceeded, with his free right hand, to drag his fingers all over my chest and stomach softly and sensually. It was very stimulating, relaxing, and pleasant. I sat looking at him expectantly, enjoying every minute of his touch.

Andrew finally spoke. He was thoughtful, insightful, yet defensive of his opinion.

"I can see your point, Dion. However, there is another side to your argument. Columbus had a terrible time drumming up financial aid for his trip to find the Orient by sailing west instead of east. He was laughed at and refused financial aid by several governments in Europe for seven years. If he hadn't persisted in his radical idea and plans despite continual rejection, we would not be here in the New World as Americans. George Washington and the other Founding Fathers of our country were condemned by many in Colonial America as rebels and traitors, and the British sought to kill them. If they had not done what the British called illegal and traitorous and what Colonial society said was wrong, we would still be vassals of England. In short, if various citizens or factions throughout our history had not defied the contemporary law, the cultural morals, or mainstream thought under which they lived, we would be a much different nation today. We wouldn't be able to eat or drink what we desired, women couldn't vote or work out of the house, we would not be flying in planes and space craft, we wouldn't be driving cars, we wouldn't have electricity, and lots of medical breakthroughs would have never been made. Government laws, religious teachings, and society's so-called moral norms are restrictive and kill positive change and innovation, sometimes to a fault or to its own detriment."

Andrew took another drink, slipped his hand gently under my tee, stroked me, and looked at me lovingly and meaningfully.

"Do you realize that, Dion?" Andrew flushed, one of the few times I had seen him do so.

I looked away, thinking.

"I mean, do you know what I am saying, Dion? Most, if not all, of societal progression, invention, and overall advancement of freedom, technology, science, and enlightenment have developed as a result of some group or someone ignoring or violating governmental laws, religious rules or beliefs, society's rules, some 'established facts', and any other so-called natural inhibitions or traditions to or against a particular thing or hypothesized fact. Hell, as I said we wouldn't be living here in America if Amerigo Vespucci of Europe hadn't realized the earth was not flat, and that there was a continent between Europe and South East Asia, Dion?!" Andrew looked at me sincerely and firmly, touching my cheek and placing a hand on my inner thigh.

"Yes, that is true... at least I cannot factually argue against it. But, Andrew," I countered, "as Christians we must recognize and honor the law higher than our laws as an individual, a family, a government, or as a society. Those laws are God's laws, and if God declares something wrong in the Bible, then it was wrong when God declared it so, wrong today, and forever wrong. Indeed the Bible says that 'Jesus Christ, the same yesterday, today, and forever.' Nothing we can say or do will or can change the Word of God!"

"I can't say I disagree with you there entirely, Dion. We will debate whether translators have skewed the Word of God for their own selfish purposes later." Andrew put his hand inside my tee, flat on my chest, and began gently and sensually massaging my chest and stomach again. "I agree that things like the Ten Commandments and the principles and morals outlined by Jesus in the New Testament transcend our laws. But I believe in areas where the Bible is unclear or silent, man must make the law based on those precepts that are specific, and set by the Bible. Things not clear or not covered in the Bible, or that are out-dated, must be legislated based on what is currently acceptable, egalitarian, fair, democratic, and based on the form of government under which we live."

"If man promulgated the laws not specifically spelled out by the Bible or upon which the Bible is silent according to the other explicit Biblical precepts, it wouldn't be bad, Andrew; but most often man doesn't do that. Most often man makes law based on the changing cultural morals and standards and on changing societal needs. It is when fallen man makes laws based on his own feelings of right and wrong, or on society's feelings of right and wrong, that we have trouble and often chaos. That kind of lawmaking leads inevitably to dictatorship and discrimination against religions and classes of people!" I stopped and gave Andrew a space for a response.

"Who is 'fallen man', or what is he?" Andrew queried. "I have heard that phrase before, but never have I heard an explanation of what it is!"

"'Fallen man' is man without God. He has no relationship with God, no use for God, or doesn't believe in God, and lives life serving sin." I answered. "Without God, man loses self-restraint. He tends to sin and continue in worse and worse sin. It is like the Law of Increasing Entropy I learned about in school biology. This law states that a system left to itself with no energy flowing into it increases in disorder rather than evolving to something better than itself. To justify the theory of evolution scientists just ignore the Law of Increasing Entropy. Fallen man, to justify himself, his sinful ways, and his increasing sin ignores the energy, God, needed to improve everything, and he spreads his sinful influence and ways to other people, groups, and areas. Gradually his sin results in total societal change. Then the society changes to approve the sin. Then the laws and governance changes to reflect and protect the sin. That is the effect of fallen man. The cycle continues without God and the chaos increases to a collapse of society."

"I can see where bad people can't make good laws. I agree with that." Andrew paused. "Dion, we have established that God created love between two humans haven't we?"

I nodded in affirmation as I looked at Andrew. I put my hand on top of his when he brought it to rest on my chest.

"We have established that two people of the same-sex share love just like two people of the opposite sex right?" Andrew asked earnestly.

"Yep!" I smiled. "We also agree that God created love shared by both opposite and same-sex couples, so therefore same-sex love can't be a sin or evil, because God creates neither sin nor evil!"

"We also discussed how condemnation of same-sex relations is in the Old Testament, and not the New. Do you remember that?" Andrew continued.

"Yes." I said. "You argue that this, along with the fact that same-sex love is not specifically condemned in the New Testament, means it is okay to date or marry a man or a woman."

"Wow!" Andrew exclaimed. "You are getting our arguments in favor of same-sex relationships and love down as well as I have them!" Andrew sat back and smiled adoringly at me. "So, I say Heath Ledger should have lived permanently with his lover once he left his wife. Why do you disagree? Why do you say we should only do that which society and the Bible say is right!? Remember, much progress in all areas of society are lost because of this belief."

"Oh, because I've been brain washed by established religions to believe same-sex love is a sin!" I smiled and sat forward. "I'm being facetious, Andrew!" I needed a refill. "I need more pop." I finished.

"I'll get you a refill!" Andrew took my glass as the news came on. "Anything for my lover! Anything for the one who completes my being!" Andrew winked at me.

My religious and moral resistance to Andrew, to us, to our relationship was slowly melting and fading. I wanted him, I needed him, and I loved him! Was it so wrong for Andrew and me to be a monogamous same-sex couple and lovers?! All that I could see about Andrew and me was our love, loyalty, honesty, integrity, passion, compatibility... everything shared by a heterosexual couple. Where was the Christian faith's leadership, proof, teaching, and influence to show us why heterosexual and same-sex relationships should be treated any differently by the law, culture, society, business, and religion? Why wouldn't or couldn't they tell us why our same-sex relationships were such a sin and so wrong and worthy of virulent discrimination?!

Andrew went to the kitchen, and I watched as he poured another vodka and mixed it with orange juice. He then poured me a glass of diet and returned to my side.

"Thank you!" I said, taking a deep swallow.

"That's all right." Andrew replied. He held up his glass for a toast. "To deprogramming you, Dion, and breaking down any and all discriminatory policies against same-sex relationships and marriages in society.

We clinked our glasses and each took a deep swig.

Andrew switched the television back to cable and selected Fox News. We both began watching a blurb about Obama's latest health care efforts. Fox News's correspondent was explaining how the health bill was thousands of pages long, Obama had not even read it, and the experts were concerned about how hard it would be to implement and write legal rules and laws for it. I watched Andrew for a reaction. Maybe tonight I could argue politics with him, we could strongly disagree, and I would be initiating the enactment of my wedge idea between us. I was not prepared for Andrew's reaction to Obama's message.

"Damn socialist!" I heard Andrew say as he shook his fist at the television screen. "I don't need the government telling me how to live healthy and what health care the doctors can or cannot administer to me!"

Andrew took a long draw on his screw driver. His sentiment and apparent beliefs were so attractive to me. I gazed at him in pleasant surprise.

I realized, with some shock and chagrin, that Andrew and I may well be on the same page with our political views!? Maybe my wedge idea was a waste of time. Maybe God was working for Andrew and me, not against us...

# CHAPTER 46

# A SUCCESSFUL SUMMIT

As Dion and I watched the Fox News channel I put my left arm around his neck and my left hand open flat on his chest. I began to massage his chest tenderly with my finger tips. I felt thankful to be this close to and intimate with Dion, but to my surprise and thrill he did me one better. He swiveled slightly so his back was toward me and laid back into me, his head resting comfortably on my chest. My whole left hand and arm now lay entirely across his chest, and Dion put his left hand up on my arm, holding it tightly. I was dangerously sexually stimulated and ecstatic!

A blurb came on concerning Obama's nationalized health care law that had passed a few months ago. As we watched it I became so pissed! I flushed in anger. Who the hell did that President, that boob, think he was?! What the hell or who gave him the power and authority to map, plan, and push for ways to get control of my health care?! The federal government and Obama had no constitutional power or authority let alone any right to destroy our nation's health care system by enacting Obamacare. The federal government was already unconstitutionally hindering and destroying our economy and everything else it regulated, legislated, or administered.

"Damn socialist!" I exclaimed angrily as I shook my fist at the television picture of Obama. "I don't need the government telling me how to live healthy and what health care the doctors can or cannot administer to me!"

I didn't know how Dion felt about Obamacare, but frankly I didn't give a shit! I had my opinion and I held it dearly. I had always been libertarian and conservative in my political views and beliefs. I believed strongly that we needed less and smaller government, and much lower taxation. Socially and morally I was more liberal, but I had never voted for a democrat for president.

I took a long draw on my screw driver as the blurb continued.

In my anger and outrage over the first tyrant's health care policies and lies he spouted during the blurb I was unwittingly tensing my arm around Dion's chest and neck.

"Andrew!" Dion croaked, pulling at my arm with both hands. "Andrew, you are pressing the air out of me! Loosen your arm please!?"

"Oh! I'm sorry, Dion!" I blushed and chuckled. Quickly I relaxed my arm. "I didn't realize I was doing that. I didn't mean to hurt you! Sorry! Are you all right?"

"It's okay! I'm okay!" Dion stroked my arm lovingly. He moved his head down into my lap and looked up at me innocently and curiously. "You look angry! Did you mean to call Obama a socialist? What is wrong?!"

I looked down at his gorgeous face in my lap and I wanted suddenly to kiss him and feel him up, but I could not!

"Damn straight I called Obama a socialist! That is what he and his cronies in corruption are up there in Washington, D.C.! I am so pissed at what Tyrant Obama and his beliefs in nationalized health care will do to destroy our nation!" I spoke with such emphasis and anger that I surprised myself. "You know our nation is in trouble with the left-wing socialist Democrat Party in control of everything!"

A huge look of relief and happiness spread over Dion's face as I flushed in some embarrassment.

"That's how you really, truly feel and believe, Andrew?!" Dion asked incredulously.

"Absolutely! I am very conservative and libertarian in my economics, politics, morals, and philosophies of government. How about you? Do you support the Democrats, Obama, and nationalized Obamacare?" I looked down into Dion's beautiful brown eyes.

Dion's smile disappeared and he frowned.

"Hell no!" He exclaimed forcefully. "I think Obama and the Democrats are communists! I too am a conservative economically, morally, and politically. Government is too big, expensive, and repressive under Obama. I just figured… well, I thought that since… well… since you are gay… according to the gay stereotype… I assumed you were… were a liberal… a democrat. No offense meant, Andrew! But you are not liberal or a democrat?"

Dion gazed cautiously but optimistically into my face.

"Hell no, I'm not liberal! I am not a loser!" I responded forcefully. "That all same-sex couples are liberal is a type-caste figment of the imagination of the media establishment and the Democrat Party! It is not based in reality! Over the years I have known gay guys and gals, some were liberal democrats. Many others who were truly politically and economically sentient were conservative or libertarian."

I took another deep swig of my screw driver. I could feel the coldness of the ice contrast with the warming sensation of the alcohol as it slid down my throat to my stomach. 'I have to calm down!' I chastised myself. 'A little more alcohol…'

I offered my drink again to Dion, and of course he refused it, but he was watching me with love, admiration, and hope in his expression.

"I'm glad to hear that your political beliefs and positions are conservative and more libertarian, Andrew!" Dion chatted happily. "I would hate for us to be in opposition to each other politically, economically, morally, lawfully, religiously…"

He raised his head toward my face and I kissed him tenderly on the lips. Then we resumed watching the news.

My political viewpoints would be best summed up as libertarian, I concluded to myself as we watched and listened. I had always disagreed with the bulk of the gay movement leaders that the Democrat Party was the ideological home of the homosexual community. I wondered who could be so blind and stupid! I knew the Democrats had for years sought to impose government regulation of everything on the nation, and I agreed more with the Republicans' stand for less government. I did not want government telling me what to do, where to go, what to purchase, what to eat, and how to live my life! Given the gay movement's resistance to any religious restraint or control I found it idiosyncratic that they would support the Democrats and bigger government. Since I had become politically sentient I had been in favor of the Republicans more times than not, but I preferred even the Libertarian Party more. I had actually voted for Ron Paul!

"Andrew?" Dion asked quietly as he gazed back up into my face. His gorgeous head rested right over my package. I wondered if he could feel me growing through my pants!? I blushed. I couldn't stop it! Dion's face that close to my family jewels was just soooo very stimulating…! I so wanted to make love to him… get naked with him… entwine our bodies together…

"Dion?" I responded, looking at him inquiringly.

"Do you have health insurance where you work?" Dion glanced at his hands as commercials played on the television.

I snorted.

"Health insurance!?" I took another swig of my screw driver. "We have the best health insurance no thanks to the damn Democrats! It provides for dental, optical, medical, and pharmaceutical coverage, $10.00 co-pay for everything. The Flamingo… I mean Bear Stearns… treats us very well!" Shoot! I had to calm down! I almost gave away the name of my real employer, Mr. Richard and The Flamingo Lounge.

"Our health insurance…" I continued, "is excellent and will also cover our spouses, male or female, or our lovers. In a while I can put you on my insurance, Dion."

At The Flamingo Lounge I had always had excellent health insurance. Mr. Richard took care of us well! In return it was up to us to use safe-sex practices at work to avoid AIDS and STDs, to be regularly tested for all STDs, and we had signed an agreement to never drive drunk. Mr. Richard asked nothing more of us. He did not seek to control our activities in any other way. I did my best to fulfill Mr. Richard's expectations and my employment contract. It was the least I could do in gratitude!

As I thought about my work and commitments to Mr. Richard, I did have to admit that I drank… a bit… well, moderately… Okay! Quite a bit! And I took the drug, avatar. However I was careful, and treated my body well in all other ways. I ate well rounded meals, I ate plenty of fruits and veggies, I worked out regularly, and I had myself checked out and tested for AIDS and STDs regularly. I took vitamin supplements and some herbal blends for various things. I figured I did quite well by my health.

I had a good record of using protection at work, probably approaching 90% of the time. I knew some fellow employees whose use of protection was maybe 40%. They walked a thin line all the time. I was not that stupid. I had had, since beginning to be sexually active at age 11, several gay friends with whom I was never involved in any way except friendship, die of AIDS, and two former lovers contracted very painful and devastating STDs. I did everything I could to protect myself because I had witnessed the consequences if I did not!

I was thankful, I didn't know any more to whom, but thankful just the same that, after hundreds of sexual encounters with hundreds of different guys, I had not contracted any sexual diseases. Considering my job was to sexually please clients at a full-service lounge, I figured that was a record of which to be proud.

I looked at my outstretched legs and feet, trying to clear my mind so I would shrink. Dion still moved his head around on my lap over my crotch, watching television, looking at me, and cleaning under his nails. I wondered if he had any idea how he was sexually stimulating, tempting, and torturing me!? Damn!

I had to 'change the subject' if I did not want to 'soil' myself. I decided to question Dion a bit.

"Do you have insurance, Dion? Or maybe I should ask… will you have insurance where you work?" I paused my thoughts and looked at Dion. Dion lifted his head and took a drink, his arm flexed against the sofa to hold him up. I reached out and gently stroked his nicely muscled arm… then his finely muscled back… I gazed back at the television.

Dion quickly swallowed, as I glanced back at him expectantly.

"Not yet!" He exclaimed. "In 30 days I will have full coverage. Medical, dental, optical, and pharmaceutical will be covered, and I'll have a $25.00 co-pay for office visits, $15.00 for drugs." He finished. He smiled coyly at me. "Your coverage sounds better! Perhaps since we are… we live together, and are… well… in a special relationship… maybe we should claim to be lovers and I should go on your insurance plans!" Dion lay back on my lap and gave me a sly, lustful look.

Now I had blubbered myself earlier into a pickle with Dion! Although The Flamingo Lounge did offer the fine insurances I had outlined to Dion, and they did extend those plans to their employees' same-sex or opposite-sex spouses and lovers, the thought hit me hard that I had thoughtlessly mentioned that to Dion. Obviously if I pursued placing Dion on my insurances I would have to disclose to him where I really worked! I could NOT do that! How was I now going to backpedal and put that idea out of Dion's mind for a while?!

"Placing your name on my benefits and insurances at Bear Stearns is a long, complicated process. First, Dion, I cannot begin the process until the next enrollment period in November this fall. Once you have applied with me we have to wait 30 business days before it takes effect, during which you have to stay residing with me as my lover. After that 30-day period we will have to sign domestic partnership papers with Bear Stearns' human resources department. They will take ten business days to process the partnership papers. After the processing period I can file papers to put your name on all benefits and insurances. Then it takes 90 days for your coverage to become effective. In short it will be a while before we can tackle that issue." I felt guilty lying to Dion. I had made it all up.

Dion nodded his head and reached up to stroke my cheek.

"I'll have insurance through Computronix long before I would get it through you then, Andrew. That's all right!"

I hated lying to Dion about the procedure for placing him on my benefits and insurances, but it was a necessary evil! I gulped involuntarily. I had dodged a bullet here!

"I am sorry, Dion." I said softly. "I would like to say you could be added to my insurances easily, but it is such a long process. Besides, Dion, your insurance sounds like an average plan. It will serve you well, I'm sure!"

"I know, Andrew!" Dion chuckled. "I was just kidding… I am… well, not yet ready for something like a lover or spousal title to our relationship… anyway!"

We watched the news a bit more.

Of course the 'All Obama all the time' media was still covering the agenda and activities of the first tyrant. Among his next initiatives was 'immigration reform', otherwise known as amnesty for millions of illegal aliens. The arrogance of going against the wishes of the majority of Americans and trying to legalize lawbreakers who belonged at home overseas was inexcusable. It was my opinion that these illegal aliens should be rounded up and sent back home! The first fool's position was infuriating! I sneered and contemplated running my fist through the television screen.

"What do you think about President Obama's position on an immigration reform plan, Andrew?" Dion inquired, turning his head to look up at me. My boner bent his ear and came up on his cheek through the crotch of my pants. I inhaled quickly in pleasure, managing again to stifle an orgasmic groan. I blushed, but Dion didn't seem to notice.

"I think it is a pile of shit… I mean it is bull crap!" I kind of gasped orgasmically from Dion's head on me… but I also needed to calm down and control my anger and passion with which I held my beliefs and expressed them. Who knows what trouble my right-wing political views might get me into!? Depending on what crowd in which I might spout off, I could find myself in the hospital or dead. I paused, and drew a deep breath. I drank deeply from my alcohol. The alcohol and avatar were probably not helping my self-restraint and self-control any.

"I am sorry, Dion!" I smiled at him and patted his firm, sexy chest as he lay resting back against my muscled legs and crotch. "I am very opinionated and I am very passionate about my beliefs!" I cleared my throat. "I do not believe that millions of people who broke the law to come to this country should be granted any kind of citizenship or a 'road' to citizenship. That isn't fair to the hundreds of thousands that come yearly to this country legally, and it only encourages prospective immigrants in the future to come in illegally to avoid delays and red tape. I believe they should be pressured to move back home by removal of any rights, benefits, health care, and jobs. Then they should be rounded up and shipped back home!"

"Well, I agree with that!" Dion's voice had a firm, impassioned, and sincere tone to it. "However, I don't believe any government reform of immigration is needed at all. I believe, based on what I've heard and read about the laws already on the books, that all levels of government, federal, state, and local, need to enforce the laws they have already in place. Additionally, I think they need to build that wall toward which they appropriated billions of dollars. You know, the wall on the U.S. and Mexico border?"

I couldn't have been more happy! I was so hot for Dion because of his intellect, physical appearance, and personality, but my only fear, one I hadn't dared to consider or voice until now, was that he and I would be on different planets politically, economically, and/or socially. Based on Dion's beliefs on health care and immigration reform, the fact that we both identified with the true conservative and libertarian beliefs and policies, and the fact that we both believed the Democrats were extreme left-wingers, I didn't have anything about which to worry. It sounded like Dion and I might be on the same page politically. That would be awesome!

I took another deep drink and sat back.

"I agree with you, Dion!" I smiled. "You know the truth about immigration. The only further government action we need in the area of illegal immigration is the enforcement of existing law." Dion and I high-fived each other.

"You know, Andrew…" Dion gazed at me. His eyes sparked due to his anger. "If I were selected to tackle illegal immigration I would do the following things. Number one, I would appropriate money to finish the border wall. Number two, I would enforce the wall and law and border agents with some military forces. Number three, I would free the states to enforce immigration laws. Number four, I would deny illegal aliens health care, rights to vote and get a driver's license, the right to work, and the anchor baby exception. Number five, I would begin rounding up illegal immigrants and sending them back to their country of origin. Number six, I would greatly increase the fines and penalties for U.S. companies that employ illegal aliens. Number seven, I would institute financial sanctions and incarceration for CEOs and company executives who knowingly or unknowingly employ illegal aliens. Number eight, I would greatly reduce or eliminate work visas and programs that allow illegal aliens to enter our country and then disappear into the society to live illegally. That would be my starting plan to end illegal immigration, Andrew. We need to get tough! Enforcing our laws and instituting all existing laws would more than end the problem!" Dion shook his fist and then sat up and hit the coffee table for emphasis.

"I agree!" I was ecstatic! Dion and I were so in sync on these issues. I felt even closer to Dion as we talked, and I was experiencing a surge of even stronger attraction to and love for him. His facial beauty, body, character, behavior, mind, and now beliefs were such a turn-on to me...

"I also believe we may even need to deploy some of our military to all of our Canadian border as well to stop illegal immigrants before they cross that border!" Dion exclaimed angrily.

"Ah, Dion! I am so... so... so glad to hear you enunciate your political, economic, and social beliefs!" I smiled happily. "I find that you and I most likely agree on a lot, if not all, of the issues facing us as a nation. It is so comforting to discover we are so compatible! You know, it greatly reduces any chance of disagreements, petty arguments, and messy fights. I love you so, Dion! More and more each day!"

Dion blushed and glanced at his feet and then his hands. He raised his head up and peeked at me before diverting his eyes out of the living room window. His beautifully tanned brown skin on his stunning face was so flushed in response to my compliments that he was bronze like a Native American.

"I... ah... well, Andrew, I... I love you too, Andrew..." Dion finally gazed back at me and we locked our focus on each other. "Andrew, I cannot possibly imagine life without you! Promise me you... you will never... ever leave me?"

"Dion, I will never leave you or abandon you as long as you still love me and never reject me..." I rubbed Dion's chest as I nodded affirmation to him.

It was at this moment that our reality really hit me. It was a reassuring epiphany.

Dion and I were more than likely completely in agreement politically and economically. If he had any liberal, socialist, or democrat tendencies, Obama's national healthcare law, illegal immigration, and immigration reform would have been issues that should have broken the back of our compatibility camel so to speak!

Dion sat up, turned to face me, and put his elbow on the sofa back about a foot from my head. He then leaned his head on his hand in a triangle facing me. He was really close. I wanted to grab him, rip his clothes off, kiss every inch of his gorgeous naked body, and make mad, passionate love to my Dion!

For his part, Dion looked like he was really beginning to get into our conversation, our relationship, and our domestic life together. He looked at me intently and hopefully. I felt now, for the first time, what a heterosexual couple must feel between them; a beautiful and comforting camaraderie, an intense love for each other, a sense of completion and oneness with my lover that transcends everything on earth! I knew I had chosen Dion well, with Someone's help!

Who did help me to find Dion that day on the bus? Who rearranged earthly events in Dion's and my life to bring us together? Was it God? Was there really a God? I had spent 20 years trying to find 'Mr. Right', attempting to meet my soul mate, my help mate, the one man who could be one with me, please me sexually, love me for who I am, and who would complete and fulfill me.

When I had realized I was coming to the 'end of my rope' in my career and actually began to look for something different, for a life-long lover, he was dumped in my lap. If that wasn't a miracle, I didn't know exactly what was! Maybe I had actually been searching for God as well my whole life!? Dion could help me in that potential quest since he was a Christian. After just a few days I knew that Dion was 'Mr. Right' for me and would meet and surpass all of my criteria for my 'Mr. Right'.

"As far as Obama's socialist nationalized health care system that is being implemented, Andrew, I too believe government at any level, especially the federal level, has no business controlling my health care, my insurance, dictating my health decisions, or establishing any standards of health care." Dion took his right hand wand, with his index finger, began drawing sensual squiggles on my chest. I wanted Dion to touch me all over… my package… my ass… It felt so stimulating I almost forgot to respond. I shook my head back to reality.

"You know, I don't know how any government board or government idiot can claim to know what health care is best to deliver, what treatments are too expensive, and how to deliver acceptable and 'affordable' treatment to the people. Nor do they know how to price what they will pay for the treatments they will authorize. What makes the government officials think that they are more qualified to run everyone's health care than the doctors and insurance companies? And, what gives the government the right to play God by rationing treatments to children and senior citizens?" I felt myself getting angry again. 'Calm down!' I told myself.

"The way the federal government screws up the various programs they start and then administer is evidence too that government health care will be a disaster. Hell, the feds cannot even balance their federal budget, let alone run a nationwide health care system that has the power of life and death over patients! Look at the Veterans' Administration and their hospitals. They deny necessary treatments and drugs to our military people all of the time!" Dion had a contemplative look on his face. "Speaking of disastrous federal programs let's take Medicare for 2000. The Medicare program was sold to Congress partially because the Congressional Budget Office estimated in ten year intervals that it would cost far less than its current cost in actual practice. Medicare is now almost bankrupt! Senior citizens are rejected for coverage who need it, and people who don't need it, or don't qualify are being covered. Large sums of money are swallowed up in the program to pay for unnecessary levels of bureaucrats. Medicare, hell the whole federal government and its unconstitutional administrative agencies are a mess!" Dion was now provocatively rubbing my chest, stomach, and down almost to my genitals with his hand flat. It was a sensual, stimulating massage like I had given Dion earlier.

"There are innumerable examples of government destruction and mismanagement of programs created by Congress or the president." I took another deep drink. "The Department of Defense, the Environmental Protection Agency, the Department of Education, welfare, Medicaid, the Drug Enforcement Agency, the FBI, and so many more. Everything the government has taken over," I took another drink, "it has run up its costs and ended up spending it into insolvency, like Social Security."

"And we're not even mentioning the unconstitutional aspect of the national health care bill. Health care is not one of the powers granted by the Bill of Rights and Constitution to the federal government." Dion sat forward again.

I was feeling pretty happy and mellow by now. I took another drink. Dion was so hot and sexy… the more he talked the more I wanted to climb up and down his bones like he was one big dildo!

"If government were to do anything legislatively to health care it should be to make it legal for insurance companies to operate across state lines, eliminate discrimination over pre-existing conditions, and offer tax-free health care savings accounts." I reached up with both hands and massaged Dion's shoulders.

Dion scooted backward so that his sexy ass was tight against my thigh. I could reach his back with my arms relaxed now, and I expanded my massage to his entire back. Dion alternately arched his spine and slumped down as I worked on up and down his back. I smiled as I worked; Dion reminded me of a cat that was being petted the way he was acting to my massage. All he needed to do now was purr!

As I worked on Dion I realized how pleasing and thrilling it would be for us to massage and touch each other for the rest of our lives. I wanted Dion to massage, touch, and hold my naked body, and I wanted to do the same to him. I also looked forward to Dion and me being celibate except to make love to each other until the day we died!

"Yeh!" Dion let his head hang and closed his eyes. "Those are good ideas for real constitutional health care reform, Andrew!"

There was a pause as we both watched television again. I stopped massaging Dion, and he sat back, right next to me. I reached out and held his right hand with both of mine.

Dion broke the silence.

"Andrew, with what political party then do you most closely identify, Republican or Libertarian?" Dion looked at me questioningly as he laid back with his head on my lap again.

"I'm registered 'independent'. I usually vote Republican, but I hold political views further to the right of the Republican platform. I am probably more Libertarian by belief." I responded truthfully.

"How about you, Dion?" I asked cautiously. "With what party or philosophy do you most closely identify?"

Dion looked seriously into my eyes.

Oh, God! His brown eyes were so lovely and tantalizing! They had… or Dion had in and emanating from his eyes… a hypnotic and sexually pleasing effect on me…

"I identify most with the U.S. Constitution Party. They are rightist, Constitutionalist, Christian, and moral. They, along with constitutional conservatives and probably libertarians, are our only realistic and effective tools to salvage this nation and get the U.S. back on the road to 'life, liberty, and the pursuit of happiness.'" Dion looked back at the television screen.

Dion's body was in a prostrate position. He had his head in my lap and, when he turned his head to watch TV, his face was right over my stuff. He had to feel my boner through my pants, as every time he turned his head his cheek rested right on it. It was so sexually stimulating to have Dion's face in my crotch and on my woody! I struggled desperately with my desires for Dion, and my love and hormones were gushing wildly for him. I was so tempted! I wanted to initiate intimate behavior with Dion, but I knew it was still too early. I must wait. Would I be able to resist my love for him and my hormones long enough for Dion to become ready and accepting of making love to me?!

"What do you think of the Libertarian Party, Dion?" I asked softly as we again met each other's gaze.

I watched Dion closely to see how he responded to my question. Dion's face registered a surprised, but pleased expression at my question. He turned to face me fully.

"Well, I don't know a whole lot about the libertarians." Dion responded, a look of thoughtfulness covering his superbly gorgeous face. "I know they oppose government interference in the free markets and the U.S. economy. I believe they oppose the federal government legislating controls and regulations on the freedom of individual behavior and human activities, and I heard they favor legalizing drugs. Other than that I don't know specifics. I couldn't really form an opinion until I learn more." Our eyes met again, and Dion shrugged.

"The libertarians are a little to the right of the Republican Party politically." I responded quietly. "They believe that the less government regulation of human activities, the less rebellion by people, and the less they will do that which is wrong. They want to control government and limit it, not the people!"

"Andrew, that sounds good to me! I know just enough about the libertarians to understand that the party is politically, economically, and philosophically opposite the Democrats, but I do not know enough to identify with their party. I'd like to learn more with you." Dion patted my chest. We both smiled at each other.

"Dion, I'd love to study the Libertarian Party or any other party with you!" I answered softly, running my fingers gently around over the sharp, stunning lineaments of Dion's face.

Presently I cupped Dion's face with my hands. Gently I pulled him up off my lap toward my face. Dion pushed himself slowly as well. He stopped, resting on his elbows. Tenderly we kissed. I was surprised when… for the first time… Dion began plying his tongue into my mouth. We played tongue tag for a minute or two. Then Dion sat up and smiled at me. I winked seductively at him.

"Dion," I didn't know how to ask this, and I hoped Dion would say yes, "would you remove, clean, and replace the bandaging and stuff on my shoulders, back, ass, and legs?"

Dion perked up more than he had been before. His face suddenly glowed and his eyes sparkled. It was like he relished and looked forward to the task of cleaning and caring for my injuries. A task that would sicken most people, Dion seemed to enjoy it! I knew I had been and would be in hog heaven to feel Dion's fingers and hands all over my backside! This proved to me that I had hit a slam dunk for my life-long lover in Dion.

"Sure!" He jumped to his feet. "Let us go to the kitchen, love!"

As we entered the kitchen, I was sexually shuddering and almost groaning in anticipation of Dion touching me as intimately as he would have to to clean and salve my healing welts!

# CHAPTER 47

# A BATTLE VICTORY!

I followed Dion to the bathroom, admiring his awesome physique, lithe, sinewy, slender body, and his cute tight bubble ass. I took some vicodin for the coming pain. Dion filled a small, plastic bucket with hot water, threw in a wash cloth, and together we gathered the first aid supplies. I helped him carry everything from the bathroom to the kitchen.

In the kitchen Dion and I unloaded the first aid supplies. Dion went about setting out everything on the counter and the table. As his manly, dexterous, sexy, and sensual hands and fingers worked to organize things and open them in place, I had a small orgasm of pleasure.

I had to get out of there or I would have to make love to Dion or relieve myself. I hurried to my bedroom and procured a mat and pillow to place on the table under my head and naked body. I then returned to the dining area. Dion was still working as I entered.

My welts and injuries were feeling much better. Amazingly, and consistent with my many previous injuries, they had stopped hurting like hell a few hours ago. I had gone through most of the day with little pain and discomfort... although I had had some help from vicodin, vodka, and avatar.

Despite my injuries, mild pain, and discomfort I had managed to accomplish my goals for the day. I had exercised. While exercising, I had received a threat to Dion from Neils. Out of love, concern, and necessity I had shared the threat with Dion. Because he was meeting with Neils on Wednesday for dinner and a discussion of 'gym membership packages', Dion and I had developed a plan for him to escape the 'date' should Neils attempt to make good on his threat to rape Dion.

The final thing I had accomplished concerned Dion and me. I had managed to establish an overt 'dating' relationship with him, and he had confirmed it. Further, our love for one another, our compatibility, and our dependence on one another were strengthening and deepening. I was on cloud nine! I could be a bit more obvious with him in private from now on about my love for him.

My next mission was to work toward a solid, irrevocable, indestructible, passionate, sexual, loving, and intense 'monogamous, steady dating' stage in my relationship with my gorgeous hunk, Dion. This true, forever love and relationship between us would be one that would always have us 'drunk' with each other. Finally, Dion and I would be one, spiritually, physically, sexually, in means and plans, in thoughts and behaviors… in goals and ambitions… Ultimately, and the thought made my knees weak and my heart leap for joy, Dion and I would culminate in becoming a monogamous, married couple as one, committed to no one else, and interested in no one except each other. I so wanted Dion for me, for us to live, to love, and to have each other forever!

I rolled the mat out on the table and placed my pillow. They lay flat on the table waiting for me to lie down.

By now I was so hard that it hurt, and I was so hot I was sweating for my Dion. I had to calm and cool down. Maybe a cold shower?!

Water! Cold water! I rushed past Dion to the kitchen sink and turned the cold water on high. Ice cold faucet water was just one of the many blessings and amenities here at Candlestick. As soon as it was ice cold I filled a large glass with water. Without thinking about anything except reversing my body's sexual reaction and hormones I dumped the whole glass over my head. The ice cold water poured down over me and wet my clothes. I shivered and focused on the cold water. Immediately I began to come down off my sexual stimulation.

I turned around and almost walked into Dion. He had approached me and was standing a few inches from my back.

Dion had a puzzled look on his stunning visage. Water dripped from his bangs, nose, and lips. The fronts of his clothes were wet and his gorgeous, masculine chest was visible.

"What the hell was that all about, Andrew?! Now you are sopping wet, and I'm wet and cold too! Why did you do that?"

I could feel my neck and face flush in embarrassment. What could I tell Dion?! Thinking about you, Dion, made me so hot I had to have a cold water shower to empower me to resist raping you? I decided to wash my hair... in the kitchen sink... with no soap?

"Andrew?!" Dion insisted. "Why did you pour ice cold water over your head and me?"

"Well... I poured... ah... I mean I... cold water..." I stammered. "Um... well... When I... You... I was thinking..."

"Come on, Andrew...!" Dion urged as he smiled. "Please answer me?!"

I decided to be honest. Dion would be scared and back track on part or all of the progress I had made with him, but honesty and truth were important between us on issues of our relationship, and honesty and truth had to be victorious in this situation.

"The truth, Dion," I began, "is that all day and evening I have been thinking about you... about us... how much I love you... how much I want you... how wonderful it is to be dating you..."

I paused. My woody was coming back.

"Anyway, all that thinking about you... about us... made me so... so stimulated... so turned on... so hard for you that I hurt. I thought cold water would help me to go back to... to go back to a... a non-stimulated condition without having to masturbate... I'm sorry, Dion... sorry for all of it..." I could feel my face flush with some embarrassment and shame.

To my surprise Dion began chuckling. When he stopped he smiled at me.

"Are you serious? Thinking of me and 'us' together gave you a hard-on that was painful?"

"I am totally serious, Dion..." as I answered I hung my head in fear, "I am so sorry, Dion... I don't want to scare you that I have such strong love, desires, and sexual attractions to you..."

I stopped. Dion interrupted me by cupping his hands around my face and lifting me gently back to look eye-to-eye with him.

"Andrew!" Dion spoke fervently yet tenderly. "I am not sorry! I am flattered… touched… proud… I am… I am… I am in love with you to…"

Then Dion surprised me… pleased me… thrilled me! He moved meaningfully and sincerely forward to my lips and kissed me. He French kissed me for a couple of minutes.

As suddenly and surprisingly as he had moved in to kiss me, Dion pulled away from me. He gazed expressionlessly at me. It was a little awkward.

"I… well, I need… I need to fix myself… I need vodka and avatar…" I smiled at Dion and motioned toward the refrigerator.

Dion smiled back and turned around.

"Okay, Andrew!" He said happily.

I fixed my drink as I watched Dion spread another towel out on the table and place the pillow right for me. I so looked forward sexually to having Dion change my bandages and check my wounds carefully to make sure they were healing as well as I thought they were.

I took my drink and crossed to the table.

"Take off your clothes, Andrew, and lie down on the table, belly first." Dion instructed as he turned his back to me and grabbed the bucket of hot water and the wash cloth. He turned back to gaze on me.

'Gladly! I will strip nude for you, my Dion!' I thought as I slipped out of all my clothes, while he watched. Meanwhile I dreamed of a time with Dion when he would strip me bare and we would then have tender, passionate sex and lovemaking… I placed my clothes on a chair. Then I lay down on my stomach lengthwise across the kitchen table. I wondered if Dion knew or even fathomed what a temptation he was to me? Did he understand what a torment it was being naked with him as he gently touched my bare flesh and I was unable to make love with him? Did it occur to him yet how strong and fierce my desire for him was? I was becoming hard again thinking about and anticipating Tyler's coming intimate touching of my naked body.

When I was comfortably lying on the table, my bare ass in the air, Dion turned to the island and began carefully making preparations for removing bandages from my back.

By the time Dion turned back to me, I was watching him intently and lying in stillness. I watched Dion look at me as he worked, a countenance of pleasure, desire, and contentment coursing his features. Then an expression of consternation came upon his face. 'What was wrong?!' I thought in alarm.

"Wow!" Dion exclaimed, touching this welt, and then that one. "You do heal fast and well!" Dion gently rubbed one scab.

"What do you see?!" I asked intently. "What do they look like!?"

"Andrew… I never… honey… What… when… I… I am… I am speechless!" Dion stammered as he gently ran his manly fingers over my back.

"What, Dion?!" I demanded, a bit alarmed.

"I can't… I can't believe… I can't believe it!?" Dion breathed slowly. His fingers and hands caressing my back were so stimulating.

"What is it, Dion?!" I exclaimed again urgently.

"Well, Andrew, it is miraculous!" Dion removed a bandage, causing me some pain, and touched other spots on my back, butt cheeks, and legs as he narrated. "The bleeding welts and injuries that did require bandaging are… they appear to be well scabbed over. Those welts that weren't bleeding or were just a little bloody are… they are fading… and healing rapidly! A few spots are entirely gone… your back, buttocks, legs, and heels are much, much better!" Dion smiled at me.

I trembled a little in anticipation and hesitation.

"Dion…" I managed.

"Yes, Andrew?" Dion was distracted as he continued checking out my injuries. His fingers on my body were tantalizing…

"Dion… what about… you need to look… it has been painful…" I hesitated over what I wanted… had to ask of him.

"Andrew, what is it?" Dion asked, his voice still tinged with awe.

"Dion, you need to look… you need to look between my… my cheeks… and check my… my anus. Please?" I managed to spit it out.

"Yes, Andrew… I will look… now."

Dion poised over my ass, took a deep breath, and gently placed his fingers. When he spread my cheeks I gasped as a wave of uncontrollable pleasure swept over me. Dion inspected my cheeks and anus, tenderly probing some injuries. My hormones and sexual pleasure went nuts with his inspection.

"Andrew…" Dion spoke slowly and in awe. "Andrew, the lacerations are healing well… scabbed over… the bruising… is fading! I see no signs of any infection anywhere!"

I winked at Dion. He smiled and shook his head.

"I cannot believe it, Andrew! The speed of healing on your injuries is remarkable… amazing… great!" Dion gushed. "I feared you would infect or not heal and still need professional care! That will not be necessary based on the rapidity of your healing and lack of infection."

"Excellent!" I responded.

Dion turned to the counter and grabbed the hot water bucket. He turned back to me and placed the bucket on the table at my side. Smiling, he picked up the hot wash cloth, and squeezed out the excess water. Turning back to the counter he retrieved wet sanitary wipes and antiseptic healing cream, and turned back around to face me, lining the stuff up next to me.

"I cannot believe how much healing you have done in the past 24 hours or so! Praise the Lord, if you continue healing this way, there should be no scars or permanent marks left on your beautiful… perfect… sexy… desirable… tantalizing skin!" Dion announced as he carefully began washing a welt on my shoulder.

"I heal well and fast." I stated, heaving a sigh of relief at the news. "Always have. I told you there wouldn't be much, if any scarring!"

"Okay, Andrew." Dion continued washing my right shoulder. "I am going to remove all bandages and wash everything first. This will probably hurt like hell!"

I gritted my teeth as Dion took a bandage off of my left shoulder and removed three large bandages on my back. He then gently removed two bandages from each leg. He carefully removed a bandage from each buttock. The removals hurt, especially the ones from my ass. However, they were done! Dion had alleviated any long suffering on my part as best he could.

I groaned and sighed in relief.

"Again, I am amazed! Pleased!" Dion stood back a little, delicately touching some welts on my backside where bandages had been. "The welts under the bandages are well scabbed and the color is fading. They have been healing fast too! I am impressed! I am ecstatic!"

I smiled with a sense of self-satisfaction. I felt Dion beginning to systematically wash the welts on my shoulders, and they began smarting and prickling.

"I have been blessed with quick healing all of my life!" I said in a fake boasting voice.

"Did I just hear you, Andrew, use the word 'blessed'?!" Dion copped fake surprise. "That is a word usually used only by Christians!"

"Not so, Dion!" I chuckled. "You have had an effect on me with your faith!"

I paused, smiling to myself, before a sense of seriousness came over me. To say what I had on my mind and to cover the increasing pain I needed some 'medicine'. I guzzled the entire glass of avatar and vodka.

Dion paused in his medical care and took my glass to the refrigerator for a refill.

I was quickly feeling much better as the avatar and alcohol began deadening the pain and giving me a 'high'.

"Dion, I… I want you to know…" I didn't know how to express my thoughts succinctly.

"I want… I do so appreciate you… ah… I appreciate and love you doing this for me! And thank you for not taking me to the ER! I didn't want the hassle and publicity of filing hospital reports and paperwork, and then filing the criminal reports, assault paperwork, and answering police questions during the investigation. I just want to get this all behind me as soon as possible!"

"It's all right, Andrew." Dion said softly as he carefully and, dare I say, lovingly cleansed another welt. "I would… I would only… only do this for you. I love… well… I enjoy… I mean, I love doing this for you."

My heart skipped at Dion's mention of love in helping me. I loved having him do this to me. My sex with men at work meant nothing to me… but Dion's touch… his massage… his love was like finding a long searched for treasure! It all was so sexually and emotionally stimulating that I still had a painful hard on!

I looked back at Dion.

"Andrew, where do you stand on the abortion issue?" Dion continued washing my back.

His touch was gentle, sensual, strong, manly, and stimulating. I knew I would have to put something over myself when I stood up, or Dion would get a sight. Hopefully he actually wanted to see me erect and ready to go!?

"Are you in favor of abortion as a birth control measure, Andrew, or are you pro-life, and opposed to abortion as a method of birth control?" Dion persisted softly.

I knew this line of questioning was coming sooner or later, and I was ready with my honest position and opinion. I had nothing to hide from Dion; at least nothing like I had to hide from many in the gay community that I had encountered. Besides, I suspected that Dion and I were more in agreement on political, social, and moral issues than we were in disagreement. I was glad to feel so confident that I could tell my true opinion on issues and not cause a major argument.

"My parents didn't want children at first, Dion. They were very set that they did not want the trouble of a child, nor did they want to bring a child into a world that had so many problems." I spoke of my real, and my fictitious parents honestly. "If abortion would have been as available when my mother became pregnant with me as it is today, and as cheap, my mom would have aborted me." Now came the lie. I remembered I had to add this. "Later, they wanted to have my brother, so abortion wasn't an option." Now it was back to honesty. "Because I could have been an abortion statistic, I am very much opposed to abortion. I am especially opposed to the federal government forcing the states to offer abortions. The abortion issue should be decided by the states or the people at the state level."

Cautiously I sneaked a peek at Dion's beautiful face. His features bore a pleased expression and he nodded in agreement as he worked on me.

When our eyes met Dion winked at me. I kissed the air in his direction and winked back. Dion grasped my left shoulder with his left hand as he lovingly washed and wiped my back.

"I'm glad they didn't abort you, Andrew..." Dion spoke softly, but emphatically. "I don't know what I would have done, or what I would do now without you!" He looked seriously at me. I knew he meant what he said. My heart bloomed into even more love for Dion, if that were possible.

There was a pause as Dion massaged some antiseptic cream gently into the welts on my entire back. I felt like I was getting a full body massage from a professional masseuse. Lord, Dion was good... perfectly created and formed... so sexy!

Dion's tender, manly touch, my strong and deepening love for him, and the fact that I was naked in such close proximity to him had me physically, emotionally, spiritually, and sexually drunk. I wanted to make love to Dion now! I was still fully stimulated sexually, and my erection was still painful because I had had it so long. I was very uncomfortable the way I was lying on the table. I carefully adjusted myself. Oh, how I wanted... and needed... sex with Dion right now!

"How about you, Dion? What do you believe about abortion?" I asked tenderly as I watched his face.

"I am also anti-abortion." Dion said softly and firmly. "I believe that abortion is murder. No one should have the right to murder an unborn child who cannot speak for itself. Abortion should be illegal except in the case maybe of rape, incest, or the endangerment to the life of the mother." There was a thoughtful brief pause, and then Dion continued. "I agree with you that abortion should be an issue decided by each state government, each state's voting population, or their courts. I think it is sad when you consider the talent this nation has lost with so many years of technology and knowledge because at least 50 million babies have been aborted in this country since Roe v. Wade in 1973. It is such a waste! We may have aborted the doctor that cured cancer, the nurse that saved a car crash fatality who became a famous senator, the lawyer who successfully argued before the Supreme Court that the fetus is human from conception, the bystander who rescued the little boy from the lake who later cured alzheimers, or the soldier who saved a platoon of pals on a military transport. We may have aborted the citizen who rescued a family from a car crash whose children became missionaries, a person who saved the next president from a pile of ruble, the women who saved the woman who later saved this nation from one world government! We may have aborted any number of very important people!"

After Dion's convincing answer he fell silent. He continued working on my back, which now felt like it were on fire.

Dion's message caused me to pause, pondering my response.

"Wow!" I breathed as the import of what he had said sank in. "I have never thought of abortion in that way before… in those terms of human self destruction before! Abortion is devastating when the true human and societal toll is considered with the actual numbers of abortions! You have just made some powerful and thought provoking points, Dion!" I was in shock thinking about it. I had never considered the secondary loss in accomplishments, technology, and life caused by the primary losses of the practice of abortion.

I fell silent, deep in thought and horror about the truth and impact of Dion's comments about the tragedy of abortion.

Dion paused as he finished washing the welts on my legs. He then took the antiseptic healing cream and began gently rubbing it into the welts on my legs. Again my pain and discomfort increased during this care, but I bit my lip, clenched my fists, and dealt with it. Several times it burned like hell, but I gritted my teeth and stifled the groans.

"I am not going to bandage anything." Dion stated thoughtfully. "There is not any reason to bandage the injuries when none of them is bleeding. You are very blessed to be so well-healed already, Andrew. I thought you were in grave danger of requiring professional medical attention. I especially worried that you may still require it if the welts were to infect and start draining. Thankfully there are no signs of infection that I can see."

"Great! You must take part of the credit though, Dion. Your excellent treatment and care of my injuries went a long way in enabling my quick healing!"

I nodded my head to emphasize my point and looked at the floor.

There was a short pause. Dion began washing the welts on my buttocks. They smarted and prickled, and it felt weird! I shuddered in almost uncontrollable sexual pleasure with the sensation!

"Do you ever want to have children, Andrew?" Dion asked quietly.

I looked back at Dion in surprise. He was thoughtfully washing my buttocks with the antiseptic cloth, and he glanced at me and gave me an inquisitive, serious look.

I had never really considered that possibility because I was gay. Having children was something that I would have to actually consider whether and how to formulate an opinion. It wouldn't be hard to answer Dion's question honestly right now. It would be equally easy to answer Dion's question honestly once I had thought about it and formed my opinion.

"I don't honestly know, Dion." I cleared my throat, as I pondered the question. "I've never really thought about it. I'm so busy in my own life, pursuing my own dreams and desires. I'll have to think about it. Then I will tell you my thoughts on the subject. It will be fodder for another interesting conversation for us later on."

"I've always wanted one of each... a boy and a girl." Dion carefully began applying some rubbing alcohol and massaging it into my buttocks. "I've always wondered, though, if I really could raise children well. I know it is challenging and hard to raise them up and train them to become up-standing, law-abiding, honest, and responsible citizens. It is especially hard in today's society what with all the corruption, drugs, crime, hate, and lack of morals and values. The media, entertainment, and adult world are so full of sins and evils that one has to be a really, really good parent to raise good, upright, upstanding, and intelligent citizens."

"I personally think you would make an awesome parent, Dion!" I patted his ass as I assured him. "I can tell you have the love, the patience, the sense of right and wrong, the ability to lovingly discipline, and more that is necessary in a good parent. If I did have kids, I would want you as their other father!"

"Thank you, Andrew." Dion began massaging the antiseptic cream into my right buttock. It felt so good having Dion touch me so intimately; I was still painfully stimulated.

"Dion?" It was my turn to ask a question. "What do you… well… do you have an opinion… I mean…" I was afraid to ask him this question, but I decided to plunge into it instead of beating around the bush. "Oh, hell! Dion, what do you think about gay marriage?!" I spit it out.

I watched Dion's face as I posed my question. Dion did a double take, and then frowned. 'This could be the first issue upon which we disagree!' I thought, regretting immediately that I had asked the question.

Dion finished the right buttock and began creaming and massaging the left. He seemed to really be thoughtfully considering his answer. I was glad he was taking time to formulate a response, because I knew he was really being careful to come up with an intelligent, fair, and fact-based answer.

"God, the church, and society have established marriage as a protected institution for a man and woman to enjoy. Inside marriage God, His divinely created agents the church, government, and society intended procreation to take place so that humanity could reproduce itself." Dion paused speaking, gently and sensually massaging my buttocks. "Marriage was supposed to establish the Biblical and moral framework within which this God-ordained procreation was to take place. Marriage was reserved for a man and a woman because God created them to be a couple, a match, and to only engage in sex inside a Biblical covenant called marriage. God believed He created man and woman to complement and complete one another, and the covenant of marriage was required to prevent complete sexual anarchy as humans tend to engage in unfettered, dangerous, and unbiblical communal sex just for pleasure."

I figured that I could see where Dion was going, and I mostly disagreed. I knew the original purpose of marriage as a cradle for having children and perpetuating the human race. But times were different now. There was no danger of humanity dying out, killing one another off, and no need to marry solely to have children and be 'normal'. I started to speak up, when Dion continued.

"You know, Andrew, I have been against redefining marriage to include gay men and lesbians all of my life while living at home. I thought the idea of two men or two women marrying and completing the other as mates was sinful, disgusting, abnormal, unnatural, and evil. Of course those attitudes and opinions I accepted early on in my development were not based necessarily on fact, the Bible, science, or anything else truly valid. They came from the opinions, comments, and rants of parents, friends, church elders, societal bias, clichés, and other people who disdained anything different from heterosexuality. Homosexuals do not need approval of society through gay marriage laws to justify their desire to be together. If I were gay, I wouldn't care what society thought of my marriage to another man. I don't need anyone condoning, embracing, and accepting my marriage to another man. If I were a homosexual and felt okay about my sexuality and relationships, then society's legalizing and accepting my marriage would not be needed." Dion began gently giving my back another massage. "But then I met you, Andrew."

I had been half listening to Dion, and preparing my response about my opinion on gay marriage. I continued half listening and planning until Dion said, 'But then I met you, Andrew'. Upon hearing this comment, I was thrilled, hopeful, and yet scared all at the same time. What did this comment mean? He was now in favor of gay marriage?! He was now fully against gay marriage after meeting me?! At that point I was paying Dion full attention, and, since Dion stopped talking, there was an awkward pause.

"What did you say at the very end, Dion?!" I asked breathlessly.

"But then I met you." Dion repeated. He continued his soft, sensual, loving, and thoughtful massage of my back.

I whirled my head to look at Dion. He had a very contemplative and serious look on his face. I knew he was being totally honest. Dion paused.

"And?!" I prompted impatiently.

"Perhaps I have said too much, Andrew. Maybe we'd better change the subject?" Dion shrugged and his expression became stoic.

"Oh, no you don't, Dion!" I snorted and then chuckled, shaking my head in the negative as best I could from the position in which I was currently trapped. "I'm not going to let you get away from this conversation and that comment without a full admission of your feelings and what you meant! What did you mean when you said 'but then I met you'?!"

Dion stopped massaging me and hung his head, looking at his hands as he cleaned them off in a towel.

"Andrew, I need to… it's time to fix you… your… inside your… ass…"

"Fine, Dion, fine!" I spoke impatiently. "Just get on with it and then entertain our conversation and answer my questions!"

Dion paused again as he gently spread my cheeks. He began washing inside me. Although I was feeling much adrenaline and hormonal urges and desires, I was also becoming more impatient.

"Dion!?" I growled as the pain became intense. "What did you mean 'then you met me'? What true feelings do you have toward me… for me?! How strongly do you feel for me? Would you ever… could you ever marry me?!"

Dion sighed as he continued working inside me. The isopropyl alcohol and creams pained me, but the alcohol and avatar I had consumed numbed me mostly. I focused on Dion and his response to my queries.

"My carnal, sinful nature immediately led me to fall helplessly in love with you, Andrew. From day one when I first saw you on the bus… I was hopelessly attracted to you… in love with you… I wanted you… in every way! Now I find myself in love with someone I cannot marry… I may be breaking my Christian faith by loving… I'm still wrongfully in love with… with you, Andrew!"

I raised up on my elbows and laid a hand open on Dion's thigh.

"Dion, honey, we can get married! You said yourself you didn't need all the legal trappings of or society's acceptance of your marriage. You and I love each other… I don't see the problem!?"

Dion continued gently and tenderly working in my ass. Despite his care and soft touch, and my current intoxication, Dion was still hurting me. But this minute, some of the hurt was emotional and mental. I moaned and bit my lips.

"Andrew, I'm sorry! I don't mean to be so blunt and honest. I also don't mean to lead you on or to become an albatross around your neck… I am, God forgive me, madly… passionately in love with you. I never knew I could feel this way about anyone! I sense that you are not so in love with me… I know this is wrong… I know I am breaking God's heart… I'll finish you up here… then I will leave. Perhaps I should just stay in Gurnee and work. I will leave, Andrew, as soon as I can pack a bag… I am sorry for coming on to you so strongly…" Dion turned to leave my side.

Coming on strongly?! He had to be kidding! I jumped to a sitting position, forgetting about my woody and my pain, and grabbed him by the arm as he turned to go. I was so thrilled to have him be so honest, and I now knew we both were deeply in love with one another. I gently pulled him back to face me. Sitting on the kitchen table, stark naked, I looked deeply, honestly, and lovingly into Dion's beautiful brown eyes.

"Dion, stop! Listen to me?!" I spoke urgently and fervently, clutching both of his hands. "Dion, you don't have to go anywhere! I do love you as much, as deeply, as sexually as you love me. I've told you that before, but it is like maybe you don't trust me?! I do so love you! I cannot imagine life without you and me together... in love together… I also fell in love with you when I saw you on the bus… so buff… tanned… hot… stunningly gorgeous! Farmer's tan and muscle, sinew, curves... Oh dear God! You were... ARE so damn masculine and sexy!"

I cupped Dion's face in my hands and kissed him quickly.

"Dion! I have been waiting for you to admit your feelings toward me completely. Now that you have, I am so thrilled and relieved!"

At this point Dion looked down. I did as well and blushed. I was still naked and hard as a rock. I grabbed my pillow to cover myself.

I stood up straight to gaze at Dion again. We almost bumped faces; Dion was so close to me.

I didn't get any further. Dion had been slowly leaning toward my face, and at that moment he moved in. We were lip-locked in a French kissing, loving frenzy that I thought was going to end up in bed. We groped each other's bodies. The heat was rising.

Dion, however, just as suddenly stopped making out with me. He stepped back, feeling my face gently with his finger tips.

"God forgive me..." Dion whispered, frowning, "I have sinned... I am sinning... I..."

I was suddenly dizzy and needed to lie down; Dion still wasn't the only thing standing up!

"Andrew..." Dion said softly, "lay back down so I can finish changing your bandages. I... we... I am sinning with you. I am not ready for this... sex... yet."

I lay back down. Dion continued his work on me.

"Dion, you aren't sinning!" I said firmly in a gentle rebuke. "You and I are simply expressing our God-created love for one another! That is a beautiful thing, not something to be despised, avoided, regretted or refused!"

"I feel... I feel so wrong... Yet..." Dion stammered as he continued massaging my back. "Yet I feel so alive... so loved... so loving... so excited! I am confused."

"Dion, we are in love!" I explained softly and with certainty. "That is something to be celebrated, not to feel ashamed about! It certainly is not a sin!"

"I don't know... maybe you are right, Andrew." Dion moved from my back and buttocks to my legs. His touch and massaging were so sexually stimulating! "I so long to be like you, Andrew! I mean you are a... well... you are a man who loves men... you are proud of it... you feel no guilt or remorse... you are just proud and confident of who you are... I don't have that! I just have the damn guilt and shame... insecurity... confusion..."

Dion turned to face me and leaned on the island counter, looking thoughtfully at me. I held his gaze.

"Dion, I was born this way, preferring men over women." I began, firmly. "I know that with every fiber of my being." (I was beginning to doubt it though!) "There is nothing hard for me to accept being a homosexual because of that certainty. If there is a God, He created me this way from conception. I am able to accept being a man-lover and I am proud of myself and proud of it because I am today who I was born to be."

"But, Andrew, that is the problem." Dion looked at me, and he looked like a lost puppy. I wanted to hold him and hug him, but I knew I couldn't being as I was naked. If I did I wouldn't be able to stop.

"I don't believe that 'same-sex' attraction and desire is inborn in people!" Dion shook his head. "I believe God when he said man to man, or woman to woman sex is a sin. I believe homosexual feelings are some things that are developed in a sinful world. To be in love with and have sex with men is a choice, a sinful choice. It is not an inevitability. How can I overcome those feelings and doubts and just have my love for you and our relationship left?! I am tiring of my conflict over us! I am tiring of the conflict between my religion and faith, and my heart, emotions, flesh, feelings, and desires... my whole being."

I lifted myself and slowly sat up, pulling the blanket over my woody.

"Dion." I said lovingly. "Don't take this the wrong way, but I don't have those inner conflicts because... well because... I don't have those problems because I don't believe... I don't... well I have never... before this... believed... I have never believed in God before..." I couldn't seem to spit it out! Truth was, Dion's presence and our talks so far were beginning to make me wonder and think about the existence of God, and what He might want for my life.

"Maybe if you... Dion..." I stumbled again. How could I reassure him?

"Dion, did you choose to have your love for me, your desires for me, and your attraction to and for me? Can you pinpoint a specific moment when you said to yourself 'I think I will be gay and lust after men today'? Every time you remember looking at another guy and feeling attracted to and stimulated by him, do you remember choosing to feel stimulated by his good looks and physique? Do you remember saying 'I think I will lust after him today'?" I looked at Dion probingly and seriously.

"Of course not." Dion replied quietly. "I never chose to feel this way or be this way that I am aware."

"That is because you were born the way you are, with whatever sexual preference you have inside you!" I slapped the table for emphasis with my right hand. "No one in their right mind, Dion, would *choose* a same-sex lifestyle. It is too hard and dangerous to live a gay lifestyle! You love the sex you were born or created to love, not the one you choose."

Dion stroked his chin and frowned.

"Are you finished with my wounds, Dion?" I asked gently.

"Yes, Andrew. You are doing fine… healing well… you can get up…" Dion was quiet for a minute. He was clearly distracted.

"Thank you, Dion." I stood up, secured the towel around my waist, and gently grabbed him.

He tried to pull away, but I grabbed him by both arms gently. I held him briefly at arm's length. He hung his head and showed shame.

"Dion, look into my eyes! Come on!" I softly shook him until he looked up and into my face.

"Dion! It's all right! We were finally honest with each other. We both know we love and care deeply for one another! There is no harm or sin in that!" I kept his eyes looking deeply into mine. "You have no reason to feel ashamed or guilty about anything! Do you understand?!"

Dion finally shrugged, then he nodded his head.

"I suppose you are right." Dion said softly. "I can't deny my feelings for you, my desires for and toward you. It isn't right to have to lie about my love for you! After all Christians are not supposed to lie are they?"

"Of course I am right!" I pulled Dion in and gave him a big bear hug. He cautiously reciprocated. "And of course it isn't right for you to lie and deny your true love and feelings! We have a right to share, love, and be loved! Our love, Dion, is right, precious, and wonderful for the two of us! We have each other forever!"

Then another thought came to mind as I wished that my anatomy would shrink.

"Dion," I bent my arms and held him close, "I am in no rush to put pressure on you to sleep with me or anything. I am content just to be with you as things are now. Your company, your love, as it is now, is enough; I love you as you are."

Dion fidgeted, but held my gaze. 'Lord! His eyes are so beautiful!' I thought.

Dion cleared his throat. When he spoke, my heart melted.

"Andrew, I'm glad too that we both know where we stand. But I'm still struggling with how my love for you does, or does not line up with my Christian faith." Dion paused. "I do love you… but you'd… you'd better get dressed now. I… I too have… desires…"

Dion turned and I let him go. He went to the counter and loaded up the medical supplies to put away. I dressed, and followed him to the bathroom.

After we both took a potty stop and brushed our teeth, it was on to bed. I pecked Dion on the lips as he entered his bedroom. I then headed on to my own bedroom.

As I crawled nude into bed, I smiled happily. I knew Dion loved me, we both knew we were in love with one another, and now I could move forward to more quickly nurture and deepen our relationship. In the days and weeks ahead I would make Dion mine, my lover, and my spouse for life!